To Ian Martin, for food and friendship

THE IMPOSTERS

By Tom Rachman

THE
IMPOSTERS

Tom Rachman

riverrun

First published in Great Britain in 2023 by riverrun

riverrun

An imprint of

Quercus Editions Limited
Carmelite House
50 Victoria Embankment
London EC4Y 0DZ

An Hachette UK company

A CIP catalogue record for this book is available
from the British Library

Hardback ISBN 978 1 52942 581 9
Trade Paperback ISBN 978 1 52942 582 6
Ebook ISBN 978 1 52942 583 3

10 9 8 7 6 5 4 3 2 1

Typeset in Monotype Fournier by CC Book Production
Printed and bound in Great Britain by Clays Ltd, Elcograf S.p.A.

Papers used by riverrun are from well-managed forests and other responsible sources.

Contents

The novelist

(DORA FRENHOFER)

HER HUSBAND IS CHATTING, his comments interrupted by potato salad. Democracy is in crisis. Another bite. Someone's friend said populism. Chewing. A woman on the radio worried.

Dora – seated opposite at the kitchen table – responds only with 'Mm', a noise of such ambiguity that Barry worries he's talking nonsense, so talks more, an abundance of words that might include something clever eventually.

On the one hand, he says.

'Mm.'

On the other?

'Mm.'

'What time did we say for them to get here?' He knows, so the question can be understood as marital sonar, probing the mood of a spouse, registering what bounces back.

Dora, who is seventy-three, spent most of her decades without a husband, intentionally so. But that preference changed when she plotted the last chapter of her life: once feeble, she'd end it. The plan presented a problem. Act too soon, and you annihilate a worthy part of your life. Act too late, and you never act at all.

So she found her solution: a younger husband (nine years her junior) to monitor her, and tell her when to act. Dora refers to Barry as her 'ageing assistant' – the kind of joke one repeats too often, which is how one knows it's not quite a joke. Someday, he'll hesitate in the next room, plucking up the courage, then will march in, declaring sorrowfully, 'It's now; probably now.' But lately, it's his physical changes that startle Dora: a stooped grey man joins her at every meal, whereas the tall craggy woman appears only in mirrors.

Barry swallows a last mouthful of lunch, and fetches his little tin of sugar-dusted French candies. He flings a purple sweet into his mouth, cheeks caving as he sucks, the bags under his eyes rising effortlessly, a melancholy man posing as a chipper one, still exuding the lonely English childhood, an engineer father who wept once, undergraduate studies hiding at a Cambridge library, followed by a series of enchantments with the charismatic, who mastered him.

Barry began as research for one of Dora's late-career novels, a melodrama involving divorce. She sought authenticity, and someone provided the number of a family lawyer. Before their first meeting, Barry read several of her books, and worried that she might convert him into a character. When she arrived, he praised her memoir above all. Everyone prefers the memoir, so she likes it least. A novel is what you make; a memoir, what's made of you. Put another way, novels are her inner life, even if her inner life rarely sells more than eighty-six copies worldwide.

Still, Dora has managed to keep barging her volumes into stores over the years, a succession of small novels about small men in small crises. As for Barry, he never did become a character in that book – he loses his temper too rarely for fiction. Instead, he morphed into an endearing companion at her elbow during classical concerts, such as those recent Bach cello suites at Wigmore Hall, when Dora enquired during the performance if he was alright, and he leaned to her ear, first clearing his throat, causing her to rear back, then: 'Scientifically, men are more likely to be moved to tears by music,' he mumbled. 'According to studies.' She pulled his arm closer, placing his hand on her thigh, causing him to look up shyly, meeting her green eyes.

Dora checks her watch – they should be here. Who are they again? She clasps her hands, arthritis-knobbled knuckles, blue veins under translucent skin. Barry leaps to his feet, and hammer-punches the table, causing the candy tin to leap in fright. Irritated, Dora looks up.

He's yanking his tweed-jacket lapel, tongue sticking out.

'What are you doing?!' she asks.

He jerks about, silent but for the squeak of his rubber soles on the kitchen tiles.

She realizes: he inhaled that purple candy. It's lodged in his windpipe.

'Barry?' She stands. 'What do you want me to do?' She grasps the cuff of his sleeve but he pulls away, both hands to his throat, thumbs pushing either side of his Adam's apple, to dislodge the blockage. He stares, wide-eyed, desperate.

Dora almost speaks. But nothing. She stands motionless before him. Finally, she turns, and walks stiffly up the hall.

Dora passes the staircase, and finds herself in the living room before tall bookcases that run down the wall. When younger, Dora stole a volume from each man she slept with: ancient intercourse flashes on the shelves among scolding classics, her own novels loitering sheepishly at the margins.

From down the hall, she hears a thud – it's Barry, lurching around in the kitchen, his shoe banging into a cupboard. A gasp follows, and loud coughs.

If coughing, he must be breathing.

The back of Barry's tweed jacket rises and sinks, his arms planted on either side of the kitchen sink, into which he spat out the candy. He twists on the cold-water tap, hoisting the purple dot slowly toward him.

'You're okay now,' she affirms.

He sits at the kitchen table, a sheen of sweat on his face, shoulders shivering with each breath. 'Well.' Another long hacking cough. 'I almost.'

'You almost what?' When Dora worked as a young office typist, she once saw a German businessman suffer a stroke. Nobody did mouth-to-mouth because his beard was flecked with pumpkin soup, still warm from lunch. He ended up with brian damage. Not 'brian' damage. That looks wrong. How do you spell it?

'Gate.'

'Pardon?'

'They just opened the gate,' Barry says. He calls to the front door a strangled, 'Coming!'

Barry, who devoted his legal career to divorces, only found his true passion in recent years, after enrolling in a part-time counselling course. On Dora's encouragement, he abandoned law, and posted an ad in their North West London community magazine: 'Couples Therapist.' At first, his clients never returned more than twice. Barry didn't help his cause by never insisting on payment – it gave an impression of amateurishness, which was the correct impression. Then, Dora crossed paths with an outgoing couple, and they lingered to gab, and the woman phoned back, asking if Barry's wife might sit in on the next session 'just to make it an even number of boys and girls'. Dora agreed: she needed fresh characters.

This afternoon's clients are still outside the closed front door, whisper-bickering before they knock.

On the inside, Barry tells Dora softly, 'I could've *died.*'

'Look, cancel the session, if you want.'

'Coming!' Barry repeats to the door, and opens it.

The male client is a frosty-sideburned Glaswegian ad exec who dresses like a hipster in his thirties, which he was twenty years ago. His wife – a plump pharmaceuticals rep of Lebanese origin in an overtight suit – wants to rekindle their romance. He prefers training for ultramarathons.

As it's sunny, Barry set up chairs in the back garden. Even before his clients sit, they've resumed their dispute from the drive over: 'You just proved my point.'

'You. Are seriously. Insane.'

'*I* am?!'

As they summarize their past week to Dora, Barry leans over his yellow legal pad, writing nothing. Clients always address Dora, for the same reason that she has often attracted people: she takes an interest, but doesn't mind if they leave. At an ill-timed juncture, Barry points out that there's a drizzle, and should they move to the living room? The ad exec is busy talking, and refuses to budge – he's fine! So Barry steps inside for umbrellas, and Dora joins to help. In the front hall, Barry blocks her. 'Do I even need to be here?' he says. 'I feel so expendable. You just walked out of the kitchen, Dora! And now we're sitting there as if nothing happened, listening to these people's sex life.'

'Or lack thereof.'

'Don't miss my point.'

'Then don't be absurd.'

He heaps three umbrellas on her arms, and opens the front door. Raindrops slice inward. He steps out, closing the door after himself. The metal gate tinkles open.

Down residential streets, he strides, wavering after a few steps – then hurrying along, knowing this is out of character, which impels him to defy character. Barry wipes his forehead, an ironed handkerchief over thinning damp hair. Humiliated: that's how he feels.

He reaches the park, formerly the grounds of an aristocrat's palace. Whenever upset, Barry fast-walks a loupe around it. But 'loupe' is wrong. Is it 'loup'? Anyway, he tries to outpace his thoughts, which keep circling back to Dora as ever, a constancy of interpretation that exhausts him.

By the duck pond, a beagle strains toward brown water, held back by the commands of its barking owner: 'No, Wally, I forgot the towel. Wally, no!' Barry presses his palm to a chain-link fence, and considers the criss-cross imprint. As a boy, he played with toy soldiers, though never on war manoeuvres; they held talks. A sense of time overcomes him, and the face of his mother, and a plunging span from then to this.

'I won't charge them for today.'

'You were in the park?' Dora asks.

'No, no – just around.'

'I pictured you by the duck pond.'

'You pictured wrong.' Pause. 'Are you going to ask where?'

'I'll keep you at the pond,' she says. 'You *could* charge them – they had the full hour.'

'It's reasonably strange, what happened.' His voice tightens.

'Exactly what, Barry?' She's suddenly ferocious, such that he'd take back everything if he could. '*What* was strange?'

He looks around the kitchen as if for a dishtowel, instead opening the fridge simply for somewhere to direct his gaze. 'Was there anything more from those two?'

She presents her page of handwritten notes, the paper blistered where raindrops landed. Barry carries the sheet upstairs to the attic office, to deposit her latest contribution in a filing cabinet. He never reads Dora's notes on his clients because he fears discovering insights more acute than his own. But he can't ignore her views this time; he missed most of that session.

He holds her page almost too far to view, giving a perfunctory scan. But his expression shifts, and the page nears his face. Barry hastens back to the filing cabinet, riffling in there for Dora's notes on previous clients. Reading, he holds still, his stomach falling.

In all those sessions, he finds, Dora never once wrote of the clients. Each page tells of the same person: an ageing man in tweed, seated beside her, posing as a therapist. Her observations are all alike, with sentences that wander, words illegible, and spelling mistakes, as she never used to make.

7

He slides all her notes back into the hanging file and locks the cabinet, needing those pages far from view. He sits at Dora's writing desk, his gaze flitting around her attic office. She's malfunctioning. He knows it.

An image from the Bach concert comes to him. When the musicians were performing a piece that he knew Dora adored, Barry glanced over. She was just staring at the seatback before her. He touched her thigh, and she turned, looked up. He scarcely knew those dimmed eyes.

Before, Dora had instant opinions on everything. She knew what she thought, what you ought to think, what everyone else should. Yet lately, when overwhelmed, she just stalls, or walks from a room, returning later as if nothing happened, and indignant if Barry suggests otherwise.

She talks of writing another novel. There will be none.

Barry tucks his chin down, breathes in and holds it, exhaling slowly. He glances at the ledge of photos behind Dora's writing desk: her daughter long before the girl grew up and ran far from her mother to Los Angeles; a faded snapshot of Dora's hippie brother in the mid-1970s with a beer in hand; a black-and-white portrait of her parents in the Netherlands after the war.

Barry has met none of these faces, yet will eventually be left here with them, he the last resident of this home, only creaking floorboards and his mutters, imagining her retorts, which made him laugh or hurt him, or both, and he'd take either, just for her voice in the room. He blinks fast, a flutter of eyelashes; he swallows. He must talk to her this instant.

In the darkened hallway downstairs, Dora awaits his footfalls, which will be sturdy until Barry reaches one step from the bottom, where – avoiding eye contact – he'll announce: 'I'm your ageing assistant, Dora. I'll tell you when. But it's *not* now.'

'Something's the matter,' she'll reply. 'With my brian.'

'Your brian is fine!'

Nobody comes downstairs. Nobody is upstairs, or anywhere else in this house. Only Dora, pondering a fictional character, this husband Barry, based on someone she met in passing once, and written into a story that isn't quite working, as none of her stories quite work anymore.

When younger, Dora populated her novels with bumblers, and depicted them with affection. Yet this story regards an unsympathetic character, a failing novelist, based on herself. It's a punishing self-portrait.

Dora regrets much about herself: that, while she wrote kind characters, she was too impatient for kindness herself; that she always spoke with honesty, no matter whom it wounded; that she rummaged through everyone to extract literary characters, who had the advantage of behaving as *she* wished, the disadvantage of being unlike anyone she met. Either she was a poor writer, or humans were poor characters.

'I need to finish this life of mine pretty soon. Don't you think?' she asks the staircase, as if interrupting Barry's descent, as if pulling him down from that last step, pressing her cheek against his brow, and spying his wrinkled closed eyelids, thus finding an ending to her story: the fading woman no longer wants an ageing assistant, only to age with this man. She does long for such a companion. Yet she'd have struggled to endure a week with him in her house.

Dora climbs the staircase toward her attic office, wincing at each impact on her sore knee. At the landing, she refuses to pause and catch her breath, proceeding straight to her desk, tense, wondering if she has anything more to do, knowing the answer.

DIARY: DECEMBER 2019

I'm jittery, this screen before me. What if the book I'm trying to write comes to nothing?

I look out my office window at other narrow London houses, populated by families growing up and down over the years. A small child appears in a distant pane. This far away, my vision is blurred: just a momentary girl, under a roof pronged with obsolete aerials.

I revert to the correct view, my desk. A computer screen, keyboard, the cursor blinking aggressively at me.

These sentences are fact. I'm writing as myself, Dora Frenhofer, not pretending to be anyone else for a change. But every other chapter will describe a different character. And this presents a problem. Readers want a book to add up to something, not to some things. So I must tie these people together. Maybe the manuscript could be about writing itself? Or about writers?

For a half-century, I've survived as one of those. I consider myself both fortunate and a failure. At the start, I had a spell of luck, and mistook it for a career.

'Maybe I need to retire,' I remarked a few years ago, walking with an old man I was then seeing.

'Retire as a writer?' he said, smirking. 'Who do you tell?'

He was right. You just stop. Nobody notices. But I panic to imagine that step. It feels dangerous even to mention. I should change the subject fast. So:

I needed glasses, and ended up with a black eye. Early for a work lunch, I was wandering down the covered arcades off Jermyn Street, puzzling over the idea of men, as depicted in displays of gents' boutiques: handmade shoes for bankers; spotted silk neckties; the hatter's yellow homburgs.

An optician's storefront presented no nameplate, just a hanging sign of a metal nose with spectacles and a magnificent moustache. I checked my wrist, near, then far, bulging and shrinking numbers: I probably had time, even if I couldn't quite see it. A clerk – unaware that I peeped through the window – removed his glasses, licked each lens in turn, and wiped them on his shirt.

'How may I help you?'

An optometrist could test me right now, though she was startled when the clerk opened the backroom door, causing her to toss aside a travel magazine as if it were smut. She trundled out a metal apparatus, half-medieval, half-futuristic, and pressed my forehead toward the battery of lenses.

'Clearer now?' she asked, as I studied the eye-chart pyramid, topped with a triumphal 'E' and descending toward a fuzz that might've been 'P H U N T D Z'. She flipped lenses. 'Or clearer now?'

I couldn't say, but felt that I must, or I'd fail somehow. 'The second one. Definitely.' Pride, it seemed, would cause me to squint for the next few years.

For much of my life, I'd navigated without optical correction, excepting a pair of reading glasses that I own primarily to lose everywhere. But in recent years, objects beyond my reach have started dissolving. How much, I asked myself, did I really need to see everything? By now, I already know what most things look like.

'As I tell clients,' the optometrist informed me, 'bifocals are like wisdom: you're finally of an age where you can see far away and near at once.'

'Isn't the problem that I can't see either?'

In silence, she rendered judgement on my miscalculating eyeballs, inputting a prescription to her database while I considered the upside-down headline of her discarded travel magazine: 'MYSTERY ON THE HIPPIE TRAIL', featuring a blurry (to me) photo of a young man among prayer flags in the Himalayas. I recall those days, when many of my friends trekked east with spiritual intent, returning with slides of Buddhist monasteries. This was when travel was still a form of disappearance, and nobody knew quite what had become of you till the handwritten letter fell through a mail slot back home, bearing a fragmentary report from your past. When my brother travelled overland to India in 1974, I gave him a copy of War and Peace for the trip. I still dreamed of becoming an important writer.

When young, I pictured writers as an intellectual tribe, toiling in Parisian garrets, frowning around New York bookshops, engaging in fiery spats in St Petersburg. Perhaps they'd invite me inside someday. Here and there, they did – and I wanted to run. When they chose not to have me back, I wondered why.

But before I get to all that, I must finish with my eye exam. For suddenly, I was late, hurrying from the optician's to my lunch on Dean Street, sidestepping the clamour of midday Soho, thronged by hipsters darting hither and thither, like a dance number involving portable coffees.

On the narrow pavement ahead, a google of media types jabbered in high-volume glee. Politely, I asked to slip through. (I want to keep these sections truthful, so must amend that. I was not polite.) 'It's not your personal street here!' I said. 'Can I get by?!'

A young woman laughed and I was ashamed, for I agreed with her. But I'd committed to indignation, so pushed by, only to misjudge the distance and stumble, my face bumping into the pole of a traffic sign. I heard gasps, and a few kind observers took half-steps forward. I refused their help, scowling up the pole as if for an explanation, and reading: 'SIGN NOT IN USE'.

One eye scrunched, I walked on, their chatter resuming behind me but not about me – I was dissolving from their consciousness, even if mine still throbbed with them. Humans everywhere, jammed together, demanding to speak. This included me. I had no case for myself over them. Why should they have moved?

Doubting yourself is no way to enter a restaurant. So I acted. Small talk followed. The menu moved back and forth.

'What happened?' my literary agent asked with concern, pointing to my eye.

I looked up from the threat of drizzled sea bass. 'A metal pole crept up on me.'

'Are you alright?'

'Actually,' I said, 'I wanted to ask your advice.'

'Get yourself a steak.'

'Oh. I'd been thinking fish.'

'For the eye, I mean.' She took a photo of mine, and handed over her phone: a swollen purple bar down my wrinkly profile, a whisp of white hair intruding into the frame.

She folded her menu, smiling in anticipation. 'Exciting: you have something new to tell me about?'

'No, the opposite. I just hoped for your thoughts.'

'Cool.'

I didn't want to say any more. But did. 'I wonder, honestly, can I justify another book? Battling with a manuscript for the next several years, and knowing there's every chance nobody will read it. At what point do I accept my situation?' My voice was jagged, for I was exposing myself.

'Wow.' She looked faintly irritated. I hadn't expected that. 'I do hate to see you dispirited like this, Dora. But ploughing ahead is part of the job. Don't you think? Unless you really can't bear to. In which case.'

'No, you're right. Fair enough.' Embarrassed, I switched to safer matters: the ugliness of politics, the prettiness of desserts.

We collected our coats. 'Look,' she said as we parted, 'what you need is to get back to work. Start a new novel!'

So I'm trying, fearful to begin, excited to: the emptiness of a page, the possibilities of a word. I could choose any of them. Come on then.

Only, I can't get the distance right, my face diminishing and growing in the screen reflection, recalling that metal nose hanging before the optician's, that sign with its magnificent walrus moustache.

So far, I have only a character in search of a story, seated at a desk, trying to type.

~~When the servant presented the newspaper and coffee at the door of his upstairs office, Mr Bhatt snarled her away.~~

Or

~~Everyone in the household leaves Mr Bhatt to steep in his rudeness.~~
~~Meals have passed, but he is too proud to march downstairs to the~~
~~kitchen.~~

Or

A grey cloud expands from Mr Bhatt's nostrils over his magnificent
walrus moustache, whose black bristles twitch with curiosity.

The novelist's missing brother

(THEO FRENHOFER)

A GREY CLOUD EXPANDS FROM Mr Bhatt's nostrils over his magnificent walrus moustache, whose black bristles twitch with curiosity. The overhead fan chops to a halt, the lazy blades slapping defeatedly at his cigarette smoke. Must be another power outage: a Hindi love song jangling in the kitchen has stopped too. For once, the Delhi electrical grid comes to his aid.

Able to concentrate at last, Mr Bhatt pushes aside spread-eagled library books and flicks empty packets of Panama cigarettes off his desk, exposing green baize where he pinions today's *Indian Express*, raising and depositing his thighs to circulate the air, his seersucker-suit trousers sighing.

Maddeningly, the newsprint has been defaced: pencil strokes under sentences, comments in the margins. Mr Bhatt propels his nose toward the page, but cannot decipher what his wife scrawled. If Meera, who rises long before he does, is going to read the newspaper first, she must leave all as it was. Or yesterday's events appear according to what *she* happens to believe important, much as when they visit the cinema, and Mr Bhatt is churning with emotion, only for her to whisper a scathing comment, and suddenly he sees all through her vinegar.

He removes his square-framed glasses, and licks the lenses, wiping each across the breast pocket of his pyjama top. With a sip of tepid instant coffee, he orients himself to the Tarzan comic strip. Next, he attempts the crossword, which he cannot complete, so curses the idiots who designed these clues. He advances – rather, regresses – through the newspaper of 13 May 1974, back to front: cricket results, business stories, lastly news. While reading, he unscrews and re-screws a jar of Brylcreem, taking distracted sniffs.

The front page is overrun with 17 lakh railwaymen on strike. Perhaps Mrs Gandhi went too far, arresting so many trade-union leaders. But she mustn't surrender now, lest another gang of rowdies rises up. Where would it end?

Mr Bhatt steps onto the balcony over Jor Bagh – by his estimation, the second-best neighbourhood in south Delhi. In the fenced park below, an ox stands with a plough fitted to its back. The caretaker – that peasant with paan-red teeth – has just left the beast stranded. The radio warbles again down in the kitchen below, and Mr Bhatt returns inside his office, pyjama lapels fluttering from the overhead fan.

While running the bath, he completes his morning jumping jacks, then enters the water with a slosh, shaving while seated, as recom-mended in the newspaper, for it steams your pores. What they failed to mention is that the bathwater becomes dotted with stubble. Mr Bhatt spends minutes pondering how to extricate himself without coating his torso in black specks.

He dresses for lunch: seersucker suit and a navy school tie that curls like a quizzical elephant trunk, owing to Mr Bhatt's habit of twisting it around a finger while considering his mission. He has much to tell Mrs Gandhi. Should he cram it into one letter? Or select a shocking fact, and place that before her?

First comes the problem of salutation. 'Madam Prime Minister'? Or 'Your Excellency'? Or just 'Mrs Gandhi'? She won't respect a man who kowtows. Madam Prime Minister, he thinks, we hurtle toward disaster! Are you aware of the work of Dr John B. Calhoun? This American scientist constructed a perfect habitat for mice, which mated and multiplied to their hearts' content with no predators or diseases; a mouse paradise. But soon, they swarmed by the thousands. The excess males lacked mates, and withdrew. Cannibalism spread, as did mouse perversity. Societal collapse next. Then extinction. That, Madam Prime Minister, is *our* future. At independence, we were three hundred million. A quarter-century later, we've nearly doubled. The density challenge will worsen this decade. By the 1980s, life will be bleak. As Delhi chapter leader of ZPG (Zero Population Growth Pvt Ltd), I propose the following simple, but firm, measures: a tax on new children; a surcharge on cribs; cash bonuses for the childless. Those who cannot resist mating should produce only one offspring, who shall be rewarded with reserved places in the better schools (provided such boys are bright). The national press must join the effort: no more news photographs of sweet babies, but denunciations of prolific parents with shaming pictures, along with a Worst Family of the Week.

Despite these cogitations, the typewriter page still contains only three words: 'Madam Prime Minister'. For inspiration, he opens a much-consulted copy of Dr Paul R. Ehrlich's *The Population Bomb*, folded on page 152, where Mr Bhatt underlined: 'The disease is so far advanced that only with radical surgery does the patient have a chance of survival.'

How, Mr Bhatt asks himself, can people amble into the future when this – famished humans swarming like locusts (or cannibal mice) – awaits us? He turns to the balcony door, his pulse quickening as if a mob clattered onto it now, sniffing at the window, crashing through, feasting on him. He flicks his lighter sideways, dragging the flame away from the cigarette, as in stylish movies. Exhaling, Mr Bhatt pictures himself not as an independent scholar but as the child of his father and mother, as if they were still in this world, and aware of the duty weighing on their son, R. A. S. Bhatt: to save India.

Suddenly, someone *is* rampaging up the outside stairs. Mr Bhatt snatches a fountain pen, and dots the nib on his fingers, the blue constellation proving that he has not been idle this morning. The office door swings open, and Ajay bursts in, giggling because he's not allowed here. The twelve-year-old bolts around and jumps, landing on his bottom, then back to his feet, attempting a cartwheel on the Persian rug, which slips, as does he. 'You'll break a bone, you fool,' Mr Bhatt warns, repressing a half-smile – until the boy grabs a book, and hurls it. This earns an angrier reproach: 'Hey! That's stupid now!'

Ajay pretends to study a battered cricket ball. He's got a runny nose.

'Where's your hankie, *meri jaan?*'

'I already blew my nose.'

'You wiped it on your sleeve. That's why they put buttons there, to stop backward boys wiping noses on sleeves. Did your mother not provide hankies? How hard can it be, no?'

Ajay is back from his first year at boarding school. Mr Bhatt was a Dosco boarder himself, unhappily so. But he believes that a young man worth his salt must endure, and Mr Bhatt is no more likely to recant a belief than to shave his moustache: he'd look like a child.

The boy is peeking at the page hanging from the typewriter, so Mr Bhatt swats his son away, then points to the mailing address in the upper corner, Safdarjung Road, residence of Mrs Gandhi. 'A correspondence we have going.'

The boy is not as impressed as he should be, so Mr Bhatt runs his knuckle up and down Ajay's ribs, which sends the boy twisting to the ground in laughter, and raises a smile on the man's face. In this room, at this desk, a monumental idea is taking shape. People will die because of Mr Bhatt. More will survive. 'Straight downstairs,' he orders. 'Enough of your nonsense.'

Ajay's wildness is a joy to Mr Bhatt but he never laughs, for it sets an example. He feels older than his years (thirty-one), and he welcomes that. What troubles him is when his son joins in Meera's condescension – the implication that a bumbling fool labours up here.

'How many minutes to cook you?' he asks Ajay. 'I want tender meat only.'

'One hour?'

'We can tell your mother to cook *naniji* instead,' he says, meaning Parvati, his mother-in-law, who is staying. 'But old meat is chewy. You would taste better.'

'What about we eat you, Baba? But my question,' Ajay adds, leaping topics as ever, 'is how does a brain think, do you think?'

Mr Bhatt takes off his glasses, licks the lenses, wiping them on his shirt, replacing them. 'A brain has an idea. How? From a pulse of blood that sends, that goes through cells,' he proceeds, with the gravity of a man who has no idea. 'And cells, they send these ideas from the senses. This is a bit complicated for you.' He escapes to the front balcony, spying a peasant in the park talking to friends – a bunch of layabouts, they are. 'How does a brain think, Ajay? I'll tell you.' He turns back. The boy is gone.

THE ENGLISH WORD 'ANCHOVY' is new to Theo Frenhofer. Even deducing it from his native Dutch – '*ansjovis*' – he struggles to visualize this fish, seeing only sea, silent on top, teeming beneath. In his imagination, the gull in this novel keeps swooping above a glossy surface, swooping and swooping, for Theo is stuck on the same sentence, distracted because the printed English words in his head are drowned out by English spoken at the adjacent table.

It's ridiculous: the guest-house courtyard is otherwise empty, but they took a table so close that he could touch that Swiss girl's shoulder or the Canadian boy's wrist. Should he move? Sun cuts between the overhead vines, roasting Theo – that could be his excuse.

The Swiss girl rests her legs on a rickety chair, bare feet inscribed with tan lines from her sandals, which lie unbuckled on the floor beneath. Her Canadian companion has a faint blond moustache and long blond hair, shirtless and fit, arms behind his head, hairy armpits on display and shoulders bulging, a belly-button hair trail disappearing into faded-denim shorts. On their table are two keys: not a couple.

Pretending to read, Theo eavesdrops, learning that they happened to check in at the same time. The Canadian boy invited her to 'take a weight off' in the courtyard café, where he crash-landed his giant yellow backpack, currently beached against Theo's ankle. On her lap, the Swiss girl cradles a purple Rajasthani sack, her slender arm atop, a beedi cigarette between her fingers.

The shirtless Canadian is asserting his travel credentials with disaster-bragging, though he has limited material – he only just arrived in India, so talks of flights, describing a con man at Delhi airport, and the drive here to Benares. The Swiss girl draws back her frizzy hair into a bun, jaw jutting, left cheek dotted with two small moles. She's a hardened trekker, six months since she and her friends left Geneva in a converted army truck, overland via Iran, across the salt desert, into Herat, watching tourists play chess on the giant board at Sigi's Hotel in Kabul, through the Khyber Pass to Pakistan, and onward.

Theo also reached India overland, though he saw little besides a bus window. His elder sister, Dora, prompted his voyage, deciding that he should leave behind his troubles in their Dutch hometown. She took the train from Munich, where she'd recently published a first novel, and she ordered her brother out of bed, telling him to come with her to Amsterdam. Theo feared contending with his sister, who suffered a common failing of the intelligent: able to dissect an animal, identify every organ, name its role – yet never wonder what the creature thought. In Amsterdam, she sought to stir her younger brother to action, assuring him that *she* knew what he must do. In a tour-company office, she forked over 299 guilders to a hippie seated at the desk, then folded more bills into Theo's breast pocket for spending money. 'But, Theodoor, I demand stories when you come back. Understood?' Her eyes shone as she slapped his hand affectionately.

When the bus pulled out, his fellow passengers roared with excitement. Theo only gripped his jeans, hands sweating. During the long ride, everyone else disembarked when possible, seeking hostels for the night and food and hashish. Theo slept in place on the bus, greasy hair over acne-starred face, large lips, large teeth. Only when the bus was empty did he get up to stretch, for he suspected that his sockless white sneakers stank. Even with nobody there, he had a shy boy's hunch.

Arriving finally at the Delhi terminus, the other passengers whooped in jubilation, and set off in groups. Alone, Theo found his way to the train station, fighting down terror: people everywhere. He bought a third-class ticket to the holy city of Benares, which Dora had mentioned, and he disembarked there, walking down shadowed lanes as bicycle bells tinkled around him, causing Theo to flatten himself against the nearest wall. The sunlight flickered on and off, causing him to look up: monkeys crossing electrical wires. He stepped on a vendor's basket, and handed over rupees in apology, ending up with an onion.

Signs pointed to Dharma Guest House, and he hurried to its entrance, climbing the stairs to the first vacant space he'd seen in a day: a courtyard café, adorned with a pink-yellow mural of the elephant god Ganesha before snow-hatted mountains. Wooden doors lined the outer courtyard, numbered and each shut with a padlock. The manager had refashioned this place for Westerners, and kept his elderly parents at a distance, though a bony old gent shuffled around, vermilion tika on his forehead, waistcoat over dhoti and slippers. In Room 9, Theo tried his lumpy cotton-stuffed mattress, and glanced around the single dwelling.

He remained there in Room 9, visiting the communal bathroom only during off-hours, and never risked the streets. His sister had convinced him that hope awaited halfway around the world. Instead, he woke in dread – within weeks, he'd have no money left. And then? Flipping between cold panic and denial, he distracted himself with paperbacks that departing guests had left by the check-in desk. Thrice daily, he was interrupted by room service: always jam toast, a metal pot of tea-leaves boiled in sweet milk, cardamom, cloves bobbing. Once, a servant grinned at him, and Theo became self-conscious, so paid his bill, and lugged his bag to the train station, intending to reach Calcutta, whence he'd venture into those holy mountains depicted in the guest-house mural. He'd find an edge of the world to peek over, and maybe lean forward.

But nobody would sell him a train ticket. An educated man hovered, and finally explained: the railwaymen were on strike. Theo retraced his steps to Dharma Guest House, and closed the door of Room 9, resuming his residency on that lumpy mattress. The other guests were always just passing through, and vacated their rooms by midday to sightsee. That was when Theo emerged, sitting under the vines, talking to himself, reading to hold back the present. He tried always to get back into Room 9 before any guests returned, but today an 'anchovy' distracted him.

'You'll get raped.'

She scoffs at this claim of the Canadian boy – already, the Swiss girl has hitchhiked around this country, and remains alive. She boasts of a plan to explore the Ganges tomorrow, taking photos at sunrise.

'How much is that?' the Canadian boy asks her.

'You find a man with a boat, and you pay him.'

'I'm up for that.'

'Good – this is cheaper with more. Maybe also this boy, who listens?' She turns to Theo, who is still pretending to read *Jonathan Livingston Seagull*. 'You?' she asks him. 'You will come?'

MR BHATT'S MOTHER-IN-LAW AND his wife stop chatting when he enters the kitchen, and they turn off the radio. He mooches about, glancing in cupboards. 'Why do you two sit at the servants' table?'

Parvati rises with difficulty, legs wide for stability, hands on hips, pushing herself upright. 'What is this on your face?' she asks Mr Bhatt, and reaches toward her son-in-law, causing him to flinch.

'What is what?' Walking into the hallway, he checks in the mirror: blue smears across his face. Before Ajay burst into his study, Mr Bhatt dotted pen ink on his hands, as proof of earnest endeavour. He must've touched his face after. Meera arrives with a wetted napkin, and cleans him. Between swipes across his face, he whispers to his wife: 'When is your mother going?' Parvati was to return to Bombay days before. Yet he already knows the answer, so gives it: 'This bloody strike.'

Whenever Mr Bhatt's mother-in-law is visiting, he gripes. Yet he is fond of her, and touched by her closeness with Ajay, which reminds him of the aunties and grannies who adored him in child-hood. 'She does no good for that boy,' he whispers, softly enough that Parvati – still in the kitchen – cannot hear. 'Does that woman know algebra? Does she know chess?'

'She raised nine children, including all her brothers,' Meera replies. 'Of course she knows how to occupy a boy. But Ajay should be back at school – you cannot keep him here forever. Jandhu can drive him to Dehradun. We are saying this for days now.'

'How I'm going to the library with no car? And what does it matter if the boy is here another few days?'

'Just now, you were saying he's a nuisance!'

'Leave me alone. And turn off the radio in daytime hours. And stop writing on my newspaper.'

'So many rules.'

As he stomps up the outside stairs to his office, the radio in the kitchen switches back on, warbling 'Chura Liya Hai Tumne Jo Dil Ko'. Mr Bhatt smiles, flushing with love for his wife – her defiance a flirt, like his grumpiness.

On the balcony, he watches faraway kites on faraway rooftops, each line swaying, leading down to another particular person. Everywhere, humans eating and sleeping and multiplying. Ajay is far below, batting a cricket ball around the front garden, nattering to himself, a test match for one.

That night, Mr Bhatt meets his wife in the hallway, she leaving the bathroom, ready for bed. He was lurking, impatient about whatever she was up to in there – then restoring the best version of himself, for he will seduce Meera tonight, the first time in months. 'You and your mother were complaining about me?'

'Why is that your question?'

'It's my question.'

Abruptly, the flirt-squabbles feel stale. They've been this way forever, but Mr Bhatt is weary of it; she is too. But if either speaks sincerely, the other mocks. At the beginning, spats led to the bedroom. Lately, they lead him upstairs alone.

Mr Bhatt transforms his wife's lack of passion for being ambushed outside the bathroom into a rejection of his life's mission. Indignantly, he consoles himself with the notion that there are upper-class intellects and middle-class ones. To fail at commonplace activities is evidence of a loftier purpose. As he once told her, 'You imagine Albert Einstein driving badly, do you not?' But even the English language, Meera employs with more facility than he. Once, she had a short story published in a British literary journal, an achievement he praised with a curling smile: to scribble tales was a girlish hobby, almost vile when mankind stood at the precipice. If she writes again, he told her, use a pen name. Also, never a character who is him. 'Besides this, anything goes!' he said, to sound liberal.

'Even love scenes?'

'I already said, don't write about me.'

If she wanted, Meera could provide his breakthrough. She'd have words to address the prime minister, a declaration to propel this issue (and Mr Bhatt himself) to the upper echelons. But the propulsion wouldn't be his. So all that he expects – and what his wife is so stingy with – is admiration. Her praise infuses him like nothing else, much as her derision empties Mr Bhatt, a plug yanked from the basin of him. She has only herself to blame. And he has only her to blame too.

Mr Bhatt touches her shoulder, his hand sliding down her soft skin to the crook of her elbow.

'What are you doing now?' she asks.

'I have to explain?'

But the plug has been yanked. He waves her away, telling her to go to her room. 'Don't let the boy bother me in the morning – I have work!'

IN DAWN DARKNESS, ISABELLE photographs a bony-ribbed cow, its tail-swat frozen by the flash. Dazzled, a passing little girl with a badminton racket blinks and sidesteps them, surveying these three young foreigners.

'You know where is the Ganga?' Isabelle asks.

The girl wobbles her head 'yes' with an authority that contains the woman she'll become. 'Now with me,' she says, and strides ahead like a teacher on a school outing. 'Hallo hallo – with me now. With me.' Finally, she turns down what appears to be a dead end with an open window in the far wall. When Isabelle reaches it, she steps through. The two young men follow.

The horizon glows orange, rising into a navy haze above the Ganges, birds wheeling overhead, a whiff of sweet rot emanating from the sandstone steps that slope down to the ghat, where worshippers perform puja in the river. Isabelle widens her eyes at Theo, and squeezes the boy's arm, which affects his chest strangely. This outing – to his two companions, just sightseeing – is Theo's most important event in weeks.

'When we get on the boat,' Steve tells her, 'take pictures of the cremations.'

'It is not allowed, I think,' she says.

'Act like you don't know.'

At the edge of the river, Isabelle turns the aperture dial on her 35mm Olympus, eye to the viewfinder, a slow shutter clacking twice, capturing blurred pandits sinking under the black with a slop, res-urrected in a burst, inhaling and brushing their fingers across their teeth. A mother and daughter in saris stand waist-deep and push out candles, then caress the river, stroking dripping fingers down their faces. A shirtless fat man – sacred white thread across his gut, palms together – clenches his eyes and bows pneumatically, splashing the water, garlands and debris bobbing.

A boatman leans on one oar, yessing distractedly to all that Isa-belle asks. When she has exhausted her demands, he accepts a thin stack of rupees, and flattens his hand to the young men.

Over the next minutes, more passengers enter. The creaky wooden boat sinks lower with each person, water squashed down, then burping back, slapping Theo's hands, which clutch the edge of the vessel. Strangers talk in languages he can't understand, but he imagines their screams, as if the boat were to flip, everyone trapped, grabbing at him. He pivots about as if awaiting someone. He must get out. But standing could overturn the boat.

The boatman dips his oars and pushes off, water twirling away, its surface winking under the low sun. The overloaded vessel glides past the stepped terraces topped by Mughal forts, gold-roofed Hindu temples, ramparts holding back the caterwauling city. The opposite bank is a flood plain, empty compared with the architectural pande-monium on the near side. Theo looks from one bank to the other, picking at his blemished face, trying not to be sick. Is that mist? A log smoulders. Stray dogs pick at the pyre.

Isabelle rises to her feet, causing the boat to wobble and other passengers to gasp, though the boatman pays no mind. She's seeking an angle on the cremation ghats. In passing, she pinches Theo's shoulder. He tries to speak but no words come. She's nodding toward the water, and her face disappears behind the camera. She photographs a floating log. Until it's the floating limb of a goat. No, the arm of a creature. Rather, a dead child's body, threads of hair fanned across the surface.

THE PROTESTERS ARE BLOCKING Mr Bhatt's chauffeur-driven Ambassador. Two stray dogs stand on the roadside, surprised halfway through mating, still attached by the genitals. Mr Bhatt gives a violent tic of his head, his muttering amplified by the driver, Jandhu, who reaches out the window as far as possible, and thwacks a protester.

Mice warring for resources, Mr Bhatt thinks.

Jandhu holds down the klaxon, and lurches the Ambassador past the demonstrators, who are bumped aside.

'The life of a man is of no greater importance to the universe than that of an oyster,' Mr Bhatt remarks.

Jandhu wobbles his head in agreement, though he understands little English. Looking through a train window from Oxford to London, a young boy surveyed fields under a drowning sky, the land seamed with hedgerows, empty of humans, the boy unsure of any single verbalized thought, just a reservoir of sentiment. Why does Mr Bhatt remember that sight? He lived in England briefly as a child, his father an Indian High Court judge on a half-year fellowship.

The car stops before the Delhi Public Library.

'Is it locked?' Mr Bhatt asks, reverting to Hindi.

Jandhu runs over to check, rattling the doors with no effect. He asks a passing student, then jogs back. 'Railwaymen,' he says.

'They run the library now? How did our country fall so low?' Mr Bhatt talks as if already in politics – not holding office perhaps but a secret eminence behind the scenes, advising the mighty. The theme of Mr Bhatt's backseat speechifying is self-sacrifice: he evokes the gallantry of Indian forces at Bogura, and how we celebrated as brothers after giving the Paks a bloody nose in Bengal. 'Then what happened? We turned on each other, our own countrymen!'

Jandhu is rungs lower in status, but every man has an intuition as to every other man's violence, and both know that the driver would be dominant. Mr Bhatt offers him a cigarette, pretending it's the last in this packet, and that he merely prefers to open a fresh one. Jandhu accepts, sliding it into his breast pocket for later – to smoke with the boss would cross a border.

When it comes to population control, Mr Bhatt explains to Jandhu, our government does have policies: implant loops in the ladies and provide rubber sheaths for fellows. But that's not enough! Not nearly. Our young men run into battle, risking death for the nation. Why not the lesser act of controlling the fly on their trousers? The sexual urge, Mr Bhatt explains, is man's lowest instinct, like those dogs in the street attached by the genitals. Thus, if reproduction is our most base drive, depopulation is the pinnacle of reason.

He frowns, recalling something Meera said, how he'd provided only one child. They'd always agreed Ajay was the start and the finish. What does she imply? That he is less than productive? Annoyed, Mr Bhatt's rhetoric grows more combative. Simply limiting offspring won't do! We've left this too late. The brave must consider the greatest sacrifice: to voluntarily leave the human race.

'Your son? You'd want this of him?'

'What are you talking about, Jandhu? Not children,' Mr Bhatt snaps.

'But when Ajay is grown?'

This impertinence reminds Mr Bhatt why some men are drivers, and should be trusted with nothing more. But that raises a concern: how to persuade the common man? What stirs a lowly fellow like Jandhu to surrender his life for the sake of another? You crack that riddle, and you've solved all.

To do just that, Mr Bhatt frequents the library, reading books and articles on the mysteries of suicide, always in an isolated carrel, shoulders high and books at his belly, as if he were consulting pornographic material. In his satchel right now, he has Hume's justification of self-murder, Montaigne's defence of noble suicide, and a mimeographed publication of the Birmingham Coroner's Court, which transcribed hundreds of suicide notes.

Misery can lead to self-destruction, of course, but valour and intelligence are motives too. Now and then, Mr Bhatt bumps into his father's friends around Delhi, and they stiffly recall the man's accomplishments, and smile to recall his wit. He was the brightest man Mr Bhatt ever met. What had he known? Mr Bhatt's own moods lack action; he would never harm himself.

Most suicide notes, he discovers, are either instructions (so-and-so gets my suits); or sniping (they never cared); or apologies (I ruined your life). Some aim to wound the living (*you* did this); others to cause minimal impact (bye). But above all, Mr Bhatt finds, suicide notes are trivial. The answer is missing, a hollow within every note. His father left none at all. That is a larger hollow still.

On the drive home, Mr Bhatt gazes out the window, hardly noticing the protesting railwaymen this time. A plan is forming. He mutters a line, read so often that he can recite it almost verbatim. 'The operation will demand many apparently brutal and heartless decisions,' Dr Ehrlich wrote in *The Population Bomb*. 'The pain may be intense.'

THE BLOND CANADIAN GUY, Steve, turns out to be wealthy – his dad owns a mine in northern Alberta. When he flew to India, Steve travelled from Delhi airport directly to Benares in a taxi, a two-day drive. Now, he must return to the capital for his onward flight to Kathmandu, while Isabelle has a thousand-mile trek southwest to meet her friends in Goa. Without any trains running, it'll be a nightmare. So Steve has a proposal: drive to Delhi together, where she can find a bus south.

'But we have no car,' she notes.

'I'll buy one.'

Isabelle leans back, impressed, and agrees – provided that Theo joins. Although he says little, conversations fizzle when Theo steps away, prompting Steve to kiss her, kneading Isabelle's small chest as if to increase its volume, she waiting for the tall Dutch boy to return. As for Theo's travel plans, he mumbled something about seeing the mountains. Mostly, he dreads the departure of his acquaintances, with premonitions of solitude again in Room 9. But they want his presence on their roadtrip; they're insisting.

Two Swedish hippies accept traveller's cheques for a papaya-orange Volkswagen Beetle that they drove all the way here from Frankfurt. They warn that its clutch is erratic, the fan grinds, and the glove compartment falls open when you hit a pothole – but it goes. Theo takes the backseat, noticing that his shirt flutters over his chest, heart pulsing. What will he do in Delhi once they all split up? On this ride, he must tell them: I'm lost – please, help me.

Isabelle wants to drive the first part. She has no licence, but her father always let her drive in the French countryside. When she sits at the wheel, Steve – in the front passenger seat – slips his hand under her backside. She calls his bluff, half-standing in the cramped VW to pull off her skirt, just underpants now.

Steve is dismayed. 'What if Indian guys see you like that, and run us off the road, and rape you?' he asks. 'How would you feel then?'

'Not so good.'

'Put some clothes on.'

'You can protect me, Steve.'

'Do you not shave your legs?'

Once they're beyond the outskirts of Benares, Steve demands a piss break, so she pulls over. Without Steve, she and Theo discuss nothing but Steve. 'He knows not very much about the world,' Isabelle comments. 'But he is a beautiful man.'

'Is this why you like him?' Theo asks.

'Is this why you do?'

She points out that there are little curtains on the side windows of this car, but not much privacy. And where would Theo go, if she and Steve made love in this Beetle?

He's back, looking suspiciously at each of them. Steve tells Theo that it's his turn to drive, and pulls Isabelle into the backseat with him.

'I can't see anything from here,' she protests.

'You know what they say: no one rides for free.'

The windscreen magnifies the sun on Theo's face. He turns the key. The wheel shudders in his sweaty hands, and he blinks hard to look more directly at the road ahead: people crossing, motorbikes veering from nowhere, trucks bulldozing by. He could make a mistake.

'Let's move, man!'

Theo pulls out, foot hard on the gas to catch up with other cars, which snaps his neck back. He slows, swallowing, and glances in the rearview. They're writhing, Isabelle whispering for Steve to wait one second. Theo watches the cracked road rush under the car. I am a pointless human. A pink lorry baps its horn. His armpits prickle, mouth parched.

'You kill us almost!' Isabelle cries, red-cheeked and laughing. She clambers over the rattling gearbox, scooching into the front passenger seat.

At nightfall, they're still hours from the capital, so they park on a dirt road, the hissing of nature all around, punctuated by distant car horns. Lit by the VW dome light, they consume leftover samosas and bottles of warm Coca-Cola mixed with Old Monk rum, which spills on the car seats.

They must've all fallen asleep, for it's abruptly bright, their surroundings transformed: not the cobra-infested jungle of last night's fantasy but a public footpath fringed with bushes that they rudely parked on. Locals keep peeping through the car windows at these hairy zoo animals behind glass.

Steve drives the last stretch, speaking only to propose places to stop and have sex with her.

'You are crazy?' she replies. 'That is a village, Steve!'

The villages grow into towns, then suburbs, then a metropolis, people crouched at roadsides, sledge-hammering rocks, swatting flies at food stalls. They've reached the edge of Delhi, hemmed in by other vehicles, yet Steve keeps searching, turning his irritation against the traffic, punching the horn, holding it down. Nearing the city centre, he veers off the road, halting on the soft-shoulder, pedestrians bounding aside, looking at him with bemusement. 'Here. Right here.'

'I don't understand,' she says.

'Nobody cares! This whole fucking country's on strike! Come on!' He's out of the car, and pulls open her door, yanking her arm; she resists. 'Under that bridge.'

'But there are people!' she exclaims. 'They are everywhere!'

He marches all the way to a stony outcrop at the water's edge that is strewn with wet laundry, washermen standing around, observing Steve with perplexity. After a moment, he turns back, shouting to Theo: 'You take lookout!'

Isabelle is shaking her head. 'It is not possible.'

Jogging ahead, Steve prowls around for a secluded space, unwilling to quit, ending up faraway – before turning back, sprinting toward them, full-speed, so fast that Isabelle tenses for impact, her shoulder turned protectively. At the last instant, he stops, crouches to level his face and hers, both hands on her shoulders. He looks to the sky. He screams. And he strips to his underpants.

'Steve? What you are doing?'

Leaving a pile of clothes at her feet, he turns and sprints back down the stony outcrop, dodging washermen and barking at ragged children, who dart aside.

'Steve!'

He leaps, appearing to levitate for two seconds – before the river crashes, an explosion of brown that bursts up, and swallows him. Isabelle and Theo watch where he plunged, the empty surface swaying, lapping against itself.

IF YOU MUST, YOU'LL kill to protect yourself. 'The threat,' Mr Bhatt mutters to his cluttered desk, 'the threat is us.'

A shiver passes through him, for he senses something potent in that phrase. He tries stating it aloud with varying emphases, finger jabbing at a different word each time: 'The *threat* is us.' Or: 'The threat is *us*.' Or: 'The threat *is* us.' Lastly: '*The* threat is us' – by which point, he has sapped the phrase of sense.

We in government (to whom Mr Bhatt addresses his thoughts), we in government are not cruel. We do *not* propose hurting anyone. The opposite. Consider this like conscription during a military invasion. And make no mistake: we *are* invaded. In this conflict, self-elimination is not cowardice but courage. Therefore, Madam Prime Minister, therefore –

He reaches an edge, the confines of his imagination. Mr Bhatt leafs through the library book of suicide notes, seeking a breakthrough, a clue, the key to what inspired such acts. But most of the notes were, frankly, written when drunk.

He drags from the typewriter roller his incomplete letter to Mrs

Gandhi, and threads in a fresh piece of paper, which wavers under the ceiling fan while he summons eloquence to match that of his freedom-fighter grandfather, who composed historic missives at this very desk. At length, Mr Bhatt holds still, hands motionless above the keys, only the flicker of a baby finger, nothing to fling steel against paper. What is it that stirs the valiant to act? They long to escape smallness, to step from the pullulating crowd, to proclaim their true soul rather than the stammering botched version of daily life. In a stunning single act, they express all that they stood for. Thus what once made them cling to life is exactly what inspires them to surrender it. Yes, *that* is it!

He jumps to his feet, then hurriedly back to the chair. Type!

But what?

The notion is slipping away. What connects Mr Bhatt to his own life? What would *he* sacrifice everything for? He pictures his beloved, and how he'd want them to remember him. Suddenly, *clackety-clack* fills the room. Black words accumulate down the white page, preceding slightly his knowledge of what they'll be, so that Mr Bhatt is informed of his own beliefs by reading the page before him. He intended merely to list what men give their lives for. But the writing got away from him, becoming a citation of those he loved, then an apology to his wife and son for his failings, weaknesses he'd never admit aloud, least of all to those so dear. Mr Bhatt confesses that he hasn't done what he wanted in life; that he isn't as clever as they think. If they heard this, it'd murder their admiration of him. He squeezes his thigh to think it – then turns with a start. 'No!'

He pulls out the page, slapping it face-down on the desk. 'I told you! You are *not* allowed!'

Ajay looks down at his shoes, mumbling that Maa wants the maid to clean up here, that she says his office is a fire hazard.

'Did I ask for the maid? Can you not see I am working?!'

Ajay registers his father's face, the wet streaks downward, so Mr Bhatt brushes down his moustache, stamps his foot, then rises in a huff, clanging down the outside stairs, unsure of his destination, inflating the fury to hide that he has no reason for it. 'Chased from my own home!' He bangs on the roof of his empty Ambassador. 'Where are you, Jandhu?' His driver is chatting with the caretaker in the park, and jogs over.

In the backseat, Mr Bhatt jiggles his leg, wanting to return upstairs. He never knows how to ask pardon. Equally, he is poor at tyranny. So he bullies a cigarette, yanking it from the packet, scraping the match so violently across the box that it snaps. Jandhu asks where to.

'I'm thinking!' A terrible thought it is: that page, still up there, face-down on his desk. What if Ajay noticed him flipping it over, and turns it back, seeing his father's barest feelings? Or if Meera reads it?

He orders Jandhu to wait, and races back up the stairs, breathlessly barging into his office, causing the maid to gasp, and bow her head. He snatches the note off his desk – must eradicate it from all existence.

Once they're driving, Mr Bhatt winds down his squeaky car window, and is invaded by the beeps of motorists, the bleating of vendors. Uneven tarmac joggles his lighter flame till it kisses the cigarette tip, a burnt-toast smell supplanting the smog. He feels far more polluted by the folded page in his pocket, as if it contained a photograph of himself in an act of filth. Yet Mr Bhatt can't just fling this piece of paper from his car window into the gutter, full of dung and spittle and soggy newspaper pages; cannot dump his heartfelt feelings toward Meera and Ajay into that. He considers himself a modern man, unburdened by superstition. Yet he harbours certain convictions about cleanliness and dirt. To efface this embarrassing page, he should dispose of it in sacred waters. The closest point is Old Yamuna Bridge, where Mr Bhatt can roll down his window, and toss the note into the river below.

Vehicles are gridlocked as they feed onto the bridge, with a steady flow of pedestrians slogging along the verges. The baby-blue Ambassador lurches, stops, lurches, until they are gulped into the bridge's lower deck, sunlight blotted out. Mr Bhatt's eyes adjust, perceiving the spans of iron, a horse-drawn cart and a flatulent Rajdoot motorbike, cars and cars, people and people. If he threw the note from here, it'd never reach the side of the bridge. He must get out, and toss it directly down. When the car next idles in traffic, he opens the door. 'You go on,' he tells Jandhu. 'You go on!' He cannot have Jandhu witnessing this.

Mr Bhatt presses a handkerchief over his nose, moustache bristling at the exhaust stench. He pushes past scruffy pedestrians to reach the girders, and flicks his note through. The folded paper nose-dives on the other side, stuck there. He kicks his shoe at the fence. The page remains stuck.

Pulsing from the heat, Mr Bhatt tries again to reach it. Cannot. Nor can he leave his intimate self exposed there. A barefooted boy offers to fetch whatever precious object the rich man is seeking over the fence. Mr Bhatt refuses, but the boy is climbing regardless, so Mr Bhatt grabs his shirt, drags him back down, whereupon an unshaven uncle snatches the youth, slaps him, and leads him away. Mr Bhatt wipes his dirtied hands with the hankie. Shakily, he climbs up the fence himself, and lowers himself to the outside of the bridge, steadying himself by clutching huge bolts in the ironwork.

He smells the river below, the effluent of his city. Behind him, a couple of rowdies laugh, and he shouts back cutting remarks, then returns to his giddy view: placid blue above, gushing brown below.

On the riverbanks, dhobis scrub undershorts, flanked by heaps of linen drying under the sun. A washerman slaps a shirt against the rocks, slaps it again. This, Mr Bhatt thinks, is why mine miss all their buttons. He stoops – still holding onto an iron bolt – and retrieves the folded note. He scrunches it up, and reels his arm back to throw the balled-up paper.

But he hears splashing down there: a tourist boy has jumped into the river, and is hollering in English to his two friends, a skinny girl and a lanky fellow who stand on the rocks, mindless that the dhobis are trying to work there. The girl hollers at the swimmer, and hands her beedi to the tall boy, who takes a puff, exhaling fast.

So disappointing, the grade of young person who visits India. Mr Bhatt's ire doubles to realize something: he can't dispose of this page now. The river below is filthy with hippie. What if a breeze caught his writing, and the swimmer collected it? Those creeps, bandying his private feelings around! Bloody foreigners – they should go back where they came from.

Carefully, he shimmies along the outside ledge of the bridge, distancing himself from the swimmer. Mr Bhatt holds to girders as he goes, one hand on iron, the other on the scrunched page.

The sun is burning him but he won't wipe away the ticklish

sweat beads, lest he smears bridge dirt on himself, and how would he explain that when home? He chortles, contemplating himself up here, imagining what his nervous mother-in-law, Parvati, would make of such a sight! He will be sorry once the trains resume, and a first-class carriage rolls her home. Ajay will return to boarding school too. Mr Bhatt suffers a pang: the house empty again.

Throughout Ajay's sojourn, Mr Bhatt has sought to impress the boy, as his own father impressed him, an eminence at a writing desk – the same desk where his father took his life. When that happened, they rushed Mr Bhatt back to boarding school, forbade him to tell anyone, but he did, and forever regretted it, that people knew.

All that Mr Bhatt wants, he suddenly recognizes, is his son near. Why send Ajay to the boarding school that he himself hated? Why can't Ajay stay at home? Mr Bhatt will find activities for the boy – they can read the same books, discuss them. He'll show Ajay everything he knows, and Ajay will soon know more. He mustn't become like me. Mr Bhatt draws a shaky breath, sweat trickling, then is distracted by the riverbank: the sopping hippie getting out, shaking like a dog. The river below is clear, so Mr Bhatt can dispose of this letter. But with his free hand, he first struggles to open the crumpled page, wanting a last look.

He stares at the crinkled paper, perplexed, as if the victim of a cruel magician. This was his confession. But all it says is: 'Madam Prime Minister.'

Mr Bhatt searches his memory: rushing upstairs to his study, the maid there, she gasping in fright, looking submissively at her bare feet, he grabbing the page.

The wrong page. He took the wrong page. His confession is still there, beside the typewriter.

His stomach muscles tighten, innards clenched. He needs to get home *immediately*.

Something else, though: he must ask Meera what they should do. He is young still. She is too. And their greatest joy is that child.

THE DHOBIS ARE LOOKING at the bridge, talking to each other. Theo shades his eyes to see. A little man in a seersucker suit stands on the outside, edging slowly down the ledge, a piece of paper fluttering in his hand. Abruptly, he loses balance, and grabs for the bridge – but drops the page. He snatches at air. The paper floats lazily down, landing silently atop the water, seconds after the man's splash.

In nervous surprise, Isabelle laughs. The washermen call out.

Underwater, bubbles fizz around Mr Bhatt, his glasses lost, a shoe gone too, cheek and ribs buzzing where he hit the surface. Each time he opens his eyes, he sees only stinging darkness.

Whatever air remains in his lungs he leaks from pursed lips, flailing his arms and legs. He can't tell which direction is the surface, and opens his eyes in a frenzied search for brightness. Guess wrong, and he'll paddle toward the bottom.

His body howls for oxygen while his mind shouts back: Do *not* open your mouth. Veins swell in his neck. Another air bubble tickles his ear, drifting sideways.

Sideways! The air is rising that way! Sideways is up!

He attacks the water, which cedes and resists at once. But he *is* moving, his starved lungs excruciatingly tight, and he. He almost. Just. Brighter. Much brighter now.

He bursts into sunlight, hitting at the water surface with force, gasping, his vision fuzzed. The river is still pulling him from below. He tries to kick off his remaining shoe, which is inundated, like a stone laced around his foot. He can't rotate his arms in this suit jacket, so tries to slough it off, but his head goes under each time, and he gasps back to the surface, coughing and spitting. A soldier stands atop the bridge. Mr Bhatt shouts for help, swallowing water.

Isabelle turns to Steve, who wrings out his wet hair, then picks distractedly at a grey blister on his foot. 'He can drown!' she says, then shouts at the dhobis, who reply in Hindi. They are calling to the man, who keeps disappearing, then bobbing up in a churn of arms and froth.

'None of *them* is diving in,' Steve tells her.

'He is in trouble!'

'*You* go then,' he says. 'It reeks in there.'

'I cannot pull a man from a river! I am not so strong! Come on, Steve!' She cups her hands around her mouth, shouting: 'You are okay? You need help?'

The man in the water turns slightly, another cough-sputter.

'He can't understand you,' Steve says. 'He only speaks Indian.'

As Theo watches all this around him, a peculiar sensation overcomes him: that everything led to this instant. That this was supposed to happen. That, somehow, it's about him.

'What you are doing?' Isabelle asks.

Theo kicks off his sneakers, pulls down his filthy jeans. He doesn't care: not ashamed of himself, not worrying about the acne on his back, or the body odour. The coldness of water shortens his breath.

It's sharp underfoot and slippery. He pushes off, chin ploughing through white laundry foam, a chemical stench that causes him to close his lips, drawing a warm breath through his nose. Long hair covers his eyes, so he ducks under, then comes back up, flicking aside his soaking locks. He spits, swimming fast, strong and certain in the river.

After a minute, he treads water to orient himself, a momentary inner tremor at the nothingness below – then he resumes, swimming the crawl diagonally across the waterway because the current is dragging that man downriver. Theo's eyes close, his face dips under, head turning, oxygen again, face in the water, head turning, another breath, kicking.

Mr Bhatt takes another coughing gasp of air. The sky is a featureless blue without his glasses. Something occurs to him: he has nothing to tell Mrs Gandhi. He deserves no public role. All his countrymen, all the coming catastrophes – he has no power to avert anything. One man can't save mankind. Not a small man.

His body still fights. But his mind is detaching.

Then horror awakens him: if he dies, Meera and Ajay will read the note by his typewriter, and it won't look like a confession of love. They'll discover his satchel of library books, and see the topic.

But it's not *that*! He would never!

He pictures Ajay, informed by strangers, as Mr Bhatt once was, needing words from his father, who is an absence of words forever.

In terror, Mr Bhatt's energy surges, a greater drive than ever in his life. He simply *refuses* to leave Ajay and Meera. It's clothing that pulls him down. If he takes the largest breath possible, and allows himself to sink, he can pull off the seersucker jacket, next his shoe, lastly the trousers. After, he'll surface, be light enough to stay afloat, and can doggy-paddle to shore.

He can do it. Right now!

He doesn't.

Mr Bhatt tries to embolden himself. Ordering himself to act.

Now.

Now!

At last, he sinks under, eyes closed, all attention on touch: first, his right shoe (no, wait: wasn't removing the jacket supposed to come first? Too late – pull off that shoe). Bending his knee, he struggles with the laces underwater. Cannot get his fingernails in the knot. He's turning upside-down, and must be sinking, for the water darkens.

He yanks at the knot, his fingers stiff, as if arthritic. Leave the damn shoe! Get the jacket off. He shakes at it, only tangling his arms in the sleeves.

His chest is bursting from need of air. He must get back to the surface, and try again. His arms are trapped behind him.

Mr Bhatt – teeth grinding, grinding, lips spreading finally – takes a sniff. His mouth opens, inhaling, throat flooding. Reflexively, he coughs and inhales, water filling his chest. Legs jutting, fists clenched, Mr Bhatt widens his jaw. His tongue sticks out, eyes bulging. His ribs shudder. Mr Bhatt goes still, arms behind him in the jacket sleeves, eyes gaping at blackness.

Theo keeps searching for that man who fell. Treading water, he turns back toward Isabelle and Steve, those from the rearview mirror, now calling soundlessly, bobbing there on the riverbank. The deafness of water amplifies his pulse. Theo flips to his back, and floats to gather his wits, haze above, chest trembling, breath out of sync.

The fallen man is gone. Theo's acquaintances are gone. Everyone is absent. He's suddenly exhausted, too far from land, drifting fast.

He flips onto his stomach, momentarily forgetting how to swim, falling beneath the surface for an instant – then back up. His vision is specked. In swimming class, a school instructor told them not to expend strength by fighting a current. Redirect yourself gradually. 'Do not panic' is the first rule. One of the students replied, 'Isn't "Do not panic" the first rule of everything?'

A ripping sensation up Theo's back and right leg – he lets out a yowl, and reaches around, running his fingers up his spine, finding a trench in the flesh, a sliver of himself gone yet without pain. Did he hit a submerged rock? Is there an animal down there, attacking him?

He kicks downward, his breaths too fast to catch. He touches his back compulsively, fetid water splashing into his mouth, the metallic taste of blood. He floats past more washermen on the bank, banging clothes on rocks. A little boy waves, shouting, 'Hallo!' The child runs along the river's edge, then is gone.

Upstream, Isabelle speed-walks along the riverbank as Steve ambles behind, she frantic for any sight of Theo. They keep passing people, and she asks if anyone saw their friend. The search assumes an unreal quality: an emergency, but nobody knows. They reach a factory installation. Nowhere farther to go. They hurry back, she scanning the water, Steve saying how dumb that guy was to jump in, if he couldn't swim well.

Suddenly, Steve shouts, 'He had my fucking car keys!'

48

'In his jeans?'

'Fuck! Everything's in that car: my passport, my plane ticket, my traveller's cheques. Why didn't you bring his stuff, Isabelle?'

'Why did *you* not?'

They run back to the promontory under the bridge, praying to find Theo's belongings. They're still in a heap: the tennis shoes, shirt, bell-bottom jeans, including the car keys. 'It's a miracle none of these Indians stole my car,' Steve remarks, and continues to the VW, popping the front trunk. 'All accounted for.' He returns with Theo's backpack, telling her, 'The guy'll be *fine*.'

'We leave his things here, you are saying? You want to go?'

'Well, what's your plan?'

'That we don't leave.'

'Come on – we can't stay here the rest of our lives. We wait a bit longer, then put his stuff on a rock or something.'

'Be quiet! I cannot think.'

'Look, I need a shower. You didn't go in that water.'

'This is what you are thinking right now?'

'Why are you shouting at me?'

'I am not shouting!'

'I smell like I took a bath in dog shit, alright? I need to get to the downtown, and find a hotel, and grab a shower. I'm not catching cholera out here. My Kathmandu flight leaves in two days.'

'Steve, you are not make sense. We are waiting for him.'

'*You* wait.'

'Fine! I wait!' She swears in French, collects her belongings from the car, and returns to the river's edge alone, smoking fiercely, counting how many beedis she has left, faint-headed.

Steve returns with their friend's passport. 'I'm stuffing this in his backpack.'

'No! You take all this to the embassy of his country! Right now! You tell them this happens. They bring people to help. Okay?'

'How am I supposed to know where the Dutch Embassy is?'

'You find it!'

'I bet you anything it's closed right now.'

'There is a railway strike, not a strike for diplomats. Come on!'

Steve walks off, amid the *thwack* of laundry hitting rocks. He guns the Volkswagen engine, and drives away.

Isabelle keeps walking along the riverbank until the factory blocks her, then back again, studying the water, each time passing the same little boy who says, 'Hallo!' Eventually, he's gone. It's dark now, and eerie.

Where are the officials from the Dutch Embassy? She can't stay here alone. It's not safe. Shivering, she walks to the road, where a sleeping auto-rickshaw driver leaps at the sound of her voice.

Over the next two days, she wanders around Delhi, brushing off touts who want to sell her a sari or change her money. She keeps looking for Steve, but never sees him. Are people searching for their friend? In a guest house in Paharganj, she meets a group of French boys heading to Goa. They offer her a seat in their camper van, if she can make herself narrow.

She mentions her missing acquaintance, how worried she is. One boy notes that it's the consulate, not the embassy, that she needed – his father was in the foreign service, so he knows. It's tough, he says: she doesn't have that Dutch boy's full name, nor any of his documents. But rest assured, he tells her, the Dutch will do what's appropriate. If it makes her feel better, he'll see if there's a consular official in Goa to check with. You did everything possible, the French boy assures her.

She relaxes into her seat in the van. She has a good feeling about Theo – just *feels* that he's safe (because she has a good feeling about her new friends, soothed to speak her language again, after too long translating every thought).

YEARS LATER, ISABELLE IS concluding a long career in human resources for a French supermarket chain. She has lived well off her salary, and owns a spacious apartment in Boulogne-Billancourt. Her granddaughter is planning a trip to India, inspired by Isabelle's hippie travels. Does she have any recommendations? Isabelle laughs. 'Oh, but the country has changed since I was there!'

For a few years after that trip, Isabelle went around claiming to understand Indian culture, dropping half-understood phrases into conversation – '*Achcha, achcha. Theek hai.*' Her cartons of Kodachrome never produced a single picture, though, due to an event that still upsets her. Upon returning from India, she couldn't afford to print hundreds of slides at once, so put the rolls of film away. Life scooped her up and deposited her in her most important love affair, a marriage, two children. In 1981, she scuffled with her husband, Charles (the French son of a diplomat, who'd enticed her to join his friends in their van to Goa). She hit him, then stormed out in fright at her act of violence. When she returned, he'd taken out all her Kodachrome from India, and stomped on every roll, pulling the black tongues of film out.

Isabelle goes online to help plan her granddaughter's trip, checking for reports of terrorism in South Asia. Gazing through bifocals at her iPad, she reads a review of a documentary by a Dutch filmmaker who went seeking a countryman who'd disappeared in India decades before. The missing youth's parents died awaiting his return. In the documentary, an Indian crook appears, variously claiming that a serial killer murdered him, or that he was kept confined for years – before the criminal admits that he knows nothing about the case. Isabelle pauses at the line, 'Nobody reported his disappearance at the time.'

What, she wonders, was the name of that boy she met in Benares? The name mentioned in this documentary doesn't ring a bell. It says he'd be in his mid-sixties, if alive. His older half-sister appears in the documentary, a minor Dutch novelist based in London, who explains that her brother had a depressive breakdown a year before his departure, and the trip was supposed to restore him. She wonders if he could be alive somewhere – not knowing has been agonizing. A photo of the teenage Dutchman accompanies the article; he's holding a beer bottle. The quality is poor, but the person looks unfamiliar to Isabelle.

At all the dinner parties of past decades, amid everyone's tut-tutting about conflict in the Islamic world, Isabelle bragged of her overland trip to India, which included a visit to Afghanistan. This was before the Taliban, she explained, before the Russian invasion even, before the mujahadeen. She saw men on mules with World War One rifles, and it was truly wild, and they smoked hash from conical pipes, and the women truly wore burkas – at the time, she'd only thought, *What beautiful fabric!* She recalled a grimy clinic in

Iran too, where she and a friend sold their blood for travel money, and girls in Tehran wore miniskirts back then – yes, in Tehran! Imagine! And an Indian rickshaw driver once picked her up near the river in Delhi, and she thought he was going to rape her, though he was merely pointing to a guest house, and this was a lesson about prejudice – an admission of humility that she declared proudly. Yet, at all those dinner parties, never once did she mention that Dutch boy whose name she can't remember.

Her granddaughter plans to roam freely in India, as Isabelle once did, not checking email or WhatsApp. She'll just post to Instagram now and then, and her family can follow her activities that way. Often, Isabelle has rhapsodized about travel before the internet. Nowadays, she says, people never really *go* to a place – abroad is imprisonment in the same packaged experience. (She herself hasn't travelled outside Europe this century, and frankly doesn't want to visit poor countries again.) In any case, she plans to set up an Instagram account as instructed, and hopes her granddaughter will be on the phone constantly.

Isabelle touches her iPad screen to see that article and the photo again. She recalls a ride down the Ganges, when they were rowed into the mist, the Dutch boy seated at the other end of the wooden boat, clutching onto the splintery sides, as if they might flip. She stood to take a photo of the cremation ghats, knowing this would impress everyone. That Canadian miner's son – what was his name? With the grey blister on his foot and the long blond hair. They didn't properly sleep together, did they? So much of her life has been forgotten.

On the bridge, there was that Indian man who fell. But was that definitely a person? Could it have been an object that looked like a person, as happened during the boat ride down the Ganges, when they agreed afterward that they'd seen a dead boy in the water, while the truthful ledger of her memory knew it was a charred log, or maybe a goat, though she talks to this day of once seeing a child's corpse floating in Benares?

The Indian on the bridge – he resembled an actor in a silent movie, a small man in a seersucker suit, tiptoeing along the girders, piece of paper flapping in his hand. A delay between splash and sound, then he vanished, the water shutting over him. And everything persisted, as if he never was.

DIARY: MARCH 2020

My taxi from Almería airport drives past arid landscape into a city that's charmless at first sight, with drab residential blocks and a concrete seaside walkway. I've rented an apartment here in the south of Spain because I'm nostalgic for how I wrote when younger. I'd go somewhere foreign, away from everyone I knew, accompanied by nothing but plot shards and character lumps. From these, I'd scrape out the contours of a book. For ten days here, I'll try again.

I open my old laptop at the dining table, sunlight glinting on silver keys. I typed fast once, but my fingers are less cooperative now, me pressing one letter, another appearing onscreen. I blame the machine. That's what machines are for.

Anyway, I'm coping, lenient about garbled words, persisting down my ramshackle sentences, a sharp turn at the end of each line, and on to the next. I'll tidy the chaos later.

Suddenly, I'm in darkness but for the glowing screen. Out on the balcony, I orient myself to the present again, the night below streaked with headlamps of mosquito-droning mopeds. During hours of concentration, I hardly noticed how crippling that kitchen chair was. I'm on a high: working and alone.

This solitary practice of mine started when I was around twenty, after an argument in Paris. I'd moved there less than a year earlier, and found a German sculptor, whose mattress I shared in a Rue Saint-Denis garret.

Klaus considered my body and my language mistakes endearing (I speak German, having grown up near the border), so he planned our summer in his native Bavaria, where we'd hike and eat indigestible sausages. But at the train station for our departure, I precipitated a row. I didn't believe my side of the argument, so grew more heated. In truth, my objection was unstated: that he wanted to stomp up pointy mountains in leather shorts within the long-lashed gaze of awkward cows, whereas I wanted nothing of the kind. I'd grown up among farms in the Netherlands, and the whiff of manure and the sight of land that went on endlessly — it felt like regression.

The result was that he boarded in a huff ('Don't come then!'), and I obliged, gone before the train whistled. All the way back from Gare de l'Est, I lugged my leather suitcase (always a strong young woman), and mounted his building's spiral staircase, its wooden steps groaning about me for six flights. Sweating, breathing hard, I closed the door after myself, and flung open the windows, wide enough to risk pigeons. All this oxygen, and it was mine alone.

But what to do? In that apartment, sloping ceilings precluded shelves, so his books were strewn across the floor. After stubbing my toes on the greats of German literature, I crouched to see what a few had to say. There I sat, cross-legged, reading. Eventually, I dragged a letter pad onto my lap, and attempted a story myself. Time lost count, replaced by utter focus. When I stopped, I held still but remained elsewhere, my cheeks hot, mind befogged.

I went slightly mad. For weeks, I produced pages and pages that I never read, fearful to break the spell. Otherwise, I walked the streets, and watched people, and ate bread. How long could I go without speaking to anyone but myself? But perhaps I was a writer – maybe an important one! Until, gradually, the isolation gnawed into me. My scrutiny of characters turned around, fixing on me now, noting how I was pitiful and devious and false. I found myself studying a plaster medallion where the light fixture hung. I imagined myself hanging there.

Nowadays, I repress dark thoughts by outstriding them in a London park, the same park every day. In the evenings, I titrate my mood with wine. Above all, I must work, or another plunge follows.

To avoid madness while in Spain, I conduct a daily outing, speed-thudding along the Almería seaside walkway toward the fish-scented port, under palm trees that have unclasped their dates, sticky beneath my functional shoes.

An Arab busker – bald and toothless, though barely thirty – is playing the musical saw, stroking a bow along the blade in a wavering rendition of 'Nessun Dorma', his tinny boombox swelling with orchestral accompaniment. A family of stray cats listens on a boulder at the sea's edge, a wave charging toward them, then changing its mind.

The busker notices me, this stiff old walker marching down the promenade. In tribute, he switches songs – 'Fools Rush In' by Elvis – and catches my smile, pleased with himself. He calls to me.

'Sorry,' I reply in passing, waving my hand, balled into a friendly fist, 'don't speak Spanish.'

On my return, he hails me again, this time in English: 'You! Coming here!' He asks my name, then makes a praying gesture, turning this finger-steeple downward, to a cup on the pavement. 'You can help me, Miss Dora?'

'I've got no coins on me.'

He shows me his smartphone: an app lets you send a contribution. He pings the details to my number, and I resume my walk, promising to register later – I'll donate then.

I'm back at the laptop, poking the wrong keys and some of the right ones, so near to the lines that they're places with people in them, hinting and scowling. Hours later, I stand, trying to rectify my bent spine by jutting my elbows backward. I'm tipsy from hope (could this book turn out well?), sobered by fact (few will care), and I want more, so sit again, knobbled hands on the keyboard, fading eyes on the screen.

Eventually, my time in Spain elapses, and I'm awaiting a flight home, seated at an outdoor patio in the airport. I wrote on a high, describing people with none around. Now I'm in a crowd again, watching an elderly Englishwoman with pink hair and befuddled gaze smoking a Marlboro, her white-haired husband toying with his nose ring. They have no reason to talk after all these years. The trip is over.

Why am I holding my phone right now? Oh, yes – that donation app. I was going to send the busker something. But a Twitter notification distracts me. My literary agent has told me I should start tweeting. Writers (we at the lower tiers) must cajole and beg the public to take an interest. But I've never yet wanted to blurt this way. Instead, I scroll past culture-war spatter, reading updates about this virus from China, which is spreading to other countries. A death was reported in Los Angeles, and a stand-up comic joked about it, and everyone is furious, except those who are furious at the furious. In northern Italy, entire cities are under quarantine, as during medieval plagues. An opera singer belts out an aria, and everyone looks irritably at me, for I'm struggling to lower the volume on this YouTube clip: a tenor serenading locked-down Italy from his window.

'. . . those seated in rows sixteen to thirty-six are now invited to . . .'

Before boarding, I drag my rolling bag to the toilets. Crammed in a tiny stall, I sit and urinate while finishing the clip, screen out of focus, which causes me to extend my phone arm, then draw it near, nearly fumbling the phone into the toilet.

'. . . any remaining passengers for EasyJet 8164 to London Gatwick please proceed immediately . . .'

Once in my window seat, I wake the laptop, considering my work of the past days. Instantly, I'm through an escape-hatch, that writerly privilege of elsewhere – till my stomach is hiked skyward, the plane's nose tilting upward, my warm shoulders pushed against the seatback.

Above a twinkling Spanish sea, the plane wheels around, turning toward England, and I peer down, insistently not falling through plexiglass, my gut fluttery from height and from hope, for I've figured out how this book could work.

I turn from clouds back to screen, and tinker with the opening of Chapter Three.

A car door slams. She cannot make out what they're saying outside.

Or

Her bare thighs are cold.

Or

She's on the toilet, reading Twitter.

3

The novelist's
estranged daughter

(BECK FRENHOFER)

S HE'S ON THE TOILET, reading Twitter. Beck never tweets –
it'd waste material or require her to stake a position. But she
does follow 3,246 accounts, scrolling down an infinite ladder of
pop-culture yammering and emotional spray.

Do men read their phones like this, given that they urinate
standing? How could they look at the screen while avoiding the
floor? Actually, they *don't* avoid the floor – but they were splashing
it long before the Digital Age.

She wonders if this could work as a bit for one of her male
stand-up comics: a middle-aged schlub at the bowl, checking notifications; he far-sightedly extends his smartphone, cutting the piss
stream, which bounces back over him. He's drenched, and on a date.

She hears a bang outside. Beck holds still, listening. Nothing
more.

What'd the guy be looking at on his phone to make it funnier? He urinates on the video for 'Baby Shark'? Nah, too cheap. What about an appeal for Afghan girls wounded in war, and he soaks them, and tries to explain it to his politically committed date? Goddamn it – she has the chorus of 'Baby Shark' stuck in her head now.

A car door slams. Men are speaking Spanish outside her house. What's that moaning?

The phone rings, and Beck fumbles it between her legs, slamming them closed just in time, pinning the iPhone, warm glass between her thighs. But she trapped only a corner. The rest dangles over yellow water.

It keeps ringing, trembling her thigh flab as she slides a hand under her legs. She raises her clenched knees, grunting, but lacks the stomach muscles. Her legs flop back down, followed by a plop-splash that chills her buttocks. The ringtone gargles.

Through wavy water, she reads caller ID – *Adam* – and snatches toilet paper: a mini-squat, swipe, unsure where to dispose of it. Not atop Adam. She chooses the basin, and yanks up her boxer briefs and sweatpants, the iPhone death-rattling against porcelain. Gotta do it: she sticks her hand in, the sleeve of her hoodie sopping. Beck wipes the phone across her chest. 'Hey, can you hear me?'

'Kinda. Where are you?'

'I soaked my phone. A toileting issue.'

'Don't wanna know,' her manager says. 'I'm just checking in with clients before we run screaming from the office. Everyone's home-working for the rest of this week – a test-run in case they lock us down.'

'They need to say this in iPhone ads, don't you think? "Takes a drippin', and keeps on clickin'." Should I rinse it?'

'What, you didn't? You're talking right now on a pissy phone?'

'I dab-dried. Can I put it under the tap?'

'What the hell, Beck! I work for Apple now? Ask a Genius. I'm calling about J.J.'

'Are you getting that crackling noise?'

'The special – we must discuss.'

'I can see my day unfolding at Verizon now.'

'Are they even open?'

'They better be. Phone people are essential workers.'

'I haven't decided if *I'm* essential,' Adam says.

'Everyone is unnecessary except the deliverymen.'

'Watch the J.J. special. Okay? We gotta discuss.'

The moaning outside is louder. Beck raises the bathroom blinds.

A gardening-company truck is parked on her street, cab doors open. Three workmen have got out, and are looking at something on the road, hands on hips. She reaches the landing window for a better view. On the tarmac, a body twitches. It's Rodney.

SHE BURSTS FROM HER house, and the gardeners take a step back. One climbs into the cab of the truck, and calls the others to join him.

Beck kneels before her bull-terrier, his hind leg kicking, as when he dreams on the couch. But the motion is off, a malfunctioning machine. His lower lip is slack, black gums bared, a thread of slobber pooling on the warm road.

The gardeners' truck grinds into reverse, backs around the corner.

Alone on her residential street in Venice Beach, she lifts Rodney onto the grass, consoling him, her voice shaking.

Minutes later, a burgundy Prius creeps up. The driver's window whirs down, and a middle-aged Persian woman unhooks her surgical mask, careful about the lipstick. 'Uber?'

'Could you open the door?'

'Where you are going?'

'I put it in the request. The animal hospital up Broadway. Open the door, please.'

'Yes, but you are not putting "animal" in request.'

'How do I put "animal" in getting an Uber?'

'You can put "animal".'

'I need to get him to the vet. This is urgent.'

'I take *you*, no problem. But not animal.'

Beck tries to control herself. 'You're out of your fucking mind!' That didn't go well. She needs this person. But something overflowed, and she can't restore it. 'You want to take *me* to the vet, without my dog? Are you insane?!'

'You can cancel the ride, please?'

'Why, so you get a cancel payment? No fuckin' way. Take me to the hospital!'

'Do not call me words. Everyone is under pressure with everything.' The driver hooks the surgical mask back around her ear. 'You can work with me, please?' She steps from the Prius, takes the long way around it, pops the trunk, and finds a pink beach towel with the image of a cartoon princess and the logo *LOL Surprise!* 'Any blood on backseat, and you are paying holstery. Also money I am losing while not drive. Is okay?'

'Can we go please?' Beck wraps the pink towel around her dog, and gets into the back, Rodney on her lap, his eyes blinking slowly, though he is limp.

The driver takes Beck's phone, and reads aloud the animal hospital's new coronavirus directives on dropping off customers. She starts the car engine. 'Why your phone smells like toilet?'

ON THE SIDEWALK BEFORE the veterinary hospital, there's a queue: a ferret on a leash; a cat box; a lime parakeet in a cage. The owners watch Beck struggle from the Prius. 'He got hit by a car,' she tells them.

'Get in line,' the ferret owner says.

'It's an emergency.'

'Everything's an emergency if it's your emergency.'

'No. Some things are actual emergencies.'

The owners of the cat and parakeet move aside for her. The ferret owner just strokes his long ponytail. Beck's arms shake from the weight of Rodney. A sign on the clinic door says: *For safety of staff and customers during this time of global pandemic, we allow only one person in at a time! Thank you cooperation!*

In her frenzied state, she reads the sign over and over. She's still second in line when Rodney dies. Upon realizing, Beck draws a pained breath, then others, trying to calm herself. She won't rest him on the pavement. She can't see clearly, her eyes stinging. Soon, she's presenting a credit card, signing a form, giving them her friend, her arms still trembling from the weight, even after handing him over. The parakeet still waits outside, its owner averting her gaze.

Beck opens the door to her house only a crack – an outdated habit to prevent Rodney from bolting. Most evenings, they'd sit on the couch, she tickling his stomach, turning to meet his gaze. Why didn't she barge into that clinic instead of deferring to a ferret?

She turns on the TV for the distraction of noise: 'I *know*, Kelly! You're telling me, girl!' Clenching her hands, she keeps noticing objects: tattered leash, a squeaky rubber chicken. She walks down the back steps into her overgrown yard, finding a breach under the wooden fence where Rodney must've escaped. Beck wonders if there's something faulty about her, something repellent: he had food and affection, but scratched his way out of her presence.

She stamps down the dirt-fringed tunnel, but is running out of tasks. No distractions in a minute. She powers down her phone to rinse it in the downstairs bathroom, the pee still unflushed, three sheets of toilet paper in the basin. When she tries to restart her iPhone, it won't. She charges it. Nothing. It's neither living nor dead, everyone she knows locked inside.

Her only internet access is a thick old laptop. She hasn't used it in weeks, and finds herself logged off Instagram and Facebook and Twitter. The 'Forgot Your Password?' reminders go to Gmail – but this too has expelled her, and will admit her only through verification on the defunct phone. So Beck is stuck, banished to the outskirts of the internet, with access to nothing but news sites with their old-fashioned 'front pages', featuring Italian opera singers performing on balconies and angry Chinese waiting outside hospitals. California reported its first death.

She surveys the couch cushions, indented where Rodney lay, and raises the TV volume. Beck can't decide whether to tell everyone about Rodney tonight, or say nothing ever. She keeps hearing moans: looking out the landing window; oh God.

What she needs is work, the distraction of watching comics perform. At the club tonight, she'll waylay a Gen Z opener, and ask her to fix the iPhone. But there's a problem: no phone, no Uber. How to get anywhere? The only comedy showcase reachable by foot is a mediocre room in Santa Monica.

Beck assumes her public look: short hair gelled and mussed into hard little shark fins; nerd glasses; roomy blue jeans and green Fluevog shoes; a button-down men's dress shirt, neck size too large, which gives the inadvertent impression of a little head on huge shoulders. She lumbers up the street, skin cool and guts roasting. Few cars are out. The stores are all shut. At the barred entrance to the comedy theatre, she glimpses a barman inside, doing inventory. He opens the door for her.

'What happened?' she asks. 'One of you guys caught the plague?'

'Nah, they shut our shit down. Everyone's out now: the Improv, the Store, the Factory, Largo.'

There's nothing to add when not discussing line-ups. 'My dog just died,' she says.

'Shit. Why?'

'Mexican gardeners hit him.'

'What, with their fists?'

'Jesus! No. With a fuckin' truck.'

'On purpose?'

'This is not the conversation I expected when saying my dog just died.'

'Sorry, Beck. I suck at sympathy. Or is that empathy?'

'Both. You suck at both.'

Long ago, back in the days when Wall Street was (briefly) ashamed of the Financial Crash and comedians were just setting up social-media accounts, Beck still did stand-up in New York, shambling up to the microphone in white Reeboks, sidestepping tables, gazes of the late-late crowd stabbing her, she more conscious of her gait than since schooldays, realizing that she hadn't yet mastered walking. She can summon it still: the metallic smell of the mic, damp with that night's stand-up spittle; dust particles in the spotlight; her airway refusing to cooperate, as if the crowd were seated on her, jumping up and down to close an overstuffed suitcase.

She was hopeless, all flop-sweat and rushed material, so dry-mouthed that you could hardly make out the words. At her final open-mic, someone in the crowd was sniffing throughout. 'So, wait,' a comic asked years later, 'it was quiet enough to hear people *sniffing*?'

She hasn't faced a crowd in years, and is unknown to the public. Yet Beck Frenhofer is among the most influential comedians of her generation.

WHEN THE COMEDY CLUBS were still open, Beck killed her day-light hours at home, snacking and lurking online until someone switched the lights out over Los Angeles, and she found a bar stool in the vicinity of chlorinated toilets, sipping a screwdriver and flinging back salted peanuts as another untalent mugged the microphone.

Each set she disassembled in her head, noting the progressions from set-up to punchline to tag, judging each comic's stagecraft too. Beck experiences comedy as a mechanical object: punchlines to reverse-engineer, premises to screw down, misdirection to hammer in, callbacks to tighten. Rarely does she laugh; jokes don't have that effect on her. But she is addicted to watching defectives expose their worst experiences for the amusement of drunks. She studies audiences too, all those cackling faces – plus the few who can't laugh, so look around, flinching if they meet her gaze.

Comics arrive in generations, the same crew at the same open-mics and pay-to-play rooms; then hosting their own shows just to get stage time, shelling out for a rental space and a sound system and nobody comes, which might be the funniest part of the evening. Despite all that, the newbies – going up at ridiculous hours, throttling the mic stand, competing with an espresso machine – come offstage wild-eyed, abuzz from a mix of fame and shame, wanting to punch, to fuck, to go again. It's a battle against the public, and the comedian *must* prevail.

Those who endure lap up years of humiliation, which makes stand-up an art in purest form: one's inner life for the applause of strangers. Eventually, a member of each generation finds a manager, books commercials, pitches a sitcom, and that person coat-tails a couple of friends along with them, while the rest panic because nobody downloads their podcasts, and it's nearly a decade of this shit, and they've wrecked their lives, so can't stop now. They hate-hug in the parking lot outside the venue, gossip about who's banging which wait staff, and smile about the ex-headliner who crashed his electric scooter on Sunset.

Gradually, each generation thins out, retreating back through the stage curtain – those who return to designing webpages full-time, or finish the philosophy degree, or raise a kid someplace with lawn sprinklers, saying Beck should totally visit, meaning it not meaning it. A handful become hacky road comics, suddenly plump, gradually old. One guy's wife and infant perished in a fire while he performed out of town, and when he returned after the double funeral, a fellow stand-up quipped, 'Hey, folks – Mr Complain is back!' At the comics' table, everyone laughed. To say 'too much' is treason.

Other comedians envy her connections, her knowledge, her income. But none wants her career. If you search the name 'Beck Frenhofer' online, the credits are minimal: a year writing for a network sketch show at the turn of the millennium; a gig in the Oscars writers' room; producer of one movie, *Bad Baby*, which was panned but became a cult hit (buying her this house).

But non-disclosure agreements hide the reality of her career. Behind the scenes, Beck has written for many of the biggest comics, those too busy or too depressed to piece together a new set. What happens is that Netflix offers a stand-up star huge money for a special, but the comic can't expend months touring a new act, especially when any audience member could secretly film it, and upload to YouTube, deflating the product right there. So Beck – whose gift is writing material that mimics anyone's shtick – will compose their sets. She's a trick of the trade, like those script doctors whose names appear in no credits but who wrote half the movies in Hollywood.

She has a second role in comedy too, this one unpaid, as agony aunt to the ego-crushed. Her greatest gratification comes from helping newcomers. Yet more than a few comics dislike her presence, she sitting there at the bar, judging them. A few months back, she was advising a young female comic at The Comedy Store, when a male headliner walked past, saying, 'Hey, hey, hey – it's the lesbo casting couch.'

Recalling this, Beck picks up her phone, which is where she goes when wanting to feel worse. Only a black reflection. On her laptop, she reaches the Verizon chatbot, and requests a replacement phone, her messages brusquer than she'd be with a human. She wonders if there's a bit in that: how rude can you be to a robot?

She hates this habit of refashioning any brain blip into material. As a young comic, her routine was a patchwork of other stand-ups' styles. What she wanted was to be admired while revealing nothing. Her work now, impersonating the foibles of others, hearing crowds holler in adoration for a guy who wrote none of that – it has levied a cost, corroding Beck, turning her cynical: that the public are stupid; that her peers are deluded self-interest machines; that we'll never fix politics; that the climate is done; that everything ends badly. Whenever she felt a flicker of hope, Beck spoke of it to Rodney, that quizzical little face looking at hers, then a lick. She just paid to incinerate him. Beck tears up, and pinches her stomach hard. Is it too late to stop them? Could she bury him in her backyard?

She googles 'dog's body in garden'. The first result is an ad for Dogsbody, an online task marketplace connecting you with free-lancers who'll do household chores. Its homepage features a beautiful woman of indeterminate race holding a plunger and beaming because your plumber is a moral choice. Dogsbody also has moral carpenters and moral cleaners, each rated out of ten. Beck clicks a name with such an abundance of emojis that she wonders if 'ROSA 😊 😄 😊

😎😌😊😹😷😇🙃😊😼' is cognitively impaired. The person has ticked every skill possible – either the most capable human in history or the least.

Beck shuts the website, and seeks a contact form for the veterinary hospital. Yet ads for Dogsbody trail her around the internet. In an attempt to stop this, she clicks one. Minutes later, she finds herself sending a price enquiry.

hey there!!!! hows it goign! Rosa replies. **What douneed?**

four hrs housework, Beck types.

?4people?

four HOURS

tuesday good;'/??

Beck almost replies, **Are you having a stroke right now?** but deletes it, and forces herself to her feet, looking out the window over her backyard. After the break-up – after Laura left, to be exact – Beck picked a fight with the housekeeper, and dismissed the woman. Her home has become a dump since, the carpeting grey with dust where it abuts the walls, the garden a jungle.

Everywhere is decay, she thinks. The global pandemic is only the start. Why are people surprised? The shock is that humans never destroyed the planet with nuclear weapons. But there's time.

She waits on the front porch till a random dude passes, and offers him a Breville centrifugal juicer in exchange for using his phone.

'You jacked it?' he asks.

'Did I steal my juicer? No, I bought it on Amazon. My phone just died, and I need to call someone.'

Uncertainly, he pulls a banged-up phone from his back pocket. She dials her manager.

Adam is suspicious at the unrecognized number, then hears her voice. 'Hey, you hung up on me before,' he says. 'What's up with that?'

'I didn't hang up. I screamed, and the line dropped. You never even tried to get in touch. I could've been in three suitcases by now.'

'If I called the cops every time a client screamed and hung up on me . . .'

'Rodney died.'

'No way! I am *so* sorry, Beck. Did I ever meet Rodney?'

'My dog, you asshole. He got hit by a truck.'

'Ohmigod! What happened?'

'He fucking died. Didn't I open with that?'

It's a problem in the ha-ha business: transitioning from ironic to sincere. Few have solved this. Adam responds by messaging an intern (his whole team is home-working; a nightmare), and the kid is ordered to drive to Beck's with toilet paper, and transport her malfunctioning phone to Verizon.

'Why toilet paper?'

'Have you visited a store lately?'

'What, there's no toilet paper in greater Los Angeles, except in the possession of your interns?'

'Correct. CAA has cornered the market.'

'Could your intern possibly take my phone, and *not* bring it back? I feel I'm done with notifications; I feel notified.'

'Did you watch the J.J. Carmelo special I sent?'

'Not yet, no.'

'Beck!' Adam has pestered her about watching this for weeks, needing her notes on the rough edit. She loathed that writing gig,

72

and has no contractual obligation to watch the result. Beck had known J.J. by nodding acquaintance before his Live+ special. The man cultivated a prickish air, onstage and off. Sometimes, prickish means shy. Sometimes, it means prick. Here, it meant prick.

He'd come from the Bronx, doing blue comedy in the 1980s, hef-Italian, hef-Puerto Rican, specializing in what used to be called 'ethnic material'. He chain-smoked, and swaggered through tales of snorting coke off Dominican hookers' backs, crashing his Trans-Am, and running from the scene of domestic assaults. In late career, he's come to resemble an ageing Leonard Cohen without the dignity, tufts of hair in his ears, tennis shorts, white tube socks, Air Jordans. He looks like a heart attack in a race-track toilet, unmissed till next Tuesday. Except that something happened: the era of unintended consequences.

Streaming-video channels need fresh content, and the cheapest was stand-up. You film a special in a night or two, the material comes audience-tested, with minimal production values, an intro of the performer plodding along a city street, entering the theatre, the crowd's hilarity filmed with three cameras, footage straight to the editing booth, PowerPoint marketing plan, release date, upload, done. In parallel, comedians' podcasts took off, hours of shop-talk that, mysteriously, fascinated civilians. Overnight, a once-seedy niche of showbiz turned hip. Plus, plenty of those podcasters grew up watching J.J., and now invited him on, providing 'Uncle Jay' with a young following for his old-guy vulgarity. A new streaming service, Live+, bought two of his classic videotaped hours, and commissioned the special. Which is where Beck came in.

J.J. Carmelo's act dried up years back, and he was filling the gap with crowd work, abusing the boozed-up for the amusement of the rest. That wouldn't work in a concert setting, where the audience couldn't see his targets. So Beck was employed to write jokes good enough for people to applaud this emotional derelict. He filmed at a small theatre in New Jersey, and Beck declined to attend. Last she heard, he'd bombed, and they weren't sure if it was even useable. Adam emailed her a screener link. Normally, she'd be professional, and watch. But it arrived just after Laura left.

'Here's the deal,' Adam tells her. 'I fix your phone, and you watch the effing special. Agreed ?'

Later, Adam's henchboy appears, bearing toilet paper. He takes her inoperative iPhone, and produces a pin, picking dust from the charging port and ignoring her questions, as if she were Mom. A minute later, he plugs in her phone. The screen illuminates; not dead after all.

That night, Beck gazes from her rooftop terrace over closed Santa Monica Pier, the beach empty, no planes in the sky, no helicopters. It's like a post-apocalypse movie, where the main character must reckon with her new reality: *I'm the only person who made it; not another solitary person.*

Adam said that all his comics are petrified, their performance income vanishing with the shutdown, and nowhere to work out fresh material. They're stuck indoors, separated from those whom they love to be loved by, societal collapse pending, their life's work more obviously frivolous than ever. On everyone's phones, the disease closes in, with national borders sealed, warnings about handwashing, families looking through windows at nurses in hazmat suits.

Already, Beck saw society as thinly protected, that optimism was disappointment postponed, that we'd run out of toilet paper. At last, everyone has figured out what she knew. Things *don't* get better in the end. You *can't* do anything that you set your mind to. Everything does *not* happen for a reason. Sometimes it happens because of a bat in China.

ROSA 😊 😄 😊 😎 😊 😊 🤗 🤠 😌 🙂 😊 🥸 rests her ten-speed bicycle on the bushes out front. Over the first month of lockdown, Beck dealt with nobody but delivery drivers. Can't recall how you do this, talking.

The words gush out: 'Move the bike round back if you want I guess there should be space though there's hardly anyone around to steal anything I don't think I don't know whatever you prefer is fine.'

'Hey!' Rosa says. 'You're Rebecca?'

'Beck, yup. You need water?'

'Would *love* some!'

Rosa is a small woman in a navy tanktop and orange Carhartt overalls, dressed as if trick-or-treating as the handyman. She rolls her shoulders, smiling, and wipes her forehead with a palm blackened from the handlebar wrap on her ten-speed. She downs half the glass of cold water, pauses for a gasp, then finishes the rest, a breathless thank you.

'You came all the way from Los Feliz?'

'Only took me an hour!'

Inside the house, Beck asks that they remain far enough apart to avoid murdering each other with micro-organisms. 'Needs a massive clean, plus some other tasks. I'll do a list.' She can't stop chattering with this weird intensity: isolation-mouth. Take it down a notch.

Rosa jots out the assigned tasks, and pulls her hair into a scrunchy, stubbly armpits on brief display.

Beck is distracted by something about this woman's features, which are oddly high-def. What *is* that? She realizes: a young person in daylight.

Technically, this gig is illegal; they're breaking lockdown. But Rosa is willing – productions are halted; even the fantasy of an audition is gone. Dogsbody earnings have fallen off a cliff too, and her other hustle – entertainer at kids' birthdays – is worse. Right now, anything is better than playing sardines with her six housemates, which is double the number she signed up for: three girls who actually pay rent plus three insignificant-others, dudes who moved in when Covid restrictions threatened to force them into celibacy. So Rosa's lockdown has been weeks of unemployed actors arguing over video games and smoking weed in her living room.

When showing Rosa around, Beck hears herself trying to impress the young woman. Because she's unexpectedly middle-class, white, and American-born? Beck wouldn't admit that, but it's so. To rebel against this fact, she acts curt, saying she has work to do, and carries her laptop to the upstairs bedroom, where she listens to Rosa singing over the lawnmower, tone-deaf but committed.

'You also do stuff like removals, right?' she calls down. 'Or you have associates for that?'

'All me.' She flexes her twig arm. 'Tougher than I look.'

'I hope so.' Beck explains what she needs removed, adding more as she goes, offering all the DVDs, the music system, various appliances in the kitchen.

Rosa proposes gathering it up, and returning later with a truck. 'I clear anything but dead bodies!'

'Could you put in the dog stuff especially? Mine just passed away.'

Rosa covers her mouth. 'I'm so sorry.'

'*You* didn't die.'

'What's her name?'

'Let's leave that out.'

'Oh. No prob. Sorry.' Rosa scours the house, gathering squeaky toys and bowls, plus the doghouse from the yard. Delicately, she approaches Beck's bedroom, speaking through the closed door. 'Did you want to see anything before it goes?'

'Just disappear it.' That came out rude, so she adds that Rosa should help herself to food from the fridge and cupboards – Adam's henchboy loaded her with bags of rice, plus other items now nearing expiration. 'Anything vegetable is yours.'

'You mean to eat right now?'

'To take, I meant. But, sure – eat it now, if you want.'

'I'm actually starving. I'll turn off the clock.'

'Keep it running. You're on a job.'

'Could I at least knock something up for you? My folks actually ran a restaurant back in Sacramento.'

'Are your folks coming to cook?'

'No, but I worked there one summer.'

'It was good, this restaurant?'

'It only lasted that summer.'

'Sounds great.'

'Take your chances, I guess!'

Before adding any ingredient, Rosa seeks permission, which gives Beck a reason to join her in the kitchen and watch, though she keeps telling her to do whatever.

They sit apart at the long dining table. Beck looks into her spoon, brilliant red with gazpacho. So strange having someone here again.

Rosa speaks of favourite food trucks around LA, and her former job assisting a culinary stylist in the Bay Area. She was a musical-theatre kid in school, so figured why not give it a try.

'Isn't New York where you break into musicals?'

'Oh, *now* they tell me.'

Rosa isn't obsessed with fame, which tells Beck that she'll get nowhere. When she babbles about showrunners she'd like to work with, Beck listens without comment, as when hearing the clumsy kid talk of the pro sports team he'll join.

Beck returns to her bedroom, lies on the floor, gazing sideways at a pillow on the carpet. For a couple of hours, thoughts float past. Should she call Laura, and tell her about Rodney, whom they adopted together? 'Liar,' she mumbles, imagining the conversation, how she'd speak, how false she'd be.

Rosa hollers up the stairs, and Beck notices the window: dark out. With effort, she climbs to her feet, knee sore, breathing from exertion.

'All done down here!' Rosa says. 'Unless you got anything left for me.'

'So I pay you how?' Beck asks, though she remembers.

'It's zapped off your card, which you entered online. So we're good.'

'What's the rate again?' All just to talk more.

'Forty smackers an hour.'

Beck would pay her just to stay longer. But you can't say that. 'And the receipt comes by email?'

'I can send it right now. Don't forget to rate me online!'

Beck asks Rosa to wait a second, and hastens to the roof terrace alone. Heart kicking, she places a call. 'Hey.'

'Hey there! You know I'm still downstairs, right?'

'I had a thought. I was just thinking. You're stuck at your place with all those people, which is not exactly healthy. I got extra bedrooms here. It's just stupid.'

'Whoa, are you—'

'Hear the ground rule first.'

'Just one ground rule?'

'Only one. No assassinating me with coronavirus. Otherwise, you stay for free.'

BECK'S OLD SILVER LAPTOP is open, a galaxy screensaver awaiting instruction, unsure of its purpose on the kitchen table except to gather milk-spatter from her Froot Loops. 'You seen this?' she asks, playing a clip of President Trump saying doctors can treat the disease by injecting patients with bleach.

Rosa snorts, shakes her head. She's the rare smart person to exist as if the mad king of America didn't. Just a shiver if the president's name is spoken. She'd rather talk classic movies or mid-century furniture or tell wending anecdotes about growing up in Sacramento and her nutty jobs since.

She has the charisma of an enthusiast, speculating about improvements that one could do to this house ('. . . you knock down that wall, and add a skylight, and . . .'). They disagree vehemently on taste, speaking over each other, revelling in the make-believe. After all, Rosa moved to Los Angeles for make-believe: acting. Yet it's hard to imagine her as anyone else. She's always herself, an ability that Beck previously viewed as if through binoculars. She pictures Rosa thirty years from now, maybe owning a bric-a-brac store in New Mexico, brown from the sun, hydrating with cucumber-infused water, enthusing over a Shaker chair that just came in.

Neither will forget this shared refuge during the plague.

Beck's phone rings, and she declines the call.

'You never pick up, do you. Such a power move.'

'I'm here with you.' Shocked that she said that.

'You're not tempted to see who?'

'It's just my agent.' Actually, Adam is her manager, but people are more impressed by 'agent'. She hates hearing herself show off – but keeps on. 'He's bugging me for notes on this thing I did.'

Rosa seeks details but Beck is vague, both for legal reasons and to sound important. Rosa has heard of J.J. Carmelo. 'What's he like?'

On Skype calls, J.J. barely looked into his camera, forcing Beck to watch the brim of a Brooklyn Dodgers cap, staring at the stylized 'B', his black-coffee sighs smellable through the laptop screen. J.J. resented that a writer had been forced on him. His idea for this special was 'political correctness', which (as Beck didn't tell him) was so hacky by now. Who even called it 'PC' anymore? When he ran through material, he didn't even try to sell it, just read as if from a grocery list. 'Got this bit on the vagina museum, how it's closed each time I visit.' He paused. 'I don't hear laughing. Something wrong with Skype today?'

'I'm waiting to see where you take it.'

'The giant tampon.'

'That's part of the museum?'

'Jesus H. Christ. Google it, will ya?'

He had no interest in who Beck was, yet she heard herself cheering him along, playing her paid role. She says none of this to Rosa. Only that J.J. was as you'd expect.

'And you did what exactly?'

'I was like a consultant.'

'Why's your agent need you to watch the special so much? You must be a big deal.'

'I'll put it on, if you're curious.' Immediately, Beck regrets the proposal, her heart sinking to view that junk again, her old self, her comedy-world self. But Rosa is thrilled to watch an advanced screener.

The special, *J.J. Carmelo: Cancel This*, begins in darkness on a bare stage. An audience of a few hundred people stirs. Onstage, a man's silhouette appears, and that is sufficient: the crowd leaps up, roaring and clapping. A woman in the crowd shouts, 'Love you, J.J.!' Everyone cheers. Still in silhouette, he launches into his opening: 'I was thinking, people. What're we gonna do about all the morons?'

The crowd bursts into laughter.

Rosa turns to Beck, wondering if she's allowed to voice an opinion. 'Why's that funny?'

Beck shrugs, and sits forward – this opening is nothing she worked on. For the next five minutes, J.J. improvises a rant about how the most oppressed group in society are the stupid. They're banned from elite colleges, they get the worst jobs, they end up with shitty healthcare – all because of nothing more than who they were born. 'This, folks, is the last acceptable prejudice. And, thank fuckin' God,' he concludes. 'Because if we ain't gonna mess with dumbasses, who we got left? We, as a people, need to come together. We need to come together, and hate as one. It's a teaching moment, bitches.' At this, music kicks in, the brassy opening of 'Crazy in Love', with Jay-Z thundering about 'history in the making', spotlights spinning around the concert hall. The audience members are on their feet again, going wild. At last, the stage lights come up, and there he is: J.J. Carmelo, mic in one hand, middle finger to the rafters, a straight white male in blackface.

The crowd seems confused: a few chuckles, awkward ones. They retake their seats. J.J. lets it sink in, then tells the audience to get used to it – this is how he's doing the special.

'What the?' Beck murmurs. 'I never worked on *any* of this.'

'Uhm,' Rosa says, 'not sure I get the point.'

Beck is silent, gripped by the awfulness of this special. J.J. Carmelo makes no attempt to explain, just baits the audience. Every bit falls flat (including a few she wrote). Boos ring out; heckles too. Any night, you can see comics bombing at clubs, but not in a filmed special. These are hardcore fans – alienating this many people that fast is tough. Now J.J. is slamming individual audience members, telling them to scram if they don't like it. Some oblige, shouting down the aisles that they want their money back, with J.J. responding that they can keep their stinking shekels. Forty minutes in, hundreds of seats are empty. J.J. tells those still left to go fuck themselves, and he walks offstage. The stragglers are incredulous. More boos. Cut to credits.

'Well, okay,' Beck says, processing this. 'That is *not* what I worked on.' She doesn't add something that she couldn't explain to a non-comic: to eat it that badly – there's something legendary about it.

She phones Adam. 'What the actual fuck?'

'You watched J.J.'s masterpiece, I take it.'

'I won't get my on-release money, I'm assuming.'

'We should be so lucky! Those idiots at Live-Plus put it out.'

'Wait, what? They went out with that?'

'Are you not on social media? It went up Thursday, and is blowing up. Not blowing up in the good way. Blowing up in the Al-Qaeda way.'

Over the past weeks, Beck forgot the jangling power of hits and losers. Adam is shoving that cultural din back at her. 'The Live-Plus guys are Wall Street – they had no idea how this'd play,' he explains. 'They figured that, with lockdown, they'd get zero new content, and they only just launched, so wanted something hot. So they threw it up there.'

'Because blackface might slip through the cracks?'

'It gets worse. A bunch of old clips are circulating of J.J. doing routines about "fags". In 1983, to be fair. But, speaking as a fag, "fag" ain't a great look in 2020. Elite-level cringe.' Adam's voice tenses, approaching something that will bother her. During the powwow with the Live+ folks, J.J. Carmelo worsened matters, going all surly and uncommunicative, so they invited a lawyer onto the Zoom call, and informed J.J. that they were taking down his special *and* the old ones they'd bought. 'His life's work, kaput.'

'Tragedy.'

'Then you came into it.'

'Me?'

'J.J. was freaking out, saying how he's not a racist, how he doesn't need to defend himself.'

'While defending himself.'

'Right. And they come back with: "White guy in blackface – slam-dunk racism. End of story." Then J.J. goes, "Why'd you hire me, if I'm not allowed to be J.J. Carmelo?" And they go, "We can't be associated." At which point, J.J. drops the Beck bomb.'

'What are you talking about, Adam?'

'This special can't be bigoted, J.J. tells them, because an LGBT person of colour wrote it.'

She needs a second to understand. Beck doesn't think of herself that way, but is now tokenized retrospectively. 'Don't put my name on this dumpster fire!' she says. 'Like, does an NDA not go the other way?'

'Beck, deep breath.'

'*You* take a deep breath! This shit has nothing to do with me!'

'I had the same exact reaction. The guy's scum. We're ditching him. Almost definitely. But I had a thought.'

'There's no version of this that's okay, Adam.'

'Listen! Listen. "Beck Frenhofer" – who's heard of that name?'

'Thanks.'

'All those NDAs keep you in the shadows. *This* would give you a name.'

'A name covered in slime. I'd get cancelled before anyone knows who I am.'

As they argue, Beck is hating her shoulders. She left the living room, and stands before the bathroom mirror, where she has taken off her XXL black T-shirt, and is trying to find the most repulsive angle on her back. She took antidepressants once, and gained a hundred pounds she never lost. This morning, she emailed the tenants at the East Village apartment she owns, telling the two comics who rent it that they needn't pay till lockdown ends. They replied without thanks, just, 'So we'll have to pay all those months once lockdown's over???'

What happens when all this ends, and life returns to normal? She can't say it aloud, but the pandemic has been her best experience in years: no panic that she's falling behind everyone, no dejection that others are living her best life.

'We turn it around,' Adam tells her. 'This dude wants to tread on you? Well, we tread on him.'

SHE AND ROSA ARE drinking bourbon on the roof. How to tell someone — especially a young person who still believes in fame — that you want no more ratings, no more contests? Beck hears herself reminiscing about her adolescence, when she listened obsessively to her dad's comedy albums, and recounts her quirks growing up. She takes another mouth-burning slug of whiskey, uneasy, because she's telling herself to someone. She only does this once every few years, and should stop. But once begun, it's like swimming toward a speck of land — you must reach it, or you go under. 'Want to hear me violate a bunch of NDAs?'

'Yeah!'

She explains the true nature of her work, her role in the J.J. debacle, and how they're trying to drag her into it because her father was black, with the added bonus that she's not exactly straight. '*Your* personality is what I want,' Beck says. 'Calm.'

'Here's what I don't get. If you write awesome comedy, why not just become a massive name yourself?'

'Serious success isn't about writing ability. You need to be a person who people want to laugh with.' Beck is breaking all those non-disclosure agreements to raise her status with Rosa, yet is now denigrating herself. She pivots. 'Know how much these guys are offering me to take the fall? Two hundred grand. All I have to do is say I wrote the one thing that I *didn't* write.'

'Two hundred grand?! That is life-changing.'

Beck doesn't say that, for her, it's not. But she recalls being hungry when struggling in New York, her outer-borough basement, almost thin, stealing leftovers from club kitchens.

'You'd be amazing onstage,' Rosa insists. 'You have a way of seeing things and saying stuff. Not, like, funny ha-ha. But, like, super-dark. And getting right to it.'

'I never stopped writing my own act actually. I have tons of material.'

'So you have a routine?'

'Hours.'

'Do something for me!'

Beck leans forward, head in hands. 'No way.' Her temples are throbbing. Adam already held a video-conference with Live+ about what J.J. calls 'the lesbian-of-colour angle'. She's getting that queasy career feeling again, as if late for something, as if people are talking about her, as if she's let someone down. The prospect of standing before strangers, saying words – she wants Rosa to reverse herself: 'Actually, don't.' To say, 'We do our own thing.'

Instead, Rosa simplifies matters: 'They pay you. You get famous. Then be whatever you want.'

It would blow other comedians' minds if she did a set. Beck could get spots anywhere once LA clubs re-open. With a phone call, she'd have a Netflix scout there. Beck imagines an audience gawking at her; her mouth goes dry.

'Who cares if people neg you?' Rosa says. 'You're way above them.'

'You know what the late great Mitzi Shore said? "You only know you're succeeding when people hate you." '

'Totally!'

Beck's upper lip itches from sweat; she wipes it. For the first time in weeks, she has a crowd in her head again. 'I don't know.'

'*I* know.' Rosa gives her a side-hug, rubs her back.

Beck goes rigid. 'Social-distancing.'

'Oh, right. My bad.' Rosa steps away.

Beck reaches for the rail around the terrace, her eyes narrowing, as if distracted by something out there.

'When you *do* do your act,' Rosa says, 'you're gonna rock.' She heads down to her room.

Beck is left on the roof, leg jiggling, looking toward an ocean too dark to see.

FOR NIGHTS, SHE WORKS on her act, poring through old note-books, alternating cold fear at how awful she is – and the possibility that she is amazing, that she'll reveal herself and people will get her.

She paces past her bed into the en-suite bathroom and back,

experimenting with the delivery of lines, shoulder pricked, eyes widening, trying to hear objectively, as if at the bar and watching herself, which jabs a shard of panic into her. She scrolls Twitter to find if people are raging yet about her role in the J.J. Carmelo special – it's frightening when the masses hate you unannounced; but provoke them knowingly, and it's a thrill. She wants Rosa to be around for this. Whenever her housemate leaves the room, Beck wants her back, even if she went only a minute earlier, and they'd exhausted the conversation, and Beck needs to sleep. Instantly, she's longing for more.

Play it out, though. After the scandal hits, comedy nerds will compile a spreadsheet on Reddit of all shows whose credits include 'Special thanks to Beck Frenhofer'. The *New York Times Magazine* profiles her, recounting the case as another sign of all that's wrong with all that's wrong. The scandal won't be J.J. in blackface. The scandal will be how comedy used her.

On Twitter, denunciations of J.J. Carmelo are plentiful, including a campaign to boycott Live+. But never a mention of Beck Frenhofer. These executives are paying to smear her name. So get on with it!

She goes downstairs. In the darkened doorway of Rosa's bedroom, Beck lets her eyes adjust, and enters softly. She stoops, her face near sleeping breaths, then retreats upstairs.

Back in her room, she's rehearsing again, downing slugs of Jack Daniels at dawn to fall asleep, then waking in her jogging pants, zipping up the hoodie, slipping on Havaianas, nearly tumbling on the stairs. Rosa left a note: *Out shopping!*

Beck herself hasn't left this house once since lockdown. She summons her image of Rosa in thirty years, running that antique store – Beck wants to be there then, not here now.

But this scandal *is* happening, right? She clicks her online-banking app, and the Live+ payment went through. All is official. Another payment catches her eye: $320 to Dogsbody LLC.

It's the same amount daily since Rosa moved in: $320 to Dogsbody. Each conversation they had, every meal, weekends included – that was paid.

'IF YOU'RE DISPUTING THE charges, I'll get you your money back,' Rosa says, hot-faced. 'Not sure how I'll do it. But fine.'

'I'm not asking for my money back.'

'I gotta make a call,' Rosa says, leaving for her bedroom. 'And don't worry,' she shouts back. 'I won't charge for today.'

'Can you wait one second?!'

For the rest of that day, Beck keeps hesitating on the upstairs landing, trying to make out whispered phone calls in the guest bedroom below.

The next morning, Beck pulls off her eye mask, and discovers a text message i left. take care.

The guest bed is stripped, towels stacked, keys atop.

Her phone rings.

'Well, how is *your* day?' Adam always talks like a stripogram when delivering good news. 'So, *I* was chatting with the Live-Plus folks.'

'Why aren't they leaking it? This is getting ridiculous.'

'Becky, my dear, something interesting's happened in that glorious place that I so fondly call the interweb: a backlash to the backlash. Before, everyone was saying J.J.'s a flaming racist, right? Which is obviously bullshit, but whatever. Then, Part Two: right-wing nutjobs start jumping in, by which I mean Trump country, all threatening to boycott Live-Plus if J.J. gets cancelled. And the free-speech folk got involved too.'

'Can you just tell me what's happening?'

'Viewer numbers for the J.J. special – exclusively on Live-Plus: hooray! – are through the roof. Half of America hates him, but who gives a shit? The other half of America is a fuckload of eyeballs,' he says. 'So, you ask: What's in it for me? That's the best part. *I* just negotiated for Live-Plus to not associate you with this hot mess – *and* you get to keep the payout. Two hundred grand of free dough, darlin', for doing fuck-all. But wait; I'm not done. Here is the best part, Beck. I. Got. You. A special.'

Her hands go cold. She puts the phone on speaker, rests it on the table. Suddenly, she wants this. Immensely. Years watching, resenting them, dying for her turn. *She* has something to say. The worst parts of herself. For everyone to laugh at. For Rosa to watch. For Rosa to know her.

'FYI,' Adam goes on, 'I'm not sitting still on the two hundred grand, either. We'll get separate terms for your director credit. Basically, nobody felt right putting you in the firing line on this, and J.J. needed to take ownership. Even he figured it was better to face the woke than to end up like Milli Vanilli. Right?'

'Wait. I'm confused. What you negotiated is for me to *direct* a special?'

'And you're most welcome, my dear.'

'Who says I want to direct for J.J. Carmelo? I thought the whole point was *my* career.'

He shifts tone, hard suddenly. 'Whoa. I don't deal with anger issues. Take that somewhere else. You don't want to direct a Live-Plus special? Send back the money. I'll give up my commission, if you want to go that route.' He means dropping her. 'What you need is to get with J.J., and work through ideas. That is what I'd seriously advise. His thinking was shooting the new special at a correctional facility: "J.J. Live at San Quentin." But who knows with Covid. I figured a selected audience on Zoom, and "crowd shots" of fans at home. You've seen his apartment in Brooklyn. It's – how to say? – characterful. Filming the intro there could work. Or a fake real apartment? Anyway, that's for you to figure out.'

'For me? Seems like everything's been decided.'

'I was expecting a bit more joy here, Beck. You keep the money *and* your reputation. You get how this works, right?' Regretfully, he must dash to another meeting, which is Hollywood for 'Fuck off'.

After they hang up, Beck finds herself staring at her list of recent iPhone calls. She presses the name, looking at this trilling object in her palm. It rings eight times, then voicemail. 'Hey, it's me. Let's not . . .' Beck begins. 'You know? I have all this space! And if I'm gonna socially isolate anyway. Right? Plus you need a place. It's crazy. Seriously.'

Some people never check voicemail. Beck follows up with a text, replying to Rosa's goodbye note, composing the longest message she's ever thumbed into a phone. She keeps adjusting wording, tweaking lines – until, by mistake, she sends it. Horrified, she reviews the note. Thank God: nothing bad, just typos and honesty. According to iMessage, *Rosa Dogsbody* is typing.

But the reply doesn't come.

So Beck messages an audio file, a few minutes of material – the most embarrassing events of her life rendered in punchlines.

She watches the blank screen.

Nothing is distributed fairly, she thinks, and forwards her entire J.J. Carmelo payment – after commissions, nearly $180,000 – to Rosa.

OVER THE NEXT WEEK, Beck limits herself to calling Rosa's number six times per day, and hangs up every time it goes to voice-mail. Adam sends details on the J.J. special, now planned for the Irvine drive-in. The Live+ team wants to crank up the edgy political material, and someone from the corporate side hatched a title that everyone loves: *J.J. Carmelo: The Great Awokening.*

Beck's phone is ringing. She snatches it, checks the screen. It's her mother in London. 'I was just listening to this radio programme on people trying to become teachers to their own kids in lockdown, and I thought of you,' Dora says.

'Thought of me?' Beck snaps. 'Why?'

'I was just remembering when I taught you to read.'

'What are you talking about? I learned to read at school.'

'No, you didn't. Sitting on my lap. You don't remember that?'

'Why are you calling?'

'Just, I keep wanting to talk with you, Beck. Have we spoken this whole time, this whole epidemic? I don't even know what you're up to. I keep imagining you there.'

Half-listening, Beck checks incoming messages. The banking app shows a new payment: Rosa returned the entire sum.

The doorbell bongs.

'I need to go,' Beck says.

A peppy guy stands before her, presenting an object. 'Don't recognize it?' he asks. 'Freshly laundered!' It's the pink beach towel, emblazoned with *LOL Surprise!* that the Persian driver gave her to cradle Rodney when he was dying. The guy gets back into the animal-hospital van, and drives away.

Beck stands in her open doorway. A trio of surfer dudes strut past her house, right down the middle of the road. They're heading toward the beach, shirts off – jogging there now, racing each other, shouting who's gonna get there first. They're the types she could never be: volleyball till sunset, beers on the sand, hooting at jokes.

For a while, everyone was hiding out, apart together, noticing how short their lives were, and that competition is a madness, and that you should probably eat too much. For a while, she felt human among humans.

But everything is returning to normal. They're running stand-up gigs on patios. She could call an Uber, and see who's performing. Her stomach drops.

Beck stands there in her front door, towel clasped. The cage is open. The animal stays in place.

DIARY: APRIL 2020

A long foreign number is blinking on my silenced phone. I wasted this morning reading upsetting news. At last, I started to work — then this number started calling.

The line crackles, a man speaking a language I can't understand.

'Wrong number,' I tell him.

His voice rises in urgency — then he screams. The call ends.

My screen remains lit for a few seconds. It dims. Something just happened to someone. I should report it. But what exactly? And to whom?

I return to my computer. I can't concentrate. I keep re-reading the same line.

I struggle to focus lately. We've been in Covid lockdown for weeks, with outdoor excursions only for food-shopping or exercise: you may gain weight or lose it, but not much else. Those with locked-down kids are in tatters. Those of us without dependants are supposedly baking sourdough and attempting yoga poses. I'm just trying to maintain my spirits, but my writing is stranded in mid-sentence.

At the start of all this, people spoke of meeting up 'on the other side'. But I can't see the pandemic ending in parades, only with a planet still hurtling toward catastrophe, a culture still ripping itself apart. Given that, what are the prospects for a manuscript like mine?

Then again, fretting about the future of the novel feels so trivial now, which is itself telling. The triumph of screens will be complete after this.

I watch the silent phone on my desk. It's blinking again, that same number, demanding me.

'Who is this?'

'Miss Dora?'

'Who is this?!'

In the background, I detect a second voice, also male but deeper, haranguing my caller, who moves away from the phone to plead in a language I don't recognize. There's a slapping, and my caller howls. 'Miss Dora?!'

'What do you want me to do?'

'You can help me? Please?'

Either my battery died, or the connection dropped, or I hung up. I'm unsure which to tell you, what each version will make you think of me. But I recognized his voice.

When I was renting that place in Almería, the busker showed me an app, allowing me to drop money in his cup digitally. He messaged me his number. But I never did donate.

I've read of scammers who target the elderly, acting as if in peril, abducted and brutalized — but they'd be spared if only someone paid the captors. Will you? What kind of person do you consider yourself?

That call must've been staged. After all, who — if truly endangered — would phone a stranger? Which is why I hung up.

I consider my phone, its invisible wires leading to almost everyone on the planet. How would I have managed this pandemic if Beck were a little girl, and still here, barging into my office as she did aged four, the door swinging open, banging into the wall, causing me to swivel from

95

my big desktop computer. She was supposed to be in bed but giggled maniacally, running circles in her pyjamas, flinging herself to the carpet, then back to her feet.

'Way too late for this,' I told her. 'Anyway, playing in my office is a reward, Becky, and we never even did reading practice today.'

'Five minutes here? Just five, Mumma? Please?'

'I only just got you into bed! The answer is no. Go downstairs. Now.' In those days, I was so bad-tempered. Not angry with Beck quite, but at a hole in myself that I only noticed because of her. I'd welcome such an intrusion now, so change my reply: 'Okay, how about this? You read me five pages of your book, then we play for five minutes. But immediately *to bed afterward. Alright?'*

The four-year-old's plump hand rests on the storybook, beside a pointing middle-aged forefinger (mine, still straight and slender then), which directs Beck to the next word. I can't recall who taught me to read, but I do recall paging through my mother's book collection, her favourite volumes spared from the fire when others were burned for heat during the war. Back then, I couldn't fathom print that small. By early adolescence, I admired books from a distance. Only in Paris did I read many. My interest was genuine but I also sought to impress, to be someone who knew all the references. I dipped into perplexing French philosophy, and noble Russian poetry, and irreverent American novels — a slow reader trying to catch up, to distance myself from a youth misspent in countryside. I never did read many works that I should have. Years later, when my first novel came out, I worried that literary types might quiz me about The Great Books, exposing me as an imposter. But they never asked; nobody knows.

When I myself had a daughter, I emphasized reading, so that she'd never feel as small as I had. Literature had become sacred to me — not only because it was my career, but because books contained many of the finest minds, offering insights into our species. Which raised a question.

Why were most children's books about animals? Another notable trait of kids' stories was comeuppance, though that was easier to understand. What preoccupied me, back when I was reading aloud from the animal-based justice system, was whether literature really could instill goodness. Wasn't one feature (moralizing) undermined by the other (animals)? We fill storytime with huggable creatures, then raise children in societies that treat animals as servants and lunch.

Another genre of children's tale, I discovered, involved the charming crook. These stories were always popular, which suggested something sinister in kids — or perhaps just the need for a breather after all that sermonizing about not thumping your little brother with a candelabra. When someone gave my daughter a picture book of a sneering fox who attended a fancy-dress party and, page by page, devoured the guests, I worried about creating a predator. On the other hand, children who dabbled in pirates and unicorns rarely became pirates and unicorns. And if they did, it was going to happen anyway; the stories appealed because Blackbeard was relatable.

Lately, a moral mission inflames culture for grown-ups too, based on the suspicion that adults themselves need educating, given the mess of our world; that hurtful words are close to violence; that oppression itself can be tackled by those who run the local theatre and the small press. If we had such sway — if novels disarmed the thugs — perhaps literature should attempt little else. But doesn't a story fizzle if proclaiming what people really ought? The jolt is seeing what people really are.

Either way, Beck never became bookish. Before lockdown, I saw reports of today's pushy parents enrolling their kids in 'Coding with Lego'. I'm unsure I'd have wanted a coder in the house. One discovery in raising a child is that a person whom you'd like is not necessarily one who'd thrive. For example, I always felt like an outsider, so encouraged my daughter to look sideways at crowds. Yet conformists seem far more fulfilled. Similarly, I wouldn't have wanted a kid who lived on a device. But the future will be.

I'm looking at my office carpet, seeing my four-year-old Beck there — before she bolts back downstairs to her bedroom. She sprinted everywhere when little. I'm alone again, and turn back to the computer.

Remind me: what was happening in this scene? I review partial drafts, suffering the gut-clenching realization that what I imagined was eloquent isn't. I mustn't fret about whether the writing is bad. Just put it onscreen, and judge it later. I'm trying.

But my phone glares at me. I check that number again, the long area code connecting to a possibility I'd rather not visualize. Even if those screams were fake, they're based in reality. Somewhere, right now, as I write and you read, people are dragged into a room to be hurt, and not just with offensive ideas.

I hit SEND on a donation, aware that I've been duped. At least I can return to work now, my bribe paid to morality. Soon, I'm lost in a scene. But something distracts me.

My silenced phone. It's flashing again.

~~A screen that you stamp on and it still works and stamp on again and it has a crack in the display but still works and then stamp on again and it works still and you stamp on it again and it never works again — a face is like that.~~

Or

~~Amir is placed into a cell the size of a wardrobe.~~

Or

He walks down a narrow corridor, staring at his feet, as ordered.

4

The man who took
the books away

(AMIR)

H E WALKS DOWN A narrow corridor, staring at his feet, as ordered. Amir's left shoulder – yanked back in this restraint – throbs, while his right knee is so swollen that it could give way. Still, he walks with full weight on both legs. Nobody should notice a weakness.

A meaty arm turns him to the wall, and a door opens. He's thrust into a confinement cell the size of a closet. Its floor is occupied by a large black duffel bag that he stumbles over, his arms shooting forward to brace himself on the cell wall. The duffel bag pushes back against his ankle. There's something in there.

The guard takes off his handcuffs, and commands Amir to enter the bag, which expands and contracts beneath him, the creature inside breathing. It's dark in this cell, so when Amir crouches, he feels for the closed zip, running his right hand across the bag contours, which jut at confusing angles.

The guard flicks a red Bic lighter, and holds it up for illumination, so close to Amir's face that he smells burnt eyebrows, the flame swerving, a shadow flickering over the bag, whose zip he finds. His left shoulder is too painful to help much – he uses that hand only to grip the canvas, gaining purchase, and he parts the zipper in a long black seam.

The face of the creature inside cannot be distinguished, only silver threads of beard hair. It seems impossible that Amir could fit, with another man already inside. The guard gives a push-kick to Amir's lower back, arching him forward, his inflamed knee landing on soft tissue of the man in the bag, who gasps, and says nothing.

Amir, suppressing grunts of exertion, folds himself inside. But he cannot close the bag from within. Impatient, the guard yanks up the zipper, needing to stamp down the bag's doubled contents with his police boot, hard-rubber treads on Amir's back and ear. The zipper teeth clench above his eyes. Inside, his bones press into someone else's. The guard clicks a padlock on the zip sliders; the two men are trapped inside. The rusted cell door clangs shut.

Only half-breaths are possible. Ownership of a limb isn't immediately clear, except by pain of impact against another. Amir gnaws his lips, realizing only from the taste of iron that they're bleeding.

When the other man exhales, it's a warm burst into Amir's nose. The smell repulses him. He wants to obliterate this person. The door opens again, and the bag is grasped. The guard stabs the bag with a ballpoint pen, struggling to breach the canvas, finally puncturing it, jabbing the other man, whose body flinches. By the fourth air hole, the fat guard is breathless, and he's lost the pen inside, so gives up. The cell door clangs shut again.

The infinite black is now spotted with cylinders of lighter darkness. Amir presses his mouth to one, torn canvas against torn lips, sucking in fresher air. Both men hold to their breathing holes. Once quenched, they remain quiet.

The other man jostles for space, which causes Amir to protect his own, pulse quickening from exertion, both of them wordless, pushing each other, crushed against the cell walls, pinching the other's flesh to make him stop. A fight conducted in silence is over. Both men lost, mashed into positions their bodies can neither sustain nor escape.

Amir has no breathing hole now. Terror swarms over him. He pushes the man, who drives back harder.

FATHER HAD A HEART attack. Amir's aunt phoned, claiming with booze-slurred insistence that he must fly out, for she could not cross the border to see her ailing older brother, owing to her medical fragility and the political danger she'd face back in her native country. She asked if he had called his father at the hospital yet. Amir intended to. Amir intended much.

At twenty-nine, he looked young to the old, old to the young. To his family, he merely looked evasive, once-bright eyes turning away. His aunt knew Amir could travel from London on short notice without professional consequences – he had no serious employment, working for a removals company that pledged to recycle but merely sifted for what its staff wanted, and dumped all the tape cassettes, filing cabinets and books at a landfill.

Upon touchdown in his aunt's city, Amir switched on his phone, and learned that his father had just died. Now he needed to rush, for the burial would be within a day. He took a cab to her place in the city centre, pressed her buzzer till his finger hurt, finally hustling into the building behind another resident, bounding up to her floor, and banging on the door. 'Where *were* you?' she asked him.

He sat in an armchair, out of breath. 'Can I even get there on time?' The quickest way was a bus. To save roaming charges, which were astronomical once you crossed the border, his aunt provided an ancient Nokia with a local SIM card, stuffing a charger into his luggage.

'Now,' she asked, 'would you like something to read?'

'What are you talking about? I have to go – I need to get there.'

Before lunchtime, he was in a packed coach, his back wet with sweat. Across the aisle, a young couple in surgical masks spoke loudly, sharing earbuds, a ticking beat audible each time the thrumming ceiling fan turned away. A little boy sat with shopping bags of used shoes. A wizened old woman scrolled a cracked-screen smartphone, rubbing her eyes. Amir told her of the reason for his trip because he sought the pity of strangers.

The bus crossed a border, entering the country of his birth, but Amir hardly saw his surroundings: talking, talking, then sleep. He opened his eyes only when the bus was stationary, the last few passengers stepping down the front stairs. A dusty road snaked around the hillside past a military checkpoint, with a barren valley below where a construction crew had abandoned digging equipment. This route would've been impassable months earlier during the fighting. But the government had 'reconciled' the area, and opened the road.

Amir exited the bus half-asleep and blinking at the daylight, landing on the road with a twist of his ankle. He massaged it as two young soldiers checked documents. His papers were in the hold of the bus, and he communicated this, but the soldiers told him to wait his turn. As they went down the line, they dismissed passengers, each filing back inside the bus. Only three passengers had issues to resolve, including Amir. The bus engine restarted, diesel fog from its tailpipe, heat radiating against his back. Urgently, Amir opened his daypack and rummaged inside to show them: nothing here. If they'd tell the driver to open the cargo door, he'd produce his documents. A soldier told him to be quiet, and disappeared with Amir's cheap phone into the makeshift office, its door wide open. A brawny moustachioed officer sat there, drinking maté, lips puckered around the metal straw, dimple in one cheek.

Amir and the other two remaining passengers waited, the sun scorching them. He could see into the office, and nobody was doing anything. Finally, a different young soldier emerged, and knocked on the bus doors, which opened. He ordered the driver to leave. The three remaining passengers shouted. An officer emerged from the office, and told them to shut up. The bus doors closed with a hiss. Amir was about to protest further, but waited because another excluded passenger – an old man whose young wife and little daughter remained aboard – was already bellowing objections. The officer swung something at this man's head. He fell sideways, arms extended rigidly, landing hard. The bus shifted into gear, turn-clicker blinking, though they were in the middle of nowhere. The officer held a hammer. The bus rolled gently up the road, around the corner.

On the ground, the old man bled from the side of his head, a dark pool expanding around pebbles, creeping toward Amir's dress shoes. The wounded man sat up, then stood, giddy, half his body yellowed from gravel dust, caked on the bloody side of his head. The officer with the hammer returned inside, joking with his moustachioed commander, whose legs were up on the desk. He changed channels with a remote control, growing annoyed with this uncooperative TV, aware that three civilians watched him as the sun watched them. He came out, remote in hand, and kicked the bleeding man in the behind, telling him to go. The man asked about the bus. A young soldier looked to the commanding officer, who gestured as if this were the stupidest request – how was he in charge of buses? The young soldier pushed the man, told him to run. Holding his wounded head, the man hurried up the winding road, parallel to tyre tracks of the long-departed vehicle.

The commanding officer pointed his TV remote at the professional woman beside Amir. She bowed her head, speaking too fast, fingers extending toward the officer, as if to reach through a cobweb without breaking its thread. As she pleaded, the officer elbowed Amir in the jaw, knocking him to the ground, his face buzzing, mind stalled. From that instant until now, another version of himself took over, as if the self-conscious surveillance camera on himself had turned off, just a body now, an insect programmed to keep existing while slowly swallowed by a lizard.

At the roadside, they put zip-ties on his wrists. He wondered whether to say these were too tight, but instead made his fingers into beaks, which alleviated the pressure. A meat van pulled up, and they slid up the metal door. Men sat on the floor, some in suits, some in shorts and flip-flops. He struggled to climb up there, arms behind him, and they shoved him in finally. He landed hard on his tailbone. Sprawled among other men, Amir watched the van door lower with a rattle of metal, daylight pushed down until only a horizontal thread remained. The van growled and advanced, the men seated around him banging into each other. It smelled of dried urine and bleach, like a locker-room toilet. Amir kept moving his jaw – it felt as if his teeth weren't aligned anymore. His phone was gone. His luggage and passport too. He'd miss his father's burial.

After a long drive, the meat van parked. The sound of shouting outside grew louder, deafening, until the metal door ripped up. In sudden brightness, Amir closed his eyes to slits, his face and clothing engulfed in grasping hands, his own still tied behind his back. Dragged out this way, he dropped off the lip of the van, hitting the ground, a cloud of dust rising, the surrounding shrieks even louder now, another prisoner from the truck landing atop him, and another. A baton struck his back repeatedly, and his mouth twice. He balled up, tucked his chin. If you cried out when struck, you were struck again. This was a lesson: don't scream. Those who couldn't stop would be stopped. Soon, the blows petered out. Only the attackers' shouts persisted. The attacked stayed silent.

In the first holding cell, Amir ran his tongue over the cracked-tooth stumps in his gums; couldn't stop jabbing at them. He pulsed variously, from jaw, hip, knee. The slightest movement of his left shoulder was excruciating. His long-restrained hands were swollen and stiff, as if arthritic. Summoned for check-in, he rose with difficulty, exerting himself not to limp. Prisoners had to wear blindfolds, but the guards had run out. So you were forbidden to look. 'If we see eyes, we take them out.'

In an office, a voice told Amir he could look now. He didn't. The voice insisted that it was fine – open your eyes! Amir found a little fellow with civilian clothing and an irresolute moustache, which matched that of the president pictured on the wall. He ordered the soldiers to remove Amir's zip-ties, and offered a chair. Amir sat, still not looking directly at the bureaucrat. He answered all questions honestly, interrupted only by sniffs, which caused the man to look up and see blood dripping from Amir's nose. The bureaucrat expressed disgust. When Amir said he was a French student but lived in London, the man appeared concerned, and asked to see a passport. It was on the bus. The man asked the destination of that bus, and noted it down. 'You *speak* like you're from here,' he said suspiciously.

'I was born here.'

The man left the office, absent for five hours, presumably checking into Amir's story. Contacting the French authorities could take a while, Amir assumed. Finally, the man returned. 'Did you fill it out?'

'Fill out what?'

The man had forgotten what Amir had said, had forgotten that he was even here. He dispatched him back to the cells. The soldiers had found a sweat-damp blindfold, and tied it around his head, knotting it with force. Amir angled his gaze down to watch his footsteps, lest they walk him down a flight of stairs for fun. He never saw the bureaucrat again.

To scare prisoners in the communal cell, the guards sneaked up to the door and crashed it open. Instantly, everyone had to assume the security position: facing the rear wall, on your knees, hands behind heads. Even when locked in the cell, prisoners were forbidden to advance closer than six tiles from the door.

The cell was built for four people but housed nearly forty, some clothed, some not, all emaciated except the newest, and silent until the guards left, whispering beneath the distant mumble of the guards' television. The cell walls were white at the top, dark at the bottom, where prisoners could touch. A neon light buzzed throughout the night.

Wake-up was 5:30 a.m., after hearing unseen birds and unseen branches rustling outside. As the sun moved across the sky, a rhomboid of daylight widened over one wall, too high to reach. On hot days, prisoners who had shirts took them off to flap and circulate air. Weeks passed, and a season changed, sunlight more and more briefly on the wall, its slant narrower, then gone one day. Each morning, blankets had to be piled in the middle of the cell. When unmonitored, prisoners stood on those blankets, straining to see over the outside bars. Mostly, they sat – you grew dizzy standing with so little food.

Once a day, the cell door opened for feeding, everyone scurrying into the security position. A guard foot-shoved an aluminium tureen of rice, olives and boiled eggs (less than one egg per man), the whole lot mixed together. They had to eat immediately – you couldn't save food, and were beaten if caught doing so. They swallowed the eggshells too and the olive pits. The cell toilet could be used once daily; you had a minute. On freezing days, guards threw buckets of cold water on them, so their clothes clung wetly as they slept. A few detainees recited religious passages. Others spoke of family. Mostly, they discussed recipes.

Amir grew alert to sounds: the 'welcoming committee' greeting another truckload of prisoners; water through old pipes, meaning it was time to use the toilet; the electronic *clack* of a digital camera to record a death.

The interrogations had no objective, except as a time-killer and workout for bored soldiers. Every room in the facility contained a photograph of the president, and they made detainees grovel before it, and call him their lord. They had to name their wives and mothers and children, and describe them, and beg the guards to fuck those family members.

The ways to hurt a body are age-old, part of a long human tradition. Much as teenagers smash a broken television, the guards were curious to see the components of a man. They rarely tortured to death. Fatigue stopped them; it was exhausting work.

You cannot remember pain itself. What terrorized Amir was its approach. Duration couldn't be understood either. He told himself just one minute more, and done, as with a medical procedure. During, he sweated more than he'd ever done, and saliva pooled in his mouth, as if about to vomit, or defecate. He wondered about saying aloud that this would kill him soon, or if that would provoke them to go harder, to show that *they* knew the endpoint, not he. He made himself boring by obedience.

During those interrogations, Amir learned why they had arrested him: on the Nokia that he'd borrowed from his aunt were satirical songs mocking the president, plus a video of ducks waddling down a dirt road, described as 'The biggest ever pro-government march'. He explained that the phone was borrowed, and named his aunt, giving her address in the adjacent country.

Under prison regulations, guards were supposed to wear surgical masks against the pandemic, but few did. Prisoners who caught the disease – that is, everyone who'd arrived without it – hid their symptoms. Amir had already suffered a mild case in London, and couldn't tell whether he was reinfected. If a prisoner was heard wheezing, or was denounced by fellow inmates, he was taken to 'quarantine', and did not return.

Some prisoners waited for relatives to pay bribes to free them. Sometimes, this happened. But Amir had purposely told nobody in London of his true destination, a country everyone associated with war and terrorism. As for his alcoholic aunt, she'd have heard that Amir never turned up for his father's funeral. She was always complaining of Amir's irresponsibility, and might assume he'd just returned to London, avoiding her again, as the rest of the family did. And even if she knew he was here, she had no way to help.

A few prisoners 'separated' – lost their minds. But Amir only stared at nothing, thought of nothing, living as if no places existed, just the tile floor. At night, everyone jockeyed for space. Waking was cruellest, the weight of not wanting this. Amir would keep his eyelids closed for as many extra seconds as possible, trying to vanquish self-pity, then distracting himself with the sight of their bodies and faces, overwritten with programmed drives: hunger, thirst, pain, hunger, fear, exhaustion, hunger, fear, hunger, hunger, hunger.

How long since he arrived here? He isn't sure. A country could've ended; he wouldn't know. Sometimes, he suffers a falling sensation, as if the floor is dropping beneath him. This place, he knows, has deformed him forever.

He swallows now, tasting thick plaque on his rotting broken teeth, the other man's breath mingling with his own. He doesn't understand why they're in this bag. You often don't know why; you just persist.

He tries to shift away, his pelvis scraping the canvas bag against the floor, his swollen knee in the other man's thigh. He can't twist around, and the effort infuriates him. The man's beard is raking his face. He wants to kill this creature. Amir's arteries swell, blood rushing around his body. The disgusting animal beside him parts those lips, leaning to Amir's ear. 'Are you hurt?' Amir recognizes that voice: his brother.

IT'S DANGEROUS TO DISCOVER relatives in this prison. They become leverage, the device of your torture, or you a tool in theirs. 'Why the fuck did you come back here?' Khaled asks.

They were born weeks apart but only met a few years later. Amir's mother – a French citizen who'd worked at an aid organization in the capital – raised him in affluence. By contrast, Khaled's mother was rearing three daughters besides him, all on the modest civil-service salary of their father. When Amir was seven, his mother moved them back to Paris, but wanted him to retain a link to his roots. So she sent him to this country every summer to stay with his bohemian aunt, a modern woman who worked on the radio, chain-smoked and drank wine imported from the next country (where she was to export herself once the war broke out).

On those childhood vacations, Amir's father turned up at least once per trip. He was proud of his French son; he was too proud in general. Shy to speak accented French, the man passed little time with Amir. The boy's aunt, when working at the radio station, deposited Amir in the courtyard of a nearby apartment block, where boys his age kicked balls and climbed walls and fell. She left him there to make friends, to figure out his meals, and she returned each evening. The first day, he was taunted by a bigger boy. Amir told his aunt, and this amused her, and she insisted that he should befriend the boy. Amir only understood later that she'd left him in that courtyard to dump her nephew at his father's feet – it was where he, his wife and other children lived, including that bigger boy, his half-brother Khaled.

At first, Amir had the impression that their family connection was secret. But everyone soon knew, including the half-sisters who came to meet Amir, inspecting him till he was dragged away like a teddy bear by Khaled. Previously, their father had been proud of his secret son. Now that it was known, he became aloof with Amir – and seemed to despise Khaled. Amir once witnessed their father kicking Khaled. The adults looked away.

On the outskirts of Paris, Amir attended a school for the children of bobos who worked at museums, in public relations, and academia. In this milieu, his non-French identity had status, so he accentuated the Arab side. But each summer vacation, this reversed. Khaled – who matured physically long before Amir – acted as guide and guardian throughout the holiday, announcing his brother wherever they went, then giving an expectant smile, as if Amir were to perform Frenchly.

When Amir attended university, he lived in a slope-ceilinged garret in the 10th arrondissement, its hardwood floor populated by empty wine bottles whose mouths were choked with melted red candles. In the middle of the room was a raft: his unmade bed, with a crystal ashtray that kept tipping over when he read paperbacks there, causing much cursing and a shake of the sheets out the window, ash floating over the elderly prostitutes in Rue Saint-Denis.

When Khaled emailed that he was visiting Paris, Amir didn't respond immediately; he wanted a way out. Finally, Amir replied that he had tons of studying, and that it might not be easy for Khaled to manage without fluent French. When Amir went out with his half-brother, he phoned those in his social circle beforehand, apologizing. Khaled hit on every female friend of Amir – erudite feminists, all. To Amir's shock, they laughed with Khaled, entertained by this specimen, the crooked grin whose insincerity was sincere, and who didn't consider the rules of this country as serious rules.

The next summer, Khaled visited again. They walked around Paris, Amir telling Khaled of various neighbourhoods, citing great intellectual figures his brother didn't know. Khaled was distracted whenever young women passed, his gaze tracking them, which irritated Amir when he spoke of Foucault dying or where Derrida resided or what Houellebecq got wrong. The only topics that gripped Khaled were money and luxury. He photographed expensive sports cars on his phone, and entrusted his fate to the God of professional athletes, that holy goalscorer and trophy-giver. Khaled believed Muslims to be more humane than Christians; mistrusted Blacks; and had a distaste for Jews (but a respect for Israelis, for their military). Much of this jarred with those in Amir's circle who embraced ethnic authenticity – provided that it was the correct authenticity: anti-racist, pacifist, non-consumerist.

Amir ended up avoiding his half-brother by hiding at the library, then sneaking out to cafés for drinking sessions with friends. From guilt, he rescued Khaled's visit at the last, engineering a boozy final two nights out, so they could hug in a selfie, and mean it.

But neither kept up contact beyond the occasional forwarded meme, plus a heartfelt email a few years back, after Amir's mother died of cancer. By then, Khaled was married, and had a boy and a girl. Amir glanced at the pictures, but children all looked the same to him.

His own life hadn't proceeded to plan. A decent American college accepted his doctoral application, and he'd expected to teach there, and fantasized about female American students. Then, without much explanation, his visa application was rejected. Only lawyers could fight it, and he had no such funds. In haste, he found a third-rate university in London, where he frequented Francophone students, and spoke as little English as possible, except with shopkeepers who also spoke little English. On better days, he perceived himself as an up-and-coming intellectual; most days, just as a video-game-playing nobody whose glance caused women to study the ground. The immigrants he'd walked past in poor neighbourhoods of London and Paris (people ignorant of what was all the rage, what was all the outrage) — they always seemed uncultured, more like Khaled than himself. But they'd understood something that Amir only learned late: weakness and power.

He expected to see Khaled at their father's funeral, and planned to apologize for Paris, though his brother would deny knowing what he spoke of. He also wanted to admit aloud that his life hadn't turned out, how he'd quit his doctorate, how he worked low-paid jobs in London, clearing junk from rich people's homes, unsure what remained in his life.

Amir grabs Khaled, unsure whether he's holding skin or clothing, only that it's damp. 'You're here.'

THE GUARDS DISCOVERED THAT two inmates were brothers. So they arranged a fraternal event, Khaled explains. They are to fight tomorrow morning. The winner must beat the loser to death. The guards are bringing friends to watch. Amir is the smaller brother, and the weaker. He has never punched anyone. 'Can we not do it?' he says, knowing the answer. Resistance is just delay filled with suffering. However, the guards could be bluffing, waiting to see if two brothers would agree to fight – then calling them scum for doing so, spitting at and hurting them. 'Khaled, you'll destroy me.'

'We'll see.'

'No, it's obvious.'

This admission of brotherly inferiority, even now, is shaming. Amir moves about, wanting to escape himself, the point of his elbow digging into his brother, who pushes back. During his detention, Amir has sought to blame something for this: his mother's idealism, for example, which led to him keep up the language. Yet it was his hatred of work that led him to travel, hoping to inherit something from his late father. Instead, he inherits death this morning. Amir pushes his knuckles hard into the canvas bag, but runs out of energy. 'If I could have a strong drink right now, I actually don't think I would.' A wave of regret overcomes him for what he never did in his life. Queasy, he finds an air hole, the frayed canvas, his pulse too fast.

'You never said why you came to this shitty country,' Khaled remarks.

'For the funeral.'

'What funeral?'

Their father died in April. Khaled was arrested two months before – he's learning only now. It doesn't upset him. He falls quiet, but briefly. 'I was wondering why he didn't pay someone to get me out. Teaching me a lesson, I thought.' Their father claimed to disdain Khaled for his line of business – a guy who could get you stuff, electronics across the border, and more besides. Khaled had a reputation for working with anyone, regardless of their side in the war. Everyone liked him, nobody trusted him. But their father's distaste never provoked Khaled's hatred, just wore him into indifference: the dead man was just someone he'd known.

'You're going to fight back,' he orders Amir. 'I'm telling you to.'

Amir turns from his air hole. 'So that you don't get in trouble?'

'There are fights where you have a big guy, and everyone bets he'll win. But then the small guy can really fight.'

'I'm the small guy who really *can't* fight. Even in my mind, I have no idea how to punch someone.'

'We can spar right now,' Khaled jokes. 'Well, *I* am gonna try, so go fuck yourself.'

'Such an idiot, you are.' A pleasure in brotherly banter. Amir smiles, wipes his sweaty face against the interior of the bag.

Khaled asks if he's got a girlfriend.

'A girlfriend?' Amir says. 'Why don't you ask if I've got a wife?'

'You? No way are you married.'

'Why not?'

'You're too soft. She'd need to propose.'

'Move your elbow, you fuck.'

Khaled swears at him in French.

Amir does the same. Lovely to curse in his own language.

Since his arrest, Amir keeps recalling something from school. His class watched a documentary on the Drancy deportations, and an elderly female survivor of the Nazi camps told the television interviewer, 'They could do anything to our bodies, but they couldn't touch our minds.' That isn't true, Amir thinks. His mind is in charge of nothing.

He struggles to extricate an arm, needing to scratch his scalp, feeling bald patches there. He dreads a mirror. All three of them – mother, father, he – will be gone tomorrow, and forever. Three years back, they'd never have imagined their time was so short; they'd have wept. Khaled will remember us, Amir thinks. But what good is that? He's the kind who can't give a coherent account of this morning, let alone recount another's life. He wouldn't think to; he wouldn't know why.

Once, when led from cell to cell, Amir passed a heap of men, eyes open like fish, numbers scrawled in marker on their foreheads. Don't think ahead. Just this, just now.

He'll command Khaled not to tell people what happened, only that he'd seen Amir in prison, and he hadn't survived. Amir can't bring himself to give this instruction. Each time he nears the thought – his coming transformation, permanent blindness, deafness, loss of taste, touch, opinion, words, disappointment, possibility, memory: eliminated, for always – he's dizzy as if flipped backward over and over, opening his eyes, closing them. Somehow, he dozes for a few minutes to the background of his brother talking.

The day before he left England, Amir did a solo removals job, struggling to find parking on a leafy street of terraced houses in North West London. He left his van far from the location, meaning he was miffed by the time he knocked, rapping hard on a red front door. This was exhausting work that he hated, but he could take shifts when he pleased. Mostly, he stayed at his studio flat in Hounslow, kitchenette in the corner, a PlayStation, junk food from a nearby petrol station, cheap Australian wine, online porn, his phone. When he ran out of money, he'd call the removals company, and accept another job discarding the artifacts of a stranger's life.

Behind that red door, a tall old woman in dark jeans appeared, maroon jumper, knobbly hands clasped, one over the other. She looked at him from a height, cheekbones like a pushy man's elbows, an indent in her temples, dull green eyes. She didn't look away, so he did. 'You're here for the work.' She backed inside to admit him, wavering momentarily when either of her legs left the ground, then landing with hard certainty, as if towers strode.

She had many belongings to discard but was not moving out, just 'rationalizing', which struck Amir as the wrong word. She had an accent, so he doubted her language skills, as she doubted his – one of those metropolitan conversations where non-native speakers silently correct each other's English. She led him around three floors, initially pointing to specific items, then wearying, and just telling him to take what wasn't essential.

'I don't know what is essential for you,' he said.

'Downstairs, I'd say the fridge, the oven, the kitchen table are essential.'

'All the rest goes? This furniture also?'

'Why not.'

'They say to me this is a small job. I need more guys for this.'

'Not *everything*. The rubbish bits, I mean.'

'Which is rubbish?'

She pointed to the music player, which Amir approached, wondering if he could sell it: an old CD player with a stack of classical discs that'd be worth nothing. The bookshelves were half-empty, a few hundred volumes lying on their sides. No resale value.

'This?' he asked, of a large framed poster.

'The Bosch?'

The print itself was worthless, a picture with heaven on one side, hell on the other, with human depravity sandwiched between. But the frame had value.

How faraway that house feels, yet the red door must be there now, existing at this exact time.

The old woman boasted about her purge: shelf by shelf, week by week, she'd been throwing away all her books, most already dumped in the blue recycling bin. Sanitation workers rolled noisily up her street each Thursday morning, flinging into their ravenous truck another alphabetized section of her past. She pulled a fallen hardcover from her shelf. 'Recognize that person on the back?' He guessed before looking that it would be her. Author photos always struck him as pathetic: the soon-to-be-forgotten posing as the long-to-be-remembered, hand on chin, gazing soulfully from a remainder bin. He was embarrassed for her, that she found it necessary to assert her status to a bored stranger holding moving boxes. Dutifully, he looked at the photo on the dust jacket – she, Dora Frenhofer, pictured decades ago at a panel event, pin-striped suit jacket with padded shoulders, a handsome middle-aged woman, red lipstick, mahogany hair chopstick-impaled.

'You had a haircut,' he remarked. Hers was white now, and badly shorn.

'I did it myself, cut with fabric scissors during the first weeks of lockdown.'

He folded boxes. All her remaining books he placed inside slowly – slow not from caution but because she paid by the hour. In other boxes he placed knick-knacks. At first, he asked which to take. But she never declined, so he just went around, helping himself. Working away, Amir pondered his father, just hospitalized then, whom he'd fly to see the next day, and this stirred thoughts of his mother, wondering how those two ever got together, which prompted a harsh judgement of his own past few years, how unappealing he'd be to any woman now, the degradation of this work, and the oddness of removals during a pandemic.

She was eating lunch, and offered him egg salad. 'You can take off your mask. I'm not worried.'

They hardly spoke until she learned that he'd grown up in France, whereupon she switched to his language. Anything he mentioned about Paris triggered the old woman to recount something about her time there, from age nineteen and into her twenties, as if his life existed primarily as a conversation-starter. While she was going on about 1960s artistic Paris, he interrupted for a smoke and insisted on going outside, though she said he was welcome to light up here. On his return, she thanked him for the company, remarking that she hadn't known how much she had missed it during all these weeks. She'd not had a single meal with a person during that time.

'No family around?'

She had a daughter, Beck, who lived in Los Angeles. But the

old woman changed topics dismissively – not a matter she cared to delve into. He resumed filling boxes, and carried them to his van. Amir appeared a final time, asking if she needed anything further, presenting a form for her to sign.

'I must admit,' she confided. 'I suddenly feel ill that those books are going. Not so much my ones that I wrote. But there are books that came from my mother and father.' Amir was ready to leave, so made unloading sound impossible.

'Have you ever slept?' she asked Amir, signing and returning the pen. 'You look about the tiredest man I've ever met.'

He didn't like her. But he dreamed of that old woman, of being looked after, of sitting silently at meals, eating her food, lodging in one of her empty rooms upstairs.

'I need a piss,' Khaled says. 'I've been holding so long that I can't go now.'

'Why'd you ask me for permission if you already tried?'

'I wasn't asking permission. I told you I need a piss.'

Amir sputters with unintended laughter.

Khaled muffles laughter too, that of someone who doesn't know what was funny but wants to join in. He squeezes his brother's knee – the bad one, and Amir curses.

'My brother!' Khaled says. 'We had a good laugh.'

'More of that. Make me laugh again.'

'I don't know how I did it.'

A cell door clangs, not theirs. A guard is hacking and sniffing.

'Brother,' Khaled whispers. 'So sad to see you.'

THE GUARDS DRAG OUT the duffel bag, and pull at the padlock — none can recall the combination. They light cigarettes. Someone finds scissors, and the blades pierce the canvas just above Amir's face, snipping downward.

As ordered, he sits up. His fingers touch something: beneath him is that pen used to poke holes in the bag. They're told to stand. He does so. Trembling, he tries to focus on counting seconds. A guard complains that Amir is wet. Someone sniffs the air, and pretends to vomit.

More guards arrive, talking about a Dubai restaurant that sells steak dipped in gold. They push Amir and Khaled toward a larger cell, where spectators can watch. But they forgot the key, so someone must return to the guard station, and they argue over who should go. Amir's brain is not processing, just stuck on a repeating fact: it's now.

It's now It's now It's now It's now

The guards are complaining about the allocation of parking spaces. They unlock the large cell. Someone mentions 'the little faggot', meaning Amir. They bet on how many minutes this will last. Tension suffuses the room, violence approaching.

Amir notices that he's clutching that pen.

'Someone left this,' he says.

For an instant, the guards aren't sure what he's doing, and someone slaps his hand, and the pen hits a far wall, and someone else says that it was his pen, and makes Amir collect it, and hand it over. This interruption deflates the guards.

A loud man works them up again, shouting about the fight. He slaps Amir across the face. Amir — gaze still on the floor — says nothing. They shove him, and he stumbles, rights himself.

'Come on!' a guard tells him.

'Now!' another demands.

Amir tucks his head down, clenches his jaw, waiting for Khaled's first blow.

'Now!' the guard repeats, and shoves Amir, and twists his face to scream in his ear: a ringing deafness. Amir's body is just a vessel in which he huddles. His eyes are smarting from drips of sweat. Blinking, he glances at his brother across the cell.

Once an athlete, Khaled is a skeleton now, his shaved head nicked and notched, a thick greying beard. His arms are extended before him, fingers splayed, as if the lights were off. His eyelids resemble black slugs. But those aren't the lids. His eyes are open. The sockets are empty, plucked.

Arms outstretched, waiting for the first blow, Khaled is mumbling something.

Amir makes sense of it. It's not a prayer. It's a single word. It's French, and meant for him. His brother repeats it. '*Merci.*'

DIARY: MAY 2020

I check the time. My event is now. I need to stop writing, and start impersonating a novelist.

What I agreed to was a literary festival in the English countryside. They promised a night of glamping, though even this failed to dissuade me. My hope was to salvage my failing literary career through networking, which I'm awful at. But all looked promising, for I was to appear onstage with two prominent writers: a fashionable young Brooklynite known for dystopian fiction of such political obviousness that it wins awards; and an Irish ex-bouncer who wrote drizzly little novels for little readership before switching to television, where he scripted episodes of Succession, *thus succeeding in the successor medium. I fully intended to disgrace myself with backstage schmoozing.*

But, a global pandemic.

Now we're appearing via Zoom, neither here nor there, with a reputedly live audience of several dozen watching on devices. While the moderator makes the best of it, I fixate on the screen, how old I am compared with everyone else, and how my resting face — limp and absent — resembles a death mask. I must adopt an expression when my attention drifts, as it already has. A respectful half-smile perhaps? A pensive frown?

There's no point in my describing people as 'young' all the time. Nearly everyone is young now, except the 'eminent'. For those neither 'young' nor 'eminent' — just white-haired and worried — there's a different word: 'invisible'. Yet today, I'm notably visible in split-screen, nodding knowingly as the moderator lists my fellow guests' accolades and genius grants and movie deals, before citing my only almost-successful book (getting its name wrong, which is fine). Behind me in the video frame, I notice, are a pair of my dirty socks and yesterday's twisted underwear, at rest against the IKEA cupboard. I should've sat before IKEA bookshelves like everyone else.

After a reading by each of us, the audience is invited to message questions. These appear onscreen, and the moderator sifts through them, bypassing crackpot queries and selecting flattering ones, most for the Brooklynite, plus a few for the TV writer.

'Guys?' the moderator tells the online viewers. 'Let's not leave our other guest hanging. More questions, folks!'

A half-minute passes.

'Come on, people!'

The two other writers gaze down, eyes flitting side-to-side, apparently checking their phones.

'Well, lucky me,' the moderator proceeds. 'I get her to myself. So tell us,' she asks me, 'what's next for you, Nora?'

After we sign out, I'm faced with my onscreen reflection, which causes me to turn away, my attention halting at the pile of unread novels on my desk. How, I wonder, can this (literature) coexist with that (screens)?

I'm absurd to persist. Or perhaps I'm just a wasp-brained algorithm, completing the programmed task. Plus, quitting would stamp my life as a failure — that I didn't resign, but bookworld fired me.

What I need is to work. Yet I'm haunted by the phantom of people watching me on devices.

Stop worrying what others think! Then again, isn't that the subject of fiction: what other people think?

It's the act of writing that infatuates me. And others' books remain among my pleasures, that anticipation before opening a cover, and anything could be inside, and you'll never quite predict it. I'm still awed at others' craft, how they patch together words, and produce people.

But all these writers, all yearning to create something of moment despite its near-impossibility — do they too wonder where this fits anymore?

~~She rarely makes it through an hour of television, so he must watch every episode twice.~~

Or

~~He stops short at the entrance to their bedroom.~~

Or

He picks his beard in perplexity at the new bedside tables, which she must've formed by stacking copies of his latest novel.

A writer from the festival

(DANNY LEVITTAN)

'EPISODE ONE'

FADE IN:

INT. DANNY AND ZOEY'S BEDROOM - NIGHT

The messy Park Slope bedroom of author DANNY LEVITTAN (around 40) and his financier wife, ZOEY (also 40). She's resting on the mattress in a leisure-wear tracksuit, lit by the television at the foot of their bed. Danny stops short in the doorway, having noticed something. She hits 'pause'.

                    ZOEY
    I'm watching. What?

HE PICKS HIS BEARD in perplexity at the new bedside tables, which she must've formed by stacking copies of his latest novel. On the bedroom wall, an episode of *Succession* is paused – Danny saw this one last night, but Zoey fell asleep. She can rarely stay awake through a late-night hour of television, so he must double-watch every show, his dreams haunted by character actors shouting, 'You can all go fuck yourselves!'

When they met two decades ago, Danny was majoring in English literature, Zoey in African studies, and neither seemed likely to own New York City property, let alone a four-bedroom in this desirable smug of Brooklyn, a short walk from Prospect Park. But upon graduating, Zoey – big-boned Irish-American soccer player with a conscience and a calculator – took a figuring-it-out job at the wealth-management firm of her best friend's dad. Seventeen years later, she's VP for social commitment, arriving daily at Connecticut headquarters with an ankh necklace under her business shirt and an endangered-turtle tattoo on her shoulder. It's *she* who can afford this place.

Danny's contribution is household chores, prompting her to remark that straight men are visually incapable of distinguishing between clean and wiped. Among his recent assignments was to find them bedside tables. But she is prone to pickiness and he prone to dithering, so Zoey took matters into her own hands, piling up those hardcover copies of his latest novel that long dwelled in Penguin Random House boxes down the hall.

'On the upside,' Danny says, 'you have twenty copies beside you every night, if the urge ever hits you to actually read it.'

'Don't you feel, at this point, that I'm pretty familiar with your writing? It's like you with your shirt off – I know how that looks. Do I need to see it again?'

'That's how you describe my fiction?'

'To be totally clear, I don't *mind* seeing your upper body.'

'This isn't what I need to hear right now.'

'Feed me lines then.'

'I thought you said dialogue wasn't my strong point.'

Her eyes remain on the frozen TV scene. 'Can I?' She un-pauses.

Danny's problem with her financial support is not pride; he swallows that with the weekly Zabar's delivery. The problem is they've lost their shared sense of mission. In their twenties, she shared in the tribulations of finding him a literary agent, and rallied Danny to keep at his writing. She was elated when he got a story in *Harper's*, leading to his debut novel, which she adored, then the second book, of which she remarked, 'I totally see what you're trying to say with this.' The third was a story collection that took her a year to get through, he watching in peripheral vision in bed each night as the pages sank toward her face. 'It's not that I'm *not* enjoying,' she said. 'I'm just exhausted.' Her exhaustion amounted to his lodgings, so he could not complain.

The next decade, Danny spent toiling at his novel-cum-bedside-table, *Babylon Lullaby*, a piece of writing more heartfelt than any he'd yet attempted. When conceiving the storyline, he watched scenes unfold behind his closed eyelids while falling asleep each night, and lurched awake in the small hours, scribbling notes, adjusting character names, fixing word choices. For years, he laboured this way, wringing scenes from everything he'd witnessed, each belief about humanity – a novel of which, if asked how long it took to write,

Danny could have pompously replied: 'My whole life.' *Babylon Lullaby* was his essence, distilled for posterity, and he daydreamed of his essence attracting a teaching position. When his agent shopped foreign rights, an Australian publisher snapped them up, and emailed him that *Babylon Lullaby* was 'sublime', and invited Danny to a book festival two years hence.

Since those thrilling days, nobody else found the sublime in his book. The *Babylon Lullaby* publication date didn't help: 19 January 2017, a day before Donald Trump's inauguration, when few cared about magical-realist historical fiction while magical-realist historical fiction unfolded on CNN. The novel was hardly reviewed – not in *The New York Times*, not *The Guardian*, only a lukewarm mention in the industry organ *Kirkus*. By the time jurors for literary awards met, they'd never heard of this novel, nor did Danny know them personally, so they saved time on the impossibly long reading lists by discarding *Babylon* without opening it. He'd once hoped that critical acclaim would compel Zoey to read what meant so much to him. At least they had furniture.

For Danny, accepting his book's death was akin to digesting a hardcover copy. He moped for months, then emailed Nell. She'd once described a literary agent's job as 'one-third contacts, one-third contracts, one-third therapy'. He required the third third, and she proposed lunch at a Midtown bistro. Her counsel was simple: stop writing seriously; write for profit. It doesn't have to be forever. Consider success a palate cleanser.

Before, such advice – to write what people wanted – would've offended him. But he was starting to suspect that the name 'Daniel Levittan' might never appear among The Great Authors. What hurt was that he'd never even infiltrated the top literary circles, where he could've made common cause with like-minded mediocrities. Instead, luck dribbled away, puddling in bags under his eyes and patching his beard white – effects that could've looked authorial in the era when he first sought glory, but that now looked nothing like a writer was supposed to look. Trapped in the right body at the wrong time, he articulated self-pity through excessive interest in the correct grinding of rare coffee beans, and by longing for the analogue past, much of which remained present if you weren't lazy. But he was: a man with a wind-up watch who checked the time on his phone.

Over that lunch, Danny and his agent brainstormed profitable plot points: the British upper class during World War Two; plucky refugee children; kinky sex; lighthouses were hot; speech impediments too. 'Endearing ones,' Nell specified. 'Not the weird kind, if that's not offensive to say.' In thirty minutes, between bites of balsamic-drizzled sea bass, they mapped out his write-by-numbers novel, which Danny composed in a five-month blur, producing a slab of brainrot so cringe that he suspected it could succeed. He emailed Nell the manuscript, *Gentlelady in the Lighthouse Window*.

She replied immediately: 'LOVE the title!' Weeks later, she read it, and raved even more, then took several more weeks prepping a submission package – she wanted to go wide on this one. They had the obstacle of his previous editor, Craig, who had a first-look deal on the next novel. But Craig was highbrow, so Nell expected he'd pass. If he did, she could stoke a multi-publisher bidding war, and Danny would feel mildly ashamed when the book came out, but able to support himself. 'Then you write anything you want!' she reminded him.

To writer friends, Danny was evasive about his current project. He planned to confess once he had the big advance. Then, as Nell was sending *Gentlelady in the Lighthouse Window* for consideration by his most-recent editor, a date on the calendar popped up: that festival.

The problem was, they had invited Danny as a serious literary author, a guise he'd spent months stripping from his soul, with much anguish. Now, he was expected to assume his former persona. Thankfully, he'd do so far from reality, Australia. But he's not sure how to feel about this, so distracts himself by checking his phone, packs stupidly early, and wanders from room to room in their apartment. 'Think I'm gonna head to the airport now.'

'Isn't your flight tomorrow?'

'I've decided to walk there.' He hoists his hiker's backpack.

'To Australia?'

'To JFK. It'll clear my head.'

A long ramble should resurrect the artist in him. Minor novelists drive; literary greats walk. (Why, he wonders, are famous authors always boasting about their walks? Do ideas come when in hiking boots? Or is it just that successful novelists own places in the country?)

His own hike – through Bed-Stuy, Cypress Hills, Woodhaven, Jamaica – proves less than pastoral, tramping for two hours over concrete, under traffic lights, past filthy vans. When not checking the Maps app on his phone, he contemplates authors whose careers he envies, and wonders if they were walkers. David Foster Wallace seemed more likely to spend hours thinking about going for a walk, then not. Zadie Smith would probably gaze down from a Manhattan window, free-associating about the quirkiness of pedestrians. Did

Kafka hike, or just pace? Virginia Woolf definitely walked: in the dim lamp of his college memory, she strides across London, and glimpses a dwarf. She walked right into the sea at the end, didn't she, rocks in her pockets.

Danny's hands are stuffed into his, numb from cold. The snow-drifts haven't melted in Queens. He's lost, turning in place. A police car bleeps once and pulls over, the officer asking if he's doin' good. Danny – round metal spectacles of a Victorian botanist, bushy beard, musty three-piece suit and neon backpack – babbles about urban hiking. Repeatedly, the cops call him 'sir', meaning it as an insult. Upon leaving, one of them mumbles, 'Fuckin' a-hole,' which shocks Danny. Did he act like a fuckin' a-hole? Was he fundamentally a fuckin' a-hole?

He reaches the outskirts of JFK, its misery hotels and anti-terror fences. An author in search of an entrance, he locates the terminal finally, takes a seat, and settles down to read. He brought *The Brothers Karamazov*, which he plans to start and finish during the estimated 34 hours, 45-minute travel time to Australia. It's a portly volume, whose cover he folds open, clearing his throat, as if about to narrate to gathered passengers the family history of Fyodor Pavlovitch Karamazov.

But the movement and voices of those passengers are a hand that slaps down the page: he must look up to see where they came from. The answer is: everywhere – twitchy humans trapped between fright and flights, primed both for a shout of 'Get to the ground!' and the shout of their names at Starbucks – the cost/benefit of the American airport. But New York doesn't equal America, as both sides are eager to confirm. Danny picks out a few venturers from Trump country: a guy wearing a T-shirt of an AR-15; a woman with confederate-flag kerchief hanging from her back pocket.

He returns to *The Brothers Karamazov*, page 3, then checks his phone, then the departures monitor. Zoey was right: stupidly early. He must kill hours more, and invokes the aid of snack food and internet. By the next morning, he has reached page 5 of *Karamazov*, and is wearily consuming a breakfast burrito when his flight appears on the monitors. At last, he can check in.

'Passport, please.'

'Wait. What?'

Suddenly, he's in a spinning clock, sprinting for the taxi stand, calling Zoey at work, telling her what an *idiot* he is. It's an oddly affectionate conversation, she explaining where his passport ought to be in their bedroom, rooting for him to still make the flight, urging him not to stress. He will get there. Festival folks will dote on him. Australian fans will swoon. 'Hanging out with book people will remind you of why you got into this.'

'Love you,' he says, reckoning with how much he owes Zoey, how she'd have wanted a family, how his moods held her back, how he wants the best for her life. He resolves that, when back in nine days, he will find an apartment of his own.

FADE OUT.

END OF EPISODE ONE

'EPISODE TWO'

FADE IN:

INT. HOTEL ROOM IN AUSTRALIA - NIGHT

An alarm clock shows 8:17. DANNY wakes, jet-lagged. He parts the curtains, low sunlight on the horizon. He calls the front desk.

                    DANNY
           (on phone)
     Hey. When's breakfast till this morning?

                    HOTEL CLERK
     It starts at six.

                    DANNY
     But till when?

                    HOTEL CLERK
     You mean tomorrow?

                    DANNY
     No, today. Right now.

                    HOTEL CLERK
     Uhm, our breakfast is only served in
     the morning, sir.

DANNY CONSULTS THE WINDOW again, inverting day to night. He splashes water on his face. It's so hot in here. He left in winter and only arrived by summer. His luggage is full of wrinkled three-piece suits, corduroys, woollen socks.

He skims his tour itinerary: the first event is a bookshop reading tomorrow at 9 p.m. Checking his phone for messages, he finds an email from the Australian publicist, Nousha, wishing him luck tonight.

Tonight? He checks the date on his phone. He's onstage in forty minutes.

Danny sprints for the lift, unwashed, panicked. He jumps into a cab waiting outside the hotel, and scrambles out at the Broken Shelf, banging his shin into a sandwich board chained to the sidewalk: *Reading tonight! Daniel Levittan, author of* BABYLON LULLABY*! Come one, come all!*

All couldn't make it. Nor could one. He stands in what looks like a barn with a small library in it, fifty empty chairs before a lectern, no humans but the cashier.

'Hey,' he says, approaching her, 'I'm Daniel Levittan?'

'You don't sound so sure. Let me get the events person. Ronda!'

Awkward wait.

'You guys hold lots of readings here?'

'Ronda's coming. I've not read yours yet.'

'So many amazing books to get to, I bet!'

She dials an internal number, and shout-whispers: 'Not my job to babysit, okay?!'

Moments later, Ronda arrives, a twentysomething with dyed-grey hair, pink cat-eye glasses, and a floor-length dress with Harry Potter lightning bolts. 'Let's give everyone a few minutes to arrive.'

'Sounds like a plan!' Danny responds, hiding his disappointment behind exclamation points.

'When did you get in?'

'Just this morning actually!'

'Too soon for a bit of lubricant?'

'Sorry, what?'

She points to a table of fifty glasses of red. 'Help yourself.'

A couple enters the store, a rickety lady propping up her prehistoric husband. Ronda hastens over to them, pointing at the stacked display for *Babylon Lullaby*, then indicating Danny, who straightens his posture, as if in a police line-up. The elderly couple shuffles over to inspect him, and the tremulous wife takes a copy, considering both sides of the cover with interest – and places the book under her arm. They sit directly before the lectern.

'My Australian fanbase in full!'

'People turn up late in this city. Others'll be here soon.'

Soon arrives. Nobody else does.

Danny – to centre himself (thus avoiding the centre of himself) – refreshes email on his phone, and finds one from Nell, who reports having told his previous editor at PRH that her client probably prefers his trashy bestseller at a more commercial imprint. It's a win-win. If Craig wants *Gentlelady in the Lighthouse Window*, he'll need to pre-empt with decent money. If not, Nell goes wide, and prods her editorial friends into an auction. 'This could move fast!!' she emailed. 'Keep your ringer <u>ON</u>!'

Ronda asks if he's ready to start. He pretends to mute his phone, and pockets it, aflutter with the Nell plan. Yes, alright, it's the end of his highbrow hopes. But with middlebrow money and – above all – success at something, he's high. If only he'd always known corruption was so pleasant. A secondary benefit is that he is bulletproof tonight, viewing this absurd situation with amusement: his walk to the gallows, a bound copy of his past decade on the lectern, Ronda there behind rows of empty chairs, giving him a thumbs-up. Danny – overdressed in a wool suit, flushed – smirks to himself.

But he must adopt the proper disguise, so unfolds his sheet of prepared remarks, sweaty hand spreading the page. 'Good to be here in Australia,' he reads. 'Wonderful that so many could make it.' He snorts, a tad hysterically, adding to the elderly couple: 'I'm glad you managed to find a seat!' Ronda gives another patronizing thumbs-up, while the cashier is audibly watching YouTube on her phone – it sounds like skateboarders hurting themselves on purpose; she claps her hand over her mouth every few seconds.

Danny explains to the massed crowd of two plus an employee what he intended artistically with *Babylon Lullaby*, how a version of that opening scene – the spider in the baby carriage – really happened (it didn't, but he vaguely believes this now). He'll give a reading of the first few pages, he warns, and clears his throat, wipes his forehead. Jet-lag sweat? Stop getting nervous. Just read what's on the page.

But spoken aloud, the words seem to smash together without spaces. Danny speaks and listens at once to this linguistic pile-up, noting that the author isn't particularly good at writing. Improvising, he edits his novel as he goes, which proves disastrous, lines ending abruptly, forcing him to track back and explain. He keeps clearing his throat, prompting Ronda to present a glass of water. He sips, and croaks, 'Thank you for your patience, everyone.' Interpreting this as the end, Ronda applauds, and the cashier looks up from YouTube and joins in, while the old couple in the front add theirs, a skin-slapping quartet that peters out.

'Do you think,' Ronda asks, 'that we might have time for Q-and-A?'

A customer enters the store, hurrying over. She asks where the travel section is, stage-whispering apologies.

'If nobody else has a question,' Ronda says, 'let me have the honour. Daniel Levittan – what *is* your writing schedule?'

The schedule of a great artist could, perhaps, be interesting. The schedule of a failure is to peep at a schmuck in private. So he obliges with a falsified version, excising the morning hours devoted to reading sports columns and watching clips of capybaras. No more questions are forthcoming, so the elderly lady and prehistoric husband try to stand. Danny rushes around the lectern to help them up. They thank him, and shuffle toward the signing table, which is piled with copies of *Babylon Lullaby*, along with three black Sharpies.

He sits, accepting the woman's copy, her husband's cloudy eyes looking in different directions, neither at Danny. She, at least, is delighted when the author asks her name, and she recounts how well they know South Africa (she seems to think he's from there), and how the part about the doctor resonated because she herself worked in the medical field for many decades at the office of her husband, a podiatrist.

'Feet!' Danny says. 'Must be great stories there!'

As he signs her copy, he marvels for an instant that the 867 pages beneath this pen are his – misspent time perhaps but meaningful in his life, a novel finalized that day when he flung hand-revised printer pages in the air, and Zoey took photos of them raining down, and she kissed him as he sat. Danny considers the elderly woman's excessive make-up, and he experiences such affection for her, a stranger who wants to read what he wrote. His efforts weren't a waste, even if the book was just for her. And if his new manuscript becomes a hit, readers might even come back and discover *Babylon Lullaby*. It's not over. He presents Edith with her signed copy, inscribed fondly.

'Oh, that's okay,' she says, returning it. 'But wonderful talk!' She directs her husband toward the exit, pausing to return their wine glasses.

Ronda approaches Danny, palms together in apology. 'If it's any consolation, *I* thought you rocked.'

'Each little bit of buzz helps, right?' he says. 'Would it be useful, by the way, if I autograph the leftover copies? I know that signed ones sell better.'

'There's actually this weird thing with publishers over here? They don't accept returns if they're signed. So maybe best to leave it? In case they don't? Sell?' She gathers them fast, as if Danny might autograph against her will. Ronda returns with a credit-card reader, and punches up $29.95.

'What's that?' he asks.

She touches the lone copy of *Babylon Lullaby* left on the signing table.

'What, the copy I signed for her?'

'We can't return it with writing inside.'

The cashier shouts across the store, 'Don't charge full price, Ronda.'

'I could offer you our staff discount?' she says, then calls back to the cashier: 'Junior-staff discount? Or senior?'

'Ten per cent.'

'Junior it is.'

In the taxi back to the hotel, Danny is ready to start his morning, which is regrettable since it's nearly 10 p.m. He enters the lobby to find the festival's welcome-mixer underway, with a blare of authors pretending to be extroverts. A young woman – shaved head, long nose, purple lipstick – holds a copy of *Babylon Lullaby*. This must be Nousha, his publicist from the Australian publishing house. They shake hands, and she thanks him for coming all the way to Oz. 'How'd you feel the reading went tonight?'

'Pretty good! Not the best turnout; not the worst.'

'I just got off the phone with Ronda.'

'So not a huge crowd. But enthused.'

'It's about building until you reach critical mass.'

'Yeah, I was pretty near critical mass tonight,' he jokes, not nearly as sour as he would've been months before. A lousy reading is a reminder: farewell to the former self.

Nousha runs through his activities of the coming days, including a writing workshop he'll teach; the big onstage event, where a major TV journalist interviews him; press appointments TBD; plus, the private dinner with Gavril Osic.

Danny steps back in amazement to hear this final item. The early novels of Gavril Osic are, in his estimation, among *the* greatest works of postwar fiction – perfectly constructed, indelible. Besides his writing, Osic was always a hero to Danny for his defiance of the despot who ran his country. Danny knew that Osic lived in exile in Australia nowadays, but nobody said he'd meet this literary idol. Nousha explains that Osic invites a selected group of festival authors to dine at his home each year. The list is submitted by the publishing houses, which propose writers of note. She put forward Danny.

Effusive with thanks, he invites her to celebrate with him at the open bar. Two proseccos and one confession follow – perhaps from fatigue, perhaps from this manic-depressive evening. 'Honestly, Nousha? I'm considering this trip my goodbye to literary life.'

'Don't say that,' she responds. 'You wrote a wonderful novel, Daniel. *That* is what matters.'

She can't be older than twenty-four but speaks with such confidence, as if it's about art not glory – an ideal that he serviced as an amateur, but surrendered as a pro. 'According to BookScan, *Babylon* sold fifty-seven copies total,' he tells her. 'That's almost hard to do. That's how many you sell from people butt-buying on Amazon.'

'I bet *some* people bought it deliberately.'

He laughs, and she's smiling back, black eyes looking right at his, as if she knows something nobody else does, polite enough to keep her thoughts to herself, to allow others to be the experts.

FADE OUT.

END OF EPISODE TWO

```
FADE IN:
INT. HOTEL DINING ROOM - MORNING
DANNY is woozy after much booze and little
sleep the night before. He hovers around the
breakfast buffet, disoriented by noise coming
from the tables, which are louder than
morning should allow.
```

HOW DO ALL THESE authors know each other?

They must've bonded at the welcome-mixer last night, and friend groups have formed. Their varied fashions – oversized heart-shaped sunglasses, sitting beside a grey suit, next to a tongue-piercing – imply recent acquaintance, though the braying suggests they've never encountered humans they loved more.

They're bidding over whether Trump is worse than Bolsonaro is worse than Boris, which morphs into humblebrags about festival schedules, and finishes with admiring citations of obscure writers from poor countries. An ageing Filipino busboy frowns – they've left an ungodly mess where pastry platter meets coffee station. Danny lifts a steel lid: porkish steam clears over mud-brown sausages.

He settles at a solo table, sipping the world's tiniest glass of orange juice, and listens unwillingly.

'Four years since Jaipur? I am *so* fucking old!'

'Wait, didn't I see you in Cartagena?'

'Oh, you're right!'

'Hate to do this, but I gotta love you and leave you. I'm on ABC in a half-hour.'

'Radio or television?'

'Christ – radio, I hope. I look like shit.'

'You look totally quaffable, babes.'

'Hotel bar again tonight?'

'I'll be the one holding the bottle.'

'Kisses, all! And good luck today!'

Constipated in his hotel room, Danny keeps refreshing email, awaiting something decisive from Nell. What would Gavril Osic make of the crass literary scene here? Danny's attention is diverted by a dozen new novels in a festival tote bag – it's a tradition to give each author a range of other invitees' work, as a way to introduce everyone. He dumps the lot into the bathroom bin, and feels cleansed.

In the hotel hallway, three writers around Danny's age are gossiping: a perfumed bald Scot in a tanktop; a jittery playwright from rural Newfoundland in butterfly frock; and a sky-high former WNBA player who switched to short stories. They notice Danny's festival lanyard as he closes the room door after himself.

'And *you* are . . .?' the bald Scot enquires, then widens his eyes at the mention of Danny's book. 'Oh, I've heard of that!' he lies. 'It's doing super-well, I'm told.'

Danny is not above sucking up or selling out; he's eager to do both. Just, he's a talentless whore, more concerned with his dimensions than theirs. But now he finds himself in the very situation that Zoey always tells him to seek. Networking is what art is about, she says. So he memorizes their names, and feigns familiarity with their work, asking about their events, and listening with furrow-browed concern as they perform anxiety about performance anxiety.

'I'm *so* bad onstage,' the Newfoundland playwright says. 'I just go blank.'

'You'll be *great!*'

'Finished,' a maid mumbles, emerging from Danny's room, dragging out the rubbish in a transparent disposal bag.

'Hey hey!' the bald Scot exclaims. 'That's my book in there!'

The former WNBA player sees hers too. 'Did you throw those away?'

Danny turns to the maid. 'I didn't mean for you to take those.'

The Scot – enjoying this – crows: 'He thinks our books are rubbish!'

The three writers fish their works from the disposal bag, flicking away chocolate wrappers and miniature liquor bottles that Danny consumed overnight.

'I rested those books *near* the waste bin, not inside.'

'Sir,' the maid insists. 'They was *in* the rubbish.'

'It's a mystery then. But I really would like those books back, you guys. I was right in the middle of them – and hugely enjoying.'

Danny lugs a dozen soiled books back to his room, bidding farewell to his new frenemies. He flops on the king-sized bed, books hopping in air, crashing to the floor, where he leaves them. According to the bedside clock, he should go downstairs for a coach to the festival site. Those three will be on it. He'll take the next. He lies back, and a wave of exhaustion flows over him. He can't stay awake. Must. He sits up.

For stimulation, he checks and re-checks email, and finds promising news. His highbrow editor at PRH, Craig, has no place on his list for a bestseller – but he loved it, and foresees great things. That opens the field: Nell can officially stoke interest, and already has three commercial imprints on the line, with nine more likely to chime in.

Zoey emailed too. He's afraid to open it because of the subject line: 'What the hell?!'

She was missing him, she explains, so glanced at the printout on his desk of *Gentlelady in the Lighthouse Window*. She only meant to read the opening – but could not stop. 'Holy shit, babe. This is <u>the</u> best thing you've done <u>in YEARS!!!!!</u>'

Yipping with joy, he leaps to his feet, and does karate kicks around the room.

Those three from the hallway went on the previous coach, so he safely boards the next behind Marlin Pratt, a parping English historian who hosts BBC documentaries, stomping around the Parthenon in open-necked safari shirt and red shorts. For those already in the coach, Marlin narrates his own entry with high irony as if for a TV audience, and the seated writers laugh obligingly. Danny is the last to board, and maintains a fake smile, nodding to Marlin, who is stretched across two seats. The man reaches up to snatch Danny's reading copy of *Babylon Lullaby*. 'You did this? Well done,' Marlin says. He flips the book, chortling at the author photo. 'Oh, you're having us on. That is *not* you!'

'It was once.'

'I don't wish to offend,' Marlin says. 'But this photo makes you look ever so slightly mentally impaired.'

'It's from a while back.'

'Like a mentally impaired sex offender.'

As the coach pulls into traffic, Danny takes back his book, and falls into a seat a couple of rows behind, not wanting to situate himself too far away, lest he appears to sulk. Finally, they reach a university campus where the festival chairwoman awaits, greeting all, but granting cheeks-kisses only to Marlin, leading him away to teach his masterclass. The other writers check in with student volunteers at a fold-out table, and are chaperoned to their sessions.

Danny is last, and gives his name and that of the workshop they've assigned him to teach: 'Freaks and Geeks: Creating Characters from Yourself'. They check the list, but his workshop isn't listed. Danny produces his itinerary as evidence, but the student-volunteers just squeeze their faces into pained expressions. He demands someone senior, and such a personage emerges from the green-room tent, eventually finding that the Daniel Levittan workshop was cancelled for low enrolment. 'It does happen, alas.'

'Maybe you should inform the person doing the event!'

'We did.'

Danny contends the opposite, and considers himself the authority on whether he knows something.

'Well,' the senior staffer responds, 'that's your truth.'

Two hours remain until his onstage interview, so he loiters in the green room, a vast tent supplied with bagels, carrot sticks, bottled water. Other writers come and go, high from workshop adulation, chattering volubly, wishing each other luck for upcoming events. Danny watches at one remove, as if in a theatrical production where all parts have been assigned, the cast has mastered its lines, and he is thrust onstage, all the other actors wondering if this guy is even in the play. Danny planned to explain in his workshop that fictional characters need conflict, and respond with transformation. But that's false to life, he thinks. In life, people face conflict, and they respond less with transformation than repetition. Gradually, you become what you were. Which is hungry.

He helps himself to a bagel, though he's still bloated from breakfast, and with a digestive tract that remains on New York. He ambles around the campus quad, and settles on a bench, soothed by exotic tweeting from the branches. Danny still thinks of himself as he was in college – except when he sees undergraduates, who shock him by being teenagers. They haven't yet staggered into everyone else's future. He wants to warn them.

A peacock prances across the empty lawn. 'What's *your* book?' Danny asks.

The animal turns, and stalks closer.

'And your agent? Oh, she's *great*. I've definitely heard of her.'

The peacock keeps advancing. Suddenly uneasy, Danny scooches to the far end of the bench, his foot raised protectively.

The bird's beak rears back, readying to peck. Danny kicks the air between them, looking around, in case he's seen losing a fight to a peacock. Is this a protected species? The fucker wants his bagel. Leaping up, Danny abandons his food, speed-walking back toward the green room, waving hello, for Nousha stands there. 'Thank God you're here,' he tells her. 'I just got assaulted by a peacock.'

'For any reason?'

'A political dispute.'

She has a block of free time, so they wander. 'What,' he asks, 'is *the* worst publicity experience you've had?'

'You want to make sure it's not you?'

'That's exactly why, yes.'

She recalls an American peacenik singer of the 1960s who wrote a

Woodstock-then addiction-then rehab memoir, and visited Australia in a baldness-obscuring orange bandana, doing major promos like an event at a cathedral, where he insisted they black out the stained-glass windows, requiring many floors of scaffolding. His rider also demanded that someone attend with an ironing board. When Nousha arrived, lugging this object, he berated her for standing there with a goddamn ironing board when what he needed was toothpaste. Dutifully, she hurried back up the long nave to go and seek some. Just as she reached the cathedral exit, the singer boomed for her to return. She sprinted all the way back. 'Is it so goddamn hard to find *toothpaste*?' he said. 'Seriously?'

Nousha's parents were immigrants to Australia, her mother a teacher from Bosnia, her father an engineer from Iran. They'd settled in Melbourne, the city where she still resides, now living in a small house with her potter boyfriend, raising chickens in the backyard.

Besides doing publicity, she writes poetry. Danny expresses admiration for that form, mentioning Wordsworth – the only poet who comes to mind. In fact, he scoffs at those who publish poems nowadays, versifying for a world that's not paying the slightest mind. But in her case, he sees a romantic, even if that image is undermined by the amount of time she spends thumbing messages into her phone. Well, that *is* her job, communications. And she must dash – another orphaned writer is wandering lonely as a cloud.

'Before you go, tell me: where do I find your poems? Have any been published?'

'I've done a couple of skinny little volumes.'

'That's not nothing! And you like it, the poeming?'

'I must.'

'You'll know you've made it once you get attacked by a pheasant.'

'Wasn't it a peacock?'

'You of all people should appreciate poetic licence. Anyway, birds evolved from dinosaurs, right? No shame in losing a fight to what was practically a dinosaur.'

A festival staffer with clipboard strides past Nousha, who calls out, 'Melanie, a peacock attacked one of my writers.'

'They're ptarmigans. Fuckin' aggressive, hey?'

Nousha asks to hand over Daniel Levittan, who needs to reach his big onstage interview. Melanie chaperones him through the crowd, and Danny confesses to nerves.

'Whatcha got to lose?' she says. 'If they're rough with ya, tell 'em to fuck right off. You got the mic. You got the power.'

'Except I'm posing as a nice human being.'

She laughs, and he's encouraged. Australians find him witty. What if this is the unexpected turn in his story? That his literary career is *here*, that he isn't finished, just that the Brooklyn in-crowd snubbed him – yet the literati of Australia see something special.

As Melanie leads him toward the outdoor festival stages, the crowd thickens. She narrows her eyes, puzzled, and stops to consult a colleague. 'Well, well, Mr Modesty,' she tells Danny. 'There's a massive bloody line for tickets. Looks like you hit the jackpot.'

FADE OUT.

END OF EPISODE THREE

'EPISODE FOUR'

FADE IN:

EXT. COLLEGE CAMPUS – DAY

A festival staffer hustles DANNY past an endless queue of people waiting to buy tickets.
He knows people are looking at him, so he
avoids eye contact, attempting a sombre writerly expression.

DANNY ONCE READ OF a little-known novelist who turned up for a book event in Japan, only to discover that he was a literary celebrity there. Imagine if that were Danny's fate here. Nousha did mention an important print review this morning, though he hadn't thought newspapers mattered anymore. Where in Australia would he live? Is Melbourne the cool city?

He spent this past year dismantling hope, and salving himself by renouncing bookworld altogether. Now, he's like an incel who finds that someone wants to have sex with him: shockingly in love.

Minutes till he goes up, Danny surveys the crowd, emotional from gratitude. But a worrying thought insinuates itself. His trashy manuscript for *Gentlelady in the Lighthouse Window* is circulating at every New York publishing house. Why didn't he use a pseudonym? Nothing ruins a highbrow reputation like a readable book. What time is it in New York? He fires off an email to Nell: 'something crazy going on here. insane buzz for babylon. mega event. lighthouse was error? talk ASAP pls hold off on taking any offers!!!'

Look at this crowd. He's not finished.

The onstage interviewer is a prominent Australian arts broad-caster, Cleo Kleeber, who joins him in the green room, giving a big smile, then fanning herself to cool down. From a ratty handbag, she produces his hardcover. 'I loved it. Absolutely loved.'

'Wow! I'm so glad to hear that. So, Cleo, do you prefer to discuss our discussion ahead? Or just go with the flow?'

'Let's keep it loose. It's always a hoot interviewing debut nov-elists.'

'Actually, this is my fourth book.'

'Nah, come on!' she says. 'What, honestly?'

Stage technicians hook up their microphone headsets. 'It's go-time.' The two walk into the festival throng, readers everywhere, milling about with just-purchased books, eating sustainable junk food and calling out Cleo's name, for they recognize her from TV.

'This way,' a festival volunteer tells him, cutting diagonally through the crowd. And there it is: a massive stage with a thousand seats before it. He has never seen anything this size for a book event. But he's puzzled. Only a few dozen seats are occupied, surrounded by an ocean of empty fold-out chairs. Wasn't there a huge queue for tickets? He saw the line.

The tech guy directs him and Cleo to the onstage couch, where they sit, he far lower than she, which forces him to talk skyward.

'Is this everyone who's coming?' he whispers to Cleo, hand covering his microphone.

A roar hits them, cheering and whooping, and he tries to sit up in the couch, looking around to localize the noise.

'Wouldn't you love to hear Malala?' Cleo says.

'She's talking now?'

'You must've seen the queue.'

'That queue wasn't for me?'

Cleo laughs, and thumbs-up the sound guy, offering a welcome to their audience (Danny counts them: nineteen people). 'Having a good time today, guys?!' Cleo asks, and reads verbatim the jacket description of *Babylon Lullaby*, then turns to its author. He's still adjusting to this let-down, and is sweltering too, pit stains on his blue dress shirt.

'Daniel Levittan, welcome to Australia.'

He unbuttons his waistcoat. 'Thank you so much, Cleo.'

'First question: why should the people gathered here today, at this celebration of great writing and great books – why should they buy *you*? Come on. Sell us.'

Sinkingly, he looks at the fourteen people in the audience (five left during the intro), and utters a few wandering sentences, barely audible because of the loudspeakers shaking on the adjacent stage: '. . . youngest person *ever* to win a Nobel Prize, author of *I Am Malala: The Story of the Girl Who Stood Up for Education and was Shot by the Taliban*, and the very first . . .'

'So basically,' Danny says, 'I guess you could dub it a novel about memory and the struggle to . . .'

'. . . couldn't be *more* delighted, *more* proud, more *honoured*, to bring up to the stage, our very special guest! Malala Yousafzai!'

Applause drowns him out, so he closes his lips to wait, a space-holder smile. The onstage sign-language interpreter shakes her head at him, cups a hand behind her ear – *Can't hear you!*

After a moment, Cleo resumes, telling the audience: 'Inside scoop, guys: we moderators get assigned events by the festival, and I only got this one yesterday. It's mayhem, going from cookbooks, to self-help, to YA. But that's part of the fun!'

Did she just imply that *Babylon Lullaby* is young-adult fiction? If anything, it's old-adult fiction – that is, adult fiction. Except 'adult fiction' sounds obscene. 'I'm just wondering, Cleo, could we get a super-quick show of hands to see how many out there have had a chance to read my book, so that I pitch my answers right?'

A huge roar from the next stage. Malala is about to speak.

'Personally,' Cleo answers, 'I'm halfway through, and I consider myself somewhat intrigued.'

He glances at her copy, pristine but for the first few pages, the corner bent around page 9. Cleo supplants his question of the audience by asking everyone to raise their hands if they couldn't get tickets to Malala. Everyone raises their hands. 'Well, you can hear her a bit from here, if you strain.' She turns to Danny. 'Soldier on, shall we?'

Sipping water, he nods.

'So, *I* learned,' Cleo says, as if sharing a confidence, 'that this is *not* your debut, which might surprise people. Tell us, Daniel Levittan, why have we never heard of you? Though I figure that might've changed after the review in *The Australian* this morning! How's it feel for a writer to read something like that?'

'I haven't seen it actually. You're making me worry now!'

'I'll read out a bit.'

'Wait – if it's not great, should we skip it?'

'You'll never improve if you don't listen to your critics, right? Like this part here,' she begins, tapping the screen of her iPad, 'saying you have a writing style that's, and I quote: "a male, quasi-autistic register".'

Danny fakes a smile.

'Shall I read on?' she asks.

'I'm not sure what's coming next! Do they say my author photo shows me as a sex offender!'

'Excuse me?'

'No, it's just that someone was looking at my author photo today, and said it reminded them of a sex person. Ignore that; stupid joke.'

'Kinda weird thing to joke about, sexual abuse.'

'Yes. I thought so.' His takes another nervous sip of water.

'You're not on a registry in America or something, are you?'

'God, no! No, no.'

'Not sure why you're laughing like that, Daniel Levittan. There's nothing funny about rape.' She says nothing for several seconds, the word 'rape' hanging in the air.

He looks to the sign-language interpreter, then back to Cleo. 'I really didn't mean to make light of that. Obviously, I'm not laughing at rape.'

'I don't know about you, audience,' Cleo says, 'but I feel a tiny bit triggered right now.' The few in attendance are paying attention now, leaning forward to hear over the noise from the next stage.

'If I made an inappropriate comment, I'm really sorry.'

Cleo takes a deep breath. 'Let's try and move on. Your research,' she resumes. 'Tell us about your process.' He begins to answer – but she breaks in, 'Because there's clearly masses of research crammed into this, right?'

'Hopefully not too much!' He sniffs and fake-laughs at once, recounting his labours at the New York Public Library, where he pored over archival material.

Cleo is fake-snoring. 'Yes, professor,' she says, and the audience bursts out laughing.

She invites Danny to move to a reading, which is punctuated by roars of approval for Malala, jarring with his scene of a deformed jester in 1730s Vienna whose companion is a one-winged canary that, mysteriously at this early point in the novel, speaks Cantonese. As Danny reads – attempting accents – he's hideously aware of the sentimentality, the devices, the falsity. He's no more an artist than all the other imposters.

A whirring noise distracts him. He looks into the audience, where a woman in a mobility scooter is driving down the aisle. She shouts to her friend, who squeaks in joyful reply. The two chat loudly, oblivious to his reading. At last, they bid farewell, and the woman turns her mobility scooter around, and whirs away. With a complicit smile, Danny tells the audience, 'At last! She's gone!'

Someone yells back, 'She's bloody disabled, mate!'

Another roar for Malala, and the echo of her voice: 'Thank you so much all for coming. I thank Australia! Thank you!'

Wild cheers ensue, over which Malala's onstage interviewer shouts that their special guest will be signing books – but no selfies please.

'You can take selfies,' Malala interjects. 'I don't mind.' More cheers.

Cleo concludes too, telling the gathered few: 'This one'll be in the signing tent too.' She drops her headset on the couch, and walks off without goodbye.

Danny stands, unsure how to exit the stage gracefully, a smattering of audience members watching him. He sees Nousha waving to him, and he descends the stairs, her expression either sympathy or gravity, allowing him to pick.

'Did you see any of that?' he asks.

'I got a taste.'

He decides to put on a good face. 'Why would anyone want to hear a Nobel laureate over me?' he jokes. 'Fuck Malala!'

A technician unclips Danny's microphone, muttering with disgust, 'The Taliban shot her, mate.'

He reaches the signing table, where three copies of *Babylon Lullaby* wait, beside stacks of *I Am Malala*, which volunteers frantically open in readiness for a signature before a lengthening line of admirers. One of her fans leans toward Danny. 'What's she like?'

'Malala? I don't work with her. I'm here for a different book.'

Finally, she arrives and sits beside Danny, smiling to him, shaking his hand. She asks if this is his book, and picks up a copy.

'You read novels?' he asks, shrinking inwardly at how self-important he sounds.

'I will try to read yours.' She glances at the queue of people before her, an apologetic head wobble, and begins signing.

Why should anyone care about his writing? It's mortifying that he wants to foist it on them. Malala's admirers are pretending not to see him, the loser with his three copies. Nousha crouches beside him. 'Act like we're having a very important conversation. Saying significant things.'

'Significant things.'

'Important comments.'

'Amazing opinion.'

'Fascinating comeback.'

'Stunning revelation.'

'Urgently but respectfully grabbing author's arm, leading him to pressing appointment.'

He follows her through the crowd, a body among bodies. The one or two novelists who represent his generation have been chosen. The hundred others who'll sign the next open letter against evil – their number won't include him either. He too wants to take a moral stand with no effect. But nobody CCs him on the emails.

He types a message to Nell, just a subject line: 'Ignore previous.'

Nousha seeks to raise his spirits, reminding him of what's ahead tonight: the dinner with Gavril Osic, whose novels will outlive them all.

```
                                          FADE  OUT.
```

END OF EPISODE FOUR

'EPISODE FIVE'

FADE IN:

INT. HOTEL ROOM - NIGHT

DANNY is lying on the carpeted floor of his hotel room, murmuring along with a meditation podcast. Eyes closed, he breathes in through his nose, out through his mouth, readying himself for the big dinner party.

GAVRIL OSIC DOES NOT suffer fools. Danny suffers fools. It's not that some people are fine with fools. It's that not suffering fools is a way of saying you've made it. Fool-suffering is the lot of the ordinary. Or maybe, Danny thinks, sitting upright on the hotel-room carpet, maybe *I'm* the fool. Maybe they're suffering me.

He vows to shut up at tonight's dinner. As the saying goes, 'Better to keep your mouth shut and have everyone think you a fool than to open it and have them know.' He resumes the meditation podcast, mumbling to himself about a fleck of dust floating through a shaft of sunlight.

A minibus will collect the eight chosen authors from the hotel lobby. Waiting around, some jabber from nerves; others hold silent, considering their shoes. Each author received a list of subjects *not* to discuss – above all, you mustn't speak to Osic about his writing. Past attendees violated the rule; it never turned out well. They came across as fans, and Gavril Osic does not tolerate those.

On the minibus, the loudest voice is Marlin Pratt, the much-gesticulating BBC historian, who is flirting with a buxom millennial chef with face tattoos, who just spent a year on a boat off the coast of New Zealand. Marlin boasts of having met Osic at a previous dinner, and declares, 'The man uses silence as a cudgel.' The face-tattooed millennial – promoting a combined cookbook and eating-disorder memoir – hopes to connect with Osic over veganism.

'You vegans, none of you can fucking cook!' Marlin says. 'You can't have morality and edible food. It's simply not possible.'

The millennial, who hosts a YouTube cooking show, retorts that she finds amazing vegan food around the country. The only problem, she admits as the minibus engine starts, is that restaurateurs recognize her now, and they're always trying to impress her with over-the-top dishes. 'Bourdain calls it getting food-fucked.'

A mousy Peruvian intellectual beside Danny asks with a smirk if he's the man who made the wheelchair person cry at his event. Others overhear, and turn with expectant smiles. 'Nobody was in a wheelchair,' Danny replies. 'A mobility scooter. And she didn't cry.'

They pull up to a stylish home in the suburbs, and everyone struggles to both rush inside yet appear casual. Last to enter, Danny finds himself stranded in the hallway. A servant takes his coat, and directs him to join the others, whereupon he clings to a glass of white wine, and glances around for another outcast, or a conversation to sidle into.

Danny always wondered about meeting a great artist, seeing up-close what differed. He's met plenty of authors in Brooklyn but most were as boring as he, particularly the successful ones. Osic is another level, a man who'll feature in literary history. It's as if this were a dinner party held by Dostoevsky himself, if Dostoevsky refused to eat animals or products derived from animals.

Danny flushes, on the verge of a breakdown in a room of strangers. 'This is vegan, right?' he asks a passing waitress, holding up his wine glass. She offers to find the bottle, and Danny follows her toward the kitchen, only to dart into a toilet to control his breathing.

He keeps refreshing email, needing something to inflate him, and finds one from Nell. She has good news, thank God: she's gone wider with *Lighthouse*, and a dozen commercial-fiction editors are gorging themselves on it. She expects bids soon.

How this crowd would shun him if they knew of his trashy best-seller! This secret transgression gives him courage. Screw them, with their essays in the *NYRB* and artists' residencies in New Hampshire. Someone knocks on the bathroom door. He opens to a finely dressed woman in her sixties, whose inquisitive gaze catches him off-guard. 'How are you coping?' she asks, looking so intently that Danny answers truthfully.

She sympathizes, condemning the rigmarole of book-promotion, which has grown so intrusive in recent years, forcing writers to become the marketing operation for themselves. He's dying to ask who she is; she wasn't in the minibus. They chat with such ease that he becomes terrified she'll leave, and he'll be marooned anew.

'I keep wondering,' he says, 'what would've happened if Dostoevsky had a book tour for *The Brothers Karamazov*.'

'Yes, exactly! Gabe doesn't do events at all.'

He twigs: 'Gabe' is Gavril Osic, and this must be his wife, she who forces the future Nobel laureate in her bed to submit to this annual encounter with the outside world.

'Gabe has a line: "Literature is lying to tell the truth about falsity." But the job of being a writer nowadays is *itself* so false. Here's my advice,' she says. 'Pick a few eccentricities, and crank up the volume. Before you know it, you'll become a parody of yourself, and be having much more fun. Anyway, we all become exaggerations of ourselves in old age, so you'll have a head start.'

'I might actually try that.'

'By the way, Gabe is *not* like they say – not silent like a Roman statue,' she says. 'Have you two met before?'

'Not yet.'

'He'd love to know you.'

She leads Danny toward the dining room, where other guests are taking seats at a long dining table, and she is drawn away by a waiter's questions about the meal. One space at the table remains, which others have avoided: beside Osic. Danny expected his fellow writers to stampede the man. Most (except Marlin Pratt, seated on the other side of Osic) seem as intimidated as Danny. He has no choice, so sits there.

After a spell, Osic tires of the unctuous television historian to his right, and Danny feels a Great Author glowering at him. Osic remains silent, hands on the napkin in his lap. This could be the only chance Danny will have to speak to one of the most important writers of his time. So he does.

But the stress is so acute that he can scarcely remember what he says as he says it, gibbering to a hollow face, blinkless eyes. Danny yammers about how festivals are not suited to him, and he scrambles for points of equivalence between them, then retracts, then repeats his quip about Dostoevsky on a book tour, which seemed witty before, but sounds pretentious now. Danny emphasizes that he's not equating *himself* to Fyodor, and is also unsure why he referred to Dostoevsky on a first-name basis, which they aren't on. Osic stares like a punitive skull, which causes Danny to blab more, both asking questions of Osic and answering them. He blurts that he's changing publishers for his next book, and asks Osic for advice on what to seek in an editor.

After a silent silent silent silence, as if Osic first had to slide off the coffin lid, he replies – but first, a slow spoonful of soup: 'Once. I had an editor. Who told me to put the beginning in the middle. And put the middle at the end. And the end at the beginning.'

'So an editor shouldn't interfere? In your case, I mean. For me, I probably need tons of editing! That's me. Not you. Is that ideal, though? In your case? Or . . .?'

Another spoonful of soup.

Perhaps the conversation just ended, and Danny should look away.

'Once, there was a book,' Osic resumes, 'with a ferry trip.'

'Is that a riddle?'

Osic glares at this fool. 'One of my novels had a ferry scene.'

'Ah, yes – I remember that. I love your stuff, by the way.'

'My editor found schedules for this ferry. The departure that I had put, the time was wrong. He told me this, and I corrected it. That,' Osic concludes, 'that is a good editor.'

'Would this apply to bus schedules too? Or just ferries?'

Eyes storming, Osic fixes on him. 'I've said too much.'

Danny is caught with an ingratiating chuckle halfway from his mouth, looking at the back of a skull.

In his hotel room, Danny punches his thigh repeatedly, mobile phone on speaker, ringing Zoey. She's at work, but agrees to eat her sandwich early. Chewingly, she tells of inept staffers and her idiosyncratic boss. 'You've gone silent,' she says. 'You still there?'

'This might've been the worst day of my career.'

'Maybe I have something to cheer you up.'

After she tells him, he makes his way downstairs to find Nousha as arranged – it's the festival-ending mixer. In the lift, he watches floor numbers descend, the doors parting upon a cackle of off-duty literature. He's expected to attend, and Nousha kindly agreed to act as his wing-woman. A photographer circulates, snapping pictures for festival's social-media feeds. Gently, Danny is asked to step aside – the photographer needs a few of Nousha Papazian alone.

Danny holds her drink, zoning out. Zoey was so disappointed after she told him, and it failed to lift his mood. He takes out his phone – he'll message her to explain. He'll claim to be excited. He finds an email from his agent with the subject line: 'Update on Book Offers.'

The Wi-Fi connection is terrible, the wheel slow-spinning. Even if they're low bids, he's taking one. He can tell Nousha about the sale, act like it's trivial, that none of this matters to him.

The email opens: words and words that he cannot turn into sense. Fifteen editors, Nell reports, have had the pleasure of reading his manuscript. Fifteen turned it down.

FADE OUT.

END OF EPISODE FIVE

'EPISODE SIX'

FADE IN:

INT. AIRPORT BOOKSHOP - DAY

NOUSHA is picking through piles of novels to
see if they have a copy of *Babylon Lullaby*
for an impromptu author signing. DANNY busies
himself seeking a volume of her poems. He
plucks out a thin volume as a BOOKSELLER
hovers behind.

> BOOKSELLER
>
> I LOVE her stuff.

> DANNY
>
> Well, I happen to have the author right
> here with me.

THE STAFF HURRY AROUND the bookstore, gathering any available volumes of Nousha's poetry. After she autographs them, Danny and Nousha walk toward the departure gates – she's flying back to Melbourne, he to New York, via Dubai. He looks at her askance. 'You,' he says, 'were on the bestseller list on their wall.'

'I know.'

'Number one. You realize that, right?'

'I've been pretty lucky with this book.'

'Why the hell are you shepherding a putz like me around? I should've been publicizing you!'

'It's been a surprise. Everything took off. But I'd committed to the publishing house till the end of the season.'

'And after?'

'I'm doing a fellowship thing.'

'What, studying poetry?'

'No, teaching creative writing. Just a thing in Iowa.'

'This is insane, Nousha. You're on the Australian bestseller list! How much poetry pulls that off?'

'Weirdly, it's on the New York one too.'

'The New York what?'

'The *New York Times* bestseller list. I'm on next week's, under "fiction" for some strange reason.'

'So *that* is why my book never made it! Your damn poems stole my spot!'

She smiles.

He is moved, not sure why. 'Seriously. Congratulations.' He takes out his copy, bought at that store. 'You need to sign it for me.'

She borrows his pen, opens the copy, and looks directly at Danny, as when they first met. She inscribes his copy. They bid farewell.

At his departure gate, he rests Nousha's book of poetry on his lap. He can't open it. He's afraid.

He wakes his phone, and googles her, looking at the images first. One photo links to a *New Yorker* article that she seemingly contributed to their website. He clicks the link – but the article isn't *by* her. It's *about* her. Apparently, she's a phenomenon, with a huge online following, massive sales. Danny, who always scorned social media, finds her Twitter account, where she has 97.5K followers. On Instagram, 340,000 people follow her. Throughout his time in

Australia, she has been thumbing stuff into her phone, which he took to be tedious publicity work. He reads a few of her posts now: lines of classic poetry; witty quips; incisive political opinions. Any time she hits SEND, more humans read her than will ever read a word by Daniel Levittan.

He feels no envy. In an unserious way, he's in love with her, as he used to fall in love at age nine, when seeking a goodnight kiss from the fourteen-year-old girl working as camp counsellor. The greats spend years among fools before they needn't suffer them anymore. He must've been one of hers. Danny always thought himself the protagonist, but he was only a character actor in a show about her.

He dreads New York, fears going home, so phones Zoey, either to save what's ahead, or to worsen it. She flares that he's still not excited about the pregnancy. If writing makes you this miserable, she says, you need to find another occupation.

'What if I try one more book? It'll be a flop. But then I can jump out the window in peace.'

'Why, though? Seriously, Danny. Why go through it? Why put *me* through it?'

Previously, when he bemoaned his writing career, she urged him to hang on, that the public would come around, that the endeavour was noble.

'I can't talk about this,' she says. 'I'm at work.'

'I am too.'

'How are *you* at work?'

After they hang up, he looks vacantly at his phone, whose screen is still showing the *New Yorker* profile of Nousha Papazian. He wonders if she found him attractive, and knows the answer.

The cliché of midlife crisis is an accomplished older man pursuing a vivacious younger woman, he buying a sports car, and wrecking everyone who ever supported him. But what if the middle-aged man can't afford his own car, has accomplished nothing, and persuades nobody to have an affair with him?

That's the real midlife crisis: you're irrelevant.

FADE OUT.

END OF EPISODE SIX

'EPISODE SEVEN'

```
FADE IN:

INT. AIRPORT DEPARTURE GATE - DAY

DANNY recognizes a fellow novelist who
attended the Osic dinner, DORA FRENHOFER, a
tall woman in her seventies. She sits by the
departure gate, rolling her left shoulder,
arthritic hands crossed in her lap. She
must've forgotten to remove the festival lan-
yard. He reads her name aloud.
```

DORA LOOKS UP, SQUINTING at him. He points at her lanyard, then locates a waste bin, and disposes of it for her.

'How did you find it?' she asks.

'The rubbish bin?'

'I meant the festival. But whichever you have opinions on.'

He tries to sound casual, yet admits his trip wasn't a roaring success.

'Literary events are spectacularly dull,' she says. 'I pity anyone who makes the mistake of attending mine.'

For her amusement, he embellishes his bad experiences at the festival. She listens, smiling.

'Tell me something,' Dora says. 'Do you actually *read* novels anymore? I mean, I know that you *have* read novels. But do you still read them?'

'Definitely.'

'Me neither,' she says. 'It's the dark secret of the literary world:

nobody who doesn't have to read this stuff still does. Why would they? My theory is that contemporary fiction is only there to be bought nowadays. Who has time to suffer through it? The funny part is that people – a class of person – still worships literature, so they buy it on Amazon, keep it on their bedside table for a few months, then slot it unread into their bookshelves, perfectly satisfied with themselves.'

'Oh, come on – contemporary fiction is still vibrant,' he counters. 'Tons of people are producing novels; think of all the creative-writing programmes. They're just not reading *ours* – or mine, in any case. So maybe me groaning that "the novel is dead" is just a way of trying to feel better, when what I actually mean is "*my* novels are dead". Could that be it?'

'You're talking about *writing*. Yes, people still want to do that. Everyone under sixty at a book event is a wannabe writer. They're scrambling for the last dregs of literary status before it's gone, the ability to drone about one's sorrows for pennies in profit. But half of those in the audience just want your seat onstage. By the way, I've not heard your name before,' she says, turning stiffly to look at him. 'Should I have?'

He cites his books.

'No. Don't know you.' She goes on: 'We mustn't complain, though. We're on a free trip to Australia, hotel and flight paid for. You realize how many people would kill for a week of our lives?'

He glances around in case other authors lurk, and witness their heresy. He confesses to his late-night habit during this festival, searching online for the words 'retraining' and 'man in his forties'. He mentions some of Google's answers: driving instructor, pet sitter, life coach. 'What even is a life coach?' he asks.

'It's someone who has ruined his life then telling other people how to succeed.'

'What kind of fiction do you write?' he asks.

'The sad kind, where nothing happens, then it ends.'

'I might be one of your characters.'

'Oh, you are. Are you only realizing that now?'

'Maybe you're one of mine.'

'Do you write women?'

'Of course.'

'Do you write them well?'

'Do you write men well?'

'Very well. Men on the verge of a nervous breakdown. Written for women who ended up married to them.'

He suggests a character truce – neither uses the other in fiction. She declines.

'You attend lots of these literary events?' he asks. 'Or you avoid them?'

'They avoid me.'

'*My* problem is,' he says, 'I'm not anyone's idea of The Author.'

'Pardon my directness, but I'm Dutch, so you must accept it. Nothing we're saying matters. If you have great talent, it comes through. But you don't have great talent, I think.'

'I don't.'

'Nor I.'

Elite-club passengers are invited to board. The festival provided business tickets to the well-known writers. They await economy.

Danny almost suggests that they sit together, but she speaks as if with an arm extended. Also, it's a long flight to Dubai, he onward to New

York, she to London. Danny fears spoiling this complicity. But he must stay in touch. When they disembark in Dubai, he'll exchange details.

At last, they approach the ticket-taker. 'Maybe it's time for us to stop, and leave this world to others,' she says.

Once seated, Danny places Nousha's poetry book in the seatback pocket before him, watching it recline into his knees when they reach cruising altitude, then leap upright as the whiff of reheated chicken pasta infuses the cabin. Finally, he opens the book, and steels himself for her dedication – where she'll urge him to keep writing, and not to be discouraged. He flips the opening pages, and finds her handwriting. All she wrote is *Nice to meet you!*

Danny watches everyone in little seats before little screens. Zoey will be in bed by now. A new lifestyle awaits him there. He tries to spot Dora across the far aisle, wondering what she's reading. He gave her a copy of his. Danny stands to see. She's watching an episode of *Succession*.

When the plane touches down, Danny stands fast. He needs more from Dora – he must ask how to resolve his story. On the other side of rumpled passengers, she rises painfully to her feet, brushes down her shirt. Overhead luggage and arms impede Danny. He cranes around, but loses sight of her.

Finally, he pushes past the laggards, approaching the toothy flight attendants saying bye-bye, bye-bye. He hurries past, lugging his bag into the long tunnel to the terminal. But that character is gone. He's on his own.

FADE OUT.

END OF SHOW

DIARY: MARCH 2021

I'm not someone who talks louder when people stop listening. So, if nobody is especially interested, why finish writing this manuscript?

Lately, I've heard this question often, posed most aggressively by the winking cursor. But I have kept poking it along, prodding approximately at my keyboard. (As another old writer remarked of his arthritis, 'If I pointed that hand at you like a pistol and fired at your nose, the bullet would nail you in the left knee.') What was that writer's name? We forget almost everything, but I worry that my blanks are no longer the normal kind.

Before, when something escaped me, I rummaged through my mental archives, flipping its pages, tracking down the wanted slip of paper. Or someone presented the missing fact, and: 'Ah, yes! Of course!' But it's more than just lost names now. I awake in the night, caught between states, frightened. Eventually, daylight seeps around the curtain edges, and I find courage. I'm coping.

I glance at my attic-office window: birds are chattering out there, a wavering tree limb hailing me. I stand, and open the window, hearing words from the street below, a man and a phone. When you can't see the talker, you realize something: speech is rarely about anything, least of all what the person means. Words are to remind someone that you're there.

During lockdowns, this street became hushed, and my eavesdropping migrated online. There, billions had something to disclose. Perhaps humans always wanted to shout their opinions, but now share the ability, so hate it. Anyway, this era of blurting has had the opposite effect on me: I want to shut up. Which is why, some months ago, I abandoned my manuscript altogether.

In the ragged time since, I've monitored what everyone else seems to care about. Gradually, something overcame me. I no longer feared that I might be insignificant; I became convinced of it. I won't matter as I wanted.

When I was small (but big enough to lie in bed until ten), my father once pulled off the covers, and warned me: 'You'll waste your life, sleeping and sleeping, then dead!' In adulthood, I assumed this horror of indolence, that I needed to accomplish, or I'd be humiliated. Most of my life has aimed at this: succeed. Writing is what I tried.

But what if my adolescent self was right? Maybe you should just make the most of your chapter. Laze in bed, and read all the books. Maybe it's my approach that amounts to a squandered life, beholden to that ever-vanishing endpoint, ambition.

So why am I resuming this manuscript today?

I could claim kinship with great artists, those misanthropes of myth who toil away, supposedly indifferent to society. But I'm nothing so brave. I've just missed the bliss of concentration: my efforts, my pages. Also, I want to see how this book turns out. I get to write the second half now.

All morning, I've typed in my dressing gown, only putting on clothing minutes ago, owing to the downpour. (Like snails, I come out in rain.) Now I'm heading outside, down toward the river, these raindrops — old friends tapping me on the head — dampening my white mess of hair.

Who's to notice? I reach the pelted, brimming Thames, which slops onto the pavement. The seas and the skies are closing in. Something has changed, but people can't.

For decades I behaved as if a contestant in this world, everyone trapped together, elbowing for position. Was it all just my imagination? Look around now: nobody anywhere in sight.

I step into the silent roadway, close my eyes, and exhale — only for a bicycle courier to burst around the corner, clipping my elbow, which I clutch.

He halts and swears but never looks back, as if I were a puddle. Setting forth, the man stands high on his pedals, and stamps down, rainwater on the back tyre spitting over my apology.

~~He bikes through London traffic at speed, on a manic high at his recklessness, silver hair rippling, no helmet.~~

Or

~~He swerves around the obstacle, cursing in English and German, standing from the seat to regain full speed, a long and lean figure when pedalling, as if mounting an endless staircase.~~

Or

On a foldable bike, he weaves down deserted London streets.

6

The deliveryman
who stood in the rain

(WILL DE COURCY)

O N A FOLDABLE BIKE, he weaves down deserted London streets, his grey hair fluttering and arms tensed from holding up this contraption, bought on eBay and forever trying to collapse under him. He turns a corner, swerving past an elderly woman who has stepped distractedly into the street. 'Stay home and save lives,' Will mutters as he passes. 'You absolute numbskull.'

Dismounting at Westerley Business Park, he rolls his bike through a complex of buildings on an artificial lake, with trees standing around like dejected security guards. Trundling past the outdoor meeting pods, Will glimpses a couple behind tinted glass, passionately latched together. The country is in another Covid lockdown, with household mixing banned – in effect, adultery is illegal. But fornicators need somewhere to sin, and he doesn't object. Will rarely musters outrage. Anyway, his eyes are smarting from smoke – without processing it, he rolled and lit a cigarette. Blinking wetly, he perceives movement near his feet, and flinches. Another rat? On closer view, a crow bouncing along the hem of a hedge. 'You lot have the entire sky,' he reprimands it, coughing in a deep rumble. 'This is our bit.'

Will finds Building 6 and, from his cargo shorts, extracts a surgical mask, the same he has used for weeks, its baby-blue front specked with pocket lint. He takes the stairs to the fourth floor, where he finds the closed offices of an accountancy firm, a television-production company, and the destination of this package: RCN Ltd. Behind its locked glass door stands a thick-necked man in black Fred Perry polo shirt with yellow-tipped collar, buttoned up to the top. He leans on a receptionist's desk, yammering to a bald man at a computer whose smile is so false that his cheeks twitch from fatigue. With relief, the bald man notices their visitor, and buzzes him in.

'Devin Doyle?' Will asks.

'You're not off to a flying start,' the thick-necked man responds, and reaches over to shake hands.

Instead, Will presents the package.

'You're just a delivery? For fuck's sake,' the thick-necked man says. Then, to his bald colleague: 'I *want* that bloke to turn up now, just so I can tell him, "You get here *this* late, you can fuck off home!"'

Will extends a digital pad and stylus. 'If you'd sign, that'd be fabulous.'

Noting Will's accent, the thick-necked man smirks, steel braces on his teeth glinting. 'It'd be "fabulous"? What are you, Deliveroo by way of Eton?'

'I'm not with Deliveroo, no.'

'Whoever you're with, you fell a long way.'

'By talking to the likes of you?'

'Ooh – banter from the delivery boy!'

Aged fifty-six, Will is rarely described as any kind of 'boy'. Yet he is youthful for his age, tall and fit, a zigzag nose from rugby at school, creases bracketing his lips. He was always athletic, a low resting heart rate and a low resting expression.

'At least you speak English. Want a job?'

'Not particularly. Who are you lot anyway?'

'Reality Check News.'

'I know nothing about journalism, I'm afraid.'

'We're not proper news. It's fucking spellchecks.'

'You pay well?'

'Give us your name first.' He wipes his nose on a plump hairless forearm, and points Will to his office at the back. Dev flops into his desk chair, googling Will's full name while chewing his fingernails. 'You don't exist, mate.'

'I'm fairly convinced that I do.'

Dev points at him. 'Take off the fucking mask. I'm not hiring someone I can't see. Or are you MI5?'

'Yes, that's right. Undercover with Deliveroo.'

'I thought you wasn't Deliveroo.' Dev notices a packet of Golden Virginia tobacco in Will's cargo-shorts pocket. 'Health-and-safety don't let us smoke up here. Come on.' He makes for the lifts, and they descend in silence to the ground floor. Before exiting into the empty plaza, Dev is already exhaling smoke, a grey cloud trapped in the revolving doors behind him, turning to a slow dissolve. Outside, he shivers and slurps a can of Diet Coke, shaking a packet of Silk Cuts at Will. 'Go on – treat yourself to a big-boy ciggie.'

Will only half-listens as Dev puffs complainingly about two fellow editors who recently quit, and how he's got all the rewrites himself now. RCN does no news-gathering, he explains, just translates foreign blog posts, slaps on clickbait headlines, and puts them out as original content.

'So you're a translator?'

'What, me? I barely speak English! That other bloke.'

'Short on hair?'

'That's the one. It's a fucking nightmare,' Dev says. 'These foreigners I got – they can't barely write. So I'm sat there, trying to make head or tails. We'd be better with Google-fucking-Translate. A proper mare, it is. I can get you four hundred a week, which is more than what Amir, my Arab up there, pulls in.'

'I'm still not clear what my job would be.'

'There's six translators between here and the other bureaus, working twenty-four-seven, giving us shite. We turn it into articles.'

Office jobs never appealed to Will. But he's become irritatingly poor, as may be inferred by close inspection: his collar frayed, its threads tickling his throat, the shorts button above his fly missing. Last night, he perused his bedroom drawers, wondering if he'd manage without shopping for clothes ever again. Twenty years more to go perhaps? Even roll-your-own tobacco is pricey now, and his savings were never saved. 'So it's proofreading?'

'Correct our Latin too, if you like.' Dev takes a last drag of his cigarette, and flicks it to the pavement, the ash starbursting. 'Ten tomorrow. I'll put you through your paces.'

A COUPLE IS COOKING in Will's house. He doesn't know who they are.

'Sausages and baked beans,' the woman explains, three pink dreadlocks swaying to the waist of her sarong. Her green T-shirt says:

Extinction

=

Everything.
Everyone.
Gone.

'Is it supposed to smell like that?' Will asks.

Her companion – a hairy young man in ironic top hat, shirtless under the wool overcoat – replies: 'They're NotDogs. It's the smell of saving the planet.'

'Way too high.'

'Who is?'

Will lowers the heat under their pan. The spit-sizzle subsides.

He has a half-dozen tenants, fervent youths with meaningful tattoos. But Will is unsure if these two belong here. Also, he's distracted by audible scurrying under the floorboards. A pest-control man offered to pull up the hardwood, and cement all entry points. It'd cost twenty thousand, which is many thousands more than Will's bank balance.

The only thing that keeps Will in this house is this house. Which is to say, tenants paying him rent. In the mid-1980s, his gentleman-farmer dad in Somerset had the foresight to buy this terraced home in North West London for his lankiest child, who'd just loafed to a disappointing degree at Cambridge. Yet this place, intended as a safety net, ended up as the foundation of Will's torpor, permitting him to loll for more than three decades now, a typical day incorporating a fleck of household maintenance, a couple of hours' low-wage labour, then carousing till late, and concluding with a soak in the tub and a book. (Will is a rare physical man who reads seriously, and he remembers the contents, though his knowledge is entirely untapped – a fact that has never bothered him.)

He has few house rules and fails to maintain them, offering to whoever he finds lurking a glass of whatever he finds bottled. He provides without expectation, is tolerant without resentment – until, every few months, he's pushed too far, and explodes. But his outbursts are hailstorms: fierce and fast-forgotten.

As a landlord, Will's chief failing is to never record who's in residence, and who is merely in bed with who's in residence. As a consequence, the house has attracted a population of scruffy piercings who affix Extinction Rebellion stickers to the front window, combat American imperialism by frequenting the Iraqi street-food van on Kilburn High Road, and atone for their white privilege by apologizing to people who aren't there. They are easy to ridicule, but Will rather admires them. Most of his friends during young-adulthood expressed political commitment by Blu-tacking posters of The Clash to their bedroom walls, buying the 'Do They Know It's Christmas?' single, and walking into impressive jobs right out of Oxbridge, married and babied and propertied by thirty.

Causes existed then too, of course. Will recalls the Rock against Racism gigs, and he had a girlfriend with a Campaign for Nuclear Disarmament ring. Years later, Will marched in that vast protest of

February 2003, a million fists in the air to oppose the pending war in Iraq, everyone shouting along Whitehall, massing in Hyde Park. How vividly he sees that scene, which he has recounted many times. Yet a muted portion of his brain suspects that he never attended, just saw footage. Anyway, they didn't stop the war, so perhaps not the best demonstration of a demonstration. Will's grandfather – a cad whose life's accomplishment was twice racing at Le Mans – always claimed that humanity's worst prognostications never come to pass because people are so devilishly clever. Never forget the Great Horse-Manure Crisis of 1894, he said: heaps of equine ordure threatened to bury every major city on Earth, the panic spreading far and wide – only for man to invent the automobile, thus saving the planet.

Anyway, catastrophes do feel rather more imminent lately. For this, Will sympathizes with his housemates' lamentation, and is patient about delayed payments, especially during the pandemic. But he can't sustain it much longer.

He himself has been relatively lucky regarding coronavirus. He caught it early, but suffered only a nasty fortnight. Two tenants developed Long Covid, and moved home to their parents. Others had fellowships deferred, once-in-a-life travel deleted from their lives, job offers withdrawn. Cooped up, fed up, and bequeathed a planet in flames, they itch for revolution, and have taken to directing their fury at Will, slandering him as a *rentier* capitalist.

As it happens, he considers himself a working man, never suffering qualms about low-status drudgery. He's taken a fiver to sweep cat droppings from a neighbour's front garden, and spent years washing dishes at a burger bar, and carrying boxes of frozen French fries from a lorry. When lockdown shut that eatery, he became a deliveryman, charmed by the vacancy of sooty old London, deserted for the first time since the Great Plague of 1665.

At first, Will drove a wine-shop van, lugging bottles to the work-from-home bourgeoisie as they embarked on panic alcoholism. Once the weather improved, he bought his second-hand collapsible bike, and took up food delivery, circulating alongside the formerly invisible: Bangladeshis on motor scooters laden with KFC; Nigerian nurses awaiting the next empty double-decker bus; that morose Romanian woman who leapt in and out of her grinning Amazon van. Essential workers served the inessential, who filled their bathrooms with anti-bac soap and hid behind locked doors, shouting through the mailslot: 'Just leave the curry! And step back, please! I'll tip you on the app!' When a few offices reopened, Will upgraded to the courier gig: important documents rather than important kebabs.

Throughout the pandemic, he has cruised through the ambient panic, asking himself if it really would be so tragic if humankind fell to ruin. At times, Will suspects that he may be missing an ingredient, unperturbed by civilizational collapse. He tends to view society as a rickety convoy, directed by rumours as much as maps, most passengers wanting only a comfy seat, while a few shriek at the drivers. But only saints and despots and the middle class believe they can change the world. As for the activist generation in his home, their zeal is close to nihilism, as if – grasping for control of that rickety convoy – they glimpse a horror: the steering wheel doesn't turn. So they overdose on the internet, they self-harm, they gorge on NotDogs.

This couple devours theirs straight from the pan, the top hat boy ashing his joint in a tea cup. They're planning to glue themselves to London monuments in protest against how the world is so depressing. However, they face a conundrum. Should they buy glue that comes off?

'Isn't that the police's problem?' the pink-dreadlocked woman says.

'That depends on the system of governance,' answers Top Hat. 'In a dictatorship, it's your problem if the glue won't come off. In a democracy, it's theirs.'

Will pictures this chap – top hat removed, scrubbed and shaven – as a guest on BBC News in a few years, live from a think tank, talking over everyone.

'The thing *I'm* kinda wondering,' Dreadlocks ventures, 'is whether the—'

'And basically,' Top Hat resumes, 'can we even call this a democracy anymore?'

'There's an easy way to find out,' Will says. 'Glue yourself to something.'

DEVIN DOYLE IS HATE-GOBBLING his breakfast from a Greggs bag, inserting rather than chewing a sausage roll whose crust showers over his gut and keyboard. He arrived late at RCN this morning, although Will was on time, admitted by members of the overnight staff – translators of Turkish, Tagalog and Russian who were kibitzing until the boss walked in. As they packed up their belongings, the Arabic/French translator Amir arrived, taking the desk of a departing Turk, adjusting the chair height with difficulty, thwacking it, then struggling with an uncooperative mouse cable.

Dev commands Will to stand in his doorway, as if to impart a lesson, though he's just watching a Facebook video claiming that George Soros and Hillary Clinton are the secret owners of Facebook, that Jeffrey Epstein isn't dead, that Bill Gates is microchipping bats. 'Why don't we have a story on this?'

'I'm not sure how to respond.'

'By making us a cuppa,' Dev says, sneering but losing his bravado upon eye contact. More sternly, he explains the workflow, how web trawlers at headquarters identify catchy blog posts, translators render them into broken English, and the day staff churns this into quasi-publishable copy, which is amplified by Twitter bots.

Will understands little of this. 'Right. Shall I give it a go?'

'Like I said, first assignment: the kettle.'

Dipping tea bags, Will watches the steaming water turn mahogany. Amir mumbles at him – he's reaching for the Nespresso machine, and asks if Will would mind making space. Up close, Amir resembles an algebra teacher, circa 1983: budget metal-frame glasses, chinstrap beard, razor burn under his chin. Hobbling around on a bad leg, he moves like a man of sixty but is probably half that, his lower lip hanging open, front teeth cracked. Will has a soft spot for the feeble, as when he saw a fox cub wander into traffic on Goldhawk Road, and leapt off his bike, ordering drivers to stop, then escorted the pup from the roadway, whereupon it scurried under a parked car, and Will resumed his journey.

He introduces himself to Amir, whose handshake is a single clammy downstroke. Seeing the two befriending each other, Dev intervenes, shouting, 'What in fuck's a "double-edge *knife*"?'

'That is not a saying?' Amir asks, hobbling over.

'No, you fucking idiot.'

185

Will says, 'Presumably, "a double-edged sword"?'

Dev – who clearly knew – hears this as if it were a revelation, and Amir confirms that this is what he intended.

'Well, put that *in* then!' Dev says. 'Nobody's heard of a double-edge fucking *knife*.' He rolls his eyes to Will, who places a steaming mug on his desk. 'Cheers, mate.'

As the morning progresses, Will notices that his boss addresses him differently than he does the translators. Above all, Dev berates Amir, whose language errors the boss shouts across the newsroom. He also treats Amir as tech support, ordering him to limp over and recover deleted files, or update the betting app on his phone. When mocked, Amir adopts the servile half-smile of one who needs the job, then enumerates the pieces that he's translating, while Dev feigns incomprehension.

'Don't spill a lung, Amir. It's pronounced with a "haitch". *Hhh-hhhhhaitch.*'

For the next two hours, Will corrects the syntax of bloggers confabulating an inversion of reality: that climate science is a plot against the poor, ethnic cleansing is the fight against terrorism, and human-rights groups are child-abuse rings. Each article concludes with a version of, 'Ask yourself this question: Why aren't the elites talking about this?'

Will is half-entertained to proofread mental illness for its respect to the laws of punctuation. This slop is so ridiculous that nobody could take it seriously. Indeed, nobody even advertises on the website, which raises the question of how RCN funds itself. Dev is vague, ranting about headquarters, how they're asking the impossible. When Will enquires about the location of headquarters, Dev just mutters about 'rich foreigners'. Dev found his way here after telemarketing in Salford, then was an estate agent at Foxtons in West London, next selling property ads for a magazine in Dubai, which is where he came across this job online. 'And the rest is history.' He turns his thumb as if hitchhiking, and jabs toward the lift. Once outside, Will forgoes the cigarette, and fetches his bike.

'Why are you unfolding that thing?'

'It's not for me, this job,' Will says, at which point his fat-necked former boss curses the empty plaza, and turns his back, still swearing as Will rides away.

HE PROBABLY SHOULDN'T HAVE done that.

After biking home, Will finds that his tenants are threatening to halt rent payments because another rat was discovered, this behind the kitchen bin. The pest-control man could lay traps and poison, Will suggests. It won't solve the matter, but it'd be affordable. An assembly is called a few weeks later in his living room, where the tenants agree that nobody should harm any animals, only capture and re-house them.

'Re-house rats?' Will says. 'Where exactly?'

'Isn't there a forest they could go to?'

Another tenant: 'I'm, like, looking around every corner now, expecting a corpse. It's seriously becoming a mental-health issue.'

'We're talking about two rats that left for greener pastures,' Will says. 'Do you have any idea how much the full remedy costs? Twenty grand, minimum. How am I expected to come up with that, if none of you pays rent?'

'Couldn't we get cats?'

'You think cats are gentle?' Will says. 'You think they'd coax our rat friends lovingly into the woods?'

'At least it'd be natural.'

'Look, some of you don't even live here!' They're startled – most haven't seen Will lose his temper. 'All of you! Right now! Write your names on a sheet of paper!'

'What is this, *Nineteen Eighty-Four*?'

'If you're not paying, you're not staying – and certainly not voting. You are, however, welcome to fuck off home. Or find yourself a forest where you can be humanely re-housed.'

'Can you just chill?'

'Absolute numbskulls, the lot of you!'

The outburst is behind him as soon as Will steps into the street. It's empty, bright. His protesters are correct: rats must fall. He really should've kept that desk job.

Will logs onto his courier app, and clicks ON DUTY. A private message awaits – a client requested him. He accepts, and bikes to the address for a pickup. Months back, he delivered a package here during a downpour. He banged on the red front door, needing a signature, then backed away, as per company policy. A tall elderly woman opened, sizing up her bedraggled deliveryman, the dripping grey hair stuck to his forehead, rain rivulets meandering down his zigzag nose. He checked that she was the name on the package: 'Dora Frenhofer?'

She accepted the damp parcel, but hesitated to sign immediately, saying, 'Why don't you come out of the rain?'

Thanking her, he stepped beneath the overhang of her roof.

'Tell me,' she said. 'How's life in the inferno?'

'Which inferno is that?'

'Case numbers soaring. The hospitals in overload. I'm safely in here whereas you're biking through it all. So? Give me a first-hand report.'

'At the moment, the inferno is raining.'

Her eyes laughed, and she retreated a step into her darkened corridor, pressing him to come inside for a coffee.

'Alas, not allowed,' he said. 'But I'll take a smoke break under your eaves, if that's acceptable.'

She encouraged it, and kept him company, speaking to Will with uncommon intensity, as if testing how to use words again. Squinting at him, she cast an appraising gaze over this sopping man, and declared herself terrible for asking what she was about to. But she specified herself to be Dutch, therefore allowed to be blunt. 'Why is a man your age and your class a bicycle deliveryman?'

'For the fresh air.' He needed to tap off the long ash on his cigarette, so stepped toward the pavement, noting her blue recycling bin, piled full of books. 'Is there anything good in there?' He knelt to inspect. 'Balzac and Kundera and Böll.'

'You're a reader?'

'And you're a writer,' he replied, raising a novel with her name on the spine. 'If this weren't waterlogged, I'd ask to take it.'

'Not worth your time! And I'm not a writer anymore. I stopped recently. After which, the funniest thing happened: I had this urge to get rid of *all* my books. I loved them for my whole life, but now? I can't even remember what's in them! Colette and Woolf and de Beauvoir and Nabokov and Gogol and who knows. What were they actually about? I don't expect it matters anymore. But damn them for tricking me!' Half-smile. 'Last chance for coffee?'

But he'd finished his cigarette, and mounted the bike.

'When you go,' she said, 'you know what I'll be doing?'

'What?'

'Staring at my keyboard for two hours, trying to spell the word "lullaby".'

'I thought you'd stopped writing.'

'I thought so too.'

Nearly a year has passed, and he expects to find her greatly aged, confined here in this narrow three-storey house. Instead, she answers in a suit jacket and slacks, lipstick on, perfumed. 'You remember me?' she asks, pleased to see him again. She recalls how they spoke of books, and says she hasn't had such a good chat in ages. Better weather than last time too. She checked the forecast (and the ever-changing Covid rules), and they can speak in her back garden, if seated apart for social-distancing.

'That's very kind of you,' he says. 'But afraid I can't on this occasion.'

'Pity.'

His goodbye is cut by the closing door.

Will has a different plan, to cycle to RCN. Although he worked there only a few hours, they still need to pay him.

Amir buzzes him in. 'You are back.'

'Only briefly. Is Dev around?'

Amir looks down. 'In fact, he is passed. Is this the right word, "passed"?'

'How do you mean? That he passed away? Well, that rather dampens my payment prospects. What happened?'

'A cardiac stop in his office. We are all very shock.'

'The man chain-smoked and ate pies non-stop. His neck was wider than his ears. How was it shocking?'

Amir stifles a laugh. 'Yes, not so healthy.'

Will looks at his watch. 'Fancy a drink? It'll almost be afternoon once we find a place.'

They walk past the fake lake, surly trees, and glass office buildings. Not even adulterers in the meeting pods today. This complex has a ghostly air, as if humans were gone, and only their saddest monuments remained.

'How'd you end up here, Amir?'

They find an empty tapas bar with an outdoor patio. The staff – surprised to have customers – rush out a wine list.

Downing an overfull glass of Malbec, Amir talks, eyes averted, telling of his bedsit in Hounslow, how headquarters pushes material that disgusts him. He hates himself for staying, but needs the money. He grew up mostly in Paris, a French mother and Arab father, both deceased.

'Why London?'

'A bit more wine first.'

Will hails a waiter.

Growing up in Paris, Amir recounts, he cultivated a passion for seedy Americana, and planned to pursue a doctorate in the United States. But Homeland Security turned down the visa application, and his life changed. He ended up at a terrible grad programme in London, and dropped out. For a while, he worked in removals to support himself. Then his father fell seriously ill and died, and Amir flew to the Mideast. While there, something happened.

'You're not saying what,' Will notes. 'Quite a cliffhanger.'

'I can't explain. Maybe I try to write it sometime.'

'Write it how? You mean for yourself? Or for people to read?'

'Who can know. We see.' Amir clutches his thigh, which stops jiggling. 'Everybody wants to say things – why people should read what I say? You know? I'm just one stupid guy.' He raises his chin, lips purpled from wine, and closes both hands around the stem of his glass. 'Maybe," he jokes, "maybe you can help me with this writing.' Suddenly, Amir is self-conscious, and changes the subject, demanding Will's story.

The life of Will de Courcy has been fine but he isn't terribly interested in rehashing it, so gives a summary in French, Amir's mother tongue – reminiscing in foreign words is more engaging to Will. After university, he dawdled in Vienna before the fall of the Iron Curtain. Did a bit of translating himself, come to think of it, including putting a surrealist Bulgarian novel into English. When hired for the job, Will pointed out that he knew no Bulgarian, but the cheapskate publisher presented him a German-language version, which he was to work from. When the Bulgarian novel proved impenetrable in any language, Will sought clarifications from the author himself, exiled in Bonn. The man was dismissive, so Will just cut and added bits to his liking. 'And thus it came out.'

'Did he learn what you do?'

'The author? Well, no. It was rather disappointing: no scandal whatsoever. My unfaithful translation even won him some obscure award for experimental fiction. They held this event with the author, and an arts critic interviewed him onstage, and kept citing plot points that actually weren't in his plot. I kept waiting for him to object.

Instead, the Bulgarian just soaked up the adulation. I don't know if he didn't care, or if he thought the critic was bonkers, or if he genuinely believed *he'd* come up with those bits.'

'The last one.'

'Yes, that's what I think,' Will says, smiling, appreciating this Amir chap, who's clearly sharp.

Will continues his story: how he grew bored of Vienna, and returned to Britain to his current house. In the subsequent years, he participated in a series of ill-judged businesses: attempting to license broadcast rights for London dog races to a Chinese television network; starting a Nepalese restaurant; selling batteries that recharge from your car's lighter port. He has a daughter in Austria, based in Innsbruck now – an oddly Teutonic child who never connected with him. His ex-wife, Will notes, once described him as 'an enthusiast with a short attention span'. The girl is thirty now.

'Around my age,' Amir remarks.

Later that evening, Will stretches out on his green futon bed, re-reading *La Vie Devant Soi* by Romain Gary, which they'd mentioned in passing. The smell of incense leaks up from downstairs, where a political meeting is in session.

Will ponders his daughter, whom he rarely has reason to mention. He rolls a cigarette, shifts to get comfortable, mistakenly sending a half-dozen paperbacks to the floor. He thinks of that elderly woman, the retired writer. The envelope that she called him to collect seemed empty, and was addressed to herself.

His phone beeps with a message from Amir, who reports having logged onto the RCN internal system: Will's payment has gone through, for £1,249.

Will frowns and leans back, reading that again. That much money for four hours work?

A car engine growls outside, then trembles to a stop. He looks from his bedroom window down at the pink Porsche Cabriolet. A petite middle-aged woman steps out, wobbling on high-heels, then brushing a hand down her red-suede skirt, followed by a second middle-aged woman who unfolds her long legs from the driver's side, and struts from view toward his front entrance. The doorbell rings; a tenant answers. Muffled conversation.

Will goes down for coffee, curious about these visitors, whom he finds in the living room, like two pointy sculptures considering the gallery staff. The taller is mother of an Extinction Rebellion activist who lives here; the petite woman is her dear friend. Both call themselves 'massive supporters of the movement'. They've handed out bottled water at eco-rallies, and dropped by today because they wanted to see an XR squat.

'Hardly a squat,' Will corrects her. 'They're paying customers. Or they were until the rent strike. It's like the October Revolution in here lately.' He blows on his coffee, whose surface ripples, then flattens.

'You're the guru then?' the taller woman asks, while her son — he of the top hat – chastises her for something, causing her face to squeeze lemonishly. She thunks toward Will in vertiginous wedge sandals, her black-leather trousers laced at the hip, with a chest and face that have clearly benefited from modern science. In such sandals, she is eye-to-eye with Will, he behind half-moon reading glasses, she behind baby-blue contacts. She's approximately his age, though her hair is shiny blonde and professionally styled. Technically, hairdressers aren't allowed to operate under Covid restrictions. But in today's Britain, rules are optional.

'Hardly a guru, no.'

He departs for more oat milk for his coffee, only to find her alongside him at the fridge. She glances around as if the house were for sale but not *quite* what she's looking for.

He still has the French novel folded over his hand, and she's impressed that he reads in other languages. 'Can I tell you a secret? I've read literally one book in my life,' she confides, pausing. 'Aren't you going to ask *what?*'

He sips.

She continues, 'I'm actually *writing* a book.'

'I haven't met anyone lately who isn't.'

After a few minutes of flirt-chatting, Will excuses himself, for he has something on his mind, that £1,249 payment from RCN. He phones Amir, who laughs, and says he was awaiting this call. They agree on another early-lunch glass at the Spanish place the following day.

Will folds his bike by the window, noting Amir already inside, the young man's face slack as a corpse's – until he looks over, lips parting in a smile, the cracked front teeth disfiguring him.

They speak in French, and Amir tells of changes under his new boss, Shannon, who flew in from the Sydney bureau of RCN. She's worse than Dev – not merely a conspiracist, but a hard-working one.

'If you ever fancy upgrading to deliveryman, you'll always find a bike for sale on eBay.'

'Not possible in my case.' Amir taps his leg meaningfully, the damaged one.

Among the stresses of Shannon is her demand that Amir tweet to 'amplify' RCN pieces. It's one thing to loathe yourself for working on vile material; it's another to become a public voice for it.

'No, you can't be known for that,' Will tells him. 'Especially if you want that memoir published of yours someday.'

'You remembered!' Amir says, palm pressed to his chest. 'I was actually thinking of showing you something I've written.'

Silence falls over them. Amir drinks more, then says how he lies in bed dreaming of quitting his job. But rent is so high. How, he wonders, do people save money? How does anyone have a mortgage?

'A better question,' Will responds, 'is whether one needs to go into RCN at all. I seem to have earned a massive paycheck for quitting after a half-day.'

Amir laughs, and explains. During Will's first shift, Dev registered him as a new employee, then considerately died before updating the system with Will's resignation. So his monthly payment chugged through the system. 'That's the problem with RCN. There's money to be made there. And who files the office accounts?'

'What, you?'

'Listen to this,' Amir says. "A few months ago, I had tons of overtime, so I put it in the system. The next month, I never adjusted my salary back, and waited to see what happened – I could've just claimed it was an oversight. But nobody noticed. Shannon is a problem, though. This morning, she asked who you were. I said a recent hire who took compassionate leave because of Devin.'

'After a half-day on the job, I needed time off? That said, even a half-day there probably merits compassionate leave.'

'If she finds out that you quit, she'll make headquarters rescind your payment.' Amir looks up tentatively. 'But if you come back, you could keep it. And get paid again.'

'What, working for a boss worse than Dev?'

'Here is what I am wanting,' Amir says, reverting to English. 'I like that we work together, me and you. If Shannon is now looking at the money, I cannot anymore do what I want. It's fine; maybe I leave this place. But let me before tell you my idea.' He mentions the Bulgarian novel that Will once translated. 'We can do this at RCN, no? I give to you my translations, and you change them, and we post online like this.'

'I'm not following you.'

'We don't make *better* the stories. We make *worse*.'

His proposal is to concoct lies even more repugnant than those RCN publishes, to slip them into articles, and keep track of how they spread, especially via Shannon's tweets, which will be composed of provable fabrications. 'Then we tell to everyone, and she is destroy.'

'And you'd be out of a job.'

'Why I care?' he says, looking at Will, like a man who wants to be brave with someone watching. 'I can *do* something!'

Neither drinks for a minute. Each is thinking.

'We could make up pandemic-related nonsense?' Will suggests. 'Claiming it's all a plot to vaccinate children, and make them gay?'

'RCN is already doing a version of this.'

'How about microchipping people at the dentist?'

'Microchipping is always nice, but nobody cares of dentists.'

Years earlier, when 'adjusting' that Bulgarian novel, Will sought only to make sense of nonsense – he was never particularly creative. He's a man who can quote a poem, but would struggle to write one.

'We must think more big,' Amir suggests. 'At RCN, they say a crazy thing like it is rumour. Then, they do a second article saying, "According to reports" – with a link to the first story, to the rumour they just made up.'

'She'd figure us out, Amir.'

'Have you work for this people?' He reverts to French: 'You know what I've learned from conspiracy theorists? That real conspiracies are almost impossible. People are too stupid to pull them off; or too distracted; or too self-interested. Usually, all three at once. And *that* is why bad things happen. But a global conspiracy? Come on! Have you met human beings? You think they could keep that together?'

'But aren't you suggesting that *we* carry out a conspiracy?'

Amir laughs. 'Yes, perhaps. So the question becomes: "Who is more stupid – us or them?" I say them.'

Will realizes he's rather fond of this chap, who's not much older than his tenants, but with another world in his head. Something cracked those front teeth; something took out his hair in a strange pattern, as if pulled out in handfuls.

'Shannon has no way of knowing where my translations come from,' Amir continues. 'She doesn't read Arabic. She can't even understand French!'

'So what's my role? Why not make up this rubbish yourself, and ship it directly to her?'

'If it comes from me alone, maybe she'll wonder, and check it. But if it comes from me, through you, they're not going to assume that two of us are duping them. Also,' he admits, 'I want to work with you, my friend!'

They drink more cheap Malbec and they plot, Amir relishing what he calls 'the conspiracy conspiracy'. Soon, he's slurring, seeking the waiter impatiently, before turning foggily to Will, muttering about when he tried to reach his father's funeral. 'But they throw me in prison. And who is there? My brother.'

'You must save this for the memoir, Amir. Which I'm very keen to read.' Will fears that the younger man is tipsy, and about to make a fool of himself.

'Okay, but I want to tell you what happened there. With my brother.' Amir calls the waiter over. 'The more wine, please?'

'Actually, perhaps we should pause there,' Will says. 'Don't you need to get back from lunch?'

They walk to the RCN office, the younger man sucking deep breaths to sober himself. At first, Shannon pretends not to notice Will, play-acting the edgy journalist, shouting across the room to the translators: 'You guys need to see this!' She storms around, slamming her fist on stacks of old newspapers. 'So,' she says finally, turning to Will. 'How was compassionate leave?'

'Full of compassion.'

'Who *are* you exactly? I couldn't find anything on social media. Are you British intel?'

'Your predecessor asked me that too.'

'Then died suddenly.'

'I must say, that's the shortest gap I've ever had between "hello" and a murder rap.'

She's distracted, messaging on her phone. 'Just DMing HQ.' She hits SEND, looks up, face contorted about whatever she just typed. 'Okay, boomer. What've we got for you?' She tells Amir to send Will something for proofing, and she'll review his work.

Will puts on his half-moon reading glasses, tilting his chin up to read Amir's first offering. It's too obviously made-up: anonymous allegations that volunteer rescuers in Syria are secretly NATO agents harvesting children's organs. He approaches Amir's desk, saying softly: 'We need to tone that down, Amir. She'll know.'

'No, that one isn't made up. I mean, it *is* made up. But not made up by me.'

'That's an actual RCN article? What am I supposed to do with it? Check for typos? Or add aliens?'

'Just make sure it makes sense.'

'It doesn't.'

Will's phone vibrates: a message from Allegra. Who in hell's Allegra? He suffers name-blindness, and must read her message five times before remembering. Ah, yes! The woman from the pink Porsche at his house, who put her number in his phone before leaving. She's flying to Spain tomorrow, and has an apartment to use in Almería, and thought she'd suggest something crazy: **u speak spanish, right? come interpret 4 me!!**

Strictly speaking, it's illegal to take holidays during lockdown, but everyone in Her Majesty's Government seems to fuck off on vacation. Will goes down to the plaza for a smoke. He unfolds his bicycle. He leaves this nonsense behind.

DOWN DOWN DOWN, DEEPER into the cold Mediterranean, then slowly back up. Will surfaces at last, the sun dazzling. He turns to locate her, for Allegra is laughing: still on the black boulder that he just leapt from. 'You're mad!' she cries.

This isn't a swimming area, just a promontory off the Paseo Marítimo. But, as soon as he glimpsed the water, he sidestepped the family of stray cats, pulled off his shirt, and jumped, still wearing his cargo shorts, flinging back his Ray-Bans in midflight.

They're staying around the corner at an Airbnb haunted by the ghost of deceased air-freshener, with framed photos of serious Spanish children from decades ago. On arrival, Will and Allegra had sex. But the bed is short, and they are tall, so they copulated diagonally. After, she longed for hash, mentioning that shady Moroccans sell it around the port. Since Will can manage in the local language, she expected him to procure for her. But he has soured on Allegra – he already had on the early-morning flight over, when she was nagging the steward for more prosecco, complaining that it was warm, demanding another mini-bottle for free.

He sun-dries while she buys endless knick-knacks from a shop on the *paseo*, more plastic to fill the sea where he just swam. Will pictures the water infested with silicon phone cases and watermelon inflatable mattresses, so clogged that he could walk across the surface. While she's paying, he grabs his daypack, and steps into a bike-rental shed. An oddball with a 'Brooklyn' cycling cap answers in fast Spanish. Will, in peripheral vision, sees Allegra walking past, scanning for him, only the Botox impeding her scowl.

He asks about bike routes eastward along the coast, and is soon pedalling peacefully. After the paved walkway, he passes an abandoned house on the beach, then agricultural lots with a trillion tomatoes under plastic, waves crashing on his other flank. They rented him a city bike with tyres as thin as a finger and a seat so hard that each time he stands on the pedals, pain surges up his blood-starved perineum. Nevertheless, it's a glorious gashing windy route toward Cabo de Gata.

Halfway up a hill climb, he pulls over, admiring the view. He's not as fit as once – ageing but unbothered. He turns a wide circle in the middle of the blacktop, no sightline around a hairpin turn. If a car were coasting downward, Will's brains – well developed, lightly employed – would be splashed across hot tarmac.

He takes the downhill too fast, with little in the way of brakes, inhaling slowly, meditating on danger. Once the road flattens, he veers onto the sand, allowing the bike to slow and sink, then flop sideways as he leaps off. He kicks away his flip-flops, and yanks off his shirt too, soon engulfed in cold liquid, swimming an athletic crawl, then treading water, wondering how deep it is, and what creatures' wars unfold beneath him.

A sandstone tower, El Torreón de San Miguel, stands abandoned on the beach. A plaque explains that it was built in the eighteenth century to survey the water for Barbary pirates. Fear preserves our species, Will thinks, which is why we need panics, why they'll never cease. The tenants embody this. But they might as well shout at these waves, ordering them to stop. Nothing really stops anything, he thinks.

His daypack vibrates – another message from Amir, wondering where he went. Voicemails keep coming from Allegra too, asking that same question, but not politely. He mutes the phone. Between those two, he knows which side he's on: the damaged. Tomorrow, he'll insist that Amir leave that job, and do something better with his life. Perhaps they can do something together. Then again, why this need to 'do something' with your life? To what end?

Biking back, he squints at the sinking sun till it's gone, and he is lit only by the headlights of oncoming cars, whose beams glint off his pedal reflectors. He passes a perimeter fence, behind which passenger jets rise from the airport where he and Allegra arrived earlier that day. He rests the bike outside, and reads a departure board. A budget flight to London leaves tomorrow at 6:20 a.m. He phones the bike shack, informing the eccentric owner that he won't return, and is leaving the bike at the airport, but the man can keep the two-hundred-euro deposit.

'That bike isn't worth a hundred!'

'I know. I've been riding it.'

BATHING AT HOME THE next afternoon, Will's buttocks sting where chafed from that pitiless Spanish bicycle seat. He's ignoring calls from Allegra and from Shannon. But when Amir messages yet again, Will thumbs a reply: **RCN wasnt for me in the end.** Bathwater beads the glass screen.

Amir replies: **But our plan . . .?**

The doorbell rings yet again downstairs: Extinction Rebellion is holding a seminar in his living room, and its supporters keep arriving. Will stands up in his tub, dripping, and types **Come over for drink, my friend!** Two hours later, deep in a preposterous debate, Will is tapped on the elbow. 'Amir!'

The young man shakes Will's hand in that earnest way of his, and presents a bottle of newsagent wine, as if this were a dinner party. He also holds out a brown package.

'Something to do with the conspiracy conspiracy?' Will asks.

'No, no. It's my memoir. For you to see.'

'Gosh, you certainly wrote a lot!' He slaps Amir's shoulder, and grips it warmly. 'And I get an early read – I'm honoured.'

'Not an early reader. The only reader.' Touchingly, Amir insists on shaking his hand again.

'Come with me.' Will escorts his hobbling friend to the kitchen, uncorking that bottle of South Australian red, filling two pottery mugs. (No wine glasses remain.)

'Is a party allowed?' Amir asks, taking all this in: fervent radicals, yapping disputes, couples kissing. 'Nobody even in masks?'

'It's a political gathering. Which is probably even more illegal. But they're all in their twenties, so presumably Covid safe-ish. Anyway, who fucking knows. It's a free-for-all in this country, isn't it?'

'I must be a bit careful. I have health conditions.' He looks to Will, hoping to be asked.

'I'd introduce you around, Amir. But honestly, I don't know half these people, many of whom probably reside here.' He rolls two cigarettes, offers one.

'Could you maybe read it soon, what I gave you? I'm feeling nervous.'

'All else is put on hold,' Will pledges. 'Tell me, by the way, if you spot a rodent. I've not noticed one in days, and I think we might've got the better of the bastards. My tenants credit their new house cat, Chavez.'

A speech is starting in the living room, and they go to listen. The seminar is 'Decolonizing the Environment', with an anti-ecocide academic explaining how the poorest countries suffer worst from climate breakdown, so white campaigners must overhaul the white-dominated movement to represent the Global South, converting it into an intersectional struggle that recognizes structural racism. Rather than clapping, people waggle their hands in approval. Amir is puzzled by this. Will explains that it's 'jazz hands' – a substitution for applause, to avoid marginalizing the hearing-impaired.

'Are there many deaf people here?'

'None, I don't expect.'

Amir keeps glancing at the brown package, which Will holds in his free hand.

'You're worried about it?' Will asks.

'No, no – I trust you. Just, I don't have a computer at home, and I didn't want this stuff on the RCN system. So I wrote it by hand.'

'Amir, I feel this document is too precious. Make a copy, and I'll read that.'

'It's fine. I want you to have it.'

'At least keep it safe for me till later.' He slides it under Amir's arm.

Cheered, Amir downs his wine – then catches himself grinning, and represses it, lest people see his teeth. Will tops up their mugs, and directs Amir to the concrete back garden. Outside, Will lights another cigarette, introducing himself to a phone-reading smoker of purple haircut and septum ring, who turns out to be associate editor at BreakStuff Books, an indie publisher in Brighton. Will informs her that his friend just completed a manuscript, and she congratulates Amir. He seems mortified, insisting that he's still working on it, and has nothing to show, and anyway this early draft is only in French. Will encourages the two to chat, and departs to tell the seminar to shush before his neighbours phone the imperialist authorities.

When Will returns a few minutes later, Amir is clutching the neck of the wine bottle – almost empty by now – and speaking too close to the associate editor, who leans back, holding a beer bottle across her chest. He's telling her that his life turned out differently than expected. He was planning to finish his doctorate, but something happened, and he's not ready to say it aloud, so he wrote it down. He looks directly at her. She mumbles that you need the right reader. Amir asks if *she* is the right reader. BreakStuff only does political manifestos, she says wearily, as if for the fourth time.

Amir pulls Will's sleeve, and forces a laugh, broken teeth on full display now, as he drags his friend into the conversation. 'Look at her tattoo – she is not telling what it means. Why you don't tell us?'

'I should find my friends,' she says.

Will leads her back inside to her cohort, at whom she bugs her eyes, whispering about the weird bald guy. Will is diverted by a bizarre exchange about how long a person can live without sleep. By the time he returns to the back garden, Amir has gone.

A few tenants are heading out for further drinking, and they want Will to come. The house cat seems to have pacified everyone for now: no more rats, and monthly payments will resume. When bundling out of the house, someone treads on a drunk – Amir, who is slumped in the front walkway, that brown parcel stuffed in the pocket of his windbreaker. Everyone else high-steps over Amir, stifling laughter each time he snores. But Will crouches, arm on his friend's shoulder, which causes the young man to blink awake, see Will, smile slowly.

'We're off for drinks at a car park in Hackney,' Will says. 'Enticing, I know. But do come if you like.'

Wobbling to his feet, Amir asks for a cigarette.

The others know that one person here doesn't fit. But decorum is such that they can't exclude Amir, the only non-white-privilege person in that house all evening.

Normally, Will would bike to Hackney. But if Amir tags along, they'll share a taxi. The others chastise Will for taking private transport, but don't push the matter – they'd probably prefer not to have this drunkard in cheap office attire leaning over them on the Tube. They bound down the street, racing each other, lit under the next street lamp, then dark, then lit by the next, then in darkness again, voices fading.

Will puts his arm around Amir's waist and helps him regain balance, recommending a steady stride till Kilburn High Road. As they walk, Will proposes something more: what if he translates the memoir into English, so that media types (obviously not that woman before, but the right person) could judge it for themselves?

'I *love* this idea!' Amir responds, and insists that Will make any changes he likes, that he fill in the gaps because the writing might not be good. He wants this to be their project together. He grips Will's forearm. 'Hope, yes?'

'Hope what?'

'I feel hope.'

Will reaches into the road, for a black cab passes. 'I do know a few people from university who became important in publishing and such. After we have a translation, I'll show a few of them. See where this goes, shall we?'

The driver rolls down the front window. 'Where to?'

Will climbs in. 'Coming, Amir?'

'I am too drunk,' Amir says gleefully, wavering in the gutter. He prefers to slog home, alone but with happy dreams. They'll talk soon. 'You read fast?'

'Fast as I can.'

The taxi driver: 'I can't drive till you close the door, mate.'

Will to the driver: 'I'm saying goodbye to my friend. Start the meter if you want.' On the plastic divider, he notes a sign that payments are also accepted in Bitcoin.

The driver: 'You said Hackney, but where in Hackney?'

'For fuck's sake. Give me a second – I'm talking to my friend.'

'Bad language now!'

'Amir, I should go.'

He hands Will the manuscript, and the driver pulls out. The passenger door swings shut.

'Steady on!' Will says. 'I'm barely inside. Could've taken my leg off.'

'*Where* in Hackney?'

Will gives an address. 'Why am I even in this taxi? Should've taken my bike.'

'Yeah, you should've.'

'You're a jolly presence.'

A talk show on the radio features a caller ranting about how elites are transfusing blood from trafficked children. Will listens for a minute: was that part of their conspiracy conspiracy? He can't recall. What bizarre animals we humans are, he thinks, and rests his tobacco pouch atop Amir's brown parcel, which sits on the taxi seat beside him.

'No smoking,' the driver says.

'I'm only rolling one. I'm not about to light up in your taxi.'

'You'll get tobacco all over my seats.'

'I won't. I'm being careful.'

The engine thrums in traffic, that Bitcoin logo staring at Will. Each time they stop, a red light on the door clicks, and the driver goes into a diatribe to his radio about how everything is hell now, and they're all paid shills, and you can't trust a word.

Will says, 'Does that red light come on to warn me when you're about to say something absurd?'

'Hey!' The driver spins around. He's alarmingly frail – he looks ill, frightened. 'I don't have to put up with abuse!'

'How was that abuse?' Will's phone is ringing. It's Amir. Will swipes away the call. 'Calm yourself, driver.'

The man slams on the brakes, jolting Will forward. 'Don't have to put up with this!'

'Steady on! I already gave one man a heart attack this year. Not trying to make a habit of it.' Will's silenced phone is flashing on his lap – Amir again. 'You're seriously throwing me out of your taxi?'

'Out! Now!'

Will opens the door. 'I see why Uber are running you lot out of business.'

The taxi roars away.

Will is on a bridge over a railway track. His lips flicker with a smile, recalling the crippling bike in Almería, left unlocked at the airport. Someone in need of a ride will find it, and pedal home.

That Bitcoin nutter wasn't well. He thinks of Amir too, pumping out tripe at that job. He *must* quit. If the only obstacle is paying London rent, Will can offer a bit of empty floorspace. Amir would thrive at the house: comrades, wine, debate.

They can work on the memoir too. Will imagines leafing through a (probably mediocre) piece of writing by Amir in the bath later, taking sleepy drags of a cigarette. But perhaps Amir is a gifted writer. What if it causes Will to leap up in the soapy water, suddenly wary not to splash a dot on what he's holding?

He recalls that beach in Spain where he dried himself after the bike ride and swim. He gazed at the Mediterranean, as if viewing the sea centuries in the past, or centuries in the future. Either side of this chapter of mine, Will thought, I'll amount to less than the specks of sand between my toes. So perhaps Amir was right: 'I can *do* something!' A strange feeling, this stirring sense of mission. Forget drinks at a Hackney car park. He'll march right back home now, and read the memoir.

But wait. Will pats his pockets. 'Fuck's sake.' He can see it there on that taxi seat, driving away into impossibility: his tobacco. Will looks up at the night sky, nearly yowling from irritation. He takes out his half-moon glasses, fumbling to unfold them in the cold, and awakens the contact list on his phone.

So, Amir is going to move into the house. After which, the tenants google his name, and find that he once worked on fake-news rubbish, not least about climate change. They discover that Will himself did a brief stint there. He's liable to end up with no tenants except the rats. Fine! He won't be bullied by revolutionaries barely out of their teens.

On the other hand, Will *has* rather grown accustomed to the right side of history, an exception to his corrupt generation, more youthful in spirit and in physique, admired by women on the premises, some of whose activism has included a week or two in his bed.

His plan had been to read Amir's memoir, then decide if he fancied slaving at it. Now, he must inform Amir that an idiot cabbie drove away with it. He plays this out: causing Amir to rewrite the whole manuscript from scratch, which rather obliges Will to work on the result.

Will scrolls to *Amir* in the contacts list, contemplating the dreary walk home, not a single cigarette for company. 'Fuck it, I'm afraid.' He blocks Amir's number, deletes the name.

Inhaling through flared nostrils, Will pockets his phone, and strides down the sidewalk, raging about that cabbie, who drove off with his tobacco, and caused all this. But with each step, Will's anger dwindles. 'Onwards and upwards,' he mutters, casting forward to what's ahead in life: a bath and a paperback. Really, what more could one want?

DIARY: APRIL 2021

Three chapters left till I reach the end. Previously, when nearing completion of a manuscript, I grew impatient. I'd revise thirteen hours a day, short of breath from urgency to be done with an idea conceived a few years earlier by an elapsed version of myself. It felt like I was finishing someone else's book. Until, at last, I'd submit my manuscript, and leap to the new idea that I rared to begin – till a few years passed, and I was once more finishing someone else's book.

What differs this time is that I've resisted any next idea; this manuscript is the last. I'm apprehensive about what's to follow in my life, blank pages I'll need to fill.

I look up from the sandy track across Hyde Park: people are shouting. I never did get those glasses, so proceed toward the commotion in a fuzzed state, mistrusting the landscape around me, which is half-imaginary – not particular trees but brown columns with swaying green lids. A pebble almost trips me. My limbs are so slow to react.

Finally, I'm close enough to identify the shouts. The Household Cavalry is practising, guardsmen in silver helmets with white plumes, red tunics and gleaming chest plates, each rider's sword drawn. 'Eyes!' the commanding officer shrieks. 'Front!'

Another civilian observes too, a blurred man to my flank. I've spoken in person to almost nobody this past year, so I try out my voice again. He's agreeable to an exchange as we walk onward, each of us commenting on those shiny soldiers, prepping for war in the wrong century, playing at battles that this kingdom could no longer win, and so consoles itself with dress-up.

The man is a TV news correspondent, whom I've previously seen gesticulating in war zones. 'Didn't you just win an award?' I ask.

He affirms this, modestly adding nothing more.

'What was it, a report on the far right?' I ask. 'Or something on climate change?'

'Those are my only options?'

'If you tell me the prize-winning message, I'll tell you the subject.'

'That nobody's coming to save you.'

'What, me personally? This is troubling news.'

Laugh lines precede the sound, his rugged face plumped by midlife, or is it the beard?

Before us, a playground roars: little buccaneers rampaging up a pirate-ship fort. The television man sighs, for he has young children himself – yet must hasten back to the studio. I'm left at an empty swing set, much like those where I once pushed Beck. She never cared for kicking back and forth, so I was her propulsion as she watched parkland swing up and down before her. A pit of sadness opens inside me.

I clasp the swing seat, and release it. The empty saddle hops away, crests, and wobbles back toward me.

~~She's an unathletic but game mother, bruised and muscle-strained as she hasn't been since schooldays.~~

Or

~~The kids are squabbling again.~~

Or

She pushes them on the playground swings after dark, her two children swooping away and back slightly out of sync.

The novelist's last remaining friend

(MORGAN WILLUMSEN)

S HE PUSHES THEM ON the playground swings after dark, her two children swooping away and back slightly out of sync, for Sofie is braver and kicks higher than her little brother, Casper.

Each time one of them whooshes toward her, Morgan – an unathletic but game mother – leaps aside, sending the kids into hysterics, each trying to flick her with their feet. She tells other mothers that, were it not for these two, she'd get zero exercise. She'd also eat less junk, bought for the little ones as treats and bribes but gobbled after-hours by Morgan in need of reward.

'Swing *yourself*!' she tells Casper. 'How did I make such a lazy boy?'

'You're my servant, Mumma,' the six-year-old replies, knowing this veers toward trouble; a late smile.

'She's not your servant,' nine-year-old Sofie objects, swinging higher and higher. 'She's mine!'

The kids are always bickering, telling each other to die, and slamming their shared-bedroom door, which the other immediately shoulders open. For short spells, they get along, usually playing Lego – until one topples a skyscraper, and war resumes.

Morgan knows each of them so well. Her daughter is imperious from fear of losing control, and hypersensitive to everyone's mood. Her son is too suspicious of peers, too trusting of adults, unpopular at school, gentle with smaller kids, rude to her, and sad at night. Do they know her? Not yet. Later. And, she hopes, kindly.

Before having children, Morgan never thought of dying, but her unexpected death has become a fixation – that they'd be raised without her, would need her, and she'd be absent. She wakes with that terror: Sofie and Casper, abandoned, under threat.

Niels talks about moving away from Denmark, that they should try her birth country, South Africa. He longs for warm weather, and isn't worried about work – he's a chemist, and would be employable down there. Morgan wouldn't return, though. She is still fond of Johannesburg and some of its people, but when she meets fellow white South Africans abroad, they tend to test which side she's on politically. *You moved away because why exactly?* Some make probing remarks to find if she's a liberal and if they'll be judged – comments like: 'It's a tragedy, what's happened to the country,' then watching her response. Morgan keeps emailing her husband articles about quality-of-life indexes, with Copenhagen always in the top three.

They met during her university study-abroad year, when Morgan came here to learn about Scandinavian epics in translation. He was playing bass guitar with friends at a party, flubbing cover songs, everyone getting the giggles. She was drunk enough to approach him, the gentle red-bearded ice-hockey player who only made eye contact when smiling. Morgan had frizzy brown hair, cheeks rugged with the final year of bad skin, and a habit in conversation of tilting back, anxious that she came across as too intense. Since age eleven, she'd considered herself fat (minus three months of a celery-and-popcorn diet in her teens), and kept her nerve only through flares of defiance – telling herself she was smarter than most, and who cared what people thought? Also, Niels found her attractive, although she feared he'd get a full nude view and his desire would evaporate, for which Morgan was always in charge of the lights. After she finished that year abroad, they kept in touch via longing letters. When she did a study programme in London, they flew back and forth to Copenhagen. At last, during his doctoral studies, she moved to Denmark, and found work teaching English. A dozen years later, she's pushing swings.

Before starting a family, Morgan worried that children would drown her own aspirations, but they had another effect. They are the location where Morgan is herself for the first time since her own childhood. Other adults comment on how close the kids are to their mother, but Morgan wonders how much is transactional: she provides sympathy and hot chocolate – who wouldn't cling? This exchange doesn't trouble her. They rank her above anyone, and that suffices.

This evening, she has cans of Coke for them in a shopping bag. Niels would object. He grew up with the food-pyramid poster in his classroom, and still recites it: egg and fish on top, vegetables next, milk and bread as your base. *Coca-Cola?* he'd say. *Why can't they have water?!* This is his country, his culture, so Morgan demarcates a corner for herself by minor infractions like this. Still, the kids become more foreign each year. Once they hit adolescence, will she lose them to their father's culture?

They're trying to kick each other on the swings now, voices rising. Previously, each has told her of hating the other sibling, and swore that this feeling would never change, that when they're grown, they'll have *nothing* to do with each other, and cannot *wait*.

The swings fly back at her, Morgan right in their path. One could hit her at full speed. She turns her back, closes her eyes. The swing seats are empty and still. Nobody is there. Just her. Years since those two died.

IN COURT, THE SUSPECTS accused each other. Conventional wisdom said one must've been more guilty: a psychopath and an accomplice. Morgan could never think this way — her hatred had room for both.

The authorities ran programmes in which survivors of crime confronted the guilty. Even if officials took precautions during those meetings, perhaps she could smuggle in something sharp. But, as Niels pointed out, if they had time to stab a suspect, it'd be only once, and that person likely wouldn't die.

'Better than nothing,' Morgan said.

'But which of them?'

The question of culpability again, whom to loathe more, the man or the woman. At first, Danish news coverage was non-stop. In normal times, you might hear of a deadly street-gang attack, or a husband who'd killed his ex-wife. But this was children. The press decided that the male suspect had been the mastermind; a minority view saw the woman as instigator.

If Morgan stabbed a ballpoint pen into one of the suspect's eyes, mightn't it go into the brain?

'This is getting too much,' Niels said.

Logically, you'd need to grasp the back of the head while plunging it in, she said. You'd never have time, Niels told her, with the person flailing around and corrections staff pulling you off. Anyway, can we stop talking about this?

She couldn't. For society had the pleasure of punishment, with the guilty in a starring role, while victims were excised, told to get on with life. That life had become two lives for Morgan and Niels, who existed in jarring time signatures, one needing dinner when the other needed grief.

Could you pay someone in prison to hurt them? But Morgan and Niels knew no criminals. And such people would just inform the police to their own advantage, or expose the plot afterward. To Morgan, afterward was little concern. To be arrested would be freedom. Plus, this was Denmark: nobody serves long in this shitty, cowardly country, she thought.

'Yes, maybe what happened came about from you in some way,' Niels said. 'But this doesn't make it your responsibility to fix.'

Whenever he made this kind of remark, Morgan erupted in fury so volcanic that she could've scratched his face, saying it was *vile*, fucking *vile*, to blame *her* for what had happened. It was a fact, though: without what she had done, their children would be alive.

THE EVENTS LEADING TO the crime hadn't even been something Morgan wanted. She allowed herself to be nudged into it, tempted by the prospect of higher status than that of schoolteacher.

Niels always encouraged her to write – when working on articles for local English-language publications, he noticed, she was easier to get along with. But her last contribution had been years back, before Casper was born. Since then, she'd done an occasional essay on her blog, which she sheepishly forwarded to Facebook friends, who clicked LIKE without reading to the end, except the retirees, who posted over-the-top praise. Niels, tiring of her dissatisfaction with the school, urged her to write again, and gave her an idea. In a rush, she pitched it to an American magazine, and heard nothing back – then a terse request for more details. The magazine might be interested, provided that she snagged an interview. This hardly seemed realistic because Jukka Arve spoke to nobody.

Arve first gained a following for pseudonymous message-board screeds, most of them taken down after his arrest, then re-posted by fans and translated into a dozen languages. In the extreme-right subculture, Jukka Arve was 'the leader we need'. When he was jailed in his native Finland, supporters compared it to Hitler's incarceration before his rise to power. The charge was terrorist conspiracy, and Finnish prosecutors cited attempts to purchase explosives and military-grade armaments.

The Arve manifesto laid out a strategy to chisel deeper into the fissures in Western culture that, he prophesied, would crack into violent conflict, much like the Second Civil War in America, which he contended was already underway. It was this striking claim that thrust Arve into the spotlight, amplified by leftist US sources via condemning podcasts and think-pieces that, in turn, provoked gleeful ripostes from far-right YouTubers. To such types, Arve was just a troll pressing the buttons of liberals who failed to realize how funny shitposting was, especially when it ended in gunfire.

Morgan sought to contact Arve at the prison. Secretly, she hoped for a definitive rejection from his team, a scattered group of young men, few of whom had actually met their leader. Their hobbies included spreading memes of hook-nosed-Jew cartoons, photoshopping immigrants as rats, and doxxing 'race traitors' by posting their mobile numbers, email addresses, even floorplans of their homes. Communicating with Morgan via encrypted message apps, they assumed a haughty tone, saying their leader was *perhaps* willing to grant her a few minutes – he was curious because she was South African, and he wanted to learn more about apartheid. His proxies went into a brief panic when it occurred to them that South African didn't necessarily mean white. She alleviated this concern, and noted that she'd grown up during the final years of apartheid, so knew plenty about it – not mentioning her leftie parents, who'd attended rallies against the race laws (yet employed an elderly African maid in a shack at the end of the garden who referred to Morgan's dad as 'master', a fact she never told anyone). So, yes, she knew something of apartheid.

When Arve agreed, Niels wanted to celebrate, which wasn't how she felt about the prospect of trekking to a prison outside Helsinki to meet a neo-Nazi. Indeed, she profoundly did *not* want to go. But the magazine had said yes, Arve waited, and Niels would look after the kids. She had to.

A running joke in their marriage was that Niels's job was to save the world (researching how to strip carbon emissions from the atmosphere), so her job was bathtime. But what Morgan most looked forward to about this trip was the hotel. She could sleep late for the first time in years. As for air travel, she'd not flown once without her kids since their births, and nearly had a panic attack when boarding, imagining Sofie and Casper growing up without her. But she reached the prison, conducted the interview, and the new Hitler surprised her: he was a bore.

Back in Copenhagen, she listened to their recorded conversation, and became frantic. She had nothing worth writing. Had she failed to ask the right questions? She was making an idiot of herself, posing as a proper journalist. An editor at the magazine in New York dropped her an email, asking how it had gone. Arve's proxies pestered her too, demanding to approve the article beforehand, which the magazine forbade. So they sought a veto over any quotes. Again, she wasn't allowed to grant that. Finally, they just asked the publication date.

She compensated for her dull interview by filling the article with background. After an all-nighter, and days of overlooking Sofie and Casper, she ran spellcheck, and emailed her piece to New York, wishing as she hit SEND that she could suck it back. Three months of silence followed. Finally, the editor replied with a fake-cheerful note and a massive rewrite. This confirmed her worst self-opinion, so Morgan fought every change, leaving both sides aggrieved. Months later, they ran the piece, buried as a Q&A, her questions rewritten, and Arve's answers condensed, often distorting the meaning, under the headline: 'Little Hitler: Behind Bars, a Notorious Nazi Talks of War and Soup'. They played up his petty whining, how Arve spoke in a high voice, that he was overweight. Also, the magazine paid only for the words published, 800, though they'd commissioned 3,000. Why was *she* penalized because they'd butchered her story? Was that normal?

The article had no apparent impact. Morgan was busy teaching, and embarrassed by her flop, but other duties distracted her. Then she found something on Facebook: strangers saying that she, by interviewing Arve, was promoting racist ideology. The degree of hostility frightened her. At school, a group of pupils complained that she had platformed a Nazi. The school administrators were caught by surprise – Morgan had used vacation time to report the piece, and they'd only been faintly aware of her previous freelancing, a few movie reviews in a local English-language publication. This wasn't that. They cautioned her never to repeat such a stunt.

This scolding incensed Morgan, who'd fallen into a skittish state regarding those personal insults online, checking her social-media mentions whenever in the bathroom. Some people defended her, saying she'd conducted an important interview with a repugnant man whom society should prepare itself against. When criticized, Morgan felt that the article had been twisted into somebody else's; when people approved, the writing felt like hers again. In this nervous state, she searched online for journalism jobs – was that out of the question? She'd studied literature and communications at university, and took adult-education writing courses after. She often contemplated the routes her life hadn't taken.

One night before bed, Morgan did the umpteenth search of her name, and discovered memes featuring her, with an image lifted from the school website, and photoshopped with a bullet hole in her forehead. Apparently, Arve was outraged by her article, which had led to the removal of several prison privileges. His comments had been taken out of context, he said. This was correct; her editors had done so. She never sought to remedy it because the magazine seemed powerful and her subject powerless. Someone known as 'the new Hitler' could hardly sue for defamation. His online supporters flooded her and the magazine with abuse.

Morgan had always been contemptuous when media types bemoaned their social-media shitstorms. But she found that when an accusation was totally unfounded, it lingered – their disgust stamped on the bruises of her introspection. The deluge peaked at nearly a hundred emails one day, some calling for her rape and death. Yet she kept checking, aching for messages of support, though these never cleansed her. Morgan kept this frenzy from everyone. At dinner, she tried to act normally with the kids and Niels, who wasn't on social media. At moments, it felt as if what animated her phone wasn't quite real, a purgatory beneath the screen, like scenes on the walls of medieval churches, with cross-eyed demons spearing the shocked sinners. Throughout each meal, her attention was fractured. His, too. They'd long ago developed a relationship of co-workers – sometimes your colleague turns up in a foul mood, so you hope for a better shift tomorrow.

His best friend turned forty, and the all-male birthday celebrations ended up at their place. They'd already drunk plenty, and those overgrown boys shouted competitive reminiscences from their ice-hockey days. At first, they spoke English in respect of Morgan's presence, but blood-alcohol levels switched the banter to Danish. How differently Niels behaved among male friends, she thought: loud and vulgar – but also a spark he never revealed with her. She checked on the kids, then returned, knowing she'd sound like the nagging spouse but: 'Maybe let's keep it down a bit, guys?'

When Niels collapsed into bed finally, they didn't touch. She fell asleep with her phone on the duvet.

TWO YEARS LATER, MORGAN was reading an article in *Politiken* about science and the justice system, under the headline 'Who Is Guilty Anymore?' The article explained the rising field of neuro-criminology, how breakthroughs in brain imaging would transform the courts. While every human has dark thoughts, the article said, scientists have proven that those who commit violent crime tend to have deficits in the prefrontal cortex. In other words, evil is a phys-ical handicap, one's body unable to stop normal anti-social impulses. If so, love, disappointment, cake – anything that feels like experi-ence or choice – is simply another biomechanical reflex. Whether drinking yourself into homelessness or landing in government, one's machinery is responsible, not the person strapped into it. Even the will is a fiction, the soul redundant. This article cited a notorious murder case, and Morgan realized that they meant her children. Hours passed before she regained her composure. This same plunge happened every morning upon waking, to remember that it had really happened, that this was her life – like a stroke patient whose memory is wiped in sleep, discovering each dawn that everything is over.

In the month after the murders, she and her husband had sex once, desperately, and never again. Morgan fell quiet when people discussed the background of the second culprit, Freja Bækkelund, a hanger-on in neo-Nazi circles who was half-Danish, half-Somali. Journalists recounted her roots, discussing radicalization in the underclass, and psychologizing about internalized racism. The male co-defendant, Jens Uhlén, preened in court, smiling and joking with his lawyers. In the media conception, he had a soul; she was 'a product of'.

Morgan, who had always leaned left in her politics, found comfort from victim-advocacy groups, most of whose members were conservative. She stopped caring if people assumed that she was right-wing. Niels grew dismissive of her fantasies about hurting the culprits, and this retreat contained all that she resented about him, how every step of their lives, from having children, to finding this apartment in Vesterbro, to furnishing it, even the ad for his current job – everything required *her* engine, she the airplane's lone turbine, he the cargo.

An argument. Many. Long into shouting, she didn't recall her original complaint, which had ramified into twenty, all boringly familiar. When they calmed one night, he approached as she sorted through mail. 'I feel like you hate me,' he said.

After a pause, she replied, 'I don't hate you.'

He urged Morgan not to blame herself. 'You are, only in the tiniest way, responsible. But you're not culpable. Nobody can say that you are. Really.'

His distinction between 'responsible' and 'culpable' suggested, not for the first time, that Niels had a more nuanced grasp of English than she'd assumed. She saw herself as the more intellectually nimble spouse, that he had the mechanistic brain of an engineer. Even in his family, they judged Niels the least clever sibling but the best at sports. But really, how could she even assess his mind? Her shorthand was 'Niels cleans the atmosphere', but she had little grasp of what he actually did. This gulf between them seemed important, and sad, as it never had before.

After the killings, she took extended leave from the school, which was a mistake. Morgan had little to do but meet her suffering every day, alone in the apartment, or in this small city where you always bumped into everyone. She came to hate the society, whose bland goodness meant that the guilty would never experience anything close to her torment. All the *hygge* bullshit of Denmark, those endless frothy articles on how this lifestyle was better than anywhere else, accompanied by photographs of cosy-socked feet before a fireplace. She couldn't leave, though – the criminal trial was here, and Niels refused to speak to the press. Once again, it was for her to look out for their kids, to inform reporters that justice required the longest prison terms possible, that these people would do something like this again. (She wasn't concerned about that last part. She just wanted them to suffer.)

At first, a Danish press organization spoke in support of Morgan, whose children had been targeted for her work as a journalist. They invited her to events, and asked her to speak once. She told of how awful it was to be on this side of a news story, especially when the media spun it to favour the mixed-race culprit. She didn't hear from them again.

Meantime, the editor-in-chief of the American magazine phoned her to offer his support, and made clear that she should consider it her home publication, that she could contribute ideas whenever. This didn't amount to a job offer, but they'd consider her future pitches seriously – and pay more per word. Yet in the two years after the murders, Morgan contributed only one more article, a first-person piece that the editor requested about what had happened. This was Morgan's selling-point. However, she wanted to write on anything but that, which meant proposing topics she had no expertise on. Awkward emails flew back and forth. They paid the kill fee on a second article, and she returned to teaching full-time. But she had lost tolerance for kids, these older than hers had been, or would be. Her work felt valueless, teaching adolescents already fluent in colloquial English, picked up from Instagram and Twitch.

Each night, she and Niels decompressed with red wine, calmer after the first glass, passive-aggressive after the second, out-of-control dispute after the third. Following that, she couldn't sleep yet again, and increased her coffee intake the next morning, not to mention the snacking and weight gain. She hadn't been this heavy since her teens, and the fat distribution was even less flattering at her current age.

Awake with insomnia, she searched the web in private mode for how to kill someone quickly, or how to pay someone to kill someone. In her imagination, the two culprits were beaten for years. First, they'd be told what was to happen, that they had no way to stop it.

SIX YEARS PASS AFTER the trial. A parole hearing for Freja Bæk-kelund becomes mandatory, and will take victim statements into account.

Morgan – furious that this is happening so soon – prepares to deliver hers. She stands before her bathroom mirror, wondering whether to avoid make-up, if it's advantageous to show how much she's aged, or if she'll have more sway if well-presented.

Morgan asked that she and Niels speak to the hearing on separate days. The officials couldn't oblige – time was limited in that conference room. They did agree to hold this part in English, until Niels specified that he wanted Danish, which she took as a personal slight. In any case, her Danish is good now, much improved since their divorce.

Morgan has left teaching, and is retraining as a forensic linguist, a field she hadn't heard of before the trial. She's midway through a PhD, her speciality parsing social media for clues to help criminal investigators. Already, she has worked as a consultant to the police when English-language slang is involved – for example, the case of a young American couple visiting Copenhagen on their honeymoon. The bride's parents in Minnesota received a distraught text message from Denmark in which the young woman said the marriage had been a terrible mistake, and that she wanted to die. They tried to reach her, but no answer. Her new husband wasn't picking up either. So they phoned the hotel. The manager visited the room, and discovered her body hanging. The husband was not present. When he returned, he sobbed uncontrollably, explaining that they'd argued, he'd left to cool off, and she must've done something insane – she had a history of depression, he noted. The lead detective was conducting a graduate seminar that week, and asked the students to review a suicidal text message sent to the woman's parents. Later that day, Morgan also pored over the bride's posts on Instagram, as well as tweets by her husband. She determined (and told the detective with greater assurance than she felt) that the husband had faked the suicide note, that its syntax and abbreviations bore his style, not that of the wife. When the pathologist's report came out, it gave the wife's time of death as before her final text message was sent.

Her phone had a face-recognition passcode, meaning that someone in their hotel room must've held the phone before her asphyxiated face to open the messenger app, then falsified a suicide note, and messaged it to her family. In other words, the husband. After this, the police department asked Morgan to participate in a programme to catch Danish men who sought to groom foreign children online, and she taught specialized officers to write English as if kids themselves, to catch paedophiles in stings.

Morgan is alone in the conference room when Niels enters. He avoids eye contact, and sits on the same side of the table, a few chairs away. He's too cowardly to address her, so she stares at the side of his face. He's lost weight and dresses more stylishly, with a hipster jacket his wife must've suggested; or perhaps he just cares again. She knows he has a newborn daughter, with a fellow Dane this time. Niels wears a wedding ring too, though he refused one when they were together, saying his father never wore one, and that he considered jewellery effeminate. Suddenly, Morgan feels old, foreign, bulky, and this collapse of confidence panics her. The officials *know* we're divorced. They said they'd respect the difficulty of this meeting. Then they just leave us here together?

'You got wet on the way,' Niels says.

'Awful Danish weather, as usual.'

'There's no such thing as bad weather. Only bad clothing.'

'No, there's bad weather.'

Niels says he never expected her to be here.

'What's that supposed to mean?'

'Please, Morgan, I'm not trying to offend you. I just guessed you wouldn't stay in Denmark.'

'You want me to leave the country now?' He must've known she was still around. She often glimpsed Niels around the neighbourhood, at an outside table for a work meeting, or on a family outing down Strøget, his infant daughter in the BabyBjörn. Morgan was always mortified to be seen alone, so hurried away.

'I think it's enough,' Niels says. 'Don't you?'

'What's enough?'

'This woman. Nearly seven years. It's a long time.'

'Are you serious?! She killed our children, Niels! She fucking killed Sofie and Casper!' Normally, Morgan avoids saying their names aloud.

'You can't say *she* killed them. Anything she did was because of the man. That's established now.'

'Bullshit. Bullshit. And it's *six* years. Not seven. Are you mentally ill?'

'Okay! Calm down.'

'Don't tell me to calm down.'

'Forget it. Forget it.' He wakes his phone.

She's quiet, but only for seconds. 'No fucking way.'

'The man, *he* should stay behind bars. But she was – I don't know. What good is it, keeping someone in a cage forever?'

Morgan is sweating to discover this betrayal. She had assumed each would tell of how their lives had been devastated, how excruciating this remained every day, and what Sofie and Casper had been like. Morgan wasn't sure she could get through that part, but had pledged to her online supporters to be brave. Now, she has the humiliation of explaining how wrecked only *her* life is, and admitting this before her ex-husband, and everyone will think she's defective, that she is shaking with wrath while he is so merciful.

Following the crime, the Danish public was gripped with horror at the murders. After a couple of years, once the guilty were imprisoned, everyone moved on. Then a TV channel produced a two-part documentary on the case, claiming to Morgan when they interviewed her that it'd simply be a retelling of the tragedy. But the documentary hardly troubled itself with her children, instead profiling the female culprit, Freja Bækkelund. The tragedy was her life, and they won an award for it. Morgan had still not watched it – she had to turn it off in the eighth minute, and broke her remote control.

'You have to forgive. At some point, you do,' Niels says, placing his phone face-down on the conference table. 'It destroys one more life to keep this going. She has parents and sisters and brothers too. She probably wants a family someday.'

'You actually don't care about your own children.'

'Come on, Morgan! Come on!'

The officials enter, smiling. It's a three-person panel: two female officials and a chairman.

Before they've sat, Morgan asks to speak first. She struggles with the zip of her backpack, and mistakenly rips her prepared statement. She reads out a first sentence, voice quavering, then clears her throat, and asks to stand.

'Whatever makes you comfortable.'

'I'm not comfortable in any way,' she says in English. 'I just feel like this is fixed.'

The older female official looks confused. 'How do you mean by "fixed"?'

'This is a hearing for the person who did the crime – to find out how she's not that bad, how she's done all sorts of prison programmes. You're looking away from me now. Yes: *I'm* the horrible sight. You want me to hurry up, and get out of the way.'

'Not true. Not true.'

'Don't you realize how *sick* this is, that you're even making me *talk* about letting her out? The mother of the victims, and I have to *plead* with you, *beg* for a minimal punishment?'

Niels, seated beside her, stares at his knees.

'You must say whatever you feel,' the chairman assures her. 'You're allowed.'

'I was trying to. Then you interrupted me.' He didn't. But nobody corrects her. Morgan's mouth is dry.

'We care what is right for society. This means you and the victims' father,' the chairman says. 'But we must also think about her.'

'Why not think about two people who aren't here? Who were *children*.'

'We never forget them. But we have her in our care.'

'Lots of people have a background like hers,' Morgan says. 'They didn't do stuff like this.'

'What do you mean, "her background"?'

Morgan's heart is pumping faster.

The younger female official raises a finger. 'You must agree, Mrs Willumsen, people from different backgrounds have different experiences. You can't blame all the same way.'

'What does that have to do with this situation?' Morgan says. 'You're saying that a person isn't responsible because of her skin colour?'

'*Nobody* is saying that!' the younger official says, offended.

Niels, still looking down, shakes his head.

'Hey, hey,' the chairman says. 'This is getting away from us. Can we please return to the question of you, Mrs Willumsen, and what you have come to say? To speak for the two victims who, you rightly tell us, cannot be here today, and whose voices we want to hear.'

'Their voices?'

The official who blurted '*Nobody* is saying that!' has pursed her lips, and placed her hands on the conference table, thumbs hooked together, as if to restrain her dismay.

Morgan reads her printed statement. After, when pushing the lift button, her hand trembles. She phones a contact at the victims-advocacy group, exaggerating how badly everything went. Her allies initiate a media campaign against parole for Freja Bækkelund. News articles come out in the conservative press. A right-wing party takes up the cause.

Ultimately, the board gives its ruling: too early to release the inmate, given the severity of the crime, and public outrage surrounding the case. The victims-advocacy group throws a party to celebrate, with a dozen activists in a community centre, drinking beneath a slow turning disco ball. Everyone cheers when Morgan enters, and a twitchy man in a Danish-flag waistcoat hurries toward her, his shiny forehead twinkling under the lights. He's smoking a cigarette, and tells her he's so grateful, so admiring of what she's been through. He confides statistics on crime, laments who's running society nowadays, how everyone's seen videos of other countries, and that's not here.

Morgan steps back but the man has hearing difficulties, so keeps moving nearer. She questions his conclusions, mentioning that she grew up during apartheid, and that repulsive evil system showed how every human deserves the dignity of equal treatment. And isn't *that* the point here? He smiles indulgently, not quite hearing, handing her a glass of prosecco, saying he's never met a lady who didn't love bubbly. He smiles wetly, urging her to drink.

When Morgan finds an excuse to leave, a pink-mascara woman with asymmetrical facelift makes pouty sympathy lips, and the Danish-flag-waistcoat man insists – insists! – on driving her home, 'Or would I be a gentleman?'

Outside her building, he switches off the engine of his banged-up Mercedes, slings his arm over the steering wheel, and pops the car lighter, pressing its orange glow into the umpteenth cigarette. He opens his lips to speak – but Morgan has the door open, thanking him too many times. She suppresses her shiver until the building door closes behind her.

THE HANDWRITING IS CHILDISH, and littered with mistakes in English. Above all, the letter is about its author, Freja Bækkelund, explaining that she'd been an immature girl trying to act like a woman at the time, how awful her upbringing was, that she wasn't trying to make excuses.

'Yes, you are!' Morgan shouts at the page, slamming it on the kitchen table, her fingertips pinning it there. '*All* you're doing is making excuses!' She balls the page so tightly that her knuckles go white, and stamps it on the kitchen linoleum, using a napkin to dispose of the letter, as if it were a squashed cockroach, dropped in the kitchen waste. She pours used coffee grounds on top, and washes her hands twice.

The parole review is annual. Morgan could tick a box, and her previous victim-impact statement would apply again. That's what Niels did. But after last year, seeing that the system wants to free this woman, Morgan plans to attend, to make her case even more forcefully.

She's hamstrung, though. You're to consider only the future; the past is bad manners. That's fine for the guilty, but do they not understand that Morgan's future is nothing but the past? Some people prefer to downplay the murder of two children for the embarrassment of its having happened a few years ago – yes, she'll say that.

In a Netto supermarket bag, Morgan brings her son's Spiderman pyjamas and her daughter's nightdress with the emoji motifs. She passes these to the three officials, telling each to take a turn holding the garments. 'That's what they were wearing. When they were suffocated. I've never washed them. That's what Casper and Sofie were in.'

Solemnly, the officials pass the items around, each unsure what degree of scrutiny to undertake, till the chairman holds the items in both hands as if sacred, hesitating to return them. Morgan doesn't intervene, for she is talking, they are listening. And she prevails, entirely in Danish. She planned to change to English if too upset, but she managed.

No party this time; she never flagged this hearing to the victims-advocacy group. On the ride home, it's jarring to resume banality, the routine of bus stops and occupied seats, that Netto bag on her lap, she knowing its contents. Morgan brought earbuds but plays nothing, overhearing pre-teen girls chatting beside her, one perched on the other's lap.

Morgan is trying *not* to consider something. But the matter recurs when she's washing dishes, working down a tower of dirty crockery. (Living alone, she cleans up just once a week; she'd be ashamed if anyone saw. Nobody sees.) She enters her study, surrounded by forensic-linguistic reference works, knowing why she feels wretched: speaking of her kids today was a recital. Down another memory corridor, she still has access to her living children. But she employs them as anecdotes now, parts of her story.

FREJA BÆKKELUND KNOWS MORGAN'S home address on Gasværksvej – the crime took place there – but she is barred from communicating directly with her victims. Only with permission will the prison forward letters. Morgan is preparing to defend her dissertation, and has no time. She puts the letter aside; she'll open this when it suits her. Or burn it, unread.

She resists only a few minutes, then opens the envelope. Freja Bækkelund is claiming to be sorry, saying Morgan was justified to criticize her in the reply. Her first letter, she admits, was inappropriate, a litany of self-pity, as if her victim should care. She wanted to explain herself. But in hindsight, it wasn't her place. Except to say that she is so sorry, also to have troubled Morgan.

Morgan speed-walks across the apartment to her laptop, impatient to type out the lacerating words in her head, a response even more pointed than the first. She has the measure of this cynical piece of shit.

After Morgan's reply, a further apology arrives.

So Morgan writes another ferocious letter, because Freja Bæk-kelund is now saying that she followed an abusive man into this crime. 'Your pseudo-apologies are pathetic, and you disgust me,' Morgan writes. 'I will do all I can to ensure that you die in prison, that you never have any joy in your life, there or on the outside, and that everyone you ever meet knows what you did and who you are.'

That night, Morgan runs a bath, still agitated. She talked down to that person, as one isn't allowed to do in normal life. But Morgan must tell herself to feel pleased; she feels something else. In recent years, she has developed such low regard for human beings, considering them delusionals who claim their good luck as utterly earned – while their misdeeds, *those* are nothing to do with them!

The next day goes better. Morgan is invited to a linguistics conference, and has a good phone call with her sister. She enjoys a healthful lunch, and a late-night walk, admiring the Danish summer sky, a twilight of noctilucent clouds. Everyone she passes is good-willed, and she notices an elderly gentleman sorting through his wallet, confounded, and she helps him entirely in Danish. He's so thankful. Once home, Morgan replies to Freja Bækkelund, a less eviscerating note this time. She knows that something as petty as her full stomach affects the contents of this letter, so she summons a little anger, mentioning in passing that when she herself is overwhelmed, she does nothing more violent than colouring in – so don't pretend that circumstances 'forced' you.

Freja Bækkelund never disputes anything. She doesn't even write words in response this time. She sends a notepad of her pencil drawings, an offering for Morgan to colour in. Morgan throws the notepad in the waste bin, then writes back to say stop sending shit like that. Freja Bækkelund responds that she has taken Morgan's advice: she loved colouring as a little girl, and it really helps with stress, which is high in prison.

Morgan scoffs at this, for everything is taken care of in a Danish prison. You live better than we do out here! Stress comes from obligations and responsibilities. Morgan enumerates her own, making sure to mention the Facebook group that she administers for survivors of violent crime.

These letters, Morgan realizes, are the sole venue where she can speak openly about her children, whose personalities and troubles and quirky joys she cites at shaming length to Freja. Morgan cannot get through writing another letter without knitting her fingers over her eyes, pressing hard against the bones of her face, as if to push herself back inside. Around the city, she glimpses classmates of her kids — some not far from adulthood, presumably thinking of university, careers, romances, perhaps even contemplating children of their own.

Freja is the only other person in the world who thinks every day of Morgan's children. After refusing it for months, Morgan asks that the criminal explain herself. Cautiously, Freja tries to, specifying that she has broken away from those people. She writes in imprecise English, never asking forgiveness. She knows that Morgan will keep denouncing her to the parole board, and has never sought to change that.

Morgan expresses anger that Freja might someday start a family while her own chance has gone, that she'll probably die stranded abroad without a single person in this country. Freja explains that she cannot have children – she struggles with endometriosis, which developed after her arrest.

Morgan asks more about this, but Freja is wary. She doesn't want to excuse herself. The facts are these: Freja was brought up in Christiania by her mother, who raised her communally, claiming this was on principle. However, it was merely practical, for the woman suffered from manic depression, and self-medicated on whatever drugs were around; often, she was unconscious in the daytime. Even before entering school, Freja had tried illegal drugs – her mother made her eat something to take a nap. By age eleven, she was sniffing glue on her own, which the prison psychiatrists said had probably caused brain damage, although she feels fine in the head. In the streets, she found older friends, adults who treated her as an adult, and she still doesn't quite believe some of those men were predators, as she's been told in counselling. They were her friends. From outside, maybe it'd be considered a violation. But she can't see her life from outside.

She certainly had the wrong companions, though, taking up with a gang of guys who made videos of bare-knuckle fights; several had self-made swastika tattoos. She became their toy, including sexually, and was subjected to constant racial taunts, mocked for her ultra-Nordic name despite the dark skin, dubbed '*Lortebrun*', meant to imply 'shit-skin'. Even she referred to herself by that nickname. As for the night of the crime, she was on heavy drugs, and remembers only her arrest. To be clear, Freja keeps saying, none of this is for sympathy. She's actually stopped petitioning for parole. Previously, she wanted freedom, but she has become low when reflecting in these letters. Thinking about it all, Freja feels that she should not get out.

To check on this, Morgan contacts the parole office. Freja is telling the truth. When the state conducts an annual review, prisoners normally send thick folders, and work for months on their pleas. Freja submitted nothing corroborating her rehabilitation, and she refused to attend her hearing.

Morgan messages Niels, asking whether he's available to drop by their old place: **I want to make peace.**

did not know we r at war! he texts back, but yes of course . . . :)

In the apartment doorway, he wears the wrong expression. He's upset to return to where the children won't grow up. Morgan planned to seduce him. Not anymore. Her ex-husband can't even go down the hall – it'd mean passing the kids' room, now her study. 'You *work* in there?'

Fury rushes back, a wave charging up the sand at her, rising to her throat. How fucking out-of-line, to imply that *she* is inappropriate, when it was she who stayed here, who slept on the kids' floor for three years, right by their bunkbeds.

'What did you want to talk about?' he asks.

'Forget it. There's no point.'

'Morgan, I came all the way here.'

'Just get out of my house!'

'Why are you shoving me?! What is wrong with you?!'

'Get out!'

After he leaves, she suffers an extreme drop in mood. The dissertation gripped her earlier that day, but she sees only pages of nonsense now. On the street, any sound of people is evidence that humanity is despicable.

The last time she felt such self-hatred was after Niels moved out. She reached out to a former friend then, her tutor in an earlier life, back when Morgan still harboured hopes for her writing, and did that programme in London. Every student was assigned an external tutor, third-tier authors whom nobody had heard of, people who'd had novels published once, but were now politely starving from indifference. Her tutor was a Dutch novelist, Dora Frenhofer, a jaded but witty fiftysomething then, whose pre-teen daughter had just moved to California to live with her father – a change that Dora mentioned with disregard: 'At last, I get to work uninterrupted again!' Art was what mattered, insofar as nothing really mattered. Morgan – still in her early twenties – wanted to be a European intellectual like that.

They kept in touch now and then, Morgan recounting her ongoing love affair with the cute Danish grad student, Niels. In handwritten letters, Morgan attempted to echo her mentor's style, mistaking amorality and sentence fragments for literary sophistication. But her correspondence was sincere in its way. So Morgan was hurt when Dora didn't come to the wedding. Still, she visited her older friend in London three times before having children. Those were odd trips, with intense talk while crossing parks and down busy streets and suddenly back home, the sharpness of Dora's remarks often funny – all followed by tense silence in her house, worsening when Morgan's departure neared, as if the older woman wanted her gone by now. When it was time to head to the train, Morgan considered an embrace, but realized that goodbye was enough. 'I need to get back to work,' Dora said. Only one of them was truly a writer, and she needed to show which.

But over time, Morgan realized that her friend's career was not as sturdy as presented, that Dora struggled to publish novels anymore, each attracting fewer readers than the last. On inspection, her private life looked different too. She'd characterized her daughter's departure as a blessed absence, yet the ledge behind Dora's writing desk contained various images of Beck: a toothless toddler; then a pudgy girl eating a peach; then an eleven-year-old trying not to smile. When Morgan asked about that girl, the writer closed the subject.

She and Dora spoke by phone only occasionally, wry observations that made them equals, until the day that Morgan offered advice. Dora went silent, so that Morgan – losing confidence to speak into a void – asked, 'Are you still there?' To which Dora said just, 'Mm,' and resumed her silence till Morgan improvised, blending apology and change of subject and farewell.

Something peculiar followed. When next they spoke (and Morgan didn't call back for a year), Dora was far the needier, speaking with such negativity about her writing, as if wanting her younger acolyte to deny this – but becoming scratchy when encouragement came. Morgan had an epiphany: she'd become one of this person's closest friends, perhaps her only friend. That made Morgan value her less. Anyway, with the birth of her children, she had no more time for phone calls.

Only after the crime did Morgan again hear from Dora, a sensitive condolence letter in which the older woman recalled how close they'd been. When Niels moved out, Morgan phoned Dora once, needing the voice of someone bold and far from Copenhagen. But nothing of the friendship remained, just old details, as when bumping into someone from schooldays, where one person cites names the other doesn't recognize anymore. Dora asked prying questions about the murders, and became strident, saying what should and shouldn't happen, and the exchange plunged Morgan even lower. Both put down the phone, knowing they'd not speak again.

The coda was that Morgan learned a few years later that her one-time mentor had actually published a novel with a character whose two children had been murdered. Morgan discovered this long after the book's publication, which showed how irrelevant Dora Frenhofer's work had become – nobody had even associated this novel with its obvious inspiration. Morgan happened across a copy in a remainder basket at Books & Company in Hellerup, and paged through with apprehension. She had to keep searching, finding no character like herself, and realizing: it was the husband. Dora had switched the sexes. Morgan didn't know how to interpret this.

She's recalling this angrily now, for everything feels insulting after her interaction with Niels at the apartment. From spite, she decides to compel Freja to join a restitution programme, where the criminal must meet the survivor in person, and seek forgiveness. Morgan will offer none. She'll do as in their letters: use this criminal to speak at, and she'll have to take it. She'll ask no questions of Freja – and will tell her to shut up if she veers from the subject of Morgan's distress.

At the prison, she is led into a 'family room': brown sofas, old magazines, individually packaged cookies, and (inappropriately, given the crime) children's toys. Weirdly, Freja tries to hug her. Morgan leans away. 'Sorry, sorry,' Freja says.

'It's fine,' Morgan replies, though it was *not* fine.

Their conversation is short. Morgan ends it abruptly.

On the train ride back, she recalls that article in *Politiken*, about how neuroscience today equates the brain to a supercomputer – that everyone is born with hardware, loaded with software, programmed to run algorithms. To explain behaviour, there's no need to cite anything but biomechanics. We are programs, never choosing anything, nobody at the keyboard, nobody moving a mouse. Condemning someone's actions is as preposterous as blaming them for their eye colour.

That can't be. It feels so wrong.

For her doctorate, Morgan must stay up-to-date with social-media apps, those that her own kids would have used, uploading shameless selfies and teen rants they'd never outrun. Technology has ruined humankind, Morgan thinks. Or maybe the internet – freeing us – is the truth about our species.

She visits Skydebanehaven, standing with her back to the playground swings, the two saddles perfectly still. It's already getting dark; Danish winter.

Morgan wakes the next day, well rested for a change. In the mirror, a different person: something of her younger self. She resumes her dissertation, even visits a trendy restaurant for a late lunch, where the attractive Swedish barman pulls up a seat and chats. He mentions a small-batch vodka made in the north of his country, and how it's unlike normal vodka, and he pours her a glass on the house. 'You drink it like that?' Morgan asks. 'On its own?'

'On its own,' he says.

That night, she writes to Freja, explaining that she wants the young woman to apply for parole again. When the letter is finished, she prints it, and rests it on her palm, the paper warm. She never sends it.

But the next day, she phones to talk Freja through this. She speaks of how this just came to her, and how she's felt light since. Freja grows emotional. Morgan declares, more forcefully, that it is the right thing; it *must* happen. She demands that Freja start considering a future outside that place. They even plan a meeting someday, somewhere in the open air — one of those cafés on the Lakes, where they could take a bench and buy hot drinks. Freja is drawn into this image, then bats away the prospect. But at moments, Morgan hears the young woman edging toward the unimaginable: free.

Morgan contacts the parole officials. They're taken aback, but delighted that she has found mercy. This puts her off, as if they were pastors, and she the humbled sinner, accepting a seat in the pew. She acts irritable about the necessary paperwork, partly to remind them who she is. They turn formal, specifying that they'll certainly consider her opinion, but other issues enter into it. First, the children's father deserves his say. Society is a stakeholder too.

A COUPLE OF STRANGE years pass, those of the pandemic. After Morgan's second vaccination, she gets a haircut, shorter than any in her life — for ages, she'd wanted to, but feared doing it. It's a shock in the hairdresser's mirror: her face is so round. She imagined this cut as grimly suited to a woman approaching her fifties. But that isn't the point. It's less bother, just as this stage of life is about fearing less that people can see inside her.

She arrives at the meeting place, ears chilly. Morgan checks what shoes she's wearing, and improves her posture, looking around: a country that was never home, where she has lived almost half her life.

They planned to meet at the outside tables of Original Coffee.

The rain has stopped, the sun meekly out. Morgan – abruptly dry-mouthed, arm over her handbag as if for balance – checks that she brought a hand towel to wipe raindrops from their benches. Anyone in the city could see them together.

She and Freja have spoken only once since her release two weeks ago. They have, however, already decided what to order. This respectful little café, which Morgan chose, sells the biscotti that she's addicted to. She promised they'd try some, along with the ginger-lemon tea that Freja cited as the soothing drink she most missed.

The state is providing Freja with housing and counselling and job opportunities. But Morgan suspects that a decade of institution-alization has made the young woman passive. Before release, Freja worried about how she'd make friends at any job, noting that one must mention the past, and it'd come up in the first conversation: *Where were you before this?* What happens when they search her name online?

She asked if Morgan's ex-husband, Niels, should be present for this meeting. Morgan dismissed that, and never looked too hard at why: that it'd make the encounter about the murders, which perhaps it should be. But Morgan is excited for another reason. This occasion affirms her humanity.

Freja arrives eighteen minutes late, jogging the last stretch down Sortedam Dossering, hand cupped over her mouth in embarrassment, apologizing profusely for her bus. She seeks a hug, which is tight and rocks side to side. Morgan abides this, but wants to push away. Finally, Freja stands back, smiling warmly. Morgan tries to smile back. This is more upsetting than she foresaw.

In prison, Freja always wore sweatpants. Here, skinny jeans

accentuate how slender she is, and a belly-shirt hangs off one angular shoulder, exposing a black bra strap. No jewellery in prison. Here, an ear full of studs, the other bare, and a nose ring, which bothers Morgan. But Freja is young, and this look is how she wants to present herself.

Morgan already bought their herbal teas and biscotti. The drinks have gone cold. Freja insists that's fine, and takes a sip, beaming. But, no – Morgan wants this to be perfect. 'You always talked about having your favourite tea, so it *has* to be hot.'

'Actually, you know what? If you're going back, I might have a cappuccino instead.'

'Really? Not your famous ginger-lemon tea?'

Once they have hot drinks, Morgan opens the bag of biscotti, which Freja expresses much gratitude for, though she takes only one lipstick-preserving bite. 'I need to stay in shape,' she remarks, patting her flat stomach. Freja talks of bureaucracy, the grind of it – it's as if they want to make it harder for ex-prisoners to adjust, she says.

Smiling, Morgan is growing distraught, and diagnoses why. Nothing is mentioned of her children. Nothing. Just filling out forms, waiting in offices.

A man passes with a large shaggy dog, and halts, crouching beside Freja, while the animal looks confusedly at Morgan. 'Is that *you*?' he asks Freja, who leaps to her feet.

'No way!'

They embrace.

'What the hell?!'

'How *are* you?'

The man shows no interest in acknowledging Morgan. Freja is

unsure how to introduce the older woman, so Morgan offers a mild greeting, then looks down to pat the dog, which allows them to resume their chat. This guy wasn't interested in knowing a middle-aged woman anyhow, and their conversation is none of her business. Yet she hears, and cannot help wondering what kind of person would ask so blithely about whether she's going to this club or that later.

Morgan looks at her phone, but is distracted by the invasive sight of her heavy breast and gut, this view downward, and how uncomfortable it was to sleep when pregnant, and neither side felt right. Was that Sofie or Casper? How can she not remember? She's blocking out their conversation, hearing only the fast breaths of the dog.

On the morning after the killings, Niels left for work without noticing that someone had broken in. He didn't check on the kids, and later explained that he hadn't wanted to disturb them. He probably just wanted to get out before anyone was up – to be free for a spell, as if he had nobody but himself, which is how it seemed sometimes.

Morgan enjoyed a late sleep that morning, a rare event, for the two kids normally burst into the master bedroom, arguing over breakfast or turning on the TV, which wasn't allowed before school, or shouting at her to punish some villainy of the other sibling. That morning, glorious silence. Morgan finally called out: 'Guys! Time to get up!'

She heaved herself into flip-flops, and clomped down the hall into their room. The children were on the floor, Sofie holding her younger brother's hand. The little girl must've reached over when they knew what was happening. Freja told them they were about to be killed; that came out in the trial.

Freja's friend is bidding goodbye, and they agree to text later.

'How weird is that? Haven't seen him in *ages*,' she says. 'Yeah, so how are *you* doing?'

'Not too bad. Not too bad.'

'I need to ask you something.' Freja touches her hand, as if to herald something important. 'There was this issue that came up.'

'Go ahead.'

'About you writing to him?'

Morgan is puzzled, thinking of the man with the dog, only to realize whom Freja means.

'Write to *him*?'

'Or he could to you, if that's better to start.'

'Wait, Freja. Sorry, I'm taken aback. You're talking with him?'

'Only recently. Now I'm out, we can. He is *not* like he was. So much was the drugs before, and a lot of mental challenges, lots of which never even got mentioned during our trial.'

'They got into tons of that stuff during the trial.'

'Well, anyway, he's still stuck in there, dealing with that place. Which is kind of like torture.'

'What is like torture?'

'Being in prison. For someone with psychological issues.' She adds, 'And he feels like shit about this.'

Morgan struggles to order her words, her throat hot, hands cold. 'You said before that – sorry, I'm in shock here.'

'No, I get that. But he's like a brother to me. He got me through so much when I was in there.'

'I thought you'd only just got back in touch.'

'We couldn't talk by phone before. Letters were always allowed. And when we got on the phone yesterday, he was *not* in good shape. I could hear he was suffering. It's not helping to be locked up.'

'He's not getting out, ever.'

'We don't know that. Who can say?'

Morgan reaches for her tea but takes back her hand, digging the fingernails into her palm. She stands.

A few people look over.

Morgan cannot identify her own state. Her mind is locked.

Freja stands too, saying, 'I'm so so sorry.' She keeps saying it.

'Stop it.'

People turn away, pretending not to listen.

'It's just . . .' Freya begins.

'Stop talking to me. You're a liar.'

'I want *you* to feel better.'

'Stop talking!'

'Didn't you say that you felt better forgiving?' Freja says. 'We're in charge of what happens, right? We all get to decide if we're happy or not, no?'

'Don't touch me!'

But two little hands won't let go of her, squeezing her fingers, needing her.

DIARY: MAY 2021

I'm tasting insects today.

I proposed this to an American travel magazine. But the senior staffer I once knew there had retired a decade earlier, it turned out, so my emailed proposal meandered among work-from-home journalists, eventually finding a commissioning editor who — desperate for copy after the barren pandemic months — accepted the pitch, somewhat to my alarm. Suddenly, I had to plan an insect-eating expedition in the Cotswolds, obliging me to rent a car (I've not driven in years), and finally buy new glasses.

I'm driving there now, the engine purring down optically sharp country lanes, sun glinting off old puddles. Every few minutes, I pull over to the grassy shoulder, hazard lights blinking, and check Google Maps on my phone. Much as I try to make this little screen comply with the arthritic finger-and-thumb double act, my pinches and pokes either do nothing, or close the app, or spin the route wildly off-track.

A van whooshes past my car, too close, the driver holding down his horn. I turn back into the road (forgetting to stop the hazard lights flashing), and drive onward, lost and late, even though I left home an hour early. At last, I find my destination, turn up a bumpy track, and park in mud.

A cheery Englishwoman — Barbour jacket over heavily pregnant tummy, rubber boots, pink cheeks — greets me at the converted beehives, which her company calls its 'test kitchen'. She's evidently surprised that the journalist is a tall old woman, struggling out of a Nissan Juke.

She offers a steadying arm, then rescinds the offer. 'We probably shouldn't touch,' she says, wrinkling her nose. 'For Covid safety.' Instead, she begins the sales pitch, from growth targets in the edible-insect business, to outlets where their products are sold, to planet-saving corporate principles. 'Sweet or salty?' She opens a packet of Sea Salt 'n' Balsamic Locust Crisps, and readies a Caramel Locust Brownie for after.

'Is everything locust-based?' I ask.

'We're developing some awesome cricket options. But locusts are the go-to. Crazy high protein.'

'These ones taste mostly like the topping flavours,' I say, chewing. 'Not sure I'm getting a strong note of locust.'

'Keep in mind sustainability,' she notes. 'Our ancestors ate insects, by the way. And people even put dried locusts on pizza!'

'In Palaeolithic times?'

'I don't believe they had pizza then, right?'

'No, I was only—'

'Actually, I'm only on the marketing side. I've never even been out here before. I work for a PR firm in London; they're our client.'

'So you drove all the way from London for this too?'

'Actually, off the record, this set-up is mainly for photo ops — pretty much all the products are made at their factory in North London. But they said the journalist wanted something "atmospheric".' She looks around: a farmer's field rising behind the beehives, barbed wire festooned with a puff of sheep's coat, a jagged stone wall up the hill. 'It is lovely here.'

'Peaceful.'

After an hour of chatting as I digest insects, she grows distracted, and apologizes: must rush back to London. She touches her belly meaningfully. 'Doctor's appointment in Peckham.'

I ask when she's due, and allude to my child-bearing, back in Palaeolithic times. She asks which London school my daughter attended, and what it was like, and whether it was hard to get into, and should she put her unborn son's name on a waiting list?

I know some of what's ahead for her. She's right to feel hope.

Driving back along the half-empty motorway, I glance in the rear-view: nobody behind me, only a bespectacled elderly woman peering into the mirror. How did I become her? I remember a green-eyed girl, smiling as I can't anymore. Somewhere, I changed. This person took hold.

Perhaps it was that I'd never matter in any domain, so preferred to retreat to my own. Gorillas do that, quitting the troop once realizing they'll never ascend. But an outcast gorilla doesn't write about other gorillas, imagining apes who aren't present, then presenting her efforts to those she might not respect but whose approval she craves.

Recently, I read about the lottery of your birth year – if it was 1935 in the United States, for example, and you were a middle-class white man, you had every chance of a good life. Born a decade earlier, you'd have survived the Depression, fought in World War Two, perhaps had a son serve in Vietnam, and would approach death just as technology was stealing the known world from you. What, I wonder, will birth in 2021 have meant for that woman's son, when he nears the end of his term?

I picture a future overcrowded, bestormed, flooded – such that a diligent upbringing, designed to prompt kindness and graduate school, leaves him unqualified for the coming hellscape. Though, even long before such fears pervaded society, I myself hesitated to have a child, worrying about what I might propel that possible person into, a world I couldn't affect, where I'd someday abandon them to cope alone.

What's strange about today is how such dread cohabits with such luxury. My insect-eating article will discuss this, how we flip between shamed horror and shameless indulgence. So: a thousand varietals of dark chocolate from exotic locales, but employing ethical cacao farmers, but poor ones, but paid well, but cute packaging, but sugar rush, but great for the immune system, but inclusive, but expensive (or how else to know that it tastes better?).

When I emailed the magazine editor this concept, she hinted that my instincts were off. 'I'd get directly into what it's like to eat insects, and how gross it is,' she wrote back. 'Then maybe a kicker on how caterpillar burritos *could* actually save the planet?'

Now that I'm back home, I email her again to ask my word count. Immediately, she replies: 'Sorry. I didn't have a chance to update you before.' She's moving jobs, and her successor wants to take the magazine in a different direction. They will, of course, pay a kill fee of eighty dollars.

I pass Beck's former bedroom, and look in, as if her six-year-old self might still be there, unable to sleep, as she often was. I'd tell her about my absurd day, driving all the way to the Cotswolds, having mouthfuls of insects, then driving all the way back – and for nothing! She'd laugh and laugh, and I'd be infused with her glee, and she'd leap on her mattress and onto me, though it's really far past her bedtime.

'If you did that today,' she'd ask, delighted, 'what'll you do tomorrow?!'

I'm not sure. I wrote books for a while, but it didn't work out.

'Well, you tried your best,' she'd say. 'Something will happen next.'

~~After decades alive, if you've paid attention, you'll see a few things more clearly.~~

Or

~~The window over the building courtyard is open, and someone down there is shouting about a delivery.~~

Or

Food and drink. Alan wants neither, though his career preys on those appetites.

The novelist's former lover

(ALAN ZELIKOV)

F OOD AND DRINK. ALAN wants neither, though his career preys on those appetites. He contributes articles to glossy magazines for Americans who dream of living where he does; he appears on National Public Radio with a whimsical (cynical) 'Letter from Paris'; and he writes non-fiction books that sell moderately: *A Poetical Journey Among the 500 Cheeses of France*; and *Broken Bread: Border Cuisines of Europe from Brittany to Borscht*; and *How Wine Saved the World*, a title foisted on him by a slapdash editor, though the book contains no world-saving, instead dwelling on an irony about the phylloxera outbreak that killed European vines in the 1800s: Old World wines come from new varietals while New World wines come from the old. He's embarrassed by this book, and keeps just one copy, turned backward on a living-room shelf. Otherwise, visitors might ask, 'How *did* wine save the world?' His answer: 'It didn't.'

Some of the above isn't true. Alan Zelikov doesn't write for glossy American magazines or appear on public radio or write books. That stopped. But he still describes himself this way, citing publications that would no longer recognize his name. When he retired, it was due. Yet he's unsure why he ever did. Mentally, he remains lucid. Physically robust too, walking sturdily and far at whatever age he is. (Alan doesn't celebrate birthdays, but is around eighty.) Perfectly bald, he has shed his eyebrows too, a saggy neck narrowing to the collar, like a lightbulb screwed into a sweatshirt.

The real reason for his retirement was the absence of his former editors, who'd died or left, sometimes in the appropriate order. Many of the magazines are themselves defunct. And those periodicals that remain are unrecognizable, led by youngsters who check his social-media footprint, and find nothing. Even before he retired, they had begun ignoring his story pitches, or they magnanimously agreed to consider pieces only for the website, which mysteriously paid a fraction of the print edition, although nobody read the print edition anymore. Those young editors weren't wrong to judge him as past it. Previously, he pursued gastronomic novelty with an ardour to match a chef's. But all his favourite restaurants are, by now, as ratty as ageing movie stars. Experience becomes a weakness: you lack the fizz to engage in another round.

Over the course of his career, he has tasted the rare and the expensive, and struggles to digest either nowadays. His last meal out was – well, he can't recall. In reviewing days, he avoided dining with the talkative because others' opinions affected his palate. His finest eating had nobody on the other side, perhaps an owner-operator in the distance, stealing sidelong glances; maybe a couple feuding in a far booth; or an after-work gathering that roared briefly, then was gone.

Nowadays, he begins each day with an apple, which he preps in slices, wary of cracking that tooth again. His paring knife hits the plastic cutting board with a repeated *clack* that is his son's alarm clock. Alan consumes the apple core and stem last, chased with a small glass of water. Around midday, he dips into a bag of mixed nuts, breaks the shells with a nutcracker, alternating left and right hands to work his grip, flicking away the rubble of almonds and walnuts. Evening is steamed chicken with zucchini, salted to excess. Lastly, a thumb-sized *pâte de fruit* from a boutique on Rue de Turenne, swallowed as if medicinally, the sweet dissolving on his tongue, eyes darting left and right as he determines which flavour: rhubarb or lychee or blood orange.

Besides a daily walk, he fetches groceries, and reads news on his sluggish computer, maddened by the world and responding with a cigarette. He retains that vice but without commitment; sometimes none a day. The purpose of smoking is conversation. His son, Benjamin, takes a break from working too, and they open the apartment windows over Rue Oberkampf, stand side-by-side, a pane apart, inhaling and exhaling in approximate synchrony.

The boy is a sports writer, pumping out thirty online briefs a shift for the news service of a gambling site. His territory is France, meaning Ligue 1, Six Nations rugby, Tour de France, Roland-Garros. He never attends the events themselves. It's quicker and cheaper to watch on TV, which allows him to benefit from his father's input. Alan has a memory for sports, can discuss jockeys who won the Arc, or rivals to Eddy Merckx, or the Yugoslav basketball powerhouse of the 1970s. History pads out a thin article, which is what Benjamin's are: word-scaffolding around an athlete's distracted reply to the post-game interviewer, copied verbatim from television. His writing is earnest in a field that is not. Consequently, his articles are dull. Alan never says this.

Benjamin looks old, a half-eaten doughnut of greying brown hair around a shiny dome. Once a month, Alan gives the kid a haircut. 'Kid' isn't the right word. Frightening to have a son this age. Frightening that Alan's existence is mostly behind him, and lost from view there. The same is true for Benjamin – but that is too rattling to linger over. Alan sits up in bed from his after-noon nap, swivels his legs around and stands, clearing his throat while – from the other side of the door in the living room – the boy clears his throat.

They communicate in English. Benjamin attended French public schools, and keeps friends from those days, corresponding via online messaging. He has no romantic life, and probably never did. Even before the pandemic, they lived a monkish existence in this two-bedroom apartment, within a nineteenth-century building that looks grand from afar, grimy from near, with an exhausted *bar à Cocktails* and a Turkish kebab shop on the street level. They prefer life up here in high-ceilinged rooms that – owing to the shape of the building – narrow into a wedge as one proceeds through the property, ending at a triangular bathroom with specialized bidet, toilet and walk-in bathtub. Neither enters the other's bedroom; they meet in the living room, where Benjamin works because of the TV. Never do they bicker. The closest is misapprehension, as in, 'Oh, I thought you'd said I should have it.'

'Sorry if I wasn't clear. Go ahead.'

'We can share.'

When the boy was around five, he told Alan: 'We do anything together. We're the best of friends.'

ALAN HAS NEVER DELVED into his son's private life, which once took place in school, then via a landline in his room, now the internet. Benjamin applies this same respectful incuriosity to his father. They've never discussed Alan's female friends, not even the boy's mother, a Dutch novelist, Dora Frenhofer, who left here too early to lurk in her child's memory.

Sometimes, Alan wonders what his son contains, plenty or little. The younger man never fights anything, not if the conditions of his job worsen, not if the assignments become preposterous. Where did he develop that? Alan's flaw is the opposite, to shoulder into conflict, something he inherited from his father, a Jewish socialist who wanted to farm without understanding farming, and moved the family constantly, impoverishing them from one American state to another. When Alan recalls childhood lodgings, it's with his three big sisters, who cannot remind him of details, each dead, first the middle, then the younger, lastly the eldest. Alan sees rooms that he struggled to fall asleep in, his father cursing downstairs, perhaps because he'd dropped the can opener, and its disobedience typified the disobedience of the world, and the man's indignation grew hotter, leaping up the staircase, till Alan pushed off his blanket, and came down, preferring flames to the sound of fire. He sees his mother at the kitchen table, smoking, asking why he's up still, and he didn't wake his sisters, did he? (All three at the top of the stairs, having egged him into going down.)

While Alan was at college, his father died of lifelong disappointment. His mother lived years more, well into her son's Paris residence, his sisters caring for her fading face. Nobody reproached him for failing to return. They knew what Alan contended with, raising his son alone. Alan tries not to think of his mother because the sorrow is too sharp, so she is erased, except when he's caught out – for example, watching classic American movies with French subtitles, and Benjamin poses questions of his father as if awaiting search results: 'What *is* a Manhattan cocktail?'

Alan will crack an almond shell, place the result beside his son, who takes it. 'My mother used to drink them.'

Looking back, Alan considers his career as an accomplishment without value. He cured no polio, built no town. He pointed the rich to overpriced food and drink. But who is satisfied at eighty with what lured them at twenty?

Some people of his age calculate how many years they have left, and make plans, and acknowledge their predicted number, as in, 'I don't expect I'll be here more than a decade!' (granting themselves a couple more years than the average lifespan). Others avoid knowing. Alan is that way. In his opinion, a man is not to be frightened in sight of others, least of all his children.

Fetching groceries that afternoon, he bickers with the woman selling roast chickens from a metal skewer, which rotates behind spattered glass. Neither is sure if the other is insolent, she calling him '*monsieur*' emphatically, he responding with an abundance of '*madame*'. When leaving, he swears under his breath, on the false assumption that American profanity remains little-understood in this country, as when he arrived half a century before. Recently, he was buying milk at the Monop', and a small child on a bike (yes, biking around a mini-market) cycled into his shin, and Alan gave a muffled yowl, exclaiming through his mask 'Little fuck!' only for the little fuck's mother to speed-walk over, and berate him in broken English. On such occasions, Alan finds it odd to still live in Paris.

He carries groceries past the courtyard mailboxes to their building, up the stairs, raising and lowering the bags as he climbs, to exercise his arms. In the living room, he's breathless, looking at Eurosport on the muted television: the pole vault.

'I have a sister,' Benjamin says.

'How?'

'She messaged me from America. She's coming to Paris.' The boy looks up from his laptop, fleetingly, then back at the screen.

'Coming here? What for?'

'For me.'

FROM A DISTANCE ACROSS Place Léon-Blum, Alan identifies her. Benjamin's half-sister, Beck Frenhofer, looks to be nearing forty, darker skinned than her mother, bulkier too, with short spiked hair, a men's suit jacket, red dress shirt, and green brogues. To Alan this combination of styles proclaims that she frequents the arts, supports progressive politics, and is open to spinsterhood. A cascade of thoughts: some people broadcast their neuroses, volunteering the stereotypes they'd like to be saddled with; how he's glad to choose clothing only by neatness and what regulates body temperature; how it'd be if people went around nude; that genitals are unaesthetic and it's strange they captivate anyone; how lust and love are genetic programming, nothing more.

Her mother's eyes.

'Can you walk?' he asks.

'Since I was a baby.' But she hastens to keep his pace. 'So. You're the vetting process?'

'Would you be able to go faster? This is my daily exercise.'

'By the way, am I supposed to keep the mask on outside?'

'Depends on your appetite for risk.'

'Purely for my information, should I expect to meet my brother soon?'

'I'll leave you on the Left Bank. That's where you're staying, correct?'

'He's there?'

'It's where you're staying, I understood.'

His daily constitutional is at least two hours, so Alan's plan is to lead her to the Jardin du Luxembourg, do a lap around the perimeter fence, then back here to the *mairie*. This grants him opportunities for an abrupt goodbye if she's awful. He doesn't dislike the young, but tires of their predictability. Above all, he is unsure what she's been told about his son and Dora.

No talking all the way to the park, except when Alan projects his arm before her like a railway barrier, protecting Beck from a turning taxi. 'I saved your life.'

'I'll owe you forever.'

As they walk, she's silent but for audible mouth-breathing – badly out of shape. He diverts them to a sidestreet shop to buy oranges. Beck removes the N95 mask, under which her face is dripping sweat – that suit jacket was a mistake, and her red shirt is untucked now, tails crumpled. She must've dressed to meet her brother.

'I never know how to buy oranges.'

'It's not hard,' he says. 'Or it *should* be hard: don't buy a soft orange.'

'Not like peaches.'

He selects one on her behalf, and they sit on metal chairs in the park. As they peel, their fingernails clog with white pith, a mizzle of citrus, the distant sound of traffic over the iron railings. He bought a bottle of water, and presents it unopened. She glugs, and gasps.

'Yours to keep,' he says. 'I'm fine.' He glances at his watch, calculating how much longer the home aide will be there – one of a public-health team that helps Benjamin bathe and with other sundry tasks. Beck mentions feeling connected to her brother, though they've never met, that she always felt someone missing in her life, and wonders if he does.

'You are in touch with him,' Alan responds. 'You can ask.'

'But what's your opinion?'

'That he can speak for himself. And Dora? She ever talk of us?'

'Only in passing. You were this sophisticated American bachelor in Paris.'

'Sophisticated.'

'Seems strange to think of you two together.'

'Every couple is strange once they're not a couple. Sometimes when they are.'

'I searched online for your last name and "Paris", and found Benjamin's Facebook profile. I figured you guys were related, and it had his birthdate. I calculated he'd been born while my mom was here in Paris and with you. She never mentioned anything like that; always just you as this bachelor. I figured maybe you had a wife, and Dora was the other woman.'

'Did you put all that to Dora?'

'I never get answers out of her. I messaged Benjamin, just to ask about you actually. He said a few things. I pieced it together.'

'So you asked Dora then?'

'She never even told me I *had* a half-brother – why would I tell her I'm going to meet him? It's nothing to do with her.'

'Did you talk to Benjamin about why his mother left?'

'Why? Does he not know?'

'For someone in comedy, you don't say much that's funny.'

'I don't tell jokes. I just write them.'

'If you promise not to tell me jokes, I promise not to laugh.'

She smiles. Against his will, he does too, then finds a way to part company.

Back home, Benjamin is clean and combed.

'She cut your hair?' Alan asks.

'It was Marc – the tall one from Côte d'Ivoire. He forgot to do my neck.'

Alan fetches the electric clippers, stands behind his son, and buzzes fuzzy hairs off his nape.

'Should I message my sister to come over tomorrow?' Benjamin asks. 'I said I'd be in touch.'

'Let me give it some thought.'

'Sleep on it.'

'That's what I thought.'

The following day, Alan fails to mention her. So does Benjamin.

A second day passes. On the third, Alan finds a letter in their mailbox in the communal courtyard. She'd like to chat about something he mentioned, and is going to be in the Jardin du Luxembourg that afternoon – she has returned there daily since he introduced her to it. Same place, about 2 p.m.?

HE CAN'T BANISH THIS woman from Paris. Nor can he stop her from knowing Benjamin. But he needs to understand her motives.

Beck sees Alan approaching, and removes absurdly large headphones. She saved a metal chair for him. He remains standing, and she shades her eyes, looking up. They're walking again.

'I'd like to apologize to your son,' she says. 'I feel it's something to say in person. On behalf of her.'

Alan is irritated. He always tells Benjamin the truth, with one exception. He said that the boy's mother turned against Paris, and that he, Alan, had been impossible to get along with, so she left. The story felt incomplete – that his mother had just gone, never once contacting her son. But which explanations from childhood add up?

The ostensible reason for a second meeting with Beck, as cited in her letter to Alan, was that she wanted advice on expat life in Paris. For now, she's in a short-term place in the 5th arrondissement that's wildly pricey. But she is unsure how to decipher rental ads in French, let alone job postings. Is she legally allowed to work here?

'No such job exists here, writing jokes in English.'

'I could do other things. Though I'm not qualified for anything else. But hey,' she says, 'I actually flew out here because I met a Parisian woman online, and came to surprise her.'

'Why not ask *her* for tips?'

'This is where it gets awkward. I was on this dating app before the vaccines, when California was in lockdown. Basically, I wanted to be anywhere else than LA, so I put my location as Paris, to see what'd happen. The algorithm matched me to Karine, and we started messaging. She wanted to improve her English, and kept telling me that – since we were both in Paris – we could meet up outside. I managed to delay for months.'

'Does she know you don't live here?'

'I fessed up yesterday. Didn't go great. But maybe I *will* live here, right?'

'My son thinks you came to meet him.'

'In part. Also for Karine. She kept saying, "Why you would come ear?" – that's supposed to be a French accent.'

'I realize. They're endemic.'

'She's only willing to see me again, she said, if I actually become the profile she clicked on. Meaning living here, a job, speaking at least basic French. She's not looking for someone needy.'

'Isn't needy what dating websites are for?'

'Maybe she was more, like, "Why you would come *ear*?" She'd actually prefer to live in California. She's into the idea of a big dog, like I used to have, and the beach outside your door, which I never even go to myself.'

'Fly her there, and you're both happy.'

'We only just met. And I haven't seen my brother.'

They cross Pont Neuf, north toward Les Grands Boulevards, Alan giving perfunctory notes on Haussmann's renovation of Paris. They turn toward Marché Bastille, where he does his grocery shopping.

Vendors stopped offering samples because of Covid, but they've known Alan for years, and make exceptions when it's quiet. He takes an extra cube of melon for her, slapping it roughly in Beck's palm, knowing how ripe it is but betraying no appreciation in order to haggle down the price, handing over euros and tipping the man all his change. He also picks up a Crottin de Chavignol, plus a *ficelle*, and a plastic-handled steak knife. Away from the flow of shoppers, he saws the bread. When the nub falls, he lurches for it, his limbs slower than expected, arthritic hand fumbling. The bread lands on the pavement.

'Should we find somewhere to sit?' she asks.

'You digest better standing.'

'Is that true?'

'No. There just aren't any seats.' He finds a statue against whose rail to lean, under a revolutionary less pertinent today than the pigeons on his tricorne. Alan chews, swallows, and his hairless eyebrows rise expectantly. 'Opinion?'

She's distracted, looking around, a visual inhalation, her eyes saying, *After so long indoors, I'm actually in Paris, and nobody knows I'm not from here.* 'Creamy?' she answers.

'Well, yes. It's cheese.'

She sputters a laugh, and he can't help chuckling, so turns away, ready to move on. Alan has the sensation — not felt in years — that this is a friendship, her expression shifting when he speaks, he amused by her snarks, and intrigued by what she says of California nowadays, where he himself spent a year when small, albeit in farmland. She isn't sure of her route back, so he extends their walk, ending before her fourth-floor walk-up by the Panthéon. He reads aloud a blackboard on the wall of Café de la Nouvelle Mairie, listing a dozen wines.

'You have better vision than I do,' she comments.

He doesn't mention his cataract surgery – it's untoward, he thinks, to speak of medical procedures. Also, he notes a second reason: he doesn't want to appear old to her. Restaurants – closed until recently by virus restrictions – are limited to half-capacity. They're lucky to find a table. He orders a glass of Ajaccio white for himself. The waiter asks for Beck's order, and she despairs at replying in French.

'Take a sip,' Alan says, handing her his glass. 'Then decide.'

'Is that Covid-safe?'

'Come on – try.' He's domineering, as if to assert that there's nothing amicable about this. She tastes, approves. 'The glass is yours now,' he says, and calls for a carafe. Bread too. The oysters that she nervously slurps are the first of her life – not an intrepid eater. He tells her to chew. 'Do it the mercy. It's alive.'

'Are you serious right now?'

'The taste comes when you chew. Otherwise, it's just seawater.'

Her mother was Alan's eating partner too, an assertive tall young Dutchwoman with large ears who'd heard that this American food writer took female company when reviewing. She wanted finer dining than she could afford, so invited herself along. Dora ate half of each dish, and he did the same, then they exchanged. Alan wasn't curious for her opinion – another's presence just helped him order more dishes, granting a broader sense of the menu. So she never talked at their meals, shaking his hand beforehand, and reading a paperback between courses. Once, he and Dora split a platter of

Gillardeau oysters and, for a change, she spoke: 'The life of a man is of no greater importance to the universe than that of an oyster.'

Alan was jotting a tasting note, and reached for another shell, emptying it nude into his mouth: fishing nets and barnacles. 'Who said that?'

'Me or David Hume,' she replied. '"The life of a man is of no greater importance to the universe than that of an oyster." Which seems an argument for cannibalism.'

He leaned back.

'If man is no more than an oyster, and we eat oysters,' she went on, 'why not eat a man?'

He deposited his shell on the ice chips, wiped his mouth with a thick-cotton napkin. He invited her elsewhere, resulting in his apartment, which was that of an established man nearing thirty. Everything followed, twisting through the decades until this stout American woman before him, who is so unlike that tall Dutchwoman, except the eyes.

Alan orders Beck the pistachio duck terrine next. He tries it first – a habit from professional days.

'Making sure the food's dead this time?' she asks.

Alan swipes another lump of terrine onto baguette, exhaling hard through his nostrils as he passes it to her, clutched by an unexpected pleasure: a person nearby, this human, here. He didn't think he needed them anymore.

Wine saturates their exchange with permission. She offers quips about her romantic flops, how she's ditching a solid career as a comedy writer to get jilted by a woman who doesn't know they're supposed to be in love; how she's tempted to bribe her prospective girlfriend into bed with the promise of a dog. A few times, she almost makes Alan laugh; he raises his brow, looks down at the food.

Alan jerks the conversation elsewhere, telling of composers and radicals and dipsomaniacs who once inhabited this neighbourhood. There's an unwanted loudness to Alan's delivery, for he misjudges volume in crowds. Remembering this, he sits back – till she comments, whereupon he leans forward to reply, and she says something, and he has an answer. For years, he quenched himself with trips outside Paris when researching a new book, visiting exquisite purveyors, driven around by them, engaging in friendship-flings for a day or two with others who eroticized taste, and whom he recollected as you do a favourite restaurant from vacation – at your peril would you visit again. But 'again' is what he's thinking, that he should re-read the books he mentions to Beck, re-try delicacies cited, listen again to the singer he cannot believe she's never heard of.

Beck jars him with insights into his former lover since Dora left, telling of her mother in London, how she has wilted over the years, gradually shedding all companions. She did this in pursuit of her writing – yet isolation only made her novels barren.

'I never hear of her books anymore; I don't see reviews,' he says.

'She goes from one tiny press to another, costing them all money. Like someone running out on the check.'

'That's unkind.'

'That was the point.'

BENJAMIN LONGS TO MEET his sister, but Alan remains vague. Another letter arrives from her with no postage stamp – Beck must've taken to heart his lament about emails and messaging, so left this envelope by hand in their courtyard mailbox. In the letter, she thanks Alan for the drink the other afternoon, though not for the live oyster, which haunts her dreams. She enjoyed his book on wine saving the world – found a copy at Shakespeare & Company. She listened to Edith Piaf too, and he was right.

Alan drops off his reply at her address but not until days have passed, to avoid seeming eager. On the way there, he exerts himself to witness Paris as she might, the surroundings projected against a screen as in old-movie backdrops, Citroëns streaking through the rain.

More hand-delivered letters pass between them, connecting his days as they've not been connected in some time. He's distracted by thoughts of Beck. It's not lust, just the intoxication from a stranger attending to his opinions, and isn't this what he always sought, why anyone writes anything? Benjamin remarks that, since his sister arrived, she hasn't text-messaged once.

Alan doesn't want them to. At first, this was because he feared that she'd hurt Benjamin, that she knew enough of their mother to say something wounding. But that reasoning has passed. Alan is disturbed by his current motive: their meeting would ruin something of *his*. Because of Benjamin's lack of spark? Or because Alan becomes elderly if presenting a son who is himself old?

'Do we look alike?' Benjamin asks.

'She's dark-skinned. I assume her dad was. Heavy-set too. The same eyes as your mother.'

'What are those like?'

'Green.'

'You're going to bed already?'

'Finish what you were saying, son. No rush.'

'No, just that I'd be curious to see them.'

'See what?'

'Eyes like my mother's.'

Benjamin is always in the living room lately, wanting proximity. He never turns in first. More than before, Alan is away, walking fast as if to stamp on what perturbs him, doubts skittering like spiders from pavement cracks.

'I wonder what I'd tell her if we end up meeting,' Benjamin remarks. 'What do you think I'd say?'

ALAN ROASTS A *poulet de Bresse*, butter and garlic and thyme and lemon zest pushed under the skin, in the oven for ninety minutes, plus Charlotte potatoes in goose fat, and purple-sprouting broccoli. On meeting her brother, Beck asks if they should hug, causing Benjamin to laugh nervously, blush. She narrates aloud her own embarrassment as it happens, and ends up seated in an armchair, with Benjamin on the sofa. They're too far apart for easy conversation, each leaning forward and back, like strangers sharing hummus.

Alan busies himself in the kitchen, but there's little to do besides watch the closed oven, its fan whirring. The conversation in the other room falters, gaps that almost prompt Alan to intervene. He mumbles to himself, to drown them out, then says, 'Five minutes!' Instantly, they join him. When he helps Benjamin into his chair, Beck stands to assist, not sure if it's an intrusion. 'Best if you just sit,' Alan tells her.

The siblings are less tense around Alan, nervous only when he steps away to carve and plate, during which they keep addressing his back. He explains the food and wine, ignoring Beck's excessive praise. Alan wants approval as much as anyone, but he never acquired the grace to accept it. So he shifts to the news, the Taliban retaking Afghanistan, the wildfires in Canada. When Alan talks, they watch. When he stops, they eat.

She knows nothing of sports, and admits this apologetically. To Alan's surprise, Benjamin says he isn't crazy about sports himself, but got into them somehow. 'I used to figure it was envy.'

Alan digs his toes into his insoles.

'Why envy?' she says.

'Just because I couldn't.'

'Oh, right. Sorry. Stupid question.'

Benjamin asks about her French classes, offering tutoring, and she accepts eagerly. Alan knows all the reports from her life – the LA stand-up circuit, her floundering affair with Karine, that overpriced Left Bank apartment. They're versions of answers she already gave him, but lacking the humour. She's unnatural because he is present.

Alan never told Beck not to speak about her mother. But she appears fearful to raise the subject. Benjamin equally so.

'One thing I was going to mention,' Beck says, slowing down, as if looking for a way out of this sentence. 'Actually I wanted to actually to actually mention something. I said to your dad before. To Alan. I said I felt that . . . I don't know.' Rushing: 'Not sure if I'm the one – if *I* should be saying this, Benjamin. If you don't want to discuss it, that's totally fine. Obviously, whatever works. I wasn't sure. Whether to message it. But a message felt wrong. I thought there are things you should say in person. To the person.'

Benjamin glances at his father, then back at his food, knife inadvertently scraping the plate, which causes Beck to close one eye.

Alan sips the Côtes-du-Rhône, stifling anger, for his son is upset. This is why he didn't want her here. Now, Benjamin has a sense of something. The boy avoids further sight of his father, or of their guest, and focuses on the chicken. Alan mentions dessert.

'Dad never eats sweet things. Just these little French jelly candies.' The boy is pleased to possess an insight into his father, and he mentions Alan's nutcracker too, and how he's always working on his grip and lifting groceries to keep up his strength so he can help me, Benjamin explains.

The boy could've died. People with his condition did. They said he'd not survive past his teens. But medicine improved, and his luck held, and Benjamin is middle-aged, though he has endured physical pain so long that he looks sixty. Alan never dwelled on his son's health, in order that the boy become resilient. In private, Alan – after indelible events, his son's agony following yet another operation, his pleas not to have another, though he'd need it – when this happened and Benjamin was still young, Alan went into his room and stuffed a balled-up T-shirt in his mouth. He never allowed grief to escape his bedroom. In the living room, you got on with matters. Honesty, he figured, was worth more than a wheelchair over time. So Alan was always truthful – except about why Benjamin's mother never contacted him: she hadn't wanted their son to exist.

The evening improves, for Beck tells appalling tales of Hollywood featuring the cellphone-throwing beasts who thrive in entertainment.

Benjamin answers her questions on French culture, always saying 'Yes, yes!' when Beck gives an opinion, all of which are misinformed. It's clear to Alan that she feels nothing of the connection with her brother that she feels with him.

He has built a fortress around the boy; Alan cannot watch more suffering. Dora never tried to know Benjamin, and his sister bore no blame. But she links to that past. She pulls him away from here.

The following day, Alan offers his son a passing remark: 'Went fairly well, no?'

'It was my best event pretty much. For as long as I can remember.'

Alan takes out a cigarette, lights one for his son. They open adjacent windows, and look out. Benjamin and Beck have plans to meet again, to work on a project, which Benjamin does not explain further. She wants help with her French too.

A WHITE FLUORESCENT LIGHT blinks above the courtyard mailboxes. You bump into neighbours there, squinting side-by-side at flickering letters. Alan finds one in her handwriting, and replaces it unopened.

'Have you heard from her?' Alan asks his son, unloading groceries. 'Has she texted you?'

'She's super busy, I'm guessing. And probably stuff with that woman she's dating.'

'Karine.'

'Silence is good news on that front, I'm hoping.'

Benjamin, who leaves the apartment only for medical appointments, cannot reach their mailbox in the courtyard. He never sees the letter to him, which Alan leaves unopened, allowing days of advertising fliers to pile atop. A second letter lands there, again unmentioned. 'Weren't you going to help with her French?'

'I'm not sure that'll come together,' Benjamin says, the television selling Gillette, a muscled athlete caressing his cheeks. 'It was nice,' Benjamin recalls, 'that evening.'

'It was.'

'Good to meet her.'

'Yes.'

'To have met her.'

A week later, a neighbour in housecoat scolds Alan for leaving his mailbox so full that fliers fall into the passage, and someone could trip. He removes everything, including the unopened letters from Beck. He dangles these over the recycling bin, pausing – then lets them drop. The most recent letter lands face-up. Alan retrieves it, and climbs to their floor, pausing before the front door to catch his breath. Cowbells from the Tour de France rattle on the other side.

'For you from Beck,' he says, as a yellow shirt pedals across the television, pursued by cameramen on motorcycles. 'Hand-delivered.'

'She didn't want to come in?'

'I didn't see her. It was in our mailbox.'

Benjamin hesitates to open it. 'I'm afraid.'

'Why afraid?'

'Could you look it over, Dad? And see what you think?'

'It's not to me.'

'It won't be anything I mind you seeing.' Benjamin returns to his laptop, pretending to work.

Alan opens the envelope. It's an apology. Her foray to Paris didn't work. The woman she was courting rejected her, and living here without the language or a job wasn't going to work. But it'd be good to say bye before returning to LA. She gives her date of departure, which was two days ago. Why didn't she text-message Benjamin before leaving? Presumably, she wasn't that desperate to see the boy again, Alan thinks.

'I'm sorry she didn't come up and knock,' Benjamin says. 'I would've been here.'

'She probably didn't want to disturb us.'

'I bet that's right. She wouldn't have wanted to.'

'No.'

'It was interesting. To meet her. Didn't you think, Dad?'

'I did.'

'I've got a sister.'

AT THE UNMARKED BORDER before sleep, Alan wavers, his bedroom window open, thin green curtains billowing. He turns and turns, overhot, the sheet twisted into a rope. From the adjacent room, Benjamin coughs, possibly in his sleep, possibly on his laptop.

When Dora was pregnant, they feared the child's condition meant lifelong care. She grew enraged at Alan, who didn't seem to grasp that *she* would end up looking after their child, and what this would mean, and forever. Not forever, Alan said.

'Years. Years!'

'Don't take any role then.'

'What's that supposed to mean?'

'Leave the child here. I'll take care of it.'

279

'Oh, please! Don't insult me.'

Doctors and teachers were always asking Benjamin where his mother was. Alan dismissed the matter, and his son learned to do the same. Alan's gruffness never hurt the boy – or he hopes it never did.

'We do anything together,' the five-year-old said, looking at his father. 'We're the best of friends.'

After decades alive, if you've paid attention, you see a few things more clearly: the pendulum of politics and culture; that each person has, at best, one chance at any stage of life. You raise your children with those insights, showing them how to ingratiate themselves with superiors, how to hold a fork. You teach *what* to want as much as how. But experience only lights the path behind you. It fails to show if that path was itself a mistake, or if your time – the near-glory and the resentments, the chosen studies and chosen ignorance – if it amounted to a life squandered.

Beck was the end of something. Something just finished for Alan: camaraderie – far less common over his life than he'd expected when a boy, when surrounded by siblings, with new kids in every place his family moved to, shouting and running and tripping and fighting and catching up. As you walk deeper into the woods, the people vanish, more elusive than deer.

Alan looks at his wall. Too few hours of wakefulness left. By statistics, about seven years. You can't say precisely. But you can say.

Benjamin is on the other side of this wall. After his father is gone, the boy will be there still.

DIARY: SEPTEMBER 2021

I'm remembering something from years ago. 'Dora,' my stepmother said, phoning from the Netherlands, 'I don't know how to explain it.'

She'd taken my father to the hospital with a gut problem. The doctors suspected an infection, and wanted to admit him for tests. He rebuffed this, yet was too ill to return home. So he sat on the side of a hospital bed, refusing to swing his legs up, growing more upset, more deranged. Finally, the nurses ordered my stepmother to leave while they sedated him. The next morning, she returned. 'He's not the same,' she told me.

The doctors confirmed that my father – despite recovering from delirium, and under treatment for an infection – was not likely to regain his faculties. How was this possible? Yes, he was into his seventies. But he'd seemed cogent weeks earlier. I couldn't query my father himself, for he refused to get on the phone. So I travelled there.

In the hospital hallway, I hesitated, taking a fortifying breath – then entered his room: a stubbly, emaciated old man. He knew me. Much else escaped him.

I kept our conversation light and fleet, as if outrunning my distress – this dignified medical man, who'd always sought to appear invulnerable (though he hadn't convinced me of that in years), and who detested embarrassment — he couldn't conceal anything anymore. Even the curtain over his door was beyond his control.

I drew it closed as I left, my chest imprinted where I'd given him a goodbye hug, unsure where to place my arms, embracing the hospital bed as much as the flat body within. Days later, orderlies delivered him home on a gurney, and helped him into his preferred armchair, where he'd read the newspaper each weekend of my childhood. Tremulously, he drank a coffee, the cup tinkling in its saucer. He was home, as he'd wanted to be, yet absent.

Later, community health workers arrived, and hoisted him onto his bed. When turned, he cried out because strangers pushed and prodded. His temporary room was on the ground floor beside the kitchen. He wouldn't leave his bed anymore, nor take food. How wretched my stepmother and I felt, eating meals with my father starving away, three steps across the hall. So we gathered around his bed with dishes to tempt him. A morsel of trout and a baby potato proved too abundant for him. 'But,' he said, his wrinkly brow furrowing further, 'is someone passing around beer?'

I rushed to the kitchen for a straw. He took one sip from the Heineken bottle, his gaunt cheeks caving, eyelids crinkling closed. After three long seconds, his eyes opened, with a sheen of pleasure unseen in a long time.

I read aloud from an old volume of Chekhov stories he once loved. I was unsure how much he understood, so tried to animate the dialogue, glancing at him as I did the voices, heartened whenever his jaw twitched in amusement. Long before any story ended, he was asleep. Soon, a half-page became his limit. Later, a paragraph.

The community health workers insisted that he turn over, but he feared falling from the bed. 'What are you doing?!' he shouted, bewildered. They called for my help. My father's dry fingers squeezed my hand, his thin arm trembling. To distract him, I spoke of the latest tales from Chekhov, my gaze locked on his.

For some reason, I recall his expression now, looking out my attic-office window over other night-time London houses, their floating rectangles of windowlight, behind which strangers eat, smile at televisions, slouch toward the stairs.

I'm guilty to describe what I have of my father, those private scenes. What do you owe those who aren't anywhere anymore, except in you?

I draw the curtains shut to obscure myself from view. I'm not what I'd hoped. But I wrote books, and thrived when doing so.

I imagine my daughter after I'm gone, leafing through what I put down on those pages. Or maybe she'll avoid my books because they're painful, and she prefers not to think vividly of me, for I'm unavailable but might be in my novels. Isn't that why I wrote them?

If my writing hurts her, I don't want her to read anything I did, only to keep copies on her shelves (if shelves are still for books in the future). My volumes could stand in the background when she's dozy from too much consumption; or joking with a partner; or looking at a child's plump hand, her own pointing at letters on a page.

The last conversation I had with my father, he spoke with awe that I'd come back to see him. He declared that, once better, he'd return to his desk. He'd write it all down.

~~Dora is travelling abroad.~~

Or

~~On the window beside Dora's seat on the bus, a wasp climbs up, climbs down, seeking escape — an organism like any machine, with its algorithms of if/then.~~

Or

She's travelling by bus, a black duffel bag between her feet. She needs little today: an apple, the sandwich wrapped in foil, a bottle of water. For company, she dropped in a tattered copy of Chekhov short stories.

9

The novelist

(DORA FRENHOFER)

S HE'S TRAVELLING BY BUS, a black duffel bag between her
feet. She needs little today: an apple, the sandwich wrapped in
foil, a bottle of water. For company, she dropped in a tattered copy
of Chekhov short stories.

Before leaving London, Dora spoke to a lawyer, designating
him the executor of her will, and stating her intentions for any last
objects. She donated her remaining clothing to a charity shop on
the high road, gave her TV to the cleaning team that emptied her
cellar, and submerged her laptop in water, then threw it away with
the weekly rubbish.

At dawn this morning, she stripped her bed – just a mattress
on a boxspring now – and showered for the last time. Dora was
pleased to find an empty shampoo bottle: she'd timed this well.
She lathered a soap bar against her head, scrubbing roughly, shorn
white hair prickling her fingers. Towelling off, she looked down at
sagging contours: me, she thought, and her insides plunged, as when

watching someone lean over a cliff's edge. She didn't respect the fear; it only interested her.

Across the bus aisle, a masked couple is speaking loudly in French – they're sharing earbuds, a ticking beat audible. A boy sits with a shopping bag full of old shoes. An Eastern European woman – mask under her chin – scrolls her cracked-screen smartphone, rubs her eyes. All these people will end, their calendar events vanishing, along with toiletries around the basin and socks in drawers, at a date to be defined. Dora's date is today.

When organizing this, she expected they'd have someone at the location to explain how it worked. But for legal reasons, nobody will attend. She expected a psychological evaluation beforehand. That never came either.

You know your own personality, she thinks, in the way that sonar knows distance, by bouncing it off what's around. According to others' reactions, your confidence shrivels or becomes bloated. Over time, this is who you consider yourself to be. Rarely, you stumble into yourself unmediated, brushing your teeth perhaps, or travelling alone.

She was in London this morning, in a black cab headed for St Pancras, not a word exchanged with the taxi driver, even when paying. She found her assigned seat on the Eurostar, which dipped for twenty dark minutes under the sea, surfacing in sunny France, then rolling across an invisible border into Belgium. At a bustling station there, she passed bakery stalls whose iced cinnamon curlicues looked like craft, while young voices commiserated with phones, and rushed to meetings with other phones. A different train took her from the city to a town, then to a smaller town, where Dora entered this bus, from which she now descends, holding to the rail, wondering if her knee will give out and she'll tumble to the pavement. A physiotherapist recommended a knee brace that sits in a cupboard at home; a doctor offered steroid injections and discussed surgical options. She limited herself to leg exercises, puffing on the carpet at home. Something must've helped: her shoes touch down safely on the pavement, paired and pointing like ducks. She holds still as a wave of pain rises from her knee, crests, withdraws.

She has no luggage in the belly of the bus, and its front doors hiss shut behind her. The exhaust pipe coughs hotly. The bus pulls away. Before her are outlet stores fronted by parking lots, not a single human.

She consults the printout of directions, and walks past a long window of sofas, each waiting to be adopted and stained. A golf store next. Dora has never tried that activity, so importantly unimportant. Golf will exist onward, and she'll never have known of it. Anything she hasn't done, she will not.

She finds the correct street, lined with new-build apartments, the kind that estate agents call 'town houses' and residents call 'small'. There's a person, the first since the bus: an old man in a navy tracksuit, plastic tubes from his nostrils to an oxygen cylinder on two wheels. He's muttering, looking around.

Dora adjusts her glasses, and checks the house numbers, seeking her destination. That man is waiting before her door. She didn't expect irritation today – she expected to speak to nobody, and has managed all the way here. Dora has no space for an old man, not for a long-winded complaint, nor to help him find keys or a daughter who has keys.

'Excuse me,' she says, in the local language. 'I need to get in there.'

'What?' he replies in English. 'I don't understand.'

From spite, she persists in the wrong language: 'Come on! You're in the way!'

He prattles about someone called Scott and a lockbox, as if his worries are her worries, that she arrived for his sake, and if he just sticks with English, she'll learn it sooner or later. In short, that *he* is the subject of this story. He is wrong.

'Fuming, to tell the truth,' he says. 'Me, sat here, and Scott driving off like that. Nobody said I'd need a password or – what's it called? – a code thing.'

'I'm not here to help you.'

'You speak English?'

'Evidently, yes. But I need to get past. I'm going in there.' Her stiff hands unfold the printout, and she finds an access number for the lockbox, and prods its buttons. A flap falls, and a key lands in her palm. She opens the front door: the plastic smell of air-freshener. The old man staggers past her, entering first, as if she worked here.

'Excuse me, but *I* arranged to be here,' she says. 'I have an appointment. I can show you the email.'

He's resting against his oxygen canister, wheezing. 'Don't know what your email says,' he responds. 'But I paid good money to be here.'

'You have paperwork proving that?'

'Scott's got it.'

'Should I know who this Scott is?'

'My son-in-law. He drove me all the way over here. He'll be back in a minute.'

'Either way, *I* have the appointment. I'm sorry, but you need to leave.'

He's stammering about a car now. She watches this half-broken machine, whose switch she inadvertently flipped.

Dora has taken pains in her life to avoid arguments with foolish men. Now, her last day, and this. She'll lead him back outside. But then? Proceed to the plan, yet with a doddering man at the front door? 'I'll call the emergency number, and they can explain it to you. Then you need to leave.'

They're in the lounge area of the apartment, with framed doilies on the wall and a boxy old television. The bookshelf contains a Bible and a pink-spined romance. In the wheelchair-accessible toilet, a hanging plant is living out its days, while the 'Peace Room' contains a leatherette couch from the superstore down the road. 'You sit there while I call,' she tells him.

A vase of orange tulips in cloudy water stands on the kitchenette table, with a letter stuck underneath. It welcomes her, including forms to sign, instructions on which order to take the drugs, and whom to call if there's a problem. 'You see,' she shouts toward the Peace Room, holding up the letter. 'This has *my* name on it.' She fails to mention that the three boxes of pharmaceuticals are all stickered with 'Mr Frank H. Ward', presumably him. She needs to prepare for this phone call. *He* must return another day, not she.

A woman answers the emergency number, caught in mid-conversation with a child or a dog: 'No, Karl! Stop eating that!' The woman offers to call back when she gets a moment, but Dora demands attention now. Both she and this old man travelled from overseas – they need this resolved immediately.

'The British person is who we scheduled.'

Dora explains that, though she speaks the local language, she too travelled here from Britain.

'Maybe that explains the mix-up,' the woman says. 'But I don't have access to Birgit's computer.'

'Birgit? I dealt with Gisela.'

'Gisela's on leave. You need Birgit.'

'Put her on the phone then.'

'I'm talking from my house.'

'So where's Birgit?'

'This is just the emergency line.'

'That's why I called with an emergency. Is there a mobile for someone who can take responsibility?'

'I can't give out that number.'

'Do you not have a calendar of who's supposed to turn up? This is unbelievable. Look, you need to get senior staff involved.'

Minutes pass. Nobody calls back.

The old man is muttering to himself in the Peace Room. Dora stays in the lounge, midway between exasperation and amusement that her last hours are this: waiting for customer service. She calls again. The same woman answers, claiming to have just spoken to someone, and that it's for them to decide.

'What, me and him?'

'You two are the ones who turned up at the same time.'

'Because you told us to! Even legally, this can't be right.' But Dora veers away from the legal angle, remembering those medications in his name. She plans to ingest them, and considers deceiving the old man, telling him the office ordered him to leave. But if he phones them to complain, they'd discover her duplicity, and could expel her.

'When is this Scott person getting here? You two can arrange to return tomorrow, alright?'

'What?' he shouts from the other room. 'Can't hear you!' He joins her, complaining between wheezes that he doesn't have anyplace to stay in this country. Scott was planning to head back to London alone tonight – he just popped out to buy something. 'There's a special wine Tina loves. He'll make out that it's from me.'

Dora pushes her duffel bag under the coffee table as if to assert her rights. Old magazines are fanned across the tabletop, their glossy covers torn: a woman presenting brownies; a tattooed sportsman holding an orange ball.

When a rat died in Dora's cellar, the smell forced her to go down, wincing in pain each time her weight shifted on the stepladder. With her bare hand, she cleared cobwebs around the light switch, and illuminated the brick-walled chamber: black droppings on the floor, and a rodent, dead on its side. She avoided the sight of its toothy grimace, and held her breath when sliding a piece of cardboard underneath, the rubbery tail hanging over. With the laden cardboard in one hand, she struggled back up the stepladder, and imagined losing her footing, with nobody knowing that she'd fallen, the cellar bulb fading. In distraction, she nearly missed a step, causing the dead rat to roll down the cardboard into her midriff. She bobbled the corpse and grasped its tail, the body swinging like a pendulum, her lips pursed in revulsion as she flung it up to the ground floor, then climbed after, polluted, her knee throbbing. Absurd shoes, she thought, looking at hers covered in cellar dust. When young, she coveted elegant footwear. These were nuns' black rectangles — among the concessions of age, surrendering bits of yourself until you look nothing like you expect. People whisper to each other, after seeing the empty-eyed elderly at nursing homes, '*I* wouldn't let myself get to that point.' But they will. The wheelchair that once seemed degrading becomes salvation. Yet the question that troubled her that day was: 'Which recycling bin for a rat?'

Dora reckoned that seventy-five years was enough, and she had reached that term. Her mother died before fifty, her father at seventy-three, which seemed old at the time. Hendrik — a country doctor — was lanky and fit until, a few years after retirement, he chopped firewood, and missed, and the axe blade severed the flesh between two toes. Despite medical knowledge, he failed to care for his worsening wound. It was a clue to dementia, which crept over him in coming years, slowly, gradually — then in a catastrophic lurch, after he visited the hospital with a gut infection, and delirium overcame him. When he regained sense, Hendrik wasn't quite there. His final months were nightmarish.

The suddenness terrified Dora. When ageing, she thought, you compromise in small measures until, abruptly, you've lost control; you're acted upon. She vowed to end her time before that. To monitor her decline, Dora compiled a list of what had failed in her father — errors and confusions that should serve as her warning signs. But if she waited for *all* those hints, she'd likely have lost the capacity to respond. So, you must act a bit too early. Dignity or time: you can't have both.

Shortly before the Covid pandemic — in those distant late months of 2019 – Dora attended a concert at Wigmore Hall alone, her bad knee mashed against the seat in front, among a crowd of white-hairs watching the young perform Bach.

Afterward, amid the polite middle-class exodus, an extrovert of Dora's age asked what she'd thought, and Dora expressed appreciation for some of the pieces – though she'd not loved the sympathy. That was wrong. What *was* the word? Other cases too. She asked a shop clerk where to find those round nuts, and he looked askance, and what're those called they're   they're

When spoken aloud, 'symphony' sounded wrong. Anyway, she hadn't loved it. Or the sympathy.

But what *is* so terrible if orderlies deposit you in an armchair, and you rave, and they clean you? Somehow, personal grooming feels fundamental. Since age fourteen, she has dealt with errant hairs, and were she to enter a nursing home, they'd ignore those, she'd grow wisps on her chin, and they'd not mind – then again, nor would she.

To be human, Dora thinks, includes dominion over your hair. But independence also means laundry, and dirty dishes, and falsified enthusiasm for younger lives that rerun the same theatrical productions, oblivious to how commonplace the dramas are. She refuses to believe that what's new today is worse than what was new. But that is how it feels. It's a lack of savour, as when she ate her sandwich earlier. She hardly remembers doing so, the buttery piggish scent of *jamón serrano* on crusty baguette. When did she have it? She unzips her duffel bag. The sandwich is still there, untouched.

Her mind needs an editor – preferably more indulgent than those who've considered her writing lately. Dora's favourite publishing person died a few years back, and a perky replacement at the imprint said she'd 'absolutely love to take a look' at the next manuscript. It wasn't a major publishing house; those had lost interest after consecutive flops. This young stranger was the last chance, lest Dora's past three years die stranded on a computer chip.

She emailed the manuscript, and waited. When she enquired as to the silence, an effusive apology leapt back. The young editor added that it'd be lovely to meet, and discuss 'your new book'. (She'd written 'new book', not 'submitted manuscript'. A promising sign?) A lunch date was set, then delayed and delayed.

Her manuscript – the late-life attempt of Dora Frenhofer to find words, to say something anyone cared about, to not worry what anyone cared about, to figure out what she cared about and hope anyone cared (then make her keyboard cooperate) – was perhaps rubbish. Anyway, the editor reached a verdict, and insisted on sharing it in person, forcing Dora to wait in agony for the woman's protracted Greek vacation to end. At last, a restaurant was selected, and a date set. Dora's literary agent (another younger woman inherited from another deceased book person) dropped out because of an auction for a novel that everyone was wild about. So it'd be just Dora and the editor.

The young woman picked an upmarket Middle Eastern restaurant in Kensington, and generously ordered too much: pomegranate-specked appetizers, spiced meat platters, rose-scented desserts. When drinks arrived, the editor confessed to not having *quite* finished reading, so she'd refrain from giving her thoughts. Dora pinched her thigh, forcing herself to tolerate the pain as long as possible, while appearing composed above the table. She praised the food and, upon parting, they cheek-kissed. The editor would be in touch very very soon.

She was. An hour later, Dora received a call from her agent: the editor had rejected it. She must've known before the meal but hadn't wanted to cancel after so many delays, thus assuaged her guilt by treating the old woman to a grand last meal.

Dora suggested phoning the editor herself, to offer changes that might satisfy her. Dora's agent dissuaded her. 'Don't want to seem like you're begging.'

'I could write an email.'

'Honestly? I'd just leave it.'

The editor and agent were dear friends, and always met for drinks, probably sighing at the mention of Dora Frenhofer – how awkward it was, how you couldn't just drop her. She'd get the message.

Dora knew before the call ended that she'd never again look at that manuscript. Her career had just ended. For the rest of the week, she tidied her house, its three floors long ceded to clutter and dust. How, she wondered, do you retire as a novelist? Do you leave a note on the kitchen table? And if you live alone?

The old man with the oxygen cylinder is talking to her, something so absurd that she listens. 'Whoever goes first,' he says, 'the other can do a spot of shopping.'

'What for?'

'They got excellent prices on golf clubs, Scott tells me. But you know what they say: you can't take it with you!'

Cliché is rough sandpaper to Dora. Yet it's his presumption that bothers her most – something enters his head, so she must kick aside whatever is in hers.

'I took my last fare the other day,' he says. 'Only lasted an hour. Was worried I'd crash, given the state I'm in.'

'Crash what?'

'The taxi. Nearly fifty years I was on the job.' He laments Uber, and says how Scott needed six years of hard work to pass the cabbies' test. 'Anyone getting through The Knowledge is impressive. Especially for him, with that thing he's got.'

'No idea what thing.'

'Where the words aren't the right way up.'

Dora knows, but can't find the word herself.

'Why anyone uses ride apps, I can't say,' he remarks. 'Would you let your granddaughter get in a car with a strange man? How's that even safe?'

'Dyslexia.'

'You what?'

'That's what's wrong with Scott.'

'Nothing's *wrong* with Scott.'

To Dora, this man epitomizes their species: lost for words, so uttering them. If he wants to keep speaking, he wants to keep living.

He brings out a photograph of his grandchildren. Dora declines to see them, explaining that she has resolved to do only what she wants for the remainder of her life. 'You're bothered by that, I see,' she notes. 'Your question was, "Do you want to look?" I said the truth.'

This directness of hers – normal where she'd grown up in the Netherlands – was especially pronounced in her father, who never softened the facts when warning ill patients of what lay ahead. They had every right, he contended, to know what he did. Whether they needed such graphic detail was perhaps arguable. Hendrik – in his unvarnished way – tended a rural patch of Noord-Brabant, a wedge between Belgium and Germany that a Dutch politician once referred to as 'a place of cows, pigs and Catholics'. However, the manners of their village owed more to Protestant modesty, every family's front curtains wide open to prove that they possessed nothing of value.

Dora's mother, Lotte – large-eared and six years older than her husband – hailed from Den Bosch, a provincial city where she grew up watching German expressionist films and reading novels about modern degeneracy, which she would've rather liked to try. She only met Hendrik in her thirties, during the Second World War, when Lotte was taking rural refuge from the fighting. During hardships toward the end of the war, they became each other's company: he, the most educated person she'd met since leaving Den Bosch.

In peacetime, Lotte accepted the role of country-doctor's wife. Privately, she viewed the village with scorn, and took this out on Hendrik. She mocked the peasants' ignorance, especially when she spoke to their young daughter, Dora, who imbibed her mother's snobbery. Lotte also took great pleasure in overexciting little Dora – wild games and late-night tickling – such that the girl forgot herself, streaking with red-faced hilarity into rooms occupied by her father. Dora sees Hendrik's slender back and high collar, his faint bald spot, and the restrained ferocity – he so full of words, and she with few, except to deny guilt (though guilty). Too late, for he'd lost his temper. Indeed, he'd lost it already, because of other frustrations, only to be presented a child-shaped occasion to discharge his outrage. When castigated by her father, Dora grew as frantic as a cat in a bag, and shouted to stop him shouting. Lotte entered her husband's study, and the sobbing girl opened her arms for her mother's comfort. Hendrik glared at his wife in warning. Defiantly, Lotte's forearm brushed her daughter's back, her fingertips dusting Dora's shoulder blades.

When Dora was six, her mother's skin yellowed, and she slept all day, behind a door that nurses sometimes left ajar. Dora peeped in: her mother disrobed and twisted, only the thinning hair on her head and the patch in her crotch identifying which side of this person was up. One morning, the door was wide open, the bed made. Hendrik returned that afternoon, stating that Lotte had been put in the ground, and earth piled atop. He knew how close Dora was to her mother, so had decided the girl ought not attend.

Dora inherited the books that her mother had not burned for heat during the war. These prized volumes became an after-life conversation between them in the form of tattered hardcovers, which she moved to every home of her life, until a removals man walked out her front door recently, lugging cardboard boxes to his van. What would her mother have thought of Dora's writing? Throughout her career, that question preoccupied Dora. Only after someone dies do you realize how different each human is: a particular space remains deserted, quiet where opinions sounded, empty where they'd have marched into the room.

Dora and her father never again shouted at each other. Over the years, Hendrik even had flashes of humour with her, particularly regarding patients. He viewed people as the greatest barrier to their own interests, all the drinking and smoking and eating to excess. So he adopted an adversarial stance, siding with their health over their will. 'I should've taken up veterinary medicine,' he commented, 'as *those* patients listen to reason.'

Hendrik busied his young daughter with activities – always what he wished, and with pedagogical intent: trees and leaves; the constellations; keeping a ledger. He escorted her to bookshops in Utrecht, Rotterdam, Amsterdam and Groningen up north. Dora was allowed to choose any volume, up to a certain price. Hendrik's interest in fiction was slight, extending only to the great Russians: Dostoevsky, for capturing the angst of life among conformists; Tolstoy, for how history shoulders into the passer-by; and, above all, Chekhov, a brother doctor who shared Hendrik's sightline on humanity, glimpsed while opening the medical bag on a farm visit.

Each weekend, Hendrik leafed through *de Volkskrant* in his armchair by the fireplace, and she'd bring in one of her mother's left-behind novels, sitting on the undersized child's rocking chair, pretending to read. He'd glance up from his newspaper, and Dora spoke for the sake of speaking, noting his unrest, and so strived (worry rising) to hold his attention – a writerly instinct years before her first typewriter.

As for moral guidance, Hendrik offered little besides his own behaviour. Dora was free to go where she pleased from early girlhood. He taught her to drive his run-down Opel Kapitän when she was nine. He let her shoot his hunting rifle without supervision.

Hendrik must've been lonely: years unmarried, a disappointment to his patients, who wished for a gentle doctor. When he found a second wife, it was a development Dora had hoped for. The local population was growing, and theirs was now a town, prompting Hendrik to employ a nursing aide. The house filled with plants, and Margriet's heirloom crucifix appeared on their wall. She was a loving woman, though Dora judged her stepmother to be simple, and looked down on her father for his preference.

Margriet often reminded Dora that her father had suffered a difficult war. *Who*, Dora thought, *had an easy war?* Also, Hendrik hadn't seen battle, and was spared the Nazis' worst crimes because of his half-German origins, his father having moved across the border early in the century. According to family lore, when her grandfather Moritz was a young man – moody-romantic son of a doctor in the German spa town of Cleves – he had a habit of sleeping in De Duivelsberg, the Devil's Mountain forest, which lay on the border with the Netherlands, and which both countries claimed. In those woods, he passed hours, smoking a meerschaum pipe under chestnut trees, listening to the creaks of bush and branch, and responding with bad poetry in a leather notebook. Once, he terrified a Dutch girl whom he took to be lost, though she was not, merely unsettled by a German youth leaping from the foliage to help her when no help was required. He must've found a way to charm Willemina, for they married and settled on her side of the border, Moritz eventually obtaining a little-desired position as country doctor – the job that their son, Hendrik, came to inherit.

During the war, Hendrik maintained cordial relations with the occupying German forces, notably by prescribing cures for venereal disease. In parallel, he gave occasional refuge to Dutch members of the resistance – though never longer than a night or two, and not to Jews. Hiding a Jew, he once explained to Dora, could have meant his death. In old age, he said something more: that Jewish colleagues – friends during his medical studies – had been deported, and he'd helped none. 'The shame of my life,' he said.

Hendrik did suffer detention once, when German soldiers and their Dutch collaborators sought locals responsible for slashing the tyres of bicycles that the Nazis had confiscated. The soldiers gathered all village males aged eleven to eighty, and forced them into a single horse stall whose doors they locked, around forty men so compressed that they could hardly breathe. If the prisoners failed to identify any culprits after the weekend, the soldiers would incinerate everyone, and they proved their seriousness by removing the horses from adjacent stalls. Grunting and screaming, the men were left for the next three days. Many died from suffocation. Hendrik survived, albeit with damage to his left shoulder, which he never again moved without pain. His older brother was among those who perished. In adolescence, Dora – casually condemning as the young are – pictured Hendrik betraying his brother. Only later did it occur to her that, if her father had been bolder, perhaps they'd have burned him alive, and she'd never have existed. Everyone owes their life to the cowardice of an ancestor somewhere.

In adolescence, Dora also heard details of her late mother's war. Contrary to the family fib, Lotte hadn't sought refuge in the village alone, but had arrived with her two small children, Sofie and Casper, whose father had been killed early in the war. When tending to her kids' coughs, the local doctor, Hendrik (more cultured than anyone Lotte had met in the area) became her acquaintance.

In 1944, the Allies launched a campaign to drive back German troops occupying the Netherlands, and this cut incoming supplies. Cold struck: the Hunger Winter. Locally, rumours spread of a hidden cow, and that one could procure milk if the farmer appreciated the woman who visited. Lotte dressed as attractively as possible, her clothing and underwear far too large by then. She set out, shivering. But the farmer and his hidden cow seemed to be a myth – or perhaps it was her poor sense of direction in unmarked fields. Crusted with cold mud, shuddering, she returned to find her two children on the floor by their shared bed, each strangled.

This account, which a village gossip told Dora, was so patchy that she sketched in the gaps herself, concocting a German military-police official overseeing investigations in the area, who learned of the murder of two local children. This Nazi, a devout Catholic, believed in law and justice, and doggedly sought the murderer (untroubled by matters just out of view, crimes in which he was complicit). But Dora never wrote detective fiction. Instead, thinking of these deaths changed something: she'd always imagined her missing mother as her closest friend, that they were alike. Now, the woman felt like a stranger.

'So you're from here?' the old man is asking.

'Here? No, not here,' she says. 'Not far, though. But I've lived in London for years.'

'London as well. Small world.'

No, it's a large world, Dora thinks, though she voices faint agreement. She's distracted, calculating how many years since she left these parts. Her father and his new wife had a young son by then, Theo, although Dora took little part in family life. After finishing school, she left, driving with a boyfriend to Paris, which was still gearing up for its student-revolutionary outburst later in the Sixties. Dora spoke French badly, with a strong accent and no fear, perturbing Parisians with her effrontery. Soon, she left the Dutch boy who'd brought her, preferring the company of older men, both for the quality-of-life and for the education. Among these was a dashing short Jewish-American food writer, Alan Zelikov, whose expense account introduced readers (and female friends) to exquisite dining. Those he brought to top eateries had no obligation to sleep with him. But they could. She pictures Alan in a fine restaurant, jaw contorting, nose flaring, jotting copious notes on a reporter's pad. What, she wondered at the time, is there to write about taste?

After one extravagant meal, she took ill, queasy to recall the three-tiered seafood platter, whose former occupants swam around her digestive tract. She convalesced for days, an anti-nausea medicine failing to revive her. Finally, a doctor confirmed that it was simple food poisoning but warned that the anti-nausea medicine was making matters worse, and could have harmed the foetus, which was a strange way to inform her of a pregnancy. She was barely out of her teens.

Alan, learning of his parental responsibility, rapped his knuckles twice on a polished sidetable, shaking the full ashtray, as if this marriage proposal were a far, far better thing than he had ever done. For the first time, Dora detected a nervous need in Alan: she, a dining partner whom he'd previously disregarded, was to determine his future. She never saw him again, but googled 'Alan Zelikov' not long ago, finding the archived obituary of a food writer who'd died of a stroke in 1997, leaving no survivors. All those years ago in Paris, doctors had no reliable way to evaluate the health of a foetus, and the suffering of a handicapped child was more than Dora could contemplate. She visited London, where men still wore bowler hats, everyone carried rolled-up umbrellas, and abortionists could be found. That child would've been past fifty now. Dora can't remain in the same air as that thought, so walks to the front door, which concentrates her on the present, the old man droning.

He's preparing tea, narrating his actions, fumbling in the fridge, spilling a milk carton. She ends up making it for him.

'My wife's gone,' he says, when she places a steaming cup before him. 'You?'

'I'm not married.'

'Pity,' he says, adding, 'Some like it that way, I suppose.'

'It's for the best in my case. Whenever I picture myself with a husband lately, I kill him off.'

'I don't follow.'

'No, nothing. I used to write stories – that was my job, a writer. Every time I wrote a husband in recent years, it didn't end well for him.'

'Whodunnits?'

'No, no. Just novels.'

'Why'd the husbands get bumped off then?'

'In the latest, I had an old woman who walks into her kitchen for lunch, and she finds this grey old fellow at the table, and wonders: How did I end up married to him?'

'What, she doesn't know?'

'She knows. But she . . . It doesn't matter.'

'Then she offs him.'

'No, he starts choking.'

'Poisoned?'

'He's eating a sweet, and it goes down the wrong way, and she sees him suffocating, and leaves him there.'

'Not believable, if you don't mind me saying.'

'You're probably right. But the idea is, her husband is the only person keeping her going, which makes him an obstacle, because she wants to end her life. When this old man – the last character in her last story – is gone, she has nothing holding her to the world. But she's frightened: wanting him there, wanting him gone. Anyway, that was the idea.'

'Here's a better ending,' he suggests. 'This husband, he's playing around on her, and he slaps her once too often, and she's had enough, and wants revenge. So she poisons him for his money.'

'Much better. You should be the writer.'

He smiles, and coughs. 'How's a person get into your line of work?'

In Dora's case, indirect blame lay with Klaus, the bearded German sculptor she lived with in Paris. A brawny man known for vast rusted artworks, Klaus aspired to write important novels someday, and loaded her with German literature that he'd equal. She was attracted to the mercurial moods of Klaus, to the depth of his voice, to his ambition. He never noticed that she had that last trait herself.

Together, they moved to his native Munich. Once, he went lake-swimming with friends, and inadvertently locked Dora in his studio. At first, she banged on the door and shouted, then fiddled with his clay and tools, irritated with Klaus, thus careless if she damaged something. Eventually, she picked up pen and paper.

Klaus flung open the studio door, shaggy hair dripping down his bare chest. She didn't respond, preferring the people on her pages, and needing to hold him back a little longer. When he realized what she was doing, Klaus laughed, as if hearing a child mangle a grown-up word. He assumed she'd be writing in Dutch, but she did so in German, which limited her to clipped prose – a happenstance that became a style.

Dora published before he did, and that ended their relationship, though she didn't realize it at the time. All she saw was how dull his drinking had become. Decades later, she gave a reading at a low-ceilinged restaurant in Nuremberg, attended by nine elderly locals, including a leonine man in brown corduroy jacket, who smiled little brown teeth. Afterward, he shook her long hand with both of his fat ones, fingers soft and warm, his gaze humbly on hers, and he expressed such admiration for what she'd become. His remarks lingered as she returned alone to the budget hotel: 'Yes,' he said, 'we must!' – one of those farewells disguised as a plan.

Her first published story paid a pittance, which was more than enough: when Dora was young, money served only to fund each week. She wanted no objects, except Italian shoes glimpsed in shop windows – but only as one admires a *château*, without expectation of ownership. After moving out of the Klaus apartment, Dora sold colour televisions, then men's ties. But secretarial work was how she earned most, and what quickened her typing. When it came to her writing, Dora preferred longhand. No rush; just a hobby. Yet it was becoming more than that. When composing scenes, Dora experienced the physiological responses of her protagonists, swallowing if they did, clearing her throat, growing upset, shouting (only realizing this when a housemate barged in, asking if everything was alright). After writing, she needed to habituate to people again; their predictability grated.

'Don't you agree?' the old man concludes.

She wasn't listening, so responds: 'Absolutely, yes.'

He nods with satisfaction, knowing they're on the same page. 'You don't say much. But you're good to talk to.'

Once, Dora's father remarked that she could be wonderful company — when she wanted. As a young woman, she did want that, becoming the one who strode up to the jazz-club doormen proposing they admit her whole party for free, and they'd smirk at her gall, and oblige. Yet once inside the club, Dora turned into the quietest, with a running commentary hidden in her head, evaluating everyone. Above all, she identified people's motives, and judged them: the successful as schemers, the failed as fools. Yet despite these judgements (which never spared Dora herself), she wrote tenderly of people in her fiction. The writing contained more humanity than the writer.

Dora sold her first novel at twenty-seven, and decided to pause while awaiting publication. She'd replenish herself among friends and a lover she'd overlooked. She enjoyed only the first day. People spoke so much slower than written dialogue.

'I can't tempt you?' the old man asks, offering that photo of his grandkids again.

Dora regrets turning him down earlier. She's tired of insisting on candour over kindness, and wants to remedy herself. 'You *can* tempt me, yes. I was distracted before — probably just tense about all this,' she says. 'Do show me. Thank you.'

She takes a long look at the grandkids' photo: all grins and missing front teeth and birthday cake. Dora almost asks if they won't miss him — it's the kind of question she'd normally pose. But it'd be cruel. Instead: 'Very sweet, all of them.' She returns the picture.

In Dora's young adulthood, the only child she knew properly was her younger brother, Theo. She'd hardly bothered with him when they were in the same house. But after she left the country, and was writing in Germany, she developed an opinion about her adolescent half-brother, whose difficulties Dora heard in telephone reports from the boy's mother, Margriet. He'd finished school with no plans, and was a mess, convinced that his peers mocked him, and somehow knew his thoughts. The reality was far less: nobody considered him at all. He'd been a minor presence at school, and they'd surpassed him since leaving. He stayed in bed most days, and Hendrik indulged this, as he never would have with his daughter. In annoyance, she decided to fix what her father and stepmother merely flapped at. She was generationally closer to Theo, and considered herself adept at wrangling complicated men.

The plan was to force her brother up and out of this funk. What'd really solve matters, she thought, was for Theo to leave that claustrophobic little town. She had an early success, persuading him to travel with her to Amsterdam. There, she took him to see tour operators selling voyages to the East. A flight was prohibitively expensive, but you could board a bus, and just go.

Theo wore a jean jacket and stinking jeans, his fingernails chewed, pimpled cheeks visible through stringy hair; a long greasy teenager. As they walked through Dam Square, he trickled with sweat at the presence of so many people, more than since school hallways.

You won't achieve anything with your life, she thought of him. You'll stay still, waste away, trying nothing.

At a canal-side café, Dora ordered him a beer, then a coffee. Theo kept gripping his shoulders, as if to protect himself from ambush. She spoke of how the world wasn't like their town, that he'd find situations where you have to manage, and thus return stronger. She mentioned friends who'd visited Indonesia, and hadn't Theo loved eating *kroepoek* when smaller? What if he went there? Other people she knew had trekked across India, seen the base of Mount

Kanchenjunga, leapt nude into a glacial lake across from China, and came home transformed. You needn't be stuck with the second-raters we grew up with, she said.

As they stepped from the café onto the road, Theo was nearly hit by a cyclist, and she grabbed a handful of his jean-jacket collar in anger, supposedly scolding him for his distraction – but secretly because she was vexed by his failure to embrace her proposals. 'Throw yourself into situations, Theo! Not into roads!' She let go of him. 'You *need* difficult times. That's growing up.' Strange, she thinks now, how that which hardened you seems the correct preparation for life, even if you're not particularly happy with how you ended up.

Cockroaches scattered across the carpet of the hippie tour agency, and a frizz-haired freak at the desk looked up from a comic book. An overland bus left weekly, including that night, arriving in New Delhi. She asked the price, and impulsively counted out the guilders from her purse. But how impulsive was it really? She'd brought along Theo's passport.

Dora expected he would be more thrilled, but he remained a musky teenage boy. The tour-company employee promised to show her brother nearby shops where everyone picked up basics for the trip. Dora gave Theo cash for this too, folding bank notes into his breast pocket, as if it were a movie scene. 'You ready?' she asked, and slapped the back of his hand with affection.

His mother spent the rest of her life trying to find Theo, taking repeated trips to India, where he'd last been seen. She hired detectives, and leads emerged over the years, all false.

'So which was it then?' the old man is asking.

'Which was what?'

'Your most famous book.'

'Mine? None is famous.'

'Don't be shy now. Give us a name.'

She mentions one.

'Never heard of it.'

An upstart British publisher bought translation rights to that book, her debut, saying they'd promote her as a Dutch version of Françoise Sagan – a silly comparison that she permitted. Dora gave London a try, and began writing in English, which sheared another layer of artifice from her prose.

The mid-1970s were grim for Britain, still in the thudding hangover of empire, its workers striking, with electricity cuts, and a mood of dejection. Yet Dora's first years there had the opposite tint: glittering book parties; taxi rides with authors of note; 3 a.m. at the electric typewriter in her bedsit, the frisson that this line before her might be superb.

Her first three novels came out too fast. They needed revision, but she resisted. Back then, Dora considered her fiction as akin to her body, and objected to uninvited prodding. Those first books were reviewed favourably, without selling favourably. She contributed occasionally to the *Times Literary Supplement*, had a few pieces in *Partisan Review*, and once in the French edition of *Playboy*. But her dealings with editors often ended bitterly. The term 'difficult', she believed, was what people applied when *they* barge ahead at the butcher's, and *you* stand up for yourself. Dora had a habit of frankness about other writers too, in reviews and in person. 'I'm Dutch,' she said, by way of explanation.

Those times belonged to another person, a character recalled with a pang – a woman who, for a decade, was mistaken for a rising star, pencilled into the family tree of important writers. But, as a fellow novelist once told her: 'A writer can be difficult. A writer can deliver late. A writer can be mediocre at writing itself. But only one at a time.' Dora was two at a time. While never late, she was difficult, and less-than-outstanding. They could pass. They started to.

'What's the word I'm looking for?'

'Is it "hazelnut"?' she tells the old man. 'That's one I can't seem to remember lately. That and "symphony".'

'We're losing it, aren't we.'

Her father's incipient dementia came during Dora's mid-thirties. Hendrik's hard edges wore away; his eyes became vague. She tried not to notice, and visited rarely. Margriet denied any decline, which bothered Dora, for it epitomized what was childish about her step-mother. Once Hendrik's mind betrayed him entirely, Margriet spoke only of prolonging his life, that he must eat well, drink enough water, stare out the window. He lost all sense of his body, and felt safe only if lying flat. When turned in bed, he clenched a bony fist, all knuckles, no threat. When Dora arrived, her voice soothed him.

'I don't know if I could do this for you,' he told her.

'You've done everything for me,' she said.

Dora needed to leave – a small French publisher was flying her to long-scheduled book promotions. Once in Paris, she sat in a hotel room, unable to concentrate on the newspaper, nor savour a croissant. She looked emptily at the *International Herald Tribune*, blinded by flashbulb images of Hendrik in bed, his toenails pointing at the sunless ceiling.

After that lacklustre promotional campaign (no journalists came to interview her), Dora was flying home, when a Brazilian academic – a man she'd chatted with at the departure gate – collapsed in the aisle, miles above northern France. She became his advocate with the cabin crew, and was still playing that role weeks later at a Paris hospital. Doctors there diagnosed a woeful condition whose treatment threatened his fertility. Gustavo was youngish, so banked his sperm for a future family. The form had a box for 'Designated Recipients', and he wrote 'Dora Frenhofer', which offended her. They had no romance, just adhesive circumstances, with Gustavo exploding into terrified rages, she turning cold, he cowering, she indulgent, repeat. His family assumed that she loved their Gustavo. She never even liked the man. Rather, Dora became addicted to virtue, all while neglecting the condition of her father.

Gustavo went faster than anyone warned. When his parents flew from São Paulo to deal with his leftover belongings, they informed Dora that she had their blessing. For? To bear his child. She winced in surprise, having no such wish. Weeks later, she saw Hendrik for the last time. He slept with his lips apart, a black hole between. Only one eye closed, he took her fingers, refusing to let go.

Dora inherited enough money to buy her terraced house, back when London property was still just about affordable. The place was in need of an overhaul that she never got to. Years passed, and Dora (who stole a book from every man she slept with) accumulated many more. She wrote several of her own too. Nearing forty, she needed plot points, so contacted Gustavo's sperm bank to research how such a place works. They had no record of him. But this *was* the place. She contacted his best friend, who revealed that Gustavo had never deposited any sperm. He just needed Dora to nurse him, and lied in order that she stay. This prompted a triple reckoning: (1) a man whose intellect she didn't respect had duped her; (2) she wanted a child now; (3) Gustavo had believed the prospect of his offspring would stir devotion, which misappraised both the qualities of Dora and the qualities of his sperm.

At an LSE public lecture, she met Clive, a Black American political economist visiting London on a fellowship. When she fell pregnant, he offered to move countries to raise their child together. Dora insisted that he stick with his teaching job and family in the Bay Area. She preferred to do this alone.

When the nurse presented a swaddled baby, Dora looked at this gummed-up stranger, experiencing only emptiness, which terrified her. She was over-drugged from her C-section, and kept slumping to sleep, waking in alarm when she nearly dropped Rebecca. This first meeting always haunted her, as if she'd botched matters from the start. Mothers, she'd assumed, instinctively know how to breastfeed, how to cradle a child, how to check a temperature with the back of one's hand – indeed, Dora saw other women doing so with natural mastery. She lacked such facility, and it rattled her. Judging herself a failure, she comforted herself by denigrating motherhood, telling friends that you were vomited on, urinated on, woken in constancy, your essence sucked screamingly from veined nipples, overwhelmed by the relentlessness of an activity that wasn't considered 'activity' but a form of self. Yet she dearly wished herself better at it, and tried, secretly reading instructional manuals that never answered her questions.

For her first post-natal outing, Dora attended a London Book Fair luncheon, standing with a glass of wine among publishing sophisticates, feeling unclean. She sought to embody her previous self, and feigned that woman's brash confidence, claiming that she still found time to write despite the newborn. She dramatized the tale of her Brazilian man on the plane, how she'd cared for him till he'd died. Misery memoirs were in fashion, and a tipsy editor commissioned one — though she seemed to regret the offer once sober the following week, and spent their next conversation enumerating all that the idea lacked. Above all, an epiphany. 'But you'll come up with one!' she informed Dora, with the costless optimism that some editors have for writerly tasks.

Dora needed income, so typed fast, hating the result, waking to the hum of the electric typewriter, or lurching upright at the wail of Rebecca, recently nicknamed Beck. An epiphany? She reverse-engineered the tale of Gustavo to make that relationship a precursor to blissful motherhood. For a change, Dora accepted every editorial suggestion. Just yes yes great yes. She fabricated sections when instructed that the true story needed more [fill in the gap], then she cut the last third, as requested, and added a phoney conclusion, so that the misery memoir ended in the mandatory glow of redemption: daughter in her arms, Dora gazing down, discovering love.

She looks up, an old man jabbering. Then to the door, exhorting the son-in-law Scott to deliver her from this purgatory. Soon, if she plays this right, her two last people will drive away. Dora's mouth goes dry, an animal reflex, programmed to resist extinction, the deletion of everything that happened.

To compose herself, she studies his face. One of us won't see tomorrow while the other swallows breakfast, considers the weather.

More could happen to you. But should it? 'You haven't said what's wrong with you,' she remarks. 'Are you dying of something?'

He answers by rattling the oxygen canister. 'Sick for bloody months. Barely get out of bed now.'

'What is it?'

'A broken heart. Jill went. All's been downhill after that.'

'Jill was your wife?'

'Course. A stroke got her.' That sounded flippant but his gaze loses focus, as if this statement is well worn but still summons her cupboard, the metal hangers tinkling. He's suffering after-effects from a savage bout of Covid, he explains. 'You name a part of my body, it done a job. Sick to the stomach. My heart beating funny – just skips a beat sometimes, and I reckon: Here it is; I'm done for now. My hands shake sometimes. Look at them! Pulling on socks takes a half-hour. When I had the Covid, I'd tell Jill: "You sleep on the sofa. I'm not making you sick too." Exhausted, I was – and still doing my shift.'

'You were driving a taxi with Covid?'

'Hang on, hang on. One of them got *me* sick.'

'You think Covid could've caused your wife's stroke?'

His eyes go black. 'I didn't give it to her, if that's what you're driving at.' He turns with difficulty, arm tangled in the plastic tube running to his nose. He shuffles to the kitchenette, and turns on the electric kettle. Over the next minute, it rises to a rolling boil, and beeps. He makes no more tea, only sits again. 'That's vicious, what you said before. Jill could've got it anywhere. Me and her, we was together since year dot – since she was seventeen and I wasn't nineteen years old. What am I supposed to do now? Sit and watch telly?'

'And your kids?'

'Dave works in Wrexham, but he don't give a monkey's. Tina's the one. Thing is, I never had a proper end with my taxi. That's what bothers me. Years I sat in traffic, looking out the window, thinking: "Wait till my last day! You'll be waving me down in the rain, and I'll drive right past!" Didn't go that way. Still, Scott done me proud. He set me up that last shift, and gave me my cab back for it. Then some posh bloke gets in, abusing me the whole way, trying to roll his tobacco, getting it all over the back seat. Finally, I go, "Get out and walk, mate!" A bitter end, that was.' The old man grimaces, pops an antacid. 'I decided, that's enough. I started talking about going to Europe, and just get it over with, given the state of me. Scott's the one had the idea of a last bash, like we done. Best day of my life. Just having everyone around me.' He's quiet, eyes welling up. He looks down. 'Kids are everything. Aren't they.'

Dora would've died for Beck. So, no: she didn't regret mother-hood. But Dora had borne a daughter under a false assumption. She'd expected they would be closest friends, them against the world. Yet they were such different characters, whether it was what they wanted for dinner, or which fashions were laughable, or what humour wasn't laughable in the least. They so rarely aligned.

Beck's father visited once a year. Dora remained fond of Clive, and always planned activities for them all: picnics, board games, the theatre. 'Might feel strange to have your dad back,' she warned Beck, mentioning fathers who returned after the Second World War with thick beards, petrifying the children who knew only a smiling young man in the wall photo. But Clive was a cuddly presence, and the two instantly nestled into each other. Dora recalls her nine-year-old on Clive's lap, just moments after he'd arrived, Beck eating a vast duty-free Toblerone, he with his ear to her jaw. 'Even listening, I can taste the chocolate!' he marvelled.

'Really?' Beck asked, smiling up at him, besotted.

Dora needn't have been there. 'You shouldn't give her so many sweets, Clive.'

After he flew home, Dora tracked down a bar of Toblerone. She promised Beck a special treat after dinner, and invited the girl to sit on her lap, which Beck did with a reluctance that weighed on Dora's thighs. She presented the Toblerone, but Beck claimed not to feel like it. 'Since when do *you* turn down chocolate?' She listened to Beck eating, but only heard herself urging the girl to stop squirming, and what is the reason for that? Beck looked away, swallowing.

At twelve, her daughter visited California for the first time. Clive – when renewing his marriage vows – had confessed to his wife about the dalliance years before during his sabbatical at LSE, and that it had resulted in an English daughter. Clive was sick with guilt that his kids in Oakland didn't know their little sister. Once the shock subsided, his wife was accepting. They'd welcome Beck to visit that summer.

After seeing her off at Heathrow, Dora took the Tube home, and climbed the stairs to her attic office, the house quieter than in more than a decade. From her study window, she looked over the backs of other terraced homes. She listened for the sound of neighbours.

Beck enrolled in an Oakland school, and never again lived with Dora, except during vacations, where she complained about London, all that you couldn't find there. Today, they're hardly in touch. Dora would never reproach Beck for this. Had Dora been any better when her father aged?

'I've been to my share of funerals,' the old man is saying. 'So I didn't want to put anyone through that. Plus, why have people saying all them nice things, if you're not there to hear it? That was Scott's point. Tina, she was dabbing her eyes through all the speeches. Poor girl had to leave early. She's like, "Can't do it, Dad." I was about to pack it in myself. But Scott goes, "Look at the turnout, Frank! All for you, mate!"'

So admiring, the old man is, when referring to Scott. Yet it sounds as if the son-in-law has taken over Frank's black cab, and moved with Tina and the kids into Frank's house, taking over the master bedroom. Scott – via his wife – presumably inherits what's left. He isn't exactly an impartial actor when it comes to Frank's death.

The old man asks about Dora's farewells, and she breezes past this, noting how sparse her family is.

'That girl of yours in Los Angeles – what's she do? A movie star?' he jokes.

'Yes, that's right.'

'What, honest?'

'No, no. She just lives there.'

For a spell, Beck did try the entertainment industry as a stand-up comic. This seemed an awful idea to Dora, who recalled how pet-rified her daughter was to speak in public. Anyway, Beck never got far, and now earns money doing odd-jobs via an app. Fortunately, her partner, Karine, makes a decent salary at a production company. Dora follows both on Instagram, sharing in her daughter's domes-ticity through photos of their bull-terrier pup, Rodney, who has grown up via trips to farmers' markets, hikes in the hills, video clips of him fetching a squeaky rubber chicken off the couch. Once, Beck and Karine vacationed in Paris, two hours from Dora by train. She imagined travelling there to meet them. But she was not informed of the trip, so restricted herself to Instagram, admiring pastry close-ups and romantic views, saying aloud what she'd have said in person: how she stood in just that spot a half-century ago. Amazing that it's so long ago.

'How long do you need?' the old man asks.

'For what?'

'Writing a book. A few months?'

'A few years in my case.'

'Years?! You need to write faster!'

'I'm not sure my arthritis would allow it,' she says, slowly clenching her hands, and unclenching.

When twelve-year-old Beck left, and Dora had her work time restored in full, weeks passed without any pages appearing. She'd taken up a new activity, the internet, which she dialled each morning from a squealing modem, pixelated images and text materializing on her monitor. Already, after becoming a mother, Dora had retreated from the London literary world, and now withdrew from the parental world that she'd frequented at the gates of Beck's school, ashamed to explain that her child preferred the father. Anyway, what was there to discuss anymore? Music lessons and uniforms and school trips? A few oddball friends of Dora lingered: gay bachelors and estimable spinsters who scythed through life, some with courage and wit, some with courage and wine.

Dora presented herself as she'd always been: assertive. But she kept finding situations where, unexpectedly, she was the weakest party, the friend invited alone. She prided herself on stating the views in public that she'd utter in private, yet noticed people finding her rude. She fell out with acquaintances, even a few close friends.

Dora started waking with an ache that wasn't digestive, simply solitude, and which she treated each morning with scalding coffee and a newspaper, repressing it further with finger-bruising activity on her laptop, and kicking it along blackberry-brambled paths outside London, where she was visited by images of her mother, of Gustavo, of her father.

Death is ordinary, organizing every news bulletin, with bomb blasts and earthquakes ranked according to their tolls. Yet few understand the act of dying itself, which is wrongly considered an off-switch to life. What Dora thrice witnessed was another process, the rendering of a person to their essence – or perhaps the vulgarization of that essence, for one never knew if the late behaviour meant everything or nothing.

Dora took notes at the bedside of Gustavo, and snapped a photograph of him after he'd fallen into a coma, which felt evil as the shutter clacked – though she later consulted the picture when writing a scene. She saw herself confined to bed someday, strangers converging around, the paid and the unpaid, though she expected no volunteers, and wanted none. Her dying, she imagined, would be subject to whatever the public health system flung out. Except, Dora decided, she wasn't surrendering control. She must obtain a dose of drugs by the age of sixty, to retain her freedom to act when the time came. Sixty passed. Seventy too. She'd never been in the same room as such medications until now, three boxes of pharmaceuticals on the kitchenette table, for him or for her.

'Whereabouts do you live in London?' he asks, and knows her street. 'One of them narrow houses? And just you there, on your own?'

Over the years, Dora considered tenants, especially after her book advances evaporated, and the memoir royalties ceased. Really, she needed to sell her home. But that would have meant leaving the neighbourhood. Or perhaps the whole country. For where? She watched the world from the internet, captivated by deranged blogs and clickbait, asking herself who read such idiocy, all this rubbish, claiming that passenger airliners emitted chemicals to control our brains; that shape-shifting reptilians controlled the world elites; that victims of war atrocities were just actors. What shabby characters sat before laptops much like hers, writing this drivel? She clicked a flashing ad for 'equity release', finding a company that paid a lump sum – approximately half the value of your home – for which she signed away the entire property, to be sold upon her death.

Dora subsisted on this cash infusion, existing as a ghost, haunting the lower rings of literary London. She contributed a couple more pieces to the *TLS*, with few readers and negligible effect, except on the authors reviewed, who wondered who in hell 'Dora Frenhofer' was, and why she had a right to pronounce on their work. Every few years, she completed another novel, published by a smaller press to a smaller print run. Now and then, she had a relationship with an old man, obtaining a few months' stimulation, though the affairs came to seem alike. The problem with wisdom is that the more you gain, the less you have in common with anyone.

She met her remaining acquaintances at galleries and restaurants, and organized her week around each occasion. Most left her worse off. They expected her to talk of writing and her daughter. Dora felt as if she'd fallen into a hole, and they stood at the top, shining flashlights at her. Other friends were stolen by grandkids; a few relocated to damp hamlets hours away; or they fell under a boulder of illness, their age doubling overnight, or ending altogether.

She had troubled sleeps, waking at the unmagic hour of 3:49 a.m., disappointed at how she'd turned out, at how she'd behaved, at what she'd devoted her life to, writing, which once seemed an exalted pursuit but had become a trivial one. Dora didn't know what she was for.

Yet she remained intellectually alert, reading *The Guardian* and *The New York Times*, subscribing to and cancelling the *London Review of Books* every few months, and growing irate about the charlatans who duped enough of the electorate to worsen life for all. She couldn't get over Brexit. She watched the climate crisis worsen.

Dora took pains to keep up with technology, which didn't interest her but whose importance she had registered back in the 1980s, when she bought an Apple II Plus, reading the instruction manual cover-to-cover. Many of her contemporaries had assumed that – as was always true before – running with the crowd meant surrendering your independence. So they skipped the digital world. But this revolution proved so totalizing that it was the resisters who lost independence, imposters in their former world, needing the young to log on, to do everything for them.

Dora refused to need the young. She never travelled without

first ensuring that she could lift her luggage, and she discarded any items that might require a strapping young chap to pity her. She did, however, gain a younger friend, Morgan, a South African whom she'd once tutored in a creative-writing course, and who'd settled in Copenhagen with a Danish husband and two blond kids in Lego-coloured jumpers. Years after that writing course, Morgan discovered a second-hand paperback novel by Dora, and read it, and found the email address of her former tutor. 'Wonderful to hear from you after so long,' Dora replied.

They exchanged further emails, and Morgan happened to be visiting London for work, so they met up, finding an instant connection – the kind that exhilirates you in mid-conversation, having accommodated poor dialogue for so long, thus assuming your best exchanges are all behind you. Never did she and Morgan suffer that plummeting insight at a café: you have nothing in common, and the cakes haven't even arrived. After that meeting, they kept in touch, Dora always adding a PS that her younger friend needn't email back – she knew how busy life was with young children.

Dora persisted with her daily hikes, and worked on her writing week after week, finding companionship on Radio 4, its patter entertainingly irritating, such as a panel discussion on whether you have a duty to leave the world better than you found it. One guest said that artistic people improve the world by showing what it is to be alive, thus expanding human experience, and this was a vast contribution. But that only applied, Dora thought, if people actually know your work.

Still, she considered her life fortunate, conducted in a time of peace, while she had gone decades without grave illness. She also saw how egotistical her pursuits had been, writing how *she* saw people, all those pages now closed darkly on one another. She searched online for her name, finding Amazon links to used copies of her memoir, bibliographic citations in library catalogues, archived book reviews, plus the defunct webpage of an Australian literary festival she'd once attended.

Dora hadn't left the world better than she'd found it, and had little chance to do much about that. But after the rejection of her last manuscript, she volunteered at Oxfam, which deployed her to a local charity shop alongside two elderly women, all competing for shifts, the others chatting insufferably, then transforming into chirpy sales clerks when someone entered, much as Dora had done in her twenties, selling ties to gentlemen in Munich (much the same ties that now came in as 'vintage'). Yet her sales in Munich involved the customer noticing her, which no longer occurred. She contacted another charity, a cause that she valued, supporting girls' education in repressive countries. The charity had a position, they said, that'd be perfect: soliciting donations in the street. One memorable afternoon, Dora urged herself to beg passing strangers but couldn't, finally stuffing £40 into the plastic container, and returning it.

What she hankered for was an extreme act – to donate her eyes, say, if anyone wanted those much-used organs. She fantasized about meeting a needy person, that she'd get it right this time. Dora found an agency seeking volunteers to teach English to refugees, and surprised herself at the rush of hope, becoming impatient to meet her pupils – not to extract details for future characters this time, just to help them. She bought ESL books online, and followed a twelve-part course on YouTube. Then someone encountered a bat, China locked down, and next the world. All classes were cancelled.

During that first Covid lockdown, she emailed Morgan, proposing a catch-up by phone. Hearing nothing after a week, Dora worried, and sent a text message: **sorry I haven't been in touch sooner but who was to know after our last talk that the world was going to implode! How are things in Copenhagen? Stuck at home here. Not ideal to say the least! Hope you and your family are ok. Dora xo.**

An answer came the next day: **Dora! Crazy busy here. Having to teach my students on Zoom. Ugh. Will get back to you when I find a free moment . . .!**

Dora skimmed the message without needing every word. Those you lose touch with during an emergency are gone on the other side. This marked an ending: her last friendship.

As lockdowns dragged on, she managed well at home, albeit picturing an inferno beyond her front door. At first, little changed besides the availability of toilet paper. But everything seemed suddenly precarious, society a weaker barricade than anyone presumed. She tested how little food she could manage on, down to 800 calories a day, and enjoyed the physical emptiness; it clarified her thoughts. Grocery shopping gave her interactions with people, so she bought small portions daily – one large orange, for example, asking the masked cashier about his day, opening her wallet slowly.

'Next customer, please!'

Along her street, delivery drivers kept clattering up the sliding doors of their vans, raising images of giant strawberries and water-splashed salads. She took the name of one company, and placed an order – a sack of basmati rice, one red onion, anti-bacterial hand-wash – and she waited. The driver chatted on her doorstep until Dora noticed that one of his shoes pointed toward her gate: he was trying to escape her. Next time (always a different driver), she had hot coffee ready, which the man declined. She offered coffee to each deliveryman, as if a pot had just brewed, saying they looked in need of a pick-me-up. When the drivers spoke no English, they'd just point at the bags on her doorstep. She responded with a thumbs-up, dragged in her purchases, and told herself not to be silly – still, disappointing, as she'd tracked that delivery all morning on her computer.

Once, a driver arrived in a thunderous downpour, a surprisingly posh-sounding Englishman in his late fifties, his threadbare white dress shirt rain-plastered to his chest. He deposited three bags, and stepped back for social-distancing, placing himself under the deluge again. She summoned him back beneath the overhanging eaves, and noticed a dripping packet of roll-your-own tobacco in his cargo shorts. 'Have a cigarette break,' she urged him. 'Actually, better yet: come in for a coffee. I was just making some.'

He preferred to stay outside, so she propped open her front door, diagonal rain pelting the hallway, his cigarette crackling as he stood on her welcome mat, sipping black coffee and sweating, for it was humid, this rain overdue, they agreed, and so heavy that it made you wonder what was happening up there (Dora growing irritable from urgency to move beyond the weather to proper subjects). She clasped one knobbled hand with the other, as if to restrain it, to shush herself till he'd finished his sentence. He lived off a patchwork of jobs, he said, and had taken up deliveries for the charm of wandering through empty London, all its mice hiding in their holes.

'Mice like me?'

'Like you.'

Baritone voices always appealed to Dora. He made eye contact and held it, or appeared to behind the rising streamers of his cigarette. She imagined him as a lover. Worth risking death by Covid for that! She suppressed a smile. But she should've been ridiculous, and asked him to sleep with her. He would've declined. So what? And who knew what he'd have said. Anyway, she missed her chance. Her regret over this festered, and it metastasized, turning into something like regret for the future: that she was beyond experiencing anything more of note, merely edging down a narrowing passage. Dora closed the front door after the deliveryman went, but she remained in place, two minutes later opening it again: the privet hedge, raindrops plopping into recycling bins, his empty mug on the doorstep.

She culled overrated books from her collection first, dropping them with satisfaction into the blue recycling bin (cardboard, paper, novels). Next, outdated works of non-fiction. Then, decent books that, realistically, she'd never re-read. After more rounds of disposal, only a few hundred volumes remained, fallen editions on dust-silhouetted shelves, including the tattered Dutch novels that she'd inherited from her mother, along with editions her father had bought Dora more than sixty years before, back when you'd still see handsome young men and know they'd done something in the war, back when writing still seemed the defiance of bullies, and books came inscribed to you, with jokes and unexpressed love, a particular copy evoking a particular person, or a café where you read it, then closed it over your thumb, and sat inside its pages, incapable of resuming the present.

Dora hired a removals man, a bald young Syrian named Amir, who boxed all the remaining books, including every copy of her eleven novels, plus the two story collections, and the memoir. Her bookshelves were empty. The next owners could pull them down, and broaden the rooms.

To keep Amir from leaving so fast, she kept adding objects to take away, amused by this farce of jettisoning more and more in exchange for extra minutes with this reticent stranger. He agreed to a free lunch, which surprised her. In her kitchen, Amir acted like a schoolboy with his great-aunt, hurriedly forking in food, leg jiggling under the table. When Dora found that he'd grown up outside Paris, she switched to French, and he became more engaged, telling her that his father – his only close family member who'd not fled Syria – had recently been buried, but Amir was unable to return for the occasion; too dangerous. He wanted her to know that he wasn't just a man with a van, that he'd graduated, and once had a conditional acceptance to an American college, until his life was derailed by a visa denial from Trump's America.

That week, her phone beeped with an NHS message, reminding her that Covid vaccinations were available to her age bracket. When she failed to book an appointment, a social worker phoned to ask why. Dora explained that this disease seemed an acceptable way to go, provided it took you alone and at home. She cited her mistake of eating healthily and exercising – her body threatened to live for many more years, if she wasn't careful.

'Mrs Frenhofer? Let me find someone who can speak to you.'

On the psychological-assessment questionnaire, Dora was candid about thoughts of ending her life. This must've triggered an algorithm, for a counsellor was assigned, a gentle sixtyish man named Barry, who (she googled him) had been a lawyer but had since retrained, and now appeared every two weeks on her Zoom.

Barry could turn on his camera, and Barry could unmute himself, but Barry rarely achieved both feats at once. The opening minutes of each session, this endearing gnome frowned on her monitor while moving his lips in silence; or a black screen appeared to the audio of stammered apologies about technical difficulties. Barry could've slipped into one of her books. But she tried to see him as other people see people: they happen, and you happen, and there's nothing to take.

He began each session by asking Dora how she was managing.

'Managing what, the end of the world? It's lovely and peaceful here. Except for hearing all these terrible things going on everywhere.'

'We *will* be done with this disease. And not long from now!'

'But, Barry, don't you think it's forever? The virus is circulating like mad, evolving, variants upon variants. There'll be other pandemics too, you have to assume.'

'You're feeling a little down today?'

'Not at all. I have no complaint. I *am* sorry for the young, who inherit all this. But I have nothing to moan about. True: I'm here on my own, and that is challenging at times. But not unfair. I left so many people in my life. Friends and weddings and birthday parties and more that I didn't want to attend. But how else could I have been? I was this.'

'You *are* this. Whatever age, we all live in the present tense.'

'Gosh, I hope not.' One should leave the field to others, Dora believes. It's greedy to linger, demanding more. She never mistook life for a children's story, never wrote happy endings. What matters about a story is that it finishes.

'Take your thoughts to court,' Barry said – one of his CBT

mantras, whereby the patient must interrogate their negative ideas, cross-examining them as a lawyer might. 'Have you taken your thoughts to court, Dora?'

'I'm hoping my thoughts come back with a plea bargain, Barry.'

This was their sixth session – the last covered by the NHS. A phrase kept repeating in her head: 'Let's wrap this up.' At the conclusion, she thanked Barry for such kind efforts. 'If we were in person, I'd give you chocolates.'

'And I'd eat them.'

The old man across this table keeps nodding off, head forward, a long strand of hair hanging free, fluttering each time he exhales. This prompts Dora to tidy her own hair, but when she cups the crown of her head, expecting a bun, she finds it shorn, and runs her fingers down to the bone at the top of her neck. When young, she considered her hair among her most attractive features. This last Christmas, she cut it off. Her fingers were uncooperative, joints too swollen for the fabric scissors. The result made her laugh at the bathroom mirror, her hand across her eyes for a second, then looking again, pleased by her own smile. 'Ah well!' When they lifted Covid restrictions on hairdressers, a stylist behind a face visor trimmed Dora to acceptability, mouthing lyrics to a beat issuing from white earbuds. Afterward, Dora stood on the street, and touched her cold ears.

Once, *he* was attractive to someone, Dora thinks, of the dozing old man. We humans live too long. A chimpanzee is dead by forty. But people outlive their teeth and their competence. A few years ago, she and this man could've fit together, and theirs would've been a freighted conversation, he wondering: 'Would she? With me?' Not because Dora was irresistible but because heterosexual men, she believes, are harassed by such thoughts about unrelated females of child-bearing age. She pities men for this narrow view of the opposite sex – such small periscopes.

A memory distracts her: a literary hero, man of the Left, who'd denounced the Stalinists when they were still in fashion, and withstood condemnation for it. When she met him, he dressed in tweed-and-tie, an émigré recusing himself from the hippie era. They sat in flirting distance at a high-table dinner in Oxford, and she ended up in his cold room, where he stripped with such alacrity that Dora hadn't yet unzipped her knee-high leather boots. Rather than shielding himself, he stood impatiently naked, as if preparing to jump in a lake. Were Hungarians nudists? She'd not known that. Normally, Dora relished quickening the breath of an intelligent man, but he had gorged on butter-dipped crevettes. The more aroused, the more garlic. Their sex was normal enough, though Dora was struck to observe that the penis of such an impressive thinker bent to the right, in contrast to his politics. Afterward, he made coffee only for himself, and she was never able to read him again.

'The end of an era,' the old man is saying, awakening.

'What is?'

'I am.' He's telling of his siblings – he's the last of four. 'And you?'

Dora mentions her younger half-brother, adding that he went missing – almost certainly dead, perhaps an accident, or he took his own life. 'We never found out.'

'If he was alive, would you be doing this?'

Immediately, Dora knows the answer. It surprises her.

In the months after Theo went, no letters came home. Dora reassured everyone: he was exploring, breaking away from childhood and home, as he should. After a few years, she accepted that something had happened — the realization came suddenly: an anxiety dream, Theo locked in a room somewhere, tormented. Even today, she has an eerie sense that he is still alive, maybe in an ashram, praying to something that isn't there. In parallel, she knows he's gone.

During the pandemic, Dora marked his birthday — she opened a decent wine in her kitchen, reviewing all that she'd known of Theo: the little boy with white-blond hair, as clumsy as if on stilts, pushing other kids because he didn't know how to get attention, till they pushed back, and he retreated for the next decade, growing ever taller, and more hunched, and she never understood his eyes. To his birthday wine bottle, she spoke in a soft voice, perhaps not speaking aloud, I wonder where you would live now. In Dad's house? I was sure you'd come back after a few months, and Dad would nod at me, and your mother would wipe her eyes in relief, and you'd tell of adventures, and mention names of friends we'd not heard of. Instead, I find you here, looking across the table. You never say anything.

A ringtone — 'Baby Shark' — causes her to jerk upright. The old man locates his device, but can't figure out how to answer the phone, which is designed for the elderly, with huge number keys. Dora responds for him, putting it on speaker: it's Scott from the taxi.

'Nearly here, are you?' the old man says, deepening his voice. He's trying to impress the son-in-law. Dora has a realization: this man doesn't want to go ahead with this. But he's trapped. That farewell party — everyone came to say goodbye. He can't let them down.

'You *can* change your mind,' Dora blurts.

Scott, voice hissing on speakerphone, responds: 'Who's that? Who's there, Frank?'

'There's a lady that let me in.'

'What, from the company?'

Dora says: 'You do *not* have to go through with this. You don't.'

The old man to Scott: 'They're saying we got the wrong day, mate. She's saying it's not my turn. Actually wouldn't mind if—'

'Bollocks!' Scott replies. 'I'm there in like five minutes tops.'

'No worries, Scott. Thanks, mate.' He puts down the phone, not looking at her.

Dora unzips her duffel bag, takes out the sandwich. She walks to the front door, and opens it. She inhales fresh air.

But she isn't hungry after all, so puts the sandwich back. She looks down the road, and walks in that direction. The old man appears behind her at the front door, leaning against his oxygen canister. 'Where you off to?'

She doesn't turn back, just raises her hand goodbye.

Dora walks along the side of the road, which is dusty from roadworks that have consumed the pavement. Every few seconds, a car whooshes past.

When she was a writer, a publisher flew her to a literary festival in Australia, and she heard peers proclaim that their fictional characters felt more alive than living people. You must allow fellow professionals a lie now and then, if it's good for business. But characters halt at the end of chapters whereas people won't stop, even once their stories are done. Dora was never the kind of writer who described the sea, just people. They obsessed her because they disappointed her. Yet now, she can scarcely even recall her characters' names.

Dora planned never to attempt another manuscript after that editor rejected her. She had the awkward Soho lunch with her literary agent, and wondered if this was how a writing career ended. Yet she left the meal with a flicker of hope, enough to sit at her laptop again, attempting stories, which expanded and contracted over the lockdowns that followed. What linked those chapters was one character: a minor novelist in a minor crisis. This was a version of herself, but with an opportunity to behave differently somehow, to solve something. Yet Dora failed to make a case for this person, who remained a middling writer, important to nobody but herself. She deleted the novel, deleted the novelist.

Now, it's only Dora Frenhofer, watching dusty black leather shoes stride beneath her, overcome by a longing for experience, a path disappearing through a field, to march into a boastful wind, her toes clutching pebbles, the coldness of water up her feet, and foaming around her ankles.

She stops to wake her phone, scrolling to a name. If she lowers her forefinger a millimetre, and her skin touches glass, signals will rush to satellites, pulses will dart along cables to the other side of this world, buzzing an iPhone on a bedside in Los Angeles.

Whenever she and her daughter speak, Dora expresses too little. Those are blocked conversations, for Beck has adopted her mother's hardness, unaware that Dora is trying so desperately to renounce it. During lockdown, Dora added more old photos to the ledge behind her writing desk, most of her daughter. Beck always hated posing for pictures: it forced her to think how she looked, who she was from outside. Dora added a picture of Morgan too, during a walk on Hampstead Heath. Beside that was a faded Polaroid: Theo holding a glass of beer in Amsterdam; plus, the only photograph of her parents together, squinting in black-and-white.

Dora swept those photos off the ledge this morning, stacking them in the hamper under her desk, among obsolete computer peripherals. Someday, a removals man will sift through the contents, and empty all those faces at the dump.

She checks for missed calls: only three in recent months, all from Beck, who tried to reach Dora during the pandemic, leaving terse voicemails to enquire how her mother was managing. Dora never called back. She always told herself: your children mustn't look after you.

She is not distressed to do this alone. Hers has been a life richly felt, tasted, investigated. This final phase, she hasn't thrived; that is true.

She half-smiles, for a London black cab is speeding down the hill toward her. Dora sticks out her arm. The driver slows to a halt, lowering the passenger-side window. 'Sorry, I'm not from here,' Scott tells her. 'I only speak English.'

'I don't suppose,' she asks, 'that you could take me to Piccadilly Circus?'

'You what?'

Dora repeats herself.

'I'm not supposed to operate in this country,' he says. 'I'm on a private thing. But we can figure out a flat fee. I need an hour first. When you looking to go?'

'I was joking. Only joking.'

'Why'd you wave me over then?' He drives off, muttering, 'Bloody woman.'

Dora passes the outlets selling sofas and golf equipment. Her knee is sore, a dull ache that is not unpleasant. She touches her cold ears, pulls on them as if they were not her, the skin and cartilage of an old woman. A deep inhalation: her chest rises. She looks up at a tower of blue air, molecules to the top of the atmosphere. How much would those weigh? It's among the facts that other people know.

At the bus stop, she eats part of her sandwich, but has no desire for flavour. She plotted this situation, came all the way here, and must find if she's a character who can carry it out.

She returns to the town house, punches in the code on the lockbox, and enters those rooms again, now emptied of the old man she imagined for company. Dora flicks on every light, reads the letter that the organization left on the table, and checks the instructions against the three medications, all labelled with her name.

'I'm a bit scared,' she says. 'Oh, come on. Don't be silly.'

She fills the kettle, listens to its rising boil. A beep. Quiet.

But she doesn't want more hot drinks. She runs a glass of water. She opens the packets.

Dora Frenhofer is falling asleep, faster than expected. Soon, nobody anymore. Not even her.

Acknowledgements

Special thanks to Natasha Fairweather, my agent, such a valued supporter of my work; your encouragement prompted me to write this book. Also, my lasting gratitude to Jon Riley of riverrun – I'm immensely lucky to have had you championing my writing. Thanks also to my American editor, Ben George of Little, Brown, who provided excellent comments and conversation; I look forward to more of both. Everyone at Doubleday Canada is a delight, from Kristin Cochrane at the start, to Kiara Kent and Amy Black – working with you is always a pleasure. Three fellow writers were exceptionally generous with time and thoughts when I researched this book: Iben Albinus, Diederik van Hoogstraten, Leo Mirani. My warmest thanks.

Lastly, I'd like to express something that can't be heard by its subject, my father, Jack, who died while I was writing this book. When I was a sloppy lad who read only magazines, he put great novels before me, and illuminated them with his passion. Mercilessly (and brilliantly), he critiqued my schoolboy essays. Later, he became the most-touching enthusiast for my novels. Finally, he leaves me with the company of Orwell and so many other writers who, like Jack himself, remain faithful guides long after they themselves have no more words.

The Sempinski Affair

THE
Sempinski Affair

W. S. KUNICZAK

Rupert Hart-Davis · London

First published in Great Britain 1970 by
Rupert Hart-Davis Ltd, 3 Upper James Street,
Golden Square, London W1
Copyright © 1969 by W. S. Kuniczak
Printed in Great Britain by
Compton Printing Ltd, London and Aylesbury

SBN 246 63995 4

FOR ARDMORE, PENELOPE AND ULYSSES
WHO STAYED ON THE ISLAND

Contents

The Sempinski Affair

PART ONE

Assignment and Departure

one

THERE WERE only four envelopes on the mail tray that day. I looked without particular interest at the first three letters: a quarterly statement from my club, where we were having lunch, an alumni bulletin (I passed it to Tommy), and a bookstore bill. But the fourth letter, in a coarse blue-gray envelope plastered with unfamiliar stamps, brought an odd excitement. It looked alien and out of place beside the opulent gloss of bulletins and statements; it seemed to intrude. The unfamiliar green-ink scrawl was perplexing; thin angular letters like a straining insect caught in the thick web of the coarsegrained paper.

I didn't reach for it right away. I didn't feel like reading letters or even like leafing through the new *Archeologie Moderne* that Zungfest, my favorite waiter, laid beside my plate. There had been just enough truth in Tommy's gentle jibes to give this day an extra dimension. We had been talking about mutual schooldays, dreams and aspirations; he had been wondering aloud what had happened to them.

I must have had a hundred lunches with Tommy in the last two years and sooner or later the subject of what we had been and where we had been heading and where we finally found ourselves came up, but it hadn't bothered me until recently. Tommy was something hush-hush with the government and pretended to work for the IRS. He was also, I suppose, my closest friend in town, the only fellow graduate of our obscure denominational college I had run into anywhere. Everyone else I saw with any frequency, other than my elegant Francesca, was a business acquaintance.

Outside our corner window I saw snow and people. The people struggled through the snow, heads down, their eyes on the gray slush underfoot and not on the snowflakes coming down around them. In a few minutes I would be among them, on my way to the unpretentious set of cubicles I shared with a literary agent. There I was Dr. O. H. Shippe, forty-two, antiquities consultant, a man who was becoming a stranger to myself. Then: work that might eventually lead to a bestowal of a gallery's *imprimatur* on an illuminated scroll or piece of statuary or an icon. Once in a while there was the discovery of a rare treasure that took my breath away . . . until I thought of the Neanderthal in whose art-littered mansion the treasure would lie. Then, home: the morning trip reversed. Dinner was at eight. A book and sherry, Mahler or Vivaldi. On Sunday nights chess with Tommy Mackin. Once in a while a gathering of people on whom I could depend to entertain each other. I saw few women other than Francesca Grey who had become something of an institution. Each Wednesday for the past four years she had come up from Greenwich to have lunch in town with her preoccupied Albert and spent the afternoons with me. It was an almost marital arrangement. And every Friday night there was the journey to satisfy a secret vice, my one incurable addiction, practiced in a Lower Eastside store converted to a *salle d'armes* where an elderly former captain of Central European lancers panted *En Garde!*

It didn't seem believable that life would never contain more than this: order without shock, adventure or alarm—and, of course, the scrolls and icons, an occasional book review for the *Sunday Times* (whenever anyone published anything dealing with the Eastern Roman Empire, Byzantium or Trebizond), occasional lectures and another book or two of my own as the years went by. Money had never seemed a worthy stimulus and there had been

4

no need to run after it; my father had also been a practical historian. And if, at times, I wondered why turbulence, excitement and exuberance had passed me by, ignored me, and left me no more than illusions of motion and adventure, I put it down to the traditional Gauguin Syndrome of the businessman. Not everyone could have a South Sea Island and, perhaps, that was just as well.

There had been a time when life seemed painted in more violent colors, but that had been almost twenty years ago. And since I still couldn't bring myself to think of that time without a sense of loss it was probably better not to think about it.

Tommy was teasing Zungfest about the alcohol content of his Chicken Marengo. I picked up the drab, alien envelope and slit it carefully and took out the letter.

I read the stilted paragraphs with astonishment, then with delight, smoothing the cheap gray sheets of gritty paper as carefully as if they were a rare and precious manuscript painted with reeds on papyrus.

I couldn't visualize the author although I had seen him often enough in frontispiece photographs of my favorite translations: the Shelf of Old Friends, the perennial favorites. The portraits never seemed sufficient. Julian Sempinski always seemed to wear the mantle of his heroes: larger than life but infinitely human. It was impossible to imagine him in his eighties, removed by so many generations from the time of his productivity and greatness. Not much of his had been translated into English, but I had read everything I could get my hands on in German or French. Novels and letters, early poetry, articles from long-suppressed liberal newspapers and revolutionary pamphlets, lectures and rare speeches. The man was a giant. Until last autumn I had thought him dead. But he had apparently survived the wars, uprisings and social upheavals that had turned Central and Eastern Europe upside down. I had read in the *Times* that he had been appointed to an honorary chair of Slavonic history at his country's oldest university. And it seemed as if the long arm of coincidence could be stretched still further because, that same week, the *Times* paragraph still fresh in my mind, I had set in motion certain other events which had now brought the unexpected letter.

I had gone to lunch with a young woman editor from a magazine which I no longer remembered, but I remembered the girl uncomfortably well. Beautiful young women have always made me feel uncomfortable, aware of qualities I do not possess. A few years ago Francesca still teased me about that, dissecting my attitudes with that easy carelessness that had become so much a part of our relationship.

It didn't take much effort on my part to feel dull, unwitty and ridiculous in front of young women, well aware that my only worthwhile currency was intelligence which never seemed enough to offer in exchange for beauty. Beautiful young women made it easy for me to remain a bachelor.

I sat through that agonizing lunch, scattering green peas, dropping silverware, and wishing that I had been anywhere but where I was then. But she had been attentive and perceptive and very well informed, so that in time I could start making sense and the lunch was not quite as disastrous as it might have been.

Her name was Kristin Napoji. I had asked her what kind of name that was, having once done a monograph on name origins. Kristin was Scandinavian; one set of grandparents had been born in Sweden. Her other name was something Eastern European. It was her husband's name. I remembered the odd touch of disappointment when I heard that there had been a husband.

We had talked about Eastern Europe and the lost treasures of the great estates—the libraries and statuary and age-old tapestries vanished in the smoke of wars and revolutions. I had wondered how many priceless objects were now doorstoppers in some cattle barn. She said that she was going to take a long vacation—a sort of unpaid sabbatical—in Europe, something to do with gathering material for a book. She was particularly curious about Eastern Europe and its ancient nationalisms, so reviled in the United States except when they helped to strain a fabric which was both socialist and international, and in the pseudo-libertarian gropings behind the Iron Curtain. Recent resurgence of official Nazism in West Germany had set everybody's teeth on edge and Eastern Europe was the place to see. Did I know anyone there, some point of reference where she could begin?

I regretted that I couldn't help her. Then I remembered that paragraph in the *Times*. Why, yes, I said; she could see Sempinski. No, I didn't know him. But if there was one mind worth exploring in the East, it would be his. And she could even do me a small service . . . No, nothing terribly important . . . more sentimental than professional. If she could get Sempinski to autograph a book . . .

She had been less than enthusiastic, I remembered. She thought that, as a leftover from the *ancien régime,* Sempinski would be hardly likely to represent new thought. Germany's new Nazis would soon be trying to put Europe to the torch again, and only Eastern Europe seemed aware of it. She wanted contact with new men, not ancient leftovers.

(But look, I said. This is Sempinski. That kind of mind never deteriorates. Nobel Prize winner. Spokesman for three generations. Granted, he's probably at odds with the system over there; he's one of the most militant liberals of our time. But won't he give you an insight unclouded by Party politics and factional bickering? He's above all that. Seeing him would be like having lunch with Dostoevsky if you wanted to look at Soviet Russia in perspective. It would be like a weekend with Cervantes for a review of modern Spanish thought. Invaluable, I'd think.)

When she agreed, still not particularly enthusiastic but willing to humor me, I rushed her to a taxi and to my apartment and handed her my English edition of Sempinski's *Chaos* and scribbled a quick, apologetic note to the old novelist.

I didn't think that Mrs. Napoji would go to see Sempinski or, if she did, that the old writer would bother to autograph the book. But here was the gray letter with the spidery handwriting and it meant more than any autographs.

Sempinski apologized for not writing sooner. But there were

certain difficulties that, he hoped, his kind American correspondent would understand in time. A new kind of project. He had
been touched by the unexpected and encouraging gesture from
America; so few people cared, after all, so few remembered the
trusted old values. He only hoped that his new American friend
would not be disappointed in his next and, he was sure, final work;
a fitting epitaph.

He had been shocked, he wrote, by the accident to his charming
new American acquaintance, and wished to share my natural grief,
and hoped that such tragedies would cease once the aftermath of
the last world war was finally erased. He would autograph the
book and send it just as soon as he could get a license to export
printed matter to a Western country. He hoped that when I got
it I would want to read it again, often and with care. Sometimes,
the true meaning of a book was never apparent the first few times
around.

The angular, green scrawl seemed to leap out of the shoddy
paper. It puzzled me with odd undertones I didn't understand.
I realized that Tommy had been staring at me curiously for
some time.

"Nothing bad, I hope?"

"A voice out of the past, you might say."

It almost seemed as though there had been two letters in one
and I had understood only the surface message. My imagination
was obviously playing tricks on me. Sempinski's troubles with
English had not been a help.

I asked Tommy, who knew about a hundred thousand girls,
if he could tell me anything about Kristin Napoji. He treated me
to the sleepy stare I had long recognized as his camouflage for
attention.

"Sure. Very beautiful but too independent for me. I prefer my
girls slightly more frivolous. She was not in my orbit."

"Whose orbit was she in?"

"Her own. As I said, this was one independent girl. But, if
you pardon a touch of the classic, *de mortuis nil nisi bonum.*"

8

"Did something happen to her?"

"Something did. She took a little trip to a Worker State and drove into a minefield left over from the war. Now, that is very odd, don't you think? Don't people mark old minefields? But that's what happened."

"A minefield! Was she hurt?"

"That's kind of the line I was pursuing here, but, perhaps, it didn't sink in. She was hurt dead, like my Latin said."

I said: "A minefield! Dead! Why didn't I hear about it?"

"That's what I was wondering. The papers exercised discretion, by firm request from the State Department, but it made page one here and there in October."

"I was in Turkey in October . . ."

"It was a very sad thing. Was Kristin a friend?"

"I met her once. I thought she was . . . very nice."

"Coming from you, O.H., that's a passionate statement. Did you know Per Lindstrom is her uncle?"

"Senator Lindstrom?"

"Do you know any other Per Lindstrom? Personally, being very prejudiced about the far right, like I'm very prejudiced about the far left, I think that one Per Lindstrom, former senator of his arid and humorless state, seventh richest man in the land of the free, founder and Führer of the Loyal Legion of American Riflemen and twice candidate for President on the Lunatic Ticket, is enough."

"I didn't know Per Lindstrom had a family."

"Did you think, like about three million other people, that he stepped down, ready-made, from heaven? Kristin was all the family the senator had. He doesn't advertise his mortal origins. She didn't like his ideas or his friends, and he went berserk about hers, but blood is blood and dynasty is dynasty, and the senator really blew his cool when Kristin was killed. Called her death an assassination, not an accident. Wanted us to go to war about it. Vowed all kinds of revenge. Got everybody extremely up-tight in Washington. The State Department got the news media to keep more or less quiet but, even so, enough got shouted

9

by the Lindstrom people to make things sticky for a while. Didn't the Turks have it in their papers?"

"Where I was in Turkey there weren't any papers. There weren't even any people."

"You knew she had a husband? A very cool, European gentleman with very curious habits. A charming man but a most unbeautiful person. Some of my business associates, in a department that shall remain nameless, had a professional interest in his activities. He was killed in a hit-and-run in Saigon last spring. Kristin was a widow for only about as long as she had been a wife, but I think she had lost a few illusions about life, marriage, decency, the pursuit of happiness and similar trivia, by the time she became a widow. She was an impassioned sort of girl about causes but her husband, although very charming, wasn't a good cause. Hence, all the people who thought that Kristin was herself a good cause, weren't particularly down about the European gentleman's demise."

"What were her causes? Surely not her uncle's?"

"She was for all the causes that people like her uncle think are un-Godly and un-American. But it was never anything organized with her. If she carried signs it was because she believed what the signs proclaimed. As I said, this was a very independent girl, a beautiful person, and a lot of people are going to miss her."

I thought a moment before asking: "It *was* an accident, wasn't it?"

Tommy looked startled. Despite our easy friendship it wasn't often that I caught him off his guard.

"Why shouldn't it be an accident? Our embassy people said it was. Her car burned right down to the hubcaps, so it was hard to tell exactly what happened, but with Per Lindstrom on their necks you can believe the diplomats looked hard."

"What about her body? Couldn't they tell from that?"

"There was no body. The story was that she was blown to bits. It's possible, you know. Certainly, our embassy people accepted the story, and they were right on the spot to ask all the questions."

"But there was no body?"

10

Tommy said: with unconvincing patience: "There was the burned car, some pieces of clothing, a part of her passport and other odds and ends identified as hers. I can't explain away the absence of a body; I'm not the State Department."

"I have a good idea of what you are, for all your cover stories about internal revenue. That's why it interests me that you don't buy that accident story yourself."

"How do you know I don't?"

"You have that inscrutable look on your face again. I've put you in check often enough to know it."

Tommy smiled, shrugged, laughed and relaxed, dismissing the subject.

"I wasn't there. I didn't ask the questions. All I know is what I read in the papers, as someone once said."

The Carter clock in the corner shifted cogs and gears and struck its first quavering note. I looked up, astonished. I had been too engrossed in Tommy's story to pay attention to the time. In a moment, the last of the morning would be over. That meant that I would be late for a meeting with Hubertus Pohl, my most important and unpleasant client, and that meant that he'd feel free to make outrageous demands.

I swore softly, not being used to swearing with conviction. Tommy said: "What's up?"

"It's Pohl," I said. "I'm late for a meeting. Now I'm in for it."

Tommy said (shaking his head, his round black face concerned): "Poor old O.H. . . . I wonder how you make it in the business jungle."

I laughed uneasily because lately I had begun to wonder about it myself and didn't want to talk about it or even think of it. There really was no reason for this odd, recurring dissatisfaction with myself; life was extraordinarily comfortable, uninvolved and safe, and only lunatics aspired to trouble.

I said: "Well, beards and poetry are gone for both of us. It's a long way from romantic dreams."

Tommy said: "Whatever happened to that swordstick you carried on campus?"

I hadn't thought about that silly stick for years. It had been part of a life I no longer cared to remember: a life of flourishes and gestures and declamation, and all the possible varieties of angers and loves.

My old briefcase brought home this gradual erosion of the spirit very suddenly. It was old, threadbare, colorless with age, although it had been a bright pigskin yellow when my father gave it to me to start the college adventure, with a variety of straps and buckles that reflected sunlight, handsome white stitching and a big brass lock. Now it was shapeless as well as colorless and reflected nothing. I couldn't understand why I hadn't noticed how weary it looked.

two

WALKING INTO Pohl's establishment I had my usual flare of wry-faced admiration for his histrionic talents. The bronze doors studded with silver-headed bosses, the saluting guards, the marble lobby with its sole display—a simple, ebony box under glass, on a catafalque draped in purple velvet—combined a sense of the religious and the profitable; a moneychangers' temple. The private gendarmerie, the hollow boom of footsteps under the vaulted ceiling, the single treasure on the immense floor, added up to stage management at its best, designed to breach the defenses of the helpless rich at a single stroke.

I took the long circular staircase to the musicians' gallery, past concealed doors that muffled the clatter of teletypes from branch offices in London, Ankara, Lima, and Tokyo-Singapore. An electric eye dissolved a section of Pohl's outer works before me, the imitation masonry slid open, and I entered the brightly lighted, modern anteroom.

Miss Gruber, Pohl's private Cerberus, took my coat and hat and indicated the *Times* and *The Wall Street Journal*. Pohl never distracted his callers with magazines that might show them treasures he didn't have for sale. I wondered what he'd have for me this time; I could think of nothing reported recently by the archaeologists.

13

I leafed through the papers.

They were devoid of stridency that morning, as if the whole world had suddenly declared a moratorium on unpleasantness.

In Europe, the Chairman of the Soviet Union was getting ready to make a speech in a satellite capital where the heads of the assorted Peoples' Governments had been meeting for a month. This was a comparatively recent chairman who had made few speeches; no one quite knew what to expect from him. The *Times* refused to speculate about the coming speech, but *The Wall Street Journal* editorialized a forecast. It would be a conciliatory speech, placating the West, possibly dangling carrots before influential satellites, promising to relax controls, pointedly ignoring Red China, and extending the Khrushchev-like hand of coexistence (minus thumping shoe).

Moscow was mending fences all over the world for the inevitable showdown with Red China, made all the more imperative by the recent military clashes on the Ussuri River. But, all in all, the *Journal* didn't anticipate new problems . . . unless the Chinese chose this sensitive moment for their long-expected stroke. Sooner or later, they'd have to make their try for the hegemony of the Communist world. Pieces would fall, then; probably on the West.

With Eastern Europe in the news, I thought about Sempinski's letter which seemed to have been written with one eye on censors. I made a mental note to find out more about Kristin Napoji's minefield accident.

My vague ruminations about Sempinski's homeland, where the Chairman was to speak, were crudely shattered by the opening of Pohl's inner door, Miss Gruber's simpering smile and a flash of brown.

The man who stepped out of Pohl's office was astonishing: lean as a stalk of celery and immensely tall. My first thought was of the Raymond Massey version of John Brown, he of the moldering body and marching soul, but this was a John Brown who, except for white shirt and a black string tie, had been dipped in chocolate from the low crown of the stiff-brimmed plainsman's hat he carried to the sloping heels of stovepipe boots. His hair

14

was wiry, close-cropped like a scouring pad, and rapidly graying. His face was like bleached parchment with flat, colorless eyes that glanced at me with absolute indifference. In that white face, the pale, unseeing eyes were electrifying. I thought them reptilian. There was the barest flicker in the narrow pupils that made me think of telescopic rifle sights and then the man was gone.

Miss Gruber whinnied and I was stupefied.

"Who or what was that?"

Miss Gruber's maiden eyes focused unkindly on my nose.

"That was Mr. Brown. From Kansas. He's an interior decorator."

"Oh, for God's sake!"

The exclamation was involuntary but the surprise was great. If ever a man failed to match job and looks it was the man in brown. Even Miss Gruber seemed to get the point.

"He doesn't look like one, does he? I mean, I always think of slim young men with odd ways being decorators. But Mr. Brown looks, well, so very much like a *man!* He looks like a fighter!"

Miss Gruber's antique lust was totally unnerving. I said: "What kind of fighter?"

"Well, he's too tall and lean to be a wrestler and not scarred enough to be a boxer. That sort of rules out fighters, doesn't it. But there is something about him that makes me think of fighters."

"Does he come here often?"

"This," she said with a Sabine intonation, "has been the first time. My first thought, when I saw him, was cowboy, of course. I mean the clothes he wears, the way he holds himself. So very still, so lithe. But he's so terribly pale. He looks as if he hasn't seen the sun for a very long time."

The buzzer on Miss Gruber's desk cut short further revelations of her secret longings and speculation about Mr. Brown. I went in to see my most difficult client.

I was prepared for almost anything with Pohl but, to my surprise, he proved to be cordiality itself on that confusing and contradictory day.

He rustled like a giant landcrab in the shadows behind his desk; the bald dome of his head caught stray beams of light supplied by a timid and uncertain sun. His face had the blue-gray tinge of a man with a heart condition and uneasy conscience, and, that day, he wore the round green spectacles of the kind favored by lady missionaries fifty years ago. They turned his eyes into opaque pools, masking all expression: the first sign that he was up to something. His smile, meant to be disarming, couldn't have alarmed me more.

"Come in, dear Doctor," he said in his throaty whisper, and I knew at once that I was in for it. Having no academic titles, Pohl despised them.

I pulled up a chair.

He said: "How long have we been working together, Doctor? When did our happy association begin?"

"It will be five years in March. You asked me to look into the Knossos controversy."

"Ah, yes . . . the Knossos scrolls. Every other expert pronounced them the find of the century. I was about to make those damned Greeks rich, until you came along. You made those expert colleagues of yours look like bumbling schoolboys. How could they make such a mistake?"

"It's easy to be wrong when you're dealing with something that might not have existed. I wasn't sure myself that the scrolls were forged until we got our hands on them and made the tests. The Greeks' aging process was magnificent."

Pohl's dry hands, protruding from the deep shadows of his wing chair, made short scampering motions about the polished desktop and made him look more like a crab than ever.

"But they didn't fool you, Doctor. You knew what to look for. That Greek wanted two hundred thousand dollars for the scrolls. He settled for fifty, when you were done with him, and was glad to get it. I sold the scrolls to the Lowenhaupt Museum for . . . well, that doesn't matter. They were glad to have such perfect reproductions."

"It wasn't any reproduction. It was a complete fraud. You can't

16

make copies without originals to copy, and anything from that period could only have survived in a known collection."

"Hmm . . . a known collection?"

"And that's also out. The only possible collection for that particular material would have been the Romanowski Library. There are no Trebizond illuminations anywhere else. And the Library was completely destroyed during the war in Europe."

"You are, of course, quite sure of that, dear Doctor, are you not?"

"No one would admit setting that kind of fire. But we are all morally sure that the Romanowski Library was burned in 1944."

"The Lowenhaupt people were willing to take the Knossos scrolls for reproductions."

"I have no high opinion of the Lowenhaupt Museum. When we broke down the Greeks' aging process, we pinned the time of manufacture of the Knossos scrolls to about fifteen years ago. That's long after the war. So, if we accept the fact that the originals were lost in the war, the Knossos find was a complete hoax."

"And you are sure the Romanowski Library was lost?"

"As sure as anyone can be. There's been no legal hearing, no investigation; no one has testified that he watched the Library going up in smoke. But we know that the material was intact in 1942. The Germans didn't steal it during the occupation because the Counts Romanowski were distantly related to the King of Sweden. Count Bernadotte visited them in 1942 and mentions the collection in his diaries. Two years later the whole region was laid waste by the Russians. The Romanowski estate was a battlefield for more than a month. If any portion of the Library survived, it can only be fragments. Some peasant has probably lined his winter boots with them."

"Hmm . . . Boots, you say."

Pohl seemed to shrink and recede behind his desk, and I assumed that whatever he was up to wouldn't be as bad as I had thought. He simply wanted information. But I was wondering when he'd get to the point of the meeting.

He said: "Tell me more about this Romanowski Library. Oh, nothing specific; just whatever you happen to know about it. Have you ever seen it? If you saw anything that claimed to be part of that collection you'd know if it was genuine?"

"It's all been catalogued. I wrote my doctoral thesis on a part of it. But what with wars, and Nazi occupations, and now the Iron Curtain, no one in this country has actually seen it since 1938."

Pohl had now all but disappeared in his chair.

"So a piece could turn up somewhere," he said softly.

"That's ridiculous. Some of these works were more than two thousand years old. You know how fragile that makes them. How could they survive a twentieth-century battle, then years of exposure and neglect or outright abuse? They probably blew up in a cloud of dust when the first shell landed in the Romanowski manor."

Pohl nodded gravely and took off his glasses and fixed his little agate eyes on me in an odd mixture of curiosity and secret amusement. Then, just as quickly as they had appeared, his eyes vanished behind the impenetrable lenses.

Talking about the Romanowski Library was a waste of time and I had never known Pohl to waste anything. All this was leading somewhere. But where? It could even be a cat-and-mouse preamble to the cancellation of my contract.

Largely to dispel my rising uneasiness, I began to describe the origins of the Romanowski Library, as if by offering this gratuitous information I could deflect the blow.

The Library had been spirited away from Constantinople in 1204 to save it from rampaging Crusaders, who had found Saracen fierceness not much to their liking and massacred the Byzantines instead. Its next home was the Trebizondian Empire, until the Ottoman Turks put Trebizond to the torch in 1461. The surviving Comneni of Trebizond took the Library across the Black Sea to the mouth of the Dnieper, then westward across the Steppes to what is now a western part of Russia. Part of the Library was lost in the various Eastern European wars of the sixteenth and seventeenth centuries but most of it had survived through 1942.

Two spots of light reflecting on Pohl's glasses moved up and down as I talked, but whether they moved because he was nodding in agreement, or in boredom, or (for that matter) because he was asleep, I had no idea.

I felt like a man groping in the darkness of an unfamiliar cellar.

Pohl said: "Has anyone responsible ever tried to buy it?"

"Responsible?"

"One of the great museums. A wealthy collector."

"The British Museum raised a subscription of a million pounds sterling in 1936 for a part of the Library."

"And those counts wouldn't sell?"

"Of course not. Anyway, their government got wind of the offer and declared the Library a national treasure. No country which has anything like that would ever let it go."

"What did the Library consist of?"

"There were four hundred separate manuscripts. And that's something of a miracle in itself. Byzantine literature is negligible and it did no better under Constantine's successors than it did under him. But when he founded Constantinople in A.D. 332, he wanted to make it the center of world learning. So he began amassing whatever he could find in older civilizations. His library included the known records of the Academy of the Immortals . . . the commentaries of Herodotus . . . Sophocles, Plato . . . the intellectual loot of an age. There were pre-Byzantine works in plenty. Hellenic manuscripts, Mythratic, Nicean and early Christian writing. Constantine's successors increased the collection after his death in A.D. 337. And then there were, of course, the Pontic Tribunals."

Pohl sighed and moved out of shadow then, leaning forward. His dry hands were clasped under his chin as if without their support his head would roll down upon his chest.

He said: "Tell me about them, Doctor."

"What's there to tell? They were scraps of papyrus and crumbling wax tablets. They represented the penance of Constantine for all the years before he became a Christian. The collection was begun between A.D. 320 and 330 and continued through centuries afterward. It consisted of one hundred and twenty-seven pieces; not one of them had been lost in all the voyages of the Trebizondian princes or in all the wars. They were a sort of Holy Grail, I suppose; no one would lift a hand against them. Until, of course, the civilized twentieth century came along.

"What were they . . . exactly?"

"The complete record of the trial of Christ."

"Everything? It doesn't seem possible they'd have everything."

"Why not? Rome was a bureaucracy. Bureaucracies love papers. It was all there, from the original complaint by the Temple to the disappearance of the body from the tomb. There is the order for Christ's arrest, the deposition of the witnesses, the transcript of Christ's interrogation under torture—verbatim, with direct quotations—and Christ's *proces verbal* itself, with the famous questions and His answers; and Pilate's decision finding Christ innocent and his reversal of his own decision; and there are the proceedings of the viceregal inquiry into Christianity—as a subversive, antisocial and unpatriotic organization, aimed at the overthrow of the established system—and the report to Rome. The whole story behind the Barrabas episode is there. Would you like to know how much it cost to prosecute Christ? There are eleven scrolls with a minute fiscal accounting that even includes the payoff to Judas. There is the equivalent of a medical death certificate, the report of the officer commanding the execution escort and police reports on Judas' suicide and the theft of Christ's body. It's a complete, bureaucratic rendering of the Passion, all the more unnerving because it's dispassionate. It's Christ's police dossier. What more can I say?"

Pohl sighed again, and leaned back in his chair where the shadows hid him.

I said: "They even had a part of the sign that had been fixed over Christ's head on the cross."

Pohl said, with immense satisfaction: "Iesus Nasarensis Rex Juditorum."

"That's the one. Hangmen are given to peculiar humor."

"What a loss," Pohl said. "What a loss."

For a moment I thought I heard him chuckle. But that would have been impossible, even for him.

Still softly, gently, he said: "Think what it would mean if somehow, miraculously, the Pontic Tribunals were found, recovered and taken to safety. You had said something about peasant boots?"

I nodded, feeling tired. I heard Pohl saying, "Curious, curious," his hands darting about the papers on his desk. He moved aside some papers to reveal the corner of a flat, rectangular box made of heavy metal.

"If you saw such material," he said finally. "And if your first impression suggested authenticity, how long would it take you to be dead sure? I'm talking about one hundred and twenty-seven pieces of papyrus, wax tablets and leather scrolls."

"I don't know. You can't set up arbitrary schedules for that kind of thing. It could take a month or ten years. It would depend on what you had to work with. You know what's involved. But if you think the Pontic Tribunals still exist you're out of your mind."

He was offhand, quite careless as he said: "You're wrong, dear Doctor; they exist. I'm going to buy them."

"I have a client," he said. "A most distinguished and distinctive man. He was in London recently. There, if you'll exercise your imagination, opportunity came knocking at his hotel door. He was approached by a man who told him a story. The man claimed to represent the heirs of an estate in Eastern Europe who have a treasure of historical value that they want to sell to an American. They want this treasure to defect to the West, you might say. Unfortunately our distinguished client detests all foreigners, particularly Eastern Europeans. The story sounded to him like a confidence trick so he had his visitor thrown out.

"Luckily, the visitor left a sample of his treasure—an inscription

21

preserved under glass. The story could have ended right there because our client is a man of action, in the finest American tradition, not an intellectual bookworm, and he had never heard of this particular treasure. But we were again in luck. Because, next day, our client saw his visitor's picture in the morning papers; he had been run over by a car outside our client's hotel.

"I must explain that our distinguished client is not only rich, powerful and distinctive, but is known for his hate of Communism. The dead man, according to the papers, had been associated with anti-Communist emigrée groups in London; thus the story of defecting treasures acquired a possible validity. Our client has little sympathy for run-over Slavs, but he began to regret his suspicious nature. The dead man's story still sounded like flim-flam but our man is a realist. He knows enough about Red terror methods to recognize the gambit of the hit-and-run. He thought the dead man's story worth checking. If it was true, he thought, he'd have a chance to strike a blow at a Communist state, inflict a hurt on its national pride that could shake it apart. So he called me. I had Hamish Potter, my London manager, put his best men on checking the sample."

"And?"

"They said it was authentic. Have a look, O.H."

He brushed concealing papers off the metal case I had noticed earlier. I took it, opened it. Inside the casket were two panes of glass, their primitive quality unmistakable. Between them lay a brown, leaflike strip of papyrus, the fibers bared, the powdery texture undisturbed. One glance could date it within two centuries of the age it claimed.

The touch of antique glass and ancient fibers were irrelevant to the certainty that seemed to come, like a current, from the papyrus itself. I had seen reproductions of this simple sign. The immemorial jeer had been made almost illegible by the centuries.

Pohl spelled it out.

I couldn't make myself believe it, despite my certainty, and said so. Pohl laughed.

"But I know you think it's the real thing. Your face betrays you. It took Potter's people three months to be sure and even then they tried to hedge. Amateurs! You know instinctively. That is expertise!"

I muttered that it was only an impression. I would still have to test.

"Of course! It's as much your reputation as mine, after all. But only you could do the work in reasonable time. Time is our greatest enemy. Each day is a threat. Who knows who's finding· out about this? Too many know now. But I was the first to know, so I can move first. And I have you, the foremost authority on Trebizond illuminations, to authenticate my treasure. Well, what do you say? Is that a good assignment?"

It was a magnificent assignment and I said so, whether or not I believed that the Pontic Tribunals still existed. The restoration of any part of this priceless treasure would be its own reward. I felt immensely grateful to Hubertus Pohl. I had misjudged him; this was a good man.

He went on laughing for some time, moving around his office. I also laughed, but for a different reason. I knew that this was probably the most significant day of my life. Work on the Pontic Tribunals would make me the best-known Eastern antiquarian in the world.

"When can you start?" Pohl asked.

"When can I have the rest?"

"As soon as we can get you to Europe."

"You know how I feel about traveling but for this I'd go to China."

Pohl said: "Imagine, Doctor! You'll be the first scholar in the Free World to see the Pontic Tribunals in their original."

"In the Free World? I understood the collection was already in London."

"Did you? I don't see how you could have. I thought I made it clear that everything was still on the Continent. Still, that's not much farther, is it? Hardly as far as China, eh?"

Pohl's voice and manner clamored for attention but I knew that the sudden warning had come too late. I knew he had me;

he had done it again. I didn't want to ask the next question but there was no way to avoid it.

"Where are the Pontic Tribunals, then?"

"In Russia. Wasn't that made clear? Still, our fellow conspirators will get them out for you. You'll only have to go a few hundred miles beyond the Iron Curtain."

three

I DIDN'T KNOW which angered me more: Hubertus Pohl's masterly puppeteering or Miss Gruber's ironic eyes as she brought in the visa application forms (all filled-out and ready for signing), currency coupons, and the supplementary papers. They had forgotten nothing, including even a pocket dictionary and a book of useful conversational phrases.

Hark, I read, opening it at random. My postilion has been struck by lightning.

Pohl had given one of his best performances. The rapid shifts from unexpected kindness to flattering attention, then to quick generosity and disarming candor, made a refusal impossible. The prize itself, and my own enthusiasm, had been used against me. Indignation would have made me look even a bigger fool than I felt.

I had no wish to play art thief, cloak and dagger plotter, currency violator and smuggler of national treasures behind the Iron Curtain where justice tends to be a little abrupt.

On the other hand Pohl's plans, as he explained them, had been laid with care. He had made provision for just about every eventuality.

First I would get a week's briefing in London, which was another way of saying that I'd have seven days to get used to

25

the idea of doing something a lot more dangerous than anything I had ever done before. Then I would fly east, to Sempinski's country, which I had always wanted to visit anyway. There I would go about my "cultural researches"—the official reason for my trip to a land few American tourists ever enter. That much had been left, as if to flatter me, to my own ingenuity. In due time someone would contact me on behalf of the Romanowski heirs. In the meantime, money would have been deposited in ten British banks that had Swedish branches. How the deposits were to be made, in view of dwindling American gold reserves, was none of my business. The purchase price of the Pontic Tribunals would be staggering; as far as I was concerned that was a job for professional financiers.

My job would start once I was taken to wherever the Pontic Tribunals were hidden. I was glad this wouldn't be actual Soviet territory; like every other American, I suppose, I had been taught to dread Soviet security policemen—an unlikely but enduring image of superintelligence mixed with inhumanity. Satellite territory didn't seem as dreadful.

It didn't seem likely that I would be able to authenticate the materials on the spot. All I could hope to do at that stage, all that Pohl expected, would be to satisfy myself as best I could that the material could be genuine. It was a risk but, as Pohl explained, the risk was worth taking in view of the probability and, he was quick to add with an insufferable smile, in view of my expertise. Once I was satisfied that the supposed Tribunals looked sufficiently authentic to warrant the necessary laboratory tests, I would send a holiday postcard to Pohl's London manager. The text would be a prearranged message. Pohl's London office would advance one hundred thousand dollars to cover the conspirators' expenses. The payment would be made in Sweden. The smugglers could, then, go about the business of bribing and suborning and the Pontic Tribunals would begin yet another journey, this time across the Baltic. I'd meet them in Sweden where a full-scale investigation could be undertaken at the Royal Institute. Time would no longer be so much of a problem once we had the treasure in our hands in Sweden, although security was another matter. Pohl was arranging a suitable cover for me with the Institute. At any rate, in Stockholm I would be able to proceed with comparative leisure. Once I was sure of authenticity I would telegraph Pohl, the balance of the purchase price would be paid to the smugglers, and that would be that. Transporting the treasure to America would be gallery business.

It was a simple and efficient plan. If there was any slip up, I was free to act as I thought best. Pohl warned me to expect no help from U.S. consuls if I got in trouble; they would be hardly sympathetic toward anyone who muddied their waters.

"But," he said with candor that would have been disarming if I didn't know him, "what could go wrong? Everything has been perfectly arranged."

Seen in this light, the adventure didn't seem particularly dangerous. The acquisition of true antiquities had always included an element of smuggling, and this assignment had just enough foreign intrigue about it to make it exciting. The secret meetings, coded telegrams and the vicarious smuggling of a treasure would flavor the job. Hindsight would make it memorable indeed.

I suppose I was a fool about it all; I frequently am. But only that morning I had wondered why adventure had passed me by, and whether anything exciting, memorable, would ever happen to me, and here was an adventure with a deep personal as well as professional meaning. To have the Romanowski Library once more available for scholars, to be instrumental in saving that treasure, was a psychological bonus beyond calculable worth. I couldn't believe that I was part of a conspiracy to rescue the Library. Dangers and difficulties didn't seem to matter; I couldn't visualize the dangers, anyway.

Only my injured pride of being manipulated remained but Pohl seemed to have made provision even for that.

He had Miss Gruber bring in a decanter of a venerable brandy and drank a toast to the success of my mission. He even went so far as to give me a present—ostensibly to commemorate the nearing fifth anniversary of our association—but, in reality, to make amends for the dirty trick.

The present was a briefcase, a black, shining rectangle of expensive leather, with my name and address embossed in discreet gold under the handle. My old, battered bag was like a derelict beside it.

The next few days were difficult and rushed. I had work to finish for clients other than Hubertus Pohl. Most of them didn't believe that I was merely taking a winter vacation, but Pohl had bound me to secrecy and I had to lie. They knew Pohl as well as I knew him and they worried about what Pohl could have been putting over on them.

I did what seemed most pressing and put off the rest. I had several more meetings with Hubertus Pohl whose distinguished client and backer had so much pull in Washington that all my papers were back in a week. I wondered about the man's identity. There weren't many men who would put up such enormous sums as would be involved here just to do an injury to a Communist state. Pohl didn't say any more about him and I didn't ask; a client's customers were a client's business; if Pohl wished to keep his backer out of sight that was his privilege.

I sent a cable to Julian Sempinski asking if I might visit him. This was my contribution to Pohl's excellent arrangements: the official reason for my trip to Sempinski's country. I was pleased to have been able to come up with something. The old writer cabled back an immediate invitation. Almost before I knew it, the preliminary arrangements were complete. I flew to London before the end of the month.

four

THE LONDON streets were dreary; gray in early evening with the rain quite heavy. We drove through a broad boulevard where trees and grass median-strips would have blazed a brilliant flowered green in summer or spring but now, in my least favorite season, there were no flowers and no grass and the leaves were dead.

The trip had tired me. The flight had been uneventful but nervous excitement had taken its toll. I couldn't get the melodrama of foreign intrigue out of my mind.

There was a time when I had enjoyed travel; now I dreaded it. I never doubted that my aircraft would get to where it was supposed to without accident, but traveling upset my sense of routine. There was always some stupid emergency about lost luggage, taxis, and hotels. And foreign air carried unfamiliar rhythms. And, more prosaically, there were cheating guides, greedy porters, confusing streets, unkept appointments and, all too often, a language like the honking of wild geese. I tried to keep my foreign travel to a minimum but, frequently, I was unable to convince a client that I could do my work easily enough in New York.

In ten years I had been five times in Turkey, twice in Greece, once each in Lebanon and Iraq and twice in Yugoslavia. As a student, I had hitchhiked across France, northern Italy and Austria— the last a mildly sentimental journey to the university town where a certain beautiful but unkind young woman had been studying. I had never been in England, never wished to go there. I admitted ruefully to myself that in this grim age of prejudices I was prejudiced against the English without any reason. I was also ill at ease with Germans, but there I could find reason. Germans set my teeth on edge to such an extent that I could hardly bear to hear German spoken without irritation and, all too often, German was the only language in which I could make myself understood. As for the English, they had their own bland way of getting under my skin. I had hoped that Hamish Potter, Pohl's man in London, wouldn't be too professionally English.

Potter turned out to be a quiet, helpful man with kind eyes and a pale mustache. He met me at the airport, and drove me to London. We said little at first but I revived enough at mid-city to thank him for coming out to get me.

"Least I could do," he mumbled with genuine shyness. "Just thought the customs, and all that, might be a bit much for you under the circumstances. They're a decent enough bunch of chaps, normally, but they can bother you a bit if you have something on your mind."

It was unusual to see a grown man blushing. I said: "You mean the assignment?"

Potter laughed a little.

"It hasn't helped my insomnia. But I'd rather do my small bit than the job you have. You could transfer all of Mr. Pohl's secret millions to my account and I still wouldn't go where you're going. Incidentally, are you up to having some dinner tonight?"

I realized suddenly that I was hungry.

"I certainly am."

"Are you sure? As you Americans say, it must have been quite a day."

"The excitement seems to have given me an appetite. If you let me invite you to dinner I can break in my expense account."

"Done," Potter said.

We drove to the Culloden in Marble Arch, a modernistic pile of glass and concrete where Potter had reserved a small suite for me. He said apologetically that it wasn't the most exclusive hotel in London; I would find fewer coronets among the guests than I could find elsewhere. But, as a compensation, the toilets were faultless and bathroom pipes were guaranteed not to bellow at night.

Potter stayed with a scotch and water in the American Bar while I followed a clerk in perfect evening clothes and was, in turn, followed by a small procession of bellboys carrying my luggage, the suite waiter with a menu and winelist, the housekeeper, a maid, and some other functionaries of indefinite title. The clerk was affable, the bellboys were swift. The rooms were not only comfortable but handsome. The view was fine despite the rain and rapidly falling darkness: Hyde Park (brown but airy), Soap Box Corner (quiet in inclement weather), Park Row with beautiful houses converted into offices but still retaining the well-bred look of old-money-rich men's homes, and the Arch itself. I could look into Oxford Street, Bond Street was not far off. Within a minute's walk lay Grosvenor Square, the Embassy, and the American Express.

I talked with the clerk while bellboys, housekeeper, and maid formed their skirmish line and attacked the rooms. Suitcases here, coat there, towels and linen checked, fruitbowl emplaced, suits taken out for pressing, shoes for shining, all bags unpacked and contents stowed in drawers.

They were efficient, quick, and sure; they wasted no motion. The show was impressive. The suite waiter stepped up on cue with menu and winelist and I ordered dinner for Potter and myself.

"Would you like to be served in your drawing room, sir? Or would you care to come downstairs?"

"Downstairs, I think."

"No need to dress, of course, sir," the clerk said smoothly. "We have a number of American guests; a business suit is quite acceptable. Besides, hardly anyone bothers to dress for dinner any more."

I tipped the maid and bellboys, thanked the clerk and housekeeper, locked the door behind them and threw off my clothes. One of that mechanized brigade had drawn my bathwater. I bathed, shaved, and felt totally restored.

In a few minutes the suite valet brought my dark blue suit from the tailor's shop, neatly pressed. I watched him laying out the rest of what he thought the well-dressed American should wear for dinner in London. After he left, I smoked a cigarette beside the window, then began to dress.

Outside, daylight had ended.

The broad mouth of Oxford Street barely intruded with its scarlet neon, but Park Row shone mistily in the rain like a page out of a history book.

The muted sounds of traffic died in this dinner hour; I felt removed from time, taken back a hundred years into an era of quiet dignity, unfrenzied and predictable, as if the floodlit Arch, that gate into nowhere, were indeed a magic portal of some kind. Hyde Park was black behind it.

I went downstairs, feeling very good about everything.

The dinner wasn't very English: Cinzano and Chestnuts Joaquin, duck broth, red mullet with a good, chilled Montrachet, a ripe, soft Bel Paese with toasted salt biscuits and coffee (Turkish, demitasse).

The duck broth brought to mind another dinner eaten long ago in Italy, when I had still thought that I could interest a certain girl in myself, and entertained some hopes, and had been younger, thinner, wearing thicker hair, less armored, more exposed, and still not having signed my own personal cease-fire with the inevitable.

It had been a dinner redolent of the Adriatic, urgency and youth when nothing was unattainable and there was time for everything in the innumerable years ahead. London and the Adriatic dinner had nothing in common. But that time had also been the start of an adventure, hopeful expectation and a quick-beating heart. I wanted to feel the old, forgotten certainties.

I enjoyed the dinner, thinking with wry amusement about the other time made distant, foolish (but still worth remembering) by the perspective of years and fewer illusions.

Potter also enjoyed it, although he seemed surprised. Polite though they may sometimes be about it, the English seldom credit an American with taste.

When he was well into the mullet, he smiled. He said: "I think I'd better make a small apology. I thought the Culloden would suit you quite well. Now that I've met you I think you would have preferred something less chrome-plated. I think I'd better learn to differentiate between my Americans."

"Do you get that many?"

"A few. Hubertus Pohl likes it here. So do his clients."

"I would have thought Pohl would have more baroque tastes in hotels."

Potter grew pensive.

"Not entirely. Mister Pohl . . ."

But he didn't finish. He would not discuss Pohl with a stranger. Still, having brought Pohl into the conversation, we could start talking about the assignment.

Potter was sure that the glass-encased sample had been the true inscription. Fraud was out of the question in this case. He had applied all the standard tests except fiber analysis and chemical composition for which he would have had to strip the protecting glass, and that could have been disastrous without a vacuum chamber or controlled temperatures. The loss of even the most microscopic fragment would have been sacrilege. But Potter had additional proof; more personal and totally unscientific and thus, he said, incomparably more convincing than any ultrasonic analyzer.

He said: "About two years ago I met a man named Danilow. I met him through a friend, an old school chum who had gone into the Army. My friend is now something rather exotic at the War Office, does the sort of work you can't talk about, if you know what I mean."

"Intelligence?"

"Something along those lines. At any rate, this friend introduced me to Danilow. London is full of former generals but there was something about Danilow that raised him head and shoulders above the others. He was abrupt, but courteous, somewhat aloof in an old-fashioned way, energetic but extremely patient, satisfied with few words unless he knew you well. At first I put his silence to a poor grasp of English. I was wrong about that. The man was trained in languages from childhood. He also had an extraordinary grasp of power politics and a particularly fine, analytical mind. I suppose I should tell you that I'm very interested in political theory and everything connected with the practice. I've made a little study, very limited of course, of the behind-the-scenes influences in European power politics in the last twenty or thirty years. It's a sad indictment: assassinations, treason, bribery, and blackmail all pointing to . . . several connected sources. Have you ever heard of a man called The Magician?"

"No."

"I suppose you wouldn't. It's one of those strange names that seems to appear every time there is trouble behind the scenes, but hardly anyone knows anything about the man for certain. Danilow had been doing that kind of research for many years before the last war. We became friends, met often, talked often. Through him I met a whole gallery of people; excellent minds, absorbing ideas. They introduced me to another world: the uneasy, quicksand world of the emigrées with its intramural strife, plots and counterplots, political maneuverings, changing allegiances and intrigues. This world of emigrée activity is like a beehive with every bee working for itself, often at cross-purposes with every other bee, jealous of its prerogatives, its own special corner. Danilow kept above the factions. He alone seemed untouched by the squabbling but in contact with all. I used to wonder how he did it. Then gradually, and accidentally, I discovered that he and his special circle were the leaders of anti-Communist resistance in Eastern Europe. Danilow was the military leader. I had no idea that such resistance existed or that it was directed by a single source.

I imagine the Communist regimes knew it well enough. They must have had large prices on the leaders' heads."

The secret war, he said, was bitter. Men Potter met one week, would be gone the next. Their friends would say that they had *gone to the provinces.* If they never came back, their friends said that they had *emigrated* or *gone to Canada.*

"Four months ago, Danilow also *emigrated.* Via hit-and-run taxi outside this hotel. His death shocked me. I began to see secret threads. These led to others. I began to understand what had been happening so long under my eyes. I talked with my school chum, the one through whom I had met Danilow. Now that the man was dead, my chum could tell me a bit more about him. His part in the secret war became clear. His executioners were, of course, either Soviet or satellite secret service agents working through the Communist underground in London. And the name of The Magician appeared again. All this is background. I wanted you to know the man who brought us our sample. You might be working with or against men of that kind."

"Then Danilow was the man who tried to contact Pohl's *distinguished* client?"

"Yes. In this hotel."

"Why didn't he come to you?"

"I was abroad. I hadn't seen him for a month. He had *gone to the provinces,* the only such trip I ever knew him to make. He was too important to the resistance to take such risks. I remember thinking, then, that whatever reason he had for the trip had to be terribly important; something no one else could do. I had a card from him at about that time, saying he would be away but that, when he came back, he would need my professional advice. I was in Switzerland when he was killed. He came back from his trip with the inscription. He couldn't find me and he could not have been expected to trust my assistants. But he must have known that he had little time left. Something must have happened in *the provinces;* the Communist agents must have been breathing down his neck. He went straight to a visiting American who, by his record, could have been expected to listen to his story.

The American didn't listen. He had Danilow thrown out into the street. Danilow was killed as he crossed the street to the underground entrance—the subway, you call it. The taxi had been waiting outside the hotel door. So you see why I had no doubts about the inscription. It couldn't be a fraud if Danilow was involved."

I suggested, as gently as I could, that General Danilow himself could have been the victim of a forger.

"No, that's just my point. If he, himself, had to go behind the Iron Curtain to meet the people who claim to have the Romanowski Library, it must have been because he knew them and could trust them, and could identify them. His people wouldn't have let him take the risk if anybody else could have done the job."

But one question still remained conspicuously unanswered. Why should the military leader of a resistance movement get involved in the antiquities business? Because that's what it boiled down to in the end: a multimillion dollar deal between private parties.

"I don't know," Potter said. "Perhaps because the loss of the Pontic Tribunals by the Communist government would have a political effect in Danilow's country, something the resistance could exploit. Perhaps because Danilow was a patriot. Perhaps because he was a Christian. Perhaps there are more practical reasons. All these things are interrelated, anyway. I can only guess and guesses won't help you."

"But you think that we can expect to find the Pontic Tribunals intact? And perhaps the rest of the Romanowski Library?"

"I think so. I trust Danilow. Whatever is waiting for you over there, it won't be fraud."

We went on with our dinner, talking trivialities while the waiters served the golden Bel Paese and the toasted biscuits. After the waiters withdrew I speculated on whom the general had gone to see at such risk and what could have gone wrong. I would be following in his footsteps in a week. Potter couldn't help me.

"I don't know," he said. "I tried to find out after he was killed. But all his friends closed ranks and mouths extremely tight."

"I would have thought that as their dead leader's friend . . ."

"But that's just it! Somebody betrayed him. Somebody identified him for the other side. His people here know it; none of them have reason to trust an Englishman or an American, anyway. They blame us for betraying Eastern Europe to the Soviets after World War II. A man like Danilow has a broader vision but I can't blame the others for being suspicious. And that's one reason why we have to hurry."

"I don't follow."

"The people who killed Danilow must know he was after something very special. If they have managed to get a spy into the resistance, someone so trusted that he would know about Danilow, they're in good position to find out what he was after. Once they know what it is, it won't be long before they know who has it. They'll have a starting point for their search, and we will lose our only advantage. That's why the quicker you get there, the better."

The worry and uneaseness in his voice urged sudden caution. I knew he was going to ask me to do something unpleasant and unplanned, and that this would upset me as much as it was upsetting him.

I asked: "How quick is that?"

He said apologetically: "I thought you might consider starting out tomorrow."

I thought, at first, I had misunderstood him. It hadn't occurred to me that the basic plan, with its comforting solidity, businesslike efficiency of timetables and schedules, could be changed so easily. I had begun to depend on the precision of Pohl's plan as a shield against the thought of the possible dangers. The murder of Danilow hadn't really registered in my mind until now. My first impulse was to say *Impossible,* or *You can't be serious,* but I could see just how serious Potter was.

"Don't you think there are enough risks involved without last minute changes?" I said weakly. "Nothing but confusion can come out of changes."

The evening had suddenly lost most of its charm.

Potter said quietly: "I'm sorry. I know how you must feel;

I'd feel the same in your place, I imagine. But things are moving so much faster than we thought they would and each day's delay increases the dangers. Of course, it's up to you; I'm only making a suggestion."

"But the arrangements," I said. "The briefing . . ."

Potter looked at his watch and said: "I took the liberty of making a telephone call while you were upstairs. I asked a man I know to join us after dinner. His name is Karpovitch. He has a lot to say about your next port of call."

"He's been there?"

"He comes from there, as a matter of fact."

"You took a lot for granted," I said bitterly. "Does Pohl know about this?"

Potter nodded.

"He didn't tell me anything about this in New York. Don't you suppose I should have been told?"

Potter inclined his head with no great conviction. Obviously he wouldn't criticize his employer but I was in no mood to appreciate this show of loyalty.

I couldn't imagine why Pohl hadn't said a word about the possibility of a speed-up. Did he think that I'd back out as easily as that? And why wait until I got to London before springing this surprise on me? I could back out in London just as easily as I could in New York; a plane could take me home first thing in the morning.

What angered me most was the lack of trust implied in this deception, this duplicity. Pohl couldn't play straight if he wanted to. I wondered if I'd ever be able to understand his devious mind and learn to anticipate his treachery.

Potter was obviously not to blame for this dirty trick and there was no point in showing him my anger. But I promised myself the luxury of very bad language next time I saw Pohl.

And something else occurred to me suddenly—a thought I would never have entertained in New York where it would have seemed crudely melodramatic. Here, it neither surprised nor amused me.

38

"Once I get over there," I said, "always supposing that I'm still interested in going, I'm to wait until someone comes and makes contact with me. Is that still on?"

"Yes."

"What if someone does come . . . but to trap me? How will I know the contact isn't a plant? I wouldn't know a police spy if I stepped on one."

Potter sighed, nodded.

"Karpovitch can answer that question better than I could. But there is something else I must warn you about."

"Oh, wonderful," I said. "What is it? Another change of plans?"

"No. As a matter of fact it's nothing to do with our business at all. It's just something about the general atmosphere you'll be stepping into. All the satellite leaders are meeting over there and as you can imagine things will be a bit strained. Their disunity is far more serious than they've let us see."

"They seem pretty united on the basic matters."

"The only reason most of them came to the meeting is because it's a Warsaw Pact Affair; that's their defense alliance, like NATO is ours. They're very careful to keep it in good shape, especially these days. They might ignore a direct summons to Moscow but they would never dare miss a meeting of the Warsaw Pact. And so the Soviets can try to organize support against China, sure that every satellite will be represented. And China is, of course, not a member so there won't be any interference."

"Yes, I understand all that. But why should that make anybody nervous?"

"They don't know what the Soviets are going to propose and they won't know until the Chairman makes his speech. It could be important."

"More saber-rattling, d'you suppose?"

"Actually, it could be a proposal for some sort of *détente* with the West. It seems logical since the Russians and the Chinese have already started shooting at each other. If that's the case, the Chinese will do everything to stop it. And they may find some very odd new European allies."

"Who in Europe could be interested in prolonging the Cold War? That just doesn't make sense. Everybody is sick of this eternal tension."

Potter looked at me curiously, then made a troubled gesture. "Have you paid much attention to Germany lately?"

I confessed that I paid as little attention to Germany as I could.

"The Nazis are back again," he said thoughtfully. "They expect to win control of West Germany in the next elections but nobody on this side of the Iron Curtain seems to want to say anything about them. If the Cold War were to end tomorrow their dreams of rearranging Europe once again would dissipate a bit. I don't think they could thrive without an East-West split. I think they'd seize on any chance to foment bad relations."

I asked if Potter didn't think he was painting a disproportionally grim picture of what could only be a minor matter at the moment. Vietnam was still keeping the Americans and Soviets apart. After all, the Cold War had existed long before the Nazis reappeared.

"Fear of a resurgent Germany is the only thing that keeps Eastern Europe clinging to the Russians," Potter said. "Those people know that only the Soviets will be strong enough to help them when the Germans come. They know that the West wouldn't be interested in helping since the Germans are, after all, our anti-Communist allies. It's that sort of a silly circle now, and it's ironic that Britain and America are helping to maintain this fear."

"And you think the Soviets are going to propose a sort of Cold War cease-fire to deal with the Nazis?"

"To deal with the Chinese. But East-West agreement would be a blow for the neo-Nazis all the same."

"Well, I suppose it's possible," I said. "But not very likely."

"Sooner or later someone will have to propose a *détente*. And if the Soviets feel they need it now, for whatever reason, they could very well propose one. Still, that's not dealing with your problem, is it? I only mentioned all that to show you the atmosphere where you're going. With everybody so nervous, I'd advise you to be very careful."

40

"I've had some thoughts about that in the last hour or so. Frankly, I'm not sure at the moment that I want to go through with this business."

"Can't say that I blame you."

"I hope you understand how I mean that."

Thought didn't come easily, yet I knew that I would have to make up my mind quite soon about the assignment. I had never before considered myself as either a coward or any kind of hero and, to tell the truth, I still found it difficult to visualize myself in physical danger. And nothing I had heard made the importance of recovering the Pontic Tribunals lesser than it had been. But the conversation had introduced an element of menace and I knew that I would shortly find myself far out of my depth. The dangers which had seemed so unimaginable in New York were very real here. The talk of Communists and Nazis was depressing because in Europe, even in London which seemed so much like an elderly New York, they possessed a presence and a substance, not just the nightmare quality of an intangible, not-quite-believable threat.

I thought it likely that Potter oversimplified the European condition but I didn't know enough about it to prove him wrong and reassure myself. As a European, even though not a Continental European, and closer to the realities of Europe than I could ever be, he could offer persuasive arguments.

To change the subject I asked about the man who was to join us later; Potter smiled as if pleased to have his gloomy trend of thought interrupted.

"I'd much rather have you jump to your own conclusions about Karpovitch," he said.

"Why? What's the matter with him? Is he odd or something?"

"Well, let's just say he's unusual, even by London emigrée standards. You can't label him; he simply doesn't expose himself to any speculation. And yet, in many ways, he's the most improbable of them all."

"You could begin with a physical description. What makes him so odd?"

"Good God, it's lack of oddness more than anything. He has absolutely no distinguishing characteristics; nothing stands out. You could spend an hour with him and you wouldn't be able to describe him afterward. There is never anything you can remember. You just get a powerful impression of characteristics that may or may not have been there."

"He sounds like a ghost."

"That's exactly right! Everybody dresses him in the kind of flesh they think he should wear. I've heard a number of people describe him; you'd have thought they were talking about entirely different men."

"What is he? Another general?"

"No. He's a retired professor of moral philosophy. He also heads what is probably the best private espionage network in Europe. Danilow thought him the most professional spy he had ever worked with. I'm sure you wouldn't think so to look at the man."

I laughed because the idea seemed preposterous.

"A Master Spy? I thought they only had those in English mystery novels."

Potter smiled gently. He signaled to the waiter.

"There are several organizations of that sort; about two dozen in Germany alone. Groups like the German Lawyers' Union, for example; they cover East Germany like a blanket. Or the Hungarian Academic League. Or the Association of Baltic University Professors . . . Each has its information network, but they're mostly regional. They seldom cover more than one country. Karpovitch's agents are spread all over Europe, on both sides of the Iron Curtain."

"Who do all these people work for?"

"Mostly for the West. But they're not an official part of the allied spy systems. And sometimes, as with Karpovitch's people, their work is for sale."

I must have looked surprised because Potter paused for a moment, then went on:

"Don't see why it should astonish you, old man. It's very

Western, very democratic . . . a typical bit of capitalist free enterprise, wouldn't you say? The chap sells a commodity to whoever wants it. Except, of course, that he's never been known to sell anything to the Communists."

"Well, that's a comfort."

"It's also sound business."

"Your friend Karpovitch sounds like a useful man."

"The best thing about him is that no matter where his people work all the accumulated information passes through his hands. And so sooner or later he knows absolutely everything."

I started laughing, then. I didn't know if this was in relief that, at last, I would be getting professional advice, or because of the collapse of the day's tensions, or the warmth and comfort of good wine and an excellent dinner. I had a sudden picture of a Master Spy: False beard and opera cloak, the smoked green glasses of Hubertus Pohl, and a fistful of tickets for the Orient Express.

I felt ease returning. The room behind me became noisier as more late-dining people came in from the theaters. I found that I was enjoying myself and said so.

"I'm very glad," Potter said. "I'm only sorry I can't tell you more about Karpovitch."

"What more could there be?"

"Something about the man himself. That's the important part. What I've told you is largely guesswork, speculation, hints dropped by friends, an odd word or two picked up here and there. The man himself remains an unknown quantity."

I watched the friendliness, warmth, and humor leave the Englishman's face, the shoulders stiffen, and the kind eyes become disdainful and cold. He stared with a particular intensity across my shoulder towards the dining-room doors. I turned to see what had distrubed him so. The surprise was perfect. Coming in, bowed-in by the maître d'hôtel and trailed by waiters, was a mountainous, bronzed, beetle-browed man in his seventies, his heavy face corroded by deep lines, stamped with stubbornness and pride. His wild shock of pure-white hair swept back to his shoulders like the poetic mane of an ancient lion. He walked as if each footstep was a declaration of personal possession.

Potter said harshly: "There's your Senator Lindstrom." But I didn't need the identification. I had seen that raging, imperious face on too many covers of newsmagazines, in too many newspapers, on too many television screens on national holidays. And it was not the sight of the reactionary fanatic that brought my sudden sense of shock and unreality. Walking beside him was the man in brown I had last seen in Pohl's anteroom.

I didn't think they saw me. It would have made no difference if Per Lindstrom saw me; he wouldn't have known me from Adam. But Brown would have known me. And suddenly the last thing I wanted was to let this strange man, with his aura of menace and his prison pallor, know that I had seen him, and recognized him and would know him again.

Confusion came next. Surprise and shock gave way to disbelief or rather a refusal to believe. Brown's presence here linked Lindstrom with Pohl and with the Romanowski Library. I couldn't understand why I hadn't guessed that Lindstrom, who possessed all the necessary money, hatred, and ruthlessness, was Pohl's "distinguished client." It was obvious now.

I turned to Potter to ask him about it and make sure, but I changed my mind. The Englishman looked upset. He was no longer looking at the newcomers but stared bitterly at his brandy glass, searching his pockets for a cigarette. I offered him mine.

The Englishman shook his head as if to clear it of unexpected cobwebs. His smile was a brave attempt to restore the earlier warm and sympathetic mood.

"Sorry if I got a bit boorish just then. The sight of your Senator Lindstrom tends to do that to me."

"He has that effect on a lot of people. Is that the man to whom Danilow took the inscription the night he was killed?"

"Yes. Foolish of him, wasn't it? The good ex-senator had him thrown out on his ear."

"Is that why you dislike him so much?"

"Dislike is a rather mild way to describe it."

I tried to think quickly. There was no point in pushing the subject and showing Potter, and Pohl Galleries through Potter, that I had guessed Lindstrom's role in the conspiracy.

I needed a little time to come to terms with this new development and I wanted to give Potter a chance to compose himself. My hand shook a little and some wine spilled on my lap. I excused myself and left the dining room.

five

THE IDEA of working for Per Lindstrom didn't make me happy. Politics didn't interest me; they seldom had any direct bearing on either my private or professional life; but vulgarity, crudeness, stupidity, and violence were another matter, and these seemed a hallmark of Lindstrom's followers. I had no wish to play even a walk-on role in Lindstrom's private wars against anything or to become a Loyal Rifleman even by a trick of circumstances.

But did there have to be any connection, despite the circumstances? My aim was to restore and preserve the Romanowski Library . . . if, indeed, it really still existed. Per Lindstrom and his politics were no part of that. I supposed that this had always been the way to rationalize an unpalatable alliance but it seemed as good as any other—always provided, of course, that I did make up my mind about the assignment.

This is what really worried me, the heart of the matter. Should I or should I not fly east tomorrow as Potter suggested? I had no doubt that I was getting into something dangerous; some complex scheme that lay outside the conspiracy to acquire the Pontic Tribunals. The presence of Lindstrom guaranteed complexities, the appearance and reappearance of the man in brown fueled my suspicions. I couldn't believe that anything was a coincidence since the moment I had found Sempinski's letter on my mail tray. Everything that had occurred since then, or that I had heard about, seemed to form some kind of a pattern. I had no ready answers, only questions. One thing I did know: if my intuition was correct, there was no place in whatever was happening for an antiquities consultant whose most ferocious skirmishes to date had been morning battles with his housekeeper about scarves and overshoes.

I needed answers, but who could advise me? Potter was obviously more in touch with a variety of European madnesses but I had only met him a few hours earlier and I was no longer ready to trust anyone completely. Besides, he was a client representative and I had learned long ago not to involve clients in personal problems. And could I trust his friend, Karpovitch, a man I had never met? Too many strangers were becoming involved in the conspiracy; I had the uneasy feeling that everyone I met knew more about it than I did.

Tommy would know what to do. He was in government service, something quite as devious as what was happening here. I could trust his advice. Perhaps he even knew someone in London with whom I could talk.

I went to the telephone. It was ten o'clock in London, four in the afternoon in New York. Tommy would be getting home in another two hours. I placed a call to New York for that time. I was very much relieved. But I found that I was still on edge and nervous when I went back to the dining room, the wine stains forgotten and apprehension mounting.

Potter was no longer alone, another man was with him. They didn't see me enter the dining room; I had time to study the new man on my way to the table. He sat with his back to the door but with his head strangely tilted and face in quarter profile, showing an undefined assembly of darkly blurred features.

It was the sort of face you'd see anywhere, the man who wore it might be anything. There was no impression of either homeliness or beauty, cruelty or kindness, or weakness or strength. It was a face made remarkable by lack of definition, a crisscross mass of fluid wrinkles that would not hold still.

The man heard me and looked around and watched me with a

blend of caution and politeness—neither a welcoming smile nor a rebuff. He was a large man, heavy, and stooped by age. His eyes were hooded. I imagined an air of suppressed violence about him. He had the delicate, long hands of a concert pianist that seemed out of place in a violent man. His eyes were watchful but the gaze had a quality that bothered me; it seemed to slant right through me.

Karpovitch went straight to the point once I had sat down.

"I've known about the Romanowski Library for some time, but don't let that either worry you or surprise you. It is the nature of a secret to become known, particularly if those who hold the secret wish to make contact with another party. In the case of something as important as the Romanowski Library, it was inevitable that the word should spread."

"Exactly how far has it spread?"

"Your secret is reasonably safe. Specialists may collect and trade information but they never gossip. It isn't economical for them to do so."

He spoke without a trace of any kind of accent, so softly as to be almost inaudible, but with a note of such cold patronage that I found myself disliking him intensely.

"And you, I understand, are the foremost specialist," I said, matching his coldness. He laughed with genuine amusement.

"I don't know what Mister Potter told you about me but some of my friends, my former academic colleagues, have made a habit of collecting bits of information. By themselves, these fragments are meaningless. Pieced with other fragments they become interesting. When you have enough of these interesting pieces they may even make up a fascinating whole. Call it a sort of hobby with us, intellectual gymnastics. We are no longer in a position to exercise our brains; our academic careers are very much over. So, we play guessing games. We make up jigsaw puzzles."

"And one day you just happened to guess that there was a plot to smuggle the Romanowski Library to the United States? That's hard to believe."

Karpovitch looked at me with irritating patience, his eyebrows moved enough to indicate a mental shrug.

48

"Well . . . Perhaps there was a little more than that."

"I imagine there was. I'd like to know just how you became so very well informed about the Romanowski Library. It might suggest who else would know about it."

This time, Karpovitch's face indicated a mild speculation.

"These things are never very clear," he said finally. "There is no way to pin down the beginning of knowledge. But references to the Romanowski Library have come up several times in the past year or so. The most important reference came a year ago. There was an economic sabotage trial . . . a man named Novotny . . . a small government official who had lined his pockets at public expense. He made a special plea for leniency and offered to expose a far greater conspiracy than his. He mentioned the Library."

"And now it's a matter of official record?"

"Not necessarily. Records are bulky, particularly in totalitarian states. Papers become lost. Sometimes they are mysteriously removed. Official memories are short without papers. Whatever Novotny might have said is now quite forgotten."

"Can't he say it again?"

"I hardly think so. He died in prison. Or, to be precise, in transit between prisons. This, I might add, interested us even more than what he had to say; it showed that someone else was interested in Mister Novotny."

My mind registered in passing the appearance of another corpse. I thought again about Sempinski's disquietening letter, the hidden message it seemed to contain. Danger was evident but its source no clearer than before. I sensed Karpovitch's continuing speculation and decided to press for an answer.

"Do the authorities in your country suspect anything? I don't mind saying that your answer will decide whether I fly there tomorrow or not."

Karpovitch spread his fingers on the tablecloth and studied them for a long, silent moment. When he spoke again, his voice was ridiculously bland.

"You're cautious. Caution is admirable. But aren't you rather close to excess of caution? You demand an answer. I am not obliged to give you any answer. It is of no concern to me where you fly tomorrow."

If he had called me a coward and a weakling he couldn't have been clearer. The insult was so calculated that even Potter made a gesture of tentative protest. Karpovitch's mild tone and suddenly understanding smile merely compounded the offense. But I had been trained by Hubertus Pohl to withstand calculated insults. Karpovitch's reason for insulting me wasn't clear unless he wished to push me into a decision about the assignment and that seemed unlikely; what would he gain one way or the other? But I had no doubt that he had a reason; he simply wasn't the kind of man who did anything without one.

I repeated the question.

Karpovitch bowed, then; a strange, outmoded gesture: half courteous, half derisive. His voice became again the dry lecturing tone of a teacher dealing with an obtuse student.

"By the *authorities,* I imagine you mean the Secret Police. They're called the NKD where you are going, or the *Nakomda.* They are unaware of your business at the moment, but this may change quickly. You must remember that it is their nature to suspect. They are superbly trained, efficient, and their leaders are intelligent. If you share the popular American belief that all secret policemen, other than your own, are mindless thugs, you might as well return to New York tomorrow."

"I'm willing to respect the Nakomda," I said carefully. Karpovitch's quick frown was no compensation for my rising anger. The interruption had annoyed him but he decided to ignore both the interruption and its source.

"We came across your secret at the Novotny trial only because we were looking for something else that might come out of the trial. The Nakomda had no reason to give it more than routine interest. Pleas such as Novotny's are common; the Nakomda ignored it. Then, later, there were other mentions. Nothing specific, of course. Such things are never definite or specific. But a hint here . . . a suggestion there . . . an inquiry somewhere else . . . In time these formed a pattern, do you follow me?"

50

This time I only nodded.

"We became interested because everything that keeps recurring with no apparent reason interests us. We watched and listened and began to put together another jigsaw puzzle, and as it grew we became *very* interested. We found some interesting ramifications. I am not going to tell you about them; they can neither threaten you nor help you if you confine your activities only to your business. I suggest you do precisely that. Furthermore, the less you know of what doesn't concern you, the less you can tell if anyone should ever question you. Do you still follow me?"

"You mean the Nakomda?"

"Not only the Nakomda." And then, with heavy sarcasm: "But, I suggest, your part in this affair is quite challenging enough. The various ramifications would only confuse you."

"I'd like to be the judge of that."

"That's out of the question. I see no need to burden you with specialized knowledge. Our interests coincide to a certain point and to that point I'm willing to help you. Beyond that we have nothing to say to each other."

I had his measure now and, again, nodded briefly. The pained embarrassment on Potter's face made me sorry for him.

"The sum total of this puzzle of yours became so interesting," Karpovitch continued, "that we decided to take an active hand. There are still many pieces missing but we know enough. The question now is this: Are you going on with your assignment, or are you returning to New York? If I may paraphrase your earlier point: whether I tell you anything more depends on your answer."

I was not reassured by Karpovitch's sudden smile, a dispassionate grimace lost among fluid lines. Nothing I had heard had been reassuring. But the man's professorial tone, his sarcasms and his contemptuous air made further hesitation impossible for me.

I said I would not be returning to New York.

Later, I would think of that night as something that only might have happened, that was never real; and that if any of it had the solidity and substance of factual experience it could have been no firmer than a dream.

There was Karpovitch's dry, disembodied voice without a clearly defined face behind it, and so it had a shadowed quality like something merely imagined. The words themselves were unreal and measured like the monotonous beat of a giant clock.

Do this and don't do that (Karpovitch was saying) and go here and there, and (under certain circumstances) do the following and (under other circumstances) this is what you must do. Later, when it was so important for me to remember exactly what I had been told, with all the accents and inflections and possible shades of meaning, I couldn't pin down one word that carried more weight or color than any other word. Each had the same uninflected grayness that blurred whatever individual meaning it might have had and made them all, remembered only in their combination, as featureless as the particles of atoms in a smooth steel rail.

I was to fly aboard a Soviet turbojet next afternoon. There was a reason for this, other than the fact that it was the first nonstop flight available from Croydon . . . a subtle shade of difference that would help to establish my neutrality . . . an imperceptible advantage. It would make it far less difficult for NKD agents to keep an eye on me, or make contact if they wanted to, than it would have been aboard a British transport. Thus it suggested innocence and that was important. Police *dossiers* were compounded from innumerable small fragments, impressions and particles of impressions, and this would be one. If it made no impression whatsoever that would still constitute an advantage. And it would introduce me, no matter how slightly, to that indescribable feeling that comes from the knowledge of constant surveillance, the inner hollowness that must be so rigidly controlled (the wondering about *who* and *where,* with eyes that can never be allowed to search, with the gestures that can never suggest tension nor be too studiously at ease); something as alien to a Western mind as deserts are to oceans; a rule of life that never becomes natural unless a man is born to it, and not always then. It would be a quarter-day acclimatization—as gentle a transition as I could expect under the

52

new ground rules. And there were certain other rules to follow, a whole vocabulary of innocent expressions to be learned, so that additional small fragments could find their way into my dossier.

"Does everyone have a police dossier? Is everyone watched?"

"Assume so. In your case, be certain of it."

"Are they always watched?"

"You can be sure you will be."

"Can anyone be trusted?"

"Never. Suspect everyone."

"Don't people ever relax? Can't they ever drop their guard?"

"They must be always careful but never show that they are being careful. Assume that even your most private moments are being observed and never let it show."

"Does anyone ever make an honest statement that means what it says?"

"You can't afford to think so. But never show that you are taking it as anything else. You may hear pro-Western comments, you may even hear criticism of the local system. Assume that it is all police-inspired no matter how drawn you may feel toward the critic."

"How do I handle that?"

"How would you naturally be inclined to handle it?"

"I wouldn't say much of anything. Can't very well disagree with a pro-Western viewpoint, and couldn't very well criticize my hosts."

"Admirable and exactly right. Take refuge in polite embarrassment. Never agree or disagree or encourage controversial comment or invite a confidence. But never fail to defend your own system if it should be attacked."

"Sometimes that's hard to do . . ."

"So much the better. Never be vehement in your defense or make comparisons between the various failings of the American system and the Communist sins. Forget that evil is only a matter of degree."

"I never thought so."

"So much the better, then."

53

And there were other rules and a timetable to follow; they were designed to give the impression of an amiable, apolitical scholar who was combining scholarship with an unorthodox vacation.

Thus there were to be three days of sightseeing, guided and alone; nonwork days devoted to the Baedeker, guidebook and city map with my supposedly vestigial American feet protesting the cruelty of cobblestones. *PABUT,* the government tourist bureau, supplied interpreter-guides to show this and that but never the other, only the clean and shining or historically celebrated; the approved New and the noncontroversial Old.

There was a standard pattern of tourist behavior, and this included violation of the regulation that forbad sightseeing without the PABUT guide, because three days of Soviet Gothic architecture, concrete-and-plateglass housing projects, dayschools and nurseries, the odd Filtration Plant and the State Opera were usually enough. Only German tourists marched in step under supervision throughout their stay; everyone else was expected to try a diversion on his own; it would make me conspicuous if I didn't try one.

"Absolute compliance with all regulations is immediately open to suspicion. It is unreasonable to suppose that absolute respect for all laws can exist unless there exists a parallel desire to conceal a crime. That is something every policeman is taught to believe."

"I'll remember."

"Be aimless in your wandering. Establish a pattern of unpredictable decisions. Let your guardian angels get accustomed to it."

"Guardian angels?"

"Plainclothesmen. The Nakomda, if you give them any reason to wonder about you."

"Won't unpredictable decisions give them cause to wonder?"

"Not if they are always unpredictable. When the unexpected is the norm, it is accepted as eccentricity. Scholars are expected to act without logic."

The colorless, cold words flowed like the metal of a ghostly right-of-way, a toneless superhighway lost in monotonous country.

Later, when it was so important to examine the shape and sound and coloration of each word, I wished I hadn't let excitement and anticipation strip me of analytical objectivity. But this was High Adventure, after all; I couldn't be analytical about anything like that.

"Establish a pattern of patternless thinking," Karpovitch was saying. "Be indecisive and make lightning-swift, spur of the moment decisions, start sidetrips only to change your mind at midpoint and go off on tangents. No one will be surprised when, later, you start in one direction and disappear in another."

"How will I get away from my guardian angels?"

"You will be told. Just make sure that you've laid the necessary groundwork."

"Tangents and lack of systematic methods. I understand. Incidentally, how should I go about contacting Sempinski? That's my official purpose, after all."

"Send him a note from your hotel. It will take a few days for his reply to reach you; that will give you time for all we've discussed. Then, make whatever arrangements you want with Sempinski."

"And my contact with the Library people?"

"Act as if there were to be none. Don't even think about them. Someone will get in touch with you at the right time."

"How will I know him?"

"His name will be Zimstern. No, don't write it down! Ferdynand Zimstern, dealer in antiques. He's a good dealer, too, with some handsome East European pieces, so it's logical that he'd get in touch with you after he reads of your arrival in the papers."

I had to admit that Karpovitch seemed to have anticipated almost everything. I wondered if he, himself, had any connection with the Romanowski Library.

"Remember: Zimstern, dealer in antiques. He has a store somewhere in the Old City. The name is easy to remember. What does it mean in English? A star of spice?"

"Cinnamon Star, I think."

And was that all?

"That is everything."

I would see the sights and inadvertently-on-purpose lose a guide and set out on some impulsive trip to one place and wind up in another, and I would set up an irrational pattern of behavior and lay the groundwork for a journey to wherever the Romanowski Library was supposedly hidden, and I would go about the business that was my excuse for being in the country and meet Julian Sempinski, and then a Cinnamon Star would appear and lead me to my journey's end.

I laughed, because it was so simple; I couldn't believe it.

"It doesn't look as if I'll have much trouble."

Karpovitch bowed his head; an abrupt gesture of assent that threw his face momentarily into shadow. And then the innumerable, mobile wrinkles and undefined angles and liquid planes that made up that extraordinary face, congealed in hard textured lines and features sculpted in granite. I was suddenly aware of diamond-hard eyes secretly amused.

The transformation lasted only a fraction of a second. Then substance melted and the rigidly defined mask flowed apart again and the quick light went out of the eyes. They had, again, the hooded transparency of windows opening on shadow.

It was well after midnight when Potter and Karpovitch left. I went up to my suite and tried to make up my mind about the call to Tommy . . . and about going East. Potter had made the reservations, but I could still change my mind and cancel everything.

Should I or shouldn't I? It seemed that I was starting to practice indecision a little too early.

Truth was, I didn't want to talk to Tommy then; I didn't want to be dissuaded from making the trip. I was too full of Master Spies, Nakomda agents and everything I had heard about that evening; my eyes were full of Cinnamon Stars, I supposed. I would go on, as planned, because I wanted to. It was my adventure. I had just enough time to get to the telephone to cancel the call before the transatlantic operator made the connection.

PART TWO

The Pontic Tribunals

six

I STOOD at the top of the portable stairway they had pulled up with tractors through the snow, feeling the sharp bite of the wind, the bitterly cold air. The world was gray, filled with falling snow as thick as the invisible clouds; enormous snowflakes slanted past my face.

I had been the last passenger to step out of the warm cabin of the aircraft into the icy wind. The soft, luxurious warmth of the huge TU was fast disappearing, and with it the memory of soundless flight high above the billowing white blanket of the two Germanys and the other borders; the forests had looked like dwarfed clumps of steel wool pressed into the whiteness; everything else—roads, rivers, villages, and towns—crouched under the snow.

It had all looked pretty much the same, no matter what the country, once we had lifted off the gray-brown mass of England and dropped the washed-out ribbon of the Channel behind us. France showed blue water and stretches of vestigial green; Holland and the forest-screened approaches of North Germany were, perhaps, less consistently white, crisscrossed with more black lines of roads and rivers than the others; but once the Elbe had drifted westward under us all land took refuge under the neutral uniform of snow. There were no borders then; no artificial lines penciled into the clean white sheet of north-central Europe; it unfolded like a fresh roll of textured Bristol block, soft and unsegmented, until we flew across the ultimate demarcation line. There the West ended and the East began.

But even this was more a matter of the senses than plain sight. I had begun to feel the approach of this most unnatural of all borders long before the aircraft commander made his trilingual announcement. The metal walls had seemed to compress. I was aware of silence and a sudden stillness; the abrupt end of forty conversations. There was no more weight-shifting from one uncomfortable buttock to another, and no papers rustled. My fellow passengers were suddenly absorbed in mindless contemplation of their own dull thoughts, and eyes grew vacant with the blank gaze of the inward stare. It was as if everyone had become locked in a drugged, hypnotic trance and had stepped far into himself, diminishing in his own, warm darkness as the line drew near.

The plane had banked gently into the southward curve that led into the air corridor above Berlin, and at once the plane commander's voice crackled on the intercom. Passengers were reminded in Russian, German, and another language that the Government of the People's Democratic East German Republic forbade air-observation of the border.

I had retreated obediently into the deep soft nap of the artificial velvet upholstery, wanting to look out, to see Berlin before it disappeared. This was the last outpost, after all. We had been flying over East Germany for some time but I hadn't felt myself carried through alien air because Berlin, with its Western Zones, had still been ahead . . . I had not yet been irrevocably carried beyond the last border. And then, there it was: Berlin, slanting toward me under the white blade of the wing, spinning away on invisible rollers and soon gone. With it went everything familiar; everything I could take for granted. From that point to the far shores of the Bering Straits lay the foreign East; barbarism began where the familiar ended.

The dull roar of the turbojets, loud in the frozen silence of this border crossing, had receded. I had become aware of new, foreign sounds as the other passengers stirred and the illustrated pages of their magazines had begun to rustle and they resumed their crackling conversations. They were no longer the wholly human fellow passengers who had come aboard with me in London; now they were trolls and ogres carried by black magic to their ice mountains in the East.

I didn't think that I had ever felt more alone. A pink-cheeked stewardess offered me trays of canapés that would have tempted St. Anthony into gluttony, but I shook my head. I listened for one word of English . . . even German . . . in the forty conversations going on around me but there was only the singsong cadence of the Slavs. They were as alien to me as the man in the moon.

I had felt as if I flew in a private chamber, the glass capsule of the absolute outsider, across the vast sweep of a brilliant sky above snowclouds. The glittering white land that flashed ice signals in the cloud breaks had no relation to anything I knew.

The crystal capsule was still around me when I stepped out of the plane into the shock of an Eastern European winter. The blue-gray light of a January afternoon was a diffused glow that seemed to give everything an extra dimension. I saw great rectangles and squares splashed with luminescent orange; dark concrete cliffs wrapped in concentric wheels of light. It took a moment to realize that these were only airport terminal buildings bathed in their own window light reflected by snow.

My crystalline shield blew up in the cold and I was once again in a time-place context, with the wind slashing through my New York overcoat as if it were paper. I hadn't got the message from the fur hats and hairy overcoats that the disembarking trolls had broken out of their luggage aboard the TU. Someone called from the foot of the mobile stairway but the wind blew the sound away. I shook my head at a snowcapped man, understanding nothing, and trudged across the surprisingly hard snow toward the orange lights. Behind me came a spattering of sound like pistol fire; icicles snapped off the tubular steel framework of the stair tower.

Inside was warmth, lights, marble, tile, potted plants, brilliant decorator colors, astonishing graphics and twisted ornamental iron shapes: a hall the size of a football field with incomprehensible signs.

A man spoke to me, his face questioning and kind, his words a senseless cacophony. I showed him my passport. He held it in both hands, looking curiously at its golden emblem, then with equal curiosity at me, then passed us both—curiosities from another planet —to a platoon of men in uniforms of gradually increasing elegance who wrote on forms and pounded them with ink stamps.

In time, my brain thawed out. I began to see the men and women I was dealing with, their various uniforms. I didn't know one uniform from another, of course, and wondered which, if any, were the Nakomda men. The faces looking up at me from the desks were uniformly square, with high cheekbones and widespaced eyes like intelligent marbles. I wondered which of these pleasant faces concealed a policeman.

One man made a more distinct impression. He did no stamping or writing on forms, but paralleled my progress from desk to desk behind the officials, occasionally looking over the functionaries' shoulders, one hand tucked neatly behind his back, the other supporting a little cigarette in an amber holder. He wore a round-crowned military cap with a dark blue band, a long double-breasted overcoat buttoned across his chest, polished riding boots, leather belt and a small pistol holster.

I was curious about everything, but careful not to stare. Everything still seemed as if it was happening to somebody else but my airtight, isolation capsule had melted away; I had a feeling of double participation, the odd detachment of an interested observer.

It was all right to stare; they would expect me to be interested. Americans were rare in their country and we didn't know anything about them. And it was all right to look nervous which was convenient because I was nervous. I found it difficult to meet anybody's eyes; Karpovitch's lecture had not included a recommended response to friendly officials.

Then I was at the end of the line of desks, a ream of forms

clutched under one arm, Pohl's elegant briefcase under the other, and my valises dangling from both hands. A herd of porters and taxicab drivers formed for their stampede and, suddenly, as I got ready for the rush, I saw them thrown into confusion: first milling like startled animals, then drifting away with increasing speed. The officer in the blue-banded cap had come up beside me.

"Please come with me," he said.

His voice didn't give anything away.

"Where?" I said. "Why? Is anything wrong?"

The officer looked at me with no more than polite attention. His widely spaced gray eyes communicated neither friendliness nor hostility, his wide thin mouth neither smiled nor scowled, but I felt coldness creeping past my knees and my anxiety broke out of control.

"Because if anything is wrong," I said, "I mean about my papers, I'd like to call the American Legation."

He asked politely: "Why would you want to do anything like that?"

I was floundering and furious about it. Arouse no special interest, Karpovitch had said. My question had been thrown out by instinct, but if I had wanted to advertise that I expected trouble, I wouldn't have been able to do better.

I said, confused and groping, "Well . . . it's customary, isn't it?"

The officer laughed abruptly.

"Nervous, Dr. Shippe?"

I started on an indignant *What would I have to be nervous about?* but thought better of it, sure that the officer would immediately tell me.

He nodded pleasantly and pointed with his cigarette holder down the brightly lighted, tiled corridor, and I set out behind him, trying to match my nervous porter's stagger to his long military stride.

Afterward there was no way to judge whether the interview had gone well or badly.

There was a small office with bright travel posters: mountains and ruined castles and craggy-faced highlanders in flat hats and capes; girls in red boots, flying braids. The office had been borrowed for the interview. A soldier with a futuristic-looking weapon strapped across his chest, and with the same blue hatband as his officer, stood outside the door. Passers-by went out of their way not to approach him or the door he guarded. I assumed that I was in the presence of the NKD.

I couldn't understand what they wanted from me. The questioning gave no clue.

The questions came, flat and disinterested, as if it didn't matter what I answered. Each answer led into another question. Sooner or later the questions came back to Sempinski.

Yes, I had come to see Professor Sempinski. I had an invitation. No, we were not regular correspondents. Each of us had written one letter and one cable. Yes, I admired Sempinski as a writer. No, I didn't know anything about Sempinski's present projects and activities, supposing them literary. Yes, I realized the writer had published nothing since 1938, but books were not produced like vacuum cleaners. No, I didn't *send* Mrs. Napoji to Sempinski; I had merely suggested that she visit him. (I gave the reasons for suggesting it.) Oh, all right, I did ask her to visit Sempinski; a personal matter. What was it? I wanted the famous writer to autograph a book. No, I didn't think there was anything unusual about that. No, it did not seem odd. No, I had written nothing in the book I sent. No, I didn't know Mrs. Napoji well; in fact I hadn't heard about her accident until Sempinski mentioned it in his letter. But now, yes, I knew about it from a friend. What friend? Would I name him? Well, all right; I named him. I was sure I could tell the NKD nothing about the accident that they didn't know. What did I mean by that? Why, nothing! I merely supposed . . . Yes, I knew she was related to Senator Lindstrom, but I had no connecton with him. None. In fact I wouldn't welcome such connections. Why? I didn't agree with the former senator's outlook, viewpoint and, well, everything; they were too extreme. Yes I was opposed to extremism in any form. No, not *violently* opposed, that's why I disliked the Lindstrom solutions.

Would I say that my philosophy was liberal? Not in the active political sense. Yes, there were other senses. Yes, I was a liberal in the humanitarian sense, I supposed; at least I hoped I was . . . No! I was not a member of the Liberal Party. Yes, I supposed Julian Sempinski was a liberal. A militant liberal? Yes, I supposed that was true. And was Mrs. Napoji also a liberal? I supposed she was; I really didn't know. But wasn't that a little academic now? *I mean after the accident* . . . No, I never got an autographed book from Julian Sempinski. No, I had never met him; I looked forward to it. Yes, I thought him a very great man. No, this was not the general opinion in the United States; few of my countrymen had heard of Sempinski . . . And No! Nobody I knew kept contact with Sempinski. Nobody had sent me.

"When is your meeting with Sempinski? Where?"

"I don't have an appointment. I plan to write him a letter in a day or two. You see, this is a holiday for me, as well as an opportunity to meet Sempinski . . . I plan to see a bit of your country while I'm here."

"What do you wish to see?"

"Well . . . I don't know exactly. I'm an antiquarian. Eastern antiquities . . ."

I stopped, beginning to feel more than just a little alarmed and confused. The security officer was looking at me as if I were already standing in the dock with the Pontic Tribunals spread in evidence on the prosecution table.

"And one of our principal antiquities is Julian Sempinski," he finished soberly.

The NKD man asked to see Sempinski's letter and my invitation. I felt the time had come for a mild protest.

"But that's a private letter."

He laughed then and looked at me with something like pity.

"That's all right," he said. "We're used to it. Like doctors, you know."

I knew that protests would be useless, in fact more than useless; they would be dangerous. Only my own pride was involved here, my right to keep my mail to myself. But he had said so gently that he was used to reading other people's mail . . . *Like doctors,* he said. And it was better for the Nakomda to go through my mail than to mark me as uncooperative and, therefore, suspicious. The quicker the interview was over the better for me. I took the letter from the briefcase and handed it over.

He read it quickly but with deep attention, as if he had already an idea about the letter's contents. He smiled a little to himself and put the letter aside. He looked at me for a long quiet moment, as if making up his mind, then nodded briefly, returned the letter to me and lit a cigarette. And it was then that I knew why the half-mocking hooded eyes had seemed so familiar. They had the same quality of secret amusement and private knowledge I had last read in Karpovitch's face.

Five minutes more of expert questioning would have finished me but, curiously, the Nakomda officer changed tack as soon as it had become obvious that I was getting rattled.

This time there was no mockery in the smile. The cigarette he offered and I took was harsh and just what I needed to pull my wits together. But for all this sudden cordiality there was still a strain. I hoped he didn't know how close I had been to panic. So much depended on keeping clear of suspicion, avoiding attention. Everything would be infinitely harder if the Nakomda kept its eyes on me; Zimstern might even find it too dangerous to attempt a contact.

The interview had been anything but routine. I didn't expect the Nakomda to offer explanations; that would be hardly according to custom. They didn't seem to suspect my real reasons for coming to their country—the Pontic Tribunals had not been mentioned—but I knew that I had failed an important test. I had not convinced the Nakomda that I had come only to see the sights and meet an old man whose work I admired. I had upset Karpovitch's foremost principle by having failed to avoid notice. Ironically, it was the cover story that was supposed to make me inconspicuous —my own smug contribution to Pohl's plans—that had earned me my Nakomda interview and interest. Who could have imagined that the Nobel Prize winner was up to something other than writing a book? Knowing that it was too late for self-recrimination didn't help me feel less foolish than I did.

The officer smiled, as if to indicate that the interview was over. "You must be tired, Dr. Shippe."

But I had learned the first lesson in dealing with security policemen: you either told them everything or nothing; there was no middle ground.

"It must be quite a strain," he went on when I didn't answer. "All this excitement. First time in the country. New language, customs. It doesn't do to overexcite oneself. You should rest for a day or two; take it easy, as your people say. We'd want your first visit to our country to be memorable. And now I'll get somebody to get you a taxi."

seven

I DIDN'T think that I would be able to sleep, but I slept like a bear. I woke on my first morning behind the Iron Curtain feeling a high sense of excitement, determined to make no new errors or repeat the old. The airport interview didn't seem so bad after ten hours of dreamless oblivion in a feather bed. I remembered everything Karpovitch had told me and went about the morning as if everything—from brushing my teeth to eating a rich and satisfying breakfast, and from an interested reading of a day-old Paris edition of *L'Humanite* to writing my note to Julian Sempinski—was done on the clear end of a two-way mirror. I was conscious of an audience in everything I did and found myself enjoying my unfamiliar role. It was exciting trying to spot possible guardian angels.

Waiters were immediately suspect, but they were disappointing; more like cabinet ministers of deposed regimes than undercover agents. The PABUT guide turned out to be a well-mannered young woman who immediately warned me not to change American currency anywhere but in official centers; it seemed that half the capital traded black market dollars, but half the traders were Nakomda agents. But there was a definitely sinister bald, fat man, who sat in the lobby behind a newspaper, and a beetle-browed, thin man who bumped into me in the elevator and passed me a note.

The note turned out to be an advertisement for a night club with unusual floor shows.

I wrote a post card to Tommy and, after a moment of hesitation, to Hubertus Pohl. It seemed a natural thing to do and it allowed me to share some of my excitement, the feeling of participation in foreign intrigue.

I had allowed Miss Jablonska of the PABUT to take me on the expected tour of the city. We rode well-bundled in rugs in a horse-drawn carriage with sleigh runners instead of wheels, while the air crackled with the cold around us. She had suggested a late-model Russian Volga with a uniformed chauffeur, but I had spotted the other vehicle plodding through traffic, with a red-nosed driver perched high on the box, oilskin cap pulled down over his ears and frost on his whiskers. She urged the warmer means of transportation but I was adamant; I had begun to think of a plan that would set me free of PABUT supervision.

She shivered like a wet kitten in her threadbare cloth coat and inadequate boots. I was toast-warm in a magnificent overcoat (lined from neck to ankles with beaver, and with a collar of solid otter fur standing up around my ears like an electric fire) and in a silver-gray Karakul fur hat. I had bought both immediately after breakfast.

The capital proved to be more than I had hoped it would be. I had read all I could about it in New York but it had been old material. Ninety percent of this city had been turned to rubble by Russians and Germans. Now, everything was new. Whatever had been picturesque or meaningful had been carefully restored, gargoyle by gargoyle and cornice by cornice. Spires and cupolas, neoclassic palaces, Italianate galleries, and urban perspectives straight out of Leonardo.

I noticed many uniforms; squads of the military stood outside the hotels. The PABUT girl explained that the Warsaw Pact conference was responsible for the security measures.

"Where is the Chairman of the Soviet Union staying?"

"The Russians haven't come yet."

67

"When will they come?"

"Who knows about the Russians? They come and go as they please."

She didn't seem particularly enthusiastic about the Chairman and his delegation.

And then we were in the Old City, and it seemed impossible that none of that sixteenth-century magic of tall, narrow buildings had been there after 1945, except as rubble. Some of the bitterest house-to-house fighting in Europe had taken place here. But now it was exactly as it had been before the war. Communist or not, the country seemed to like its history within reach.

I was delighted with it all; from the worn thresholds, hollowed into basins, to the coats of arms carved among the gargoyles. The ancient cornices and the steep-roofed buildings that seemed to spread and settle on the cobbled streets like old dowagers, the huge gates studded with enormous nails, hung on ornamental hinges, the narrow alleys with opposite roofs practically rubbing lead rain gutters and copper spouts overhead, steep limestone stairs no wider than a fireman's ladder plunging between houses from the ancient market square to the riverbanks: all these appealed to my sense of history, the continuity of the human serial. Even the ancient city walls had been reconstructed, complete with holes that had been pounded into the defenses by Swedish cannon in the sixteenth century. These were streets made for the heroes of Sempinski's novels, fashioned for swordsmen and plot and intrigue. Time seemed to stand still here; yet it was moving softly in the dark doorways, through the winding alleys. It would be here that I would be taken by the conspirators, at least in spirit, no matter where they actually led me.

"Magnificent," I said.

The guide said something inaudible and sad.

She had begun to sniff among the plate-glass and concrete boxes of modern avenues; she sneezed and coughed among the cupolas and spires. In the Old City she was hoarse and fevered. I took pity on her. I suggested coffee. She led me to a cellar restaurant under the traditional wreath of a sixteenth-century tavern where, in the steam of Turkish coffee, she had to lean on my arm going down the stairs.

I couldn't face her accusing eyes and felt my resolve melting like the Napoleon pastries on my plate, but it was too late to turn back from my plan. I suggested that if she was ill she should go home; I would find my own way back to the hotel. The poor girl shook her head.

I looked around and saw the fat, bald man whom I had last seen in the hotel lobby. He had his back to us but I was sure that there was no mistake. His polished head caught the light like a billiard ball and seemed to flash signals. He sat like a gleaming idol, his beefy back encased in shining serge that made me think of stuffed sausages.

Back in the sleigh, I peered about with all the eagerness of a sightseeing tourist, but if the beefy guardian angel was on the job he kept out of sight. He would be in a taxi, of course; there were many taxis. Streetcars clanged and grated. There were horse-drawn drays. Quick crowds moved on the sidewalks hampered by the snow. We went on, the coughing girl and I; she pointed, whispered, and I looked obediently but I could no longer hear the explanations. I almost forgot to ask about the famous ghetto, but finally I did, and she made an odd, resigned gesture as if that wind-swept, icy wilderness was too much to bear. She stood beside me, huddled in her light coat, while I looked at the ruins that had been left untouched to serve as a memorial. I hadn't thought they'd have any effect on me; I was not a Jew, and without some bloodlink one battlefield is much like another. These foreign acres of uncleared, snowsheeted rubble should have meant nothing to me. But somehow, as a human being, I found myself awed and incredibly moved. There was a gaunt magnificence about the pyramids of broken masonry; the wind, shrill in this wasteland, booming in the canyons of a hollow town, wrapped this monument in a Gregorian chant and peopled it with shadows. I felt no pain, no personal involvement. But the desolation sheeted my mind with lead. I was glad when the ghostly battlefield vanished in the snow that had begun to fall.

By midday, my guide had a burning temperature. Another hour of the icy tour would send her to bed. She would be too ill in the morning to take charge of me, but I counted on her Communist sense of duty to keep her off the sick list until the last possible moment. By the time PABUT could send reinforcements I would be on my own.

The alien city no longer worried me. I had it in perspective. If anything, it was this totally foreign air, the lack of anything familiar, that sharpened my pleasure.

The sleigh glided through narrow backstreets behind the Market Square, across pale pools of yellow lamplight between banks of snow. It was a silent, shuttered quarter, unpeopled and empty; its tall, narrow windows had the hooded look of sentries guarding secret meeting places.

I looked up and out and sat up with a start, caution forgotten and recovered too late. Above a dark window and a gaunt doorway hidden in the shadow of a narrow passage hung a wooden sign. It spelled the name of FERDYNAND ZIMSTERN, DEALER IN ANTIQUES.

Coincidence? I wished I could afford to think so. There could have been no mistake about the PABUT guide's sudden movement against me, the quick pressure that had made me look up at the sign.

I forced back an exclamation only just in time, but my surprised start had been exclamatory enough. How could she know that Zimstern's name would mean anything to me? Who was she? How much did she know?

I forced myself not to think of answers. That way lay danger. I would do my thinking when I was alone. There were implications here that made me suddenly feel as if my furs had turned into paper in the fierce cold of the darkening afternoon.

Occasionally I glanced at the girl. She kept her face averted, her head down; she seemed hardly conscious. I thought that she had kept her head down even as she had made that quick, insistent movement. What had it been, anyway? I was confused and shaken.

The icy afternoon swept without warning into evening and then into night. Snow fell in silent masses; soon the streets were a flickering dark haze of indistinct shapes smeared with pale splashes of yellow light and multicolored neon. I was alone, shut off in a private cubicle of darkness and snow, carried on hissing runners through a cacophony of Klaxons, streetcar bells and the whine of motors straining in first gear. Danger seemed very near in the spotted darkness.

I got rid of my furs in the downstairs cloakroom, not wanting to go up to the false privacy of my room. I would have given anything to be at home: dry and warm with apple logs burning in the fireplace and Mahler filling my study with a hurricane of sound. Thought would be calm and orderly with the sherry a mahogany red in the cutglass decanter, and the day safely locked outside. I ordered dinner, thinking that eating would be an ordeal, and enjoyed a sort of combination cabbage-roll and carpetbag steak: an envelope of delicately cured veal stuffed with brown rice boiled in red wine, mushrooms, a shellfish of some kind and herbs in a white-flour sauce. Tension gradually left me as I ate.

Why had the PABUT girl drawn my attention to Zimstern's sign? If the Nakomda suspected me of dealings with Zimstern they wouldn't need to confirm their suspicions by staging an elaborate confrontation. And how could they have linked me with Karpovitch's man? Only Potter and the Master Spy himself knew of my connection with the antique dealer.

It would be good to know just what the Nakomda had on Zimstern. A hookup with Karpovitch was one thing; the Pontic Tribunals were another matter. The Nakomda could link me with Zimstern only if they had got wind of the conspiracy. But, if so, why warn me by tipping their hand?

I wondered what to do. The easiest thing was to do nothing, and wait. If the police were setting a trap my best course was to play the tourist and take no chances; sooner or later someone would contact me and tell me what to do. If Zimstern was in trouble, he could be replaced. If he was not in trouble, he would show up when it was safe to do so.

But this simple course wasn't good enough. Perhaps it was too reasonable at a time when not much made sense. Zimstern had to be warned. He was my only sure contact in the capital; I couldn't afford to lose him. But I knew, even then, that the real reason for what I had decided to do lay in my own curiosity. I was drawn by the magnet of the dark night, the mysterious doorways and the shrouded windows of the Old City backstreets.

I took my time about leaving the hotel. I got my briefcase so as to have all my identification, then read the *Continental Daily Mail* in the dining room until it started emptying. No one followed me into the lobby cloakroom where I picked up my furs. My spirits rose as my excitement mounted. My fat bald guardian, his back to the lobby and the revolving doors, was in a heated conversation with a desk clerk. A crowd of young people pushing in, loudly and suddenly, out of the windswept street, provided a diversion. I was through the revolving doors in moments, struggling into furs.

"Taxi!"

The wind caught my voice and carried it away. But a familiar dark shadow broke through the curtain of falling snow and plodded toward me. The swaybacked horse staggered up to the curb. Behind him gleamed the oilskin cap and the frozen whiskers.

I gave the address by shouting *Old City,* the only words in the language that I could pronounce. The driver looked behind me, as if expecting another passenger, then grinned and slapped the reins and made a kissing sound with his lips and the old horse looked up, sadly but resigned. I climbed into the sleigh and spread the wraps about me. It was bitterly cold. The sleigh swung away from the curb and then we were weaving in and out of traffic, still heavy despite the snowfall and late evening. I thought I could hear the old driver chuckling above the tinny sound of the small bell on the horse's harness, the whine of motors, blare of horns and clang of streetcar bells. The sleigh moved nimbly through a fleet of similar vehicles and taxis. Anyone trying to follow us would have an awkward time; it was obvious the old man on the driver's box had done that kind of thing before.

Streets followed streets, and then the ancient, steep roofs began to crowd together, and the modern streetlights gave way to ornamental iron redolent of age, and windows narrowed and alleys became darker, and then we were in the Old City and it was time to stop.

The driver looked down at me, grinning, and winked conspiratorially and nodded toward the street behind us where whoever might have been trying to follow us would now be lost and cursing.

I was at once surrounded by small boys begging for foreign currency. The few odd dimes and nickels I had in my pockets quickly disappeared and the sight of a quarter quickly provided me with a voluble small guide and shortly afterward I was knocking on the antique dealer's door.

There was no answer, no sign that anyone inside had heard me or would hear me. I listened for footsteps. I imagined a small, stooped, myopic man coming through the store, silent in felt slippers, an unassuming man in bottle-bottom glasses who would blink in the sudden brightness of the streetlamp. And now I was anxious to get out from under the bright glare of the lamp, into the darkened store. I knocked again, louder. I listened. I heard nothing. There was only the soft hiss of snow falling around me and the distant sounds of disembodied traffic far beyond the dark mouth of the street.

The windows were dark. I supposed I might have imagined the gleam of light I thought I had seen moving between the shutters. I knocked once more, then tried the door. It swung inward with a slow, painful creak and a small bell sounded overhead. I stepped inside.

There was a smell of dust and dryness. Dark shapes retreated from the sudden light, resolved themselves into counters and tall cases, ancient metal, the dusty sweep of hangings stirred by the icy wind blowing from the street. Light from the lamp outside lay in shallow pools among small coffers, stacked canvasses and frames, disfigured plaster busts, bronze heads. Darkness clung to the corners among squat suits of armor bowed like crippled robots.

I heard a rustling movement on my left and thought of rats

and mice and then I thought I saw a larger shadow. I asked: "Is anybody there? Hullo . . ."

At once a powerful white light struck me in the face, blinded me. I fell back from the door as a foot came from the darkness and kicked it shut, and the tall shadow behind the white glare began to move swiftly backward through the store.

"Herr Zimstern," I began . . .

A harsh, cold voice said: "Don't move. Stand still." Then added, unnecessarily: "Close your eyes."

The man was an American. He backed away toward the rear of the store, shielded by the high intensity flashlight that made him invisible. He kept the light trained squarely on my eyes. Then a door opened in a corner and both the light and the man were gone. I heard light footsteps leaping over stairs.

eight

I WAITED in the darkness minute after minute, trying to recover my night vision and to make some sense of what had just happened. The startling presence of my vanished countryman had been the last thing I had expected to find in Zimstern's store. Who was he? His voice had been too coarse, too nasal and violent for an antiquities consultant and, anyway, I knew all my colleagues very well. I had never heard that unpleasant voice before.

But the man had seemed to know me. He hadn't asked who I was, or why I had come. He hadn't asked my name. I had spoken in fluent, unaccented German but he had known that I would understand his commands in English. And he had made sure that I wouldn't be able to see him behind his blinding light.

I heard footsteps behind the back door, on the same stairs that the unexpected American had mounted so quickly. I supposed that the stairs led to living quarters above the store.

Someone was coming down, carrying a lantern; I saw a wavering light frame the rectangle of the door, grow brighter, steadier, and then the door was flung open and a man came in carrying a hissing carbide lamp high over his head. He was a small, round man in a glittering pince-nez, black alpaca jacket and a wool scarf that masked the absence of a collar. His wispy hair stood on end

75

as if he had just been roused out of bed; it gave him the appearance of unreasoning fear.

I took a step forward, said: "Herr Zimstern? I . . ."

He uttered a peculiar strangling sound and fell into the room as if propelled by a catapult. The lamp was shaking in his hand; it threw drunken shadows down his yellow face, past the thin lips of a petulant child to an angry chin. He peered at me with sharp little eyes.

His voice was shrill with anger and alarm.

"What are you doing here? Why did you come?"

I said: "I'm Dr. Shippe. I came . . ."

"I know who you are! Why did you come? Weren't you told to wait in your hotel? Oh, this is madness, madness!"

This wasn't the reception I had been expecting. The angry round man wasn't the unassuming dusty little figure I had imagined as the antique dealer. He placed the lamp shakily on a bookcase and ran to the window.

"I'm sorry," I began, but he cut me short.

"Madness! Insanity! Are you trying to get us all shot?"

I said that No, on the contrary, I hadn't wanted to get anyone in trouble. I had come to warn him about a development that seemed significant. I had thought I would be rendering him a service. And, I said: "I wasn't followed, if that's what's worrying you."

He turned on me quivering with anger.

"How would you know if you were followed or not? Are you such an expert?"

"No," I said, "but it had seemed to me that the cab driver, a man of experience, had known what he was doing."

"A cab driver? You came here by cab?"

"How else was I to come? Look," I said, hoping to reassure him so that he would listen, "I made sure that no one followed me out of the hotel. No one saw me get into the cab. The cab took me to the Market Square. A little boy brought me the rest of the way."

"And why should anyone follow you when the man most likely to be your guardian angel brought you here in his cab?"

He had me there. It hadn't occurred to me that the picturesque cab driver could have been a spy. Why not? He hadn't looked the part. What do police spies look like? I didn't know that either. It seemed that there was a great deal that I didn't know and that I was making too many dangerous assumptions. Once again, like some sort of undercover Icarus, I had tried my wings and the wax had melted.

I said that I was sorry; I had not meant to endanger anyone. My apology seemed to mollify the angry round man. I told him why I had taken such a foolish chance to see him.

He listened with attention and, gradually, his humor improved. He chuckled when I told him how I had disabled poor Miss Jablonska of the PABUT. He found my fears about the guide especially amusing but, when I pressed him for an explanation, he merely shook his head.

He was less amused when I asked him about the mysterious American who had given me such a blinding welcome.

"That's nothing to do with our business," he muttered uneasily. "An unexpected guest. Another matter. But it is not good that he saw you here."

"He seemed to know me."

Zimstern became suddenly evasive. "Did he? You are a well-known man, Dr. Shippe"—he pronounced it Sheep. "Perhaps that's the answer. But now that you have given me the unexpected pleasure of meeting you, perhaps we can do business. I had hoped to arrange a different meeting, elsewhere, in a day or two, but your precipitation of the matter would make that difficult. So, perhaps, we can proceed from here, eh?"

"You mean you'll take me to the Romanowski Library tonight?"

He cocked his head, as if listening for a sound upstairs, then treated me to a yellow-toothed smile.

"Why not? Sooner or later I would have to take you. The Library will not come to you, so you must go to the Library, eh, Doctor? Isn't that why you have honored our country with your presence? If you have not been followed here, and I believe now that you have not been followed, at least not by anyone who means to do us harm, we could go. You like the idea?"

Events had begun to move far too fast for me. I didn't understand Zimstern's certainty that I had not been followed, but something in my story must have reassured him. I wished he would explain his unexpected American guest. I thought he had dismissed my concern about the PABUT guide with excessive swiftness. But all these matters lost significance beside the prospect of seeing the Library.

"Yes," I said. "Of course!"

He took me to a little office at the back of the store: a dusty room lit by a pale desklamp, heaped from floor to ceiling with crates, boxes, and bursting bales out of which protruded stone limbs of statues; racks of rusty halberds; furniture piled with long abandoned objects; none of it worth the cost of salvage from a rubbish dump. A row of bronzed, cast-iron heads of Napoleon Bonaparte lined a waist-high shelf like criminal remains above the gates of a medieval city.

I sat at Zimstern's open rolltop desk while he left me to, as he put it, make necessary arrangements. The Library wasn't in the city. We would go by car.

Now that I had come so close to the end of my mission, it seemed impossible to believe that I had been part of a conspiracy. Considering my blunders, errors in judgment (if *judgment* was the word for my impulsive descent upon Zimstern), and the near-panic that had gripped me during my Nakomda interview, I knew that foreign intrigue was out of my depth.

If all went well I could be back in the capital in a day or two and on my way to Sweden by the end of the week. It would be enough for me to satisfy myself that only a few pieces of the lost collection had an authentic look; one item, proved authentic, would repay Pohl his hundred thousand dollars several times over, even supposing the rest of the material was a downright fraud. And even if my tests in Sweden showed the whole thing to be

78

a gigantic hoax, my client could still make a substantial profit on an academic curiosity.

I didn't really think that I would find the Romanowski Library where Zimstern would take me. The odds against authenticity were astronomical. I had accepted the assignment because no odds were too impossible to dismiss a chance; a mere suspicion that the Library could, possibly, exist would be enough to call for an investigation.

I had every reason to feel satisfied. I had done what had been professionally expected of me; no matter what the outcome of my research, my client could make a reasonable profit; neither I nor he would lose anything, and . . . I had a savored moment of the kind of life that had eluded me.

I had met a Master Spy and had been questioned by the NKD, and something could always be made out of poor, frozen Miss Jablonska, the picturesque cab driver, the fat man in the blue serge suit, Zimstern, Brown, Lindstrom and the mysterious American upstairs. Before I left for Sweden I would meet Sempinski, and that was quite enough to repay me for any frights I might have had along the way. Perhaps I would find out a little more about Kristin Napoji's accident.

There was nothing that I could regret. I was glad the adventure was coming to an end; I'd had the best of it—and just enough to know that any more would have been too much. When Zimstern, bundled up in furs like a diminutive fat bear, brought his car to the front of the store, I was in the best spirits that I could remember.

We drove through the silent streets of the sleeping capital, then crossed the river over a collonaded bridge and headed east. The night was still black when we left the city, but graying before us, so that the hushed streets and deeply buried country roads acquired the sudden look of water under ice. We flowed along this icy river without talking, each of us thinking his own thoughts. The sky was full of brilliant, pale stars that promised a clear day.

White fields gave way to black woods; silent walls of trees, diminishing in distance, bowed under their heavy winter canopies. Icy shrubs formed glittering cages among tree roots. Long, lonely lines of pug-marks trailed into the trees; I wondered what animals lived there. I supposed that there had been strayed cattle trapped in the snowy wilderness, perhaps even people. There would be timber wolves. Possibly wild boar and black bear in spring. There would be deer, lynx, wildcat, and the red fox. The prewar tourist guides I had read in New York had much to say about the bisons of the Eastern forests. I wondered if any of them had survived the war. At one time the bearded aurochs had crashed through these woods, but not any longer. So, maybe no more bisons either. Besides, this wasn't the forest that the guidebooks had been talking about; this was another country. During the war, fighting had been heavy in this neighborhood; I looked for war scars in the deep, unbroken wall of trees, some indication that the land remembered, as people always seem to remember, that there had been a war. But if there were scars, they were hidden under the white bandages of snow. And, anyway, scars had a way of healing, the land never failed to renew itself.

I looked at my watch as the white, icy miles sped away under us. It was 5:30, time for the sun to rise. The sun broke out of the mists and fog beyond the wooded dunes that made the open country like a frozen sea; it flooded the black forest with a scarlet light. The sun climbed, unhurried, as if unwilling to speed the new day and hung, without warmth, like a dull red bulb in the copper sky.

The lodge stood in a deep, dimlit clearing where an outcrop of limestone marked the convulsive heave of the ridge.

The biggest oak of all clamped its roots around a snowsheeted ruin at the far end of this undulating space, the white boughs swooping over the massive, wooden structure, foursquare and solid, built to resist time, spreading at the base, and now buttressed by ice. The lodge and oak were both elephant-gray in the indefinite light that threaded its way down from the snow canopy overhead. The air itself seemed frozen here; it shimmered with fine particles of light, suspended like a shield between the earth and the sun. It was a false light, distorting and dwarfing, as was the stillness on the forest floor.

An animal screamed deep in the forest, resenting the human invasion, and the forest wall answered with a belling chord: a violent protest stabbing the false silence. It made my vision shake. It rolled down from the depth of the retreating forest, splintered and dissipated seeking echoes.

We left the car at the mouth of the track which ran like a tunnel under the heavy-laden canopies of trees, and plunged into the deep snow billows in the clearing. Zimstern had brought a strange assortment of tools: hacksaws and chisels and a hammer as well as his lantern. We burrowed through the snow dunes crashing through the icy crust up to the waist and, occasionally, chest-deep, our progress marked by frantic heavings and thrashing as if the snow were quicksand. The lodge resisted our attempts to enter. We had to shovel aside the snow with our hands, tramping it down so that the door could open, and then the solid oaken door had to be freed from its seals of ice one chiseled inch at a time. The tinny hammering, the click of the chisels, were unnaturally loud in the breathless stillness, and when the chisel slipped, or the hammer missed, the house itself boomed a hollow echo that reminded me of violated crypts.

Inside was a powdery dry darkness and a quick illusion of impenetrable mass that seemed to fill the ancient dining hall from one invisible end to the other. The oak walls, bleached dead-white by time, tinder dry, caught up the hissing glare of our lamp and threw it into massed layers of cobwebs, turning the cobwebs into a furry whiteness that seemed as solid as cotton packed around a gem.

By midmorning, we had cleared a working space around the refectory table and the stone steps that, Zimstern said, led to the cellars where the treasure was stored. I was cold and hungry but Zimstern wouldn't allow a fire laid in the fireplace that looked big enough to accommodate a bear on a spit. We ate the black bread and goat cheese that Zimstern had brought and washed it down with the sweet wine of the country, and I looked up at the parchment skulls of long-slain animals that hung from the lintel the length of the hall, wondering how many rough and boisterous hunters' suppers they had witnessed with their hollow eyes. The lodge was older by several centuries than the country from which I had come. The heraldic device carved into the mantle had lost its identity years before the little fleet of Christopher Columbus had sailed from Cádiz.

But there were newer relics buried in the dust dunes: a rust-brown bayonet, a gaping leather ammunition pouch; during the war this island of antiquity hidden in the forest had been used by the partisans. It had been a band of partisans which had attacked the German column that was carrying the Romanowski Library away from its home a hundred miles to the east, or so Zimstern told me, but the treasure had not brought them luck. Each of the men who had helped to turn the lodge into a treasure house died violently in the ensuing years: in ambush, accident, betrayal to the Germans, mysterious illness, postwar anti-Communist resistance, show trial and purge. Ill fortune seemed to follow even the few members of the band who had been driven into exile.

The stairway was a narrow well spiraling deep into the rock on which the lodge had been built, with a small iron door, no wider than a coffin-lid, barring the way beyond the bottom step. We broke the padlocks and pried the heavy door open and entered the cellar.

The impression was one of a burial vault: long wooden cases branded with the Nazi swastika and eagle, stacked in dim rows the length of the cellar, frayed leather handles, rotted rope. The martial hieroglyphics of the Wehrmacht were still legible on the dusty wood: caliber designations. I had expected dampness but the air was dry.

We broke open the first of the cases. Nestled inside were five lead cylinders too heavy for one man to carry, hermetically sealed like time capsules. I thought that if I had ever wanted to store perishable materials, I couldn't have done better than this dry cave tunneled into solid rock and the lead containers. Whatever lay inside would survive anything. We carried the cylinders upstairs one at a time, and then took turns sawing off their ends, but the lead filament clogged up the hacksaw blades and I broke several before I got the hang of it. It was slow work; we had to be careful. Zimstern assured me that the contents were further protected but I took no chances.

Despite my skepticism my excitement grew, and when the first cylinder was finally open, and we had picked out the powdery wood shavings, and carefully lifted out one of the sealed glass display cases, I was certain that its contents would be genuine. If the dark brown fragment of papyrus between the fused panes of glass were a forgery then I had just inspected the most elaborate and believable stage setting in the history of antiquarian fraud. I was sure that if anyone measured the depth of the dust on the ammunition cases, and analyzed the age of the wood, lead, shavings, glass and even the crumpled dry newspapers wadded up for padding, he would discover nothing to contradict the story of when and how the Romanowski Library had come to be stored in the lodge. Zimstern had brought a jeweler's eyepiece and a magnifying glass and I went over every millimeter of the papyrus in the bright glare of the carbide lamp. The inscription was in ancient Aramaic, with that peculiar juxtaposition of clauses that went out of the language about a hundred years after the crucifixion. Much of it was no longer legible but enough remained so that I could follow this police report about a meeting of a group of Galileans at which wine had been drunk and bread had been eaten and strange words had been said about the Blood and the Body. I had no doubt that my microscope would confirm what my eyes accepted.

I wanted to open at least another cylinder—not to inspect the contents but merely to see them, read them, feel the medieval glass around them—but I had ruined all the hacksaw blades in my first attempt and, besides, the day was coming to an end. Still, having waited for so long to see the almost-legendary manuscripts and still unable to make myself believe the truth of what I saw, I didn't want to be parted from them. I wished that I could risk taking the spy's report on the Last Supper with me, just to have it near. But I knew that I would have to wait until it was delivered to me at the Royal Institute in Stockholm. I repacked the case and plugged up the cylinder with a part of Zimstern's car blanket, and then we carried all the cylinders downstairs, replaced them in the case and nailed it up again.

Simply to delay departure, and to have something to poke around with while I waited for the manuscripts to arrive in Stockholm, I had scraped some filaments off the cylinder, broke a splinter off the packing case, swept up a few of the dehydrated shavings and chipped the glass panes. I would leave no part of the story unchecked. Zimstern asked if Dr. Sheep was satisfied; I told him he was. He acted as if he hadn't expected any other answer.

We drove back to the capital while a desultory snowfall drifted down and covered our tracks. The skies were heavy with dark clouds that promised a snowstorm.

nine

I BOUGHT a stack of brightly colored postcards in the hotel lobby: castles and monuments and urban perspectives; and wrote my message to Hamish Potter over a dish of wild strawberries, whipped sourcream and powdered sugar. I wondered where they got the strawberries in the middle of winter.

The dining room was empty so early in the morning, but the fat, bald man had come bustling in close on my heels; he didn't look as if he had slept well. I knew I might have some explaining to do to the PABUT people but a sheepish story about girls and cabarets would take care of that.

I wished Pohl had concocted a more imaginative message but I supposed he knew what he was doing and wrote *Having a Wonderful Time, Wish You Were Here,* on the back of the restored throne room in the Royal Castle where, at that moment, the heads of the various Peoples' governments were probably meeting. Just for the hell of it I sent the same message to Pohl and to Tommy Mackin, adding to Tommy's postcard: *Hark, my postilion has been struck by lightning,* out of my book of useful conversational phrases.

But I didn't mail the postcards right away. To do so would be to acknowledge the end of the adventure and I wanted to savor it a little longer. I felt foolishly like a small boy walking on a fence, daring himself to do something he wanted to do anyway, knowing that he could jump down to safety anytime he wished. My fat, bald guardian angel was an adequate audience.

I went upstairs to file my postcards for use later in the week, and couldn't find my briefcase, and suddenly remembered that I had left it in Zimstern's office before the trip to the lodge. He had brought me back straight to the hotel, dropping me off with correct conspiratorial procedure some distance away. My mind had been on the Romanowski Library, I hadn't missed my briefcase until I needed it; it was too new to have become a habit. But all my documents were in it, including my passport and my traveler's cheques, and while I had enough currency on hand to last for several days the passport was another matter. This was another urgent reason for contacting Zimstern.

I had seen an old-fashioned telephone on his desk, the kind with the mouthpiece on a post and the earpiece on a tangled cord. But I couldn't identify the dealer on the page of Zimsterns, a dozen of them Ferdynands, in the telephone directory, and I didn't think the cautious conspirator would appreciate a call. That meant another trip to the Old City after dark.

This time I didn't want to go. There didn't seem to be any sound reason for reluctance. Perhaps it was a premonition of some unspecified danger, or the rising awareness that I was beginning to push my luck too far, or the anticipation of fresh blunders, or a combination of the three. My reluctance mounted throughout the day, matching the gloomy gathering of snowclouds, so that when night fell I left the hotel with all the enthusiasm of a convict ascending the scaffold.

No one followed me into the icy wind and snow that had begun to obliterate the city during the afternoon and now acquired the swirling dimensions of a minor storm. The city had a white, abandoned look. I walked three blocks before waving down a passing taxi, suddenly warmed by the checkered stripe painted around its side; it made me think of home. The taxi took me to the Old City. I paid and got out. I looked around to get my bearings and spotted the cafe where I had taken the frozen PABUT girl, and wondered why Zimstern had been so amused by that part of my story. The taxi driver made an impassioned speech, pointing to himself, to me, to his watchless wrist and to the street, but I shook my head. I would walk from here. I entered the cafe setting myself a fifteen-minute limit for comfort and warmth, to give the taxi time to disappear and to see if I had picked up a guardian angel somewhere along the way. Several people looked at me and one or two smiled. I knew I looked foreign. Sooner or later someone would talk to me. I started looking forward to the conversation, then remembered that I had not come here to attract attention or enjoy myself. I had a job to do. I waited for my fifteen minutes to go by, looking, in the meantime, about the low-ceilinged smoky room, intimate as an oak-paneled hunting club, with animated faces bent toward each other through the blue haze of tobacco smoke and the steam of coffee, and the sweet, almost tangible smell of confections wheeled among the tables.

No one looked like a police spy, not even the waiters. The customers were either young (late teens and early twenties; the boys in turtleneck sweaters, with too much hair falling across their foreheads, gesticulating, laughing; the girls scrubbed clean of makeup except around the eyes, long-haired and wholesome) or in their mid-forties, with that used look of Central European faces, sharp-featured and intelligent. They made me think of Hubertus Pohl who was nothing like them. Students and intellectuals, I concluded. I wondered if the animated young people were talking about me, if they had taken part in the recent student demonstrations in the capital, and if I'd have an opportunity to talk to them. It would have been pleasant to sit here and talk.

But my fifteen minutes were soon up. I went outside. The snow fell more thickly. The wind cut like ice. They made me wish I could have spent the night in the cafe. Still, it was not far to Zimstern's from here, I remembered. I began to walk. The taxi was gone. I walked, looking into windows, at snow-covered coats-of-arms carved into door lintels, at the traditional signs hanging over doorways. I wondered if the fat, bald man was anywhere about. It would do no harm to confuse the trail. I turned as quickly as the icy sidewalk would allow into a dark alley, then cut into another. I thought that Zimstern's street lay around the corner. I chose a dark angle of ancient doorway and buttressed cornice to stop, and looked back along the empty street behind me, a ghostly thoroughfare spotted with pools of orange light that seeped through falling snow. No one was there. I rounded the corner. I didn't recognize the street at all. Well, if not that corner, then the next; I was sure of that. But the next corner and the next and the one after that were all unfamiliar, and I could see no trace of the secretive doorway, shuttered window and the peeling letters of the antique dealer's sign. Well, if I had made too many right turns, a few left turns would mend the situation. I went on in the face of thickening snow that piled ramparts and glittering white mounds against the silent walls, through empty alleys that looked like all the other alleys, and soon the street lights began to thin out and disappear, spreading long corridors of blackness before me. I stopped, then, knowing that I was hopelessly lost.

Well, what now? The cold cut through my furs. My feet were numb and my ears seemed on fire. So much for masking trails, confusing pursuers. I swore. I felt like an idiot. To hell with it! I would find my way into the light of a major avenue, flag down the first cab in sight and have myself taken back to the hotel. Whatever my talents as a foreign agent, finding my way about a foreign city—at night and in a snowstorm—wasn't one of them. I'd telephone all the Ferdynand Zimsterns in the morning until I found the right one, whether he liked it or not, and have him send my briefcase to the hotel. At least, I thought, disgusted, I couldn't lose my way in the dining room. I went on. But now the storm settled above the city and threw down mountain-loads of snow into the dark, empty canyons of the streets. The gaunt, lifeless houses suggested wartime ruin, left like the ghetto as a monument to terror. I had no idea in what direction I was going. I peered at tall, drab houses in what might have been a working class district, an abandoned slum. There'd be no workers living here now. Who would? As if in sudden answer, I realized that there were men about: singly and in small, silent groups in the black tunnels that led to the inner courts of the ancient tenements; unsmiling men wrapped in shabby cloth, switching their eyes away as I passed the doorways. I tried to hurry, feeling more and more flat stares centering on my back, cursing my damn stupidity; each alley grew darker, narrower and seemed to take me deeper into the menacing quarter. And then I knew that I was no longer alone among the silent buildings; a man in a shabby leather coat had detached himself from a black doorway behind me, and another man in what looked like a broken military cap fell into step with me across the street. Both men turned where I turned, stopped when I stopped, hurried when I hurried.

Sweat soaked through all my clothes. I had to get out of this maze of alleys into the light, among decent people. Now Leather Coat was closer, coming faster, and Military Cap was gone. Where was he? Had he taken a shortcut to head me off? Street followed street, all dark, all narrow, all alike. I peered into alleys for the bright, saving glare of an avenue at the other end, and heard the quickening pad of footsteps crunching behind me in the snow, and turned one more corner under a blown-out streetlamp into a street I seemed to know—still narrow, dark and silent, housing secrets, but incomparably broader than the others—and there like a beacon at a harbor mouth was the sign with the peeling letters. I stopped there and looked back. The dim forms of the two men halted at the border between light and darkness, then withdrew.

I laughed, enormously relieved, and waited to recover both my breath and composure. It had been a narrow escape but now I was safe. The bright light of a lamp directly in front of the antique dealer's door gave warmth to the unpopulated distance of the street. I saw a fleeting gleam of light between the wooden shutters. Zimstern was still up. I stepped up to the door and knocked.

When no one answered, I pushed the door open, wondering with mild annoyance why the conspiracy-minded dealer never locked his doors, and went inside, calling out for Zimstern.

This time no one blinded me with flashlights. But I saw the pencil-thin stream of another light along the bottom edge of the office door at the far side of the deepest shadows. I slammed

89

the street door and shouted Zimstern's name in the sudden darkness. The light from the streetlamp was now locked outside. No one came in reply to my calls. Perhaps Zimstern was out. But then, I thought, suddenly uneasy, why was the door unlocked? I called again and this time the sound of my own voice disturbed me in that still and unresponsive darkness. I stepped carefully through the dark, object-littered store, feeling my way along dusty tables, brushing the cold shoulders of suits of armor, like empty husks of petrified dead men. Then I was at the door of Zimstern's little office. I pushed it open and stepped into light.

Afterward, it seemed to me that I saw everything at once: the old and the new, the discarded and the usefully familiar: a man's jacket and vest draped over a chair; a folding cot piled with tangled bedding; the suitcase and the flat brown hat; the open desk and books and ledgers and the small, oddly deflated figure sitting at the desk. The gray, balding head was cradled in its arms between the ancient inkwell and the miniature Copernican globe.

"Mr. Zimstern?"

There was no answer; I knew there wouldn't be one. I felt curiously detached, as if the dead man had nothing to do with me, as if he were no more real and no more a man than the empty suits of armor in the store behind me.

I looked from him to the telephone receiver swinging on its cord, buzzing with the insistent hum of distant wires. The soft smoke of a cigarette curled out of the ashtray.

None of this seemed to mean anything to me; I couldn't believe it. I had never seen a corpse before, never bothered to imagine what a corpse might look like. The dead were ancient: potters who had shaped Byzantine amphorae, painters of parchment with papyrus reeds. I looked at this modern corpse, wondering why I didn't even feel curiosity; to feel curious seemed to be the least I could do. Obviously, the man had been alive only recently. There was the evidence of the cigarette laid only shortly before in the ashtray. How long ago? A minute? Two? How long does it take for a quarter of an inch of ash to form in an ashtray? There was the softly humming telephone still swinging off the hook. Whom had Zimstern been calling the moment he was killed? To whom had he been talking when he died? It didn't seem to matter. And who had killed him? Why? That seemed to matter even less. The wispy hair that had given Zimstern a look of perpetual panic lay across the black, polished rectangle of familiar leather.

Time passed. The drone of the hanging telephone receiver sounded like a far-off hive full of aggravated bees. My brain came gradually alive and accepted the unacceptable evidence of the corpse and briefcase that the dead man clutched with such desperate affection. It was my new briefcase, that unexpected gesture from Hubertus Pohl. With this thought came awareness; dispassionate coldness vanished. I had to get away at once before someone found me with the corpse; I would never be able to explain what I was doing here.

I felt a violent aversion against touching the dead man. But, damn it, why not? He was dead, he wouldn't mind. I took a cautious grip on the edge of the briefcase and began to pull it from under the dead man's head. The balding head moved with the case. The dead hands clung to it. They wouldn't let go. I got out a handkerchief and wiped my face with it. I stared at the dead man. The deflated face had turned toward me while I tugged gently at the briefcase and now one wide, strangely bulging eye regarded me with astonished outrage. The mouth was ajar, showing yellow teeth. The dead wrists showed the pinpoint scabs of fleabites. Small black specks like animated, frantic punctuation marks leaped among the papers scattered on the desk.

Fleas, I thought, astonished.

I had never seen a flea. I found myself frantically wiping my hands with my handkerchief, then threw it on the floor, then backed away from the frenzied asterisks as far as I could, then jumped as a spearpoint pricked me in the back. A rack of halberds tilted like a hedge of spears against one of those cavalry charges Sempinski wrote about, brought me up short.

I caught sight of my face in a mocking mirror: a shocked, disgusted grimace in an ornate frame.

I turned once more toward the desk and, suddenly, stood still. There had been no sound in the cavernous store, nothing to suggest that anyone else was there, but I was sure that I was not alone. I felt the cold certainty of danger, the inexplicable knowledge. Later, I could never tell how I knew or even what I felt; there were the frozen senses and the racing brain, the urge to shout, the crawling scalp and all the other signs. Someone was watching me. Who? It made no difference. Thieves, spies, police spies . . . they were all the same. Danger was the same. The watching man was the murderer. It was so obvious that I didn't know how I could have missed it. The murder was so fresh that the murderer wouldn't have had the time to get away. The murderer was still here.

Well, all right, I thought. The murderer's still here. What will he do? If I just tried to leave, would he let me go? Why not? I hadn't seen him, wouldn't be able to identify him. But supposing he didn't want to leave? He might think I'd bring the police down on him.

I forced myself to move toward the desk. I looked in the mirror. The mirror faced the open office door and reflected darkness. Nothing moved in the mirror or in the store but I thought I could hear a man's heavy breathing. Imagination, of course. Where would he be hiding? Back by the street door would be the best place. Out of those dark corners he'd be able to see most of the back room: a narrow aisle formed by the crates, bales, junk, spears and halberds that penned me between the desk and the cot. Like shooting carp in a pool. Well, there's no help for it, I thought. Must get the light out. How? Knock the lamp over and duck, and hope the fellow hadn't brought a flashlight. Maybe he wouldn't want to use a flashlight anyway; it would give him away. Once the light's gone he'll know I'm on to him. Then he'll come after me. He'd come after me anyway, with or without a light, so might as well make it difficult for him . . . even things up a bit. He knows where I am, I can only guess where he might be. But he can't move through that junkpile without making noise. He must be made to move. Meanwhile, I'll keep still. He'll have to do some guessing himself. That makes it almost fair.

I sighed, as if resigned to a long session with the scattered papers on the dead man's desk. I took off my furs, glad of the dark suit that would help to hide me once the light was out. Now, how to play my hand? It didn't seem likely that I would be able to outmaneuver the murderer and get to the street. And had I guessed the killer's intentions? I had to assume that I had. Very well. I thought over what my tactics were going to be. The agility learned in fencing lessons, silence and a cool head were all that I could pit against the other man. I wouldn't have a dog's chance unless I worked out a plan and stuck to it.

I had the advantage of the first move, provided I moved soon, but that advantage would be gone as soon as the move was made. I didn't worry about weapons for the moment. My best chance lay in outthinking the killer, forcing him to play into my hands and disarming him by making him strike only second blows. He had to come to me when I was ready for him. I had the tactical advantage of interior lines. I could reckon on the man to feel out if he was up against firearms, then to work his way carefully through the dark maze of the littered store and then to try to force me into breaking cover. He was somewhere between me and the outside door and he'd be careful to stay on that line. One way or another, he had to be kept moving. Unless he was the man who slept on the cot, he wouldn't know the geography of the store any better than I. All that seemed sound enough. I'd play the rest according to the way the game developed.

I stooped over the desk, measuring the distance to the cot; I'd dive for that as soon as the light went out. I was no longer concerned about fleas and dead men. All my attention was on the hidden man. And then I heard two slow, careful sounds of metal scraping metal: the bolts on the door. I hadn't reckoned on the door being bolted. Well, anyway, so much for the murderer's intentions. The contest would take place inside the store.

And now I heard the soft sigh of a sleeve brushed against furniture. The killer was coming. The game had started. Let's get on with it. I seized the lamp and threw it on the floor.

The bulb exploded. In that narrow space it sounded like a cannon. I dived. I heard the hiss of air rushing over my head, the sharp crack of the exploding mirror and ringing of glass shards. I inched across the floor on my belly, as a last shard of glass slipped out of the mirror and shattered behind me. At once there came a soft *ping,* like a hushed guitar string, and a projectile flew past me, low enough to hit me but wide of the mark, and struck against metal. Metal on metal, I was sure of that. Thrown with incredible power. Then from the darkness of the store came another ping and the whisper of the hurled projectile was loud in my ear.

What the devil was it? A mild ping and a gentle whisper. But the crash of the projectile against the brick wall settled all doubts about velocity. Some sort of catapult? A crossbow? Something automatic. Judging by the havoc the whispering missiles were causing behind me, they struck with the force of an elephant gun. And they came low! The killer had clearly anticipated my position; he was down on the floor, shooting at shin level. And that changed everything. I had to move fast. I hadn't thought of anything like this. At a cost of an initial slow-up, the killer had won the interior lines. His misses were so close that I felt them rushing past like miniature express trains. They smashed stone statuary, clanged into a cast iron head of Napoleon Bonaparte and sent it thundering down, heavy as an anvil, to the floor.

I started getting ready to jump up. I had already got my hands flat against the floor and drawn a leg under me, when a soft, slipping sound came from the direction of the desk. I didn't know what it was; perhaps the dead man had sagged against the briefcase. But the killer's response was immediate: two shots pinged and hissed and struck flesh with the nightmare sound of wet clay hit with a croquet mallet, and the dead man spilled out of his chair with a wooden clatter. And then the dead man sighed. I had heard about this kind of thing: air trapped in the inner cavitites, leaving a corpse long after death. The sigh became a gurgle, then expired.

The silence went on for what seemed all of a half hour. I didn't dare to stir. I prayed that the killer would think he had hit me and would come in to see if I needed finishing off. He made no move. He watched and listened, as I watched and listened. I couldn't understand what was holding him up. The sound of pierced flesh, the sigh and the gurgle, had been unmistakable but the killer's waiting indicated a doubt in his mind. This was clearly an old hand at the ambush game.

And then a floorboard creaked just outside the door. I had become accustomed to the darkness enough to spot the shadow of the man against the infinitesimally lighter background of the store. He came on cautiously. Something was puzzling him. He seemed to sniff the air. Then, all at once, he made up his mind. He stepped into the room and I charged him from the ground with a speed and force I wouldn't have believed, feeling my shoulder smash into the small of a lean, muscular back, hearing the sharp, short cry as the man was thrown into the desk and as he fell over the chair in a cascade of papers.

I was out of the door and running through the store in moments with plaster busts and furniture scattering behind me. I had to reach the street door before the killer recovered his senses. I didn't think I'd have time to get into the street. Getting the door un-bolted would be enough for now. Everything depended on how quickly the murderer could get himself disentangled. I found the bolts and drew them, hearing furniture clattering in the back room, and something smashed against the door with a force that numbed me. I scurried among crates, trying to keep quiet. Then I stretched out behind a bale of carpets and struggled to control my breath.

Resting, I took stock. The honors seemed even. Perhaps I even had a bit of an edge. At some risk to himself, the killer had found out that I was unarmed and still very much alive. He'd also watch out for surprises from now on. On the other hand, I was out of the box, with better cover and space for maneuver, I had got between the killer and the outside door, and I had drawn the bolts.

But, for the first time, I realized that there would be no quick end to the duel. I had gained stalking-space, true, and I had turned the tables on the murderer and I had got back my interior lines, but the door was still as good as barred as long as that pinging, whispering cannon could be brought to bear. The weapon gave the killer a permanent advantage. He could keep me pinned down until daylight came and robbed me of my only shield.

I needed time to put together a new plan of action. It was no longer enough to keep the other man on the move, wasting ammunition. It was pointless to try guessing how many more deadly pings-and-whispers he was good for. The weapon was a mystery. The duel had to be forced to conclusion before daylight. That meant that the killer had to be enticed within reach of whatever weapon I could devise. Evasion and delay were no longer the point.

I wondered if I could be cold-blooded enough in the final moment to go through with murder. There was no way to tell. The idea was so alien that I couldn't fit it into any conception I had of myself. But I wasted no time questioning the morality of what I had to do. I knew that I should be frightened and fought against resignation and an acceptance of defeat. That way lay disaster. I prayed that my nerves would serve me just a little longer. The killer had me, unless I kept a tight grip on myself.

How did the killer see it? What would be the last thing he'd expect? He didn't know that I was changing the rules of the game.

I had to bait an irresistible trap. I had to make him think that my nerves had gone and I no longer knew what I was doing. It wasn't that far from the truth, anyway. He had to think that he had me boxed again, and there had to be only one way for him to reach me. Knowing the axis of attack would be my one advantage. I wouldn't get more than one chance to strike. That meant the back room again, the only site for ambush where the killer wouldn't be able to come in from any angle he chose.

I took off my shoes and lined them up with pointless care behind my bale of carpets. Time seemed to slide into a new order. Everything slowed down. Each of my movements unfolded with dreamlike precision. My hands and knees had begun to tremble. I couldn't control them. A deep breath would help but I couldn't risk it. I heard a sound in the street but I didn't bother to identify it; it seemed to have no relation to time and myself.

I stepped away from my protecting rampart of carpets and crates. I wasn't sure of my bearings in the darkness. I had the uneasy feeling that the killer knew what I was up to. Nervous laughter threatened to shake me apart. Shippe the Antiquities Consultant and Shippe the Hunter found each other hysterically foolish. I had to stop and recover control over myself. My eyelids seemed to weigh a pound apiece. My nerves were finally going, there wasn't much time left. Sound reached me through a filter.

The killer was on the move to my right, about midway between the office and the out ide door. He made no attempt to keep quiet, advertising confidence. But there was something not quite right about the way the killer was acting. His movements made no sense but they had a pattern. He seemed to be circling in the middle of the room. The closer he got to the back room the less noise he made.

This could have been an attempt to lure me out of whatever ambush I might have prepared. I thought that was likely. The killer was playing right into my hands.

I went on, step by step with agonizing caution, until my hands found the hard edge of the office door. My knees sagged then, and the killer charged me.

I knew in one shocked moment of paralyzing truth that I had walked into the perfect trap. The murderer was on me in three leaps, coming straight down the path he had cleared while I had been wondering how to draw him out. Everything else he had done had been a diversion.

He came in with a shout. One hand crushed my throat, the other swept up. And then the street door flew open and a black shape launched itself into the store in a flood of light, and I had time to see the long colorless face a foot from my own jerking around in astonishment and rage, the upraised hand with its black, metal cylinder suspended over my head. The charging shape struck us both and I flew backward into the back room. I hit the wall with the top of my skull.

I struggled back to consciousness in a bitterly cold wind that swept through the store. The street door was open. My head was full of anvils. The light from the streetlamp hurt my eyes.

I got up and focused my eyes. The office was a shambles of scattered junk and papers. Broken glass and plaster crunched underfoot when I pushed myself away from the wall. Zimstern was stuffed into a narrow crevice between his desk and the rack of halberds. The killer was gone.

It had been Brown, the man whom I had seen in Pohl's anteroom and later with Lindstrom, and whose plainsman's hat I had failed to identify on the cot in the office. I could still see that dead-white face and reptilian eyes, and feel the fingers tightening on my throat.

I began to cough. The effort sent me staggering into the cold wind sweeping through the store. Snow had begun to form mounds inside the open door. I closed the door and bolted it, then went back to the little office, righted the lamp and tried to turn it on. It took me some time to remember that I had smashed the bulb. But I had a lighter. By its light I found a candle end. I lit the candle and sat back on a moldering pile of old books and closed my eyes. I began to tremble.

And then I heard the groan.

At first I couldn't understand what it was; then I saw a dark form on the floor. It was a man, the fat, bald man, my guardian angel, the polished skull no longer a symmetrical pink egg but a crushed red shell. The eyes were open. The eyelids trembled in the light of the candle. A drunken, bubbling voice brought out a word in English.

"What did you say?"

"Tell . . ."

"What?"

"Tell . . ."

And then a name.

"What was that? Chafield? Was that it?"

"Tell . . ." And then with dreadful clarity: "Dr. Shippe . . ."

"Who are you?"

But the bulging eyes were no longer blinking. The fat man was dead.

I took my candle end back into the small room. The first of my two corpses regarded me indifferently from the narrow cavity where Brown's missiles had thrown him. I righted the chair and sat down in it, and put my elbows on the desktop and my hands around my head. Afterward, I supposed that I had sat there as long as an hour. It took me at least that long to pull myself more or less together. The drowned voice of the fat man bubbled in my ears.

I went through the rest of it in a mindless dream, retrieving the briefcase, brushing it absentmindedly, unable to remember what it was that I wanted to brush off.

Light caught a gleaming object on the floor. I picked up a small dart, no bigger than a woman's ball-point pen, the kind sold chained to matchbox-sized address books. I wondered what it was. One like it had gone right through Napoleon's iron skull. Then I found the pistol. I supposed that Brown must have dropped it in his struggle with the fat man. It was the strangest pistol I had ever seen: a dull, black cylinder about eighteen inches long, with the muzzle narrowed by concentric black rings to the diameter of the dart. Two bright tubes ran under the barrel into the oval handle. Unthinking, I pulled the trigger. At once there came the familiar ping, the weapon jerked a fraction of an inch, and across the store a suit of armor clanged, toppled and fell over.

I threw the gun and dart into the briefcase. I was too tired to know what I was doing. I knew that I should try to identify the fat man but that meant going through his pockets, and that was too much. I wanted nothing more to do with corpses. The last thing I remembered was to find my shoes. Eventually, I got into my furs and went into the street, carrying the briefcase.

The snow still fell as thick as frozen oatmeal, but the storm had subsided. I headed up the street toward the Market Square. In no time I began to lose momentum and strength; each step became an individual engineering project. The inner slowing down, that had begun while I was circling my invisible adversary in the store, became complete. I had to stop and rest in the icy wind after each dozen steps. The snowdrifts became insurmountable. And then, as I was at the point of final resignation, the thin sound of the sleigh bell approached me from behind, and there was the familiar sleigh, the ubiquitous sad horse and the old man with the oilskin cap and frosted whiskers. A small voice at the back of my exhausted brain began to question the coincidence of the sleigh, always magically appearing when I needed it, but I refused to give it any thought. I had none left to give.

I didn't know then, or ever afterward, how and when I had got to my room that night. The elevators had shut down at midnight. The night-clerk handed me a key and a letter and told me something about visitors. Somebody was waiting. All I could think of **with** any clarity was bed and oblivion.

ten

THE MAN who waited for me in my room, and rose politely as I entered, was the Nakomda officer who had questioned me at the airport.

I didn't recognize him at first in civilian clothes. The surprise was perfect. But I hadn't the energy to make a response.

I struggled out of my furs, wondering if he'd give me time to get them on again when he arrested me. Arrest would bring the night and the whole impossible adventure to a logical conclusion. But he did nothing threatening. He sat back comfortably in my sole armchair and lit a cigarette.

He said: "You're quite the night-owl, Doctor, aren't you?"

I didn't reply. He smiled and began to inspect the glowing coal of his cigarette.

He said: "I've come to have a talk. No, don't look alarmed. You're not on trial and I didn't come to trap you into anything. But I don't have much time so don't waste it with protestations of innocence. Believe me, if you were a candidate for an NKD cell no protestations would help you."

I started brushing the sleeves of my coat. My hands were still trembling but I thought that I might have them soon under control. The Nakomda man was careful not to look at me, a nicety

I didn't understand. He spoke in a relaxed, amused voice as if to give me time to pull myself together.

"When my department wants someone behind bars, it doesn't send its district deputy commander to spend half the night in the victim's room. Let me tell you how it's done; a tip for the future. There are four men. Don't ask me why; the reasoning behind this mystic figure is too complicated. But we, the Soviet MVD and the East German Abteilung always send four men. Your FBI uses two, with two in reserve. The Gestapo used three. Each country has its own pet theory on how many men it takes to put one frightened man in jail. In Mexico, I understand, it's ten to a victim. The favorite time is two hours before dawn. A man isn't likely to kick up a fuss when he is tangled up in bedclothes. And the last two hours of the night are supposed to be the time of the deepest sleep. Psychologists call it the nadir of oblivion. A man is helpless then. It takes most men twenty minutes to reach full consciousness if they are awakened at that point. Believe me, it's all been statistically computed. Thus you would have four visitors two hours before dawn. You would be given exactly three minutes to dress. That means no more than shoes, overcoat and hat; there is a psychological advantage to questioning a man dressed in a nightshirt. You would be taken to a small black car. It's always a small, black car. You would be in the interrogation room long before your twenty minutes of confusion were up. No one would chat with you in your room, as I am doing. Talk gives a suspect time to get his wits together. And it's an international principle with security policemen to have their victims as witless as possible. Silence suggests that the arresting agency knows everything. The victim feels helpless. Helplessness means terror. And without terror, Doctor, even your FBI would be no more than a society of muscular young lawyers. So, you see, you're not going to be whisked off to Siberia. I'm here to talk business without witnesses, stenographers or electronic gadgets. And I made sure this room isn't wired. I know what to look for."

I was done then with my hat and coat. I turned from the

closet. But the Nakomda man still kept his eyes off me. He was staring out of the window with quiet concentration, his fingers drumming a military march on the arm of the chair.

Very well, I thought. So the surprises of the night are not over yet. The stalking game goes on. My hands still trembled slightly. I put them in my pockets and sat down on the bed.

The officer nodded, whistling soundlessly. His face was turned, as if to invite a study of the sharply carved profile, the thick black hair with a touch of gray, the small-pored, dusky skin. It was a lean, ascetic face but the eyes were cynical and the line of the lip suggested consciousness of power. I thought that he was, probably, the most dangerous man I had ever seen. Despite all efforts I felt my pulse quicken.

He said quietly, softly: "Where were you tonight? At Zimstern's? There is hardly anywhere else that you could have been. He told me you had left your papers at his place so I suppose you went to get them, since you have your briefcase. I wish you'd stay put and follow instructions. You really make it difficult to keep you out of jail."

I blessed my slow reflexes, my exhausted brain. But even so, I started to mumble an incoherent protest. The officer cut me short.

"Please, Dr. Shippe; I have no time for amateur dramatics. I appreciate your conventional terror, but I must really get on with our business. Zimstern was my man, although I had recently begun to suspect he had other employers. He was connected with Karpovitch, which is how Karpovitch comes into this business."

I said: "What business? I . . . don't know what you're talking about."

The Nakomda man made an impatient gesture.

"I am the man who is selling you the Romanowski Library."

This time all I could do was to shake my head. I was lost and I knew it, but the knowledge seemed far less terrible than its anticipation. The main thing was to make no admissions, no matter what the Nakomda man said to reassure me.

"I had hoped to stay in the background," he continued. "But Zimstern's death makes that impossible."

I said: "Who is Zimstern?"

The Nakomda man gave me a look which was frankly bored.

"Still clowning, eh? I know he is dead because he was talking to me on the telephone at the precise moment that he was killed. He had told me all about your visit to the lodge."

It was my turn to shrug. The less I said the better. The Nakomda officer went on:

"You've heard of General Danilow?"

"Never," I said.

"You're a rotten liar. The general was my uncle. During the war, under the German occupation, he was a leader of our resistance movement."

I shrugged again as if to imply that none of this had anything to do with me.

"I led a small and highly irregular group of partisans," my visitor continued. "In one of my more successful actions I inherited the Romanowski Library."

"A handsome inheritance," I said. He laughed.

"Since there were no legal heirs left alive an accidental heir seemed as good as any."

Carefully, I asked: "What did your uncle think about all that?"

He grinned with sudden candor.

"My dear uncle, whose motives were always noble and impractical, didn't know anything about my inheritance. Needless to say I didn't advertise my windfall. I admit I had some patriotic notions about restoring the Library to the nation but fortunately common sense prevailed."

I said cautiously: "How fortunate for you."

"Yes," he said. "Wasn't it? The war soon took a course which meant the end of the old order in this part of Europe. Men like my uncle chose exile. I chose a connection with the source of power. But life at the source of power tends to be unstable; the competition is rather intense."

"And now it's getting a bit too much for you?"

"Not yet, dear Doctor. But from the beginning I could foresee a time when warmer climates would be more appealing. I took steps, some of them quite painful, to ensure that I became the only man who knew that my inheritance had survived the war."

"Are you telling me that you're planning to defect to the West?"

He was hugely amused.

"Wouldn't that be silly?"

I said: "I don't know what you'd consider silly."

"Defection is silly. You merely trade one hopeless situation for another. No, I have better plans. About a year ago I realized that the time for my retirement was approaching quicker than I had expected. Something quite critical was beginning to happen. My instinct for survival has always been remarkable. I decided to part with my inheritance and put out the necessary feelers."

"And is this one of them?"

He laughed, elaborately at ease.

"Well, you ought to know. I used Zimstern whom I knew in my official capacity as a fairly harmless Western agent. I also used my uncle."

I said, feeling danger near: "I thought you said his motives were noble."

"Nothing but the noblest. I convinced him that our national treasure should be sold on patriotic grounds."

It was my turn to laugh but the Nakomda man didn't take offence.

"You don't see it, do you. The Library has been more than just a treasure to the people here. It has been a symbol, and we tend to set high value on symbols in this part of the world. For many people it has a deeply religious meaning. For others it's a relic of this country's history. I convinced my uncle that the Library wasn't meant to be hidden from the world. The relic, if you like, had to find a setting in a country where it could continue its symbolic role."

I said: "And so America? A strange choice for you."

His yawn was ostentatious but his voice remained bland.

"Did I sound as if I didn't care for America? My error. I

wouldn't like to live there but I enjoy my visits. And anyway it was my uncle's reaction that mattered."

"So it was he who wanted the Library sent to America," I said.

He nodded. "Look at it this way. The presence of this symbol in a country is enough for many of our people to look upon that country as a kind of shrine: the home of faith, courage, decency and justice. D'you get the idea? Men like my uncle want America to have that kind of image."

"Why would they?"

"In order to maintain a spirit of resistance. If there were no difference between the moralities of the West and of the East why should anyone struggle over here? It wasn't difficult to show my uncle that the installation of our symbol in America would turn that country into a sort of Holy place. A Mecca where the faithful could address their prayers."

"And he fell for that?"

The Nakomda man shrugged contemptuously.

"He was an idealist."

I thought that my adversary's purpose was quite clear then: to goad me into a damaging admission. I struggled to show no sign of my awareness. If this were some extraordinary, devious trap, as it seemed to be, it was being laid with a master's cunning. Even the tone of the revelations was right for the job: cynics are always more convincing than moral enthusiasts.

Sooner or later the angle of attack would suggest itself. Until it did there was little I could do.

I said: "What happened to your uncle?"

The Nakomda man didn't reply immediately. He stared out of the window with intense ferocity, drumming a military march on the arm of his chair, then said coldly:

"He was killed. He came to see me here last autumn to verify that the Library existed. Somehow . . . I don't know how . . . he was betrayed and killed."

"Who killed him?"

"It wasn't my colleagues, if that's what you're thinking. If

106

the NKD had uncovered his identity I would have been able to protect him. Have you ever heard of The Magician? No? Somehow The Magician is involved in my uncle's death but I haven't been able to get to the bottom of it."

I thought then that the time had come to strike back a little. I wanted my disquietening visitor to know that I, too, had resources for resistance.

I said: "You tell a good story. But I'm not interested in your stories. I want to go to bed."

He said, grinning fiercely: "Your innocence is almost convincing. If I didn't know better I might think that I had made a mistake."

"You did," I said.

He said, amused: "And you've really never heard about The Magician?"

"What's all this nonsense about magicians?"

"It isn't nonsense. The Magician is a very real person. Every intelligence officer in the world has been looking for him . . . at one time or another. He's a sort of private consultant in disaster. I don't like the idea of his connection with any part of our business. It's quite dangerous enough without him."

I said, as calmly as I could: "You're quite an expert on fairy tales, aren't you. Well, what's the rest of your fable?"

"You know the rest. My uncle went back to London, found Lindstrom and died. And here you are."

"And here I am," I said. "And now if you're all done, I'm going to call the embassy. I hope you don't mind?"

He shrugged.

"I don't have much time, Dr. Shippe. Don't waste it with bluffing. Nothing is going to happen to you anyway, if I've a say in it. So just let me finish what I came to say and wait a few days before you shout for help. If Zimstern hadn't been murdered and if I hadn't been obliged to handle the negotiations myself, you would have had no reason for panic. As a realist I can't expect you to trust me. Unfortunately I must make you trust me. Certain events are taking a very dangerous turn and there is no time for gentle parlor games. Tell me this, what in the world made you choose Sempinski for your cover story?"

I said: "Why don't you go home and let me get some sleep?"

"All right, consider that a rhetorical question. Because of your connection with Sempinski, you are under surveillance. I don't know who is watching you. The agents are NKD men from the personal entourage of our General Rauss. Rauss is the head of State Security and a most unpleasant man. God only knows how he survived the de-Stalinization circus we all went through here, but his survival instincts are as good as mine. In fact, they're better. Only Rauss knows what the Sempinski Affair is about; I have no idea."

The Nakomda man crushed his cigarette in the ashtray and immediately lit another, working it into his short, amber holder. He leaned back heavily in the armchair and crossed his legs, and closed his eyes, letting his arm dangle dramatically over the side as if to demonstrate how weary and vulnerable he was. I thought him about as vulnerable as a locomotive.

Despite myself, I had begun to like him. He would have been a personable, utterly believable rogue if there had been one word of truth in what he had said. I couldn't afford to think that he was anything but a clever liar; still, I found myself enjoying his cynical frankness.

Obviously he knew everything about my business in his country. I had to assume, for safety's sake, that this astonishing meeting was part of some Nakomda machinations too complex for me to understand; to trust the man would have been insane.

Oddly enough I didn't feel afraid. My earlier shock and feeling of entrapment had given way to a peculiar calmness that made me almost eager to accept the challenge of the situation. I had made some blustering noises, transparent denials, largely to bolster my own collapsing resolution, but now I thought I could fight back a little. Not that fighting would do me any good if the Nakomda officer was simply amusing himself at my expense. But both my fencing and chess had taught me that a wholly defensive game had little chance of success in the long run. As far as I

108

was concerned, the time had come to invoke the emergency clauses of Pohl's plan; the assignment was too dangerous to continue. Morally, I was free to cut and run. Every instinct dictated a precipitous retreat. There was no hope of help from any quarter here or at home; but a meek surrender was out of the question. Sooner or later some opportunity would present itself.

I began to concentrate on my opponent's moves and, for the first time, quietly advanced a piece of my own.

I said: "You mean this business about Julian Sempinski is too much for you?"

He gave me a curiously appreciative look.

"When Rauss goes to the trouble of throwing a full security screen around something, it's a superb performance. A flea can't squeeze through. I know just enough about the Sempinski Affair to stay as far away from it as I can. In fact it only took one faint whiff of it to convince me that it was time that I became a wealthy coffee planter in Brazil."

"What could a man like Julian Sempinski have done? It doesn't make sense."

"Any conspiracy is the art of the improbable married to the unexpected."

"Maybe you're letting nervous imagination run away with you."

The Nakomda man laughed openly.

"Imagination is my stock in trade. How do you suppose one survives in my kind of jungle? Instinct and good reflexes are the first requirements of an intelligence officer. But in this case I do have a little more to go on. What counts, though, is to make sure you keep your nose out of Rauss's sticky little business. I have no intention of missing out on three million dollars simply because you blunder into something that's too much for even the best professionals. We have to move quickly on our deal. The time's just about up. Unfortunately, your involvement with Sempinski, and Rauss's interest in you, make quick moves sheer suicide. You would lead Rauss straight to me . . . and that is something I wouldn't enjoy."

"Then why did you take the chance of coming to see me?"

"It's not as big a chance as you think. Give me the credit for some expertise. But I don't intend to come near you again. Your next contact will be through that poor, unfortunate little girl you refrigerated. She is something of a friend of mine, though not as dear a friend as she might suppose. Still, she can be trusted for the moment."

I said: "You forget that I don't know what you are talking about."

He smiled. "And you forget that your life depends on my interest in you. I can't afford to lose you until you send a certain telegram from Stockholm. I will protect you as long as I can, provided you do exactly what you're told. But if you put me in the position of choosing between the life of a Brazilian millionaire and a penniless exile, I will be the most high-minded exile you have ever heard of. The only reason I'm still trying to shovel some sense into your head is that I would rather write checks than manifestos. Is that clear so far?"

I nodded and said that his words were clear.

"And just in case you have doubts about our General Rauss, let me say that he had his training in the good old days, in Russia and in China . . . when they threw people into locomotive boilers. Don't ever fall into his hands. If you do, I will have to kill you before you can talk. So I have this advice for you: Make no effort to contact Sempinski. Don't visit him, don't receive him if he visits you, don't write to him and don't accept his letters. Have nothing to do with him or with anyone who is sent by him. Don't underestimate Rauss since he is totally beyond your comprehension. And don't underestimate me."

I said that a threat of murder was hardly the basis for trust.

"Nonsense," he said. "I have nothing against you, and every interest in keeping you alive. I am even willing to respect you as an intelligent and courageous man. I know your type. I've known Americans like you. I also know that you are probably stubborn; once you start something, you want to finish it. You'll take my warning for a Nakomda trick; in your position I would do the same. But don't stir from the capital where I can protect you. If you go near Sempinski you are a dead man."

Then he got up, yawned, stretched, rubbed his graying temples with a slow, gentle circular motion of long fingers, looked at the graying light outside the window, picked up his hat and coat, and left.

I collapsed on the bed.

Escape was the answer.

Zimstern was dead. Brown was the murderer. He had come within a fraction of a second of murdering me too. With two murders to conceal he'd probably try to get at me again. And the Nakomda knew about the Library.

In formal spy language, I was burned—finished. The various hounds were in full cry. All that was left was to run for my life. I had never been on the run before; I hadn't the first idea of how to go about it. And where was I to run?

The first thought was: the airport and home. But if the Nakomda were after me, and I had every reason to suppose they were, I'd never get past Passport Control. All legal ways out of the country would be closed to me.

I could hardly expect gentle treatment at the embassy if the criminal police demanded my surrender for questioning in a sordid, back-alley murder case. The Nakomda would see to it that I was implicated.

That left Sempinski, an old revolutionary who knew all about illegal border crossing, who had the necessary wisdom and experience and the rare humanitarian impulse of his disappearing kind. Maybe Sempinski was my only answer.

This much I knew: I could no longer stay in the capital where either Brown or the secret police could get to me at leisure.

I tore open the envelope that the clerk had handed me downstairs and read the hastily typed invitation to come at once to Sempinski's home near the southern mountains. Sempinski even suggested the train I might take: the crack Prague Express that left the capital at seven in the morning.

I didn't hesitate. I put one suit, a pair of slacks, a sweater and three shirts into my smallest suitcase. I threw in the darts and the pistol. I thought I would be able to find an opportunity to get rid of this evidence in the country.

Money and documents went into the briefcase. Everything else would keep where it was. I wasn't abandoning anything that couldn't be replaced once I was safely back on my side of the Iron Curtain.

PART THREE

The Sempinski Affair

eleven

SEMPINSKI'S MAN was to meet me at the Corn Exchange, an easy landmark in the heart of the ancient border city where I had left the train. I bought a picture postcard of this relic of the Middle Ages to show to my cab driver and, eventually, found myself outside a cafe that fronted the cloisters—an old place with bulging windows covered by steam. I would have liked to go in, out of the cold, but I was afraid of upsetting Sempinski's arrangements. I waited on the cobbled sidewalk, looking at passing cars. The wind was like a blade of ice laid along my neck. Time passed but I wasn't worried; I had followed my host's typed instructions to the letter; sooner or later someone would pick me up. And if we should miss connections I would always be able to hire some kind of transportation to Sempinski's famous estate near the mountains which, even on this gloomy afternoon, I could see towering in clouds to the south. In a few hours I'd be with Sempinski.

As far as I was concerned, the Library conspiracy was over. To go on with it, even if I had known how to pick up the broken threads, was suicide with the Nakomda in full possession of the facts. Even Pohl would understand this, after a suitable period of mourning for his lost commission. Besides, I wasn't sure that the whole affair hadn't been some intricate Communist attempt

113

to capture world headlines. I remembered Potter's warnings about the satellites' restlessness and need for some unifying incident. I wondered if the Library affair would have been enough to cause the necessary indignation. It seemed a little weak but then I wasn't a Communist theoretician.

Anyway, faked or on the level, I was through with it. The deal was off and I was going home: to apple logs in my fireplace, Mahler, the chess and the sherry, and Zungfest's goulash. That was enough to make me feel content.

The chill awoke my hunger. I remembered that I had eaten nothing since the night before. So much had happened since that first dinner in the capital: treasures and corpses and secret policemen and my escape from it all . . . I couldn't quite believe that all that had been crowded into only two nights and a day. I wondered about the connection between Brown and Zimstern. What was Lindstrom's henchman doing with Karpovitch's agent? What was the link? And who was the bald, fat man (if not a Nakomda man) whom Brown had murdered instead of myself? And what was all that business about The Magician?

Then I remembered that I wasn't going to worry any more about spies, plots, counterplots or secret policemen. That was all in the past; I meant to keep it there. I started looking about eagerly for my transportation to Sempinski's home.

I saw the horses first, probably because I had always liked to see good-looking horses. This was a gray dappled pair pulling a boat-shaped sleigh. Two men were in the sleigh; neither looked particularly reassuring. The driver was a broad, scowling peasant in a tall fur hat, hugging himself against the sharp bite of the wind in a long sheepskin coat with the wool turned out. Straw spilled out of his sleeves like the stuffing from a ruptured scarecrow. The other was a big young man in heavy furs, half buried in the rugs and traveling robes in the back of the sleigh.

They drove past me, staring, and then the young man spoke sharply, gesturing toward me, and the peasant nodded. He brought the sleigh to the curb, stopped and got out, stamping his greased, untanned boots for warmth. The young man shouted and the

114

peasant shrugged and came heavily toward me. He looked me up and down with dull hostility, picked up my suitcase and jerked his head in the direction of the sleigh.

My cheerful optimism slipped a little as I stared at the unfriendly pair. This wasn't a reception that I had expected. I hesitated at the curb. The peasant grew impatient.

"*Kommen sie,*" he said. He spat into the snow.

"Are you from Professor Sempinski?"

"*Ja. Ja.*"

He threw my suitcase into the front of the sleigh. The big young man stirred just enough to make some room for me under the fur robes in the back. His face communicated nothing except arrogance. The sullen peasant and the arrogant young man seemed an odd pair to send after a houseguest.

I asked how far we were going.

The young man's head turned with the deliberate slowness of a clockwork mannequin.

"Far," he said.

"But how far?"

"Four hours. Perhaps five."

"That far? I thought Professor Sempinski lived closer to the city."

The man ignored me. The cold face turned away. He ordered the peasant to start, shouting his quick command in contemptuous German. The peasant flicked his reins, the sleigh moved away from the curb. It was an astonishing reception.

The town slid out from under us, street by street, and soon it fell away altogether. We were in open country, flying down the white highway fenced in by telephone poles and snow-thickened lines of cable, past frozen fields that disappeared in the low gray clouds on either horizon. Small towns and villages went by, woods rose and sank in the unlimited white space.

At first we met other sleighs, wagons and some motor traffic staggering through the snowdrifts, but in an hour the highway was empty. There was no sound then beyond the whistling of the wind, the soft hiss of iron runners on fresh snow and the hard drumming of galloping hoofs.

The white miles went on. But by midafternoon the horizons narrowed into broken country: sudden black walls of rock, ghostly eruptions of old burial mounds, snowsheeted ruins, deep gorges floored by frozen streams, and thickening woods. The road rose and fell. Soon there were no more telephone poles or cables to show that there was a road.

I felt frozen to the bone despite the traveling robes and furs. I watched the black walls of a forest advancing toward the sleigh from either flank. Darkness came with it. The plain constricted. Soon the trees would be upon us, bringing their shadows with them. I watched the shadows, suddenly convinced that my eyes were playing tricks on me. The shadows were moving. They seemed to have a motion and direction independent of the marching treewalls. The shrubs and bushes and black, ragged vegetation had pulled up their roots; they ran in a swift, silent mass under the trees, parallel to the road.

I rubbed my eyes and shielded them from the wind, but they kept lying to me; the loping undergrowth came near with increasing swiftness as the white belt of snow narrowed between the closing walls of the forest.

And then the trees ended, brutally cut off. We were among fields. The dark, running forms spilled out of the forest and into the fields. I heard the long, baying howl.

Wolves!

I didn't believe it.

I turned to the others with astonished eyes but they paid no attention to me. The peasant driver was on his feet in the narrow neck of the sleigh, slashing the air with his braided whip. The young man was methodically loading an automatic shotgun. One of the horses stumbled then, and the driver laid into both of them with cracking leather. They ran with their ears pressed flat against their heads, stretched out like greyhounds in a terrified gallop.

"Uh-ha!" the driver shouted. "Uh-ha!"

The sleigh seemed to lift in the wind. The dark, howling mass came on behind us like black water rushing through a broken dam. White space shrunk before it as if devoured on the run. The deep baying was resonant and clear.

Then both horses stumbled.

The driver caught them up with the reins and his whip cracked like a flurry of rapid pistol shots. The horses recovered. But the white space between the wolves and the flying sleigh had narrowed by a dozen yards. The wolfpack was gaining. Its howl belled with triumph. I could see individual animals forge ahead of the tight, ragged mass: long gray beasts with maniacal eyes, taller than a calf.

Space vanished under us.

Acres fled. The wolves came on swiftly.

"How much farther?"

I had to shout in the big man's ear, my voice torn by the wind. He did not answer, but stretched out in the back of the sleigh and leveled the shotgun and, for a wild moment, I remembered that I too was armed and looked desperately about for my suitcase trying to remember where I had put the pistol and steel dart. But it was too dark to find anything in the wild-swaying sleigh. We were now deep in shadow, among trees.

"Are they gaining on us?"

I could see that the wolves were gaining. They were enormous.

One more stumble from the horses, I thought: That's all it'll take. And what if either horse ploughs into the ground? The rhythm of the hoofbeats had become ragged; I could hear the horses' whistling breath. They were beginning to falter.

Oh God, I thought: this didn't make sense! Sleighs . . . wolves . . . what century was this, anyway? Such things didn't happen any more!

"How much farther?"

The shotgun roared twice in quick succession. A dark shape leaped and tumbled and the pack boiled across it like a convulsed wave. The shrinking white space suddenly expanded. The booming shotgun beat out a steady rhythm. The wolfpack split, milled, and lost ground, then came together again in pursuit. But with each shotgun blast it hesitated long enough to lose a little ground.

Now the big young man laughed.

"You like this? Is that enough for you?"

At first I didn't know if the man was shouting at me or to the wolves. Now I could see what the wolves were up to each time the shotgun knocked one of them over.

And now the horses staggered. The sleigh snapped back and forth across the road like a loaded whip.

"Here they come!"

What happened then was so fast that I couldn't grasp it until it was all over. First there was the narrow white road rising among trees, the driver's heavy back and nodding heads of horses up ahead and the horrible dark mass coming up behind, the rattling breath of horses, the crack of the whip and the booming shotgun. That was all one picture, seen and heard in parts but possessing all the unities; making its own mad sense. And then a dozen individual dramas were being played out at lightning speed with no relation to each other but each possessed a terrible clarity.

A horse screamed and the two madly pumping heads disappeared. The driver shouted in a frantic voice. Trees spun, the lowering black sky revolved. The sleigh swung around so that for one, insane moment it looked as if we were about to charge into the wolfpack. I was down in the bottom of the sleigh, entangled in robes, then up, then down again as the sleigh ran broadside into a kilometer marker buried in the snow. I heard the desperate grating of the iron runners dragged across the stone, a crack of parting boards. Then the sky tilted. It was no longer spinning but hung crazily askew with the shaggy tops of trees spilling across the lower half of it, while the sleigh slid with agonizing slowness back to the road, off the embankment it had climbed after the kilometer stone.

God damn it all to hell, was all I could think of. One horse was down. The other was up on his hind legs, front hooves flaying, throwing himself violently against the leather traces. A broken chain described a lazy arc overhead.

The driver was out of the sleigh, up beside the horses. His whip rose and fell too swiftly to follow in one whistling motion, so that there was no interval between the hiss and the crack of rawhide exploding on horseflesh.

Then the fallen horse was back on his feet and the weight of the sleigh dragged both the horses back onto their haunches. The young man was up in the narrow neck of the sleigh, in the blunted prow, shooting across the horses. The horses were streaked with blood where the shotgun pellets scored their necks and flanks. The shotgun blasts tore long gaps in the dark mass of the milling wolfpack.

And then, as quickly as it had begun, it was all over. The sleigh was on the road, slanting through the snow. The peasant driver was half in, half out of the sleigh, pulling himself up over the side like a swimmer clambering into a lifeboat. The young man was beside me again, in the back of the sleigh, fumbling with shotgun shells. The wolves came behind.

"Can you shoot?"

"What?"

"A pistol, fool! Can you shoot a pistol?"

"Yes!"

Could I? I had never tried it.

"Here!"

And the man threw me a dark, heavy object, and I held it, wondering if I had lost my mind, understanding nothing. There it was, in my hands, with the blue-black metal cylinder tapering in concentric circles at the business end, the oval handle—much too long for pistols—and the silvery rods under the barrel.

"Compressed air!" the young man shouted. "Makes no noise, no recoil. Just aim and squeeze, aim and squeeze. You have thirty rounds."

Aim and squeeze.

Ping! Only there was no ping or whisper this time; the wind picked up those delicate sounds and carried them away. Without

119

the sounds I couldn't tell if the damn thing was working. Aim and squeeze. So Brown had had thirty chances to nail me in the store. How many had he taken? *Ping!* That was two down, twenty-eight to go. Each one good enough to down an elephant. Tore hell out of armor, pierced cast iron heads. *Ping!* Twenty-seven. Brown hit the mirror with his first one; he drilled his cowhide suitcase, that was two; two into poor dead Zimstern, dealer in antiques, junk dealer and Karpovitch's agent, also double agent. Who said he was a double agent? My Nakomda tempter who had also talked about a Sempinski Affair. Aim and squeeze. Twenty-six. What was the story about Brown and Zimstern? *Ping!* Twenty-five to go. I don't believe in coincidences any more. Brown was the man who slept on the cot behind Zimstern's store. He was the man with the blinding flashlight, Zimstern's *unexpected guest.* Nothing to do with our business, Zimstern had said. But what about Karpovitch's business? That meant that Zimstern, Brown, Per Lindstrom and Karpovitch were together in something, and whatever that is I don't want any part of it. Except that (*Ping!* Twenty-four) I'm already in it. And Brown is after me. He would have got me if the fat man hadn't rushed into the store. Poor man, bald head caved-in like an eggshell. He knew my name . . . a dreadful voice but American. Good God, the man had been an American. I've got the accent now, why didn't I catch on then? Who was he? I could have found out if I had searched his pockets. Damn squeamishness, anyway. What the devil had he been doing there? I had thought he was a Nakomda spy but he wasn't, was he? Aim and squeeze, and there goes one of them; I've got the hang of it now. Aim and squeeze. Twenty-two to go. And now the shotgun's going again. *Ping!* Brown had put one into the cast iron, vacant head of the first emperor of the French, a boon to historians. He sent two to my left at shin-level (or what had been my head-level) on the floor, and two to my right, and then three into the outside door while I had been fiddling with the bolts. One, two, then two again, including Napoleon's. Four on the floor and three into the street door. I let one fly when I picked up the thing from beside the dead man. Five, seven and one make thirteen. An omen? Thirteen gone; seventeen still left. I picked up one of the darts in the store. How do you load these things? I've never heard of them; they can't be as common as all that. How did Brown get one? Why did this man have one? Why did they both have one? This man is a German. You don't hurl commands with such an accent unless you're born to it. The peasant's not a German. He hated the German. Hates me too. Probably thinks I'm another German. What's all that about? What's Sempinski doing with a German servant? And if the man's a servant I'll eat my fur hat. A serving German is the most servile servant in the world; ersatz butter wouldn't melt in his mouth. Servant, my suffering aunt! And armed to the teeth. The shotgun is for wolves; very well. But the crazy, futuristic pistol? The silent, secret, armor-piercing pistol is nothing that anybody can pickup in a pawnshop. It's an assassin's weapon. It is a firm connection between Brown and Sempinski's arrogant German servant . . . who is not a servant. It doesn't matter at the moment what he is. As with the splintered drama on the road, everything here was a part of everything else.

Now, everybody that I had come across since that day in Pohl's anteroom was linked and locked solidly together in some mystery that, I knew, had nothing to do with the Romanowski Library. Perhaps there was a Sempinski Affair after all; and perhaps it was as desperately serious as the Nakomda officer had warned me that it was; and perhaps he had been warning me, not laying some complicated trap.

Well, it was too late to think that way now. Wise or not, for good or for evil, I had come . . . I was here. A half hour's talk with Sempinski could clear up everything. Sempinski had asked me to come to his house. He wanted me there. I had come . . . or rather, I was on my way. It was up to the old writer to set his guest at ease. Aim and squeeze.

And that was twenty.

And suddenly it was over.

The narrow white neck of the road sprang open, the trees fell away. The forest vanished. We were on a hill, coming down. Ahead was a plain, the infinite white miles flattened out by distance. Below us lay the black ribbon of a river, glittering with the jagged scales of icefloes like the armored spine of a prehistoric monster. A narrow, wooden bridge pilloried the river. Beyond it were houses: twelve wooden cottages thatched with snow, lined up behind fences, with cartwheels nailed flat on top of wagon tongues set into the gound where storks could come to build their nests in spring, with chimney smoke spreading among the eves; and there were men in the village street. Trees made a black horizon.

We drove across the bridge with the hollow rattle of an express train. The wolves didn't follow.

I lay back against the cloth-and-leather seat in the back of the sleigh, an awkward, ill-designed bench with wrought-iron curlicues for armrests, feeling fatigue settle about me with the danger gone. I didn't really believe that there could have been danger. Relief had made me lightheaded, I supposed. I lay as still as the sleigh would let me, laughing to myself.

Even the German didn't bother me. It was too silly to worry about odd-looking people with odd pistols; road company mysteries. Sooner or later everything would have a logical explanation.

The German took his pistol back. I watched him snap open a tubular magazine in the oval handle and load half a dozen steel darts. His exaltation seemed to have left him as rapidly as it had come. But I thought I had better start someone talking as soon as possible so that some fragment of the truth might suggest itself. I made a comment about the gun being interesting, but he only grunted. Then, with an inspired bit of flattery, I asked: "Is that a German invention?"

He said, with unconcealed pride: "It was designed by Otto Skorzenny himself."

I had, of course, heard of Skorzenny but pretended vagueness. "Let's see . . . wasn't he the German commando leader who rescued Mussolini from an allied prison about the time the war ended?"

The young German treated me to a look that was half pity, half contempt.

"That was nothing for Otto Skorzeny. The allies had the fat Italian hidden on top of the Alps, with twenty thousand men around the mountain. With no way up except by cable car. We crashlanded two dozen men in a glider on top of the mountain. Do you know what a *Fiesler-Storch* is? A small plane. Artillery spotter. Like your Piper Cubs, only better. We put Mussolini in a Storch and dived it off the edge of the mountain. He was shaking hands with Adolf Hitler before the amis knew what had happened. But that kind of thing was just routine for Otto Skorzenny."

"Tell me more about him."

"Why, he invented a whole concept of warfare! He terrorized the whole Anglo-American army with four hundred men! He showed the world what a handful of men can accomplish if they have the audacity and imagination. Nothing is impossible if the coup seems impossible enough!"

"He sounds like quite a man."

"He is a man! Do you know what he did when the Hungarians started getting nervous in 1944? He kidnapped their Regent right out of his own castle in the middle of his own capital! He had the Hungarians back in line before they knew they were supposed to change sides. And what about the Ardennes? You know about that?"

"You mean the Battle of the Bulge?"

"The Rundstedt offensive. If the traitors around Adolf Hitler had only let him do what he wanted he would have won the war! It would have been just like that!"

He snapped his fingers to show how easy it would have been.

"We had the amis running like dogs after their own tails. Four hundred men in ami uniforms changing road signs, spreading rumors, starting panics. Ah, if only we could have got as far as Paris!"

"Paris? What could you have done there?"

"Killed Eisenhower, of course! What else?"

"Ah, of course. What else . . ."

"Listen, you think this is funny? You think that killing Eisenhower wouldn't have stood the Anglo-Americans on their heads? You think the other ami generals wouldn't have started shaking in their boots? They would have been so busy looking under their beds they would have had no time to think about the war. All you need is the audacity for the one great stroke. Cut off your enemy's head, tear out his heart, and what does he have left?"

The German slapped the cylindrical magazine into the pistol butt. It made a quick, conclusive sound.

"One man can change the course of history," he said. "You kill a president or a country's leader and you are telling everybody in the country that nobody is safe. With one shot you have wounded everybody. There is Hysteria. That gives you the necessary Terror. Terrified people don't think. They bite like frightened animals. They bite anything you tell them to bite no matter what happens afterward. For the price of one bullet you have won the world."

"Were you with Skorzenny?"

He hesitated, as if tempted to tell me that he had been, but he could not have been much more than a child when the war had ended.

"I was too young," he said, as if ashamed.

twelve

NIGHT CAME before we stopped outside the iron gates of a walled estate. I was too tired, cold and hungry to pay much attention to surroundings; I wanted to get up to the house, in and out of a bath, into clean clothes and to a dinner table as swiftly as I could. I was uncomfortably aware of my crumpled clothes and wilted linen. Sleep would be good. I hoped Sempinski could spare me some time early in the morning. But I had a moment of uncertainty at the gate; that undefined uneasiness that had served me often in suggesting danger.

A wild moon galloped through ragged black clouds in a spectral sky. It threw its dead white light on turrets and towers, a precipitous moat floored with glaring ice, and the insanity of the flaying tree crowns.

I heard the savage anger of big dogs, then saw them: three coal-black mastiffs hurling themselves against chains.

The horses backed away from the gate, their ears flat. They made mewling sounds. The German laughed. Then two men armed with rifles appeared on the parapet of the crenellated wall. The wall had fallen, in places, into the moat, giving the gray mass of ragged granite the look of a stormed castle after a massacre . . . a kind of haunted starkness. The gate was a giant grille hung on heavy hinges from two flanking towers that were clearly several centuries older than the gate itself. The two men came off the wall to open the gate and pull back the mastiffs, and the peasant driver guided the sleigh and horses across a heavy-timbered bridge.

We entered the park: The dogs were down, green-eyed and menacing in the angled shadows between the wall and a crumbling buttress. They made the horses mince as cautiously as if the ground before us was covered with eggshells.

We went up to the house—a monumental stone pile with a square tower like a Norman keep, round towers and turrets reminiscent of the fairy-tale castles of the Rhineland, and an irregular pattern of exaggeratedly pointed roofs radiating from the massive granite centerpiece. It was a blend of many centuries but neither incongruous nor disturbing; a historical document in granite, stained glass and what would surely be copper-sheet roofs under the covering of snow and mirror-bright ice. Light blazed through mullioned windows at all levels, gilding the snow on archers' galleries and the icicle beards of gargoyles brooding over rainspouts. A cluster of enormous chimneys was stark against the sky.

I knew just enough about Sempinski's picturebook retreat to understand the mixture of centuries. This was *Hetmanska Gora*, the Hill of the Chief, presented to Sempinski by his nation on the twentieth anniversary of the publication of his first book, a proof of affection, but sinister on first sight under a spectral moon.

It had been a small castle in the twelfth century—the keep, the moat and the crumbling outer walls testified to that—raised at the foot of the mountains to watch over the passes. It had played many roles in its country's history. When given to Sempinski, the castle was restored and more or less modernized by public subscription.

Judging by the number of lighted windows I guessed that the old writer had other visitors.

I asked the young man about my fellow guests. He didn't even pretend to listen but yawned and stretched and got out of the sleigh as soon as it had stopped, and another man, who could have been his surly replica, led me through an ecclesiastically

126

gloomy refectory hall with a groined, painted ceiling of blue and gold diapers made dim by the centuries, supported by granite columns with carved capitals. A hammered iron torch-ring, grim and heavy as a millstone, hung overhead with Damoclean menace.

We went up a baronial staircase, down another, through innumberable corridors and vaulted passages—some dark, others dim-lighted with electrified gasoliers—in cavernous chill. This was the coldest house I had ever been in. I thought it strangely silent for a country house presumably filled with guests. And yet the silence wasn't absolute; it was a modulated hush composed of many sounds. Stony-eyed servants stood motionless as statues in the corridors. All seemed more or less of an age that could have been anything from twenty to thirty. All seemed to be of a size, as if they had been stamped out on the same press. In the rectangular shadows cast by granite pillars, under stained glass and the Gothic gloom of vaulted ceilings, their uniformity seemed almost monastic. But they had none of the patient serenity of monks; indeed, they seemed to suck serenity out of the air and to replace it with a current of violence.

None of them looked at me, as if they knew everything about me and didn't think me worth another glance. Servants? Not on your life, I thought, irritated. Anything but servants. And there were other men (glimpsed through open doors and through the arches of a gallery that turned the library into a shadowed cloister): with books and newspapers in armchairs, studying the lay of a billiard table, talking. Quiet voices, perfectly assured. Cold faces, austere and professional. My fellow guests? They could be nothing else; they bore an air of authority that raised them above the servants like insignia of rank.

I looked at them with curiosity. They were Sempinski's guests, presumably his friends; a clue to the man and to whatever was taking place in his extraordinary house. I wanted some idea of who and what they were; I needed reassurance after my reception. These men would be, in effect, my allies against rising uneasiness. But what I saw puzzled me; I wasn't reassured. I couldn't fit these men into a familiar category any more than I could explain the improbable servants.

Priests? Surgeons? They could have been either but, obviously, they were eminent. They looked as if it had been a long time since anyone had questioned their authority. Power made natural by exercise, no more remarkable than breathing; the habit of command . . . and there was something more that defied identification. What? I didn't know. Whatever the quality had been, it was something in keeping with the ageless quality of the house.

Some were Orientals. Most were European. But there was an underlying similarity about them, more subtle than the graven uniformity of the servants. It was as if in their case the blueprints had been more complex, the mechanisms more delicately geared and the workmanship infinitely superior. Even their austere calmness—the detachment of the Grand Inquisitor they all seemed to wear—had been refined to the needle sharpness of the icicles glittering outside.

There were perhaps a dozen of them in the library, each one distinguished enough to focus all attention on himself, lifted above ordinary people by an absolute assurance, a sense of belonging and a peculiarly inflexible quality of face: polished, with the high gloss of metal filmed over imperceptibly by a pale dust. I thought that if I were to put my hand on one of those faces I'd feel an unyielding surface.

And then I saw the man who sat apart from the others in a deep armchair placed in the brooding darkness of an alcove formed by the angle of the monumental fireplace where no light intruded.

He was a huge man, hunched forward between the sweeping wings of the tall-backed armchair. His massive head was covered with thick, close-cropped hair like a helmet fashioned out of steel wire. Enormous shoulders and a packed, shaven neck leaned out of the leathery gloom. He stroked the air with incongruous fingers, like rubber truncheons glittering with polish. His face had a hard, gray hue with vertical lines, sharp furrows; he might have been a soldier. He smoked a cigarette in a long ivory holder. The delicate holder, cocked across his knee, looked as if he might have borrowed it for the evening.

He looked up as I passed the open arch and I felt frozen needles sliding over me, as if I were being stripped and dissected.

I hurried past the arch, heart pounding.

Perhaps it was the damp chill of the ancient walls inadequately heated; or the platoons of hostile servants; or the sum-total of my bleak impressions that made my stomach lurch suddenly with a certainty of danger. It wasn't anything that could be grasped at once; nothing was that obvious. But I knew the danger in the watchful sharpening of my senses.

I thought I would do well to find out what I was up against. I asked again how many other guests there were in the house.

"Guests?"

"Yes. Like me."

Suddenly the young man laughed.

"Like you? There is one like you and one something like you."

"I asked you a question."

I heard in my voice the odd, faulty note of an angry man.

"So? You asked and I answered."

"Answer me properly. What about the others? The men in the library?"

"Oh, they're nothing like you."

"What kind of servant are you, anyway? What's your job in this house?"

"It isn't answering questions."

It had taken me many years to learn how to control my explosive temper. I supposed that few of my associates had ever suspected me of a capacity for anger and, to tell the truth, I seldom allowed myself to lose self-control. But if there was one thing that could demolish all my carefully constructed barriers of restraint—the barriers that allowed me to make just about limitless allowances for other points of view—it was gratuitous rudeness.

I wanted to attack the arrogant young man. I had always been able to control the impulse and clamp a tight lid on my indignation, remembering who and what I was and what was involved. But that was *then and there:* home—where you could understand the motives, where you could weigh your personal dignity, your civilized essence, against these motives and, inevitably, find that even verbal violence on your part was an affront to you as a human being. I eschewed violence in any form because it was an indignity, the last resort of an animal. For the same reason I had avoided involvement in Causes; because all causes sank into violence of some kind sooner or later. And no cause seemed sufficiently personal or important to risk the humiliation of being violent.

But that was then and there; this was here and now. I felt myself close to the boiling point, following the German.

The corridors narrowed, the ceilings drew perceptively closer to the granite flagstones. The vaulted passages had become progressively colder with the damp, truly penetrating chill of old tombs. I had been in enough crypts to be familiar with their curious duality: dry enough for the undisturbed dust of centuries to form its miniature Saharas, damp enough to cut through any clothing deep into the bone. The echoes were hollow, now. Clearly we had come to the old part of the house: the original fortress.

My room was a granite chamber as long and tall as an indoor squash court. Daylight would make small headway here against the heavy gloom, seeping through the armorial stained glass of three lancet windows, little more than loopholes. A man could hardly thrust his arm through them. Now, the solitary light of a dim bulb threw shadows out of a cast-iron trefoil bracket chained like a prisoner to the naked wall. Stone walls, stone floor; I had expected them. They were as much a part of this tower chamber as the battlements outside. The fireplace was like a thirteenth-century tomb—big enough to roast an ox and a pair of sheep—and equally expected. It looked as if it hadn't felt the heat of a fire in a hundred years. What heat there was, came from a porcelain stove in a corner; this century's addition. There was a huge, carved bedstead on a dais, under a canopy, some old chests studded with oxidized black iron, and heavy furniture. But the ceiling was fifteenth-century coffered wood, painted in white and red chevrons, with heraldic lions (rampant in goldfoil on sky blue) and crimson griffins (on canary yellow) in alternate squares. Elsewhere and at another time I would have been delighted with this rare find.

I put my bag and briefcase on a banded chest at the foot of the bedstead. I felt immensely chilled. The German youth leaned against the fireplace with quiet insolence.

"Does the gentleman find everything satisfactory?"

I nodded. "It will do."

He laughed. "That makes me very happy. We wouldn't want the gentleman not to enjoy his stay."

I turned my back on him. The granite walls were without ornament. The lancet windows were black with the night behind them; I supposed that they would offer a fine view of mountains that could be no further than twenty miles away. Beyond the mountains lay another country; I couldn't immediately remember which country it was.

The German asked if I wanted anything to eat but hunger was the last of my problems, even though my last meal had been an excellent dinner eaten on the train. When I refused a tray, he shrugged with indifference, heading for the door.

I said: "When can I see Professor Sempinski?"

He didn't answer as he left the room.

thirteen

I SAT DOWN in the nearest chair, grateful that my stomach was empty, hoping that no one would bring me dinner after all. I didn't think that anybody would.

After a while, I got up. I had a violent headache. I didn't care any more about seeing Sempinski; I wasn't interested in any explanations. I knew that I had to leave Hetmanska Gora as fast as I could. I started walking up and down the chamber, counting flagstones. There were two hundred flagstones in ten rows of twenty. The clatter of my leather heels thundered in my head.

I thought I heard a faint noise outside and went to the door and found the door locked. Locked? I pumped the ancient iron handle up and down and pushed against the black oak boards and bruised my shoulder on one of the rose-shaped iron bosses that studded the door. But the door *was* locked. The keyhole was empty. I put my ear to the keyhole and heard a man's breathing; the door was not only locked but also guarded: I was a prisoner.

Whose? Why?

I had no idea.

But I knew now that I had been brought to Hetmanska Gora by design. Nothing about this visit had been accidental—from the first letter from Julian Sempinski. But what the devil did they want from me?

I wandered about the room with no clear idea what to do. But gradually thought began to crystallize into a decision to escape.

How? Where? It didn't matter where. What mattered was to end the nightmare. I had been stalked, shot at, tricked, threatened, insulted and imprisoned. I had had enough.

I had read somewhere that condemned men experienced moments of terrible elation; as if (like moths heading for open flame) their destruction was coincidental with attainment. Having decided on escape, with no illusions about either the dangers or my chances, I was aware of a comparable sensation; relief—short-lived but consoling—sustained me for a time.

I had a perfect right to be afraid. What I proposed was little short of madness: a desperate journey through a hostile country, alone in the dead of winter, and definitely pursued. I had had several samples of what to expect; the wolves and the conspirators were only a part of it. I didn't know the language of the country which seemed paranoid about the only other language I could use here. I didn't have much money. I couldn't ask the simplest directions without making myself conspicuous. And my pursuers would probably know exactly where I was heading, and every step of the road I had to take. It wasn't a bright picture.

And to start this journey I had to escape from a castle in a snowy wilderness, past guards who wouldn't think twice about killing me, and killer dogs who'd do their best to tear me to pieces.

That had the sound of a damn poor start but there was nothing I could do about it. Daylight escape was out of the question. Only night offered any kind of chance. There would be fewer men about the corridors, none in the park if the dogs were loose. I might get out of the house undetected. Once out of the castle, I would have to make my way quickly across the park . . . by no means a gentle stroll by moonlight. Moonlight meant danger. I would have to keep carefully to the shadows. I didn't know the geography of the wooded acres, and darkness would be sure to add to my confusion. And there would be no time for any confusion. I would have to keep away from the well-used paths to get to the wall, then get across the wall and the moat (sure to be patrolled), and make my way as surely as a homing pigeon across the snowy wilderness of open country to the village road. In that cold, with those mountains of snow, in that bitter wind, I wouldn't last a half hour away from the road. Keeping away from the drive and the well-used paths was taking a chance on losing my bearings. But the mastiffs would be on me in a minute, otherwise. I had to take my chances with them anyway; it was a large park and there were only the three mastiffs . . . they couldn't cover it all. If they did sniff me out, there was always the compressed-air pistol. I hoped I would be steady enough to use it if I had to. I had been steady enough in the sleigh but I had no illusions about my prowess there; it was one thing to ping away at a dark, indivisible mass of wolves—who seemed utterly unreal anyway—with the shotgun booming and frantic horses hauling me to safety, and other men involved who knew what to do; it would be something else for me alone, nerves taut, jumping at every shadow, with silent killer dogs padding invisibly behind. The mastiffs were a deadly danger but the men were worse. It was the men I had to worry about. They would pursue me far beyond the walls.

But if I got away early enough—say, around midnight, with the household sleeping—I could have as much as six hours before anyone realized that I was gone. They would find me missing when they brought my breakfast. Add another hour for a search of the castle and the grounds. Perhaps another hour while they got a pursuit party together and on its way in the right direction. That was eight hours. In eight hours I could be well on my way to the ancient city where the sleigh had met me. With luck I could be getting on a train for the border before the hunters started after me. It wasn't very likely but there was a chance . . . if, I concluded bitterly, I ever managed to get out of my room.

It was at this point that the pretty tapestry of my little dream filled with gaping holes. The *ifs* and *mights* collapsed. Because escape from the castle was about as likely as a rescue party of United States Marines landing on the roof. The door was locked and guarded. The windows would defy a fugitive cat. The walls and floor were solid. That left the fireplace. The fireplace could give me access to the roof—*if* the chimney wasn't blocked by a hundred years' accumulation of debris or even other optimistic fugitives. Once on the roof, I could presumably flap my arms and fly.

I leaned against the wall, wondering how I could have been stupid enough to hope for some way out. My addiction to mystery novels and historical romances was to blame.

My headache came back, magnified. The stone floor was cold under my feet. I sneezed. I sat on the bed and tried not to think.

But thought persisted. I couldn't give up quite this easily; I had to try something. The fireplace wasn't much of an escape route but it was a start. Perhaps it would take me past other fireplaces and, thus, into rooms with unguarded doors. And if the chimney only took me to the roof, I might be able to find a way down the precipitous walls, or spot an entrance into another part of the house where no one would expect me. I wouldn't know until I had explored it.

I put on slacks and sweaters and took off my shoes and put on all the spare socks I had. I remembered gloves. Before I entered the fireplace and began the climb, I wedged a heavy chair under the door handle. I draped a towel over the door handle and the keyhole.

Later, I would think of that moment and what came after it as a monument to the incredible, a not-quite-possible experience that I could view with clinical detachment—a form of amnesia in which I had a vivid recollection of a variety of terrors but could not remember the terror itself.

The fireplace looked more than ever like the mouth of a crypt. I didn't know what I would find in the icy darkness, hearing the soft rustling and scurrying high up in the tunnel, seeing red pin-point lights glittering in pairs like clusters of splintered glass. It was all something I recalled afterwards as a nightmare of darkness and dryness that went far beyond infinitely powdered dust, as though I had been drawn into the gullet of a science-fiction monster

135

or the airless mouth of space itself. I rose hand over hand, peering into absolute blackness and now and then I looked down between my feet at the shrinking rectangle of light: my fireplace and granite prison chamber that seemed an embodiment of safety. And all too soon the light shrunk into nothing. I went up through pillow-thick cobwebs made solid with powdered brick and mortar, with the squeal and rush of rats like a loud river around me, lifting myself from ledge to ledge, feeling ahead with fingers that were gloved with dust. I couldn't see my hands against my face. The tunnel walls seemed to contract and expand about me like a living throat; I felt as if I was crawling into the earth itself with mountains settling over me, enormous weights shifting, pressing down. I fought panic. Blinded, I began to doubt my sense of direction. I couldn't tell if I was climbing or moving headfirst into a bottomless pit. I clung to the brick ledges, fighting vertigo and the certainty that the walls were moving down on me. I passed the open mouths of other tunnels, like caves in the subterranean passages, but I couldn't tell if these led up or down or even if they were horizontal. It was soon apparent that I was in the shaft of the main chimney, like the interior of an ancient, fossilized tree trunk, with an infinity of branches leading out of it to other parts of the house. The gaping mouths breathed with the torrential sounds of rats rushing from my approach. Or . . . were they rushing at me? My body tried to shrink into itself; I fought to keep from screaming. I had an overwhelming desire to let myself drop down the shaft. It would be so easy . . . Just let the fingers open on the ledge above . . . keep eyes closed . . . Drop. Straight down and away from your own contaminated skin . . .

A rush of cold air brought me to my senses. My hands were numb; I no longer felt the woven mat of cobwebs parting about me. The river-sound of rats fell away. No power on earth or beyond it could have induced me to open my eyes; I sniffed the ice-cold air, hoping for direction, then went on up (or was it down, or sideways?) hand over hand.

It went on like that for a time that had no relation to minutes or hours. Each moment was a small eternity. My body seemed to alternately shrink and balloon between walls, within the endless core and gut of a time without boundaries, the essence of darkness. But time did pass. Each of its subdivisions became progressively colder. Eventually I felt ice on my face and opened my eyes and saw the roundness of the night framed in the mouth of the chimney, and the incredible glitter of a star.

I lay above a world of ice: sharp-angled cliffs of roof, precipice of walls. Turrets and towers like the fluted columns of glaciers high above the treeline, festooned in icicles like frozen waterfalls . . . the furry rolls of gutter and drainpipe and spire and lightning rod grown heavy with snow.

Getting here seemed to have been an end in itself; I couldn't immediately remember why I had come.

But the coldness helped. The icy wind stroked me into motion. I raised myself out of the mushroom-shaft of the huge chimney, and slipped over the edge to the ridge of the roof. I went down on my hands and knees, feeling myself fill up with the cold. I knew I would be frozen solid in minutes. I had to move. But where? Anywhere. There were the turrets and the sharp slope of dormers soaring toward the torn and raging sky. Anyone of them would do if it had a window.

I edged away from the supporting mass of the chimney, inch by inch astride the icy ridge of the roof. The couloir of the ridge was a yard wide with ice and perfectly rounded, with polished sheets falling as smooth as water to the dark edges of the precipice, high-angled like the glazed roof of a house of cards. The wild sea of the tree crowns boiled in the wind far below. There were no handholds anywhere on the sheets of ice; one slip and I would rocket to the frozen ground. Ice burned my legs like fire. I crept out into the middle of the roof, making for the white wall that rose across my path: the central mass of the ancient fortress with a high archers' gallery above turrets. If I could climb up there . . . But I couldn't. The wind kept me pinned to my icy saddle. I began to freeze. I had to go back.

Again time slipped into its own private subdivisions with no regard for man-made labels of seconds and minutes. There was a sort of rhythm to the backward progress I made on the roof, the push-and-slide motion of retreat; I supposed this could have been a way to measure the seconds. But, toward the end, each of these seconds felt like a quarter of an hour. I had no recollection of reaching the shelter of the chimney, or getting up and over the high lip or sliding inside. But suddenly the wind no longer cut into me, the rocking buffet had stopped and, in the odor of ascending dryness, I dropped down inside.

I felt no disappointment then. That would come later. Sinking into the tight throat of the tunnel I felt and thought nothing.

I started making my way down and saw at once that the descent would be much harder than the climb had been. My feet were numb; they registered no contact. My hands were not much better but, at least, they could still signal the difference between handholds and empty, black air. I had to turn around and try it headdown. The shaft was slanted at sharp angles, I remembered; vertical drops were infrequent. And, going down headfirst, I would have my face farther away from the rats gathering behind me.

I eased myself into a side-tunnel and crawled out headfirst. I moved out cautiously across the crumbling edges.

The descent was also something that I remembered later in incomprehensible fragments as an exercise in horror; not my horror but an impersonal case history.

It was the same nightmare of ancient dust and darkness, giant rats and spiders, the dry smell of pulverized mortar, blindness and hallucination; but, going up, I had had hope and purpose. The roof had been a magnet, escape was the spur. Coming down, I had only the knowledge of defeat.

In no time I was sure that I had taken a wrong tunnel and lost the main shaft of the chimney. I had no idea where I was in reference to the shaft. The tunnels narrowed. They branched off in innumerable passages, each narrower than the one before. Soon I was moving with the crumbling stone brushing against my back, and there were bricked-up exits and holes that opened up suddenly between my hands, and there were blocked tunnels and masses of rubble that forced me to back off. I entered new tunnels, took new directions and eventually knew that I was hopelessly lost. Breathing became difficult. Small white stars began to revolve under my closed eyelids. I was starved for air. I scrambled forward, face-down against scampering soft bodies, trapped in the claustrophobic labyrinth.

My fears ballooned; doubts overwhelmed reason. I found that I was biting my own hands. A furry river of animals ran over my legs; my nostrils filled with their fetid smell. I thought I was drowning.

I didn't know how I got myself back under control. I was a bit mad then, I supposed. But the cold pushed me forward. Nothing else around me had any relation to anything I knew; but the chill summoned instinctive reactions.

And suddenly my eyes were open and saw what obviously couldn't be there for me to see: a white light knifing through the blackness, a pencil-thin beam of incredible brightness.

I heard human voices.

I didn't believe what I saw or heard.

And then the walls seemed to lift and fall away. There was space around me. There was a seeping rivulet of warmer air and the intoxicating smell of tobacco smoke. Threads of light dressed the walls in cobwebs. I lay on the floor, on my back, breathing the warm air.

fourteen

I WAS IN a small, vaulted chamber behind a fireplace, a stone closet angled away from the wall, tucked behind bricks. The brick curtain between my hiding place and the room on the other side was nominal at best. The bricks were crumbling, old. Most of them had fallen away on the inside, leaving one layer in the fireplace. Their mortar was fine dust; I could pick any of the bricks away with two fingers. The light and voices came from the room through this porous curtain. At first I didn't listen to the voices; it was enough to hear them. Hearing them, I knew that I was not going to die in the tunnels.

After a while, I rolled over on my stomach. There was plenty of room in my hideout for moving any way I wanted. I got to my knees and put my eyes against the broadest of the innumerable cracks between the bricks and looked into the room. I saw perhaps a dozen of the so-called servants but many more seemed to disappear in the shadows where the light of the lanterns didn't reach.

The room was enormous. Light from a half dozen lanterns fell on a long trestle table and the glass partitions of a conservatory beyond it. There were chairs, armchairs, chests, carved pilasters, partially dismantled suits of armor; these looked bloodily dismembered in the reddish glare of the lanterns. Debris of food littering the table, spilled papers and outdoor clothing piled without care,

140

turned the hall into a stage setting for a guardhouse and the ready-room of a military task force. Pistols and rifles on and against the table among gnawed chicken bones. Fur robes and uniforms. Coarse voices. Odd packing cases spilling straw and metal. A greenish mound of ammunition boxes. Liquor bottles, red in the violent light. Light thrust with difficulty through the shifting streams of blue tobacco smoke.

I heard words and, at first, that was all I could hear: words without meaning. I could sense the jubilation of the laughing men, their soon-to-come moment of fulfillment. I didn't grasp much more than that. But gradually the words acquired meaning; I recognized their general direction. I heard my own name. Mention of The Magician also made me sit up and pay attention. It took me some time to understand how my name could possibly fit-in with what the so-called servants were so darkly pleased with.

Two of the nearest voices, a young one and an older one, were discussing murder; a political assassination. The men sat near the fireplace, out of my line of vision, but I thought that the younger voice belonged to the man who had met me with the sleigh. A note of respect and a kind of anticipatory, boyish excitement made his voice difficult to identify; I had heard only his arrogance and berserk exaltation.

The murder under discussion was not (as I had first supposed it to be) a gruesome fact of medieval history, but something still to come—a forthcoming event.

And then I understood that this assassination was to be more than an ordinary murder (thinking, even as I became aware of this, that I had surely come far if I could think of any murder as being ordinary): somehow the United States were to be implicated.

And I heard that I too had had an assigned role in the assassination plot. I had helped, apparently, to provide a vital ingredient: the undeniable evidence of American involvement.

I thought then that the terrors of the journey through the chimney tunnels must have scrambled my senses.

But this much was clear: the plot was the brainchild of The

Magician who was on his way to Hetmanska Gora to supervise the final detail of the operation—a detail of which I formed an important part.

"Tell me about The Magician," said the younger man. "Is he as good as they say?"

"He is the best, he's always been the best. Who else could organize an operation like this? Who else could bring together such a mass of detail? The man is a genius."

"Have you ever met him?"

"No. Nobody knows who he is. I don't believe his own men know who they're working for. Even to us, who have watched him operate for years, and who used his services in the days of the Reich, he never seemed to be more than a legend. But we'll both meet him in a day or two."

"You used to be with Skorzenny. Did you ever work on an operation as big as this one?"

"No. Oh, there were some fine times, some great operations. But our Otto was all dash and fire, a great man with the hand grenade and the submachine gun . . . This kind of subtlety would be beyond him. Look how long and how carefully The Magician spun his web around the amis. Look at the proof we have lined up against them. Each thread is strong enough to enmesh the amis, but spliced together, these threads make a hangman's rope. There is the old man upstairs, the girl, the letters, and now this new American has brought us the money. Who else but The Magician could have netted our big fish in America and even got us an American assassin for a scapegoat? We have everything tied up as neatly as you please and right on schedule."

"Are you sure that the American brought the money?"

"If The Magician said he was bringing it, then he brought it. We'll know where it is when The Magician gets here."

I couldn't understand what money they were talking about. I had brought very little cash to Hetmanska Gora, and only about a thousand dollars in travelers' checks. I didn't know what other

142

role I had played or was supposed to play in this new conspiracy but there was *some* role and that was enough.

The scope of the affair put me in a mild state of shock, I supposed. This was a matter for professionals. Nothing like this was ever supposed to happen to an ordinary man, a private citizen who paid his bills and taxes, crossed streets on a green light and fed parking meters, met his responsibilities as best he could and tried to make a reasonable living for himself.

I didn't want to have anything to do with this affair, but I had little choice. Some kind of a conspiracy was being aimed at the United States; I couldn't just stand by and watch it unfold, although I had no idea what to do about it.

Was this the awakening of a latent patriotism? That word had always had a rowdy, dull-witted sound for me; it smelled of beer and sweaty auditoriums and the comic-opera uniforms of paunchy old men. I had my own, quieter definitions of America. But what it all boiled down to now was that I'd be damned if I'd let a bunch of reconditioned and pubescent Nazis get away with some propaganda stroke against my own kind without, at least, trying to upset their plans.

This put the whole affair in a new perspective. Escaping from Hetmanska Gora just because I resented being pushed around was no longer the point. My feelings weren't important. I had to unravel at least a few of the threads the two Nazis had been talking about so that the embassy in the capital could be told about the Sempinski Affair.

To start, I had to find Sempinski. I didn't believe that Sempinski could be a party to the plot. He had been used by the conspirators as I had been used. He might be able to provide the necessary details that would illuminate the entire plot. Once I knew exactly what I was up against, I would find a way to reach the capital.

I started looking about the room with greater care, noting details. A plan began to take shape in my mind. The Germans had now found a new subject for discussion—the girl they had mentioned earlier, some other dupe. They made coarse jokes. I didn't have to listen to Teutonic humor. I took the opportunity to fix the layout of the huge hall firmly in my mind. The glass doors of the conservatory captured my attention. They were incongruous in that medieval chamber, an Edwardian addition. But beyond them would lie the greenhouse and it would abut on the park and, since glass was a lot easier to break through than granite, it could be the way out of the house that I was looking for.

Almost at once, another piece of luck presented itself. A new man entered. Someone asked him what he was doing away from his post.

"I got hungry," he said. He found a piece of cold chicken and began to eat.

"Who's on the old man's door?"

"Nobody. What's the matter? You think Sempinski can get to the door? Besides, Grossmayer can see it from where he is sitting."

"Grossmayer has his own job."

"Then you better get up there and wake him, before his American crawls out through the keyhole."

An hour seemed to pass before the men started to leave the hall, taking their lanterns with them. In the sudden darkness, the echoing click of the closing door had a grim finality.

I felt a return of panic; the black walls seemed to close on me again; I was once more entombed underneath the mountain. I struck against the bricks, feeling them shift and grate under my knuckles, hearing their clattering fall in the room on the other side.

I heard the thin, melodious chimes of a musical clock striking the opening measures of Mozart's Little Music of the Night, then beating out the hour.

I sat back on my heels, breathing deeply. I brought my body and mind back under control; I couldn't afford panic. I counted the ringing strokes of the chimes: there were eleven of them. I had been in Hetmanska Gora exactly four hours.

Soon all sound ceased; the household was asleep. I forced myself to wait in the darkness, adjusting my vision to the moonlight.

The terrors of the journey through the chimney tunnels were

still very much with me but they were no longer a matter of the moment. My thoughts were orderly. From the exchange I had overheard, Sempinski's room was off the same corridor as my own in the central fortress, close enough for one guard to watch both the doors. The guard on my door had fallen asleep. By the time I got there, Sempinski's guard could also be sleeping, having stuffed himself with chicken before my eyes. And even if I didn't get to Sempinski tonight, I would manage to pinpoint his door for a try at some other time. Sooner or later I would have to see him.

I was cold and hungry; my muscles were cramped. But I began to pry out the bricks until the hole that I had punched in the wall in my earlier panic was big enough to crawl through. The various darknesses of the moonlit hall did not confuse me; I had the room's geography fixed firmly in mind; and so I moved quickly among the litter of supplies, making no sound on the cold stone floor in my stockinged feet. I had one bad moment when a black, formless shadow leaped at me out of glass: but it was only my own soot-smeared reflection.

The double doors to the conservatory were bolted and locked but the key was in the keyhole and the bolts were oiled. I was inside the abandoned glass house in a moment, taking care to leave no telltale footprints between the doors and the exit to the park.

The outer door was locked and keyless but the ancient lock was rusted and ready to crumble at a touch. One good kick would send the door flying off its hinges. Beyond it lay the black wilderness of the park, threatening in moonlight.

I came back to the hall hardly able to believe my luck. I had found the way out of the castle. The chimney tunnels would be the escape route; the greenhouse would be the final exit. I'd have to blaze some kind of trail in the chimneys, and that meant going back into the catacombs, but there was no way to avoid that chore. Besides, I knew what to expect in the tunnels; once faced, a terror lost much of its bite.

This new excitement had wakened my hunger.

There was enough leftover food on the table to feed a small

army. I attacked the sour black bread and garlic sausage as if I had never eaten anything better, and washed down this explosive dinner with a fair wine. The wine sent warmth into my numbed arms and legs. I lit a cigarette. My spirits rose. My vision sharpened. Everything became marvelously clear and defined. Nothing seemed impossible.

I searched through the piles of the conspirators' equipment until I had found a powerful flashlight and some lengths of thin but strong nylon line. These were just what I needed for exploring and marking the tunnels off the main chimney shaft. I didn't bother with any of the weapons; they looked too complicated for me. Clothing was more to the point: short sheepskin jackets, fur-lined boots and hats, quilted gloves . . . I noted what I would need but left it alone. It would be right here when I needed it.

I was tired then. The wine began to make inroads on my senses. My arms were suddenly extraordinarily heavy. My head filled with a gentle, soporific humming.

It had been a long, brutal day and it wasn't over; there was a great deal more that I had to do. I set about repairing the breech in the fireplace, sure that I was doing it all wrong. Whatever my manual skills might be, they didn't include masonry. I got the bricks together more or less the way they might have been before I had disturbed them, hoping it was a good enough job to hide all traces of my break-in. I swept up the dust and pocketed the small debris and risked a flash of light along the fireplace. The wall looked all right. A bricklayer would laugh himself sick at the sight of it but I didn't think the conspirators would spot my mistakes. I took the nylon cord and the flashlight and went to the door.

The corridor was silent, dark, empty and unguarded. There was no threatening sound inside the house; only the creaks and groans of old timber, the unremitting ticking of large clocks and the sad echoes of the wind speeding down the ancient corridors. Out of the heavy shadows rose the familiar granite pillars of the refectory hall, so that I knew where I was and which way to go.

146

The clocks were striking midnight by the time I felt the dank walls of the granite fortress closing about me, and saw the dim lantern of the sleeping guard outside my door. There was another light farther up the corridor, where a second guard slept, head-down, at the head of a stone stairway that curved into the black arch of a tower entrance.

This would be Sempinski's door, the one I was seeking. It was partly hidden in a deep, black recess not much wider than the lancet windows and less than half their height. It would be a tight squeeze past the guard who sat under the arch of the doorway, growling and muttering in his sleep. His chair took up more than half the space on the landing.

The guards seemed sound asleep but getting past them was an alarming proposition. Each had his lantern. These made twin lakes of light. Once I was out of shadow I would be totally unprotected. If either guard should wake while I was in the light, the game would be over before it had properly begun.

It took all my sagging resolution to get going. Each step within the pools of light was a minor miracle. With each I listened for the yell of an awakened guard. But the men slept. My good luck seemed to be continuing. I crossed the trembling pools of light that seemed like crimson quicksand and reached the new shadow on the other side of the curving stairway. There I could rest, taking time to pull myself together, hearing Sempinski's guard yawn and stir on the stone platform above me; his hobnailed boots hung over my head like a pair of clubs. But the man settled back to sleep and I started the soft, slow climb toward him. The steps were worn and hollowed into basins. The wall was cold and dry against my back. My hands left wet marks there. I took one step at a time, eyes fixed on the cretinous face crumpled in sleep above me. A dozen times I thought he would awake and see me. I couldn't understand why he didn't sense my approach. I thought that the air around was filled with so much tension that some of it was bound to penetrate the guard's stupor. He muttered restlessly but did not awake. I edged past him, brushing the thick oxlike

147

back and pressed myself into the alcove of the door. The key was in the lock and the lock was shining with oil. I unlocked the door, pushed it open one millimeter at a time, and entered the room. I closed the door behind me with infinite care.

fifteen

THE NEAR half of the room was bright with multicolored moonlight that slanted through the leaded stained-glass windows in chaotic beams, but the far corners were in opaque shadow. The towering catafalque of a fourposter bed advanced out of darkness as the torn clouds struggled with the moon outside; the sudden flat gleam of gold curlicues around gloomy portraits, dark wood and colorless iron shapes, retreated into unexpected distance. The measured breathing of the man in the bed seemed to come from everywhere at once.

I looked down at the gray, ravaged face and knew it at once; I would have known it anywhere. Even in its terrible disguise of time and disease it was the same face that used to stare at me from the frontispiece portraits of my favorite historical romances, different only in texture like a bad translation. The savage wing of white hair had become a deathly gray in the uncertain light, the mouth had fallen into stricken hollows, and two weary trenches had been driven into the gaunt escarpments of the cheeks. But there the difference ended; the thin nose still leaped like a violent beak out of its ambush of innumerable wrinkles and the famous eyebrows spilled across imperious eyes like chalky tree roots overhanging the banks of a river.

I started explaining who I was, how I had got into his room

and why I had come. There was no way of proving to the silent, watchful old man that I was anything more than part of a bad dream. I felt like giving way to tired hysteria; everything seemed so absolutely senseless; I had been a fool. My experiences had acquired the unreal quality of a nightmare from which there is no way to awake.

"There is a chair behind you, Dr. Shippe."

Sempinski's soft voice would have gone unheard if there had been another sound. But after my hoarse whispering, the sound seemed explosive. I threw a wild glance at the door, expecting the bleak mass of wood and ornamental iron to erupt into pounding boots and violent light, but it remained closed. Sempinski's eyes had followed mine.

"There is no need to whisper."

"Can't the guard hear us?"

"The door is oak, ten centimeters thick. Nothing that happens in these rooms can be heard outside."

"I'm a bit jumpy, I'm afraid. This is all very new to me."

Sempinski smiled. His head remained rigid, pressed back into the pillows. Only his eyes and lips moved.

I asked: "What about you? Are they keeping you a prisoner in your own house?"

He nodded, said softly: "I'm paralyzed. My prison is this bed."

"I had begun to think that you didn't believe who I was. I know I don't look very reassuring."

"Why shouldn't I believe you? I knew you had come to Hetmanska Gora. As for thinking that you might be part of some kind of a trap . . . well, my keepers don't need to set any more for me."

"How did you know I had been brought here?"

"They had shown me your letter from the capital and the answer that they had written in my name. They take good care to keep me informed about their successes. It's one of their most popular amusements."

"Who are they, sir?"

"An ironic combination of young Nazis and the original breed that had found refuge in the East German police in the Stalin era. There are also important local Stalinists among them, men who had lost power in recent years and want it back. I'll tell you all about them in a moment. What is important is that they underestimated you. Our only chance lies in the mistakes they may make. They would never have thought you capable of doing what you did tonight."

I said: "Neither did I."

"You are planning an escape, of course? You have to warn your embassy about this as soon as you can."

"I'm going to try it, as soon as I know what this is all about."

"The quicker the better. These people are professionals. Have you found a way out of the house? You seem to get around quite freely."

I explained about the chimney passages and the conservatory. Sempinski laughed then: a clear, almost youthful sound.

"I can help a little. There are some blueprints and architects' drawings of the house in my desk. The National Historical Society took measurements before the world war. We can go over that. And I can help you plan your route across the park. But what about the other side of the wall? Do you know anybody who can help you?"

"I had hoped you would know someone."

"No," Sempinski said. "I can't trust anyone any longer. The old friends are dead. The new men are largely . . . reconstructed; I can't vouch for the way they think."

I was too upset by this revelation to say anything; I had counted on Sempinski to arrange my entire escape out of Eastern Europe. Now that the situation had become so very much more dangerous, and my plans so much more involved, he could barely help me get out of his house.

I told him what I thought I might do if I managed to reach open country beyond the park walls. Light seemed to leave his face as he listened to me.

"That has damn little chance," he said finally.

"What else can I do?"

"Nothing. That's the trouble. Damn, but I wish I hadn't brought you into this."

I said quietly: "I wondered why you had me come."

"I didn't want you to come at all. I wanted to send you an autographed book, and in that book to include a message which you could take to your government, I had no idea you were coming here until you sent your telegram from New York. Our keepers cabled you the invitation. They wanted you here."

"But why choose me?" I asked. "I don't know anything about this kind of thing."

"You were the only man, anywhere, to whom I could write. I had to make some contact with the West . . . any contact. These murderous animals would never allow any other letters. They had their own reasons for wanting you here, so they permitted a letter to you."

I couldn't keep the bitterness out of my voice.

"And I walked right into their trap."

Sempinski said: "If it's any comfort, you're only one of many to have done so."

"But what the devil could these people want from me?"

"You sent Kristin Napoji here. You knew where she had gone. You could have directed possible searchers to this house and that would have exposed the whole conspiracy."

"But why should anybody search for her? She is dead, killed in an accident. Her case is closed. Even the American Embassy has gone along with that."

Sempinski sighed, smiled. He said: "There never was a real accident. Kristin is in this house. She has never left it since she brought me your letter and my book."

I couldn't believe that I had understood properly. Sempinski laughed a little.

"No accident?"

"Oh, there was an accident, yes; but she wasn't in it. Don't look so stunned, Doctor, so bewildered. If these mad animals could conceive their incredible conspiracy, it would be child's play for them to hoodwink a bored embassy official. Kristin's so-called accident was undoubtedly a magnificent production."

"But she wasn't in it, thank God!"

"That was one detail they couldn't supply. It must have hurt their professional pride; they glory in detail. Which, incidentally, is another reason why they wanted you here."

"I don't understand."

"You had become an unexpected detail, an unraveled thread. You had brushed against their conspiracy and so you had to be tidied up. These people leave nothing to chance."

"Couldn't they have dealt with me in New York? Why have me come here?"

"That I don't know. Perhaps you are to be an exhibit . . . as I am to be. I only know that you're important to them."

He had begun to look very tired then.

"Are you finding all this too hard to believe?"

I didn't know what to believe. My all-too-brief sense of well-being had evaporated. I was too tired to think clearly, anyway. Too much had happened: the night, its terrors, disappointments, revelations and astonishments pressed down upon me like a suffocating cloth.

I urged the old man to go on but it seemed as if Sempinski wasn't listening to me. He had stepped deep inside himself, out of range of voices. Clearly, he was approaching a moment which would be both painful and difficult for him.

I said, as gently as I could: "Well sir, what is this all about?"

His voice had become low and uncertain.

"Forgive me if I don't come to the point at once. This can't be done quickly. There is only one sequence in the telling that makes any sense. And there is also the matter of my own pride—because, you see, I am responsible for much of this."

"I can't imagine how you could be to blame."

"I have been a gullible old fool. The bitter truth is that you will be risking your life to undo the damage that I helped to cause. Perhaps that is why I find it so difficult to start telling you about it."

I said: "I can't believe that you could ever be involved in something like this."

"Why not? I can be fooled as easily as anyone. And probably easier."

The multicolored beams of light swept away then, as the clouds covered the moon, and left him in darkness. His face was suddenly luminous against the banked pillows.

"You overheard a fragment of a plot and this fragment shocked you. No, perhaps not shock. Anger and indignation would fit you better than shock. You were indignant. Shocked too, of course, but in a different way . . . It's a preposterous plot, you said . . . These people must be absolutely mad . . . Isn't that right?"

"Yes. More or less. How could anybody be made to believe that the United States could be involved in an assassination?"

"A few years ago it would have been impossible for anyone to believe it," Sempinski said gently. "But now there are precedents. Political assassination isn't so far removed from the American scene, is it?"

I wanted to protest that the assassinations he was talking about had been the work of deranged men. The conspiracy aimed at implying an official American involvement. But the difference seemed morally uncertain . . . only a matter of degree. I waited for Sempinski to go on but it was some time before he could continue.

He said, simply: "I call myself a patriot . . . In this country patriotism is still considered a virtue. In many ways we're old-fashioned, with old-fashioned values. Some of us love our country more foolishly than others, I more foolishly than most. The system under which my country lives today is an insult to me as a human being, an alien imposition. You have to know what *we* mean by freedom to understand how far we would go to secure it and why I became involved in this conspiracy."

I nodded in the pause that followed, growing aware of what had apparently been happening for some time: a gradual cooling of the atmosphere in the room, a change in the air, as if the physical balance and chemistry of atoms had been carefully altered. An inarticulate warning began to form like a shadow in my mind.

154

"Freedom to us is individual freedom," Sempinski continued. "We think that the individual is the ultimate defense against tyranny. Individual freedom creates; everything else destroys. Everything that creates the dignity of the individual is freedom, but its particles are fragile . . . perishable. They can be made to disappear quicker than a dream. Even in your America, that fragile prop for our hopes, this freedom is gradually eroding. It is a gentle killing . . . you neither see nor feel this terrible erosion . . . in fact it can be made to seem pleasant and desirable. We are more fortunate than you. No one bothers to make our loss seem painless. We have neither dignity nor importance as individuals, but no one pretends seriously that we do. Time is against you because you still have freedoms you can lose. But it can't erode a particle of what we don't possess. And so we have a special kind of patience, like a kettle kept carefully on the boil. We nurse the fire and wait. Do you understand me?"

I said I did and watched the old man anxiously; his face had assumed a waxlike quality that made him seem depleted. He lay with eyes fixed rigidly on the shifting shadows as if they were assembling judges and he the accused.

"I also waited," he began again, his voice growing harsh. "What was I waiting for? A signal, a sign that the West had not forgotten us . . . that is what we wait for. There have been many signals through the years but never the right one . . . First the Hungarians, then the Czechs . . . And then, suddenly, I thought that the years of waiting were over. Foolish? Perhaps, in view of experience . . . But when you want something very badly, Doctor, when you have prayed for it and waited for it for a generation, you do not examine it as carefully as you might when it it finally handed to you . . . Can you understand?"

"I think so," I said. Then seeing the other's pain, I added quickly: "Of course, sir. Yes."

The sign, Sempinski said, had been more than he had ever hoped for: an American plan to overthrow Communism in Eastern Europe at one blow: the signal for a general uprising of all countries east of the Iron Curtain.

155

"But that's impossible," I said.

"To seize the Soviet leaders," Sempinski continued as though no longer believing he was saying anything. "And with this act to signal the beginning of the slaves' revolt . . . No longer just one country making its hopeless protest, but all our countries simultaneously in arms. The Soviets shocked and stunned . . . confusion and chaos . . . and in this chaos the whole might of the West coming to our rescue. Do you think this an idle dream? Nothing could be more practical and realistic . . . This is exactly what causes nightmares in the Kremlin. Think of the unrest in the Red Empire . . . the whole, vast structure shaking . . . the time had seemed perfect. It was easy to believe that the time had come. I had no reason to doubt that the people who brought me this signal were CIA agents."

"How could you?" I said despite myself.

Sempinski stared at me with something like pity. I felt foolish, like a bluffing schoolboy with his hand raised and no answers ready.

"I only mean that we've never done anything like that," I finished lamely. "That isn't our way . . ."

Sempinski nodded gravely.

"Forgive me," he said. "I've made this too abrupt. Certainly, every man believes his country innocent of spying, treachery, broken promises . . . That is the way your enemies go about survival . . . Your hands are always supposed to be clean; you are—how do you say it—St. George in silver armor . . . No, please don't interrupt; I am not mocking you. In fact I envy you this innocence. But only Americans see themselves with American eyes. In Europe, we don't listen to your clergy and your politicians, we do not read the reassurances in your daily press . . . We know that a man does not need absolute purity to stand for a just cause; we have all recognized rust on our own armors. And, in this corner of the world, we know better than most how well your country plays the game of practical politics. Believe me, I had no reason to doubt the source of the plot. And I allowed my patriotism to trap me into organizing violence that, even if it had been inspired by our friends, could only have brought disaster for everyone here. It was an honest act of patriotism, but a form of patriotism that does not belong in the twentieth century."

"But the conspiracy was not American-inspired?"

"No. My first contact was one of our people, a member of an underground organization which works for the West."

I said, feeling a sudden certainty: "Was his name Zimstern?"

"Yes. How did you know?"

"I was sent here to see him by a man called Karpovitch."

"Professor Karpovitch is the famous Magician. A brilliant man. I've known him since he was a child. A truly evil man. But that's a recent discovery of mine. When Zimstern came to see me I had no reason to doubt either him or his master."

"And you began to organize the conspiracy on their word, sir?"

"I received letters from prominent Americans. And, of course, British and American agents began to arrive."

"What agents?"

"It isn't easy to confess that I was a fool . . . My Western agents are our present jailers. But they had been well schooled, their credentials faultless, and those who came as Germans, not as Americans, were vouched for by the others as West German agents of the CIA."

A fit of coughing silenced the old man. When he resumed, his voice was practically inaudible. I leaned forward to hear him, sure that he must soon reach the end of his strength.

"Behind that portrait of the man in armor is a safe. It is open. There's no need for my keepers to lock it from me. The letters are in there for the proper aging and the required dust. That's where they're supposed to be found after the assassination. Get them and read them, Doctor."

I took out a thick package of letters, feeling the familiar opulence of good American bond. I thought that, surely, this white handful of expensive stationery should enjoy extraterritorial rights like embassies; it seemed incongruous in the black tomb of the little

157

vault behind the portrait, with the dungeon coldness of the room laid on its glossy surface.

I took the letters to the window, where the light was better. My tired eyes and the pale conspiratorial moon combined to defeat me; the typescript blurred, words advanced and retreated on the textured pages, but I had no trouble deciphering the sprawling signature of Per Lindstrom.

The letters told the whole story: the conspirators' version. In one letter, Lindstrom wrote "for the President"—as his friend and unofficial agent. Even those typical cautious White House platitudes about freedom took on a sinister ring. In another letter Lindstrom underwrote the coup with half a million dollars. He implied that behind him stood all the American treasure and resources. In yet another letter he urged the execution of the Soviet leaders as the signal for revolt. He undertook to provide the assassin, and promised to advance fifty thousand dollars as the killer's fee. And there were copies of memoranda to and from directors of various United States and allied agencies and the supposed nerve-center of the conspiracy in London—each circumspect enough, as they should be, no single paper deadly in itself, but in sum-total an unanswerable indictment.

Even I, knowing what I did, and sure that these papers could only be forgeries, thought for one nauseating moment that they were authentic. I could imagine how this "proof" would sound and how it would look in the hysterical pages of the world's newspapers.

"The bastards," I said. "Oh, the miserable cunning bastards . . . They really think they can get away with this, don't they?"

"They do."

"The dirty little forgers," I said and threw down the papers, and Sempinski said: "They are not forgers. These are not forgeries."

And I said in a wobbling voice: "They couldn't be anything but forgeries!"

"Perhaps the memoranda. Lindstrom's letters to me are genuine enough."

"Nonsense! Of course they forged the letters! Without the letters they wouldn't have anything, would they? But with the letters, and with you, and with these other forgeries to be found with you after the murder . . . ! Well, they'd have everything, right? Do they have the money?"

"I don't know about the money," Sempinski said gently. "If they have it, it's something very recent. All I know is what they have told me. They have laughed about it. They've said that the money is coming by carrier pigeon."

"I am the carrier pigeon but I certainly didn't bring them any money. Oh, well, I suppose they could always say the money had been spent, although cold American cash, shown as the intercepted payment to the killer, or found on the killer, would really give them an airtight case. And, of course, they'd have the actual assassin."

"I understand they have one," Sempinski said.

"It's Brown, of course, a man who tried to kill me with an air pistol, the same kind of pistol that one of your Germans was carrying. I don't know why he tried to kill me unless he didn't know that I'm also supposed to play some role in this plot. Perhaps the plotters are keeping the two conspiracies apart: their own and Lindstrom's. And Brown is Lindstrom's man . . . But if Brown who is Lindstrom's man is also their assassin, then Lindstrom must also be in this thing . . . And if he is in it, then the forgeries . . . are not forgeries, are they?"

"No. They are not."

I said, cried or thought I did: "How could he do it?"

Sempinski said: "Perhaps he couldn't help it."

"Couldn't help it?"

"Perhaps he thought that he was using *them*. Later they could bring pressure he couldn't resist."

"What pressure? How? What kind of pressure could they bring?"

"They have Kristin here."

159

"Oh," I said, no longer doubting but still unwilling to believe. "That would do it, wouldn't it? Would that be enough?"

"I think so," the old man said. "If Senator Lindstrom is that kind of man."

"He is that kind of man. Oh, they don't miss much, do they!"

"They are professionals."

But wait a minute, I said, still pleading because there had to be some way out of this. "Wait a minute. This is too complicated, too involved for what they'll get out of it. They aren't going to get that much out of it! It's only a cold war gambit, isn't it? It's only propaganda. Why should they go to such infinite trouble for such trivial gain? That's what I don't understand about this whole business. And whom are they going to kill?"

Outside, the wind picked up and the ragged clouds fled before the storm and a vast chill came from the stone walls of the chamber, and this, and the unspoken fear of what was coming next, make me shake inside.

Sempinski said, quietly: "The intended victim is the Chairman of the Soviet Union. He is to be murdered as he speaks this week in the capital."

I was silent, overcome I suppose.

"My good friend, I wish these letters were a forgery. But they are not. They are what convinced me. But in the end it wouldn't have mattered who had written them. What matters is the authorship of the plot itself."

"Old Stalinists . . . new Nazis . . . it doesn't make sense."

"Why not? They were partners once before. Nothing is impossible in practical politics. They're both after the same thing, the continuation of East-West hostility. But there's more to this conspiracy than that."

"What more could there be?"

"This is China's attempt to destroy Soviet authority among the satellite countries and to win control over them. America is the target of the plot only as part of this Grand Design. She must be dishonored, her alliances shattered, her leadership rejected by the

160

Western world so that she can not interfere with Chinese ambitions. But the main purpose of this murder is to show the Eastern world that a *détente* with America and the West is impossible. Every Communist government will feel as mortally threatened as the Soviets themselves. At one stroke, the Chinese will sweep us all into their camp, and destroy you as a moral force in world politics. What more could they want for now?"

"But surely," I said, arguing as if I could force reason into madness, knowing that what I was attempting was hopeless but doing it anyway because, as long as I could resist belief, the truth seemed unproven. "Surely the Chinese involvement will become apparent? The Russians are no fools."

"The Chinese used fools like me, dupes like Lindstrom, Nazis, Stalinists masquerading as CIA agents, and a professional terrorist from London to organize it all. Every thread of the conspiracy leads to the West."

"But what about the Soviets? Surely they'll know who is attacking them."

"If they attempt to ignore or explain away this ultimate blow, no Communist will ever feel safe in their hands again. Besides, no one will want to listen to any explanations."

sixteen

THERE WAS little more that I and Sempinski could tell each other after the novelist's final explanation: the killer's target named and the conspiracy fleshed-out. Now that I knew who was to be murdered, there was even a kind of natural logic to everything that had happened to me, as though by identifying the eye of the hurricane I could see its whole dimension and follow its entire course. Even Lindstrom's involvement on behalf of China made a kind of nightmare sense that needed no particular explanation.

We studied architects' drawings and blueprints made during the reconstruction of Hetmanska Gora and looked at photographs and watercolor sketches of the park and the surrounding country—done in the lost days, Sempinski observed, by long-lost friends. I gave up wondering where the old novelist stored his reserves of strength.

"Once you have left the house," he said. "Cross into the woods here at this point, by the giant oak. You can not miss it even in the snow. It is magnificent . . . I wish you could have seen it in the autumn . . . Then follow the path to a grove of pine . . . there used to be a wooden summerhouse beyond it. Then leave the path. Go west. It will be difficult . . . snow, vegetation, fallen timber . . . Can you read the stars? Good. I hope the night is clear. The park is thickly overgrown at this point but it's the best part of the park for you. It is the closest part to the village. The

162

wall is about a kilometer away. It's far but, again, it's the best wall for you. It's the oldest, in the worst repair. The ditch should be filled with rubble and easy to cross. Once you're across the wall, turn north. Walk across the fields. Don't stop no matter how tired you are; you would freeze in moments. In half an hour you will reach the village road."

I wanted to destroy the letters but Sempinski stopped me. I would need them at the embassy; without them, no one would even bother to believe my story. I put them back in the safe with misgivings.

"Take them when you come to say goodbye to me," Sempinski said quietly.

We took particular care to avoid the subject of Sempinski left alone to face the conspirators' vengeance. He was calm, seemingly untroubled. His face was marked with a kind of exaltation as if whatever lay in store for him had been preordained. I did not pity him; he would have disdained pity. Also, I sensed his need for expiation.

Then, because this was another matter that was very much with us, I asked Sempinski about Kristin Napoji. Abandoning the ill old man to the plotters' anger was unavoidable; leaving her behind would be inconceivable.

Sempinski was adamant about that.

"You can't seriously think about taking her with you? That is out of the question."

I said: "I'm not so sure."

"You have no right to jeopardize your chances. They are miserable enough as it is. Surely you can see that? Nothing can be allowed to burden you or distract you or load you down with additional responsibility. She'd tell you that herself."

"Perhaps she would. But I'm still responsible for her being here."

"So it's a matter of your conscience, is it? Is that more important than what you have to do?"

"I have to live with it."

"Be wary of it. A conscience is the hobble of the intellectual man. If she were my own daughter I wouldn't allow her to jeopardize your chances."

"Would she really do that?"

"You'd never reach the capital if she were along."

I didn't want to offend the old man or to have him disappointed in me. It seemed a good idea to distract him.

I asked: "What kind of girl is she?"

"I see her often. It amuses my keepers to let her visit me. We've talked a great deal. She is the kind of young woman that young men can dream of. But no matter how fine she may be you can't take her with you. A man can lose himself in crowds if he is lucky and if he knows how to go about it. But anyone who had ever seen her would remember her."

"I don't remember her too well," I said.

"Then leave it at that."

I left Sempinski's room soon afterward through the huge hearth and chimney, armed with plans and blueprints, and found my own chamber without any trouble. I marked my several secret roads through the labyrinth and moved my furs, pistol and briefcase to the bricked-up hideout. I thought that I would transfer my passport, papers and money to my pockets later, and abandon the briefcase but, for the moment, the briefcase was an adequate container. I burrowed with the stolid assurance of a mole, a resident of long standing, through the black tunnels that had meant such horror. They were still a foul, infested maze of web and glittering eye and softly undulating ceilings and hungry, pulsing walls. But once mapped and measured they were no longer menacing with the dark promise of the utterly unknown. I made work for myself despite my exhaustion: folding the furs, counting money. But I was conscious of fraud as I did it and, in the end, after I had run out of hairs to split, I had to get on with what I had been trying to put off. I studied the mapped maze where, at the end of yet another tunnel, there was a granite chamber similar to my own: the young woman's room, one floor below.

It would be up to me whether I took her along or not but I

didn't want to make any decisions just then. Everything that Sempinski had said about jeopardy was probably true; our trail would be marked as clearly as a highway for the pursuers to follow. And the girl, no matter how fine or brave would call for special care and compromise with hardships. But everything that I had thought about my responsibility for her predicament had also been true.

I half hoped that I wouldn't be able to find her room but Sempinski's drawings had been accurate. Her room, like mine, lay off a main shaft easy to find and follow. I hoped I'd find her fireplace bricked-up and thus have no need to make any decision. But the granite cave was open, clean and dry. She had an iron lantern splashing light off her bedside table. I could see the glow long before I got close to her room, crawling much slower than I had to and making more noise. I dropped into the fireplace and the light, rising slowly, aware of a particularly soft smell and a whispering sound to my right and above me, the motion of swiftly parting air, an object descending. And then my head blew up and the light withdrew into a pinpoint rainbow nucleus turning like a wheel with multicolored spokes.

Cold water revived me. I saw her face above me: whiter and thinner than I remembered or thought I remembered, not quite sure what there was to remember. My head was pounding like a copper kettle.

She had spread a cold wet facecloth on my forehead, and put a pillow under my neck, and all too soon I had no more excuse for lolling about in semiconsciousness. She helped me to sit up and to lean against the carved brackets of the hearth. I took my time about speaking, not sure I could do it. I looked about the room, focusing my eyes experimentally on the delicately fluted columns of her bed, the dark hangings, the maroon richness of an inlaid hardwood dais, iron-studded coffers, benches heaped with a barbaric profusion of cushions, and the blue and gold checkerboard of the painted ceiling. I had expected to see a barricade in front of her door: chairs, chests, tin basins and that sort of thing; it was the kind of thing I thought a woman would construct under the circumstances. But she had piled nothing against her door. Well, I thought, no wonder. My head felt as if the girl (now so quietly attentive, waiting so patiently for me to start talking, neither anxious nor afraid) had pulled the ceiling down on it; paint, molding, coffered squares and all.

"What did you hit me with?" I asked. I groped with cautious fingers around my aching head. I didn't care about her choice of bludgeon but an acknowledgment was due.

"A shoe."

"A football boot?"

"A sensible English shoe. Is your head all right?"

"I can't say."

"It looks all right. A little sooty, and there's a small spider walking on it, but it looks all right."

"I can feel the spider. He's wearing the boots."

She brushed the spider gently into the fireplace.

"He's really very small."

"Large feet, though," I said. "What size shoes do you wear, anyway?"

"Six and a half," she said smiling.

I looked at her then, feeling as if my face and head were covered with feathers.

She was fine drawn; her face seemed smaller than I remembered and terribly young: the richly textured, smooth face of a beautiful young woman that, I thought, should be worn in lockets. There was the start of a troubled line above her left eye; an astonishing brown eye like a brightly lit intelligent almond that was suddenly no longer brown but deep gold; a very large, thoughtful eye seated calmly over a delicately angled cheekbone, reaching out toward the dark frame of hair with a small starburst of humorous wrinkles. Small shadows under the cheeks, small but firm chin. Her hair was brown but, I thought, there had to be a better way to describe it because it was a great deal more than simply brown hair. She had worn it like a red-gold cap in New York but now it was combed out and brushed past her shoulders: two even wings of

166

chestnut made bright by the yellow-red light of the lantern. I wondered why I should have thought of her as having been blond. I suppose that I had been too full of Sempinski during my lunch with her to get more than a general impression of summer-light hair, the deep gold tan that comes from tennis and the foredeck of a catamaran in the Sound, thoughtful eyes and an odd tranquillity. The lunch had been business and she an interviewing editor. I had thought her particularly well-read and interested, and her questions had been not only pertinent but intelligent and that, in itself, was such a revolutionary change for an editorial lunch that it would have crowded the other impressions aside.

Beautiful, yes; she was that, I could see. But there was no one feature or set of features that made her beautiful. Nothing intruded, nothing said: Here, this is beauty, this couldn't be improved upon, take note and pay attention and never mind the rest. Perhaps her hair and the delicately arched nose and finely turned nostrils could have made some such statement. They seemed independent enough to say anything, but I had the feeling they would say nothing of the kind.

Nothing was truly perfect anyway, anywhere. And beauty is a joint internal and external production. Her mouth might have been too broad, too generous, but I thought it splendid. Her face was possibly too small and young and unmarked; the laughing starburst and the gentle lines so hard to credit on her forehead were more ornaments than blemish. I would not argue with a beauty expert about her, I supposed, but I would demand proof of expertise if there was an argument. As for the rest, she wasn't gaunt, bony, concave or cadaverous enough to model for high-fashion magazines. She had a fullness quite as generous as her mouth but it was not intrusive, so that, at first glance, I would have thought her more delicately constructed than she was.

In total of face, features, body, bearing, the lessons she had learned and those she had rejected, her manner and the sense of quiet awareness that she seemed to wear as naturally as her hair, I thought her extraordinary.

There was no longer any question in my mind that she would

come with me from Hetmanska Gora. All that mattered was to have her out of the madman's dream of plots and castles, back where nothing could do her any harm. It was as if I had come to that country for no other purpose.

And, in the meantime, I was in her room, and the bottle-bottom panes of mullioned windows had become dull and ill-defined, and there was a pale blue edge along the hem of the sky.

She asked, again, if I was all right.

I said that I was.

"I didn't know who or what you were," she explained. She gestured toward a serviceable, low-heeled walking shoe. Then she laughed. "You sounded like a bear in that chimney. I didn't know who you were until I washed your face. Does your head still hurt?"

"Yes," I said, feeling stuffed with sawdust. I coughed to clear my throat. "I suppose it does."

I watched her push the shoe out of sight behind her. She sat back on her heels and put her hands carefully in her lap and waited. And I was suddenly aware of the deep, unnerving V of her robe where it had become disarranged a little: a tawny, tailored garment of cashmere or camel hair or Shetland wool trimmed in small dark flowers, making her look both coolly competent and vulnerable: a young girl home for the holidays. (To be what after school? An actress? A writer? Something that required both dedication and illusions.)

Listen, I'm not a dull, witless clod, I wanted to say. Instead I said: "We haven't much time."

"Yes," she said.

I stared. "Yes what?"

"The time," she said. "I was just agreeing that it's getting light outside. You have to get back to your room before morning."

I nodded and at once my head threatened to roll off my shoulders. My eyes slid out of focus.

"Your head is really bad, isn't it."

She looked at me steadily and with particular care as if aware of a new and unexpected quality. Then she smiled, the eyes warmer, bigger. She said that sunrise was at six. The pale light outside meant that there was not more than an hour before breakfast. I should be starting back to my own room.

"You've had a bad bump. Probably a mild concussion. I'm sorry about that. I put my heart and soul behind that shoe. Next time I'll make sure I have the right victim. You obviously don't feel like talking very much and, besides, you must be asleep in your bed before they bring your breakfast. You mustn't let them suspect anything."

"Yes," I said. "Of course."

"Will you be able to sleep? I mean, really sleep. They are so terribly clever, you see . . . I'm just afraid they'd catch you if you were pretending."

"Are they that good?"

"Quite first rate. They've caught me every time I tried anything. You will try to sleep?"

"I'll try."

"They mustn't catch on to what you're going to do."

"We," I said. "We are going to do it. I'm taking you with me."

She didn't comment. Instead she said: "Do you know what this is all about?"

I told her about my visit to Sempinski.

"Oh, of course," she said. "That's how you knew where to find me. God, I am sorry about that damn shoe."

"It's all right," I said.

"The devil it is. You don't know how glad I was when I recognized you. A bit late, I admit. We waited for you as if you were some kind of a Messiah, and the first thing I do is bop you with a boot."

"Shoe," I said, dull.

She laughed then; a clear, open sound that was remarkably good to hear. It didn't bother my headache at all. The dull pounding roar in my head began to subside.

"You're too forgiving. But I'm glad. When can you come back so that we can talk?"

I said: "Let's talk now. There might not be another opportunity."

She looked doubtful but agreed that we could try to talk now if we kept one eye on the graying windows and one on a watch. She had a lot to tell me. Was there anything about the plot that I didn't know?

"Two things," I said. "The Zero Hour for the assassination and the money. Did they ever get that half million dollars?"

She said that she didn't know but didn't think so. She and Sempinski had wondered about that. None of the guards had boasted about it, which they would have done if this last necessary piece of evidence had been acquired on schedule. As for the date of the assassination, that would depend on when the Soviet Chairman was to speak.

"Has he already arrived in this country?" she wanted to know.

"I think he was expected this week. I wish I knew how much time we have."

"How much do we need?"

"Three or four days to reach the capital. That much again for the embassy to check our story, contact Washington and get their instructions. Or perhaps Washington will take over the job from then on. Then a few hours to get the security people in this country going. I've no idea what the embassy is going to do to get the officials in the capital to believe them. Frankly I don't care. I just want to get all this into competent American hands and forget about it. Ten days wouldn't be too much for everything that has to be done."

"I am sure there is at least that much time. Do you know anything about the American assassin they are supposed to have?"

"Yes," I said, suddenly uncomfortable. I told her about Brown and the episode in Zimstern's store, then about the wolves and the air pistol.

"I don't think there can be any doubt that that's our man." Then, because her pallor was extraordinary and her eyes bleak: "Do you know him? He works for your uncle?"

She nodded.

"I'm sorry," I said. "I wish your uncle wasn't mixed up in this.

Perhaps there's still some explanation for his part in it. The letter could still be a forgery."

She shook her head. She said she knew her uncle's signature too well; and she knew her uncle. He could have written such letters, knowing what they meant.

"Because you are a hostage?"

"Yes. But the first letters were written long before I came here. You see, Uncle Per wants a war with Russia. To his way of thinking it would be a sort of Holy War . . . provided America got the chance to strike first. He could have been blackmailed into writing some of the later letters and reports. But his offer of money was made almost a year ago."

"I see."

"Do you really? I wonder. You probably think him either mad or evil."

I didn't want to cause her any pain. I said: "Perhaps he is less evil than misguided."

"He's not misguided. To be misguided a man must be led. Uncle Per has never followed anyone; he would always do anything to have his own way. And since he thinks that his way is the only right way you can't call him evil. He is a dedicated man. Terribly wrong but not evil."

I nodded to change the subject and watched her warm, impassioned face, the intense eyes, and shoulders straight and rigid under the soft robe. I saw the fragmentary tremor on her lips. I thought that I would give a lot to see her come to my defense as readily as she had come to that of Per Lindstrom.

But time was passing all too rapidly and there were still arrangements to be made for the escape. I told her quickly when we would escape, and how. And she said quietly: "You know that you don't have to take me with you, don't you?"

"That's what Sempinski tried to tell me."

"He's right, you know. You don't owe me anything. The plotters would have got me into their hands one way or another. They know Uncle Per's weaknesses and I am one of them. They would hardly have missed the best possible pawn for their blackmail games. That's why you shouldn't blame yourself for sending me here. And besides, I planned an escape of my own. Now that I know a way out of the house I have a chance to try it. Don't worry, I'll do very well."

I laughed then, feeling better than I had felt all night. Her face flushed quickly, her eyes alight and wide to meet this challenge that I had not meant as a challenge at all. Her breast rose, the shoulders lifted, the round chin came up. She stabbed the cold, dank air with small fists.

"You don't believe I've thought about escaping?" she demanded. "Who do you think would have had to do this job if you hadn't come? I really don't need any help from you."

I said: "Maybe I need your help."

She was immediately silent. Then her shoulders bowed and her hands moved once more into her lap and folded there. Her angry flush receded. I watched her thinking how beautiful she was in or out of anger. I wished that I could make my voice less hard and impersonal but everything I said sounded abrupt and cold.

"I'll come for you early. Perhaps in the meantime we can find out about the money and the timing. We'll start a little after nine tonight. We'll go down into that bricked-up fireplace and wait until the guards have cleared off. Then we'll try the greenhouse and the park."

I laughed then because there was a question that I had to ask and it made everything seem ridiculous: the night, myself, my plans and even the girl.

"Any questions?"

"No," she said. "No questions. Except one: Are you sure that you want me along? If you have any doubts about it, I'd rather not go."

"No doubts," I said aware of several. "The problem will be to get to the village and to hire a sleigh. From then on . . . well, it will be up to luck and to whatever gods look after fugitives."

"I'll have to make a special sacrifice," she said, then laughed.

"Sacrifice?"

"This is an old house and there are all sorts of very ancient gods to get on our side. I'm an expert on them, thanks to Professor Sempinski."

"I hope they're not reconstructed gods."

But she was no longer laughing. I supposed that she might have been thinking about the old man who would not go with us. I listened to the silence of the house.

The corners of the room had become light blue and the lantern dimmed. There was a particular coldness in the room, the chill of the morning. Outside, black clouds fled before the wind. I thought that there might be heavy snowfall later in the day. I heard the sound of my own breathing and the low humming of the wind high up in the chimney.

"Well, I'll go now," I said.

She nodded, quiet.

"And about tonight . . . Don't pack anything. Wear everything warm that you have. And listen" (I went on, leaning forward, suddenly anxious to see her smile or to hear her laugh, and troubled about it): "Do your best with the *Lares* and *Penates,* will you? I have a feeling we'll need everything they've got."

Back in my room I washed myself from head to foot in the cold water basin that, along with an enameled white jug, a towel and a chamberpot (a porcelain cauldron bordered with hand-painted forget-me-nots) was my medieval bathroom. Scrubbed clean, the black water carefully poured into the deep cracks between flagstones, dressed in fresh pajamas (the grimy debris of my clothes stuffed high onto the first ledge of the chimney) I lay in bed under the reassuring canopy and watched the gray day stalk across the tree-tops.

I waited for sleep, sure that it wouldn't come. My hunger returned and with it an extraordinary thirst. But I didn't waste time thinking about discomforts. I reviewed the night, not quite able to believe anything about it. I was, at best, a mildly interested observer watching myself go through the mental motions that would have puzzled me if I had understood them.

seventeen

GUARDS WOKE ME with breakfast: one slice of black-brown bread crusted with yellow flour, a peeled cucumber, coffee stiff with sugar. I was instantly awake.

Outside my window, the clouds were thick and black, an oily mass twisting bitterly overhead. Under them, the day was crisp and clean. I could see a long way toward the purpling towers of the southern range.

The house stood on a mound. The park fell steeply away from under my window into an ironed flatness. Tree crowns were globular with packed snow and ice. Beyond them was the plain. The land was still, and desolate and dreaming.

I drank my coffee while I shaved and dressed, taking my time. I took my time about everything that morning. The snow began to fall; soon I could see nothing through the window in the new, gray light.

I didn't think about the coming night. I supposed that I hadn't had enough sleep: no more than an hour. My head felt heavy but there seemed to be surprisingly little in it beyond a gray dullness. I didn't think that I would be able to come up with anything new to do with the escape; it seemed less real with each passing minute.

The sour black bread tasted like damp putty. I was about to

start on the cucumber when locks ground and grated behind me, the door opened and struck against granite, and there was the harsh clatter of heavy boots more or less in step. The doorway filled with men: my escort of last afternoon, my inefficient guardian —looking well-rested after a good night's sleep, and a dozen others. I noticed that my guide of last night, the insolent young man who had so annoyed me, wasn't there. The men wore the holiday faces of Roman circus-goers. Behind them was Karpovitch.

He wore a faultless suit of English country tweeds and a pale mustache. His hair had been cut short; it was no longer nondescript as it had been in London. He looked younger, fresher and infinitely dangerous.

"Good morning," he said. He sat on my bed and lit a cigarette. "Don't let me interrupt your breakfast."

He waved a careless but imperious hand toward the others. My former escort snapped to attention behind me. The others began searching the room. They wasted no motion. My suitcase was emptied on a sheet, the clothes and toiletries were fingered and probed. I thanked whatever providence looks after secret agents for my foresight that had allowed me to save and hide my briefcase and its contents in the bricked-up fireplace downstairs; escape would have become impossible without my passport, papers and the little money that I had. The searchers worked in disciplined silence that was broken only by the soft tapping of Karpovitch's elegantly shod foot on the granite floor.

"Continue with your breakfast," Karpovitch said easily. "I'm sorry we can't compete with gourmet fare, but it's good, nourishing food. Peasants thrive on it in this country."

I said: "It's hardly first-class service."

Karpovitch laughed.

"But that's the way of the world, isn't it? The world is a cucumber, like the one you're eating. Just as you think you have it in your hand, you find it has been rudely pushed up another portion of your anatomy. But, I must say, you don't seem surprised to see me?"

"Surprised? Yes, I'm surprised."

175

Karpovitch studied me with quiet curiosity and I felt my heart beating up a little. I knew that this was the principal adversary, the enemy-in-chief; I found myself shaken despite my best efforts.

I tried to look into the cynical cold eyes, and the sharp fox-mask, without showing fear. Everything about Karpovitch made me think of foxes: the angular thin face with protruding cheekbones, the thin mouth and the yellow mustache streaked with white and stained with nicotine, the narrow forehead receding under the tight cap of close-cropped pale hair, and the sleek impression of a winter pelt in his russet clothes. But if this was a fox, it would have to be a particularly cynical and cruel animal, with a touch of the wolf.

The trick was not to panic. I thought that Karpovitch would expect me to act both surprised and angry but I had little faith in my histrionic abilities. I had no wish to underestimate him; more than anything, I needed time to arrange my tactics. I stared at Karpovitch with worried indignation.

"Yes, I'm surprised," I said again. "Although nothing should surprise me about this damn place."

"You don't care for it? I find it picturesque."

"This is a madhouse. I don't know what's going on here but someone had better be ready to explain my locked door and these incredible housemen. What are you doing here, anyway? What's your connection with this?"

"One question at a time, Dr. Shippe. Let's just say that I am here to taste a moment of triumph."

"You're mad," I said. I hoped my anger sounded and looked convincing. "I don't know what you're talking about but you're stark raving mad."

"You've made your point, Shippe. Now do be quiet. This is necessary. A faithful servant expects his little moment of strutting and crowing. I find it quite amusing not to disappoint my critical employer: he must be made to realize in full the importance of my contribution. Also, I expect an interesting reaction from you. But go on with your cucumber. I'm sorry we could not get you an egg for your breakfast but there is a temporary shortage of dairy products."

"A necessary sacrifice, I'm sure."

The wooden platter was too far away to reach with the cucumber, and I didn't think that I would be able to walk the necessary three or four feet without betraying how frightened I was. I started eating the watery vegetable; it tasted clean and cool.

"Good of you to take this attitude," Karpovitch said coldly. "I agree that the servants here are incredible. But they are only temporarily in domestic service. The older men, in fact, are really high-ranking officers of certain government departments in East Germany and here. Once a colonel, always a colonel, you know—whether the fellow is driving a taxi or polishing silver. You must have met several types like that in London."

When I said nothing, Karpovitch nodded to himself, smiling a little.

"You never met the good General Danilow, did you? No, he was already an *emigrant* when you came to London. Gone to Canada, as they say. His own fault, you know. He had stumbled on a clue to my identity during his visit to the capital last year; our friend Zimstern slipped up. I think you might have liked Danilow. Whom else did you meet? Let's see, there was Potter, an unimportant cog. There was Brown. You'll have an opportunity to meet him again. That really answers most of your questions. As for your locked door, that's easy to explain. You are a very special guest."

"You mean I am a prisoner."

My voice, I noted, was quavering a little, which was the correct sound for the impression I was trying to convey. Something was going to happen and I realized that I was too tired to cope with it; I felt as if my mind was falling off a hillside.

"Well, yes, if you insist on a specific definition. A little patience, and you'll know everything that might interest you."

One of the searchers said something then in a voice that promised nothing good, in a language that I didn't understand. Karpovitch listened carefully. His knowing eyes were amused and curious but also watchful now, as if he had sensed a distant possibility of danger. His thin lips formed a speculative circle.

"Where are your papers?"

"In my briefcase," I blurted out, trying to play for time.

"And where is your briefcase?" Karpovitch asked softly.

"Downstairs," I said. My stomach turned slowly over and over. I tasted the muddy coffee and the sour black bread. It had been sheer afterthought that had prompted me to take the briefcase to the bricked-up hideout.

"Where downstairs?"

"I don't know," I lied. "The man who brought me here took it away with him. Something to do with reporting my arrival to the authorities. At least that's what he said. I don't know anything about it."

"I think you're lying."

"Why should I be lying?"

"There's something wrong here," Karpovitch said slowly. "No one reported taking your briefcase from you. I don't like coming up on unreported facts . . . they have a way of proving quite significant. I think we had best send for the man who brought you to this room."

He said something quickly to his men. One of them answered with a prolonged shaking of his head and a gesture indicating both his watch and the white distances stretching outside the windows. Karpovitch became very still. He barked an order and my former escort left the room at once.

"The man who brought you here has already left for the capital," Karpovitch said quietly. "Another surprise? But you couldn't have known that he wouldn't be here. Are you bluffing, Shippe? I truly hope I haven't underestimated you. That could prove dangerous to us both. You are, quite frankly, not what I expected."

I felt a tremor start along my upper thighs. I couldn't control it. I was terribly afraid that I had given myself away. I tried to calm myself, counting numbers and keeping my breath shallow.

I was afraid of Karpovitch's brain more than of any possible violence or pain. It was a brain that had survived decades of international plotting and maneuvering; I was no match for a man like that. Be calm, I told myself. Make your mind blank. Communicate nothing. Karpovitch will sense it.

Two more men left the room on Karpovitch's order. He had lit a fresh cigarette and I suddenly realized that he was under extraordinary tension. His calmness was a fraud. I couldn't help admiring his iron self-control even though I didn't understand the reasons for his tension. I was aware of my own heightened perceptions and my growing calmness as I weighed and evaluated Karpovitch's inner turmoil.

"Something about you puzzles me," Karpovitch said. "You're not as stupid as you should have been. There is a feeling of, what shall I call it, awareness? about you . . . a cold emanation . . . I wonder just how much you've guessed and what you're up to. I have a feeling that you're trying to fool me. You had better not try. I'll have you flayed alive if I should think that you represent the slightest danger to me. Make no mistake about that. You are among men who kill people as easily as you might kill a fly. I am beginning to regret that I had you brought here."

He got up and began to walk about the room. He looked at his watch and ordered two more men to go downstairs and to join in the search for my briefcase. I couldn't understand his interest in my luggage.

"It's all gone so well," Karpovitch said more to himself than to me and his remaining two men. "Everything is ready. The Chairman landed in the capital this morning. He'll speak in three days. The press of the entire world will be there to hear him and see him. I've worked too hard to have anything go wrong now; there's too much at stake. And something has already slipped a little. The CIA has come into the picture. How? What could have happened?"

He turned suddenly toward me.

"I have an idea that you know something about that. I had

Brown hidden at Zimstern's store, exactly where he should have been hiding if he had been a Western assassin. But something went wrong, he had to run for it. He left two dead men behind him and one of them was a CIA agent. What was he doing there?"

I said: "I don't know what you are talking about."

"Oh, you don't, eh? Well, I'll tell you, since we have a little time. In three days we are going to kill a man in the capital. We've gone to great lengths to make sure that this murder is blamed on your CIA. Brown was to be the weapon found at the scene of the crime, along with his host Zimstern, a known Western agent. Why did Brown suddenly kill Zimstern and a CIA agent who had no business knowing about Zimstern? The puzzle is beginning to assume dangerous proportions."

I said: "As I remember, you are fond of puzzles."

"You didn't have anything to do with Zimstern's murder, did you? You wouldn't be, by any chance, an agent yourself? But no, that's impossible. If you had been an agent, suspecting anything, you wouldn't have walked into this trap. And you wouldn't have sent me Lindstrom's girl. I'm grateful for that. I had that megalomaniac well in line but she made all the difference. With her in my hands I could give the orders . . . You should have seen Lindstrom's face when he finally knew who was the tool and who was the master. How quickly he collapsed . . . We could move rapidly after that. There was no question, then, of getting all the necessary papers and, of course, the money. And that is something else for which I must thank you."

"Money? What money? What in hell are you talking about?"

"Whether you know it or not, you've brought me half a million dollars. It's in your briefcase, in large denomination notes easily traceable to Lindstrom. It's the last evidence that I needed to hang your precious United States."

"What do you have against the United States, Karpovitch?"

"Absolutely nothing. I don't like Americans but that is merely a matter of taste. Hardly anyone likes Americans except the Americans themselves and that, of course, is useful to my plans.

But, unlike everybody else in my conspiracy, I have no ideological involvement. Nevertheless there'll be a certain satisfaction in knowing that I shall be instrumental in the overthrow of one of the greatest powers on earth."

"If you're so confident about that, why are you so nervous?"

"I don't know why I am uneasy. It must be the strain of this climactic moment. We'll find your briefcase and we'll find Brown in time to leave him dead, shot by security men, with the murder weapon in his hands and American money stuffed in all his pockets. And we have unanswerable documentary proof that Brown was sent and paid by Lindstrom to murder the Chairman and that Lindstrom was acting for the American government."

"You'll never get away with this. This proof can be repudiated."

"Who'll repudiate it? Lindstrom is committing suicide day after tomorrow, on the eve of the assassination. The horror of America's crime will have proved too much even for that fanatic. Do you think that I am such a fool, such an amateur, as to leave a single thread unraveled?"

"Somebody will stop you."

"Shut up. You bore me. If I didn't need you here as Lindstrom's courier and Brown's paymaster I'd have you killed right now. So don't, as your people say, push your luck, Shippe."

"But I didn't come here as Lindstrom's messenger. I've had no contact with him, have you forgotten that? Pohl sent me here to inspect the Pontic Tribunals. Or is he also working for you?"

"Peripherally, yes. He is quite adequately linked with Lindstrom, Brown and Zimstern as far as your being sent here is concerned. He doesn't even know that I exist. All he knows is that Lindstrom ordered him to give you a certain briefcase and to see to it that you took it with you. Besides, is your Mr. Pohl likely to kick up a fuss once he knows what kind of conspiracy he has been involved in?"

"You didn't miss a thing, did you?" I said. Karpovitch started laughing.

"You look so damn forlorn, like a child who finds out that Father Christmas is a fake, like Lindstrom looked when he saw himself as a witless tool . . . Of course I didn't miss a thing. And in your briefcase is the most spectacular proof of my efficiency. I want to present this proof to my employers and earn my place of power in the sun."

Karpovitch no longer paid any attention to me. He walked up and down the chamber, occasionally stopping to look at his watch. I supposed that nothing was important to him at that moment except the contents of my briefcase. But what contents? Where could they be hidden? I was sure that I had not brought a fortune in dollars in my briefcase.

I heard footsteps in the corridor, the quiet drone of voices. Karpovitch became still.

A dozen men came in, followed by the heavy, commanding individual whom I had observed in the library. I was aware of an air of menace, an almost tangible emanation of antagonism rigidly repressed.

The new arrival sat down in my only chair. He took a short black cigarette from a silver case and worked it carefully into his ivory holder. One of his men hurried forward at once with a burning lighter.

The man said: "Proceed."

Karpovitch said carefully: "Shouldn't we wait for the Chinese delegate, General? For the rest of the staff?"

"They aren't coming."

"I had hoped . . ."

"I know what you had hoped."

"It would be simple to take the briefcase to the conference rooms," Karpovitch said, his words unnaturally precise. "I am sure that the whole staff would be pleased to see what we have, General."

The heavy man's yellow and strangely flat eyes centered on Karpovitch. He blew a careful smoke ring and watched it drift, dissolving, across the agent's face.

He said, as if unaware that he was speaking: "What you are sure of and what you are unsure of can be of interest only to yourself. I caution you against putting undue strain on my patience.

182

You've done competent work, you are in fair standing. What is it that you want? Praise and salutes?"

The general raised his cigarette and holder slightly in the air, and inclined his huge head a fraction of an inch.

"Consider yourself saluted. Now proceed. I have come here despite an understandably busy schedule as a token of my appreciation for your work. I have no time to waste."

A nerve had begun to work spasmodically in Karpovitch's cheek.

He said: "We have to wait a moment, General."

"Wait?"

"We must find the briefcase. In this briefcase lies the last strand of the conspiracy . . . the absolute proof of American complicity . . . the money used to pay the assassin and back the revolt . . . in notes of $10,000 traceable to the emissary of the American government."

"We are quite aware of the importance of the money," the general said. "Please don't waste my time."

"Yes," Karpovitch said with deceptive mildness. He would not look at any of the others who now began to stare at him.

"Without this money," he said. "Without the documents . . . But yes, I know the general has no time to waste. I will not waste his time. The money, then. We shall shortly have it. I have sent men to get it."

"Where is it?"

"Downstairs, sir. It had been left downstairs. A man will shortly bring it."

"I will wait one minute," the general said.

"The briefcase will be here in a moment. It is a special case with a compartment built into the lid. Absolutely foolproof . . . a part of the case itself. There are no secret locks, no such amateur devices. The case was built for this specific mission. It is clearly labeled with this man's name and address. When it is ripped open before the correspondents . . ."

My former escort came into the room, his lips fixed in an idiotic smile.

"Herr Professor . . ."

"The briefcase," Karpovitch said sharply. "Well? Do you have it?"

"No sir. We've looked everywhere."

"Everywhere?" Karpovitch's voice was heavy with elaborate patience. "Obviously you haven't looked everywhere, idiot. Go back and find it at once."

The German said: "Maybe it's here somewhere."

"It isn't here! Go back downstairs and get it!"

"Where shall we look, professor?"

"What do you mean, fool? Look everywhere that you've already looked and everywhere you haven't!"

Karpovitch's voice and manner had lost some of their calmness. The general leaned forward. One set of fingers whitened on a knee. The other grasped the carved lion's paw that ornamented the arm of his chair.

Karpovitch seemed to bend as if a heavy weight had settled on his shoulders. His silent lips moved with terrifying slowness. They had lost their color.

The general said icily: "You have lost the briefcase?"

Karpovitch said nothing.

"Five hundred thousand dollars is a substantial sum," the general said as though bemused. "Enough to tempt most men into treason. I am prepared to hear any reasonable explanation. You have one, of course?"

Karpovitch slowly shook his head.

"This wouldn't be another of your magic games, would it, Magician? I don't believe that even you would dare to jest with me."

"I am not joking, sir," Karpovitch said quietly.

"I see," the general said. His voice was soft and distant. "Then I assume that you have failed to procure the money. That is the most charitable assumption I am able to make. Is that what happened? You've failed? You blundered?"

Karpovitch said nothing. He stared with the mild expression of a disillusioned child over the general's head, past me and the others, at the soft mounds of snow transfiguring the windows.

"You were a famous man, Karpovitch," the general said slowly. "You were a legend that even I had been tempted to believe. That is why I recommended you to Pekin. And now you put me in a difficult position. I have never been known to fail at anything. I'm sure that you're familiar with my record. I can not, therefore, admit that I have failed. The only explanation I can offer to our Chinese allies is sabotage and treason. I hope I've made myself clear?"

"I've not betrayed you," Karpovitch said quietly.

The general gave a dry, unpleasant laugh.

"Astonishing how alike all you intellectuals are. How ready to swear undying loyalty as soon as a sword hangs over your heads. Your oath is hardly worth five hundred thousand dollars. Your head, at this moment, is worth about five cents."

"Then give me five cents' worth of opportunity to repair the damage."

"You mean you have an explanation after all? Perhaps you will produce a magic briefcase for me?"

"The briefcase was brought into this house, General. It can't have flown away."

"Reassuring. I think that you are merely playing for time, Karpovitch. But I will give you five cents' worth of mercy. If by tomorrow morning you can produce the money, you will keep your head. That's a fair exchange. As you know, I am leaving for the capital as soon as we conclude this ridiculous performance. I shall be in my office at seven in the morning. If you are there at seven-thirty with five hundred thousand American dollars, you will be alive at seven-thirty-five."

"That's only slightly more than twenty hours . . ."

"Damn you!" the general shouted. "Do you think you can bargain with *me?*"

He was out of his chair and on his feet with speed I would never have believed possible for such a heavy man, and gone from the room as if a hurricane had swept him through the door. His men backed out behind him.

Karpovitch uttered one sharp, violent exclamation. I tried to keep absolutely still so as to draw no attention to myself. Despite my fear and awareness of terrible danger I looked at him with a fascination that bordered on pity.

As far as the top echelons of the conspiracy were concerned, Karpovitch was finished. He had less than a day to find the missing money and he wouldn't even suspect where to look for it. And that meant that when I fled the castle with Kristin and Sempinski's letters, I would have the money. The plotters would lack their evidence. Even the spent old man up the corridor wouldn't be useful to them.

This wouldn't mean the end of the plot, I knew well enough. But it might slow it up a bit; it might gain time for Washington and local officials to move against the plotters. If nothing else, I would be able to upset the schedule.

My God, I thought, silly with relief. It might work, after all. They're not infallible. They can be defeated. I might just manage to get the job done.

eighteen

THE REST OF THE day passed in a blur of conflicting thought. I swung from wildest optimism—seeing myself and Kristin safe in the embassy, the Lindstrom papers and the money turned over, the plot exposed and the conspirators scattering for cover—to the deepest doubt. Karpovitch wasn't a man to give up that easily. And he was not a man ever to take for granted.

I couldn't help feeling a grudging admiration for the Master Spy. The Nazis and their middle-aged compatriots had fallen into bewildered pieces with their hopes demolished but Karpovitch had stood his ground before the menace of the general.

I wondered who the general was and where he fitted into the framework of the plot. I was sure that he was one of the highest leaders, in power in the capital where he had an office. The embassy would have to be told about his complicity. I hoped that I would never come across him again or have to face him.

I tried to put myself into Karpovitch's place to guess how he would go about recovering the money. The only reason he had not guessed my part in the disappearance of the briefcase was that no one knew that I had found a way out of my locked and guarded room. It wouldn't take him long to get on the right track; all he had to do was contact the man who, I had said, had taken the briefcase. I had no doubt about what would happen then: Karpovitch would find a way to persuade me to tell him where his money was.

I waited for the day to pass counting interminable hours. I expected Karpovitch to return at any moment. I couldn't keep my eyes away from the door; each second was an eternity of dread and waiting. I grew progressively more nervous about the escape; it was all right to think about as something that I would have to do in the unspecified future, but each of the terrible slow minutes brought that future closer. I was sure that I had forgotten something vitally important.

Guards brought me my midday meal: boiled meat and a boiled potato. I hadn't seen these men before, they didn't look German. I had heard several cars driving away from the house in the morning; there was an impression of great activity going on around me but the thick walls insulated me from anything that might have told me what was going on. I supposed that with the Chairman of the Soviet Union already in the capital, the conspirators were moving their forces into position for the coup. Loss of Lindstrom's money wouldn't change the plan. In my brief and now forgotten moment of relief, I had thought that they might hesitate or falter with the money gone, but there was no reason why they should. The money was Karpovitch's problem. Everything else must have been proceeding according to plan. And that would still call for the assassination to take place in three days—an impossibly short time for everything that I had to do. But there was one bright spot on the otherwise dismal and threatening horizon: Karpovitch had said something about the CIA. The fat bald man whom I had thought to be a Nakomda man had been, apparently, an American agent. But why had he been following me around the capital? And how had he been so miraculously at hand in Zimstern's store? There was no use even thinking about that, far less seeking answers. But if the CIA already had some inkling of the plot it would make my job at the embassy infinitely easier. All I had to do was to get there with Kristin, the letters and the money.

Night came eventually. I forced myself to eat my evening meal —thin soup, another boiled potato and another slice of the sour black bread. Outside, the clouds had covered up the sky. Desultory snow fell past my windows; there were no stars, no moon. I heard the mastiffs baying in the park. I sat still for a long time after eating. I did not think that I would be able to move.

The time had come. Now there was no more future to consider as far as the escape was concerned.

I supposed that if there had been some way to back out, I would have welcomed it. But Sempinski was expecting me in his room. Kristin was waiting for me. The thought of Karpovitch's vengeance on her was unendurable. Outside, the mastiffs and the guards were probably also waiting; but there was nothing I could do about them.

Nine o'clock came all too soon—the time I had assigned to myself for the start of the escape. I stared with painful concentration at my watch, counting off the seconds as if it mattered whether I began to move before this arbitrary deadline. But it seemed suddenly important to make the escape precise and defined as if some guarantee of security could be found in time tables. The sweep of the second hand wiped thought from my mind. It implied order and routine and normalcy in a situation where nothing was normal. It was the only lifeline that connected me with reality.

My heart beat heavily and my mouth was dry.

Very well. I had gone over every step so often in my mind that it became as automatic as the marching seconds. Cold. Must be ice cold about this, can't have any nonsense. No thinking or planning now more than a second or two ahead. I got up. I went to the door and listened at the keyhole. No sound of any kind. I nodded profoundly as if this silence were some kind of revelation. I pushed the heavy iron-studded coffer against the door and jammed it securely in the doorway. The armchair came next, on top of the coffer, the cruel lion's paw pushed under the door handle. I reinforced the barricade with the nightstand; it gradually acquired a comforting solidity that would defy the efforts of several men, more than the pair who would bring my breakfast. That would mean fifteen, possibly twenty extra minutes before the alarm. I had no reason to despise any extra minutes. My tactics were clear. I put on all my clothes: three shirts, a sweater and my suit. No shoes. They would be useless in the snow outside. I would replace them with the felt-lined winter boots in the guards' ready-room downstairs. Now there was nothing to keep me from leaving. I couldn't think of anything that I hadn't done that might delay discovery and pursuit. I looked at my watch. It had taken me seven minutes to build my barricade and to dress. The time was nine-oh-seven. It would take me eleven minutes to reach Sempinski's room. Allow five minutes there to collect the letters and to say goodbye. Formal and cold, of course. No emotional claptrap. Nerves were uncertain at the best of times and this was, certainly, not one of those times. Iron control of nerves, time, all the faculties was mandatory. Mandatory. I savored the word. It had a comforting and reassuring sound. So, five minutes for the old man. The trip to Kristin's room would take eighteen minutes. Eleven from the old man's room back to the level of my own, then seven more to drop down to hers. She would be ready for me, all ready to go. No need to waste time there. In forty minutes more we would be in the cave downstairs behind the guards' bricked-up fireplace. That made it seventy-four minutes. The time was now nine-oh-eight. We would be in the cave at 10:22. We wouldn't have to wait there more than half an hour if the guards closed up shop at eleven as they had last night. Germans are creatures of remorseless habit; no reason to suppose that their bedtime would be different this night. I thought it likely that Kristin and I would be out of the house by 11:15.

And suddenly the room, the cold granite chamber with its gray patina of age, violence and danger looked so warm and welcoming that my knees buckled under me with longing for safety. The fireplace and, by association, everything beyond it looked more than ever like the yawning mouth of a cavernous tomb.

I leaned against the cold marble and granite. I tried not to think. Then I began to climb.

I moved through the chimney shafts, following the knotted white nylon cord, with an impatience bred by familiarity. Rats, spiders, matted cobwebs no longer perturbed me. I smashed slow-moving spiders and hissed at the rats. Everything that could do it, ran away from me.

I wasted no time in Sempinski's room. I dropped into the old writer's fireplace with the agility of a paratrooper. I nodded to him, making for the safe.

"Everything all right?"

I meant the contents of the safe and the old man knew it.

"Yes," he said. "The papers are there."

I went quickly through the letters and other documents, wrapped them in a handkerchief and stuffed the bundle between my second and third shirt, away from my body. My fingers were like nervous sausages fumbling with the buttons.

I said: "I'm ready. And listen, professor: I've got the money. We have everything. After I'm gone the plotters won't have anything."

The old man looked up, questioning, then smiled, delighted. He nodded, asking nothing. He looked at me with a quick and quiet admiration that made me suddenly ashamed. Only I knew what a fraud and what a coward I was.

I said: "Goodbye, professor."

"Goodbye, Dr. Shippe. Good luck. Or as the Germans say: *Hals und Beinbruch.*"

"Actors say that in the United States."

"Well, there's a point in common."

The old man turned his face carefully away as if to study the violent shadows moving in the windows. The room was darker and more threatening than it had been the night before; the

191

shadows were deeper. I thought I could detect a certain hopelessness in the novelist's collapsed body and turned-away face.

I got back into the fireplace and made my way rapidly back to my own roomlevel and then down to Kristin.

She was ready as I had thought she would be but I was too nervous to notice immediately how pale she had become. She was dressed perfectly for what she had to do: ski pants, wool socks, several bulky sweaters and heavy skiing boots. Her hair was stuffed into a knitted helmet that fell in folds like a medieval shirt of mail over her neck and shoulders. It left only a fraction of her face exposed.

"All right?" she asked, smiling.

"You mean your uniform? Couldn't be better. I wish I had thought to get outfitted for skiing before I came here."

"I came here on a holiday," she reminded me. I noticed that she packed a small bundle that looked like towels wrapped in a pillowcase.

"What's that?"

"My battledress," she said still smiling. I noticed her pallor then. Her hands seemed more nervous than they had been the night before. But her eyes were bright.

I said abruptly: "I told you not to pack anything."

She looked at me steadily, then shrugged. She undid the bundle and showed me flimsy underwear, stockings, fashionable shoes, a purse and cosmetics. There was a dress as well, something bright, full of greens and yellows. The sight of this pretty trivia angered me out of all proportion. I knew that I was too nervous to keep anything in perspective but this reminder of her femininity seemed suddenly too much.

Women. I knew that I didn't know anything about them but, at this point, with what lay ahead, what I knew seemed enough. Perhaps taking Kristin with me was an invitation to failure and disaster; I had been a fool to hope that it could have been anything else. The trouble was, of course, that I hadn't thought; I had refused to think after having seen her. Oh well, damn it, it was too late now to do anything about it. That's how it always is, I thought: you see a beautiful young woman, Dr. Shippe, and you send your brain on a permanent vacation.

I barricaded her door as I had my own. That, anyway, could be done according to plan. The similar barricades in the empty cells would be as good as an announcement of our joint escape but the conspirators would link the two disappearances together, anyway. The point was to delay discovery and, therefore, pursuit. She helped me with the barricade, saying nothing. When we were done with the fortifications I moved toward the fireplace and she followed me.

"Keep close behind me," I said, my voice harsh. Its harshness surprised me.

I didn't know how to go about being rude to women, and no one can be rude for long to a beautiful young woman for whom one begins to feel an idiotic longing and attachment. And, anyway, what would come next—the rats and the spiders—wouldn't be easy for her. I remembered the horror of my first·encounter with the tunnels:

I smiled as best I could and said:

"How did you do with the household gods?"

"I did my best," she said.

"Then it should be all right, shouldn't it? They ought to be glad to do something for you."

"They are a nice bunch of old gentlemen."

Her voice, I noted, had steadied and so had her hands. Good nerves, I thought; perhaps I had been wrong to doubt her for a moment. I wished my own nerves were as good as hers. Either that or that my memory had been better. What the devil had I forgotten to do? I had been so letter perfect in my calculations, but I knew that there had been something that I hadn't taken into account.

Time was passing, more than I had allowed for this part of the attempt, but this didn't worry me. I had saved several minutes in Sempinski's room. I wanted to say something to her to prepare her for the chimney shafts and for what lived and scurried inside them, but I could think of nothing that might do.

"All right," I said. "We'd better get started. Now remember to keep close behind me. I'll have the flashlight but I won't use it much; it might shine through some crack in the wall and give us away. And don't allow yourself to get upset by anything. It's not a long trip."

She wanted to know how long it would take us to reach the bricked-up fireplace and looked unbelieving when I told her.

"Forty minutes?"

"They'll seem like forty hours. But don't think about it. Try not to think about anything. It's . . . well, it's not going to be pleasant but try not to mind it."

She nodded then, looking serious and vulnerable.

"Let's start," she said.

Later, when clear thought was possible again, I would think that this had been the easiest and the safest part of our attempt. I wondered why I had been tense and nervous and upset because, not in my grimmest calculations had I been able to include all the elements. How could I have calculated something that I could not imagine? I had made up schedules and time tables, and I had assured myself that I would not think more than a second or two ahead, so as to avoid panic, and I had hardened myself against emotional distractions. I crawled through the colonies of spiders and rats with a girl who was frightened and distressed by the horror but who crawled bravely in the shower of mortar and old stone, in the squeal and rush of rats, trusting me or perhaps only hoping that I knew what I was doing and that the dreadful journey would come to some end. I was tuned wholly outward like a cornered animal and so I could not help her. This was the first proof of my miscalculation but I pressed on because (I told myself, sententious with fear) I had no other choice. There was a brief confirmation of my calculations because we did reach the bricked-up cave behind the fireplace at 10:23 and by 11:45 we were in the empty, no longer festive hall of premature German celebrations, and there were all the boots and sheepskin jackets to spare for the next stage of the escape. I had my own furs and pistol and the precious briefcase. A hunting knife made quick work of the briefcase. I had a moment of blinding unreality as I looked at the long notes which amounted to more money than I had ever seen . . . the savings of lifetimes. Kristin was overjoyed, and hugged me enthusiastically at the sight of this last piece of vital evidence that we were stealing from the conspirators. I packed this fortune in a soiled napkin inside my shirt and after I had thrown all the scraps of briefcase into the fireplace, and repaired the breeched wall again to hide our escape route, I felt that I had accomplished everything that I had set out to do.

I couldn't understand why I wasn't able to congratulate myself on an accomplished mission. But the deathly pale, bright eyed, admiring and enthusiastic girl beside me served as a reminder. She urged me on into the cold outside where a storm was raging. And then, of course, I realized what I had forgotten to do while making brilliant calculations and composing schedules; I had not thought to look out of the window at the storm outside.

The night was unbelievable. I couldn't force myself to go out into it. My resolution, or whatever had carried me so far in the nightmare, suddenly ebbed away, and it was only when Kristin took the lead that I stumbled out into the frozen whirlwind.

I had not thought that there might be a storm. I had assumed there would be a moon and stars to guide us; I had studied landmarks. But as soon as the bleak castle disappeared behind us we were flung into the raging night and I was immediately and absolutely lost.

There wasn't one star in the mad black sky to show us the way. We had to shout to be heard above the wind. I felt the blinding snow freezing on my face.

What happens to your calculations then? The clouds which had brought twilight at noon show what they can do. The icy wind cuts and a thick cold mask spreads across your face. You haul the girl along, or perhaps she hauls you, it is impossible to tell;

and within minutes you can't tell whether or not you are still together. The only way to tell is by the weight dragging against your arm or by the stumbling collisions of two bodies. But the weight vanishes when your own body becomes too difficult to drag through the snowdrifts, and the collisions are with trees as often as not. There is no sense of direction. There isn't even any sense of motion. For all you know you may be standing still despite all that effort, pounding along on an icy treadmill. It goes like this hour after hour or, perhaps, minute after minute; there is no way to tell. There is the battering cold and blindness. There is no terror because for terror there must be understanding and you understand nothing. You suspect that you are going to freeze unless you find shelter. Indeed, you feel yourself beginning to freeze. The body refuses to respond and that is a signal. Everything slows down. Thought processes dissolve. There is a lack of air despite all that wind. You feel that you are drowning but there doesn't seem to be anything that you can do about it. You settle down to a mindless contemplation of your own destruction. Time dissolves. Well, well, you say and Oh well, and you fall and stumble and drag something along—something shapeless and unrecognizable—wondering what the whole business is about. There is a vague thought about guards and mastiffs; that makes you keep going. Legs like white logs sinking into snow, coming out and plunging. The snow grasps and holds like quicksand. It has formed walls and corridors among the trees and deflects the wind upward, and you are in a maze of wild toboggan runs carved out of ice mountains, and this too drives you on with the thought of the pursuing danger. You have to keep moving. The walls soar and fall; white buttresses and castles in the blue-gray light. Moats and pinnacles. Everything is white and frozen and unsympathetic; still more blue than white in the new blue light but beginning to glitter: diamond studded hills in the spreading whiteness. But the hills sink and flatten and begin to spread like melting confectionery, and soon you wonder what has happened to the trees, and you recall climbing over something that had the hardness of stone under the snow and the ice and that appears to have been a wall other than an ice wall, and since you have a vague idea that a wall and ditch contained the trees, you think that this phenomenon might account for their disappearance. You are out of the park and it is broad daylight. You see dunes of snow sweeping across fields. The park is far behind you; you experience an upsurge of thankfulness and gratitude that makes you want to fall onto your knees and rest. You want to give thanks for a storm that had kept the mastiffs skulking in their kennels but you remember that you must go on because to stop in that cold is not to move again. Daylight is no friend. You should have been in a village long before daylight. Time is suddenly important again, but there is no sign of any village in the windswept plain. There is a small black object moving rapidly at the extreme edge of your field of vision and you focus your inadequate eyes upon it, and it resolves itself into a sleigh, a horse and a man. The foreshortened sleigh looks like a lifeboat plowing through white waves, with snow spume sweeping up and sideways and falling behind. There is the white steam of a horse's breath and a man's red face. The man makes distant, incomprehensible sounds which seem sympathetic, as if finding you in the open fields after a storm explained everything. You croak the name of a town and the man nods, pointing with his whip, and you lose consciousness under the revolving gray sky.

Pain brought me back to consciousness. Warmth made a gradual return under the straw and sacking in the sleigh and as my body thawed out the pain strengthened its attack on me. I had never experienced anything like it.

My hands and face were particularly painful, being rubbed with snow that Kristin scooped up as the sleigh carried us along. I tried to focus my eyes on her to tell her to stop it but my eyes were tired. Their pain was white and sharp. Everything blurred when I looked at it. I'm snowblind, I told myself as though this was a remarkable discovery. I thought I felt the quick pulse in her icy hand even though I couldn't feel the hand itself. My voice sounded extraordinarily remote and I suspected that my ears were frozen.

I muttered the name of the ancient border city where we would have to board a train for the capital, and Kristin said: "It's all right. The driver knows. We're going there. Move your arms and legs. Can you move them yet?"

"Of course I can," I said but I couldn't do it. When my eyes had steadied I studied Kristin as she worked on my wooden fingers. She had taken over. I was astonished that she was in command.

"Where are we, anyway?" I asked. "How did we get here?" She gave me a curious glance that I didn't understand.

"We're on the road to the city. You got us out of the house and through the park into open fields and the sleigh was there. I wouldn't have believed anyone could have got through a storm like last night's."

"We didn't get to the village, then," I said, beginning to remember.

"No. If we had we would probably have been caught by now. They must be searching all over for us by this time. The village is the first place they'd go to, don't you think?"

"After they've searched the house," I said. I struggled to sit up and to look behind us. "They must be coming after us."

"But that's just it," she said. "They are not behind us. You took us out of the park on the side away from the village. If they went to the village they will be on another road. When did you change your mind?"

"About what?"

"About not going to the village but trying the other side."

"I didn't," I said. "I got lost."

She laughed in an odd, disbelieving way.

The peasant driver cracked his whip and called out cheerfully to his horse and the sleigh rushed headlong over the icy road. Sooner or later, I knew, I would have to give some thought to how we were going to get aboard a train. I was sure that our pursuers would beat us to the city and watch at the turnstiles in

198

the railroad station. But there was still a little time before I had to think. I lay back and tried to ignore the sharp pains in my thawing body.

I looked at Kristin bending over me and found it difficult to recognize her. The small circle of exposed cheek was crimson, the deep eyes underlined in frostbitten white. I supposed that the snow and wind had scrubbed us both clean of the black traces of the chimney shafts but, even so, she looked a far cry from the beautiful young woman who had so distracted me before our escape. She must have understood my glance because her back stiffened, her chin went up, and she attacked my face with a particularly ungentle handful of snow.

"That hurts!" I said.

"It's meant to. Or would you rather have your nose and ears fall off? You'd be a little less critical about other peoples' appearance."

"It feels as if you were tearing them off anyway."

"You have a lovely case of frostbite."

"Didn't you get frozen?"

"No. At least not as badly." (Then her voice softened.) "You must have shielded me from the worst of the wind. I never thought we'd get through."

"Neither did I. It's lucky this sleigh came along this morning. Are you sure the man is taking us to the city?"

"I told him you would pay him if he got us there. He thinks we are lost tourists."

"He's not far off. But can you speak the language?"

"Enough to make myself understood about meals, soap, money, things like that. This is the country where my husband came from. And Professor Sempinski taught me a few phrases when I was planning my own escape. That poor man . . . what will they do to him?"

"They'll kill him," I said. And then, to soften the impact of brutality as much as I could: "But I think he knew that. It's what he wants now, I think."

"Why should they want to kill him now that he's useless to them?"

"For revenge. Or perhaps just because he's useless. But we'll make them pay for it, won't we?"

"That won't bring Sempinski back to life," she observed.

"Perhaps not. But it will give me a great deal of pleasure to make these animals suffer."

She looked at me carefully and paused as if she wished to say something more. But then she changed her mind. The pinpricks of returning feeling were stabbing my fingers.

"That's good now. I feel fine. Why don't you get your hands under this straw and sacking and get them warm? And get down out of the wind. The storm is almost over but you can still get frostbite."

The flat land slid past us in a hiss of snow under the runners of the sleigh and the steady pounding of the horse's hoofs. Our front horizon was blocked by the driver's patched sheepskin jacket. I was conscious of the girl beside me and her clean, snowy smell.

I said: "This could be something out of a Sempinski novel."

"This kind of thing?"

"The sleigh should have three horses and it should be driving through a forest. The hero and the heroine should be in love with each other. Other than that we just about have it."

Almost at once, as if by command, woods surrounded us. She laughed.

"There is your forest."

"Well, it's a start. But I'm afraid the hero is supposed to be a fiery young man, resourceful and brave. He has come back from the Tartar wars covered in all kinds of glory."

"And the heroine?"

"She is a beautiful, proud and high-minded young woman who knows her own mind. She hasn't seen the hero since he was a boy. They had been betrothed as children by their parents and she has been wondering what he would be like as a man."

"Does he disappoint her?"

"He does at first. He's a bit wild, I'm afraid; keeps rotten company. But in the end he recovers his reputation by magnificent, patriotic deeds."

"And she, of course, has loved him all along even though he had been a bit of a bastard."

"That's right. Have you read anything by Sempinski?"

"I never even heard about him until you sent me here. But I think I'd like to read him now. You have a lot of his things in your library, don't you?"

"Everything that he ever wrote."

"Good," she said. "Then I'll be able to read him."

She laughed then; a quick, pleased sound.

"What is it now? Changing your mind about Sempinski?"

"It's not that at all."

Then we were silent, conscious of each other. I thought about my books and about her reading them in the warm apple-glow of my library and Mahler's thundering music. New York had never seemed as far away as it was then. There were innumerable dangers and uncertainties between us and New York. I had no guarantee that there were no pursuers coming fast behind us although it seemed more likely that they would be on the village road. The snowstorm would have covered up our tracks but they would assume that we had headed for the village; anywhere else would have meant disaster. The hunters would be puzzled in the village where no one had seen us. I almost wished that I could be there to watch their confusion. It all depended on Karpovitch and what he was up to.

I told Kristin about Karpovitch and the scene with the general in my room. She said at once that she thought Karpovitch had left Hetmanska Gora before our escape.

"My windows overlooked the stables where they kept their cars. Most of the Germans left yesterday morning. The man you described left early in the afternoon. He seemed in a hurry."

"That means he might be waiting for us in the capital. And

if he figures out where we are heading, which he is sure to do, he'll block our every route."

She said, smiling: "You'll think of something."

"Damned if I know what. We've had a streak of luck so far but we need more than that. This is like playing chess in a blindfold; you can counter one move, perhaps two. But we must have some idea of our opponents' game to know what moves to make."

She smiled and pressed my hand; a warm reassurance.

"I think you've done beautifully so far."

"And anyway," she added after a while. "Didn't you say that the CIA was in this already?"

"That's something I can't understand at all. But I don't think that we had better count on anyone to help us until we get the letters and the money to the embassy."

"But you don't doubt that we'll manage, do you?"

"I'd feel a lot better about it if we had more time. The assassination is planned for the day after tomorrow; that doesn't leave us much space for maneuver."

"Something will happen," she said fervently. "I know something will."

I laughed, partially relieved. "That's a very Slavic way to look at it."

"How's that?"

"They're always looking for miracles to get them out of trouble, always waiting for some sign from heaven. I don't think we can afford to count on miracles although it'll take one to get us to the embassy in time. Still, maybe you made some points for us with those household gods?"

"I didn't try very hard," she confessed. "I'm afraid I've given up believing in miracles."

"That sounds a little bitter . . ."

"I don't mean to be bitter or cynical about it. It's just that I no longer believe that good things will happen simply because one wants them to."

"Did you ever think that?"

"I used to think that before I was married. I thought that if one really wanted something and believed in it and worked for it too, then it would come. But it never did come, not completely. And if it looked like what you really wanted, it didn't last."

I said: "Are you still talking about your marriage?"

And she said quickly, looking up: "What made you think that's what I was talking about?"

"Nothing," I said. "I had heard that you were married and that your husband was killed. I'm sorry if that sounds abrupt."

"That's how it should sound," she said quietly. "We were only married a year when my husband was killed."

"In Saigon, wasn't it?"

"Yes. He was sent there by his government as an election observer. He was hit by a speeding car, you know. The car never stopped. And no one seemed to care very much about it."

I said that I was sorry.

She said: "I couldn't understand why they had to have him killed."

"Had to? You mean it wasn't an accident?"

"Oh no. It was a political matter. The Vietnamese were very bland about it. It seems they're used to that kind of thing. Our own people wouldn't tell me anything. They were only interested in getting me out of Vietnam and back to New York."

"Then you had your own reasons for hating Communists."

"It wasn't the Vietcong who killed Jan. It was our own people. They thought that Jan was a Communist secret agent. He could have been. It doesn't really matter. They couldn't prove anything against him so they had him killed. It seems that's the way it's done all over the world."

"My God!" I said. "Are you sure? That's terrible . . ."

"I couldn't believe it for a long time. I never thought our side could do anything like that. But it all added up after a while when I remembered small incidents, little things that I hadn't paid any attention to before. It could have been as they said. But I didn't care. All I cared about was that it had been our side

203

which had murdered Jan. After that it was hard to believe in miracles."

"My God," I said.

She smiled, squeezed my hand. "You're a nice man to listen to all this. I've never really told anyone about it. It isn't the kind of confidence that one can share easily. But you can see how I could accept Uncle Per's letters without a sense of shock, of how I could believe that poor Sempinski could have been fooled into thinking the CIA responsible for the conspiracy."

"No wonder you looked at me in an odd way when I talked about revenge on the plotters."

"They are everything you called them."

"But so are the people who murdered your husband. Don't you hate them for it?"

"No. I never did, I suppose. At first I was too shocked, too bewildered, and later it didn't seem to make much difference what I did. Hate doesn't help anybody. You can't hate something you can't even understand."

"My God," I said. "I had no idea."

"About me and Jan? No reason why you should have known anything about it. Things like that aren't supposed to happen to people like us."

"But they do happen, don't they? We get caught up in things like that whether we like it or not."

"Not often. Most people wouldn't believe any of this if it happened to them. People have a way of living their own lives and seeing only what they want to see no matter what happens to anybody else."

"So what does it all amount to then? A choice between two evils?"

"Oh no. The systems are on the surface and that's where people live. They have nothing to do with what goes on under the surface; it's not their concern. We make our choice from what is available where we can see it. The rest . . . well, that's for the murderers on both sides."

I sat quite still then, my thoughts awry. I had been badly shaken by her story but my sense of shock had little to do with her husband's death. I was quite willing to accept the fact that no one faction had a monopoly on evil. In fact, I agreed with Kristin's summary that under the surface of systems and slogans moved another world peopled by creatures who had no relation with the world of ordinary men. What made me pause was the realization of her knowledge. She seemed so young and vulnerable, so capable of naïve hopes and ideals. She couldn't have been older than her middle twenties but she already knew what I had only begun to learn at forty-two. I was ashamed that I had been so complacently naïve, and that I had misread her so completely. Her youth and beauty had dazzled me but now she had allowed me a brief glimpse of depths underneath the surface. I wanted to know more about her; it seemed suddenly important to find out everything that mattered to her. The only starting point for questions was her husband's death and I didn't want to talk about her husband. I supposed that I was jealous of the dead man. The odd, diffused feeling of disappointment that I had felt when I had first discovered that she had had a husband came back, magnified.

She took my silence for worry about the uncertainties ahead and went on to encourage me with quick words that showed confidence and trust in my judgment. I had no reason to share her trust in my abilities; on the contrary, I had every reason to think the opposite. I cautioned myself against being optimistic about anything. I had been lucky, certainly; a fool's blind luck, a beginner's luck. It wasn't anything to bank on in this league.

I was aware of quickened feelings toward Kristin and told myself at once not to be a fool.

The woods ended shortly afterward; trees gave way to the familiar windswept whiteness that seemed to slant upward into the gray sky, and then we drove into and along a highway thickening with traffic. The distant spires and towers of the ancient city rose clear and defined in the odd blueish light.

I looked down at Kristin to comment about that and saw that

she was sleeping. The night and the storm had been enough to drain anyone of strength. I felt the gentle rocking of the sleigh on the hardpacked snow and longed for sleep and rest, some mild oblivion. But that would have to wait until I had got Kristin and myself safely aboard a train.

The sleigh slowed down and then crept off the road onto the snow enbankment. Ahead of us, other sleighs and trucks began to lurch and spill into the highpiled drifts among the telegraph poles, and then I heard the furious bleating of a Klaxon horn and the roar of a powerful engine driven at top speed. A huge black car splattered with the grime of a desperate journey hurtled past in a spray of snow. I had a momentary glimpse of streaked windows and tense, glaring faces, and in the fraction of a second that it took for the mass of metal to fly past the sleigh I recognized my former escort, the insolent young man whom I had blamed for the disappearance of the briefcase, and Karpovitch.

All thoughts of rest and sleep went down the road with the car, driven at mad speed for Hetmanska Gora. I was seized with an icy chill far deeper than the cut of the wind. Whatever margins of safety I might have wrested from the situation earlier in the morning had now shrunk into practically nothing.

PART FOUR

On the Run

nineteen

SNOW CAME IN from the south, from mountains, carried by the wind. It piled minarets and ice towers on the train sheds, and blotted out the pale light in the glassed-in concourse, and shifted restless dunes between the tracks, and drifted along platforms in the false heat of steam that froze when it touched stone. The wind smelled of mountain passes and wet granite.

Time, like the snow, hissed through cracks in the windows. I looked at my watch; my eyes were blurring with anxiety. I walked through the concourse peering through the crowds in search of the hunters.

My arms and shoulders, back and thighs ached as though I had walked long and far carrying a burden. My eyes stung; they were red-rimmed and the flesh under them was gray. I didn't recognize myself in the mirror of the ticket window, looking haggard and a little mad. I had lost my fur cap in the night and now my tangled, overlong hair stood stiff on my head like a frosted mane.

"Two first class tickets for the capital," I said to the clerk, a pig-eyed little man with a sharp pointed nose. He gave me a look of bored distaste, hearing me speak German.

"Returns?"

"No. No returns. One way."

The clerk pushed the ticket coupons through the grille, looked at the single banknote that I held out toward him.

"I've nothing smaller," I said. I wondered what the clerk would think if he knew that I had a fortune in dollars stuffed inside my shirt. I asked when the train was due to arrive.

"There will be an announcement," he informed me.

"What platform will the train be on?"

"It will be announced."

"Is the train on time?"

"It is winter."

"Does that mean that the train might be late?"

"All trains are late in winter."

I moved as quickly as I could into the crowd. Time had become an implacable enemy. It had been several hours since Karpovitch's car had passed our sleigh and that meant that we could expect the hunters at the terminal at practically any moment.

I stooped as I walked, knowing that without this cramped bearlike stagger I stood head and shoulders taller than most men who passed me. I had to make myself inconspicuous. My face astonished even me when I caught sight of it in glass. My furs were matted and dirty. I thought that I must have looked like a demented bear.

I passed a group of children, then some foreign tourists whose sudden bursts of English made me sick with longing for security, but whose name tags proclaimed them all to be a cultural congress of British workers. The children had red winter faces, bright pebble eyes and wool stockings and quilted coats with fur collars. They chattered, pointing at the trains, with a peculiar mock adult restraint. Everyone seemed unnaturally strained. A small boy looked at me, solemn as a fledgling owl, then hid his head behind the shoulder of another. Soon all the children were silent and watching. Their round eyes followed me across the concourse. I kept my eyes carefully away from the English tourists who wore the puffed uncertain look of jungle explorers: half anxious indignation and half dysentery.

"An hour late. Terrible. So inconsiderate."

"Terribly inconvenient. I suppose we'll have to wait *another* hour."

"Still, I suppose the snow . . ."

I edged past them, keeping my head averted as they stared at me, and made for the stairs. Outside, the wind smashed into me. I crossed the square into a narrow street, no more than an alley. The snow lay deep here, undisturbed by footprints. The wind rattled toward me. I searched for the workmen's canteen where I had left Kristin and knew sudden panic when I couldn't find it. Somewhere around here, surely? Where the devil was it? The narrow doors, thick walls, ill-smelling corridors were dreadfully familiar and all looked alike; bare, cheerless sheds with ancient furniture, gray windows, iron stoves and the smell of sour cabbage, dishwater and mushrooms. Dour men sat hunched over cooling bowls at tin-topped tables under naked bulbs. I wished that I could have taken Kristin elsewhere to wait for the train, a clean place where she wouldn't be the only woman. But everything that had seemed cheerful and pleasant was too far from the terminal. And so I had taken the instinctive course of the fugitive and looked for a dark place, a hideout among people who would pay no attention to anybody but themselves. They had seemed less men than ragged heaps of clothing, old rags and wornout furs held together with string. Bleak faces with sliding eyes and chins buried in cloth. There was a modicum of safety to be had among them. They wouldn't lift their eyes to watch a murder at a neighboring table.

I pushed old doors, peered into gray shadows, and finally found the place. I was too tired by then to feel relief. Kristin moved in her corner; I saw her at once. Even in her dark skisuit and bulky sheepskin coat she had a luster that made her vivid and impressive. I sat down beside her.

"All clear so far," I said. I put the ticket coupons on the table. She studied them as if a little puzzled, then smiled.

"They haven't got here yet?"

"I didn't see anyone I knew."

"When is the train due?"

"Nobody seems to know. They say the trains are always late in winter."

"But approximately?"

"I don't think there'll be anything for another hour. We've missed the morning express anyway. But there's a local train."

"Another hour," she said. "Do you think they'll be here in an hour?"

I hadn't told her about seeing Karpovitch and the others in the speeding car.

"It's possible," I said.

"Perhaps we should take the first train out, no matter where it goes."

"We have no time to go anywhere but straight to the capital."

"You're tired," she said. "Why not rest for an hour? Nobody will notice if you sleep right here."

"No, I can't sleep right now. Was everything all right here?"

"Nobody bothered me. Nobody went out or came in while you were gone. I don't believe that anybody even looked at me. I don't know if I'm too happy about that."

"What? Why?"

I was aware of a pounding headache. I had considerable trouble keeping my thoughts in order.

"I may be on the run and I may look like hell but I'm still a woman," she said. She laughed. "Or have you forgotten that too?"

I assured her that I had not forgotten, my voice cracked with fatigue. I was more conscious of her now than ever before.

"You ought to get some rest," she said. "You need it."

"I can't sleep here," I said. "There isn't time to sleep. We'll sleep on the train."

"At least we're not going to sleep together," she mocked. "That's a prim arrangement."

"What?"

"The tickets, coupons or whatever they are. One is for the

first class and one for the third. Isn't that carrying propriety a little too far? And which of us gets which?"

"What? Let me see . . . That goddamn clerk!" I was suddenly enraged. She stared at me astonished and, I thought, oddly pleased. What in hell would she have to be pleased about? "The son of a bitch did that because I spoke German."

"Go to it," she said, laughing.

"Are we quarreling? What are we quarreling about?"

"We are both tired," she said.

"That's right." I felt the anger crumble and a great weight seemed to collapse on me.

"You need some coffee," she said and waved her hand at the old woman who sat, mountainous and greasy behind the zinc-topped counter. She had a face like a bag of walnuts and hands like drowned hams.

"One other thing has occurred to me," I said. "I don't like to carry all this money in my shirt."

"Why not mail it to yourself in care of the embassy? Then we can pick it up as soon as we get there and hand it over."

"I'm not sure about that. I have a feeling embassy mail is watched, particularly if it comes from inside this country. I'd rather mail it to myself at my hotel. I still have my room there."

"Would that be safe?"

"I don't know. But that's what I'd like to do. Then if anything should happen to me at least the money will be out of reach of the Karpovitch gang."

She said quietly: "You still think that Karpovitch will catch up with us, don't you?"

I was sure of it but said evasively:

"It's not only that. This money is a fortune, more than anyone in this country can earn in a lifetime. It's an invitation to robbery and I'd rather not take any more chances than we have to."

"Then let's send it off. Although I still vote for the embassy rather than your hotel."

Then she added:

211

"I've been thinking about the train. Do we really have to go by train? Isn't there another way?"

"What way? Why?"

The train to the capital had been such an important part of my planning that I couldn't think of anything that might replace it. And why replace it? I clung to all my plans, futile as they seemed to be, with the unreasoning stubbornness of a child. Elimination of the train from my painfully worked-out equation of safety seemed as revolutionary as an elimination of the embassy itself. But she said reasonably:

"Karpovitch will expect us to take the train. His people will be watching at the terminal. They can't help seeing us. They'll follow us aboard. But what if we don't take the train? What if we rented a car? The PABUT people advertise car rentals."

"A car? Well, yes, a car. That solution wouldn't have occurred to me," I said.

"You've already blazed a trail at the terminal," Kristin went on. "You've bought the tickets. Karpovitch's men will be sure to board the train even if we did manage to slip past them somehow. Let them take their train ride by themselves and, in the meantime, we can drive. Well, what do you think?"

"But what if Karpovitch doesn't take the bait? A highway can be lonely if you need some help."

"Would anybody help us on the train?"

"All right. We'll do it. They've pretty well run us into a corner as it is; we've nothing to lose."

She laughed and clapped her hands, delighted.

"That's the spirit!"

I found myself laughing with her, too tired for control. Besides, I didn't feel like controlling laughter. She was so obviously delighted and so impressively right with her suggestion. It was the only sensible thing to do. She seemed particularly pleased when I told her how impressed I was and how lucky I felt to have her along.

I had an AAA International driving permit, thanks to Miss Gruber's efficiency, and the PABUT clerk provided both the AIT and FIA carnet and required insurance. I wondered what good it would do me if Karpovitch ever caught up with us. The car was a five-seat Volga. It would be ready in an hour. Was I sure that I didn't want a driver? Only a little bit more. Yes, I said I was sure. The clerk assured me that the journey would be much more comfortable with a driver but if I wished to drive that was up to me; a PABUT guide or driver were no longer mandatory equipment for tourists. In the meantime, while the car was being prepared, would Monsieur and Madame care to tour historic landmarks in the city? The clerk seemed offended when I declined the offer.

I used the time to buy a heavy manila envelope and to stuff the money into it, address it, and take it to the post office. I felt totally unreal mailing half a million dollars to myself at a foreign hotel. Kristin still opted for the embassy but she said nothing when she saw me scribble the address.

We drove north on an old Imperial highway, with the land suddenly desolate around us. Ahead rose the dark misty battlements of a minor range of wooded mountains.

The car rocked through the icy blue coldness with windows starred and webbed by frost. Outside the windows the world was hushed and white. Inside, there was warmth.

I drove stupefied, all my senses blunted. My body moved in odd spasmodic tremors as if no longer willing to obey my brain. I swayed in would-be sleep, conscious of Kristin's cowled head heavy on my shoulder. My brain sent down weak and garbled messages like a defective telegraph key. I had to keep myself going if our escape was to have its desired if illogical conclusion. The logical conclusion was disaster but that was not desired. What was desired more than anything was sleep and rest and an awakening in which the day and the preceding night were erased from memory so that the shocked brain and the weary body could come to terms again.

A village slid by, then another. A warning sign leaped out of gathering darkness. Steep road and narrow road, snowdrift and broken pavement. I worked the car down into second gear feeling the back wheels sliding under us.

Then the day vanished in surprising blackness. There was no moon. Snow started falling heavily again. The road was empty. No traffic. No sign of anything alive. The road began to climb in short, angry loops among sudden hillocks. Pinewoods descended on the road from towering escarpments. I was aware of a rhythmic drumming in my head. My feet were heavy, leaden; and it was only the wild slide of the wheels on sudden hill corners that brought me back to partial consciousness and reminded me of the weight of my numb foot on the accelerator.

A sudden lurch threw Kristin's head off its perch on my shoulder and she woke with a quick cry. It took her several moments to locate herself within the time-place continuum of car and night.

"I fell asleep," she said as if apologizing. Then she peered around. "Where are we?"

"Mountains," I said. "Road. I'm not sure, exactly."

"Have I been sleeping long?"

"About an hour. Maybe more. I don't know. I think we've been driving for more than two hours."

"You must be dead tired. Let me drive a little."

"No," I said. "I'll do it. I want to get through the pass. Then you can take over."

"You've got to rest."

"I'll rest later. Got to get on now, make time. Can't stop now. Road is terrible. If we stopped now we'd never get started again. Just keep talking to me."

"I wish there was a radio," she said. "Yes. Then we'd be able to put on some music. What kind of music do you enjoy the most?"

"Mahler," I said. "Oh I don't know . . . anything."

"So you're a Mahler enthusiast too? That's a revelation. There's something very special about Mahler people."

"How special?"

"Well, let's say distinctive. They seem to be a quiet, self-contained lot, rather introspective. The sort of people who keep to themselves a lot. Is that how you are?"

"Yes. I suppose so."

"You don't go out very much at home, do you? What do you like to do? Whom do you see? Do you have any friends I might know?"

"I like to play chess," I said, and suddenly the idea of chessboards seemed ridiculous. I didn't want her to think me ridiculous. But having started talking I couldn't stop myself. "I study fencing," I added. "I'm not very good."

"Jan was a fencing-master," she said, suddenly reflective. "And we both liked chess."

"Did he like Mahler too?"

Kristin sighed and reached out and pressed my shoulder.

"He didn't know anything about Mahler and I don't know enough. But I would like to know. And I'm a good chessplayer if you need a partner."

"Do you fence too?" My slow words surprised me. I could not make myself believe that the high, trembling voice was mine.

"No, I'd be rotten at it. I'm terrified of knives. People with swords awe me and mystify me. I'd be an awful flop in the seventeenth century. I'd be far too impressed with all the gentlemen."

"I would be too," I said. "Ah, it's a silly pastime in our time."

But she said no, it wasn't, on the contrary. It seemed somehow moving to study fencing in the twentieth century; it reaffirmed some kind of faith in the human future. Didn't I think so?

"I used to. I used to think a lot of things like that."

"And now you don't?"

"There is so little time for thinking outside the practical."

"But your work is more than merely practical, isn't it? You're a scholar. Don't tell me that takes no thought. I know how eminent you are in your field. Believe me, I had all sorts of qualms before I had that lunch with you in New York."

"And after the lunch?"

I wondered what she'd say. I thought it suddenly important that she would think very highly of me but couldn't see why she would.

She said: "After I met you I thought you were a very nice, very gentle man. I thought it would be nice to know you a lot better."

"Well," I said. "Your wishes certainly came true."

She sighed and laughed a little. "They certainly did."

She was quiet for a moment after that and I felt the weight of my fatigue pressing down on me again. My eyes, I thought, were playing tricks on me. The clouds seemed to have blown apart and threw a scattered mass of stars across the sky and the car seemed to be heading straight up into them as they leaped and turned, advanced and retreated. The stars were yellow-green and oddly paired in darkness. And then I heard the long chilling howl of wolves deeper in the darkness.

My foot hit the accelerator in quick, vicious panic and the car leaped crazily around a sudden bend and spun, flying straight for the ghostly suggestion of a wooden guardrail along the highway's edge, with the black cavern of the night beyond. It took all my strength and wits to hold the wheel steady and to leave the brake untouched. Instead, I geared down, hearing the unsynchronized mechanism howl, and Kristin's quick alarm. The car spun, slid; a fender crunched against splintering wood, and I sat frozen into sudden immobility watching the darkness rush toward me, waiting for the precipice to appear. But the car had bounced clear of the railing and stopped in deep snow at the foot of the escarpment, lights tilted crazily to bare naked branches. I sat there trembling. I put my head into my hands. I was too tired to go on any longer.

Kristin asked if we were stuck, too deep to get out.

I said: "You take the wheel and I'll get out and push."

I got out feeling as if I had been broken in half, legs and brain completely disconnected. I thought it took me an incredibly long time to gather up the fragments of the broken guardrail. I pushed them under the rear wheels.

216

I signaled and she put the car in gear. With infinite care and patience she put in the clutch, then let it out and engaged the motor. The wheels spun madly. Snow flew, the rear of the Volga sank into the snow. Stop it, I shouted, Easy! But she couldn't hear me above the roaring of the engine and the whining tires. Too late, too bad, no good. Again! The car sank deeper then, with a slow lurch; it slid like a tired prehistoric monster into the six foot snowbank. She tried again and again. I paid no attention. I sat in the cold wind feeling my sweat freezing. I couldn't feel the metal of the car with either hand. After a while I got back inside the car. I hunted for a cigarette with hands that felt nothing.

"I'm sorry," she said. "Are we dug in for good?"

"I'm afraid so. But it wasn't your fault. The back wheels were hub-down in snow before you even tried."

"So now we're stuck," she said, oddly reflective.

I sighed, swore quietly. "That we are. And we can't stay here. We're all right as long as the engine and the lights are on. Once the motor cuts out we're out of a heater and we'll freeze in minutes. What are we like on fuel?"

She checked the gauge, shook her head. "Nearly empty. Where are we exactly? We seem to have gone about a hundred kilometers. Aren't we close to some town? Somewhere we could walk to?"

I found a road map in the glove compartment but it defied my cold fingers for a moment. I couldn't feel the edges to open the map. I said: "There seems to be a sizeable town ahead of us. It could be five or six kilometers away."

"Couldn't we walk that?"

"Can't you hear our company?"

With the tires silent and the motor idling we heard the lonely calling close and very clear.

"What is that?" she whispered.

"Wolves." I saw her shudder.

"Oh God," she said. "What else will there be?"

"I don't think they'll come to the car so long as the lights are on and the engine's going."

An icy chill ascended through the floorboards. She tucked her feet under her on the seat and massaged her ankles. I tried to follow suit. It took me a long time to hoist my feet up and fold them on the seat. The effort left me breathing in white clouds and hunchbacked with effort. The cigarette fell out of my hand and I watched it stupidly burning on the floorboards. I was too tired and indifferent to bend after it.

Whether it was the horror of the plaintive howling, or the beginning of a strong feeling for me or plain rebellion against meek acceptance of disaster so early in our bid, Kristin refused to give up. I had a momentary pang of doubt, a sense of hopelessness and sorrow when I thought about her and all the odds that were still stacked against us. I cast about for some plan that would save her, if not myself, with further struggle useless. But she seemed to have no doubts. This was the strong, impassioned girl Tommy had talked about.

"We can't just quit! We can't just give up. We have to do something. Too much depends on us for us to quit now. Think of Sempinski. Think what he is going through now. Think of what will happen if we don't get to the capital before tomorrow. We have to go on. There has to be some way. Can't you think of something?"

I grunted, tired. I tried to shake off the torpor of cold and fatigue. I knew that I could not allow myself to fall asleep; and there was nothing that I wanted more than sleep.

"Something . . ." I said.

"Perhaps someone will come along," I thought I heard her saying. "Some other car. We can't be the only people traveling by this road tonight."

I mumbled something in reply, felt my head sinking, my chin on my chest. Felt nothing. I was immediately asleep.

twenty

SLEEP MUST have been a matter of no more than moments. I was numb throughout as I awoke but oddly aware of her voice, her hands and her excitement. She was pummeling my arms and shoulders to get me to awake and she was shouting at me. Words without sense. Sobbed out more than shouted. Chaotic words tumbling into the fog that had enveloped my brain.

"What . . ." I said, waking. "What happened?"

"It's a car! There's a car coming up behind us. Look! You can see the lights."

Perhaps a mile down the road, at the foot of the hill winding up toward us, a pair of headlights stabbed through the spangled darkness with flat orange beams. The wind brought the thin wail of the Klaxon horn, the drone of the motor.

"I think that's wonderful," I said also laughing. "It's a miracle. You must have done an A-One job on those household gods."

"Good old gods," she said. "Wonderful old gods! Oh, I knew they wouldn't let me down."

We got out of the car, stumbling in the snow, with the strange headlights suddenly vanished around a bend in the road far below us. The night was darker than before with the lights gone. But the black escarpment was bordered with silver. The snow had stopped falling. The clouds had blown away. The sky was dusted over with bright stars and there was a moon. In the white light of the moon the road had a peculiar cleanliness and smoothness, and I could see it clearly all the way to the bend where the light grew stronger. Come on, I urged it, laughing. Come on! I couldn't understand such a stroke of luck.

The lights came on, unsteady, at great speed on the treacherous surface of the snowpacked road, with the Klaxon blaring. There was an oddly chilling note to the Klaxon and the roar of the motor as if they meant to clear the road ahead of any obstacle, living or dead, or fling them aside in passing. Then the headlights burst into a white glare around the last bend, wavered in a wild skid, steadied and came on, and the great black car hung in uneasy profile for a moment at the edge of the road. Black lights danced madly along bespattered sides. The strident cry of Klaxon, widespread wheels churning up a silver spray of snow . . . It was an eight-passenger Opel Admiral, its shining bulk unmistakable in the moonlight. And I said No, numb beyond understanding, frozen in disbelieving shock.

"It isn't fair," I said, now blinded by the white, triumphant lights coming up the road, hearing the gears pushed down, the motor roaring.

"What," Kristin said. "What?"

I shook myself free of paralysis.

"Come on!" I shouted and jumped off the road, heading into trees. She ran after me, uncertain.

"What? What's the matter!"

"Karpovitch!" I shouted. "It's them! It's their car! Come on!"

We scrambled up the slope, plunging in and out of the snow like horses swimming across a river. Behind us on the road tires screamed, the horn blared, the motor protested.

"Karpovitch . . . But how could you know . . ."

"Come on!" I shouted.

There were shouts behind us.

I ran.

I fled. It was a leaping, soaring superhuman flight. Branches smashed into me but I didn't feel them. Kristin had caught up with me, still clutching her bundle, and had seized my hand and I pulled her along as if she were weightless. We topped the ridge and dived into darkness among trees and gigantic bushes, a tangled cage of vegetation made soft and doubly treacherous by snow. Trees closed about us, skeletal in the moonlight. Heavy black shapes boiled at the edge of vision. What now? Good Christ, what now? A blaze of light blackened the trees behind us as if the hunters meant to follow us up the steep escarpment in their car. Not fair hunting out of cars, I thought idiotically. I should have known. Those stabbing lights had come up so fast, they had been so urgent. They should have warned me, I thought, feeling the hot sweep of fear and self-pity. Instead I had jumped up and down in the road shouting like a child. And now Karpovitch's killers were coming up the slope using the tilted headlights for a path. How many are there? Two had gone with Karpovitch to Hetmanska Gora. How many had come back? I ran and then I fell into a sudden opening in the ground, a deep dry hole of leaves and rotten branches only slightly salted with snow under a heavy canopy of trees. Kristin rolled over me, gasping. Snow showered on both of us from the disturbed branches. My nostrils filled with a sharp acrid smell of fur and of wetness; a fetid animal stench that made me struggle for breath. And then I heard both the wolves and the hunters.

The wolves were near. They had withdrawn before my stampede and the shouts of the hunters. But their paired yellow-green lights blinked in the shifting shadows as they studied both the hunters and the hunted. They wouldn't wait long.

The hunters had stopped on the ridge, at the edge of the tree-line, and now peered into blackness. There were three of them: Karpovitch and two others whom I didn't know. I saw them clearly outlined by their headlights on the white sheet of snow. They were too far away from me to hear what they were saying but there was no mistaking Karpovitch's angry gestures and his men's reluctance. It would be only moments before they made up their minds and ventured into the darkness. Once they got some light on our tracks we would be as good as caught.

And suddenly I was cold in a manner that had nothing to do with temperature; thought became frozen and defined. There had been three men in the car as it sped toward Hetmanska Gora: Karpovitch, my former escort and the young man whom I had accused of taking my briefcase. Now there were two new ones. The Germans who knew me by sight would be on the train. I didn't think Karpovitch had brought further reinforcements. That meant that I was up against the trio and whoever had been left in the plotters' car.

I pressed my mouth against Kristin's ear and began to whisper.

"They've made a tactical mistake. They've split their forces. They don't know where we are but we know where they are. They've given us every possible advantage. We'll stalk them just as they think they are stalking us. We'll circle behind them. They'll come straight in along our tracks as soon as they've found them. Meanwhile, we'll go around them, get down to the road and steal their car."

"And leave them here?"

"Can you think of a better idea?"

"I was thinking about the wolves."

"So was I."

"They terrify me," she whispered.

I assured her that she was not alone in her fear of the wolves. But there was no time to wait precisely because of them.

"They'll move in any minute now. They're used to us now and they'll soon lose their fear of the lights. Ready to go?"

She nodded, her hand tight on mine.

"I love you," I said. My heart was hammering.

"I love you," she told me.

"Thank you," I said, not knowing what else to say.

We crawled to the lip of the hole, rolled over into snow and moved into the darkness of the bulbous shrubs, walking hunched over as if there was a guarantee of safety in making ourselves small. From one dark patch of safety to another. Hearing large forms moving. The creak of snow under our boots seemed as loud as unoiled hinges. Karpovitch shouted something from the edge

222

of light, a question muffled by distance and scattered by the wind. One of the searchers replied from less than a hundred feet away. We were abreast of him then, moving toward the edge of the escarpment as he moved deeper among the trees. I hoped the German would have eyes only for the darkness and for the yellow eyes of the wolves that massed and stared in an unblinking wall behind us. With each step I thought that I could hear the start of their inevitable charge.

I stumbled and almost fell when a searcher's shout came suddenly from behind and I waited, every sense alert for the moment of discovery. Instead there came a sudden wave of terrible swift sound. The wolves were gathering for the rush. I heard the lone searcher shout again and then start running panic-stricken through the undergrowth, and then the savage baying. We ran across the naked ridge, sliding down the slope in a cloud of snow. No thought then of searchers. I heard a pistol shot behind me and then another and a furious howling, and then a terrible short scream drowned in growling sounds and snarls. Some black form was leaping down the slope beside us in its own cloud of snow. I struck the hardpacked snow and ice of the road on the run with both feet together, Kristin in my arms, and then we were running like madmen for the black Opel Admiral whose huge spotlights illuminated the ridge and the black waves of animals boiling over it. Then we were in the car, slamming doors, hearing another door slamming behind us and then a pistol shot blasting in my ear, and Kristin's muffled scream and Karpovitch's voice raging in white passion:

"Drive! Drive!"

I released the handbrake, flung the car into second, trod on the long accelerator pedal and the machine leaped across the ice. The night tilted, suddenly askew, trees spun out of sight. The white slopes revolved and the road itself twisted and bucked; white rails, telephone poles and milestones crisscrossed every window. My eyes saw nothing then, seeing everything. I was aware of the raging tide of animals crashing against the car and falling behind. The flat snap of Karpovitch's pistol was very loud. The hill-road rose and fell and suddenly the car was on a straight and level stretch of tolerable pavement, a dizzying transition with the hills behind it. The wolves came on. There was a rush of cold air and sudden loss of balance as Karpovitch flung a rear door open and emptied his pistol into the milling pack. The wolves stopped. The car went on. Karpovitch shut the door and the air stopped rushing in. The wolves and trees and towering escarpments had fallen away.

I drove headlong between huts and houses and the lighted windows of a little town. My face, when I caught sight of it in the rear-view mirror, wore the stricken look of slack-jawed idiocy. I began to tremble violently. I heard my own dry sobbing and Kristin's stillness and the labored breathing of Karpovitch behind me. Resigned and not at all surprised, I felt the cold muzzle of a pistol pressed against my neck.

Small towns passed in sad procession of black and gray buildings streaked with tearful moistures. Then there was a provincial administrative center jammed with horse-drawn drays, then the massif of the mountains, more gaunt and lonely than any mountains I had ever seen, and then, with sunrise, we had crossed the pass— a wild, disturbing place designed for inarticulate destructions.

I drove until I could no longer see or feel the wheel in my numb hands. I gave a hopeless sideways glance to Kristin and saw her huddled in the corner of our seat. She was terribly pale, despite the fresh bite of the morning air. I brought the car to a gentle halt at the side of the road and shut off the motor, not caring about Karpovitch's reaction. He seemed as tired as we were and as glad to rest. Too much had happened to us all, including Karpovitch; we were beyond mere tension. It would take several long moments of silence and lack of motion for anything to start making sense again, I thought.

I lit a cigarette and passed it to Kristin.

I wondered if she had meant what she had said about loving me. I knew that I had meant it. All my life, I supposed, I had looked for someone with whom I would be able to share whatever life provided. There was so much to get out of life, I knew now. It didn't have to be sterile and empty, uninteresting and gray. I had it in perspective now that the future looked as brief as the short barrel of Karpovitch's pistol, no longer than his interest in keeping us alive. Once he had got what he wanted from me, there would be no future to worry about.

But now, wondering if Kristin really loved me, if she could love me (and wondering why she should), I was desperately interested in having a future. And I wasn't going to give up what I had found so unexpectedly without at least putting up a fight. The gentle, amiable and unoffending consultant on antiquities seemed a shadowy figure whom I could no longer picture clearly to myself.

To start with, Karpovitch would be even more tired than I. His reflexes would have become blunted by tension and fatigue. He couldn't risk hurting us until I had told him about Lindstrom's money. Thus his hands were tied by the necessity of keeping me alive; I had no such problems in relation to his health.

I hoped to make good use of all the lessons the plotters had taught me; choosing the moment of attack was a more ticklish matter; I didn't think that Karpovitch would give me more than a solitary chance. I had to be careful not to force matters until I was ready.

It would be safer to start defensively and get the feel of the enemy's offensive, but I already knew the general line of Karpovitch's wishes. Defensive play would only delay the final violent conclusion and each minute worked to sap my strength faster than Karpovitch's.

I said: "All right, Karpovitch. It's your game; I know when I'm beaten."

Karpovitch's voice was harsh, broken with fatigue. "Wise of you. I've no time to waste. I want that briefcase. What did you do with it?"

"It isn't here."

"I know that, you fool! Do you think you'd still be breathing if you had it here? I want to know where the money is, not where it isn't! What have you done with it? Quick, or the girl gets it in the head."

"I'll give it to you if you let us go."

I thought that Karpovitch would expect only my immediate and unconditional surrender but he had clearly learned not to take me for granted.

He said: "I'll let you go when I have the money. Now, tell me: Where is it?"

"I'll take you there."

"Where? Where is it? Tell me now or I'll start hurting your young woman. This pistol fires an eight-millimeter bullet that spins at two thousand revolutions per second. At such close range the laceration is severe, the flesh tatooing is extremely vivid. It will have the same effect on this young woman's beautiful face as a high-speed drill combined with a blowtorch. Am I quite clear?"

"What guarantee do I have that you won't kill us as soon as I've told you what you want to know?"

"My word!"

"That," I said, calm, "is not good enough."

"All right," Karpovitch said, his voice difficult. "I know what you're up to. You're trying to drive me out of control. You think that if you enrage me I'll make a slip and give you a chance. A chance for what, you fool? Do you suppose there is anything I wouldn't do to get what I want? Killing you painfully has been a dream of mine for several hours and yet you're still alive. Obviously, I've decided to let you live but don't test my patience. I am tired and under considerable pressure. You should know by now that I must be taken seriously."

"I know it."

"Very good. Now perhaps we can understand each other. I want the money. You want yourself and the girl safely out of this country. Between the three of us each of us can get exactly what he or she wants."

"Aren't you working for the plotters any more?"

"What business is that of yours? Besides, you know what I'm

up against; you're the man responsible for the pressure. Oh, I would give anything to be able to kill you!"

"With that, how can you expect me to negotiate with you?"

"To hell with that! You have no right to expect anything!" Then he passed his hand wearily across his eyes. "All right. You push me too much. I am not used to this position of partnership by necessity."

I started laughing.

"You're on the run, aren't you, Karpovitch. You've broken with the plotters. They're after you as much as after us now, aren't they?"

Karpovitch swore and suddenly brought the sharp muzzle of the pistol hard on top of my head. It was an expert blow; the pain was astonishing.

The pistol slid, trembling, about my head. Karpovitch's breath was labored; he had clearly come to the end of his road. I fought to ignore the pain, the clouds of fatigue. I had to seize control of the situation. Karpovitch was helpless without Lindstrom's thousands if the conspirators were after him, but doubly dangerous with himself in danger. I had to disarm him.

"Let's talk," I said. "I've mailed the money to a place in the capital. I can't give it to you until we get there. So let's talk. We're in the same boat, more or less. Let's see if we can help each other a bit."

"I don't need your help," Karpovitch said slowly.

"I have the money you need to save your neck. You have the contacts to get us to Sweden. Let Kristin drive us to the capital and we can talk about it. Well, what d'you say? Or would you rather sit here until your former buddies catch up with us?"

"All right," Karpovitch said. "But no tricks. I still have a pistol."

"I'll keep that in mind."

I walked around the car and got in beside the Master Spy in the rear seat. Out of the car I felt suddenly alone and everything was clear; it was a moment that could be savored. The icy air felt clean in my lungs and my boots were springy on the hard-packed snow and, for a few seconds, I was vividly aware of the remote possibility of success. I asked if the plotters were on the road behind us. Karpovitch shook his head.

"They're looking for me in the capital."

"They'd kill you even if you did get them the Lindstrom money. What does loss of the money do to the conspiracy?"

"Nothing. It goes on as scheduled; three o'clock tomorrow afternoon in Napoleon Square. It is too big to stop just because a part of the plan went wrong. It's too late to stop it anyway; everything is in motion. You'd have as much chance stopping the Prague Express by standing on the track."

"Couldn't you stop it?"

"Why should I? It doesn't concern me any longer. I'll be in Sweden an hour after you hand me the money. Then South America. I have a few friends there."

"And what about Sempinski? What have you done with him?"

"Nothing. Why should I do anything to him? Let him be found where the conspirators want him to be found. He has a role to play in the conspiracy . . . some letters to back up."

I thought quietly for a moment, then I said: "I have those letters with me."

Then it was Karpovitch's turn to stare and to start laughing.

"You have the letters? You really wrecked everything for them, didn't you? I really misjudged you. I had no idea how dangerous you were."

"Do you still plan to kill us once you have the money?"

"What for? Revenge for wrecking the conspiracy? I am all done with that. Personal revenge? I have more pressing problems. To keep you quiet? The only people who might want my skin are the conspirators and you're not likely to go to them with news."

He relaxed then, and sat back in the seat for a moment and even closed his eyes. It was a fragmentary dropping of his guard; his eyes were immediately open again and fixed on me intently. But the movement had suggested the possibility of further relaxation. Clearly this was no time to alarm the Master Spy or to put him on his guard again.

I sighed, pretending to relax. I watched Kristin's rigid shoulders hunched over the wheel. I wondered if she knew how dangerous our situation had become. When the time came to attack Karpovitch in the speeding car, success would depend on her nerve as much as on mine.

I closed my eyes, yawned. I smiled at Karpovitch.

"I'd like a little of that money," I said conversationally. Karpovitch grimaced. His pistol hand relaxed.

"You are about to propose an American deal?"

"There's plenty to go around."

"Not for me, there isn't. I got that money out of Lindstrom, it belongs to me. If I leave the conspiracy, the money goes with me. You're getting enough as it is."

"I am? I didn't know that I was getting anything out of this."

"How much is your life worth? That's what you are getting."

Karpovitch laughed. He passed his hand across his eyes again. He seemed to have trouble with his shoulders; they appeared too heavy for his tired, thin frame. I knew that only moments separated me from the final act.

With infinite slowness I gathered myself together, too nervous to think. I got my legs under me, testing the suddenly slack muscles against the limousine's rich carpeting. I could throw myself sideways into the Master Spy. The problem was: how to make my body get on with the job. I could not clear my head of the image of the small black pistol.

I felt my resolution ebbing and forced it to stay. I felt my arms push off, my body going sideways and turning toward the staring spy; I heard a shout spiraling in a harsh blend of fear, and a wish to frighten; my left hand clutched and closed upon Karpovitch's wrist with a strength I didn't know I had; my right hand smashed bruised knuckles into Karpovitch's face.

I heard Kristin's shout, oddly thin in the chaos of other sounds around me. I twisted the wrist I was clutching and heard the dry snap of a bone, a wild yell, and the fall of the pistol. I felt another hand closing about my throat. Then the car rocked and swayed, thrown into a sudden swerve with the brakes pushed down hard, and I was hurled off the seat hauling Karpovitch with me. Karpovitch lost his grip on my throat. I drew back my fist and let it fly blindly, conscious of nothing beyond terror and despair, and felt the sharp pain of cracked knuckles. Then there was a struggling body under me and I was hitting it and kicking. The car swerved again and rode up on the bank. Kristin was shouting something that I couldn't understand. I beat the spy until I could no longer find the strength to hit him again. Then I sagged back. I sat on Karpovitch, jammed between the seats. Only then did I realize that my eyes had been tightly closed all the time.

Kristin was calling, laughing. I felt her hands around my painful face and then her arms around me. The car doors were open and I was bitterly cold.

"You did it! Oh, I love you, you wonderful, mad scholar. You've got him out cold. Could there be anybody like you?"

I tried to say something but my teeth were chattering. I couldn't stop shaking. Then a quick pain burned in my face where, her hands were resting.

"You're hurt!"

I tried to tell her that it was not serious. Just cuts and bruises. But I was too spent to argue with Kristin. She shook her head and looked concerned.

"How does it look?"

"Awful. You're all bloody."

I was suddenly delighted.

"Stop grinning," she said. "This is serious."

I went on grinning. "I am in good hands."

She kissed me quickly. "We have to get you a doctor. Something might be broken."

"No, it's just cuts and bruises."

"I can clean you up with some of that useless stuff I bundled up in Hetmanska Gora but you must have proper treatment."

"I'm getting it," I said. I felt pleasantly luxurious and didn't want to miss a moment of it. "That was some pretty fancy driving, incidentally."

"I used to wreck a sports car a year," she said. "I'm an expert at it. It's one of those skills you never forget."

230

Then she began to rip up silk and linen. "Now hold still. Oh, sorry. Is it hurting now?"

I admitted that my face felt a bit tender, particularly the nose.

"I almost expected you to say that it hurt only when you laughed. You're an incredible man, do you know that?"

"I'm willing to have you tell me all about it."

"Oh, I will, I will. You can be sure of that. Now, is that comfortable? It's the best I can do. It doesn't look very professional I'm afraid."

I touched the white cocoon she had spun around my face and head. It was trimmed with lace. I knew better than to laugh although I had a devil of a time to keep my face straight.

"That's beautiful," I said. "You make a splendid nurse. And you're a scary driver. Do you think you could take us on to the capital? Where are we, anyway?"

"We have a little less than a hundred kilometers to go. We can be there in a couple of hours if you can stand the bumps."

Then we both looked at Karpovitch's bloodless face. His eyes were vacant. His nose was blue and swollen wide across his cheeks. His mouth was partly crushed. His wrist was obviously broken. Kristen looked at me without saying anything, but she shook her head. I felt uncomfortable then, as if suddenly ashamed.

I said: "A pretty murderous job. He looks as if he had tangled with a madman."

"A rather wonderful madman, I would say."

"I feel a bit sick about that. I'm afraid I'm not much good at this kind of thing. What are we going to do with him?"

She thought a moment, shook her head.

"We can't leave him here. He'd freeze in half an hour. Or maybe more wolves . . . no, we'll let him out nearer the capital. There isn't much harm that he can do us now. He'll be too busy saving his own hide to cause any problems."

We tied Karpovitch with his own belt, with my belt and with strips of Kristin's slip. We left him lying on the floorboards of the car. I got into the passenger seat beside Kristin and sat back on the cushions, my head suddenly heavy. I put Karpovitch's pistol in my pocket. Kristin got in behind the steering wheel. She got the car back on the road.

We drove a long time, with the white countryside broadening and opening into fields as the hills and slopes and violent escarpments fell away behind us. The day was brilliantly clear. We could see far toward the horizon. Small towns and villages went by at irregular intervals. I slept a little, lulled by the sound and motion of the car.

The day began to end at midafternoon. Darkness came quickly. The sun hung for long reluctant moments behind the thick clouds piling up on the horizon, turning them purple, then vanished. In the sudden darkness, the chill seemed particularly penetrating and the night unfriendly. The road flowed under us narrow as a stream tunneling through mountains; I longed for daylight and its broad horizons.

As we got closer to the capital, traffic became heavy; cars, trucks, antique excursion busses, horse-drawn drays moved out of snowy side-roads; and soon the highway filled with dark, unlighted shapes swaying dangerously out of gloomy blackness, and then began occasional long moments without motion. Far ahead of the lurching column, I saw waving lanterns and the long tongue of a barrier swung upward in the white beams of innumerable headlights.

"What do you think is going on up there?" Kristin wished to know. "An accident?"

"Looks like some kind of roadblock."

We heard distant whistles and shouts of command. Behind us, Karpovitch drew a long groaning breath and moved on the floorboards. I looked into his disfigured white face; his eyes were wide with pain and hatred, faintly luminous.

I said: "We'll have to dump him here. We'll never get through a roadblock with him in the car."

Kristin said quietly: "What about my papers? Isn't that the first thing they want at a roadblock?"

I had forgotten about Kristin's lack of papers. I said: "We'll just have to try to talk our way around that. Maybe they aren't

232

as hard on foreign tourists as they're on their own people. After all, that's how they get hard currency."

"What do you think that roadblock's all about?"

"God knows. But I don't think it's anything to do with the plot. In this country, it could be routine."

She said: "Perhaps it's something to do with the Chairman's visit? Security precautions?"

I thought it was likely.

Kristin drove slowly and I climbed over the back of the seat to our prisoner and got him sitting upright on the floorboards. He said nothing to me but his eyes were eloquent. I covered him carefully with his own pistol while I tugged at the knots and buckles that had him trussed up. As an afterthought I went through his papers. Some looked imposing, with seals and heavy signatures. He didn't answer when I asked him what they were. I put them aside.

Then the column of traffic staggered again to a chaotic halt. Kristin pulled up behind a ladder-truck piled high with sacks out of which spilled dark mounds of winter potatoes, and I threw open the car door on The Magician's side and pushed him toward it. He shrugged off my hand with abrupt violence, got out and walked slowly to the walls of snow piled at the roadside. There he turned, cradling his injured arm, and looked toward us. Instinct told me that he would not try to reach the roadblock ahead of us. He was not yet ready for a public confrontation. For the moment he was in check. I closed the car door more hastily and locked it.

I sat back on the cold leather cushions, Karpovitch's papers on the seat beside me, wondering how to solve the problem of the roadblock. The traffic edged persistently toward the small group of soldiers and the striped pole they raised and lowered across the road, and then I saw trucks and cars stop before us, and dark forms started dragging bundles out of them and threw the bundles, packages and other odd objects far into the snow. Kristin began to laugh.

"What's the matter?"

"Looks like there are some others worried about the roadblock," she said. "I wonder what they're throwing away."

"Can't imagine. Could be black-market stuff. But that reminds me about something I'd better get rid of."

I threw Karpovitch's pistol across the roadside snow bank. I said: "Now all we have to worry about is passport control. Are you a good actress?"

"Not good enough to be paid for acting. How about you?"

"Oh, great. I used to play the Train in Shakespeare's historicals at school."

"What train?"

"You know where they say things like Enter Gloucester and Train? Well, I was the Train. It won't help us here."

"It might," she said. "Are those Karpovitch's papers you have there? Could you do anything with them? If the conspirators are as highly placed as we think they are, there ought to be some passes."

I looked through the papers. Karpovitch had a Swiss passport which was useful; I would be able to speak German at the roadblock. His photograph was unrecognizable. With luck and in the wavering light of hurricane lanterns it could have represented anyone, possibly even me. I thought that if the signatures on the passes were important enough the guards might not scan the photograph too closely.

"Well," Kristin said. "What about the passes?"

"There are a couple of papers here that look authoritative. National emblems on the letterhead, big black signature and a red seal. Looks like the Nakomda."

"Well," she said, laughing. "That ought to do, don't you think?"

I said, uncertain: "It could be a traffic ticket, for all I can tell. Well, what else is there? We can't risk getting stopped for any questioning or a search for passports. I'll try it if you're game."

"I'll do it all," she said. "You just relax and look important in the back seat. It looks better that way. I'll be your secretary and driver. In this country that's a common combination."

"How the devil do I act important?"

She laughed. "That's very easy. You keep your head motionless,

234

eyes fixed ahead except for a flicker when the soldier shows up at the window, and say nothing. Think yourself a millionaire driving past his plant guards."

"They look stuffed."

"Exactly. See how easy it is?"

Then there were only two vehicles, a truck and a small car, between us and the striped barrier, and a soldier began to move heavily toward us, bulky in furs, with the odd, futuristic submachine gun they all seemed to wear, strapped across his chest. He gave Kristin an appreciative look and saluted, smiling. She handed him Karpovitch's documents."

"How far is it to the capital?" she asked in German, her voice pleasant. "My employer is an important Swiss comrade on special business. You know who is visiting the capital, of course?"

"Oh," the soldier said, unconcerned. "That's why we are here, to have a look at whoever's coming into town. It's a cold night but it'll be worth it."

"You mean if you catch someone suspicious?"

"Hell no," he said. "Didn't you see the speculators tossing out black-market stuff a mile back? Who do you think is going to pick it up tomorrow?"

Kristin laughed. "No wonder you don't mind the cold."

The soldier went on grinning. "Best duty there is. You don't catch me missing roadblock duty." And then, about the papers: "These look fine, miss. Drive carefully, there's a lot of ice ahead."

He raised his arm and, ahead of us, the striped pole went up and Kristin trod on the accelerator and we were through the roadblock.

twenty-one

WE GOT to the capital in early evening, with the day long gone and the night grown dark. Snow started falling again heavily. The people hurried with heads down along gloomy streets, whipped by the wind and the snow, blurred and unreal.

We drove through a pleasant, nineteenth-century suburb with its parks and gardens now hidden under snow, old royal pleasure grounds sheeted over as if for temporary storage in the owners' absence. Then into the city proper: tall houses, steep roofs and ornamented balconies and then the broad expanse of a glazed boulevard bordered with palaces.

We passed the university gates and the Fine Arts Palace and eventually the opulent façade of my hotel. On a sudden impulse I told Kristin to pull over and stop.

"But shouldn't we hurry? The embassy will be closing up for the night soon. It's almost five o'clock."

"That's the trouble. Can you imagine anyone letting us in to see the ambassador? Looking the way we look? With our kind of story?"

"But we can't waste the time asking for appointments."

"I don't intend to ask for one. I want to call the embassy and get a name. Someone we can ask for. I have a friend in New York who works for the government. I've picked up enough from him to know how to make contact with his kind of people. Maybe I'm wrong, but I don't think we'd get anywhere just barging in with a wild story about murder plots."

"We have the letters."

"I can imagine the reaction to the letters. We'll have a better chance once we have the money. Nobody can dismiss half a million dollars without, at least, a second thought. Let's see if the money has come and call the embassy right now. And maybe you would like to freshen up a bit and put on your dress. That's if you have anything left to put on after playing nurse."

"I'd like that, thank you. But do you think it's safe?"

"I don't see why not. The plotters wouldn't be looking for us here. And we're not in trouble with the authorities. On the contrary, we are trying to do them a service."

"That's right," she said. "What could happen now? This whole nightmare is over!"

"Well, not quite over."

"Well, as good as over! I can't believe that we've finally done it. Or rather that *you've* done it. I don't believe I've ever known a man like you. I don't believe that there is anything that you wouldn't be able to handle. And don't start being modest. Don't tell me how lucky we've been. Luck's had damn precious little to do with it; it was all your doing. It was your courage and ingenuity that got us here safely, and I'll be the first to crown anybody who talks about luck."

"Then I'd best keep my mouth shut," I said, also laughing. "I still remember that shoe in your room."

"It might be wise to keep it in mind," she observed.

Coming into the marble lobby I was uncomfortably aware of my battered and unshaved face, tangled hair and dirty, rumpled clothes. Kristin's appearance seemed only a little better. The desk clerk looked hostile, then astonished and finally dubious until he saw my passport and checked his registers. Even then he looked unhappy about surrendering my key.

I sent Kristin upstairs so that she could bathe and change and went to the bar. A stiff brandy helped steady me a little. I asked for the telephone and, when it was brought, called the embassy.

I could imagine the cool, marble pillars, the efficient lobby with its burnished Marine sergeant and uniformed doormen, the crisp click of high heels, and the candy-striped flag with the golden eagle—so reassuring in the foreign city. That was, indeed, another world and for a moment I wondered if I had the right to intrude.

Certainly, my reception, so close to the end of office hours, indicated that I had no rights. But I managed to impress three Midwestern women in succession with the importance of my mission and, eventually, I was explaining my implausible tale to a Mr. Stevens—speaking guardedly, conscious of an audience. I was alone in the bar but God only knew who was listening in to the conversation.

Stevens cut me off as soon as the general drift of my story began to present itself. He took my number and said he'd call back after checking with someone in another department. I offered to come to the embassy to see him but he hastily assured me that my visit would be unnecessary. What made him pause was my announcement that Kristin was with me.

I heard the murmur of a conversation at the other end: soft American voices over the insufficiently shielded telephone, and then Mr. Stevens told me that someone would shortly come to see us at the hotel. In the meantime, I was to make no more telephone calls. Was that clear?

It was and I said so, grinning to myself. Tommy Mackin had taught me several valuable lessons.

I checked with the desk clerk to see if I had any mail and found, to my surprise, a letter from Tommy and a postcard from Hubertus Pohl.

Tommy wrote that he had heard that I was taking an Eastern European vacation and that he hoped I'd be careful not to drink the water. He had some friends in the capital, he wrote, whom he had asked to keep an eye on me. He hoped I wasn't taking any silly chances on the ski slopes. Hubertus Pohl wanted to know when he would hear from me.

238

The bulky envelope containing Lindstrom's money hadn't been delivered. I cursed myself for not having taken Kristin's advice to send this vital piece of evidence to the embassy. The clerk's assurance that one more postal delivery would be made this evening depressed me; I was sure that I would never see that money again. I hoped the letters would be enough to intrigue whoever was coming from the embassy. I had no faith in my ability to convince the man.

Kristin came downstairs shortly afterward, looking so little like my recent fugitive companion that, at first, I didn't know what to say to her. I delayed my own cleanup to enjoy her fresh, new brightness longer; it was as good for me as the Russian brandy. And before I could go up we were joined by the embassy man.

He was tall, thin and stooped like a questionmark, with thinning gray hair. His hands were deep in his pockets, his tie was askew. He shook my hand and smiled enthusiastically at Kristin. His name, he said, was Field and he sold vacuum cleaners. The vacuum cleaners confused me for a moment; now that the time had come to tell what I knew I didn't know where or how to start.

I blurted out: "Are you CIA?"

Field smiled quietly. "I've always been a salesman of one kind or another."

Then Kristin shrugged and closed her eyes. Her face was suddenly terribly drawn. Field nodded to her, at ease like an old friend, but I thought him watchful.

"Well, Doctor, supposing you tell me all about it. Start at the beginning and just run through the whole thing step by step. I gather that you have a pressing problem but we'll save more time than we'll lose by getting the whole story on the table before we decide what to do about it."

I said: "All right."

I heard my thin tired voice begin the story and wondered where the voice was coming from; it didn't seem mine. Pohl and Per Lindstrom and the Library deal, Karpovitch, Brown, Zimstern and the fat man who died in Zimstern's store, General Danilow's ruthless but endearing nephew, Sempinski and Hetmanska Gora, the Germans and the plot, and the brutal, powerful man who had so quickly destroyed The Magician . . . none of these people and places and events seemed to have anything to do with me. Telling the story I thought that I would never believe it if Field and I were suddenly to change places. I told it all from my lunch with Tommy Mackin and the arrival of Sempinski's letter to my escape with Kristin from Hetmanska Gora and our coming here. And out of the entire account only Kristin mattered; the Pontic Tribunals were only crumbling bits of parchment; the Sempinski Affair a matter for the professionals to handle. I was no longer concerned about anything except ending the nightmare so that Kristin would be safe.

Field listened intently, his face noncommittal, but I could sense his interest wax and wane with certain names and places. The Library affair didn't interest him except for the part apparently played in it by the Nakomda officer. But the awesome general who had condemned Karpovitch, and Karpovitch himself, brought instant reactions.

He didn't tell me anything about anyone involved in my narrative but, when I was finished, he watched me for a long moment with curiously appreciative silence. Then he read Lindstrom's papers and folded them and put them almost reverently into his inside pocket.

"That's quite a story," he said and laughed uneasily. "You don't happen to be a mystery writer on the side?"

I said that I wasn't.

"We would have problems trying to convince anyone important that all this could be true."

"Then you don't believe me?"

"It doesn't matter whether I believe you. Oh, I can pass the word to some friends and they could start checking, and, in enough time, they would check it all out. But if your story is true there is no time for that. How can we be immediately convincing?"

"I thought the letters and the money . . ."

Field shrugged. He tapped his breast pocket. "I can predict the

240

reaction to the letters, Doctor: forgery. A clumsy attempt at blackmail. Possibly an attempt to discredit an important American citizen. The ambassador is a personal friend of Senator Lindstrom. He would never believe that these letters could be genuine."

"The CIA does not report to ambassadors," Kristin said coldly.

Field nodded, smiled. "Quite right. We have the privilege of going our own way. But we must pay our rent, you know; the ambassador would have to be the first to know what's going on in his bailiwick. And you don't get to be an ambassador without a few friends of your own. He could be obstructive."

"So now we have to play nursemaid to your ambassador?"

"Be reasonable, Dr. Shippe. If the ambassador's personal friend and political idol turns out to be a traitor and a fool, the ambassador must be given the opportunity to cover himself. Otherwise he'll stall us. We can't afford delays. He must be on our side from the start."

"Would the money help?"

"It might. Can you get it?"

"It hasn't come yet. I expect it after dinner."

"You must get it for us. But tell me a few things more. You say that Senator Lindstrom is about to commit unplanned suicide?"

"That's what Karpovitch told me. He has people in London. He had no trouble murdering General Danilow there."

"And this Karpovitch is here? He is The Magician?"

"He admits it. But let me ask you something. Why are you so willing to listen to my story? You don't even know me."

"Oh, I expected to hear from you sometime. Your friend, Mr. Mackin had mentioned you to some mutual acquaintances. He said you might need looking after. I think he'd be surprised to see how well you can look after yourself but, to oblige him, we kept an eye on you."

"You had me followed to Hetmanska Gora?"

"I wish we had. But you dodged us along with everybody else after the Zimstern murder. The fat man whom Brown killed was a friend of mine."

"I thought he was a Nakomda spy tailing me because of the Library affair."

"That's how it goes sometimes. Everything is pretty much a misunderstanding until it's too late."

"And what do you think about that Nakomda officer who told me he was the man with the Library for sale? Could that be true?"

"If your talking about Colonel Danilow, the Nakomda deputy commander for the capital, I wouldn't put it past him. But he is just about the last man in this country I would trust. Next to his boss, of course. Anyway, Doctor, will you get me that money as soon as you can?"

I said I would, but there was a condition. I wanted Kristin out of this whole business immediately. If Field would take her to the embassy and protect her there from the conspirators, Karpovitch or whatever other danger could still threaten us, I would wait at the hotel until the money came.

I said: "I don't suppose you want me to deliver it to the embassy?"

Field shook his head quickly.

"That's the last place I want to see you in until this affair is over. We don't want any link between you and the embassy until everyone has a chance of smelling like a rose."

"I thought embassies are supposed to protect American citizens in trouble," Kristin said bitterly.

Field smiled. "That's the theory of it. In practice that could prove a secondary matter. As you see, I'm being quite honest about it."

She said, contemptuously: "That's nice of you. Is there still some danger?"

"I wouldn't discount the possibility," Field said.

"Then why don't you wait here and get the money? Why must we get it for you?"

"Only Dr. Shippe can pick it up without arranging a burglary. That's hard to do in a country where the authorities don't share our point of view."

"It's not hard to do in Saigon, I imagine," she said bitterly.

Field inclined his head.

She said: "You can arrange all sorts of mischief in Saigon, can't you? I remember you now. What was it you were selling in Saigon? Earthmoving equipment? I'm not going with you to any embassy. I'm staying here until we get the money."

I said: "Go with him. As a favor to me."

"What makes you think I would be any safer with him than with the other killers?" And then, with quiet intensity to Field: "What difference is there between you and Brown and Karpovitch or the others out there?"

"None, really," Field said calmly. "We are all pretty much alike if that's how you see it. But I think you know what your husband was doing in Vietnam. You didn't know at the time, of course, but you must know now."

"It makes no difference what I know," Kristin said. "What you did is what matters."

"Jan Napoji was a very dangerous man," Field said.

"So are you," Kristin said. "I have no reason to think better of you than of any other murderer."

Field said: "I'm sorry, Mrs. Napoji. I can't say more than that. I would be glad to see to it that you are taken care of at the embassy tonight. You're not directly linked with the conspiracy, as Dr. Shippe is linked, and besides we owe you something for your accident. But I can't force you to come with me."

"No you can't," she said. "And where is Dr. Shippe going to spend his time until all the plotters are jailed? Sitting in the hotel lobby like a target?"

"I'll find him a place once we have the money."

I said urgently: "You must go with him."

"Oh God, I don't know," she said. "Will you be careful, though? You can't trust these people any more than you can trust the others."

"I'll be careful. But there isn't much to worry about now."

"You know better than that."

"I'll get the money as quickly as I can and hide somewhere

until everything is over. I'll join you at the embassy in a day or two and then we can go home. That isn't much to worry about."

She said: "I just don't like it. I have a feeling that if I lose sight of you something terrible will happen."

"Nothing will happen," I assured her, then said to Field: "Well, where am I to meet you? And how do I get there?"

"When you leave the hotel don't use the front entrance. By the time you have the money your Nakomda friend may have a tail on you. Get to the Old City. There is a wine shop on the south side of the square."

"I know it," I broke in.

"I'll wait there until midnight. When you come into the wine shop, come straight to my table, without any fuss, sit down and act as if we had a date for a drink and a talk about vacuum cleaners. From that point on I'll look after things. All clear?"

I nodded.

"Then we'll leave you now," Field said. "You've given me a lot of work to do between now and when I see you later. If you don't get the money tonight just don't show up and don't stir out of the hotel."

"Why not?"

"If what you say is going to take place tomorrow, all of us are going to be dodging lynch mobs. If you're not out in the street nobody can hurt you."

It didn't occur to me to wonder, then or later, why Field had seemed so anxious to leave the hotel. An hour's wait could have provided him with Lindstrom's money. I supposed that he had a lot to do and couldn't spare the time. Kristin went with him reluctantly. I was glad to see her in safe hands; I couldn't quite convince myself that Karpovitch was now completely out of the picture.

I told the desk clerk that I expected mail and left him my sole remaining dollar bill—a week's wages for the clerk, according to the black-market exchange rate, an hour's wage by the official scale. He was to bring the envelope to my room as soon as the mail was delivered and sorted. I wondered if I would ever see either the clerk or the envelope if he had had any idea of what the envelope contained.

My room seemed just as I had left it. Nothing looked disturbed but I had an uneasy feeling that everything I touched would transmit a signal to a hidden listener. I thought of a hot bath and the warm feather bed and the thought came close to unnerving me completely. I chose the least comfortable chair in the room and sat down. I don't know how long I sat there. Perhaps I slept for a time. Finally there was the expected knock upon my door, and when I flung the door open there was the clerk and the bulging envelope. I didn't look inside it, afraid to open it before my imagined or real observers, and equally afraid that the contents would not be the money but some kind of fraud. I put the envelope on the dresser and backed away from it and watched the trembling lamplight give the envelope a semblance of life; it appeared to breathe. My tired brain was playing tricks on me. I hoped that I would be able to hang onto my wits long enough to get the money into Field's hands.

I threw off my clothes, feeling as if I was peeling off my skin and, with it, my old identity which spelled danger. I must stink, I thought. I stole the time to wash, shave and finger my bruises, explaining the time-waste to myself as a need for cleaning-up, changing my appearance, putting on disguise. I dressed in fresh underwear, a clean soft shirt and my warmest suit. I couldn't touch my filthy furs again and stuffed the envelope into my New York topcoat pocket, and put on the topcoat, feeling momentarily free of conspiracies and Iron Curtain winters.

There were room-service waiters in the corridor, wheeling a guest's dinner cart and champagne bucket from the service elevator, and I took the stairs to the floor below so as to have the service elevator to myself. I got out in the basement and left the hotel through the freight entrance without seeing anyone, as Field had wanted me to. The envelope felt incredibly heavy in my pocket. Each moving shadow increased my alarm.

The snow came down like an avalanche in the alley behind

the hotel; I could see nothing ten feet in front of my face. All lights were blurred and diffused into an unreal orange glare, forms were dim. People loomed through the thick white snow curtain like wavering ghosts.

I rounded the hotel building and came into the main boulevard without a thought of taxis, and headed north toward Castle Square, guided by the statue of an ancient king that rose high above the rooftops in that part of town. Floodlights made the lone bronze figure appear suspended in an inward flame, unsupported above the falling mass of snow. I was aware of many men moving near me but I couldn't see them. And then I was in the Old City again and the ancient houses closed about me with their welcome sense of permanence; a partial reassurance.

I supposed that I was quite completely frozen at this point, moving by instinct, numb; feeling nothing, quite sure that I was being followed. I wondered which of my many possible pursuers had picked up my trail and hurried, feeling time narrowing about me, into Market Square, then down the stone steps into the cellar wine shop where music was playing.

The place was crowded. I peered through the smoke until I saw Field waving from a corner table, and made my way toward him, hearing a cacophony of languages around me. I hung my topcoat on a hook behind Field and sat down across the table from him.

He said, with unexpected bonhommie: "Hi there, O.H."

I said: "Been waiting long?"

It seemed like the correct question for the role I thought we were playing.

"Oh, maybe an hour."

"Who are all these people?"

"The world's press in for the big show tomorrow."

"You mean the Chairman's speech?"

"That's the one. The speech is billed as a major Soviet policy announcement. It looks as if the whole world had been invited to a grandstand seat . . . I'm glad you gave us that call when you did."

"You mean that all your doubts about my story are resolved?"

"There's no doubt about it."

"What settled it for you?"

"We heard from the London office as soon as I got back to the shop. I had to give your fiancée some bad news about her uncle. It seems he just couldn't take the strain, just as you said he would not. Nobody could have made that up without prior knowledge."

"So you got things moving?"

"Right away. The word went out from head-office an hour ago; we're all busy as hell. But the competition's had a long time to dig in and it's hard to uproot them."

I said, thinking about Lindstrom but unable, even now, to drum up sympathy for him: "So they did it, did they? That makes it look as if they're going on with their plan despite everything."

Field said: "It looks that way. They must be pretty sure of themselves. But right now I have a couple of other small problems and finding you a place to stay is one of them."

I started laughing, too exhausted to resist hysteria.

"So you didn't need the money, after all? I had to play the part of a clay pigeon for nothing? And don't give me that bit about there being no danger to speak of. That was all right to set Kristin's mind at rest, but you and I both know how much danger I'm in. You people really are a ruthless lot."

"Of course we need the money. We can't have the competition get its hands on it, can we?"

"What are the chances of stopping the plot?"

"Too damn tight, but we'll do our best. The trouble is that our government and this one aren't on speaking terms, so we can't take our story to the local boys. We're trying to do the whole business ourselves and we're damn short-handed. Anyway, I hope this report cheers you up a bit?"

I said, tired: "It's a nice change to have everything in professional hands. How's Kristin?"

Field looked away, then, suddenly evasive. I waited, feeling suddenly sick with premonition. A waiter came up and Field quickly ordered two double Russian brandies, crackers and caviar.

After the waiter left, I said: "I asked about Kristin."

Field nodded: "I heard you."

"Well, what about her?"

"Fact is . . . the fact is she changed her mind about staying with us. We couldn't hold her. She said she was going back to the hotel to wait with you for the money."

"You let her do that, knowing the place might be watched? My God, she was right about you!"

"Stop shouting. You'll attract attention."

"The hell with attention! You and I are going right back to the hotel. I'm sure somebody got onto me there, and if she walked into any kind of trap there . . ."

Field said, his voice calm but firm: "Shut up and keep still. I tried to argue with her but she didn't listen."

"Oh, that's just fine," I said. "That makes everything perfectly all right. She was damn right that we couldn't trust you."

Field said: "Hey, listen, don't you have that twisted around a bit? Who walked out on whom? Stop worrying. If your colonel friend picks her up before we get to her it won't do her any harm. The Boss is her late uncle's friend, remember? We'll have somebody at the proper place the first thing in the morning."

"And what if it's somebody else who picks her up first? Like Karpovitch?"

"Listen," Field said, no longer cold, smiling, his eyes sad but friendly. "I know how you feel. But you mustn't complicate the situation. It could be a lot worse. She has her papers back, she's all in the clear. There is no reason for anybody to hold her after the Boss gets on the phone tomorrow. Now relax, sit back, listen to the music. Enjoy your canapés, they taste pretty good. You've more than earned a little relaxation."

"But dammit, Kristin . . ."

The brandy clouded whatever clear thoughts I had had, except a feeling of immeasurable fear, despair and an anxiety that exceeded any worry I had ever had.

248

"She'll be fine, I tell you," Field went on. "She may get a bit frightened if Danilow picks her up but that's all that'll happen. When an American citizen gets in trouble in a foreign country, even a country that is not as friendly as it might be, there's usually little to worry about if the embassy takes immediate action."

"I've had an example of the care that I could expect."

"You're not the niece of a Per Lindstrom, friend," Field said reasonably. "Besides, at the moment the ambassador is very anxious to make a good impression. As for Karpovitch, don't worry about him; he has to stay low until he has managed to get his demoralized Krauts together again."

"How long will that take?"

"At least a day, Doctor. By that time everything will be over. So for God's sake disconnect that fuse and relax. That's it, that's much better. Want another drink?"

I shook my head, too dispirited to care. Field looked casually around, sighed with satisfaction and signaled a waiter.

"Well, thank God the shouting is all over, anyway. I don't think anybody noticed . . . they're all too busy anticipating the Chairman's speech and reshaping the world. I'll make a phone call in a minute and see if our people have some news for you. Will that help?"

"Yes," I said. "Oh, I don't know. I'm too tired to think."

"That's good. Don't think. Let me do your thinking. I'm far more concerned about you than Kristin at the moment. Everybody seems to be looking for you tonight. Your friend, the colonel, is turning the capital upside down to get to you before anybody else. His people have barged into just about every place where I thought I could hide you. I'm embarrassed to admit that he must have known my business for a long, long time."

I didn't want to think about the Nakomda man or the Romanowski Library or anything else. Field went on, reflectively:

"Why should he be so interested in you? There are just too many unknowns in this case; it's the damnedest can of worms I've ever come across. Maybe we ought to let him find you. Maybe he had been on the level all along and you have an ally you don't know about. Danilow would be a good ally to have in this situation. We'd have no trouble stopping the conspiracy if he took a hand."

"Then why not tell him all about it?"

Field looked shocked. "You want *us* to cooperate wih *them*? I wouldn't trust Danilow if he gave me directions to the men's room. What an idea . . . the Nakomda and the CIA working together to save the Soviet Chairman! I almost think you might have something there; it's just ridiculous enough to be the best way."

I shrugged, weary beyond reason. "Do what you want."

"What I want is to have you on ice, out of the way, until this mess is over. I guess it'll have to be the embassy, after all. But I've got to have your word that you won't try to beat it out of there, like your girl friend."

I said: "Why don't you just leave me alone?"

He sighed. "It's a tempting thought. Except that you'd make things difficult for me if you disappeared. Well, Doctor, what about playing ball and going to the embassy with me? Do I have your word that you'll stay put?"

"I don't know," I said. "Give me time to think."

"There isn't any, friend. You know what's involved. I know it's easy to give advice but you're in no shape to make any decisions and I want you out of this business right now."

"All right," I said. I didn't want to think even if there had been something that I could have done about the chaos of disjointed images and confusion in my tired head. Whatever resolution I might have had throughout this whole affair had finally left me.

"Fine," Field said. "You just sit right here. I'm going to telephone the shop about your girl friend. That should cheer you up a bit."

But suddenly his grin dissolved and he said sharply, urgently: "Where's the money?"

"What?" I said.

"The money, Doctor. Give it to me now."

"It's in the coat," I said. "Behind you."

He got up and quickly put on my coat. pointing to his own. "We'll trade for now, if you don't mind," he said. "Just in case the roof caves in or something. And remember, whatever happens you have nothing to worry about from this point on."

I nodded and Field left at once. I watched him walk away among the crowded tables, and suddenly I knew that something was terribly wrong. The dancing couples who had been moving like ships in a fog to the plastic strains of *Winchester Cathedral* began to disappear. Talk died down rapidly and the music blared in the sudden silence. I saw Field's stooped figure vanish behind a group of waiters near the kitchen door.

And then I was aware that a group of men in leather trench coats had appeared at the main door, and that another group was moving quickly through the room toward me. I half-rose as they came around my table, looking desperately for Field, who would know what to do, and they grouped around me so that the room, the smoke, the people and the silence were obscured by the blackness of the polished leather. Someone took my right elbow and someone the left, and I was propelled swiftly across the room among the hushed tables and up the stone steps to the bitterly cold street where a small black passenger car without markings stood with open doors.

I was inside the car, crushed between two heavy men with impassive faces, and before I could gather a fragment of my wits about me, the doors were slammed shut and we were rushing through the streets. My silent captors did not look at me.

PART FIVE
The End of the Affair

twenty-two

THE CITY WALLS were gone in this part of the bleak antiquity but the huge gates still stood astride their narrow streets, guarded by the barbican that Mongols had stormed in the eleventh century, and the gray walls and towers of a royal castle perched on a black rock, as they had hung suspended over the heart of the city for a thousand years. Twelve hundred years of human progress were on display here: from loopholed barbicans and bronze bells cast from Turkish cannon, to the roar of a turbojet slanting invisibly overhead, and the headlong rush of the black car which carried me, as so many terrified captives must have been carried through these ancient streets, to a threatening destination. The city was like an old family house, in the same hands for fifty-seven generations, built to defy time, furnished with what each generation thought best in its time; each adding something but subtracting nothing, finding room for its own fancies without disturbing whatever it inherited along with the house. It was a world far removed in concept from my own, and yet I was ironically aware of how hard I had tried to reproduce this world in my apartment with its books, scrolls, old maps rolled up in Morocco, my brass telescope and Dick Turpin pistol, the chandelier, Flemish tapestry, dark oak and beeswax candles, goulash and red wine. I had found so much to resent and avoid in my world and had sought the sense of permanence that history could give me, and here I was: enveloped by history and longing for the reassurance of my own time. I looked at my frightened face in the rear-view mirror, half-hoping that the rumpled image would give me a clue. But the face was a suddenly unfamiliar arrangement of mismatched oddities: gray eyes puffed with anxiety, broad mouth drooping at the corners, ears fattened by the glow of frostbite and my prize-fighter's nose—a souvenir of freshman intramural boxing. It was an incongruous element in an otherwise ordinary and undistinguished face, a kind of badge, like the names I had been given with more hope than aptness: Oliver Hazard Shippe. There had been an attempt at school to call me "Battle" Shippe but it hadn't lasted beyond freshman year. Now friends, and even strangers, called me O.H. as if the appropriation of the first and middle names of the defender of Lake Erie, a distant ancestor, were too broad a joke for politeness. I had accepted the abbreviation as a discretion; I had not earned the names and I had wished that I had really done something to earn the nose, something more than to walk into a boxing glove held up with more hope than skill by a fellow freshman. Since that time I had walked into few fists of any kind; each year there seemed to be fewer to walk into in my world.

The thought of secret tribunals was only a dim shadow in my mind. I felt an odd sense of exaltation mixed with my bewilderment and fear, as if my seizure had decided something, given me direction. Terror would come later, I knew, along with despair, but I didn't think about them in the speeding car. Wrapped in the icy darkness, rocked along the silent, secret streets, I could feel only a weary if anxious relief. The music of the interrupted dance moved sluggishly in my head.

I wondered if Field had noticed my arrest; he could have hardly been able to help seeing it, everyone had seen it. He had, in fact, made himself scarce with suspicious speed as soon as the Nakomda men had appeared in the restaurant. Perhaps this had been regular procedure for CIA agents, but I could not help thinking myself abandoned and betrayed.

I wondered where the Nakomda men were taking me, a gradually crystallizing curiosity, largely academic at the start. Prison? It could be prison but I didn't think so if, as I had begun to suppose, Colonel Danilow had had anything to do with my arrest. This was his district, after all, and he was in charge, and he had told me that he would be able to protect me in the capital, and there was more reason now than ever before why he should want to protect me. The Sempinski Affair would probably destroy him; its threat would make his defection urgent, and only I could get him the money he needed. The more I thought about it the more I believed that the cynical colonel could have been everything that he had said he was. He had known everything about the Romanowski Library. All his warnings about Sempinski and Hetmanska Gora had proved so terribly correct. Nothing would have happened to me if I had stayed in the capital, as Danilow had urged me to do, if I had not panicked after my early-morning interview with him and run to Sempinski.

Seen in this context, my present situation made a sort of sense. Danilow could have sent his men after me to get me safely hidden from the conspirators; I was his only key to money and defection. Thus, instead of being a catastrophe, my arrest could be a form of salvation.

That was the way to think of it. This thought meant hope. Hell, I thought, suddenly ebullient, it was more than hope; it could be the solution to everything if Danilow, with all his connections and manpower, could be enlisted to help against the plotters. He could be drafted to help in the crisis if for no other reason than to save himself and to keep secret the Library affair.

The Nakomda car slowed down, hissing like a rubber-tire hearse through the empty streets, wrapped in its own peculiar darkness that seemed to make it invisible. It stopped before a heavy gate of wrought iron reinforced by steel bars, and rolled between striped sentry boxes into a floodlit courtyard full of hurrying men. My captors pulled me out of the car and herded me up long stairs, through lobbies where typists and clerks were busy and along innumerable echoing corridors full of armed men in uniforms and

254

civilian clothes. I felt as if I was in the middle of an armed camp on the eve of battle. The vast building which formed three sides of the courtyard seemed an amalgam of a corporation headquarters, medieval fortress, barracks and a communications center; a humming, clattering world of modern machinery and old stone. I supposed myself in the headquarters of the Secret Police, still not as worried as I might have been, although some of my earlier ebullience evaporated. The huge guards set a headlong pace and, tall as I was and used to striding out, I had a difficult time keeping up with them. The stairs rose and fell, long corridors unfolded becoming gradually more luxurious, and finally there was a kind of modern opulence about me that made me think of a Sultan's anterooms transported into the heart of an industrial empire. I was now in the executive section of the building and my hopes went up. Soon I would be face-to-face with Danilow, a possible ally. I didn't need the guards' impatient urging to hurry me along.

My escort halted before a heavy door of polished walnut gleaming with brass fittings, and here the sentries seemed to glitter more brightly than at any other door. The double doors swung open and I was quick-marched through a vast but delicately hushed office where uniformed men and women worked behind steel desks, and then there was another portal with sentries who cradled submachine guns in their arms. Behind them lay a richly paneled room hung with brocade draperies.

"Inside," one of my escort said in sibilant English. The sound of English was shockingly unpleasant in this place.

I stepped into the inner office, feeling the soft carpeting sink under my feet, confused by the oriental profusion of barbaric luxury, Chinese vases, Persian hangings, rich rows of books in leather, ornate furniture. I saw the battlement of the enormous desk at the far end of the room and the men grouped behind and beside it. They stared at me without curiosity or interest, as they had done when I had caught their eyes in Sempinski's Library. I searched for Danilow with suddenly anxious and impatient eyes but I did not find him. And then I saw the man who sat, dark in a brilliant uniform, apart from the others. I thought that he would always be apart, no matter where he sat, reducing all others; stained with darkness in the alcove formed by the angle of a massive fireplace, looking just as he had when I had first glimpsed him in the leathery gloom of an armchair at Hetmanska Gora. No one spoke within the undefined borders of his presence; even the air around him seemed cowed into stillness as if a deep mesh of a transluscent material, an impenetrable barrier of energized crystals, hung between him and the other men. He drew the others despite their apartness as though the barrier around him was their sustaining force. I thought of moths and fire, but that was wrong; fire had warmth, this man's presence provided an icy chemical incandescence. It seeped through the invisible wall into every corner.

I looked at the graven, gray-hued face with its vertical furrows and felt all my composure, strength, courage, or resolution abandon me at once.

I was lost and knew it, and I also knew that everything was lost. Nothing that Field or anyone else could do, could save me, or prevent tomorrow's public murder and its consequences, if the Nakomda itself was in on the plot. No miracle could take me out of the hands of this man who had destroyed Karpovitch with such ease; even Danilow had been afraid of him.

So it had all been for nothing, I thought. I would have fallen if two of my guards had not held me up.

Everything was finally in place and clear but the explanation would do no one any good. I would never be able to tell anyone what I now knew. I waited quietly for the conspirators to tell me what they wanted from me.

Someone was speaking to me. I listened with polite attention; it seemed suddenly important to be courteous now that all my other principles had failed me.

Yes, I said quietly. I was Oliver Hazard Shippe, aged forty-two, American, antiquities consultant. No, I was not an American intelligence officer; the idea would be quite preposterous. I had never been connected with any agency of the United States. No, I would not admit that I had violated the hospitality of the country or any of its laws, and I had not been officially involved in subversive activities anywhere. But yes, it could be said that I had been unofficially involved. I had come to the country to visit Sempinski and had, thus, come upon the conspiracy. Yes, I quite realized that I was on trial.

I didn't waste either my time or that of my judges by claiming the prerogatives of a visitor; the embassy had no value in these circumstances. Besides, I realized that the trial was a game with a specific goal. The goal had nothing to do with either law or justice.

The man who read my indictment in a language that I didn't understand wore the close-shaved, disciplined look of a Russian officer, his voice unmarred by either inflection or emotion, and the small, neat, murmuring civilian who droned a translation provided counterpoint so that their joint performance had the quality of a musical arrangement. They did not look at me and my eyes were drawn as remorselessly as theirs to the brooding figure of the general which loomed, impassive and motionless, out of the ecclesiastic shadows of his tall-backed armchair. He smoked a Russian cigarette in an ivory holder, as he had done in my room in Hetmansaka Gora, and the pale drifting of the smoke rings provided the sole movement in the air around him. This was the man who, Danilow had told me, used to throw people into locomotive boilers.

The voices of the military prosecutor and, I supposed, the civilian counsel for the defense, provided a bizarre background for my thoughts.

"This is a special tribunal of the National Security Commission of the People's Democratic Republic," my defender droned. "You are charged with conspiring with persons both known and unknown, to prevent the execution of a known deviationist from the original Marxist-Leninist revolutionary principles, with an attempt to halt the progress of the democratic peoples' revolution and with interference in the internal affairs of the People's Party. You are charged with having committed these crimes against the people with full foreknowledge and of your own free will, with the connivance of the capitalist espionage apparatus, and traitors both known and unknown, and with the assistance of, and in service

257

of, foreign-based reactionary-terrorist organizations and, both directly and indirectly, in the service of the espionage and subversion agencies of the United States. You are hereby informed that witnesses have been examined and depositions taken and that you have been found guilty as charged on each count of each charge, and that the legally prescribed sentence of the tribunal on each count of each charge is death. You will be informed in due time as to any clemency provisions allowed to condemned criminals by regulations governing the tribunal. Do you wish to make a statement at this time?"

I said: "No, thank you. Are you my defender?"

The droning voice went on as if I hadn't interrupted.

"You are informed that the privilege of examining prosecution witnesses is not extended to criminals condemned on capital charges. But because of the extraordinary nature of this special tribunal and its attendant circumstances, by permission of the convening authority and president, General Karol Rauss, here present, you will be supplied at this time with the names of the witnesses who testified against you. These are: General Karol Rauss, here present; and Kristin Napoji, widow, not present."

"I don't believe that," I said.

The defense counsel frowned with obvious irritation.

"The tribunal is not concerned with what a condemned criminal believes. However, because of the extraordinary circumstances attendant on this case, you are permitted to confront the witnesses if you wish. Do you wish to confront General Karol Rauss?"

"I believe I am confronting him," I said quietly. I nodded toward the silent figure seated in the corner.

"That is correct. Do you wish to confront the witness Napoji?"

"Yes," I said. So they had her, too.

"You are warned that you are not permitted to speak to the witness who is, herself, a condemned criminal."

"What are the charges against her?"

"That is not your business. However, again due to the nature of this special tribunal, and by permission of the presiding officer, I am allowed to inform you that her crime is treason."

258

I said, disbelieving: "Ridiculous. Your country has no jurisdiction over her."

"Under the law she is a citizen of this country by marriage. She has committed crimes against her people."

"You are not her people!"

"The prisoner will be silent!" defense counsel shouted.

"Very well," I said.

The small civilian no longer translated whatever the military prosecutor was saying, as if the prosecutor's speech had nothing to do with either him or me, as if those harsh, clipped words addressed to the silent group behind the desk were unrelated to me. All semblance of reality slipped from the proceedings.

"The prisoner is warned to follow rules of conduct governing condemned criminals. He will speak only if directly addressed by an officer of the tribunal with the president's permission. I am now directed to inform you of clemency provisions allowed in your case. The sentence of death passed upon you by this special tribunal may be commuted to imprisonment at the discretion of the presiding officer. I point out that this is an extraordinary act of clemency in itself, under the circumstances."

I said: "You must want something very badly from me. Under the circumstances."

"You are impertinent," defense counsel said.

"Does this clemency extend to Mrs. Napoji?"

"Are you trying to bargain?"

"It seems that I'm in the position to do so," I said.

Neither the military prosecutor, nor the general, nor any of the others seemed to react or even notice this exchange between the civilian and myself. But the civilian became agitated.

"You have been warned about speaking only when addressed. Another such breach of prescribed conduct will be severely punished. But I may answer you, under the circumstances, that such clemency may be authorized at the discretion of the presiding officer. Such clemency is contingent on your conduct before this

259

tribunal. You are obliged to make complete confession of your crimes, naming all persons, agencies and governments who have participated in your crimes. Such a confession has been prepared for your signature. Will you sign it now?"

"No," I said.

The military prosecutor finished his speech abruptly and now turned toward me, and I became aware of the newly charged atmosphere in the room. The general's huge head turned slowly in the shadows and I felt his icy eyes upon me.

"You!" he said.

The small civilian reacted as if he had been stabbed.

"Sir?"

"Make it clear to him."

"Yes, sir," the small man said. And to me: "You are warned that your refusal is tantamount to a dismissal of any possibility of clemency either for yourself or the criminal Napoji. Is that understood?"

I said nothing.

The small man said: "Silence is agreement."

I said: "I won't sign anything."

The general shrugged and made a brief gesture. A side door was opened and Kristin was led in between guards.

Her face was dead-white, and the shadows under her eyes had the dark stain of those who are bereft of hope. She looked up at me and her eyes narrowed as if she was unable to bear even the softly muted lights in the tribunal room.

It didn't matter any longer what would happen to the world tomorrow afternoon. The world was an enormous concept; too broad and impersonal for me to comprehend. And it was presumptuous of any man to think that anything he did or didn't do could have a permanent effect or bearing on the world. I could continue to resist the plotters as a kind of patriot, but I could not make decisions as a patriot, only as a man. Only Kristin truly mattered to me. I could not trust anything the conspirators might promise but I could not allow her to be killed without some effort on my part to save her, no matter how unreasonable and how hopeless.

I had robbed the plotters of all their evidence and now they wanted me to replace it by confession. There was the possibility that if I replaced it Kristin would not be killed. It was up to me whether I allowed her this shade of opportunity to live.

What would confessions matter anyway? What mattered was my own decision. I could not hide from making it. Nothing could intervene to save me from the need to make the decision, whether or not there really was a chance that the conspirators would not kill her.

Kristin was gone from the room as quickly as she had appeared in it, taken out by her guards. I was alone with the conspirators and with myself.

I heard the prosecuting officer, the little civilian and the somber men behind the desk continuing with the ritual but I paid no attention. I wondered why they had bothered to put on the show. Why did they need these vestiges of legality to blackmail and murder? Why not simply forge my signature and put a bullet in my head? Was it because men who are above the law always took care to shield themselves with law? Perhaps they never would put a bullet in my head but break me and keep me as a witness to my signature, their only evidence. That too was possible.

Time was no friend, no matter how much time they might give me for reflection and I knew that they wouldn't give me much. The ritual came to its conclusion. The prosecutor finished whatever he was saying. The officers conferred. The general rose and slowly left the room. The guards formed their moving wall around me and led me outside. Then it was the former ascent-to-luxury in reverse: the well-appointed rooms and corridors fell away, darkened, became colder. Passages narrowed, grayed. There was an elevator falling like a stone, and then an icy coldness and the dead white light of an unshaded bulb trapped in a wire cage and a steel cell without furniture or windows. The cell door boomed with hollow echoes, closing.

twenty-three

TIME PASSES. Night flows on. The muffled sounds of prison have sunk into silence, the anxious silence of unsleeping men staring into darkness.

My thoughts were calm and orderly like corpses in a morgue; I could examine them at leisure, almost without feeling. I thought, at times, that I could hear footsteps in the corridor and waited with quiet resignation for the conspirators to come with their confession for my signature and, perhaps, with their instruments of torture.

I had got away with it too easily so far; bluffing and luck were an unrealistic set of crutches in this league. I had expected that Karpovitch would have had me beaten to within a millimeter of my life at Hetmanska Gora—a realistic price to pay for my deception in the matter of the missing briefcase—but there had been no beating. Granted that Karpovitch may have had too much on his mind with his own life in danger, and also granted that it wouldn't have occurred to him that I could have outsmarted him even by accident, and further granted that my lie had been temporarily supported by the absence of the German whom I had accused of taking the briefcase, sheer frustration at being deprived of his moment of triumph, and his humiliation before the general, should have been enough for Karpovitch to vent his spleen on me. I had no reason to suppose that Karpovitch, despite his brilliant mind, was any less a vicious animal than his assorted Germans. My bluff had worked too easily. But now I could expect no bluff to succeed. I could expect all the punishment that I had escaped before.

I thought about Kristin, with whom life would have promised so much good. I didn't think that there was any hope to save her. I hated the conspirators; all plotters of all sides and factions. It had been their games that had got out of hand, and people who had had nothing to do with conspiracies would be paying for them. Well, perhaps the innocent non-participants could have done something to prevent the games; I didn't know. But I didn't want to feel the blame for what would happen the next afternoon; it was easier to hate the Rausses, the Karpovitchs, the Fieldses and even the Sempinskis for starting their games.

Midnight came and passed. There were no more footsteps or other illusions about sound. And then I did hear footsteps: a quick energetic echo that stopped outside my door. So they have come, I thought, and began to shiver.

I heard the bolts slide free on the other side and then the door opened. I saw the Nakomda uniform, the boots and the badges. The man's face was shadowed by the dark peak of his military cap. Then I recognized Danilow leaning toward me with an extended hand.

"Quick," he said. "On your feet. We have no time to waste."

What kind of trap was this going to be? I got to my feet. The colonel put both hands on my shoulders to steady me.

"Have you been questioned? Beaten? Have they given you an injection? Anything like that?"

"What? No . . ."

"Can you walk?"

I nodded.

"Come on, then. The guard will be away for only two minutes."

Danilow looked out into the corridor, then went through the door and motioned to me to follow.

We came out of the cell into a white-tiled antiseptic passage, and now I could hear the soft humming of an air ventilation system and the drone of hidden generators. So there had been sound all along; the silence had been an artificial lie. They would have tried to rob me of sound, of course; it was an old technique. You take away sound and a man's consciousness of time and, eventually, you dislocate a man's identity. Once you have undermined a man's identity you can make him do anything you wish. The corridor was cut by many black steel doors. There were no guards in sight but I thought that they were probably watching. I followed the quick-striding officer down the tiled tunnel; I didn't care where he was taking me. This, like everything else I could expect in this place, could only be some kind of trick. I didn't believe that this could be any kind of rescue. To believe that would mean starting to believe in the impossible again.

The corridors unfolded in surprising turns and loops and unexpected length. I tried counting cell doors just to keep some kind of a hold on reality but there were too many and any figure beyond ten seemed astronomical to me.

Then the condition of the corridor changed. It became drab and the cell doors gaped vacantly open. This must have been the old, abandoned section of the ancient prison: old brick and crumbling stone and stale air. We seemed to be falling, as if on a gently sloping ramp. The corridors narrowed. Soon we could barely walk abreast through the tight passage between glistening wet walls. And then there was a rusted iron door that groaned and grated as if a long time unused, and then our footsteps were echoing under the vaulted ceiling of an ancient sewer. The air was cold here, but redolent of antique stenches, and the pavement under our feet was slippery with old slime. Rats moved in cautious masses at the edge of vision, running before us like a shadow. I almost laughed with pleasure, seeing the familiar red pinpoint lights staring at me again, unblinking, in the dark.

"Stop here a moment," the colonel said.

He went on alone and I watched his shadow melt into the general darkness. I heard the officer's grating footsteps, then a clang of iron and the deep breathing of a silent struggle with a weight. Then came the clatter of cast iron rolling over cobblestones and a flood of suddenly icy air. Fresh air? I couldn't understand the meaning of this portent. The colonel's voice came to me from somewhere on the ceiling.

"How does that smell to you?"

"What . . ."

"The fresh air. Smell good? This is an old sewer, a road we used during the occupation. The Germans used to pour gasoline down on us through the gratings. Well, come on Shippe, climb up."

I stepped forward and walked into the bottom of an iron ladder. My shins burned from the sudden contact with the icy iron. I began to climb. Each rung was solid with a coat of ice. Each scorched my hands. I looked up and saw an impossible star winking at me from the roof of darkness. The colonel's impatient voice urged me on.

Then I was out of the manhole and standing in an open street among silent ruins, gaunt pyramids of brick, a snowswept wilderness where the wind made plaintive weeping sounds as if lost generations had come there to make their complaint. The obelisk of the Heroes of the Ghetto rose above the rubble.

"Are you all right?"

This was Danilow again. I felt the firm touch of his hand on my shoulder.

"I'm all right. Where are you taking me?"

Danilow pulled me toward a small car hidden under the arch of an ancient gateway. I moved toward the car as if that, too, was less an undeclared friend than an enemy. And suddenly the rear door of the car was flung open and Kristin was there . . . running toward me . . . putting her arms around me. She was laughing. The colonel's hand applied heavy pressure to my shoulder blades.

I said: "I don't understand this. What is going on?"

I thought I could detect a note of weary hysteria in Kristin's broken laughter.

"He got us out! He's on our side, darling."

"Don't trust him," I said. "We can't afford to trust anyone."

"Get in! Get in!" Danilow urged me impatiently and we got into the car. The car lurched across rubble.

"Where are you taking us?" I said to Danilow.

The colonel laughed softly. Kristin said:

"We're on our way to a hideout where we'll be safe while the colonel tries to do something about the plot. I've told him everything I knew about it."

"You told him . . ."

Danilow went on laughing, then said:

"Dr. Shippe has learned to be cautious. He thinks that Rauss is going to pop out of the trunk at any moment. And he still doesn't know what to make of me."

I said: "You can't blame me for that."

He said with deceptive lightness: "I found out where they had you locked up only about an hour ago. Mrs. Napoji is more spectacular, she was easier to track down. There was no time to organize anything properly but sometimes an *ad hoc* action is as good as a plot of a year. I ought to beat you to a pulp for causing me this trouble."

"I thought someone would get around to that by this time."

Danilow laughed.

"Do you feel deprived? If you had stayed in your cell four hours longer you would have had all the beatings you could wish for. I told you when the Nakomda does its questioning. The nadir of oblivion, remember? The hour before dawn."

"I can hardly remember anything you've told me."

"That's obvious. Don't you Americans ever do what you're told?"

"We're not conditioned to instant obedience."

"That's also obvious. But, I suppose, if you had done what I told you and stayed in the capital, I would never have had the pleasure of meeting Mrs. Napoji."

"Or finding out about the Sempinski Affair," Kristin reminded him.

"Yes, there is that. I'm damned if I know what to do about it."

I said quietly: "Why should you want to do anything about it?"

Danilow made a rude, impatient gesture. "The situation must

be restored to normal. Rauss must be muzzled. We still have some unfinished business, Dr. Shippe, remember?"

"Good God, are you still thinking about smuggling out the Library?"

"Do you have anything more pleasant to think about? I've survived a great many plots and conspiracies but this Sempinski business is too much. I've told you, it's time to retire. I don't want any post-assassination hysteria to interfere with that."

I said: "I didn't think you were helping us for any high-flown motives."

He laughed. "I haven't had one of those since my sixteenth birthday. Well, is our deal still on?"

It was my turn to laugh. "How on earth would I know? Lindstrom is dead."

"But his money is waiting in Sweden. Your Mr. Pohl has the authority to spend it. So let's clean up this Sempinski mess and get on with something profitable, eh? I've been doing a lot of reading lately about growing coffee."

I shrugged, said: "Have it your own way. I haven't thought much about the Library lately."

"I can well believe it. But you can take another look at it, that'll revive your interest. We're going to the lodge where you went with Zimstern. And, for God's sake, stay there, will you? You've given me quite enough to do without searching the country for you again."

I nodded.

"How are you going to move against the plotters?"

"That's a good question. Rauss is well entrenched even though most of the Nakomda is unaware of the conspiracy. But that's neither a help nor a hindrance to us. I must go to the Premier about this and I can't go empty handed; my word simply wouldn't be good enough to overthrow Rauss."

"Can you get to see the Premier?"

Danilow laughed without amusement.

"In this uniform I can get in bed with him if I wish. The trouble is to convince him that I am not out of my mind."

"There are some papers that might help," I said.

"Well, I don't have them. But you had better tell me the whole story. Something new might occur to me. Your young woman was very impressive but she was so concerned about you that her account of your adventures was more a paean of praise for your ingenuity and courage than an intelligence report."

"All right," I said.

Danilow listened carefully and, when I had finished, I knew what troubled him. My story, even if it could be believed without evidence, was simply hearsay. It would not be enough for him to take to his government.

I hesitated for only a moment.

"There is a man called Field at the Embassy. Do you know him?"

"Counterespionage happens to be my business."

"He has the letters and the money."

"It'll be nice to see five hundred thousand dollars. So you propose that Mr. Field and I join forces to save the Soviet Chairman? The novelty itself should be enough to get us to the Premier."

"But will Field work with you?"

"He won't have a choice. You can leave that part of it to me."

"There's one other thing," I said. "I know who killed your uncle. It was The Magician. Your uncle found out his identity. His name is Karpovitch. He's somewhere in the capital. He's after us because he wants the money."

"Good God," the colonel said. He laughed. "Is there anything that you haven't found out? If I ever come out of retirement and back into the business I'll only employ amateurs."

Then he said softly: "Yes, it must have been Karpovitch."

I said: "What now?"

"I found your Mr. Brown in the capital at about the time you were being arrested," Danilow said. "It was a routine matter of an unreported alien, with routine surveillance. But we lost Brown almost as soon as we had found him. He disappeared with another man. It must have been Karpovitch."

"Then Brown is also out of the conspiracy. What do you think he and Karpovitch will do?"

"Search for you and the money, I suppose. It might not take them long to pick up your trail."

"How could they do that?"

"Have you forgotten that Karpovitch knows about the Library? Zimstern might have told him where the Library is hidden. It won't take The Magician long to add two and two once he knows about your escape. And, don't forget, he might still have friends on Rauss's staff. We must take care of him, permanently, as soon as we can."

The sun rose shortly afterward. The morning was cold. We entered the forest. Danilow stopped the car at the edge of the clearing where the narrow trail sunk under the snow. I could see no track on the crisp, unmarred surface of the snow to show that Zimstern and I had ever been here. We walked the rest of the way to the hunting lodge, carrying the provisions and equipment that Danilow had brought in the trunk of the car. There was a rifle wrapped in an army blanket, canned food, a kerosene lamp and a transistor radio.

"It's not for entertainment," Danilow explained. "It's to tell you what is happening in the capital. If I fail to stop Rauss and the conspiracy you'll have to make some rapid decisions on your own. I won't be able to warn you."

I thanked Danilow for this thoughtfulness but he only gave me an amused glance and shrugged.

"Thoughtfulness has nothing to do with it," he said.

Inside the lodge, the dry chill of the crypt enveloped us at once.

"Quick," Kristin said, shivering but smiling. "Light the fire."

"No fire," Danilow said. "The sight of smoke might bring someone here. And this place is as dry as a tinderbox. It would go up like a bomb at the first misplaced spark."

"The Library would be quite safe in the cellar," I observed.

"What good is the Library to me unless you are safe?"

"You have a point there," I said.

"You have to do the best that you can with blankets to keep warm. There are more in the car."

I laughed. "Is there anything that you forgot?"

He said, suddenly annoyed: "Lots of things. But the less I tell you about that the better for your peace of mind."

"All right, no fires," I conceded. "What else should I know?"

"I'm going to leave you this rifle and my pistol. Do you know how to use them?"

"I've never seen as many guns as I've had thrust at me, one way or another, in the past few days. What will I need guns for?"

Danilow said, impatiently abrupt: "For . . . emergencies. Protection. Rauss knows by now about your escape. In the next few hours he'll turn this country upside down looking for you and Kristin."

"Didn't you say that only a small circle within the Nakomda is in on the plot?"

"What difference does that make? Rauss can call out the entire army for a manhunt, and keep his reasons to himself. He doesn't depend on just his fellow plotters. What a fool you are, Shippe! Did you really think that you were out of trouble?"

I said nothing because I had begun to think so. Danilow went on:

"And then there's The Magician. Would you like to fall alive into his hands?"

"No," I said. "I wouldn't."

I was enormously tired. I tried to focus my unsteady eyes on the dark, intense face bent impatiently toward me.

I asked: "When will we hear from you?"

"The only thing you'll hear is the radio. That will tell you whether the plot has succeeded or not. If it succeeds, you will know that my career as a Brazilian millionaire has been indefinitely postponed, and that you had better start running as fast as you can."

"Where should we run?"

"Toss up a coin. You have five hundred miles to go before you reach a border. Any border. You could try the coast, that's

270

the way most of our defectors take. It doesn't really matter where you go if Rauss is after you."

"You don't sound very confident about stopping him."

"I happen to know him."

There was no longer anything appealing in his saturnine face. The gloss of cynical amusement had long worn away and the sardonic eyes were clouded over with a reflection of my own depression.

I followed him up the dusty stairs to the second floor where massed cobwebs and a litter of wartime debris blocked off the entrances to three yawning rooms. It was ice cold there, a ghostly emanation of forgotten years inhabited by God-only-knew what memories for the Nakomda man. He brooded in the doorways, touching dusty lintels, as if recalling faces and hearing voices and reliving unspeakable events.

I remembered what both Danilow and Zimstern had mentioned about the bad luck that had seemed to follow the partisans who had rescued the Library from the Germans; all had died violently except Danilow, the ruthless inheritor of the treasure. I seemed to feel their presence in the icy coldness of the empty rooms. Danilow also seemed to sense it; he shuddered suddenly and passed a slow hand across his eyes. I wondered what he saw in the lowering dark rooms, beyond the curtain of cobwebs and dust, what memories had thrust themselves upon him. What had he been like as a young leader of partisans? What had been his hopes and how had his men died?

We went back downstairs and into the cellar where he stood for a long time staring at the cases, touching the near edges with lingering fingers, nodding to himself.

He said remotely: "This should all be safe, no matter what happens here . . ."

After Danilow had left us, I stood for a time at the window—staring but not seeing. I felt remarkably alone.

Morning passed in silence. Kristin and I sat side-by-side on a wooden bench, huddled under two blankets. I had set and wound

271

the ornate clock that occupied one whole corner of the downstairs hall and now the clock haunted me with its persistent ticking. I wished that there had been some way to halt the passing minutes and extend the deadline of the afternoon.

For all I knew, Danilow might be heading straight for a waiting firing squad in a Nakomda cellar. It wouldn't have taken Rauss long to discover how we had escaped and, even if Danilow did manage to avoid immediate arrest, the escape had been so hastily arranged that innumerable telltale threads must have been left unraveled for the conspirators to follow. Also, I couldn't put aside the thought of Karpovitch making one last attempt to secure the money which he so desperately needed to survive the plot. It would be unlike him to give up either the loot or the revenge. It was, I was sure, only a matter of time—time counted in hours—before one manhunt or the other swept us up again and, this time, there would be no miraculous deliverance from prison, only a savage enmity to be faced in a lonely forest. Time, that implacable enemy, threatened us everywhere I looked.

I was too exhausted to eat any of Danilow's provisions. Kristin nibbled on some bread and cheese. Later she held my hand as we listened to the radio hoping for a sign of change in the Chairman's program, some indication that the plotters' plans were going awry, but we heard nothing that could have suggested a change in anybody's plans. Even the weather, threatening in the night, had cleared up into a brilliant morning at the capital and, early as it was, a quarter of a million people had already started massing in the square where the Chairman would speak.

As noon drew near I could no longer doubt that the plotters were still in control and in full command. There was an interview with Rauss about the security arrangements for the Chairman's visit. His voice reflected only satisfaction and icy confidence. How could I have supposed otherwise? How could I have been so stupid as to hope? I stared at the white clock face as if to will the hands into immobility but the remorseless minutes ground on with a soft scraping of unoiled gears.

I was no longer willing to believe in miracles. I forced myself to walk away from the radio. The crackling bulletins followed me the length of the hall. My slurred footsteps frightened me a little; I knew that I was close to nervous exhaustion, the near limits of endurance. I smiled at Kristin, feeling as if my face were carved out of soapstone.

"Let's light a fire," I said. I didn't think it mattered any longer what happened to the lodge. We would soon be on the run again. I thought that a cheerful fire in the fireplace would take the chill off the way we felt, the chill that had nothing to do with temperature. Kristin did not object. So she has also ceased to hope, I thought; a fire could no longer threaten us since everything appeared to be over. I built the fire and lit it. The dry tinder blazed high into the chimney.

"Won't that make lots of smoke?" Kristin asked carefully and looked at me as if to make sure that she had read my mind correctly as to why I was disobeying Danilow's instructions.

"I don't suppose it matters any more. Do you?"

"It would be nice to think it did. Are you sure that it's now too late to hope for success?"

I pointed to the clock.

"Well," she said. "A lot could happen in three hours. Haven't we been through too much to give up now? Isn't there still something that we could do?"

"I don't know what. I think that we had better start planning how to get away. We have no transportation and nowhere to go. It's not a very encouraging beginning."

"We didn't have much more at Hetmanska Gora," she reminded me.

"We had a purpose and we had direction. The embassy was a goal. Now we'll be simply running for our lives."

"It would be silly to start running until we knew that we had no other choice."

I agreed that we would wait and listen to the Chairman's speech. Besides, I had no idea how to set about our second escape. We could, presumably, walk out of the forest along the buried trail, but that would only take us to the capital highway, the one location where the manhunt would be sure to begin. True, we were armed but, the thought of weapons seemed repellent and unrealistic; we could not allow our plans to depend on weapons. Fast transportation, warm clothing and a guide were what we had to have; these I could neither hire nor provide. I had no more money and, anyway, where would I find a guide and horses in the forest?

Kristin was right about the smoke, of course; it would soar high in the still and snowless air and attract attention. Our future visitors would be sure to spot it. But did the smoke need to draw only enemies? Why couldn't it do the same for a curious woodsman, woodcutter or peasant who might come to see what was going on in the abandoned lodge? They would have sleighs and horses since no one would be able to walk far in this snow, in such cold. Sleighs meant transportation. The peasants could provide sheepskin coats and hats, felt-lined boots and warm straw. They could be persuaded to guide us to the coast.

I felt excitement begin. Here was a chance, weak as it might be, but I had had no more than that at Hetmanska Gora. What would I use for money? Unsurprised, I found myself looking at Danilow's pistol, a clumsy-looking revolver of shining black steel.

I picked up the pistol, weighing it experimentally first in one in one hand then in the other; it felt awkward, heavy but not out of place. A month ago the thought of hijacking a sleigh would have been impossible for me. Now I found it logical and simple. If we were lucky, we could force someone to take us to the coast. There we could look for a sturdy fishing boat, one large enough to take us across the Baltic Sea to Sweden in the teeth of winter and the fierce winds that swept out of the north at this time of the year. We could obtain the boat the way we would obtain the sleigh; the thought of piracy was now no more foreign to me than that of hijacking and robbery on the highways.

For the time being I decided to keep my new excitement to

myself. There was no point in raising Kristin's hopes if my solution proved unrealistic. And, just in case our smoking chimney drew the wrong, unwelcome kind of visitors, I went outside to look at our defenses.

twenty-four

OUTSIDE, I was immediately frozen; colder than I had ever imagined possible, even colder than during our escape from Hetmanska Gora. After the mild warmth of the fire in the lodge, the dry coldness of a winter noon seemed to scrape my face. My breath hung motionless behind me as I moved. The corners of my mouth began to ache at once.

I walked around the house, inspecting the windows. They glowed a pale pink with the fire behind them. Snow and ice had begun to shift their patterns on the window panes, offering fresh shapes and textures: frosted branches, thistles: a miniature white forest.

I fingered the heavy shutters: three-inch planking seasoned to the hardness of iron, with a small heraldic device carved into the center. I peered down to read the motto under the device but it had been obliterated by years and weather. I thought it possible that the heavy shutters might stop a rifle bullet. I didn't think the conspirators would bring anything heavier than rifles. The door was even thicker, blacker with age and weather, and reinforced with brass studs and thick iron bosses. All this seemed satisfactory. I worried about the flammability of our would-be fortress, remembering what Danilow had told me and Zimstern had implied, but I decided that the danger of fire would be worse inside where the walls and flooring were bone dry. Outside, the snow and ice could foil arsonists.

All in all, I was satisfied. If Kristin and I were forced to fight for our lives in this place, I thought we could do it. I wouldn't let myself think beyond that.

I looked at the smoke, pieces of flying white ash and burned wood no bigger than snowflakes, and the myriad whirling sparks high in the branches of the giant oak. I thought that the smoke should be blacker and thicker to attract attention as far as the highway. The wind smeared it brownly under the vast-spread canopy of icicles and snow packed among the branches. Well, there was wet wood in plenty to throw on the fire.

I walked around the house and noted the ravine which tumbled precipitously to a frozen stream behind the house. The back wall was blank, without windows, nothing that invaders could use for an entrance. The ridge and the gulley would defy them if they tried to approach the lodge from this sheltered direction. There were two windows facing from the wings, one on each side of the building: small, narrow, glassless, solidly iced loopholes in the upper floor: too high for anyone to reach, too narrow to enter. Only the front of the lodge offered a way in with three shuttered windows on the upper floor and one each flanking the door downstairs. I decided that I would shutter both the downstairs windows and shoot through the door. The upper floor may have offered certain advantages for defense but I felt oddly ill at ease about it, as if a human presence in the empty rooms were an intrusion. I could see no obstacles, other than rolling dunes of snow, to mar my field of fire as far as the trees. My new vocabulary amused me: fields of fire, indeed. Very military. I felt an odd sense of elation, dismissed it as foolish, but didn't particularly mind when it returned at once.

The sound of birds startled me; I paused for a moment. A huge black flock had risen cawing in the forest, raucously indignant. At once the tree-wall answered with its cough and snarl; the silence was over. The harsh, riverlike murmur of the forest began again. In fact, I realized that there had been no silence at all;

the thick winter air had been full of dry, remorseless sound: grinding and whirring and so penetrating that it seemed to come from within the blood, chipping the bone with an abrasive whisper. I had scarcely noticed it, but now the persuasive sound of this collective menace filled all the space under the vaulted canopy of the trees.

I stamped my feet to warm them, moved my arms inside their difficult cocoon of clothes and fatigue. The dark chill of the forest had penetrated my bones. I listened to the distant anger of the crows.

All the events since my breakfast with Tommy Mackin at the club appeared momentarily before me and were understood. Neither the people nor the plots surprised me or mystified me any longer. I didn't question my involvement in conspiracies. Neither Hubertus Pohl, nor my work nor my way of life—the comfortable routines of so many years—interested me any more. I viewed them coldly and dispassionately like objects behind glass. I didn't think that I would ever again choose such a simple, selfish, uncommitted way of living, not even if there was a future to consider. I realized that whatever I did from now on would be something that I had never done before. Life, as I had thought of it in New York, no longer made sense. I would never again go hunting after relics, let relics stay buried. That's where they belonged: in the past, in their own time. If Kristin and I survived what was coming, our time would be the future.

And so with the Pontic Tribunals and the Romanowski Library. Let them remain a scholars' Holy Grail that is never found. After the Chairman's speech, in less than an hour, the world would have a need for Holy Grails; faith could become important again.

I looked at the brooding solidity of the lodge with mild astonishment. I had come so far to find the treasure that was hidden here, and the start of the adventure seemed so very long ago, that I could hardly believe that the treasure waited for me in the dry old lodge. I knew that I would look at it again with Kristin, to share with her the experience of touching and seeing the source

278

of faith and inspiration of so many centuries. But I would not allow the library to be moved from here.

Why should it travel to America? Why should any one place be picked out as a sanctuary for human aspirations? Who really deserved to possess this treasure? No one played the game of international power politics with clean hands, no one seemed to be beyond reproach. It was only the degree of dirt that mattered and even that was impossible to determine at first sight.

I had been commissioned to insure the Library's preservation; I was to make it available to scholars. Well, I was a scholar of a kind and I would always know where the Library was hidden. And if the world ever returned to sanity and there was time, again, for beauty, reverence and inspiration, I could produce the Library. It seemed unlikely that I would ever want to. Let it stay where it is. The Library, and what it represented, could wait for more appreciative times.

I turned toward the house, again aware of the crows and ravens which now rose from near trees and circled the forest. I was very cold. I found it difficult to breathe in the suddenly still air.

twenty-five

WE SAT before the radio. Kristin was pale. Her face was stony, a beautiful white mask with staring black eyes.

"When is the speech due to begin?" she asked.

"Any minute now."

We were listening to an American commentator, one of a Delphic pair heard throughout the Western world. His broadcast, like a hundred others, would be simultaneously translated into every language. Orbiting satellites would bring it into every instrument in the listening world.

The day is clear and cold here, at the foot of the giant building, the Palace of Culture and Communication, the gift to the people of this capital from the Soviet Union. Millions are flocking into the snowy square. There is an air of tense expectation. The Chairman of the Soviet Union is expected to make the most significant announcement of Soviet policy since the beginning of the Cold War, the end of World War II. The whole world has been invited to attend through the modern facilities of international radio and television . . . It is, in effect, as if the whole world had come to this city today . . . a momentous occasion.

Total press, radio and television coverage . . . (the commentator said) facilities never before offered to Western reporters east of the barrier which, up to this day, had so bitterly divided the East from the West.

It is believed here, in this city, that what we shall shortly see and hear may well affect the future course of human affairs. More than a million people stand within sight of the draped balcony from which the Chairman will speak. They stand in silence, heads raised, waiting. As all of us are waiting. They have come from far as we have all come today to see . . . whether this will be, indeed . . . a day to remember . . .

Nothing like this had ever happened before in the long, troubled history of the world and of East-West relations, the commentator said.

He was reminded of another historical moment . . . the return of Neville Chamberlain from Munich in 1938 . . . *the assurance of peace for our time* . . . even though that assurance preceded World War II by only a few months.

But there is a feeling here today that the time has come for all men to live together no matter what their systems and . . . perhaps . . . something of that feeling has gripped the world today. Peace has been too long absent.

I could imagine the tense, waiting crowds.

The preliminaries of the program were under way: minor speeches, welcomes and introductions, a concert by massed military bands, hopeful commentaries.

I got up and went to the window. Something about the scene (white glare of snow in the early afternoon sun, blue shadows sloping among roots and deadfall) brought a vague warning, an unspecified alarm. The wind had fallen away, and the suddenly unburdened air was particularly still. The silent tree-wall mocked me with its artificial stillness, the false and watchful lack of motion and sound. I had the feeling that each time I took my eyes off anything, inside the lodge as outside, intense activity broke out silently and that this stealthy frenzy, somehow touched with malice, ceased at once when I swung my eyes toward it.

I wished that I had closed the shutters while I had been outside.

I turned and saw that Kristin had come up to join me.

"Nervous?" she asked.

I could see how very frightened she was then. I put my arms around her. She did not tremble but she moved against me. She said that hers had been a stupid question: "I should disregard it."

"I wish I could answer it. But I don't know if I'm nervous or not. I can't really feel anything. Nothing makes sense now."

"I'm terrified," she said. "I can't believe that it's going to happen in just a few moments. And we'll just sit here and listen to it happening and won't be able to do anything about it."

"Oh," I said. "You mean the assassination?"

"Yes, of course. Wasn't that what you were thinking about?"

"My mind has slid away from that entire subject."

"It's all I can think of."

"That's why I can't imagine it. Who could?"

"How could it ever be allowed to happen?"

"It didn't happen overnight."

"That's just what I mean! How on earth did we all come to this? Why couldn't someone have done something to prevent this? Couldn't anyone see where we were all heading? Oh, I don't mean the Chinese . . . and this conspiracy. I mean all the conditions that make war possible, whether hot or cold. Where do these terrible things start, anyway? Why can't the starting point be clearly recognizable to all? There ought to be a warning sign somewhere, but there isn't, and we all march ourselves, over and over again, step by step, into this kind of horror. And now we've really done it, haven't we?"

I pulled her toward me.

"Oh God," she said. "I can't believe it. Step by step. Each one taking us a little nearer, a little closer to the precipice. All that talk about peace . . . all those politicians! Didn't any of them know what they were doing?"

Oh my dear love, I thought. I asked, gently:

"Couldn't you find an easier question?"

"But it's so stupid," she said. "So thoroughly stupid! Why do we elect stupid men?"

"They haven't all been stupid, have they?"

282

She said: "I don't want to get hysterical. If there was only something we could do!"

I kissed her.

And then the commentator's voice spiraled with excitement. We heard a quick, roaring flutter of anxiety from the gray masses marshaled in the square as the commentator reported an unexplained shooting in a neighboring area. Some kind of malcontent, rumored to be a possible assassin, had been trapped and shot.

What happened, Kristin wished to know.

"Somebody has been shot."

"It has to be Brown!"

"Well, no," I said gently. "It could have been Field just as easily . . . or Danilow, if he was still alive. This could be part of Rauss's preparations to set the stage for terror and hysteria."

I heard a wavering note of fear in the commentator's voice, a voice made famous by its bland assurance and kindly authoritativeness. Now it climbed an octave and fell uncertainly.

There have been rumors of a plot to embarrass the Chairman. Several persons were arrested last night and this morning, some prominent . . . One report implicated a high-ranking officer of the Security Police. Police activity has been heavy in the past few days . . . it was unusually heavy last night and this morning. In an interview three hours ago, General Rauss, the national security director, said that every precaution had been taken to protect the Chairman. But here in this historic square where a million persons have waited since daybreak the air is charged with tension. Rumors run from person to person . . . anxiety is mounting. Another such incident could be catastrophic.

The murmur of the crowds had now become a sustained roar.

And now the mood of the thousands gathered here has changed. It's an explosive, almost angry mood. The tension has reached an unbearable pitch. No matter whether these uneasy masses are Communist or not, they have come here to hear a message of hope. The rumors, the extraordinary security precautions, reports of arrests and even executions that have been circulating through the capital this morning, have set everyone on edge. And if an attempt were to be actually made on the Chairman's life, the consequences could be beyond comprehension. Everyone knows that no matter what measures are taken, there is always someone . . . somewhere . . . some deranged mind . . . which can . . .

I could imagine the assassin waiting among the cornices and ballustrades on one of the placid, neo-classic roofs that had so delighted me. I imagined him as Brown; the cold white face would be settling close to the stock of his rifle. I supposed that it would have to be a rifle rather than a pistol, and wondered if the conspirators had compressed-air rifles in their arsenal. I didn't see why they shouldn't have them.

The thin black cross of the telescopic sight would be moving now back and forth across the draped balcony that the commentator so meticulously described, as if to stroke the scarlet hangings, massed banners, golden wreaths of wheatsheaf, the hammers and sickles.

I listened to the nervous roar of the waiting crowds.

Kristin's eyes, her face, indeed her whole body, were turned to the radio. No part of her appeared to be moving; she did not seem to breathe. Only her eyes, fixed with absolute intensity, wide and unblinking, betrayed her with tears. She cried without a sound, motionless as if her narrow body had been marbled over.

And then an inward tremor passed over her. A scarcely noticeable shift in lighting and color showed that her lips had begun to tremble and the tremor spread to the stiff muscles of her face and the dilated eyes. The shadows underneath her cheekbones began to move, compressing and expanding. Her eyelids fluttered faster than eyesight could follow. Her body moved violently forward and she was suddenly out of her chair and on her feet.

"Is there one chance that Danilow . . . Field . . . could still . . ."

I shook my head.

"I don't see how they could. It was a wild chance at best. If they had succeeded we would have had some evidence by now."

"What about all these arrests the man just talked about? Couldn't that mean something?"

"Rauss was still in command when they interviewed him."

"But that was more than three hours ago. Everything could have changed in three hours."

"That's true, but I wouldn't hope."

"Why not?"

"I don't think we should build up any more illusions. I think hope would be unreasonable at this point. I think it's better to simply accept what is going to happen."

"Accept it! I can't even believe it!"

"Nobody ever will."

"I think I'm going mad," she said. "This is impossible."

"Yes. But it's true. Can you accept an impossible truth?"

"Oh God, I don't know."

I could imagine the festive balcony with its flags and ornaments and its dark interior that had begun to fill with the shapes of men.

The welcoming roar of the crowds and the nonprofessional excitement of the commentator told me that the Chairman and his entourage were beginning to emerge, pacing with easy majesty, like sated banquet guests leaving the midnight hall. The Chairman's position would be in the center, flanked by the national president and premier, with many others taking their places behind, filling every corner of the balcony. I could imagine the cold eyes, hard faces, stern shoulders in boxlike greatcoats, heavy furs. They would stand in smiling rows, eyes resting with the serenity of undisputed power on the crowd below, while the crowd welcomed them. There would be that angular polished sameness to their Eastern European faces under the hats and fur caps: faces made familiar by the public prints but, in mass, undistinguishable from each other. The announcer named them in order of appearance on the balcony; he also named Rauss.

I looked quickly at Kristin to see if she had noticed, but if she had she gave no sign of it.

I listened to the speculative roar of the crowd: tense party regiments brought from every secret corner of the world to hear the new standing orders for mankind and to witness what was going to happen. I heard their sudden silence and then the brilliant speech. I listened to the wasted rhetoric, the promised pacts of friendship that had come too late, the call for open borders (soon to be permanently closed), the call for destruction of all nuclear weapons. I strained to catch the moment when the Chairman would falter and choke on his words. There would be no gunfire with the compressed-air rifle. The mild *ping* would be lost beneath the roar of the stricken crowds; their cry of anguish would rock across the world.

The lifting of restrictions on freedom of expression . . . freedom of conscience everywhere . . . freedom to seek new social and political forms . . . Peace . . . end to the Cold War . . . coexistence brought to its only logical conclusion in cooperation . . . the wealth of the world to be thrown into service of all humanity . . .

I listened, waited. I could not look at Kristin.

And now, I thought, the assassin is taking aim. The thin black cross of his telescopic sights moves across the body of the stocky man who stands with upraised arms on the blood-red balcony.

The crowd had gone wild. Their roar drowned out the high, excited voice of the commentator. And then there was another sound.

As if unable to transmit the excitement of the moment, the radio blew up; all its multicolored components were momentarily visible: tubes, coils, wires, small bulbs, odd shapes disintegrating.

A breath of silence was followed by the rattle of machine-gun fire which burst in with an icy blast of air from outside. The windows splintered and the great skull of an ancient elk sailed off the wall which was suddenly pitted with rows of dusty explosions.

Glass showered down. I threw myself face-down on the floor with Kristin beside me. I couldn't see in the dust and smoke. Where had the smoke come from? I had not noticed it before.

But the fresh air rushing through smashed windows blew the smoke about in thick clouds.

"Are you all right?"

This time she heard me. "Yes."

The crash of falling furniture, the exploding mirror, and the remorseless hammering of bullets on the walls and door, had deafened us both.

I looked at Kristin's face under mine; her eyes were enormous. I pulled my upper body over her while shards of glass and splinters sharp as razors spattered the floor around us.

And suddenly the sound was over; the silence seemed explosive in my head. I felt the wind sweep over me through the broken door. It took me several moments to find my voice, to whisper:

"You're not hurt? You're sure?"

"Yes. Are you all right?"

"I think so." I looked up at the bullet-pocked walls, the ruin and debris and at myself. What blood there was had come from cuts, all minor.

"Who are they?"

"Rauss's men, Karpovitch, what's the difference?" Then I choked on smoke. "Goddamit! I wish I could have got you out of here."

I thought: If only breathing wasn't so difficult in the smoke. Where had the smoke come from? Perhaps a part of the house had been set on fire. Well, if that's the case, we're really in for it.

Kristin said: "What are we going to do?"

"I don't know. Can you use that pistol?"

"I used to fool about with a twenty-two on Uncle Per's ranch. It was a long time ago."

"This thing looks like it might work the same way. Could you . . . shoot somebody?"

She looked at me soberly and nodded.

"I think so."

"Then watch the left window. If anything shows in it, shoot at it. I've got to look outside. I'd like to know how many we are up against."

"Are we going to fight them?"

I looked at her, touched her face.

"If it's Karpovitch, there isn't any choice. He means to kill us. Maybe there is some kind of a chance with Rauss, maybe not . . ."

I crawled to the door which hung grotesquely askew on one hinge, and put my eye to the crack formed by the splintered black oak and its icy frame.

"What do you see?" Kristin asked. "Can you see anything?"

"Not much. The clearing. There's no one out in the open. I see a little smoke. It's almost like a mist rising around a few trees, about waist high for a normal man."

"Is that where they are?"

"I suppose so. There seem to be four positions, about ten yards apart. We couldn't hope to leave the house without being spotted."

"Can you see anyone?"

"No. Wait. Yes. There's one. He's looking up from behind a tree. Now he is standing up!"

"Be careful!"

At once machine-gun fire raked the lodge again, downstairs and upstairs. The bullets whined about us. I ducked down. When I looked up again, the man I had seen earlier had moved into the clearing. He disappeared suddenly behind the snowdrifts. Then the barrage lifted and a man shouted: "Shippe! I want to talk to you!"

It was Karpovitch's voice.

twenty-six

NIGHT CAME so swiftly that neither of us noticed it until it was there. The white plate of a crooked moon, and another light that we could not at first identify, lit up the glazed trunks of huge trees. An animal roared nearby and crashed through the thickets; the sound of its passing died fastidiously in the absorbent darkness of the forest roof.

Stray shots thundered against the forest wall from time to time. The riflemen were hidden. Their silhouettes showed occasionally near the fires they had lit at the edge of the clearing.

I sat on the floor under the right window, raising myself up on my haunches to peer into the moonlight. I had put out the kerosene lantern so that the pink glow would not betray us to snipers. I had hoped that, with nightfall, there might occur an opportunity for escape. But the moon had lighted the clearing and turned its snow surface into a white sheet on which every shadow stood out stark and black. The light grew rapidly as if an auxiliary red moon had been hung in the sky where I couldn't see it. I knew that a great fire was burning nearby. Sometimes I even thought that I could hear its hungry roaring in the wind. Smoke seeped into the lodge; it lay in acrid strips under the ceiling. And yet the lodge was nowhere on fire, I knew. I had gone over the house to make sure of that much shortly after nightfall.

I looked at Kristin. She was facing the window, the gun in her hand, her head and hair bright against the scarred walls and shattered furniture. I felt a deep resentment, knowing that I had finally found a reason for working and living. It struck me as particularly cruel to lose her so quickly: a spiteful and gratuitous piece of mockery. I was determined that she should survive.

And now a strong ground-wind swept up so that the fire, where ever it was, burned fiercely. It roared like an express train through the forest. I supposed that the besiegers must have built a bonfire in the ravine on the blind side of the lodge. They had tried arson earlier; a man had run up with what looked like a five-gallon gasoline container. I had shot at him and missed but he had dropped the can, which now lay blackly in the bright-lit snow, and dodged back under cover.

Snow swirled into the house through the glassless windows. I saw sparks spiraling in the clearing. I thought that ice and snow would probably protect the old building unless the fire was so close that it melted the snow and dried the old timbers. Then the lodge would become a furnace in moments. But the smoke was the more immediate problem.

I lay down on one elbow, closer to the floor. Here I could still find some unpolluted air. I could no longer feel Danilow's rifle in my freezing hands. Hunger, exhaustion and the ache of my small wounds had driven me close to my limits. My eyes felt as if they had been rubbed raw with sandpaper then sheeted with lead. I had no doubt that Karpovitch's next attack would be the last; all my resources had been expended.

I propped myself up by the window sill, peered out. Karpovitch was still in the hollow behind the nearest snowdrift. He had a cheerful fire going. He had been quiet for some time. Now he began to call again:

"Shippe! Are you still alive?"

I said nothing. Images without substance moved across my eyes.

"Shippe! I want to talk to you! Come out!"

My frozen hand on the rifle stock jerked in a sudden reflex. A single shot thundered into the sky.

Karpovitch laughed.

"What are you shooting at? Come out! I have news for you! How would you like to know what happened in the capital? Or don't you care about that any more?"

Care? No, I thought. I don't suppose I care; everything is over.

"An old friend of yours is here," Karpovitch went on. "Brown! He saw it all happen."

The image of the pale face and flat eyes filled with an unseeing malice shook me back into consciousness.

"How come Rauss didn't murder him?" I cried out in a cracked voice wobbly with hysteria.

"So! You can talk! Come out and stop being a fool! Nobody knows where you are, none of your friends can help you."

"What happened to Danilow?"

"He is dead. We met him on the road."

"How did you know where we were?"

"Easy! But I'm tired of shouting. Either you come out or I am going in. And don't try anything heroic!"

Then he began to laugh again. "Shippe! Your roof has just caught fire! I thought that old tree would never burn down. Well, you'll have to come out now, whether you like it or not."

I sank back to the floor. My eyes were watering with smoke and my throat was raw. Kristin crawled nearer to me.

I whispered: "Did you hear him?"

"Yes. What are you going to do?"

I stared at her, then shook my head. I didn't want to make any more decisions.

"Let him come in," she urged.

"In here? Karpovitch?"

"Yes. Have we really anything to lose?"

The smoke had blotted out the top of the stairs. I wondered if the fire had now broken through the roof to the upstairs rooms.

"Shippe!" Karpovitch shouted. "Your last chance!"

"What chance?" I asked. "What is he talking about?"

"Perhaps he wants something."

"And is that a chance? We've nothing to trade."

"Perhaps he thinks we have. Let him come in."

I shook my head, then nodded. I heard the swelling roar of the fire and thought that I could feel a gradual tremor starting through the house as if the old building was also suddenly awakening and seeking life aware of its danger.

"All right!" I called. "Come in!"

Karpovitch was laughing.

"None of your tricks now, Shippe! No more idiotic heroics! My men are coming around the house. They'll blow you all to hell if you don't behave. We have about ten minutes before your house caves in. You give me what I want and I'll let you go."

"He won't," I told Kristin, wondering where my odd voice was coming from. "He'll kill us."

"Perhaps he won't. Perhaps something will happen to give us a chance."

"What could happen now?"

"I don't know. But there is no chance at all unless we get him within reach."

I watched Karpovitch coming clumsily through the deep snow, thick in his coarse furs like a menacing animal, his head grown hugely in a bushy hat. One of his arms was in a black sling. I had forgotten that I had broken his wrist while we had been struggling in the car; I didn't think that he had forgotten. His other arm cradled a submachine gun. I wondered how he could fire it with only one hand. He kicked the shattered door and it fell apart.

"Smoke's getting thicker, eh? Your upper floor is well alight. I know these old houses. The ceiling will come down on you in about five minutes."

"On you too," I said.

Karpovitch shrugged, smiling maliciously.

"It was your fire, Shippe, that dried off that old oak. Then sparks got the tree burning. That got your roof nice and dry and now your house is burning. Well, it was time that one of your stupidities caught up with you."

I said nothing, unable to think.

"How do you do it?" Karpovitch went on. "You are a clumsy, incompetent amateur . . . you blunder into situations that would defy the most experienced agent, ruin the most painstakingly planned operations, and somehow you blunder out again. You survive everything. I am beginning to think that you are the real magician."

"What do you want?" I said.

"But it's all over now. There is no escape for you this time. It's all finished in the capital and my time is short. Rauss is shooting everyone who had anything to do with the conspiracy. I have no doubt that he'll remember about me."

"Rauss?" I said. "Rauss is shooting the conspirators?"

"Of course! What do you think? Washington warned the government here. As soon as Rauss saw that the game was up he started covering his tracks. He has an instinct for survival. Last night and this morning he rounded up, court-martialed and shot everyone connected with the plot except you and me."

"So there was no assassination?"

"Not even an attempt. Rauss will probably get a half dozen medals."

"Don't his superiors know about his part in the conspiracy?"

"What kind of fool are you? Who is alive to tell them? Perhaps you told someone in your embassy about Rauss but do you think the CIA would give away a blackmail plum like that? They probably have Rauss working for them already."

Karpovitch's laughter was laden with a dark intensity. He was wholly coiled within himself. He did not seem to hear the violent roar of the fire upstairs or see the scarlet lines which had begun to spread between the ceiling timbers. All his senses were totally focussed on the dark game he had come to play.

"And so by virtue of mutual allegiance, Rauss is now almost a countryman of yours. Doesn't that make you proud? You could have saved yourself, your woman, and even Danilow if you had simply stayed quiet in your embassy. But you're a stupid, virtuous, idealistic fool and so you had to go blundering about until you had accomplished what virtue and stupidity and ideals invariably accomplish and that's the destruction of everything that has meaning for you. Now do you see yourself, Shippe? Where did it all get you? What good did you do? Officially there never was any conspiracy. No one is ever going to admit how close they came, this time, to blowing up the world . . . not Washington, not Moscow and certainly not the Chinese. They'll simply try it somewhere else at a better time. Nothing has changed, the same old game goes on. Nothing you've done will make any difference."

"What do you want?"

"The money, fool. Did you think I'd let that get away from me?"

Karpovitch's face hung like a disembodied narrow fox mask in the smoke before me. I could no longer hear him through the roar of the fire and the deep groaning of the house as beams parted and gutted timbers shifted.

The house shook and quivered. Restless pools of light began to appear on the walls and along the stairs. The red lines overhead began to part and rivulets of flame spilled out of the ceiling.

I was aware of men running outside and calling and of Karpovitch shouting. Kristin's white face swam into view as she stared at the cascades of flame splashing the floor around us. My lungs seemed on fire. I heard as if from an immense distance the sharp explosion of disintegrating walls. The ceiling had vanished. A mass of flame hung overhead, suspended by its own whirling vacuum. I felt flames brush my face; my clothes would be burning in a moment. I had the unreal sensation of watching an interminable silent film running in slow motion. Karpovitch shouted and retreated into the doorway, his furs smoldering. His mouth moved but I heard no sound. The short barrel of the submachine gun came up. And suddenly I felt blind rage. I ran at Karpovitch pulling Kristin with me through a stinging red and yellow shower, and saw the barrel of the submachine gun twist upward in Karpovitch's one uninjured hand, and heard the crash of the bullets sprayed over my head. Then I was upon him, and the submachine gun was torn from his hand and he fell heavily into the fire. A man loomed in the doorway and I turned the weapon upon him and saw him blown out into the snow. Then a twisted, colorless face swung in front of me, the reptilian eyes no longer flat but oddly bulging in the firelight, and I went on shooting as I ran toward it and this face, too, vanished suddenly.

And then my lungs were full of icy air. Kristin was behind me. We ran through the fire-tinted snow. The submachine gun fell out of my hands. We heard a booming sound and looked back. The lodge had vanished. In its place stood a column of fire that rose beyond the glittering canopies of ice, snow and branches, shooting a whirling mass of stars into the sky.

I heard myself ask in a grave, stiff voice if Kristin was all right, if she could walk to the track where, undoubtedly, Karpovitch had left his transportation. She wished to know where we would go in Karpovitch's car.

"To the capital. Once we get to the embassy, Field will know what to do."

I got behind the steering wheel but Kristin pushed me gently to the passenger side. Neither she nor I had anything to say.

The sloping countryside around us was gray with the light of a new day; the night was over. I thought about the night. I saw again the swaying pillar of fire which had destroyed the lodge and which had been a funeral pyre for Karpovitch. I wondered how long the fire would burn before the new snow that had begun to fall would stifle the embers and bury the ruins.

Then the woods thinned out, the flat open country spread in front of us. I looked for the spires of the capital in the cold red light of the new day.